Leona —
   Thank you Aunt E———— ————l, in the rain, the day your twin cousins were born. Had you not this book may not have been written.
   I hope you will read and enjoy this tale of Lucy from Twin Willows. It is a strange yarn mixed with truth and memories.
   I am blessed to have you for a cousin on this journey through life.
   Have a peace filled Christmas
      Love Verna Lee

Vlee. of Twin Willows
   12-2011

IN THE SHADE OF A SHADOW OF REASON

A VLEE OF TWIN WILLOWS NOVEL

Verna Lee Hutton-Ely

Copyright © 2011 Verna Lee Hutton-Ely

All rights reserved. No part of this book may be used or reproduced by any means, graphic, electronic, or mechanical, including photocopying, recording, taping or by any information storage retrieval system without the written permission of the publisher and the author except in the case of brief quotations embodied in critical articles and reviews.

WestBow Press books may be ordered through booksellers or by contacting:

WestBow Press
A Division of Thomas Nelson
1663 Liberty Drive
Bloomington, IN 47403
www.westbowpress.com
1-(866) 928-1240

Because of the dynamic nature of the Internet, any web addresses or links contained in this book may have changed since publication and may no longer be valid. The views expressed in this work are solely those of the author and do not necessarily reflect the views of the publisher, and the publisher hereby disclaims any responsibility for them.

ISBN: 978-1-4497-2043-8 (sc)
ISBN: 978-1-4497-2045-2 (hc)
ISBN: 978-1-4497-2044-5 (e)

Library of Congress Control Number: 2011913128

Printed in the United States of America

WestBow Press rev. date: 10/03/2011

My heartfelt gratitude to:

The very talented Richard Biffle – for allowing me to use his painting *Respite* on the cover. I believe the same muse that inspired his creation of the little man inspired my vision of Angus.

Thom Foy – My Editor, My Lance – who found me sitting in a field of despair and made me Queen of a world where Love is possible.

Vern & Irene Ely – My Mom & Dad, abiding now on the other side – for fostering the enchantment that is Twin Willows.

Stacy Munn – My Cosmic Sister and creative advisor – without whose dogged encouragement my dream of completing this book would have gone unfulfilled.

Professor Nicole Pitts – My composition teacher– who encouraged me to write.

Lynn Cardemon – My Dearest Pal – whose courage and determination has been an inspiration.

Veronica Sue Ely Yankovich – The Good Twin (who never lets me forget it) – for sharing the egg that made me us.

Vern Michael David Yankovich – Gorby Guy – for his countless lessons in kindness.

B. Michael Ely & Dustin Ely – My Sons – who listened to my stories on long rides to Grandma & Grandpa's and told me to write them down.

Nancy Newton and Pat Ker – My Readers – for their patience and encouragement.

Mia Kania, Joy & Lauren Courtney – My Frog Sisters – for their examples of friendship regardless of guilt.

Norwood – Sir Woody of Catron – who let me know that he's watching from the other side.

To Alex the Brave, Princess Lia, Buster Boy Charlie, and Sweet Pea Chloe – You light up my life.

The Friends of the Serpent Mound, Delsey and Jeff Wilson, and Larry Henry – Seekers and Guardians.

The staffs and volunteers of the Southfield, West Bloomfield, and Oak Park Public Libraries.

Michael, Lance, and Lucy – I will miss you.

Angus – who wanted his story told.

Most of all Jesus – for His unconditional Love.

Contents

1 – It Begins Again..1
2 – First Meeting...14
3 – The Fairytale...24
4 – Moonlight Becomes You..39
5 – The Fairytale Continued.......................................56
6 – The Painting..64
7 – Benefit of the Doubt..76
8 – Glen Eden...93
9 – Secrets in the Study...108
10 – The Butler..120
11 – Time Times Seven..133
12 – Facing the Truth..142
13 – Waste Not Beauty..155
14 – From Magic Garden to Stonehouse.............................167
15 – Dreams in a Midsummer's Night...............................179
16 – What's Love Got to Do with It?..............................181
17 – A Straw of Hope...185
18 – Fred, Chants, and Charms....................................202
19 – The Knowing Ledge...221
20 – The Great Serpent Mound.....................................232
21 – Angel or Devil, or No Good Deed Goes Unpunished.............246
22 – Brutal Honesty..259
23 – Roller Coaster..277
24 – Look into My Eyes...288
25 – Tuatha De Danaan..300
26 – Confronting Demons..311
27 – Time and Again..319
28 – Shalala...332
29 – Serendipity...342

30 – Resolutions. 353
31 – What Cost Free Will 368
32 – The Day Gets Stranger. 382
33 – Waiting 397
34 – Birthday. 408
35 – Leaf Message 416
Epilogue. 424

1 – It Begins Again

Lucy sat staring into her teacup at the spent tea leaves lying about the bottom. She lived alone, and with no one to talk to she spent most of her time remembering things from days past. Today she remembered that her grandmother used to read tea leaves. After taking the last sip, Grandmother would turn her cup upside down on the saucer and spin it around three times. She'd then turn it upright and peer into it, studying the pattern the leaves had formed on the bottom of the cup. She would say things like, "Oh look here, we are going to have a visitor." Later, when the Fuller Brush salesman showed up at the door, Grandmother told him the tea leaves said he was coming. Grandma told Lucy the tea leaves could show things from the past and from the future. One time she read Lucy's cup and said, "Oh my, there's a strange little man with a message for you." Lucy didn't know what she meant by that, but it was great fun listening to her.

Her grandmother was from Ireland and had been raised having tea every afternoon. This was not tea in a tea bag. No, it was loose-leaf tea that was spooned from a tin into a teapot full of boiling water. There it would steep until it was dark and strong. It was then poured steaming into a cup. Not an ordinary cup and not a mug. A teacup. One made of china with a saucer. "This is the only civilized way to enjoy tea," her grandma would say.

Tea in the late afternoon was a ritual that continued with her grandmother all the days of her life. She passed it on to her daughter, Lucy's mom, who would ofttimes, but not so diligently, sit down to a cup in the afternoon.

Lucy had never been fond of tea as a girl; although when she stayed with her grandparents, she would gladly suffer through a cup so that her leaves could be read. As she grew older, she learned to love the times spent with a good cup. She would now sit in the late afternoons having a cup brewed in the old style. This somehow made her feel in touch with her mother, her grandmother, and all the other generations of women in her bloodline who sat sipping their tea on winter afternoons, perhaps thinking about their mothers and grandmothers.

She carefully placed the old cup adorned with pansies, which had been her mom's favorite, upside down on its saucer. "One, two, three," she said aloud, turning the cup with each count. Carefully uprighting it and placing it again gently on its china mate, she looked into its bottom at the green-brown dregs resting there. The leaves had formed a barn. Not just any barn, it was her Uncle Claude's barn. In her mind's eye she saw the big, old wooden structure painted a bright red. She loved to play in that big old barn with her cousins when she was young. Her Uncle Claude and Aunt Nellie lived on the farm adjacent to her grandparents. On summer days when Lucy and her sister stayed with their grandparents, they would make the quarter-mile walk down the gravel and dirt road to visit their cousins, who had come from a neighboring town to spend time with *their* grandparents.

In the magic of the tea leaves she saw herself climbing up into the loft and jumping down onto the haystack below. She recalled a day in a summer long past when her sister Sue and their cousin Bobby made a ghost out of a sheet, tied it with a rope, and hung it from the rafters. Bobby, who picked on his little sister Deby mercilessly, laid a plan to scare the beejeebers out of her and Lucy. On this day he had talked an accomplice into his mischief. He would take the ghost up into the loft while Sue, Lucy's twin, went to get the other girls to come with her into the barn under the pretense of taking apples to King, Uncle Claude's plow horse, who was old, gray, and worn for as long as Lucy had known him. Once in the barn, Sue would lag behind the other girls and swing shut the big door, chasing out most of the light except for a ray or two that might peek in through missing knots in the old boards.

It was all going quite well. Lucy and Deby entered the barn slightly ahead of Sue who, undetected, switched directions and ran back outside. She slammed shut the old, hinged door and made eerie "Woooo Woooo" noises. Deby clutched tight to Lucy and was just starting to whimper when Bobby let fly the ghost. It worked as planned: both girls screamed in fright. Then something else happened that wasn't in the plan. The ghost and the screams spooked old King. He let out a whinnied scream of his own and kicked a big hole right in the side of the barn. Old boards shattered and went flying in every direction as he took off on a dead run right through the hole and into Aunt Nellie's flower garden, trampling and uprooting rows of her county-fair-blue-ribbon-winning Gladiolas. He then ran amuck through Uncle Claude's blueberry bush nursery, trampling and snapping the young and valuable twigs under hoof.

When Aunt Nellie heard the commotion, she came running from the house. Waving her apron over head, she managed to chase King back to his pasture. When the horse was safely corralled where he could do no more damage, she learned from Deby the mischief that had taken place. She sent the twins back to their grandparents, pointing a finger at Sue and admonishing her with a "shame on you." She led Bobby into the house by his ear with the promise of "a darn good lickin'" when his grandpa got home.

Lucy threw her head back and laughed out loud, recalling this adventure from her childhood. When she looked again into her cup, the barn was gone. In its place the leaves formed something different. She struggled a little to make it out, turning the cup this way and that until… there it was: a magnificent horse rearing on its hind legs. On its back sat a handsome warrior. "Hello there," she heard herself say. Again she laughed.

She carried the cup and saucer to the sink. Turning on the water and reaching for the sponge, she gazed up and out the window. The snow was fresh and bright and lay in blankets on the yard between the house and the blueberry field behind it. Something caught her eye, a movement in the snow. She thought at first it must have been a rabbit and fixed her gaze on the spot under the big evergreen that stood at the far edge of the yard on the border of the field. That's when it happened.

It was that glance, that innocent little curious glance, that would change and rearrange her life forever onward. She didn't realize it at the moment. At the moment she merely thought her eyes were playing tricks on her. She stood still as a stone, staring at the spot in the snow under the evergreen. "No, it couldn't be," she thought, squinting now to make it out more clearly. But the more she focused, the more amazed she became. She blinked and stretched out her hand to wipe the window.

It couldn't be, yet there it was, a little man waving to her from under the tree. Her eyes widened and she bent closer to the pane, holding her breath and pressing her nose against it. There it was all right. He stared back at her for a moment, doffed his hat, jumped under the low-hanging branches, and disappeared. She stood up straight with her mouth agape. She was trying to dismiss what she had just seen. She rolled it around and around in her mind evoking a conversation in her thoughts:

"I must have been daydreaming."

"No, that was no daydream; it was real. I saw it plainly. It was real."

"Real, but what was it? Grandma Cavanagh used to talk about the little people in Ireland. Were they real? Could this be one of them?"

"Now wait a minute! Those were fairy tales, weren't they?"

While this argument was taking place in her head, she stood staring, hoping to get another glance at what caused this breach of her peace. Finally realizing it must be gone, she turned away and turned her thoughts to what she should do about it. Should she tell someone? Who? What would she say? Her head was spinning. She sat back down at the table. She thought it all out again, trying to understand what had just taken place. Had she really seen a little man under the tree? Her mind gave her no doubt; yes, she certainly had. She knew what she saw, but what was it? It defied logic. She was always so logical, and this, well, this was beyond anything she had thought of for quite a while. As a child she had played with make-believe fairies. They *were* make-believe, weren't they? She tried to remember, but she had been too young. There were too many years and life experiences crowding her mind for her to remember clearly anything of that early time. Maybe there was something to those fairy stories she had heard as a child. There was of course Tom Thumb. He was real, a human anomaly. Lucy had seen a picture of him in the World Book Encyclopedia. But Tom Thumb at his full-grown height of forty inches was a giant compared to what she'd just seen.

She wanted so badly to tell someone. Maybe she should call her son, Dustin. No, he'd be at work in some meeting or on the phone with a buyer or colleague.

She was always uncomfortable calling him at work; he was always so busy. Besides, what would she say? "Hello, honey. I just called to say I saw a little man under a tree in the backyard." No, she couldn't do that. He was already set against her decision to move into the country all by herself. If she told him now that she had seen something this odd, he would probably insist she move back to the city. She wouldn't tell anyone right now. But she would write it down, document it. Maybe someone else had seen this thing, or something like it. It could be important, and she wouldn't want to forget about it. Not that she could. She had seen it, and it had captured her thoughts. Though she didn't know it right then, she would not be free from thinking of it until someone else filled her mind. She found a pencil and an old notebook with a green, brushed velvet cover. In it she wrote this:

> *January 19, 2008*
> *I saw it under the evergreen tree in the backyard. It appeared to be some sort of little creature, man-like. I have no idea just what it was, or exactly how big it was, probably only the size of a small rabbit. It was dressed in odd garb: an earth-brown colored jacket, dark green pants, high brown boots, and a tall red hat whose point flopped forward. It had a long gray beard that tapered down to its waist or somewhat lower. I only saw it for a long moment, yet I am sure I saw it, and I believe it saw me too because it waved and then jumped out of sight under the low hanging branches.*

After she wrote this, she went back to the window to resume her vigil, barely moving. Finally, she dragged a stool in from another room and sat it in front of the sink so she could maintain her watchfulness in some comfort. She climbed atop and waited for another sighting. But she saw nothing else, save for a rabbit that ran out from under the same tree. It scurried forth as if something had frightened it and ran into the blueberry patch where it finally disappeared from her view.

The thought came to her during her watch that she should go have a look-see under the tree. She soon dispensed with that idea, reasoning that by the time she dressed for the below-zero weather and ventured out through the knee-high snowdrifts, any good light from the sinking sun would be gone. Besides, what would she do if she did find this little visitor? Other questions occurred to her: had it waved or had it beckoned? Should she be afraid? It didn't seem to be threatening. How could a little thing like that hurt her? Yet there is always fear of the unknown. But was it unknown? Something else crept through her mind: although on one hand she was quite sure she had never seen such a thing before, on the other she was beginning to think of it as familiar in some way. "How odd," she thought.

The dark settled in around six p.m. and she could no longer see past the big bridal wreath bush that sat close to the house. Reluctantly, she gave up her post. She wandered into the phone room and sat upon the daybed. Dustin might be home from the office now. She picked up the phone and dialed his number. But before she heard it ring, she slammed the handset down. "Better not," she thought. She wanted so badly to tell someone, to share this incredible event. If only her husband were alive. He would have believed her. He would have shared her excitement, and together they would have made an investigation of it. She closed her eyes and imagined telling him.

"God, I miss you," she let herself say aloud.

He was a fine generous man with a heart of gold, though she had not always thought of him so. He had provided her with a good life and had given her two wonderful sons. They had been happy together. He died when the small plane he was piloting crashed and exploded on impact on an island in the Outer Hebrides. Dustin had just graduated college at the time and was still living in Dublin. He was supposed to return home with his father after his father's business was concluded. Their other son and his new bride were on a mission trip to Siberia. Since there was no body and not even ashes could be found in the debris, especially after two weeks of a torrential downpour at the remote site of the accident, Lucy opted not to have a funeral. Instead, a Mass was offered at the university chapel at Dustin's school, of which his father—and his father before him—were alumni.

Lucy returned to the States with Dustin, and Dustin's brother flew back to the mission field. After two years, Lucy sold the big house where the family lived on Grosse Ile and moved back to Twin Willows, the house her father built and where she had lived as a child.

"Stacy," she thought. "I'll call Stacy." She thumbed through her address book until she came upon the number. Stacy had been her friend since she started Junior College in Grand Rapids. They shared an apartment for a short time until Stacy moved back home to help care for her dad, who was dying of cancer.

It was at that same time Stacy met a tall handsome soldier just home on leave from Vietnam. He walked up to her and announced, "You are the woman I want to marry." Although at the time she thought it was just a clever pick-up line, it proved true. They dated for a brief period, and he went back to the war. He wrote to her frequently, always proclaiming his love and his intentions for when his tour of duty was over. The day of Greg's release came, and he went straightaway to Stacy's father, who had his whole life been a devout Catholic and insisted his daughter marry within the faith. The answer was as Stacy expected: Greg must convert so they could marry in the Church.

Greg, who believed in God but not organized religion, told him that if he did convert just so he could marry Stacy, he would be a hypocrite and that would not bring honor to their marriage or to God. So a stalemate took place, which Lucy was instrumental in breaking.

She, in those days, had also been turned against organized religion. As a result, she applied for and received an ordination from the Universal Life Church.

This gave her authority, the same as a minister from any other denomination, to go into jails and hospitals and talk with people she may not have otherwise gained access to. This was during the period of the horrendous war in Vietnam. The nation was terribly divided, and a lot of young men were fleeing to Canada or being sent to jail for refusing to report for the draft. Lucy wanted to be able to minister to the ones in prison and to the ones who had been sent back horribly wounded to convalesce in understaffed, ill-prepared V.A. hospitals.

Lucy mentioned to Stacy that she could legally marry them in an outdoor ceremony that might appease both Greg and her father. Greg went for the idea right away, but Stacy's dad took a little convincing. Lucy agreed to meet with him to show him her credentials and talk about her beliefs and the type of ceremony she would perform. Although still a little skeptical, he gave his consent. He realized that his time was growing short, and if he wanted to be at his daughter's wedding and see her happily married, it needed to happen soon. Besides, as Lucy pointed out to him, Greg was a really good man who loved his daughter deeply.

On a beautiful summer day, the wedding was held in the far backyard of Stacy's parents' home, where the lawn brushed the banks of a sweet little stream. Friends of the bride and groom brought guitars and sang folk standards, with gospel and other love songs mingled in. Lucy selected passages from the New Testament and read from Khalil Gibran's *The Prophet*. The bride and groom exchanged vows they themselves had written. And so it was that in the presence of God, friends, and family Lucy pronounced the two officially and legally wed. At the end of the ceremony, Stacy's father embraced Lucy and thanked her for the beautiful service. With tearful eyes, he proclaimed he now felt at peace knowing his daughter was married, in the eyes of God, to a good man who would take care of her.

"Hello, this is Stacy."

"Hey, kiddo, thanks for the lovely meditation you sent me."

"No problem. Did you get the book I told you about?"

"No, not yet. I'm going into South Haven tomorrow, so I'll see if they have it at the library."

"Oh Lucy, you just have to read that book. I mean, Lucy, you have to! Promise me you will."

"Stacy, I promise. If South Haven doesn't have it, I'll have Dustin get it in the city and bring it to me."

"Okay, that's good because it will blow you away. I mean totally blow your mind." Stacy was always urging her to read some book or another, and vice versa. They each considered the other to be a soul sister, closer in likes and dislikes than their own biological siblings.

"I *want* to read it. I'll get it, I promise. But I've called to tell you something pretty strange."

"Oh yeah, what's that?"

"This might be a little hard for you to believe, but I swear it happened. I've been dying to tell someone. I didn't think anyone would believe me. Then I thought about you."

"Oh boy, this should be a good one. Come on, let's have it. My curiosity is piqued."

"Earlier today... well... I saw something."

"You saw something? Okay, what did you see?"

"It was a little man." Lucy recounted the whole event, including that she thought it may have beckoned to her. Stacy was silent when she finished.

"Stacy, did you hear me?"

"Yes, I did."

Lucy waited for more but it didn't come. She worried because her friend had become uncharacteristically quiet. "Well, what do you think?"

"What do I think? Hmm... let's see. I think that it's good you didn't go outside. After all, you don't know what it is or what it wants."

"So you believe me."

"Sure, of course I do. I mean, I'm not saying I could see it. Maybe only you can."

"So you think I'm crazy?"

"No, Lucy. Come on, that's not fair. I know you all too well for that. I don't think you're crazy." She cackled a wicked little laugh then added, "I know you're crazy."

"Thanks a lot, girlfriend."

"What I mean to say is there are all sorts of stories about people seeing aliens, people seeing angels, people seeing fairies and stuff. I have never seen anything you could term as unearthly or supernatural. But that doesn't mean I don't believe they exist. I think certain people may have the ability to see things that others can't. I wish sometimes I could see more or know more. But I believe God gives us the sight or insight He wants each of us to have. He wants us to seek the truth, but if we are truly in His will, then I think He will reveal what we need to know. Get my point?"

"I do, I guess." Now Lucy was uncharacteristically silent.

"Lucy, I'm telling you, you have to get that book. It's very weird that you're telling me this now. I don't want to say any more. Just get a hold of it, okay? I have to go. Greg is tapping his foot by the door; we're picking up a friend of his and going to a full moon celebration bonfire. I've made a Thermos of your special hot chocolate to take with us."

"Love that hot chocolate," Greg yelled from the background.

"Call me and let me know when you get the book," Stacy said.

"I will."

"Oh yeah, and call me if you see your little friend again. But promise me you won't go outside alone looking for it. Promise?"

"Promise, with my fingers crossed."

"Fine then. I know when I'm talking to a stone. We have to go. Love you."

From the background Lucy heard Greg shout, "Love you too, Lucy girl. Come see us."

"Love you both. I'll come down in the spring."

Lucy loved going to their cabin on a mountaintop in North Carolina. They bought the land years ago and used it for a camping site until one time they decided they didn't want to be anywhere else. So they disposed of all their property and obligations and stayed right there. They lived in a popup camper until the cabin was complete enough to move into. God was good and provided both of them with jobs in the area.

Lucy prayed silently as she hung up the phone. "Thank you, dear Lord, for my good friends. Watch over and protect them and draw us all ever nearer to you. Amen."

Well then, there it was. She had told someone. She felt better somehow. She walked out into the breezeway and stoked the fire. Sitting before it in her grandmother's old rocking chair, she thought of possibilities. If it was a little man—and she was sure it was—where had it come from? Exactly what was it? An alien? Some other sort of race that shared this planet with us yet was previously undiscovered or forgotten? Was it a fairy? Fairy stories used to be quite common; although in recent years she hadn't heard any. Even in Ireland and Scotland, where fairy legends are plentiful, people only recount tales of things their parents or grandparents said they'd seen. After what she saw today, she had to rethink everything. If the little guy was a fairy, or even something else, it made her wonder what other old bedtime stories were actually real. Maybe there *were* fairies, and if fairies then elves, trolls, goblins, maybe even unicorns. After all, like Stacy said, just because only certain people could see them didn't mean they weren't real. She thought of all these possibilities until sleep summoned her, and she went off to bed.

The next day, she braved a very cold Michigan winter day to drive into South Haven to do some grocery shopping and meet a friend for soup at their favorite little restaurant. Lucy and Lynn had been very close through their high school days and for a year or so after. They'd lost touch when Lucy moved to California. Years later, when she moved back to Twin Willows, Lucy found Lynn working at McKenzie's bakery cafe in town. It was great renewing a friendship with someone who knew her from her life long ago, a life that she had mostly forgotten.

Lynn had never married, though she came close a few times. Each time, a tragedy befell her intended. After they graduated from L.C. Mohr High School in South Haven, Lynn got engaged to a guy she had gone steady with for most of her senior year. He had gone to Holland to a basketball game with some buddies. He was supposed to meet up with her later at the Edgar Allan Poe teen dance club, an old converted funeral parlor where Lynn had gone dancing with Lucy and their friend Jane. But he never showed up, and later they learned he had been killed when the car he was in tried to beat a train through a crossing.

Twice again over the years, Lynn came close to marriage, but each time some foul act ended the life of her fiancé. One drowned at a local swimming hole where he had gone swimming since he was a small child. A crack in the old dam caused a vacuum that sucked him under. And even though he was with a bunch of friends, they didn't get to him until it was too late. Her last fiancé was blown away by a shotgun blast as he strolled out of a bar where he had stopped to use a payphone to call her. He didn't even drink. It had been a case of mistaken identity. The man that shot him thought he was a guy that had hustled him at pool the night before. It was a classic case of being in the wrong place at the wrong time.

After that, Lynn resigned from trying to find happiness, thinking she must be cursed and would only bring disaster to anyone who loved her. She opted instead for a life of service to her family, taking care of her older sister who had fallen ill with encephalitis after a mosquito bite, and then later caring for both her mother and father in the ravages of old age. Now she lived alone, except for her dog Molly, who accompanied her everywhere.

Lucy hadn't intended to mention the little man to Lynn, thinking it might be a bit much for her to accept. But they soon settled in to their comfort zone, chit-chatting over a cup of hot cocoa. And by the time the soup was at the table, Lucy had delivered her fantastic tale and waited to see what reaction would be forthcoming from her old friend. She was shocked when Lynn asked, "Is it the same little man you saw with that strange guy you dated before you left for San Francisco?"

"What on earth are you talking about?"

"The guy you were all gaga over before you left for the coast. Oh, what was his name? You met him up in Saugatuck, remember? It was an odd name. I mean, uncommon. Oh gee, what was it?" She went silent trying to think of it.

"Do you mean Ashley?" Lucy questioned, not that she had ever been "gaga" over him. At least she had never admitted it to anyone.

"No, no, not Ashley."

"Who then? Who are you talking about?" Lucy pressed.

"Geez, Lucy, that was a long time ago. How do you expect me to remember if you don't?"

Lucy felt a chilling sensation creep into her bones. She knew she had lost parts of her memory after suffering a blow to her head from a fall while visiting Cornwall with her husband. She had gone out hiking alone to take photos while he attended to some business. When she didn't return as planned, he searched and found her unconscious near the base of the dolmen Chûn Quoit. They assumed she had been climbing on the boulders and taken a tumble. She wondered if this was why the little man had somehow seemed familiar to her. Had she encountered him before?

Lynn could recall no further details and was getting annoyed by her friend's insistence that she try to remember, so Lucy left it drop.

After lunch, she stopped by the library to check for the book Stacy had mentioned. As she had suspected, they didn't have it. After gassing up the car, she found herself anxious to get back to Twin Willows. Her thoughts kept drifting to the little man and the possibility that maybe she had seen him before. Maybe, crazy as it seemed, he had some sort of message for her. Isn't that what her grandmother had read long ago in her tea leaves? *A little man is coming with a message for you.* She admonished herself for this thinking and tried to chase the thoughts from her head. She turned on the car radio, already tuned to a local Christian music station, and sang out loudly the words to a popular praise song. It almost worked.

Back at Twin Willows, she put the groceries away, never failing to glance out the window over the sink every time she strolled past it. But there were no new sightings.

One day passed, then two, then three, one week and on and on. Still she would catch herself standing and staring out the window; she rather enjoyed thinking about the possibility of seeing it again. After all, she had seen something quite extraordinary, something that maybe she had seen before but simply could not remember. On any count, she was determined that, if she did see it again, she would signal somehow to let it know she would like to communicate. What secrets could she learn from such an encounter?

When after three weeks there had not been another sighting, she worried that she'd never see it again. This made her feel unsettled, sad in some way. She had started to hope that it had come especially for her, to deliver a message maybe, or impart a secret wisdom. She liked thinking that. It made her feel special somehow, something she had not felt since her husband died. She didn't think she was being unreasonable. "After all," she told herself, "it saw me and signaled instead of just running off."

The end of February neared. The snow from the lake effect around Twin Willows was piled high, and the days were short on sunshine. She bundled up to walk to the end of the driveway to fetch her mail. This exercise was her daily early-afternoon routine. If the weather would allow it, she would walk all the way to the old school on the corner, a quarter mile away.

The little one-room brick schoolhouse she had attended as a child was the same little school where her mother and father had met when they were young. Crow school had been one of the last of such schools to operate in the country. Although closed and boarded up since the early seventies, it contained some of her fondest childhood memories. It was these memories she would conjure on her walks. She had made this same trek every day of her school life, from kindergarten through twelfth grade graduation. Though the little school was only through the eighth grade, even after she left it to attend high school in South Haven, the bus would pick her up right there on the corner in front of it, right by the massive stone boulder to which she now walked.

She had consumed many peanut butter and jelly sandwiches while sitting on that old stone, had played many games of king on the mountain, had crouched behind it for games of hide and seek, had gotten her first kiss from Glenn Cole, and had sat atop it weeping when her older sister left home to elope. Though it stood right there on that corner for years, Lucy always thought of it as her stone. Davy Kilpatrick told her once that his grandmother warned him never to sit on it because fairies had enchanted it, and if you sat on it you gave them permission to take you. "Huh?" Lucy murmured out loud, remembering this long forgotten story. Nevertheless, she walked over to it and gave it a fond pat as was her custom on these walks. Then she turned and headed for home.

She walked briskly as the wind picked up and blew the powdery snow into drifts across the road that had been freshly plowed that morning. The banks at the sides of the road were piled so high in some places that the wind blowing across them hurled little ice crystals right into her face. The muffler she had tied across her nose and mouth was already glazed, and the visibility in the swirling white was getting worse. She never tired of this walk, as there was always something to see, some sort of wildlife scampering, flying, bolting, or bounding here or there, be it cardinals, wild turkeys, squirrels, rabbits, or deer. She looked forward to these walks, especially this time of year, to get fresh air and much-needed exercise.

Back at the point where the drive met the road, Lucy stopped and collected the mail from the very same box her father set when he first built the house. The wooden post that held it up had been replaced several times through the years. Since it sat so close to the road, it was an unwitting target for the county snowplow once snow drifted high enough to cover it from sight. The box itself had a few dings and dents from the same calamities, though it had been carefully bumped back into shape and received a fresh coat of paint every few years to conceal the scars from snowplow and age. The most recent layer of paint, applied just last summer, was still a crisp white coat. The words TWIN WILLOWS had been written in Lucy's best paintbrush script in forest green across both sides. From inside the box, she pulled out a sales flyer, the electric bill, and a postcard inviting her to her cousin Kathy's Tupperware party a week from Tuesday. She casually strolled back up the drive to the garage.

She and Sue had helped their father build the old garage when they were eight. The twins carried lumber or fetched nails or helped in whatever way they could because they loved being with their dad, even though that usually meant working hard. He was never one to sit still.

For thirty-one years he worked the early shift and most Saturdays at the National Motors foundry in town. He'd arrive home at 3:30 every afternoon, black from the smoke of the furnace that he stood by, chipping the slag from automobile motor heads as they came smoldering past him on an overhead line. He'd wash his face and hands, have a cup of coffee, and head for the fields of his small farm. There was always something to do. He loved farming, but there was just no way to make a living at it as his father had done before him. So he surrendered his days to the heat and smoke of the factory.

It was a two-car garage, though she never remembered two cars ever being parked in it at one time. "Not fancy but functional," her dad said when he eyed the finished building.

When she was ten, her dad, again with the help of his family, built the breezeway portion of the house. It was a large room, almost doubling the size of the family's living space, connecting the formerly freestanding garage to the house. It had windows across the east and west sides. In this room, you could sit having your coffee in the morning and watch the sun's ascent over the woods to the east. When dusk approached, you could sit sipping your tea while viewing the magnificent colors filling in the spaces between the blueberry rows to the west as the sun retired for the day. The double glass storm windows that kept out the harsh winter wind were taken down and replaced with screens in the summer months to catch the cool breeze blowing from across Lake Michigan. This room had seen many changes over the years. It was the one most utilized by the family.

Her father, with the help of his brother, laid the fireplace on the south wall of the breezeway with stones they had collected through many seasons of plowing their fields. Here and there a special stone was mortared in place, one not gathered from the farms nearby but collected as souvenirs from different places family or friends visited. There were two stones from the badlands of South Dakota that her Uncle Claude brought back from his vacation there. There was a stone from Roswell, New Mexico donated to the cause by a neighbor who drove the distance to see a new grandchild. There were several puddingstones from Drummond Island where her Uncle Leo had a hunting cabin. But the one stone that her father was most proud of was a large black polished-looking stone with two crystal clusters in it. He said it had fallen out of the sky and landed at his feet while he was hoeing cucumbers late one Sunday afternoon on the back of his farm. He claimed it was an omen because the twins were born nine months to the day later. Moreover, he and his wife believed they could have no other children because it had been eleven years since the twins' older sister was born.

Lucy decided to grab the shovel and push back some of the snow that was still drifting across the drive. As she scooped the white fluff and threw it up on the steadily growing mounds at the sides, she noticed funny little marks in the snow. She bent down, trying to make out what kind of little animal or bird could have made them. A chill of excitement ran down her spine as she realized just what she was looking at. They weren't animal tracks at all. They were tiny boot prints! They laid a trail out to the old barn and beyond. "This trail must have been made by the little man, or one such as he," she thought. Without giving any consideration to what she was doing, she threw down the shovel and began following the tracks. She trudged past the old barn and followed them through the berry patch, through the old apple orchard, up the hill, into the pine glen, and down the hill until they led into a thicket that she could not pass through.

Her excitement of possibly seeing the little man again kept her attention focused on the trail she was following and not on how far she had wandered. When she looked about, she didn't recognize where she was. The wind was swirling the snow around her and covering even the tracks she had just laid. "That means," she reasoned, "the little guy must be just ahead of me, or his tracks would have been covered. She called out, "Hello... Hello." She listened hard but heard no reply. Her feet were freezing and her forehead was beginning to sting. She pulled down the hood of her coat to shield her face a little more, but the wind's chill blew right through her. She called out again, hoping to hear a strange little voice. But when no reply came, she turned and started walking in the direction she thought was home.

She grew up wandering these hills—these woods—yet now she felt lost, out of place. She picked up her pace. She remembered the time when she was nine and was playing in these woods with Sue. A storm came up much like this one. They became disoriented and wandered in circles. Their dad went out to search for them while their mom stayed home to honk the horn on the canary yellow 1956 Ford station wagon that had been her father's first brand new car and the reason he built the garage. They heard the horn and followed the sound toward home. She wished she could hear that horn now.

She kept her head down and leaned into the wind as she battled it to move forward. She hoped she was going in the right direction. The visibility in the swirling snow was pretty much nil. She felt fear creep upon her, but she knew what to do. She offered a silent prayer: "Lord, lead me home."

No sooner had she made this request when something grabbed at her arm. "Oh, thank you, sweet Jesus," she said aloud when she realized that it was the branches of a big old blueberry bush that had grabbed her. She walked down the long row praising her Lord. The massive old bushes she helped her father plant as tiny twigs were shielding her now from the harshness of the winter wind and leading her home. She left their protection and came out of the field into her backyard right by the tree where she first saw the little man.

Once in the house, she brewed a cup of tea. Sitting at the table sipping it with her feet in a pan of warm water, she wrote once again in the old green journal just below her first entry.

February 19, 2008

Found tiny boot prints in the snow. I followed them for nearly two hours until they disappeared into a thicket. I have the feeling that he knew I was following and that he was leading me somewhere...

She thought a moment and wrote

...maybe to my doom.

2 – First Meeting

◦᥈◦ Years ago she found herself in a meadow with no recollection of how she had gotten there. The sky was a brilliant blue with puffy white clouds gently floating here and there. She squinted up at the sun and beheld something she'd never seen before. It was approximately one of her hand lengths below the sun's position in the sky. She shaded her eyes, trying to get a good look at the shrinking phenomenon. To her reasoning, it appeared to be a hole in the sky, and around it were two colored bands, one pink and one blue, like two shades snatched from a rainbow. They framed the oval opening in the heavens, which continued to grow smaller. The inside of the hole appeared to be a milky whitish-blue, not at all the color of the sky or clouds. It was more like the color of a lace veil across a doorway. As she strained her eyes to watch it, it shrank to a mere spot and then, poof, it was gone.

She heard a voice: "Hey there, are you all right? Do you need help?" She looked in the direction of the voice to see a man standing on a hill in the distance. Her eyes were adjusting from the brightness they had been staring into, so she couldn't see him clearly. She was dazed and confused. She didn't know where she was, let alone how she had gotten there. He called to her again, "May I come over there? I don't want to frighten you. Are you hurt?"

"I... I'm fine, I th... think," Lucy managed.

As he walked toward her, she saw he was dressed in hiking clothes: khaki shirt and shorts with boots. He wore an Outback-type hat with a pheasant-feather band. She started to stand up, but her legs were too weak. Noticing her trouble as he drew closer to her, he said again, "Are you all right, miss?"

Lucy's senses were waking up. She felt a burning on her right elbow and noticed it was bruised and skinned in a patch the size of a quarter. As her head cleared and she looked about, she began to recognize her surroundings. She was in a meadow where she often came to gather wildflowers. It was in a state game reserve about seven miles from her apartment. She stared at the stranger walking toward her and noticed how good-looking he was. He was tan, about 5' 10" with an athletic build. He had blond, wavy hair that hung almost to his shoulders, a mustache and a short beard. Around his neck hung a silver cross on a silver chain and a small leather pouch dangling from braided thongs. But what she noticed most were his eyes: they were the greenest eyes she had ever seen, the color of oak leaves in the spring.

She stood up, but her legs were shaky. As she started to swoon, he caught her by the arm. "Ouch," she cried, pulling away.

"Oh, sorry. I'm sorry. You *are* hurt," he said, looking at her wounded elbow. "Let me see that. Here, sit down." He gestured her toward a log not far from where they stood. She took a few steps, sat down, and stretched her arm out for his inspection. He knelt on one knee in front of her and gently examined her wounded extremity, moving it carefully up and down and turning it from side to side. "Well, you've lost some skin and have a nasty bruise, but I don't think it's broken. What happened to you?" he asked with concern in his voice.

Lucy was still foggy on that point and replied, "I wish I knew."

He offered her a canteen he took from a pouch on his belt. "Would you like a drink of water?"

"Yes, please," she replied, feeling very thirsty all of a sudden. She took the canteen, tipped it toward her open mouth and swallowed several times. "Thank you," she said, handing it back. "You're very kind."

He smiled broadly. "Yes, well, I'm trying to convince the Good Lord to install a Jacuzzi in the mansion he's building for me." He pointed with one finger to heaven.

Lucy giggled; she liked that odd response. She began feeling like herself. She tried to remember what had happened. She had seen something out the window of her apartment and ran outside. Just what she saw and how she came to be in the meadow was still beyond her. She related these facts to him, and when she finished added, "I'm sorry. I know this sounds strange."

"You are talking to the wrong person to judge strange, my lady." His words seemed genuine and sympathetic.

This guy is a charmer, she thought, looking into his beautiful green eyes. He raised his hand toward her face, pulling a small twig from her hair. She held her breath as he did, feeling a sudden strong attraction to him. She looked away, almost embarrassed, and said, "Really, I can't remember anything. Isn't that silly?"

"Do you think it could be a dream, then?" he asked. "Because I think I'm in one."

"Maybe," she heard herself say, looking into his eyes again. They both smiled. He turned away this time and sat on the log next to her, handing her the water again. She took another drink, and they sat quietly for a moment or two. Lucy felt oddly safe—here in this beautiful meadow with this man she had never seen before—even in these strange circumstances. "Maybe this *is* a dream," she thought.

A rabbit suddenly darted out from the hollow end of the log where they sat. He jumped up and shouted after it, "Angus, you old scut. What have you to do with this?"

"You talk to rabbits?" she asked.

"That one I am acquainted with. But that's a story for another time. Do you think you can walk now?"

She rose as if commanded and stood before him. "Well, I know the rabbit's name is Angus, but I don't know yours."

"Lance McKellen at your bidding and service." As he spoke he removed his hat and bowed to her. "May I have the pleasure of knowing you by name, then?"

"You may, kind sir. It's Lucy." She smiled, offering her hand. "Lucy Cavanagh."

"Lucy," he repeated, returning his hat to his head and taking her hand in both of his. He smiled into her eyes and gave a nod. "I'm certainly glad you dropped into this meadow and into my life." He loosed her hand and repeated, "Do you think you can walk some?"

Lucy suddenly felt confused again. "Dropped into this meadow? What do you mean *dropped*?"

"Well, how else did you get here? You haven't offered a better explanation, and I did see a heaven hole closing up right over the top of where you were sitting."

"You saw it too?"

"Aye, I did. I thought to myself, 'she must be an angel then, and dropped down to bless my life a bit.'"

This talk made her smile. "An angel? I'm no angel. I am quite sure of that. Are you sure you aren't the angel dropped down from that opening to save me?"

"So you need saving, then?" he asked. "And just what is it you need saving from?"

"I don't know. I don't know anything for sure right now. I don't even know how I got here. I can't remember." She was beginning to feel anxious. Tears welled in her eyes. "I can't... I can't remember," she cried.

"Hey, hey," he said, putting his hands on her shoulders. "It will be fine. It's not how we get somewhere that counts, but what we do after we get there." Once again he had calmed her with his voice, and once again he repeated his question, slowly this time: "Do you think you can walk? My truck is parked about a mile up the trail. I could give you a ride somewhere, if you like."

Lucy sniffed, rubbed her eyes and nodded. She liked his voice and the unusual way he had of talking. "So, what now?" she jested. "Are you going for a deck on that mansion of yours?"

"Would be nice." He threw his head back and laughed. "I like you, Lucy Cavanagh." He reached for her hand and they started hiking through the tall grass. She still felt dazed as he led her. She didn't mind that he had taken her hand; she liked it. When they reached the clearing of the trail, he asked if she wanted to rest.

"No, I'm fine. Just confused. What time is it anyway?"

Lance glanced over toward the horizon. "It must be going on five."

"What?" she gasped. "Five?"

"About that," he replied.

She started feeling a little dizzy again. "I think I ran outside about ten this morning."

"Lucy, what day do you think this is?" he asked over his shoulder as he pulled her along.

"Day?" She strained to recall. "It's Tuesday."

Lance stopped and looked at her. This time she saw concern on his face. "Lucy, it's Thursday."

"What? Thursday? Oh!"

He saw her go white. Again he put his hands on her shoulders. "Hey, don't panic. Let's just get you home so we can figure this out."

She shut her eyes tight. She was trying to remember so hard it made her brain hurt. She swayed a little.

"Lucy," he said, shaking her gently. "It will be okay, I promise."

She didn't know why, but she believed him. She opened her eyes and saw his.

"Come on now, take a deep breath and talk to me."

"I don't know what to say."

"Then maybe I'll share something with you. Are you listening?"

"Yes," she said.

"I don't believe I found you by accident. I believe I was meant to find you. Is this too much?"

"Meant to? What do you mean?"

"I'd like to go on, but it's sort of a long tale, and I think we'd be better for it if we put some distance between us and this place right now." His glance darted from side to side. "I don't mean to scare you, but if you could just trust me on this."

"I'm not sure why, but I do trust you," she replied.

"Good, then let's go." He tugged her hand again and bolted off at a quicker pace. She did her best to keep up, and in less than ten minutes they were at his truck. It was old but in good shape. It was silver—a bright, shiny, metallic silver. He pulled out his keys, unlocked the door and opened it for her. She climbed in as he reached behind the seat and produced an Indian print blanket. "Here," he said, "put this around your shoulders. You are shaking."

She did as she was told and noticed for the first time that she indeed felt cold. She also noticed for the first time that he had a large hunting knife, sheathed, hanging from his belt. He shut her door and ran around to the driver's side. He hesitated before climbing in. He looked down and toward the back of the truck and said something low in a language she didn't understand. She surveyed the area as he backed out and drove away from the parking spot, but she saw nothing save for a rabbit. She wondered if it was the same one, Angus.

As they reached the main drive he looked over at her and asked, "Which way now, Miss Cavanagh?"

She was still dazed and not paying attention. She was just letting him transport her. "What?" she asked.

"Which way do I turn here?"

"Oh, right." She looked around. "Go left."

"Left it is." As soon as he completed the turn, he reached over, put his hand on hers and squeezed it a little. "You are still pretty cold. I'll put up the heater for you."

"Thanks," she said, not moving her hand.

"This isn't the first time, is it Lucy?"

"What?"

"The first time you have lost track of things?"

"What?" she repeated, with a little more surprise in her voice. She moved her hand.

"I'm guessing here Lucy that this isn't the first time you have found yourself off somewhere that you couldn't actually remember getting to. Am I right?"

"What?" she said a third time, more indignantly. How could he possibly know that? Who was this guy? "Who are you?" she demanded.

He smiled and winked at her. "Have you forgotten me so soon, darlin'? I'm Lance. Lance McKellen. I'm the one that found you sitting in the middle of the meadow back there."

"I know that," she said sharply, "and you know very well what I meant. How did you know that I've had other… er… there'd been other times when I…" she stuttered, "when I, uh… couldn't…" she paused.

He finished for her: "…couldn't remember how you had gotten somewhere?"

"How did you know that?"

"Angus told me."

"Angus? The rabbit?"

"The very same."

"Look, Lance, you seem to think this is all very funny. But to be honest, I have had a rough day, or I guess three, and I'm not finding any humor in this at all. I'm tired and I'm confused and I'd like to know how a perfect stranger knows so much about me."

"Perfect?" Lance repeated. "You think I'm perfect?" he asked with mischief in his voice and a twinkle in his eye.

"Perfectly maddening," she shot back.

"Well now, that might not be too far from the truth. Is it here that I turn, or would you like me to keep going?"

Lucy looked up and realized where they were. "Yes, turn here. Or did you know that already?" She was being sarcastic now.

"I guessed you might live in Saugatuck from the 'Butler' insignia on your shirt."

Of course, she thought, *the Butler shirt. I'm an idiot.* "I work there." Her voice softened. "You know the Butler?"

"A buddy of mine used to tend bar there: Ashley Randall. Do you know him? Is he still there?"

"Sure, I know him. All the girls who work there are in love with him."

Lance laughed. "Of course they are. He can cast a fair spell. He has the gift of eloquence, you know. He's kissed the Blarney stone. I watched him do it."

"And you, Lance, have you puckered up against the cold rock and received the gift yourself?"

Lance looked at her with a big smile and said, "Well now, darlin', since I've gone and told a tale on ol' Ashley, we'll let him tell you one on me. If you care, that is, to mention my name when he is around."

"This is my place," she burst out, "the grey one." They had come down the big hill off the main road toward the heart of the little town. Lucy lived just around the last bend before the road headed straight for the river. It was a big, old, one-family house built in the late 1800's that had been converted into three apartments sometime in the 1950's, two downstairs and one up. Lucy's was on the bottom east side of the house. It was a small but cozy two-room place. It had a big kitchen and a large living room with a hideaway bed.

Lucy showed Lance where to park his truck since there was no driveway. When these houses were built, the only access was along the river. Years later, a portion of the hill was cut away to accommodate a two-lane road, and what used to be the houses' back doors became their fronts. He pulled up on the opposite side of the road at the base of the big hill where every two to three houses a space had been scooped out for parking spots. An old church sat atop the hill. The access drive to it was further up the road and wound back and forth up the hill before emptying into a parking lot behind the building. The church was built facing the southwest so boaters entering the river off Lake Michigan could see the imposing steeple. There were stone steps near where Lance parked that snaked up the incline for those who wished—as Lucy always did—to walk up.

"Grand old church," Lance said, craning his head in the windshield to look up.

"The bells chime out hymns. They're beautiful, really, though I used to hate it when I first moved here. I work every Saturday night and usually help close the bar, so I don't get home till around three a.m. By the time I'm off to sleep, it's near four. And every Sunday at seven sharp the bells start tolling every half hour. Then at nine o'clock they go constant with hymns, ending with a call to worship at ten." She slid out of the truck, folded the blanket and returned it behind the seat. She shut her door and started to cross the road. She noticed he hadn't gotten out, and she remembered she hadn't asked him in, said goodbye, or even thanked him.

"Lance," she said, walking to the driver's side of the truck, "would you like to come in for a while, maybe have a cup of tea?"

"I was hoping you would ask." He hopped out of the truck and grabbed his pack from the bed as he passed. He took her arm as they waited for the traffic to clear so they could cross the street. As they walked up to her door, she stopped short. The door stood slightly ajar. Lance dropped his pack, pushed her aside, and swung it open with one hand while his other reached for his knife. He went through the little apartment quickly, checking behind every large piece of furniture and in every nook and cranny big enough for someone to hide. "We're okay, then," he said, returning to her after only a few moments. After sheathing his knife, he picked up his pack and took her arm again, coaxing her inside.

Since there was no one in the apartment and there seemed to be nothing missing or out of order, Lucy guessed she had left the door open when she ran outside to see... to see... She still couldn't remember. She let out a long sigh and sat down in her grandma's old rocker. It was the one piece of furniture that was hers; the rest came with the apartment when she rented it. The furniture was old but of good quality, antiques most. The walls in the living room were knotty pine on the bottom half and wallpaper in an off-white, flowered motif of burgundy, mauve, and yellow roses on the top half. The ceiling, which was unusually high, had ornate, mauve-colored molding encircling it. On the east outer wall was a big stone fireplace with a highly polished oak mantel and bookshelves on both sides.

Lucy put her head down with her face in her hands. She was trying to clear her thoughts.

"Hey now, how are you doing?" he asked, squatting down in front of her.

She looked into his beautiful eyes and sighed again. "I'm tired, I'm cold, I'm confused," she said in a tiny voice just above a whisper.

"I know, I know, darlin'," he said, patting her hand. "What say you go take yourself a nice, hot shower. I'll build a fire to take the chill off this room and put on a pot of tea. How does that sound?"

"That would be wonderful. The tea is on the shelf over the range." She stood and walked almost zombie-like through the kitchen and into the bath.

She stood in the shower letting the hot water flow over her. She jumped a little when it first hit the skinned part of her arm, but she soon got used to the sting and stood with her head down, her arms steadying her against the wall. She wanted to rest her brain and just feel the water. She breathed in the steam as she rubbed herself slowly with Bonner's peppermint soap, letting its scent refresh her. She tried not to think. She held her breath a moment and moved her head under the spray. She gave her hair a quick wash, also with the peppermint soap, then switched to cold water for a rinse and wakeup jolt.

When she turned off the spigot, she could hear the sound of whistling coming from the kitchen. It was a happy Irish tune. She dried her body, wrapped her hair in the towel, and slid into her rust-colored chenille robe. She became anxious to see Lance again, to see if he was real, to see if all of this had been real.

Coming out of the bathroom, she could already feel the warmth from the fire filling the small apartment. Lance wasn't in the kitchen, so she hurried through it to the living room. As she rushed in, she was relieved to see him leaning on one of the bookshelves beside the fireplace. He was holding an open book in one hand. He looked up and smiled when he saw her. Raising the book, he read aloud:

> *To the bright east she flies,*
> *Brothers of Paradise*
> *Remit her home,*
> *Without a change of wings,*

Or Love's convenient things,
Enticed to come.

Fashioning what she is,
Fathoming what she was,
We deem we dream—
And that dissolves the days
Through which existence strays
Homeless at home.

"His voice is amazing," she thought, "so soothing and gentle yet full of strength."
"Emily Dickinson," he said, shutting the book and replacing it on the shelf.
"Yes," she said and then repeated the lines:

We deem we dream—
And that dissolves the days
Through which existence strays
Homeless at home.

Lance's eyes locked on hers. A sadness filled the room. The tea kettle whistled. "Well then, I'll see to our tea. I hope a pot of Earl Grey is to your liking this evening."

"Yes, that's fine. Thank you." She sat back down in the rocker and took the towel from her hair. Her long auburn locks tumbled out, and she pushed them behind the back of the chair to dry in the heat of the fire. She sat rocking with her head back and her eyes closed when Lance returned a few minutes later with a tray. He set it on the table in front of her and sat down in an old, overstuffed chair next to the door. He sipped his tea, watching her and watching the street outside. From where he had positioned himself, he could see the yard and the walk up to her door.

When her eyes opened again, she spoke. "So you aren't a dream then, because I wake and here you are."

"That I am, right here, watching over sleeping beauty and making myself at home. I'm afraid your tea has cooled down. Shall I warm it a bit?"

"No, it will be fine, but thanks anyway. Why on earth are you being so nice to me?"

"You know, the Jacuzzi thing," he said, pointing up with one finger.

"Oh yeah," she chuckled, "and the deck."

"Aye, would be nice." He smiled his beautiful smile.

"Lance, I want to be serious now. You said a few things earlier that I need to ask you about. I have so many questions in my head I don't know where to start."

"I'll tell you what I can, Lucy, but there are a lot of questions that don't have answers, at least none that I can tell."

She took a deep breath, let out a sigh and began: "Lance, how did you know that things like this have happened to me before?"

"If you remember, Lucy, I already answered that question. It was Angus who told me."

"Oh yes, that's right. Angus the rabbit told you."

"Aye, he did. He told me just before I got into Quicksilver when we were leaving the wildlife reserve. He said, and I quote, 'They've been taking her to school, preparing her.'"

"Wait, what? Quicksilver? School? Who are *they*? What on earth are you talking about?"

"My truck. That's her name, Quicksilver. Sorry. I guess you know what school is, and *they* are—well, I'm not totally sure—fae folk, I imagine."

"Lance, please," she pleaded. "Don't tease me. I need answers. I feel like I'm losing my mind." Her eyes welled with tears again.

He moved to the edge of his chair and leaned toward her. Taking her hand once again and looking into her eyes, he began. "You saw a rabbit because that is what he chose for you to see. I see him for what he is."

"And what, may I ask, is that?"

"He is a fairy. Well, part elf actually."

"A fairy? An elf?" Lucy scoffed, jumping to her feet. "Lance, don't jerk me around. Things like this have been happening to me all my life, things I can't explain, things no one would believe. I have paid plenty for it, to be sure. People think I'm nuts; they make fun of me." Lucy was sobbing now. "I thought you were going to help me, but you're just teasing me."

He stood before her. "No. No, Lucy. Please sit down and listen to me." His voice was soft yet firm. "I *am* being serious. I am not making fun of you or your situation. Please, please sit back down." He handed her a tissue he pulled from a box on the table beside her chair. She took it, dabbed her eyes, and slowly sat back down.

Lance returned to his chair. Again he took hold her hands. "Please, Lucy, just listen to me. Listen with an open mind. Don't be like those people who hurt you. I'll not lie to you, and I do know what you go through."

"I'm sorry, Lance, but how could you know? Oh, that's right. Angus must have filled you in."

"Actually, that's right; he did."

"Lance, stop it," she said, pulling her hands out of his. She glared at him through her tears. "Fairies and elves? Lance, I'm trying to find the truth, and you're talking fantasy."

"Am I?" He leaned back in his chair, letting out an exasperated sigh. He sat quiet a moment and gazed out the window. When he looked at her again, she thought how sad his eyes looked now. "Lucy," he began softly again, "we don't have to talk about this. Maybe you aren't ready." She looked at him but said nothing. After a few moments he said, "All right then, I'll leave you alone. I'd like to have one more cup of that tea before I set out, if you don't mind."

"No, of course I don't mind. Please help yourself. I... I..."

He interrupted. "Would you be having a hot cup with me?"

"Yes, thank you." He gathered their cups and walked into the kitchen. She didn't know why, but sadness filled her heart. The tears that were running down her cheeks weren't for herself now, but for him. She sniffed, used her tissue and after a few moments followed him into the kitchen. She sat at one of the two chairs at the table as he emptied the old metal teapot into their cups. "That teapot was my grandmother's," she offered, as a way to break the silence between them.

"Was it now? And a fine one it is." The smile returned to his face. As he looked over at her, his eyes twinkled and he gave her a wink. It was almost magical, she thought, that wink of his, the one that made her feel like everything would be all right.

"Lance, would you care for some Irish in your tea? There's a bottle in the cabinet there to the left of the range, if you'd care for a taste. I believe I could use a touch tonight."

"That's a fine idea, lassie. A touch of the Irish it will be, then." He splashed some into each cup.

He brought the cups to the table and sat across from her. She stirred in a teaspoon of honey and squeezed in a wedge of lemon she'd taken from the fridge. She breathed in the steam from the mixture and looked up into the green lands of his eyes. "My dad would fix me this whenever I was under the weather."

"Would he, now? Sure, it be a fine old cure."

She nodded and took another sip. The sun was going down, and as they sat at the table they gazed out the large window in the adjacent wall as the Kalamazoo River flowed past. The water picked up a reflection from the sunset-painted sky and carried the colors atop its deep darkness like a banner blowing in the wind.

"Well, darlin'," Lance said, pulling her back from the river's enticement, "are you ready to hear my Fairytale?"

3 – The Fairytale

"A Fairytale," Lucy repeated. "Sure, why not. I mean, a nice yarn over a cup of the blend from a handsome storyteller on a cold spring night, that's a fairytale already." She looked up at him; had she said that out loud?

"Handsome storyteller, is it?" he smiled. "You better take to just sipping that brew darlin'." They both laughed, she blushed, he began: "Do you remember this afternoon when we were in the meadow and I told you that I thought I was in a dream? I wasn't kidding, Lucy. I think I am in one, have been for a long time now, if that is what you call walking through a world that is different from the way most people perceive it. Sometimes it's more of a nightmare, but I'll not tell that part right now. I just want you to understand something, Lucy, something that not everyone can or even would try to understand. Some people, like you and like me, are different than most. We, well, we aren't really from here."

"What do you mean *not from here*?" she asked.

"I mean not from the same reality most people perceive."

"Lance, I don't know what you're saying."

"We are not from this reality, this Earth."

"Good grief, are you telling me I'm an alien now?

"Elysian."

"What?"

"Elysium is the name of the realm we come from."

"Oh boy, that *is* what you're saying. You are as nutty as people think I am."

A scowl came to Lance's face, yet he said softly, "You are not one of those people, Lucy."

"Lance, look, I think you should know this before you go any farther: I am a Christian. I believe in Jesus Christ and what it says in the Bible. I don't believe in magic and aliens. Those are just things of the devil."

"Are they now? And you have read this yourself? And that truth has been revealed to your heart, by and through the Holy Spirit? Or are you quoting to me what *they say*, the so-called Christians that have hurt you. Are you telling me another man's interpretation, or is it really yours?" She sat staring at him, not knowing what to say.

"I don't believe it is yours, Lucy," he continued. "I am a Christian too, and by that term I mean that I believe that Jesus was the Christ, the anointed one, the son of the One Great Creator God, and that He came into this realm to help people, to teach them how to live the way His Father had intended, to offer them grace for the forgiveness of sins if only they would believe and extend that grace to others." As he spoke, it seemed to Lucy that his countenance changed. He spoke with authority and conviction. "Lucy, you can't let narrow-minded men—who have a religious spirit in them that perverts the Word of God—tell you what you should think. They make their God so small that he can only deal with creatures that fit into their narrow perception. Anything outside of that they deem of the devil. They say they believe their God has power and that they are heirs with Jesus, yet they don't assign any of that power to their own lives. They don't know how to love their neighbor let alone extend one iota of grace to anyone else. They don't know how to use the mustard seed measure of faith that God has given to them. If they did, they could use it to do this world some good. They could move the mountains of pain and oppression that hold so many people in bondage. The Truth is He is the God of Creation, all Creation. He has created everything: the heavens—plural—the billions of stars, planets, galaxies, including earth and all the dimensions above, under, in, and through it. He created time and space and he has put in them exactly what he wants whether that fits into any man's narrow scope of understanding or not. He created man—human beings—and every other creature, be it extraterrestrial, inter-dimensional, elves, dwarfs, fairies, dogs, cats, bugs, germs. He created them all.

"The Bible tells us to get knowledge and with it understanding, but they search out knowledge like it is God. They don't even bother with understanding what to do with the knowledge or why he has given it to them. They label things as evil just because they don't understand them. They call people with vision crazy. It has been that way since Christ walked through this dimension with his disciples. Even some of them didn't get it. But He extended them His grace anyway to teach others how to love.

"The truth is, Lucy, you have a gift, a special gift. People who sit under a religious spirit will do their best to see that you don't use it. They will put you down and call you crazy because you are dangerous to them. You open up possibilities that they are afraid of. They don't have the mind of Christ, and they don't want it; it would mean they would have to give up their self-righteous ways and actually love people for who they are and not for what they have obtained, be it status or wealth or both."

Lucy sat mesmerized by his words. The things he was saying had long been in and out of her thoughts.

Her mind drifted back to a time when she was seven years old and attending the Lacota Methodist church, a small country church near her folks' farm. One Sunday after listening to a message the pastor had given on sending missionaries to the Pygmy tribes in Africa, she approached him to ask a question: "Why, if God is so loving and forgiving, would He send Pygmies to Hell just because they don't know about Jesus?" The answer she got never made sense to her.

"Well now, Lucy," the pastor began, "that is the reason we must all tell the world about the sacrifice of God's son. It is only by belief in him that they will be saved."

"But pastor, what about the ones who have died already and no one told them?" Lucy, the child, cried.

"Then we have failed them, haven't we, Lucy? God told us to go forth into all the world and preach the gospel. It is our fault then if no one told them, not God's. We must all work harder."

Lance saw that she was lost in her thoughts and used the opportunity to drink down some of his tea. "Lance," she said when she became aware again of the silence, "I'm sorry. I *was* judging you the way others have judged me. Please forgive me for that."

"There is nothing to forgive, darlin'. I know the knot your mind must be in right now, but hang in there with me for just a while longer. I'm afraid I'll be tugging on that knot a little more if you will allow me to continue with my Fairytale." He spoke softly and his eyes twinkled in the dim light of the kitchen.

"I am your captive," she said.

"If that is true, then I would like to offer food to my prisoner. What say you to this: get dressed, and Quicksilver and I will transport you to the Blue Nile. You should get some food down you. I think they close at ten, am I right?"

"My goodness, you do know this town," she said. Now that he spoke of it, she realized she *was* hungry. She hadn't eaten anything, save a slice of whole-wheat toast, since early that morning. No, not that morning, it was the morning of the day before yesterday. No wonder she felt so hungry; funny how she hadn't noticed it before he mentioned it. "I'll hurry," she said, standing up and rushing into the living room where she grabbed a clean pair of jeans, socks, and a long-sleeved pullover from the wardrobe. She hurried back into the kitchen, but Lance was gone, and the teacups were cleared from the table. She held her breath a moment, not wanting him to be just a dream. She turned around and noticed the door from the kitchen leading into the garden in back was ajar. She walked to it and through the opening saw Lance standing in the twilight. She breathed deep with relief. She hurried off into the bathroom and dressed. Her hair was still damp, so she took a moment to dry it with the blower. She slipped into her shoes and rushed out to join him in the garden.

"Hey, that was fast," he said. "I expected to be out here a spell longer. 'Tis a bonnie night." The first stars of evening were just coming out. "I'd like to give you something," he said, taking her by the shoulders and turning her toward the western horizon. A lone star shone brightly. "I give to you the light of this star. Will you accept this as a token of my appreciation for the honor of spending time in your light?"

"Yes," she whispered softly. "I will accept this gift. When I see this star, I will think of you, of your kindness." They stood side by side gazing at the brilliance of the beautiful star. The scent from the lilies of the valley that bloomed here and there about the garden wafted through the air. She turned toward him once again and spoke. "I, in turn, for the help you have given me and the kindness you have shown, would like to present you with this." She pointed to the crescent moon lying on the horizon in the east.

He turned toward it, bowed his head and in a voice softer than the gentle evening breeze whispered, "The honor is too great."

"No," she said. "The full moon at harvest would not be too great an honor for one such as you. But, alas, it is not now mine to give." He looked up at her and in her eyes could see the star that he had given her. Face to face they stood in the garden with the sounds and scents of the spring night all about them, and in his eyes she beheld the light of the very moon she had given to him. They drew into one another, breathed in breath from one another, and softly, gently, slowly, they kissed. Time stopped and the earth passed. They traveled beyond the starlit heavens and came upon a land of golden green.

A window creaked opened and a voice cried out, "Lucy, Lucy is that you?" Lucy left the golden green land and came back to the garden. "Hello? Hello, who is down there? Lucy is that you?"

Looking up, Lucy called out, "Yes, Mrs. Garrett, it's me. Can I help you with something?"

"Is there someone there with you, dear?" Mrs. Garrett asked. Lucy looked around, but Lance wasn't to be seen.

"No, I am alone," she said.

"I haven't seen you in a couple of days dear, and, well, I've run out of my medicine. Do you think you could get up to the pharmacy before it closes and pick some up for me? I need to take it first thing in the morning, you know."

"Yes, I know. Of course I'll go get it. I'll pick it up on my way to dinner tonight. I'll leave it in the basket on the hall table outside your door when I get home. That way you'll have it in the morning, and I won't have to wake you if I come back late."

"Oh, you are a sweetheart. I don't mean to be a bother. I don't know what I'd do without you, Lucy dear. God bless you, child."

"Think nothing of it, Mrs. Garrett. I'm happy to help you. But I better get going. Good night now."

"Good night, dear." As Lucy walked back inside, she heard the old lady's window slam shut.

Lance was standing by the front door, his hat on his head and his pack slung over one shoulder. "We better hurry to make the pharmacy before it closes, you sweetheart you," he said.

"I'm sorry, but Mrs. Garrett doesn't get out much, and she sort of depends on me to get her medicine for her. You don't mind, do you?" she asked. "You must be hungry too." She picked up her purse and hurried out the door past him.

"I don't mind her request," Lance murmured, shutting the door and checking that it had locked, "just her timing."

They sat next to each other on big pillows on the same side of a small, low table at the back of the restaurant. The Blue Nile was sort of an oddity in the area. Downstairs housed an Ethiopian restaurant while the upstairs housed a bar known locally for its jazz. It was also one of the first gay bars in the area. The big barn-like building, now painted a bright blue, sat on the same side of the road along the river as Lucy's apartment. She had herself never been inside it before, though she walked by almost every day on her way to or from work at the Butler.

Lucy allowed Lance to order for her as everything looked wonderful and she knew it would take her much too long to make up her mind. She was also afraid she wouldn't pronounce the menu items correctly. He chose for them that evening's special, Yatakilt Wat, for two. He reasoned it would be especially nutritious and the fastest to the table. The dish consisted of fresh, lightly cooked carrots, potatoes, string beans, and peppers seasoned with turmeric and other spices. Their waiter was a tall, thin lad with a heavy Ethiopian accent. "I am Asad," he said, placing water on the table before them. He seemed new and nervous. As Lance spoke to him, he relaxed and smiled.

"Lance McKellen, Asad; pleased I am to meet you." Lance took hold of the waiter's hand and shook it firmly. "And this is the lovely Miss Lucy Cavanagh, who has honored me with her company this fine evening."

"Hi, Asad," Lucy said, waving her hand at the introduction.

"Miss Lucy." Asad bowed in her direction. He returned his attention to Lance. "May I bring to you and your lady a liquid refreshment?"

"What is it you would suggest to go with our meal, Asad?" Lance asked.

"Enat. It is the house wine and it will go very well with what you have chosen. It is a wine made from golden honey." Asad seemed pleased to help.

"Aye, mead," Lance said, "a favorite of the elves. Am I right, Asad?"

"Yes, that is right, Mr. Lance," he replied, grinning widely. "The elves they drink mead. Asad has only learned that tonight. Mr. Lance knows of the elves? Asad wishes to meet one of them."

"Well, maybe you already have and just don't know it," Lance replied. "There is still a remnant of that race left here as guardians. They are very clever, and it would not bode well for them to go about undisguised in this world. They do get hungry and they do love vegetables and the fact that you serve mead wine would surely bring them in here." Asad stood wide-eyed, grinning from ear to ear as Lance spoke. "Would you be a good lad now and bring Miss Lucy and me each a glass of that golden nectar? We will drink to the Guardians this night."

"Yes, Mister Lance, right away." He turned and rushed off.

"Now that was a strange conversation," Lucy said.

"Was it now?" Lance chuckled.

"Elves, mead wine. How would you know, and how would he know about such things?"

"Ask yourself that, Lucy. How would he know about elves and mead wine? Think about it. It will come to you."

"Come to me?"

"Sure. You're a very smart lass and well read, from the books I saw at your apartment. Your powers of observation may be a tad off because of the ordeal you have been through, but they are growing sharper. After you get some food down you, it just may come to you."

Asad hurried back with a carafe wrapped in a brightly colored cloth. He poured a small amount in Lance's glass and waited while he tasted it. "Are you pleased, Mr. Lance?" he asked nervously.

"Aye, it's like tasting a sunbeam." Asad broke into another wide grin as he filled both their goblets.

Lance hoisted his glass to Lucy and issued forth this toast: "We drink to the Guardians this night and to the secrets and dreams that they protect. May they all enjoy a warm meal, a good cup, and the company of a beautiful woman." Lucy touched his glass with hers and felt a warm glow come to her cheeks.

They sat talking, as people who are hungry often do, about favorite things to eat. They were both mostly vegetarian, though not strict. Lance admitted to enjoying a fine roast at the table of hospitable strangers or hunting and fishing for his dinner when restaurants were not an option. They found they both had a fondness for stout beer, his favorite being Beamish and hers Murphy's. He told her that a friend of his owned a pub in Grand Rapids called the Green Dragon and the Little People where he was certain both brands were served. "If you haven't had enough of me by then, maybe on your next free evening you would accompany me there."

Lucy didn't hesitate. "I'd love to. Monday is my next scheduled day off." Reality rushed at her and she added, "That is, if I even have a job. I was supposed to be at work tonight, though this is the first time I've even thought about it." Worry and questions began to take the lilt off, and her posture sagged. She had lost other jobs in the past when time slipped away from her.

He picked up her chin with two fingers and looked in her eyes. Softly he whispered, "It will be all right; I promise." Her heart grew light again as she held him with her eyes.

Asad returned just then with the big platter of steaming vegetables, which he sat before them. He also placed on the table a low, flat, covered dish. It contained injera, a pancake-like sourdough bread. Lance served Lucy and then put food on his own plate. Before they ate, he asked if he could offer a blessing. "Please do," Lucy said, bowing her head.

Lance looked to the heavens, placed his hands in the air as if to surrender, and said quietly, "*Tika wa potu noturum. Aved noturum. Da avid tika nu da avid camra tiju.*" When he finished, he took Lucy's hand and gave it a squeeze. "Did you understand?" he asked.

"Yes, Lance," she said almost breathless, "I think I did. I'm not sure how, but as you were speaking, in my mind I saw the earth barren, then the Sun came, and then it rained. The sprouts shot up, then turned to plants, and the vegetables grew. I saw people too, Lance; they came and harvested the vegetables, and other people washed them and prepared them, and Asad sat them before us. It all came in flashes. Lance, how did I know this?"

"It was in the prayer, Lucy. Our life is sustained by accepting the life force of other living things. These vegetables have received their life force from the universe, from nature, the sun, the earth, the rain. We must never take this great gift for granted. We are sacrificed for every day, the Creator's life force poured out of one vessel into another's."

"But how did I understand what you were saying?"

"Because, Lucy, it is your language too. You will remember it." She wanted to ask him more, but she was starving.

Lucy had never felt so much in love: with the food she ate and the wine she drank; in love with life and the moment; in love with this man. They didn't speak at all while they ate. She thought of every bite and of every portion she laid upon her tongue, as if it were a sacrifice on an altar. She felt strength from each morsel flow into her as she swallowed it. Never before had food satisfied her so.

When she finished her plate, she slid it forward and looked at Lance. He was sitting back against a big pillow pushed against the wall with one knee up. His hand, holding his glass of wine, was resting on it. He was watching her and smiling. His plate had already been removed. She didn't know when.

"Feeling better, are we now?" he asked.

"Oh my goodness, I was lost in that food. It was delicious," she said.

"Well, you were sort of grazing like a cow," he laughed.

"What!?" she shrieked. "How dare you." She jabbed him with her finger, causing him to almost spill his wine.

"Hey, hey, quit that," he laughed. "I was watching you eat and thinking about Florica. She eats in much the same way, chewing each bite very well. It's a very healthy practice, I might add."

"Oh yeah, well, just exactly who is Florica?" Lucy demanded with fingers in the air poised to attack.

"She is my dad's milk cow," he replied.

"What!?" Lucy shrieked again, and again started jabbing at him. He caught her hands with his, for his own protection, looked her in the eyes, and said ever so innocently, "She is a very beautiful animal, very contented."

They both broke out laughing so loud that she thought they had surely disturbed the other patrons. But when she looked about, she saw that they were alone save Asad. He sat across the room at the same table he had been at when they first came in, reading the same book.

"*The Hobbit*," Lucy burst out loud. "That's how Asad knows about elves and mead wine. He is reading *The Hobbit*." Asad looked at her, held up the book, smiled and nodded.

"Very good," Lance praised her. "You see, your powers of observation are returning." He picked up the check from the table. "I guess we better move on out of here so they can close up. Do you feel like doing a little walking? I could leave Quicksilver here and walk you home. It will do us good to get a little exercise after that great meal, if you're up for it?"

"Oh, I get it. The shepherd boy leading the milk cow home from pasture."

"Something like that," Lance laughed.

By the time they reached Lucy's apartment, Lance's moon had climbed high in the sky. He stood by her door and waited as she disappeared into the main entrance of the building and climbed the old hardwood staircase that led up to Mrs. Garrett's apartment. She put the package she had picked up from the pharmacy in the basket on the beautiful mahogany table that stood in the hallway outside Mrs. Garrett's door. A large crocheted doily lay atop the table and on it, at the table's center, stood a marvelous old lamp. Its base was porcelain with hand painted fairies dancing in a meadow, peeking out from behind dandelion puffs and swinging on ivy vines. The lamp was always on at night, as it was the only light in the hallway. Every time Lucy saw this table with the fanciful lamp, she thought about her own grandmother's house. It had been full of such treasures. Her grandmother had been of the Fairy faith, as she called it, and many were the times Lucy sat spellbound listening to tales about the "Good People."

"Grandma would have loved Lance," she thought, because he was rugged and adventurous as her own grandfather had been. Lucy had only one memory of her grandfather being a vital and independent person. She had been taking a nap with her twin sister in a large hammock that stretched between the two twin willows that grew in their front yard. He drove up in a big black car. She was at first afraid of him, until her mother came out and embraced him. He bent down and smiled at them. 'Hi there, little ones. I'm your grandfather, and I am very happy to meet you.' He had silver-white hair and twinkling eyes. He picked them both up, carried them over to his car, and showed them a big crate of sugarplums in the back seat. 'Look here what I've brought for you,' he said. From that day, every time Lucy ate a sugarplum she thought of her grandfather and his twinkling eyes. She had other memories of him but not so happy. She remembered him being chairbound and shaking so drastically that he couldn't even hold a spoon. Her grandmother would spoon-feed him all his meals. Her cousin told her that he had contracted some type of palsy after being bitten by a black widow spider while out looking for gold in California.

Lucy's grandmother had had eight children that she raised mostly by herself while Grandpa Will was trying to make their fortune. He had gone on numerous adventures—quests for riches—over the years they were married. Each time he returned he would only stay a year or two until the money was almost gone and wanderlust tugged at him. Grandma Josie was usually pregnant when he left. He would be faithful to send her money whenever he could, though it was never enough to clothe or feed the ever-growing family. So Grandma would take in wash, ironing, and boarders. The children all helped by caring for their younger siblings or getting jobs themselves. Even with all his roaming, his wife and children remained totally devoted to him. Lucy wished she could have gotten to know him better.

She rushed back down the stairs to rejoin Lance. He stood leaning against her door jamb, arms folded across his chest, his backpack at his side. He looked up as she walked toward him, and even in the dim moonlight she saw the sparkle in those beautiful green eyes. "There's my good girl now," he said.

God, is he good looking. He's like a handsome hero from a tale of old, she thought. *I've never known anyone like him.*

"Will you be coming in with me for a while to tell me the rest of your Fairytale?" she asked as she came up next to him to put her key in the door. She brushed against him and immediately her knees weakened. She would have fallen right down had he not caught her. He picked her up with little effort and carried her into the apartment. He laid her gently upon the sofa. "I'm sorry," she said. "I don't know what's wrong with me. I feel so weak."

"Maybe you are just tired, darlin'. You've had little rest in the last couple of days."

"Oh," she said, remembering the events from earlier but still unable to recall where she had been or what had happened to her. "I still can't remember." Her emotions began to flood over her. "Why can't I remember?" she sobbed. He knelt down beside the sofa and cradled her in his arms like a child and let her cry. "Lance, I'm so confused. I'm so tired."

"There now, you just need to get some rest. Let me build up the fire for you before I go. My Fairytale can wait for another time."

Lucy felt panicked thinking he might leave her. She clutched his shirt. "No, Lance! Please don't leave, not yet. I don't want to be alone. I don't want you to go yet. Please stay awhile. You've done so much for me already I hate to ask, but I'm afraid Lance. I'm afraid of what I might remember. Please stay for a little while. Please," she begged.

Stroking her head gently, he said, "Sure it is I won't be leaving you now. It would be my pleasure to sit with you for a time. Just try to relax. Don't force your thoughts; just let them come when they may. How about if I brew up a pot of that mint tea I saw in the kitchen earlier? It might help you relax a bit, and it would be a good aid on our full stomachs. What do you say to that?"

"Thanks, Lance," she sniffed. Releasing him, she settled back on the sofa. "You must think I'm mad."

"No, Lucy, I don't think that, not at all. I think you are in trouble, and I'll be here as long as you need me." He kissed her gently on the forehead, rose, and tended the fire. He then went into the kitchen, tossing his hat on the chair by the door and putting his backpack beside it.

Lucy woke at 9:20 a.m. Her shoes had been removed, and the quilt her grandmother made was over her. Lance was gone. She feared he had been just a dream. The phone rang and Lucy sprang up to answer. "Hello," she said, hoping it was Lance, forgetting that she hadn't given him her number.

"Lucy, where have you been?" She recognized the girl's voice.

"Hey, Jann. What day is this?"

"What?"

"What day is this?" Lucy repeated.

"It's Friday. That's why I'm calling. Are you coming into work today? The boss was a little steamed you didn't show up last night. I covered for you, so you owe me big time. I told him you called me and said you weren't feeling well and—since he sent me home last week when we didn't get busy—that you were just going to stay home unless we called and needed you. Thank God it was dead in there last night. And thanks to me you are still Saint Lucy in his eyes."

"Jann, that was sweet, but I don't want you lying for me."

"Sure you do. That's what friends do; they cover for each other, right? I must have missed a pretty good party if you don't even know what day this is."

"No, well yes, I mean no. I mean, you don't have to lie for me. I don't expect you to do that. Lying is one of the things our savior hates the most." As she was finishing her sentence, the door opened and Lance came walking in carrying a bag of groceries. He was whistling a peppy Irish tune. He kissed her atop the head as he strolled by.

Jann picked up on the background sound right away. "Who's that?" she asked.

"No one," came Lucy's quick reply. She didn't want to have to explain things just then but realized her mistake as soon as she said it.

"No one, huh? Just a little song bird? Well tell me this, girlfriend: is he good looking?"

Lucy was flustered now. "Very," she said. "But it's not what you think."

"Oh, it isn't, and how would you know what I think, Saint Lucy? Maybe there are a few other things on that 'our savior hates the most' list that you should be reminding yourself of."

"Jann, cut it out. I really don't want to talk about this right now."

"I bet you don't. Well, have fun. I'll see you tonight at work—unless, that is, you will be too occupied to show up again."

Lucy just wanted to end the conversation. "See you tonight, Jann. Thanks." She hung up the phone and gave a sigh of relief. She turned and strolled into the kitchen to see Lance busy breaking eggs in a bowl. He was still whistling. He stopped when she entered and said, "You really were exhausted last night. You were out before I even came back with the tea. Are you feeling better now?"

"Yes," she said, "I'm just a little embarrassed by the way I acted. I'm surprised that when you left last night you didn't just keep going."

"Lucy, I didn't leave you last night. I stayed right in that chair, and I have the kink in my neck to prove it. I didn't go out till the sun was high this morning. I left to find a grocery. I had to walk back to the restaurant and retrieve Quicksilver first. I had an old friend guard your door while I was gone."

"Old friend?" Lucy asked, but Lance ignored her question.

"So would you like to try one of my famous drunken goat cheese omelets?"

"Famous, huh?"

"Well, my mom likes 'em."

They both laughed. Lucy brewed a pot of coffee and went to wash up while Lance played chef. He cut up and sautéed a red pepper, an onion, and some mushrooms. When they were cooked to his liking, he poured in the eggs and let them firm on one side then flipped it all over. He added the chopped-up goat cheese before folding the whole thing in half.

Soon they were both sitting across from each other again at her little table. He reached across the table, took her hand, and offered gratitude to the Lord for the food He had provided them. Lucy could not help smiling. "Wow, this is really good," she said. She didn't mean just the omelet; she meant the time they were sharing together.

"It is pleased I am that you like it. May I place you alongside my mom on the list of its endorsers?"

"That you may, sir," she chuckled.

While they ate, she asked him questions about himself. He told her he was raised on a farm in southern Ohio where his mom and dad still lived, that his younger brother and his wife lived with them. He spoke fondly of his family and of his home. He told her he had not been back there for over a year, though he did contact them as often as he could. He told her he had attended several colleges and earned degrees in both theology and anthropology, and since then he had been traveling around the U.S. and Canada researching places of power. He said he was planning a trip to Northern California and Oregon in the fall before going on to the U.K.

When they were finished eating, Lucy gathered their plates and flatware and carried them to the sink. She brought back the coffee pot and refilled their cups. "You must be rich to be able to travel like that."

Lance laughed at this. "Rich I am in the love of the savior, and rich I am in having the love of a good, supportive family. Actually, I am in this area to meet a man who might want to finance my research. God always provides the money as I need it. So now then, let's hear about Lucy, for all that I know is what Angus has told me and the knowledge I gained while I guarded your sleep."

"And just what knowledge would that be, may I ask? My shoe size, perhaps?"

He threw back his head and laughed out loud. "Well, I already knew you were kind hearted."

"Oh, I get it: big feet, kind heart."

"So my mom says," he chuckled again.

"Okay then, so what else do you know about me besides I graze like your father's milk cow and have big feet?"

He reached across the table and took her hand. He looked into her eyes. Earnestness replaced his smile. He took a deep breath and said, "I know you are beautiful for me to behold, that your eyes sparkle with secret and magic, that the lights from the moon and the stars dance from your hair and crown you as their queen."

"Lance," she sighed.

But as she said his name, he raised a finger to his lips and held it there while they became lost in each other's eyes. When the light of his gaze became so bright it was blinding to her, she blinked and looked down. He took his finger from his lips and stretched his hand out to touch her face. Softly he caressed her cheek while her glance returned to his. He smiled, breathed aloud long and hard, removed his hand from her cheek, and said, "Lucy, you are my Queen—Queen of Elysium—and I am your liege and your servant."

A chill ran through her as he spoke. She loved his way of speaking, the sound of his voice, yet what he said troubled her. Now again he had mentioned this Elysium. He was different from anyone she had ever met. She felt so safe and comfortable with him. Was this just a poetic way he had of speaking, or was he some sort of lunatic lost in a world of make-believe? To break the spell and grasp reality, she grabbed hold of her coffee mug. She brought it to her lips and took a sip, still looking in his eyes. She put down the cup and said, "Then, sir, as your Queen I issue this command to you." Her voice was stern as she mimicked the Queen of Hearts from a movie she'd seen when she was little: "Tell me how you knew that I had had other episodes of lost time."

"Lucy, you mock me," he said, looking down. "But nonetheless I shall do as you command, for I am not mocking you, and I have only been truthful in all I have said. You are my Queen."

Lucy felt embarrassed. "Lance, I'm sorry. It's just a little hard for me to buy all this. I'm Queen of Elysium? That's like this fictional place, right? You're playing a role?"

Looking again into her eyes, he said, "We all play roles in life, Lucy. You need to decide for yourself what is real. I'm still searching for much of the Truth myself. I will tell you all I know. I only ask one thing, that you will sit quietly and listen to what I have to say with an open mind—but most of all with an open heart, for truth is first known in the heart."

"I promise," she whispered.

"As I told you, I have been traveling around looking for places that native people call 'places of power,' which exist in many parts of the world. Legends and myths surround them. Probably the most famous is Stonehenge in England. Do you know of it?"

"Sure. It's one of the places I've always wished to visit."

"Have you, now? Well, maybe you will have your wish sooner than you think. But let me continue. Near my folks' farm in Ohio is another ancient place of power, the Serpent Mound. Have you heard of it?"

"The Serpent Mound?"

"Aye, that's what it is called. It's a geometrically perfect mound, a quarter mile long, spread out in the shape of a slithering snake with its mouth wide open around a smaller circular mound, which people refer to as an egg."

"I've never heard of it."

"That's what I thought. I'm learning that not many people have. Strange it is to me that a place of power could be right in the heart of America and only a handful of people know about it, outside the Native Americans. They have long considered it a very sacred place. Amazing, otherworldly things can happen in such places. Maybe that's why the powers that be here in America don't publicize it." He took a sip of his coffee and continued: "I think I may have come from that egg." He paused because he knew, even though she promised to listen to him quietly, this was bound to bring a response. It did.

"You mean you think you were hatched?" Her eyes were wide like saucers.

"No, not hatched, transported. I've learned a few things about the Mound: it well may be a portal. As I have told you, I feel as if my existence here is as but a dream. I don't belong in this realm, yet here I am. There are those who think there are at the least a dozen portals scattered about here on earth, each leading to or from a different dimension. And from those dimensions other portals leading to yet other dimensions.

"I believe I do have a purpose here, or a calling if you will. I thought at first it was for the clergy, but as I studied theology and the religions of the world, I came to realize they all contain only part of it. Since the Fall, humanity—no matter what the ruling religion—has fallen far short of the glory God intended for them.

"I believe now I am more a seeker, here to glean and gather truths that have long ago been hidden, for whatever reason, by the leading religion of the day or powers of the world, whoever they are. Some are wholly wicked, crafted to seize power from the everyday man to enslave him to the intentions of a ruling class. But some truths were hidden and guarded by the angels or other beings because not all men are able to accept them. Jesus embodied the Truth. I believe that if a man's heart is good and his intentions are pure, then he may obtain the enlightenment he seeks. The Bible does tell us to seek the truth while it may yet be found."

"Yes, it does," she nodded.

"I have already told you that I believe that the Great creator fashioned not only the heavens and the earth but the stars, countless universes, realms, and dimensions. Man in his arrogance sometimes forgets how great a God we have and believes himself to be superior to all other species and virtually alone as an intelligent creation, a fact that I do not think can be proven anywhere in the Bible unless it is misinterpreted and misconstrued as often it is. I know for a fact there are countless other beings that walk among the men of this realm. Some are from places in the stars; others are from dimensions both similar and diverse from this one. Some of these beings can be seen yet go unrecognized by all; this is probably because they can exercise some sort of mind control that makes you forget about them as soon as you see them. Others that are here can go unseen save by just a few who have the Second Sight, as they say. I have this gift, if that is what you want to call it. I can see things that most can't. Take Angus for example, yet he is not the only creature who reveals himself to me."

She sat as if in a spell listening to his voice, her mind wrestling with her heart. She wanted to believe him, but this was a bit much.

He went on, "There are others—and this is where I think we come in—that exist here. They live, work, go to school just like everyone else. Only they are not really from here but from—"

"Elysium," Lucy chimed in.

"Exactly," Lance acknowledged. "We are here, yet we really don't belong."

"Then what are we doing here and how did we get here?" *Oh God*, Lucy thought, *that sounded like I believe all this.*

"That is exactly what I am trying to find out. I would probably think that I were mad had I not learned I am not the only one who believes this. All throughout the history of this planet there have been people who have believed this way, people who have guarded the secrets, even with their lives. There have been secret societies like the Illuminati, the Knights Templar, the Priors of Sion, and religious orders like the monks of Sel Mar who have guarded ancient manuscripts and passed down oral truths that not all men have access to." He paused and asked, "How are you doing?"

She breathed out a deep sigh. "Tell me more about Angus."

"He has actually been with me for a very long time. The first time I can recall was when I was about nine. A robin fell from a tree dead at my feet. I picked it up and asked God to heal it. It shook in my hand and then flew out. As I watched it fly away, I heard someone say, 'Be careful not to use these powers in front of anyone. They will not understand.' I looked down to see the little guy standing on a rock. He was just a wee thing, even to me then at my small stature. He was odd looking, but I was only a child and had not seen much of the world, so I did not quite realize how odd he was. He told me his name was Angus and that he was there to keep me safe until it was time for me to return.

He told me that I was not from this dimension but from another, and that as I grew older he would reveal more to me. Of course I didn't understand any of it at the time. When I heard my father's voice, I turned to call to him. When I turned back, Angus was gone. A rabbit hopped from the stone, and that is all my father saw."

"The same rabbit I saw?"

"The very same."

"Lance, if I am from Elysium like you are, then why can't I see him as a little man?"

"I'm sure you will one day, Lucy, but that day will be up to Angus."

"Is Angus from Elysium?"

"No, Angus is from another realm, but for sure he travels where he may. He is what is called a Guardian elf, though he is not full elf but part fairy."

"He's good then?"

"Well, he has always been good to me. I think he can have his rascally moments, and I think he rather enjoys them. In not all things would I trust him, but in matters of my safety he has proven himself time and again."

She sighed again. She didn't really know what to believe. All of this was new to her. At least she believed now that he believed it and wasn't just messing with her mind. But was it just crazy talk? How could she judge? She wanted to believe him if only for the reason that he believed her.

His voice broke into these thoughts. "Lucy, I was wondering if I might use your shower. As I said earlier, I have an appointment with a man who may finance my research. He lives not far from here, and I have an opportunity to see him today."

"Of course you may, Lance. By all means, make yourself at home. I am so much in your debt that I am happy to help you in whatever way I can. Who's the man you are going to meet. I know a lot of the locals. I may know him already."

"Yes, I'm sure you do; however, he has asked to remain anonymous, and I must acquiesce to his desire."

"Oh, I see. All right then." She felt strange by his refusal to share this information. She felt somehow like he had already trusted her with so much, and she with him, and now a line was drawn.

As if he could read her thoughts, he said, "Lucy, there is a lot more I want to share with you, if you will allow it. But on this matter, I have given my word."

4 – Moonlight Becomes You

After Lance left, Lucy busied herself around the apartment cleaning and tidying up. She normally washed her uniforms on Tuesday, but since that was one of the days she couldn't account for, she needed to attend to that task today before her shift at five. As she worked around the apartment, she couldn't help but think of him.

He had taken his shower and came from the bathroom fully dressed. His hair was tied back, and Lucy saw that his ear was pierced with a silver post set with a small greenstone. "It matches the color of his eyes," she thought. He had changed clothes and now wore a denim shirt and blue jeans. She was standing at the sink doing up the breakfast dishes when he walked up close to her. She felt her body grow weak. He kissed her gently on the head and said he'd be leaving. "Will I see you again?" she asked.

"Of course you will. I've not yet finished the Fairytale. You do want to hear more, don't you?" His hand was on her cheek and he turned her face toward his. He watched her lips as the words came out.

"Yes, more than anything," she said.

"Good. Then you shall. But I must be off for now. Seek the Creator this day and let His spirit speak into your heart. Look inside, Lucy, and you will find many answers to the questions you have." He let his hand slip slowly from her face as he backed away from her. He picked up his hat and pack and strolled out the door.

Lucy stood as if frozen, watching him go, and as the door shut she finally took a deep breath. "God protect him," she whispered atop the air she released from her lungs.

She finished the dishes, gathered up her uniforms along with towels and a few other personal items and stuffed them in a small duffel bag. Before she set out for the laundromat, she ran upstairs to check on Mrs. Garrett. The elderly woman was always happy to see her. She had what she reported as "wonderful news" to share with Lucy: "I've received a letter from my daughter Fiona. She wants to bring my granddaughter here for a visit and stay with me a spell. That no-good cad she has for a husband has been straying again."

Lucy wondered why Mrs. Garrett thought of this as wonderful news. Her daughter's heart must be breaking. Their family is in danger of being destroyed. "God, help me extend your grace," Lucy prayed silently. "I know Mrs. Garrett is lonely and is only thinking of her own needs in this situation; help me not to judge her. Father, I pray for this family and for your intervention in hearts and minds."

Mrs. Garrett continued, "She's hoping that coming here to America will shake him up and make him realize what he's going to be losing if he doesn't change his ways. Thanks be to heaven that a man with means is buying the tickets for them or they couldn't afford to come."

"That is fortunate," Lucy said while her suspicious mind wondered if this "man of means" might just have an ulterior motive. She knew from her own experiences that there is always at least two sides to every story. Mrs. Garrett addressed this suspicion with her next comment.

"He is a good friend of James, went to school with him he did, and he is my little Maggie's Godfather. I wish Fiona would have put on her bonnet for him instead of that no-good, lying sneak of a man she married."

"There, there, Mrs. G, don't get your blood pressure up. Remember, what Satan intends for evil, God can use to do good."

"Well, it would take the hand of God to do any good with that one." As Mrs. Garrett sat chattering away about a rose bush she bought and wanted Lucy to plant in the garden out back, Lucy's thoughts strayed to Lance. She wondered again if he had been real or if soon she would wake up in another meadow. He seemed so perfect, so different from any man she ever knew. She reflected on the kiss in the garden, and as she did her hand strayed to her mouth. She closed her eyes and searched her memory to feel his lips there.

"Are you all right, dear?"

"I'm sorry, Mrs. Garrett. I guess I'm just tired." Lucy jumped up and headed for the door. "I have a lot to do before work today. I'm happy for you that your daughter and granddaughter will be coming soon for a visit. I look forward to meeting them. I'll pray for their safe passage."

"Will you, dear? That's very sweet."

"And for healing in that marriage."

"Well now, only if it's God's will."

"Of course," Lucy said as she bounded down the stairs. "I'll see you on the morrow then." She picked up the laundry bag and hurried off down the sidewalk. It was a beautiful late spring day. The sun was high overhead as she walked past the Blue Nile with Lance filling her thoughts. He stayed there even as the Butler came into view.

Up until last evening, she couldn't see the old hotel without thinking about Ashley. She had had, she guessed, a crush on him. What girl that knew him didn't? Lucy and Ashley had fun at work by playing a little joke on their co-workers: They kept up a provocative banter that made everyone around them think they had something more than just a work relationship going on. She was only being realistic when she thought that he could get just about any girl he wanted. But he probably would never settle on any one woman, and if he did she was sure it wouldn't be till late in his life.

Their relationship had made it fun for her to work at the Butler. Working in a bar can be tough at times. It was nice to have someone there to watch her back, especially when one of the patrons got a little too "hands-on." Ashley had actually jumped over the bar with one fell swoop and knocked to the ground a burly deck hand who had had one beer too many and grabbed her as she walked by with a full tray of drinks. That of course started a chain reaction. Lucy was thrown into an adjacent table, knocking it over, spilling drinks and patrons. The deck hand's buddy decided he would deck Ashley. That action was thwarted when big Rick the bouncer got involved. She was certain that that was the night her crush began. It was nice to see someone act gallantly on her behalf. Many of the girls who worked at the Butler had broken lives, but Ashley treated them all with respect and demanded that everyone else do the same. At one time she thought maybe he did have some special feeling for her, but that was the charm of him. He made everyone he talked to seem special. It was fun, anyway, having someone to think about, and she always thought of him while walking by the grand old building where they worked. But not today. Today someone had totally crowded him out.

Lance consumed her. Despite all the odd things he had told her, she thought she had fallen in love with him. She felt strange admitting this, even if just to herself. "God, how can that be? I've known him less than twenty four hours. He thinks he's an alien, and he thinks I'm one too. I'm not even sure if he's real. Lord, you know all my secrets, even the ones I don't know. Please guard my heart and help me to rightly discern all this."

She thought by inviting God into her thoughts the ones of Lance would somehow wane. But that was not the case. He was even more present than before. She was infatuated, enamored, and she knew exactly when it had begun: it was the moment his green eyes penetrated hers. Had he cast a spell? The kiss was affirmation that something magical had indeed taken place. It was unlike any kiss she had ever been given. It was as if with that union of their mouths they had surrendered one to another the essence of their existence. That kiss had been more real, more intimate, than any sex she had had with her ex-husband.

With that thought, the spring fell away from her step and that whole ugly weirdness climbed back into her mind. It wasn't that she hadn't loved Ray—she had—but not the way a wife should love her husband. She knew she had married him for all the wrong reasons. She married him because she felt sorry for him and to alleviate her own guilt. She was raised to keep herself pure for her husband, and she had wanted to do that. But one night he got drunk and raped her.

She had borrowed her father's car, the yellow station wagon—which by that time was nine years old and rusty—so they could go roller-skating. Sue and her boyfriend were supposed to go along, but at the last minute they decided instead to ride with another couple and meet them there. Lucy never liked going out alone with Ray because all he wanted to do was park somewhere and make out, and that always led to an argument. She picked him up and let him drive. Instead of driving straight to the rink, he drove to a make-out spot near a small lake. He produced a bottle of whiskey and tried to convince her to drink. She refused and told him he couldn't drive her dad's car if he was drinking. He said he didn't care, though not in such polite terms, and proceeded to guzzle down the spirits. After a while his mind was captured. He crawled into the back and started sobbing, repeating over and over again that no one ever loved him. She got in back to comfort him. These ugly little scenes had happened before, always when he was drinking. But this time it was different. This time he wanted more than consolation.

They made out for a while, but when he started to get aggressive, she tried to call it off. Her protests seemed to make him more determined to take what she did not want to give. She begged him to stop, but he was a man possessed. It wasn't tender and it wasn't beautiful, the way she had dreamed her first time would be. It was painful and awful. She felt dirty and ashamed. He laughed at her tears and told her she needed to grow up.

Though they had been dating for over a year, she never thought they would be getting married. She tried several times to break up with him, but each time he would come back begging to be given another chance, telling her she was his salvation. His mother had been killed in a train wreck and his father severely injured when he was only seven. He was raised by his teenage sisters, who weren't ready for and didn't want the responsibility. He told Lucy stories of being locked in a closet for hours at a time with only his pillow and a peanut butter sandwich so his sisters could go out and hang with friends. With no real guidance in his life, he dropped out of school and fell in with the wrong crowd. He spent most of his time with an alcoholic stock car driver who was at least fifteen years his senior and who would exploit his young protégé by using him to con people. Ray told her that he knew what he was doing was wrong, but if he had the right person to care about him he knew he could change. All of this made Lucy very vulnerable to him. He was a master at playing on people's sympathy, a survival trait he learned at an early age.

After he raped her, he managed to make her feel guilty for it, telling her she had let it go too far before wanting to call it off. "It was as much your fault as mine, you know. You just can't do that to a man, sweetheart. You got me so excited I just couldn't help myself. Besides, it's not a big deal. You have to grow up some day. And hey, I love you."

She felt dead inside, ruined. She didn't tell anyone. He came to her a few days after and begged her to forgive him; his excuse was that he had been drunk and didn't really know what he was doing. He produced an engagement ring, proclaiming his love and professing that she alone could change his miserable life and make him a better person. She felt like her fate had been sealed and that she had to marry him. Even as she was on the way to the altar, she knew it was a terrible mistake. She asked God to help her be a good wife. She tried to make it work, but his drinking only got worse after the wedding. He blamed her for his life not getting better. He soon began taking out his frustration and disappointment on her. He slapped her on more occasions than she could now remember, always when he was drinking. After each episode, he'd storm from the house only to return when he had sobered up, begging her forgiveness, vowing it would never happen again.

She let him have her whenever he wanted, thinking that was her duty as his wife, but she never felt any tenderness or love. On her nineteenth birthday she came home from work to find the house trashed and beer bottles broken against the walls. She was cleaning it up when he returned home with his old stock car buddy. They were both bloodied and drunk. She asked if they had been in a fight, and he told her to shut up and fix them dinner. She soon learned that he had lost yet another job. This one her father had gotten for him. She was sorely disappointed but tried not to let it show. "Don't worry," she said to encourage him. "You'll find something better, and until you do my job will keep the bills paid." That was the wrong thing to say.

"You think you are so goddamn much better than I am, don't you?" He grabbed her by the throat and raised his hand.

"No, no that's not what I meant," she cried. "I just don't want you to worry is all."

"Go ahead and pop the bitch," his buddy said, lifting another beer to chug. Ray had told her during one of his sober periods that he didn't like hanging out with this guy because they would get wasted and hurt people. He even admitted to being a little afraid of him at times.

"Rayme, please," she begged. "I didn't mean anything, really."

"Rayme, please," the other man mocked.

She thought she saw a softer look come to his face, but she knew he would act macho in front of his friend. "Please," she whispered. He lowered his hand and threw her hard to the ground.

"Shut up and fix my goddamn dinner." He stomped off into another room. The other man laughed and offered her his hand to get up. She took it. Another mistake. He pulled her up then pinned her against the refrigerator. His hand roamed over her as he tried to kiss her.

"Stop it. Stop it," she cried. She slapped him, and he backed off.

Ray heard the commotion and stumbled back in. "What the hell is going on?"

"Your bitch slapped me," he said. "Put her in her goddamn place, or I will."

Ray grabbed her by the hair and dragged her to the basement door. She was afraid to tell him what really happened because she didn't want him to get hurt by fighting with the monster of a man. He backhanded her once, pulled open the door, and pushed her into the dark. She tumbled down a flight of rough-hewn stairs onto the damp dirt floor. She lay there listening, afraid to move. The dark, old, Michigan stone basement was full of mice, spiders, bats and cobwebs. She wondered if he had shoved her there to protect her from the older, stronger man. When she was sure they had left, she picked up a piece of loose cement and broke the glass out of a small window. She could barely squeeze through it, but when she was finally free, she ran up the road not really knowing where to go. It was dark and she knew she was a sight. She didn't want to get her parents involved, nor did she want to call the police. Ray's sister's house was about a mile away, so she decided to go there.

As usual, after they had finished dinner Kathy and her husband Todd were drinking cocktails. They acted very standoffish when Lucy appeared at their door. They didn't want to get involved; she could understand that, but she didn't know where else to go. When she told them what had happened, Kathy responded, "You better stop pissing him off. He just might kill you next time." She realized they were right. It was his low self-esteem and his drinking that caused his rage. Neither could she do anything about. She had to divorce him or end up dead.

This was yet another one of Lucy's secrets.

As she walked on, those bad memories were pushed from her mind by thoughts of Lance and the gentle way he had touched her face. She felt his light again and her face showed it.

"Now that is a mighty pretty smile you are wearing, Miss Cavanagh." It was Lance. He came from out of nowhere and was walking beside her. "Here, let me carry that for you." He took hold of the laundry bag and lifted it from her shoulder.

"Lance, what are you doing here?"

"I went by your apartment, and when you weren't there, I decided to drive up to the pharmacy's soda bar and have a root beer float. I saw you walking here, so I parked at the Butler and caught up. Would you care to join me in celebration?"

"I really need to start my laundry first, and then I'd love to."

"My fortune gets better."

"So I take it your meeting went well with your mysterious benefactor."

"Praise to the Almighty, it went very well. He is a very wealthy, wise and powerful man and has pledged to give me not only the monetary support to continue on with my quest, but also access to ancient manuscripts and artifacts that I would not otherwise be afforded."

"Oh Lance, I'm so happy for you." She took his arm and gave it a little squeeze. She felt his strength and warmth flow into her. "I'd really love to hear about your work if you would care to share it with me."

"It's more of a mission, really. I will share with you what I can." He stopped walking and turned to face her. "I look forward to it. I know now that I will be staying in this area for a couple of months while I study with the Keeper—that's what I'll call my benefactor so I may talk more freely with you and still not betray his trust."

"The Keeper," she repeated. "Because he keeps secrets?"

"We all keep secrets, don't we?" He tilted his head and looked deep into her eyes.

"Yes," she whispered.

"Because he keeps certain things from falling into the wrong hands."

"What things?"

His eyes moved from her eyes to her lips. "Come here." He pulled her off the sidewalk and behind a big elm tree. "I have an overwhelming desire to kiss you again. Would you allow it? If I am being too bold, I apologize. But I have been unable to think of little else all day. Even when I was talking to W... the Keeper, you kept dancing through my thoughts."

"I have been thinking about you too, Lance. I would love for you to kiss me." She closed her eyes.

He put the laundry bag down and took her face softly in his hands. He came at her slowly, barely touching her lips at first, just brushing them softly with his, then pressing slowly, ever more firmly parting her lips gently with his tongue. She touched it with the tip of hers and sighed quietly. He filled her mouth and she accepted willingly, tenderly sucking the muscle that helped form his words, as if she wanted his whole story inside of her. She lost touch of her senses and floated upon a wave of desire. She didn't want this kiss to end. When it did, and he slowly withdrew his tongue, she felt as if she were being pulled into him. His lips gave up the pressure, sucking ever so softly on her bottom lip and then releasing it. He stood with his forehead on hers. They opened their eyes at the same time. She was breathless. "Wow," she whispered.

"I'll second that," he said. She blushed. "I'm not sure that one has cured me. It's just left me wanting more."

"Me too," she said with a breathless sigh.

"Good," he whispered, taking a deep breath and letting it out slowly into her ear and on her neck. Quietly he spoke: "We best get on with your task now and have our ice cream. We'll let our desire ripen, like a berry in the sun, until it's time of harvest. It will be a luscious sweet fruit if we don't rush to pick it."

He took her hand, and they were back on the sidewalk before she could take another breath. She felt like she was floating beside him. He was whistling now and she was smiling so broadly her cheeks hurt. She was so wonderfully happy she was afraid she might wake up to find she had been dreaming. Real life had not been happy for her for a long time. Only in her dreams had she been able to find peace and contentment like she felt now. "If this is a dream, I don't want to wake up," she said softly.

"If it is a dream, then we will live in it. Waking is overrated—unless, that is, you've conjured yourself up a nightmare."

She went into Wash the Time Away while Lance waited for her outside under the shade of another elm. She hurriedly stuffed two washers with her clothing, separating the whites from the colors. After adding the detergent, she closed the lids and placed her quarters into the slots. She pushed in the metal device containing her coins, saw the lights come on, and heard the water flow into the machine. She read the instructions carefully so she knew how much time she had before she needed to return to put her things into a dryer. Happy the procedure was over so she could rejoin Lance, she turned to see a puzzling sight.

A county sheriff's car was parked in front of the building. She caught a glimpse of a handcuffed Lance being pushed into the back seat. "What on earth," she thought. She had a sick feeling in her stomach. She ran outside just as the patrol car sped off. "Hey! Hey!" she called, running after it in a mismatched chase. The car turned the corner and vanished from her view. She stopped running and glanced about the empty street. She bent over and put her hands on her knees, trying to catch her breath. She felt as if she'd been punched in the gut. *Oh my God. My God,* her mind's voice repeated over and over. *What on earth could the police want with Lance?* A chill came suddenly upon her. The sun ducked under a cloud and the whole sky turned gray. She felt like she was falling, falling from a high place, falling and about to hit the ground. She staggered back into the laundromat and slumped down on a cold, hard, wooden bench. Her mind raced. *There has to be some mistake, or some reasonable explanation. What on earth could the police want with Lance? He's such a good guy. Isn't he?* She knew she had fallen in love with him and that she barely knew him. "I know enough," she determined. "I simply could not be so attracted to someone who is evil."

His words came back to her: "…unless you've conjured up a nightmare." He did seem too good to be true. He had told her some pretty weird stuff. But was it any weirder than the things in her own life, the things she was afraid to tell others?

Ray had been arrested three times in the two and a half years he was in her life. The first time was for forging someone's name to a check and trying to cash it, a stupid stunt he had been prodded into doing by his stock car buddy. For that he was put into juvenile detention for three months and ordered to pay restitution. He had also been arrested for underage drinking, and finally for failing to show up in court for a summons on a speeding ticket. None of these she reasoned were horrible crimes against humanity, and so it gave her an odd hope as she sat there that what Lance had just been arrested for was merely some minor infraction. But even that didn't fit into her made-up character of this man, made-up because she had to admit that no matter how strong an attraction she was feeling for him, she simply did not know him well enough to have any real handle on his character. "I don't care," she resolved. "Lance *is* a good person. I just know he is. I will not think of him any other way until some proof is offered to the contrary." She would trust Lance to sort it all out and come back to her. Really, there was nothing else she could do.

"Oh God," she prayed, but it ended there. She could still taste his tongue in her mouth, feel the tenderness of his lips as they brushed hers, and sense his breath on her neck. "Oh God," she offered again. "Help him. Help me." Prayer language filled her mind and soon, with her laundry done, she was on her way home.

She wasn't floating now. Her steps felt heavy as she purposed each foot in front of the other. The sun chose not to penetrate the layers of gray clouds that gathered around it to steal any brightness from the remains of the day. She noticed as she passed by the Butler again that Quicksilver was parked in the front lot. That vision, seeing something that belonged to Lance, made her feel better. She picked up her pace and got back to her apartment with little time left to prepare for work.

She brushed her hair, pulled it to the top of her head, banded it and twisted it into a Tinker Bell style, securing it with hair pins. She gave it a shot of hairspray and attached a little black bow in the back. She pressed her uniforms, chose the one she'd wear that night, and hung the others in front of her wardrobe.

On her walk to work, she formulated a plan to find out what had happened to Lance. She was fairly sure it was a county sheriff's car she had seen carrying him off, so that meant it had to be either Sheriff Carter himself or one of his deputies.

Deputy Clyde Pearson was the one who mostly patrolled Saugatuck. He was a former marine who had worked for the sheriff's department since he left the service ten years ago. He was a serious sort of fellow who had never married. To earn a few extra bucks and to help him out, Lucy ironed his shirts. He took his dinner at the Butler on most nights. Verse White, the owner, liked having the police come in, and he instructed all his employees to give them a fifty-percent discount on all personal food orders. Even on his nights off, Clyde would show up, have a drink, and talk to the locals. He never had more than two beers, and he always acted a perfect gentleman.

Ashley teased Lucy that Clyde was in love with her. "He only comes in here to sit and watch you." She secretly suspected that may be true, but she teased back, "It's you he comes in here to keep an eye on." Clyde asked her to dinner once when he came over to pick up his shirts. But she politely refused, telling him she was feeling under the weather. He must have gotten the hint because he hadn't asked her again. He would from time to time pick her up in his patrol car to give her a lift, if he saw her walking to or from work. She appreciated the attention but was always careful not to give him the wrong idea.

Tonight, though, she would use his affection for her to try to get information about Lance. She had to go about it the right way. She felt better knowing that she had a plan. It gave her something to think about other than just waiting.

When she got to work she noticed right away Quicksilver was gone. "Lance must have come back and moved it," she thought. "But why hadn't he stopped to see me?" She tried to stay extra busy at work so as not to have to answer too many questions of her own. Jann was all over her about the guy she had heard in the apartment when she called her that morning.

"He was someone I met at the wildlife reserve. We hiked together for a while and he gave me a lift back to my place. We had tea and he asked me out to dinner."

"Wow, he's a fast worker. So that's why you didn't show for work last night, or even call, you little devil. Everyone thinks you're such a goody two shoes. Tell me more."

"There's no more to tell."

"Come on girl, fess up. I want to know all about this guy. Did he spend the night or just show up for breakfast?"

Lucy hated being questioned like this, especially since she couldn't come out and tell the whole truth. "He spent the night," she admitted, knowing that it would probably be taken all wrong.

"What? Oh my God! This is big. I mean B I G."

"What's B I G?" Ashley asked, walking up to the waitress station to replenish the lime wedges, lemon twists, cherries, miniature onions, and olives they would need to garnish the drinks he would make for them.

"Lucy slept with a guy last night!" Jann blurted out.

"What?!" both Ashley and Lucy gasped simultaneously. "I didn't say I slept with him."

"Sorry, you said he spent the night. I just sort of assumed he hadn't sat there guarding your door from boogiemen."

"Who is this guy?" Ashley asked. Now Lucy had the questions coming from two directions.

"He is this really nice guy I met. I was having a little trouble and he helped me."

"What kind of trouble?" Ashley was quick to ask.

"I'd really rather not say right now. But Ash, he said he knows you."

"Really, what's his name?"

"McKellen."

"Never heard of him."

Lucy felt sick. She wanted to believe in Lance. Had he lied to her? "Ash, are you sure?"

"McKellen? Doesn't ring a bell."

"He said he watched you kiss the Blarney stone. Now do you remember him? Lance McKellen."

"Son of a bitch," Ashley cursed as he cut his finger with the small curved blade he was using to make the lemon twists. "Oops, sorry girls. That lemon juice smarts."

"Ashley, do you remember him?"

"Lance. Sure, I remember him. I wouldn't be standing here right now if it weren't for him. I didn't recognize his last name right off. What's he doing around here?"

"He has some business in town."

"Maybe he's having a little pleasure too," Jann piped in.

"Jann, there are two guys sitting in your section dying of thirst. You are still working here, aren't you?" Ashley snapped.

"Yes sir," she replied. As she turned to walk away, she mouthed to Lucy, "He's jealous."

"Ash, what do you mean he saved your life?"

She had to wait for his answer because the Friday night crowd started coming in and three guys had just bellied up to the bar. She had two tables seated almost at the same time, and from then on they were crazy busy for the rest of the night. But she did manage to get an answer from him, piece by piece, through her many trips to the waitress station that night.

It seemed that Ashley and his brother had taken a road trip through Europe after Ashley finished college. She had heard parts of this story before. The part that was new was the part where his brother met a girl at a pub in Killarney and sort of abandoned him, telling him they would meet up at Rosslare Harbor in three days where they were to catch the ferry to France. Ashley decided to take a bus to Blarney castle to see the famous stone. What most people don't know until they go there is that the Blarney stone is actually a part of the wall under a window on an upper floor of the old castle. If you want to kiss it, you need to climb to the floor just above it and lean backwards out an opening in the wall, contorting your body to get your lips in position. Usually there is an old man from the nearby town who sits by the opening and offers to hold on to you for a small fee, which helps him buy a pint and his dinner at the end of the day. On this particular day, it was raining and the old man who was to hold onto Ashley had already had a couple of pints too many. Ashley lay on his back, stretched out of the opening and puckered up against the cold stone. Right after he gave it a kiss, his hands slipped, and the old man's grip failed. He went plummeting head first toward the ground.

"I don't know where he came from or how he happened to be standing right where he was, but Lance grabbed me just before my head hit the rocks. We both tumbled to the ground. I tell you, I was shaken up more than just a little. He told me the last bus to town had already left the castle and there would not be another until morning. He said he was camping nearby, and I was welcome to come with him. He took me to his campsite, and I ended up spending two days with him. He hunted rabbits for our dinner, and we went fishing. It was the grandest part of my whole trip, really. It was almost like traveling back in time or to another world or something. I'm surprised he's here. I've sort of thought of him these past years as not being real, like he was my guardian angel or something like that."

Lucy was glad the night was so busy; it kept her mind off Lance. She felt better knowing he hadn't lied to her about Ashley, though she was a little ashamed of herself for thinking, even for a moment, that he had.

Clyde came in and sat in her section as usual. He was in uniform, so she knew he was still on duty and had come in just for dinner. She carried a big glass of water over to him instead of his off-duty draft.

"Hey Clyde, how are you?"

"Mighty fine, Miss Lucy. Thank you."

"Would you like the catch of the day, or are you going to have a burger?"

"A burger, and make it to go. You know the way I like it. We sort of have a situation, so I need it fast so I can get back out there. Can you bring me a bowl of clam chowder while I wait for it?"

"Sure, Clyde. What's going on?"

"Plenty, Lucy. Listen, I don't want you walking home alone tonight. Try to get a ride from someone or wait until I can swing over this way."

"Come on, Clyde, I'll be fine. I do it all the time."

"No, Lucy, not tonight. Promise me," he said sternly. He had never talked to her this way before. "There's an escaped loony running around out there. The sheriff had him for a while this afternoon. Picked him up right down on Main Street here and was transporting him to county when he managed to get out of his cuffs and jump out the back seat of the squad car. Darnedest thing. It has Sheriff Carter plenty pissed off. He's called in the state boys. We won't stop till we get him."

This was easier than she thought it would be. But she was getting the sick feeling back. "Just what is this guy wanted for?"

"Well, that's just it. The sheriff picked him up because he fit the description of a guy who escaped from the criminal detention floor at Nine Hills Sanitarium in Kalamazoo last week. The guy is a real nut case. He was in there for killing a waitress a couple years back. He met her on a hiking trail and molested her. We found her hanging by her feet from a tree, naked. He'd stabbed her repeatedly with a hunting knife. He said the little people told him to do it because she wasn't really a woman but an alien changeling."

He reached his hand out and took hold of hers. "You're shaking. I'm sorry I upset you with this talk. We'll get him, Lucy. I promise. And in the meantime, I don't want you walking anywhere alone, especially after dark. Understand?"

"Sure, Clyde. Thanks. I better put your order in so you can get back out there. I'll tell them to rush it." Lucy walked away from the table with weak knees.

Lance is not a killer she heard her brain shout. It was answered by *He met you on a hiking trail, he was carrying a hunting knife, he was talking to a rabbit.*

"All right Satan, I'm not going to listen to any word you whisper in my ear. I will not believe this awful story has anything to do with Lance."

"Come on, it has to be Lance. Clyde said the sheriff picked up the killer right up the street. You can't explain that away."

"Clyde said the sheriff picked up someone that fit the description. Just because Lance might look a little like the guy doesn't make him a killer."

"Then why did he jump out of the squad car?" God, she had a headache. She couldn't think straight with this argument going on in her brain.

Ashley noticed something was wrong when she ordered a Tom Collins and had to bring it back for a John Collins. "Number One, what is going on with you tonight?"

"Nothing. I just made a mistake, that's all."

"Come on, Lucy, this is the second one in ten minutes. I already drank the gin gimlet you had me make in error. You're acting like a rookie."

"Screw you, Ashley," she snapped.

He knew he had struck a nerve because he had never heard her curse before. "Pat," he yelled to a girl sitting at the break table in the room behind him, "take over Number One's section. She's going on her break."

"I still have ten minutes left on mine, and I want to grab a smoke," said a voice from the break room.

"Pat, if you make me say *please*, your breaks will be ten minutes short for the rest of the week. Now get your butt out here."

"Okay, Ashley. Don't get your shorts in a bunch."

"Ashley, I'm fine. Let her finish her break," Lucy argued. "I apologize for my harsh words."

"Deliver those drinks and get your tail into the break room," he barked at her. She knew not to argue with him when he was in his take-charge mode.

She closed the door of the break room and turned down the light. She knew Ashley was right; she did need a break. She wasn't herself. How could she be? "I don't think I'll ever be myself again," she thought, and she let the tears flow. She needed to clear her head and go before the throne. "Lord, forgive me for letting you down once again. Calm my mind and my spirit and help me to have faith, faith to endure till you call for me. Give me the peace that passes understanding."

She heard the door open and raised her head to see Ashley standing beside her. "Here, eat this. Tweedy made it fresh at lunch." He sat a bowl of chicken noodle soup in front of her. "Have you eaten anything today?"

"I had an omelet this morning. Thanks, this looks good."

"Jann told me you called in sick last night. Maybe you should have taken tonight off too. You were looking a little pale out there."

"Thanks, Ash. I'll be fine."

"Lucy, maybe it's none of my business, but you know that's never stopped me." He chuckled. He was trying to make her feel better. "You said earlier that you were having a little trouble and that Lance had helped you. Well, I want you to know that... I mean, I hope you know that, well, if anything comes up you need help with, you can call me."

"Thanks, Ash. That's sweet. Do you think you can give me a lift home from work tonight? Clyde made me promise I wouldn't walk."

"Sure, no problem. I already told him I'd do it. He told me about the psycho that's loose out there. I think our deputy is smitten with you, Miss Lucy."

"Ashley, stop. He's just a nice guy who doesn't want to see anyone hurt."

Ashley sat with his chin in his hands watching her eat her soup. *I don't know who it was that knocked her self image down by her ankles,* he thought, *but whoever it was just may have done mankind a favor. If she ever starts to see herself the way Clyde and about a dozen other guys I can name around here see her, she would be a real man killer.* Almost like she heard his thoughts, she looked up and smiled. *Lance, huh?* Ashley thought. *Well, maybe he is the only one who'll ever be good enough for her.* Ashley realized he was staring at her and told himself he was just drunk from throwing down her mistakes all night.

She felt better after her break. God had calmed her mind as she'd asked. She managed to suppress the paranoid thoughts about Lance and focus on serving her customers and cleaning up afterwards.

Ashley gave her a lift home as he promised. He sat in the car until she was in her apartment and the light was on, and then he hurried off to the Friday night poker game. Every Friday night without fail bartenders from the various bars around town met at the apartment of the bartender from the Coral Gables' Rathskeller and played poker until one of them had everyone else's tips from the night.

Lucy walked in, flipped on the light, and kicked off her shoes. She decided to put on the kettle for tea. While she waited for it to boil, she took off her uniform and wrapped up in her housecoat. As was her routine, she set her tea to steep while she went into the bathroom to take a quick shower to wash away the tobacco smoke and whiskey smell. That accomplished, she came back into the kitchen, drying her hair with a towel. She stopped cold when she saw something on one of the chairs at the table. It was a hat, Lance's hat. Her mind was racing. Lance was in her apartment. She didn't know what to think or how to act. She froze in these thoughts: Was he the man she thought she loved, or was he some crazed killer? How had he gotten in when the front door was locked? The garden, she thought. She heard him now in the living room and started to back away. But he heard her and called out, "Lucy, don't be frightened. I'm here. I saw your light and knocked. When you didn't answer, I went around back and found the garden door unlocked. You really should keep it locked, you know. I called to you, but you were in the shower, so I decided to build up a fire. Lucy?"

"Yes, Lance," she squeaked in a voice she didn't even recognize. She couldn't move.

"Are you okay?" She heard him walking toward the kitchen.

"Lance, stay right there. I'll join you in a minute. I'm drying my hair." Her initial shock was gone and her courage was coming back.

"Was it all right that I let myself in? I've been thinking about you all day. I'm sorry we didn't get to have our ice cream."

She stood trying to hear his words over the pounding of her heart. "It's fine. I've been thinking of you too, Lance." She saw his backpack now. It was sitting on the floor near the back door. The hunting knife was in it. "Lance, what happened? I saw them put you in a police car."

"Welcome to my nightmare," he said.

"What?"

"They thought I was someone else, an escaped killer. I wanted to pick you up from work, but there were police all over the place."

"So why should that bother you?"

"Well, that's sort of complicated. Are you almost done? I'd rather talk to you face to face."

"Yes. Just another moment, please." She had to think fast. She tiptoed over to his pack and pulled the knife from the sheath. She slipped it into an inside pocket on her robe. "I want to hear all about it. I've been worried."

"I was a bit worried myself, but God is good and it's working out."

"God," she thought, "'God is good,' he said. He knows God is good. He *can't* be bad."

"Even the devil knows God is good," came the voice she hated in her head. "Good God," she prayed, "what am I doing? What am I thinking?"

"Lucy, look in the fridge. The ice cream may be a little melted, but it will make for a good float, if you want one now. But I notice you have a cup of tea steeping."

She yanked open the fridge door to see a bottle of Dad's Old Fashioned Root Beer sitting on the top shelf and a pint of Borden's vanilla ice cream stuffed into the small freezer section at top. The happy thoughts she had had earlier that day spilled back into her. She turned around and tiptoed back to his backpack to replace the knife in the sheath. But when she did, he was standing in the doorway. "Lucy, what did you want with my knife?"

"Lance, I… I…" She bit her bottom lip trying to think of something to say.

"You what, Lucy?"

"I just wanted to see… I wanted…" She didn't want to lie.

"You wanted to see my knife." He walked over to his pack and pulled it out. He turned toward her and she jumped backwards, nervously bumping into the sink.

A loud pounding came on the front door.

"Who's that?" he asked. "Are you expecting someone?"

"No."

The pounding came again.

"Late for a visitor. You better get it."

She hurried by him to the front door. "Who is it?" she asked.

"It's Clyde, Miss Lucy. May I come in for a moment?"

She turned to check with Lance, but he wasn't there. His backpack and his hat were gone. He'd slipped out the back door.

"Clyde," she said as she opened the front door, "what are you doing here?"

"I was just going home and saw your light on. You were so upset when I told you about the killer tonight I wanted to come by to let you know we got him."

"You got him?" she asked. The reality of what her fear had done came heavy to her heart.

"Yep, someone called the station and said we'd find him tied to the elm tree in front of the laundromat on Main Street."

"Was it the same guy the sheriff picked up earlier?"

"Nope, about the same height and build though."

"So what about the guy who escaped, is he wanted for anything? I mean, the one that jumped out of the sheriff's car earlier."

"Well, this is the funny part. According to the description the killer gave us, that's the guy who tied him up to the tree."

"What?"

"Yep. Strange, isn't it?"

"So you aren't looking for the other man anymore?"

"Well, the sheriff is still really steamed about him escaping like that, but we don't have anything on him. I say we should give him a medal. He made our jobs a lot easier tonight."

Tears started falling from her eyes. "What have I done?" she thought.

"Miss Lucy, what's wrong?" the deputy asked, taking her arm.

"I'm a terrible fool, Clyde, a terrible fool."

"No, now don't say that. Everyone gets scared now and then. Heck, even me, and I've been in some real tight spots before. I ought to be used to it by now."

"Clyde, thank you for coming by to tell me."

"Sure thing, Miss Lucy. I didn't want you to worry yourself none. A woman hadn't ought to have to live in fear of creeps like that. You best try to get some sleep now." He backed away from the door putting his hat back on his head. "Good night now."

"Good night, Clyde." He started to walk away. "Clyde," she called.

He turned toward her and removed his hat again. "Yes, Miss Lucy?"

"Thank you for being out there night after night and putting yourself in harm's way to keep people like me safe." She took a step forward and kissed him on the cheek.

"Yes, ma'am, you are welcome," he beamed. "Go on in now and lock your doors." As she backed into the house and shut the door, he replaced his hat and hurried to his patrol car.

Lucy watched from the front window as the deputy drove off, and then she turned and hurried into the kitchen. She had a sick feeling growing inside her. She opened the back door and peered into the garden. Her eyes confirmed what her heart most feared: Lance wasn't there. She stepped out into the chill of the night. Though her robe was warm and thick, her hair was still damp from her shower, and she shivered as the breeze danced around her. She took a long, deep breath. But when she exhaled, it left her body in short, broken spurts of silent sobs.

The river that flowed just beyond the garden was a wide, black ribbon dotted with small orbs of light that traveled billions of miles to dance on its surface. She walked slowly toward the bank. She heard the rush of the water as it hurried past the rocks that hadn't been totally swallowed up by the river's rise after the winter snowmelt. They jutted up here and there along the bank, giving a voice to the waters that would have otherwise moved along in silence. Tonight the river's words taunted her. Her mind was tired and her heart felt so heavy that she fell to her knees in the thick, damp grass that carpeted the flat land before it yielded to the power of the watercourse.

As the wind ushered in heavy clouds to veil the stars, the dancing orbs blinked out one by one until only one or two survived faintly on the surface of the river. Across the river now Lucy saw black figures. They were darker than the night itself, and they were beckoning to her. She had seen them before. They were the captains of despair, and her heart had been shredded many times by their daggers. She knew what they wanted; they wanted her. The voice she hated disguised its vileness by offering her comfort: "There is rest in the black water. It will carry you to a place beyond all pain." She rose to her feet and inched forward, stopping for one last breath before giving herself to the promise of the bourn. The wind blew against her, and the cloud that had been hiding the moonlight gave way to the crescent she had given to Lance just one evening before. It shined on the surface from directly over her head, dispersing the utter blackness. Its reflection penetrated her eyes and carried an elixir to her troubled mind. She raised her head to behold it.

The wraiths left the far bank as if threatened by an approaching danger. Lucy turned away from the bank to make her way back to the garden. As she did, Lance stood before her. The moon was back in his eyes, and she rushed into his arms.

The kiss they made was one of fairytales. It was a kiss that could have awakened a princess who had slept for a hundred years. It was a kiss that could have turned a cursed frog into a prince. It was a kiss that would seal their fate one to another until the end of all time.

5 – The Fairytale Continued

  Back inside her apartment, Lance sat on the carpet before the fire, leaning against her sofa. She sat leaning against him, his arms and legs surrounding her like a fortress, keeping her safe. The chill was leaving her bones as the warmth from the hearth dried her hair and reached her scalp. There was so much she wanted to ask him, so much she wanted to tell him about herself, but none of it seemed to matter right now. The only thing that seemed to matter was his nearness. Not near enough. She pushed against him and felt his desire for her. She had never felt like this before. She was desperate to have him, desperate to have all of him. They kissed again—this was not a kiss of fairytales. This was a kiss of passion, a kiss that asked and a kiss that granted permission, a kiss that ignited fires in their flesh.

"Lucy," he breathed in her ear, "I don't yet know where my path will lead. I cannot promise anything beyond this night, though my wish would be for an eternity, and my heart will be locked to yours forever. If we bond this night, it will be without promise for tomorrow. I will not have you deceived. I saw what hunts you from your past, what called you to the river's edge. If my love can be your armor, then pleased I am for you to wear it. But Lucy, I could not bear it if it would give strength to what seeks to destroy you."

"Lance, if this is all we have, then it will be enough, though your promise for as many tomorrows as you may give is my true desire."

"Then you have it my love; as many as God may grant will be yours."

He found her mouth again and drank the nectar from her lips. He found all of her that night. He tasted every inch and marked it as his own. His tongue was as a wizard's wand, sending shock waves through her. His tenderness drove her to delirium, and then he became the killer. Not the killer she had feared him earlier to be. He became the killer of the captains of her despair. He drew the sword of his flesh and stabbed her over and over again until she screamed for his mercy and he finished the job. She laid, dead in his arms forever, the torment of the rapes and brutality that had been the only sexual encounters she had known. He took her to heaven, and together they touched the face of God, and He smiled on them.

They slept as babies wrapped in the warm womb of love. Awaking, they were born into a world where they were more than who they each had been. Their desire was also born anew. Over and over again they pleased each other, rising and falling on magnificent waves of pleasured frenzy. Their honeymoon was delicious. About one in the afternoon they made their way into the shower. They tenderly lathered each other as a new excitement washed over them and once again they joined.

Now they had another appetite to satisfy. "Are you as hungry as I am?" she asked.

"Hungrier, I'll wager, since I skipped dinner to hunt down a madman and duct-tape him to a tree."

"I knew that had to be you. How on earth did you catch him? And how on earth did you get away from the sheriff?"

"Let's get dressed, and I'll tell you all about it on the way to the Knife and Fork. I need to throw down at least a dozen eggs after what you did to me last night."

"After what I did to you?" she laughed, "And just what was that?"

"You captured my heart for all time and eternity."

She couldn't help herself. She had to suck the last drop of honey from his lips. He let her have her kiss and then pleaded, "We best go get that food now before we start down a different path."

They dressed quickly and then hiked up the hill to the church parking lot. Lance explained that he'd moved Quicksilver there after Clyde showed up at her door last night. He had originally parked across the street from her apartment but thought it might be better if he moved to a more secluded spot to avoid anyone questioning her.

The Knife and Fork sat just off the Blue Star Highway across the river about a mile and a half from her apartment. The locals knew it as "The Greasy Spoon." It was a small, no-nonsense place where a working man could get a big plate of food for a reasonable piece of change, the type of small diner where breakfast is served 24-7. Lance ordered two grilled cheese sandwiches with fried egg, grilled onion and tomatoes on them and a stack of hot cakes. Lucy decided to try one of the sandwiches to see what it was like. She loved it. Of course she did; she loved everything about this man.

As they sat waiting for their food, they each drank down a large glass of orange juice. Lance answered all of Lucy's questions as to the events that transpired after she saw him being tucked into the back seat of the sheriff's patrol car, though his answers left her with even more questions.

"The sheriff pulled up and asked me for my ID. I told him I was out for a walk without it on me. Right away he pulled his gun. He told me that he already knew who I was and that I was under arrest. I asked him just who he thought I was, but he told me to shut up, put my hands on the car, and spread 'em. He was very dramatic. I could tell by his macho vibrato that he was really into his role, so I did as he requested. He patted me down, cuffed me, and shoved me into the back of his car. Fortunately while he was distracted with me, Angus, who had seen the whole business, hopped into the front seat and lifted the keys to my cuffs."

Lucy stiffened at the mention of Angus. It was like he had poked her mind.

"He hopped into the back seat and hid under a jacket. He unlocked my cuffs while the big guy was telling one of his buddies over the radio that he had just nabbed the 'Jogging Path Killer'. When the sheriff stopped at the sign on Lee Street, Angus jumped into the front seat and hit the switch that unlocked my door. The sheriff saw him do it, but I bet he'll never admit to it. I jumped out and scurried through some backyards, jumping a fence or two and making for the woods. I counted on the fact that a man who carries around as much weight as the sheriff couldn't run fast enough to give a decent chase. He tried to compensate for that fact with his gun. Fortunately for me, he is not a crack shot. I cleared his view, jumped behind a tree, and let him run right past me. I heard him yell 'halt' and start blasting away. For all I know, he bagged a good-sized buck for his dinner," Lance chuckled.

"I'm just glad he didn't shoot you," she said, stretching her hand across the table and covering his. "I don't understand why you just didn't let him take you in and get this all cleared up."

"Because, Lucy, they would ask me questions and not care for my answers. My quest does not allow me the luxury of time. It would take me too long to explain the truth to people who don't particularly care to hear it. I cannot allow myself to get tangled in their web. I figured the only way I had to stay around these parts without being hunted was to go out and catch the guy they were looking for."

She didn't fully understand, but she didn't interrupt.

"I doubled back toward the car to look for Angus. He stayed behind when I bolted. He took care of the radio—yanked a few wires—to buy me some time. I reclaimed my backpack, and we made off for the Keeper's, who agreed with my plan and brought me back into town to retrieve Quicksilver. I only regretted not having time to find you, but I had to make haste to snare my doppelganger."

"But how did you know where to find him?"

"I saw him at the wildlife reserve. I spotted him in the woods just off the trail. He was watching something. When I looked to see what it was, I saw you. When I called to you, he slunk away. His demeanor at the time disquieted me. That's the reason I wanted to get you out of there as quickly as possible. I figured he would still be hanging around that area, and I was right. He had a camp set up not far from where I had seen him. I asked Angus to go up and have a little chat with him. He was more than happy to go with me after that, poor guy."

"Poor guy? Lance, do you know what he did?"

"He didn't kill that woman Lucy, a Draconian did it."

"What?"

"He didn't kill that woman. She was already dead. He killed a Draconian that had abducted and assimilated her."

Lucy suddenly couldn't swallow her last sip of OJ. She couldn't even breathe. As if he could sense her panic, he reached out and took her hand. "I know this all sounds very strange to you but you need to trust me. There are many things I would like to bring to your mind. I pray God will allow me the time. I trust now you know that I am not the deranged killer you thought me to be last night."

Her eyes widened. "Lance, I didn't… I mean, only for…"

"Hush now, I saw the fear of me in your eyes when I asked you why you wanted to see my knife. It hurt me Lucy, but I understood. There is much I have not told you, much you do not know, but knowing is both a blessing and a curse."

"Lance, I'm so, so sorry."

He kissed her hand. "Your friend showed up at the door, and I couldn't risk sticking around. I sensed you just might give me over before I had a chance to explain. There is a lot at risk for me now, Lucy. The key to understanding what it is I must do is closer than it has ever been. I cannot allow anything to keep me from learning the Keeper's secrets. I have a feeling the sheriff won't take kindly to me from now on, even though I did him a big favor. I also made a monkey out of him, and he'll not soon forget that. He is a boastful, prideful man. Men like that and in his position usually have a hidden agenda. I don't want to spend any of my time explaining things to him, time I could be spending with the Keeper or with you, so I have to be very careful. It may be best if you do not tell anyone about me for a while. If he gets wind that you have taken up with a stranger, he may want to get a look at me. He may even have your place watched. You do understand, don't you?"

"Of course," she said with a smile, though in her heart she felt disappointment. She wanted to shout his name to the four corners of the world, to proclaim "This man—this beautiful, wonderful, amazing man—loves me!"

"Lucy, the wraiths, they won't bother you again. Angus has promised me that."

"Angus?" she questioned. "Just what has he to do with them?"

"He is a Guardian, Lucy."

"A Guardian? You mean, like the elves we drank to at the Blue Nile?"

"Very good, now you are remembering."

"Remembering? Lance, it was just the other night. Why wouldn't I remember? And just how is it that you could see them, the wraiths? I thought they were just part of my sick imagination."

"Your imagination isn't sick, Lucy. To the contrary, it is well, healthier than most of the beings' I've encountered here. It's not your imagination you have to worry about. It is your doubt and your fear. Because you are different, you have been made to feel inferior. But I speak the truth to you Lucy; you are august. God has created you for a very special purpose. There are those who wish to see that that purpose is never fulfilled. You must remember we have a savior, and through him we have power over evil. You know that, but what you may not know, what is not stressed in the churches here today—what has been omitted from the Bible by the suppression of sacred texts—is how much power he has given us against evil. Most people take that to mean power over our thoughts and power to choose to do good. It is that certainly, but so much more. It is power to fight evil manifestations no matter where they come from. It is important that you remember that, Lucy."

"Excuse me, folks." A man in a greasy white apron approached their table carrying three plates. Their waitress was busy with another customer, so the cook, not wanting the food to get cold, brought it out himself. "Here are your sandwiches and hot cakes. Enjoy."

"Thanks, Lyle," Lance said. "How's that son of yours?"

"Oh, it's you," the man exclaimed, setting down the plates and shaking Lance's hand. "He's doing just fine, thanks to you. I can't stand to think about what that bear might have done to little Joey if you wouldn't have come along when you did. It was just a miracle, simple as that, and I thank God."

"Good," Lance said, "Glad to hear it."

"There's no charge for this food, mister. You can eat here whenever you want. It's the least we can do for you."

"Well, thank you, Lyle." Lance released his hand and he went back to the kitchen.

"Now what on earth was that about?" Lucy asked.

Lanced winked. "You don't think you are the only one around here that needs savin', now do you?"

Their attention turned to the plates that were before them. They were both ravenous. Lance again offered a prayer in the language that only she and the angels could understand.

On the ride back to the apartment after they'd eaten, Lance told her that he needed to spend as much time at the Keeper's as he could, but he hoped to see her after she finished work. "We only have two more safe days. After that I better stay away until you're safe again. I don't know if I can trust myself not to have you if I stay. Our desire is strong and our flesh is weak. We cannot put our trust in man's forms of protection for something this important, and I'll not have you taking that poison pill the doctors are pushing at women."

"Lance, what on earth are you talking about?"

"Your safe days Lucy, the days when you cannot conceive."

She felt like she'd been slapped. "Wait... wait a minute. How do you know when my 'safe days' are?"

"Trust me, I know."

"How?"

"That's a story for later. I don't have time to open that can of worms just now." He pulled up in front of her apartment.

"Okay, then answer me this: don't you want me to have your baby, Lance?" Her voice was breaking. "Because the love I feel for you is all about wanting your children whether you stick around to help me raise them or not."

The voice in her head, the one she hated, answered the question for her: "Why would he want someone like you bearing his children? He knows about the times when you go missing. It was nearly three days last time. What would your baby do if you just up and disappeared?"

Lance answered differently: "Darling, of course that's what I want. More than anything that's what I want." He pulled her close to him. "But it is not about that. It is not about what I want or what you want. It's about what we must do. It always has been about that."

"What must we do, Lance?"

"Well, right now what you must do is trust me. Will you do that please? Just trust me until I have time to explain. I know it's hard, my darling. Please just give me some time."

"You have the rest of my life, Lance. Is that enough?"

He brushed a tear from her cheek with one of his fingers and looked deep into her eyes. "I hope so, my love. God knows I hope so." The kiss they made alleviated all doubt from her mind and she yielded to his will.

She sighed deeply as he drove off. She had a promise to keep to Mrs. Garrett: the rose bush needed planting, and she thought this would be a good time to do it.

When she returned to her apartment after work, she was disappointed Lance was not there. She built up the fire, put the kettle on for tea, and took a quick shower. She sat now in the rocker staring into the flame, sipping her tea and letting her hair dry. She realized that she was smiling and had been doing so all day long. Jann had commented on this fact at work: "Gee Lucy, you seem to be extra cheerful tonight. You haven't stopped smiling since you got here. Is there something you want to share with me?"

Lucy tried to take the smile off her face, but it didn't work. "Share with you?" she asked coyly.

"Yeah, girlfriend, like who's the guy who put that twinkle in your eyes? Is it your little songbird?"

Lucy wanted to tell her. She wanted to tell the world that she had fallen head over heels in love, but she remembered what Lance had asked of her, so she just said, "I had a really good day, that's all. I planted a rose bush for Mrs. Garrett."

Jann was suspicious. "Gee, maybe I should take up gardening," she said. But they were busy, so she let it go.

Lucy finished her tea and braided her nearly dry hair, trying not to look at the clock to see how late it was getting. "Maybe Lance got busy at the Keeper's and decided not to come back." Her heart sank the moment that thought came to her. "After all, he only said he *hoped* to come back this evening." She closed her eyes and thought of him, and the smile came back to her face.

"Hello," he said. "Are you having a good dream there?"

"Yes," she answered, keeping her eyes closed. Her smile widened.

"Then maybe I'll be off and just leave you to it."

"Don't you dare," she said, jumping into his arms. "It's only good because you are in it." They kissed and he held her.

"I'm afraid I cannot stay long. I only came by to see if you were missing me."

"I think you know the answer to that." They kissed again and he carried her to bed.

Spring slipped into summer with Lucy happier than she had ever been. On the nights she had to work Lance usually met her somewhere along her walk home but was very careful not to be seen by anyone. If a car came along, he would duck into the bushes or behind a tree. He told her it was absolutely necessary that he not be discovered or his work at the Keeper's would be jeopardized.

Sheriff Carter had circulated a composite drawing of him with the caption "a person of interest." When he showed the picture to the staff at the Butler one night, Lucy was afraid Ashley might tip him off. But when Ashley was asked if he'd seen the guy before, all he said was that the picture looked something like a guy he'd met in Ireland. Lucy managed to hide away in the break room while he was there so she would not be questioned.

Toward the end of August around dinnertime, a knock came on her door. It was one of her days off and she was half expecting it to be Lance. She ran to the door, but to her surprise it was Deputy Pearson accompanied by Asad.

"Clyde, hi. What are you doing here?"

"Miss Lucy." He removed his hat as was his custom when he talked with her but then put it back on his head. "I'm here on police business."

"Oh."

"This here is Asad Shinaka. He works at the Blue Nile up the street."

"Yes, I know. Hi, Asad. How are you?"

"Miss Lucy, I'm well. I hope that I have not caused you any trouble."

"Trouble? I'm sorry but I don't understand. Would you like to come in?"

Clyde took over the conversation and was all business. "Thank you, no. What I have to ask you will only take a moment."

Lucy had a knot in her stomach. "Sure, Clyde. What is it?"

"Well, Miss Lucy, do you remember a couple of months ago when I came by to tell you we got the guy who'd killed that waitress and then escaped from the nut house?"

"Sure, I remember."

"Well, the sheriff had actually arrested another man earlier that day thinking he was the killer. But on the way to the station the guy got out of his cuffs and jumped out of the squad car. We believe he is the one that actually caught the killer, duct-taped him to a tree, and then tipped us off."

"I remember, Clyde. You said they ought to give him a medal."

"Yes, ma'am, but you see Sheriff Carter won't let it go. He's on a mission, obsessed with bringing this guy in."

"But why? What did the guy do?"

"We don't know, but the sheriff, he says he must be wanted for something or he wouldn't have been so anxious to get away. Anyway, I showed a composite to our friend Asad here, and he told me that he remembers this guy." Lucy's heart raced, but she tried to look unaffected. "He says it looks like a guy who brought you to dinner one evening."

"The picture, it looks like Mr. Lance," Asad said, looking very much like he had done something wrong.

"Here, Miss Lucy, I'd like you to have a look at this. Have you seen this man before?" Clyde took a folded 8-by-10 piece of paper from his shirt pocket and handed it to her. She slowly unfolded the paper, expecting to see a likeness of Lance. Her head ached and her stomach churned. She didn't want to lie but resolved she'd have to. She stared at the image.

Clyde waited and then asked, "Well, Miss Lucy, have you seen this man before?"

"Yes, Clyde, I have. But I don't understand."

"Do you know where this man is now, Miss Lucy?"

"Clyde, is this some sort of joke?"

"No, ma'am. Can you tell me where he is?"

"Sure, he's right here."

"Here?" Clyde put his hand on his firearm and looked around. "Where?"

"Right here, standing in front of me." She handed the paper back to him. His face turned bright red when he looked at it. It was a perfect likeness of himself, dressed in uniform complete with hat. Asad grinned widely. Over Clyde's shoulder, Lucy saw a rabbit dash across her yard. Clyde nervously searched all his pockets and checked in the car, but he couldn't come up with the other picture. He apologized to Lucy for bothering her and said he would see her at the Butler when he got his hands on the right picture. Lucy felt sorry for him but was totally relieved that she didn't have to divulge her relationship with Lance, at least not this night. She watched as the embarrassed deputy and Asad walked back to the squad car. Then she closed the front door and strolled back into the kitchen. Lance was sitting at the table.

"Lance, did you hear?"

"Aye, Angus saved us this time. But things are getting too hot for me to stay around much longer. I've nearly completed my studies at the Keeper's."

"You aren't thinking of leaving, are you?"

"I must. Lucy, you know that."

"When, Lance?"

"Very soon, I'm afraid. But not tonight." He rose and took her in his arms. "Darling, you will be brave? Our time is not at an end."

"Yes, Lance, I'll be brave."

6 – The Painting

Walking into the room, Daniel saw Lucy standing perfectly still, pale as a ghost, mouth agape, eyes bugged. "Lucy, what's wrong?" he asked.

She didn't answer. She stood mesmerized, staring at the wall.

Leaving his cart, he went to her side. "Lucy?" he said again, this time touching her shoulder.

She jumped and—shaking her head as if to clear her thoughts—gasped, "It's him."

"Who?"

"It's him," she repeated.

"Who's him?"

"Oh my God! That's him. That's him," she said excitedly.

"Lucy, what are you talking about?"

"Him!" She pointed to an old painting hanging on the back wall. She ran up to it and studied it closely. "Who did this?" she wondered out loud.

"You mean, who painted it?"

"Yes! Yes! I need to find out," she exclaimed, examining the bottom corners, searching for a signature.

"It *is* pretty cool," he admitted, coming to her side. "What is that, a leprechaun?"

"Part elf, part fairy," she muttered, not taking her focus from the canvas.

Daniel eyed it thoughtfully. A little man was stretched out beneath the shade of a large plant leaf. The setting was a forest that appeared to be in the throes of winter. Ice encased the limbs of the trees and icicles hung from their bare branches. Yet where the little man lay, all was as mid-spring; the grass was green and mushrooms grew nearby. Daniel stepped back and looked at Lucy, who was still visibly shaken. "Lucy, do you mean you have seen this painting before?"

"No, I've never seen it."

"But you said you have seen him."

"I'm talking about *him*. I have seen *him*."

"Lucy, you're freaking me out. That's a painting of an elf—or some other little creature—in some sort of fantasyland."

"Part elf, part fairy," she said again, "and you don't understand: I have been there."

"Where?"

"Right there, Danny, right there!" she said, pointing with emphasis to the center of the circle of stones that ringed the plant the little man reclined under.

"Okay, okay, take it easy, Lucy," Daniel said as he backed away. "I'm trying to understand."

"Oh Danny, I'm sorry. I know it sounds nuts, but listen, I have seen this little man. I have seen him many times, only… not for a while." She saw the disbelief in his eyes.

"Are you feeling all right? Maybe you better sit down a minute. Do you want me to get you a pop or some water?"

"No one ever believes me," she sighed under her breath. Then a new thought seized her mind. She grabbed his shirt and shrieked, "Lance! Oh my God, Lance!" Her eyes opened even wider. "He was there with me. Right there inside that circle."

Danny had enough. "Lance again," he thought, "her elusive lover." He took her firmly by the shoulders. "Lucy, stop it," he ordered. "It's just a painting. Maybe you have seen it before, but…"

She cut him off and spoke with stern defiance: "I know what it is. I'm telling you, I have never seen this painting before, but I have been in that circle, and I have seen that little man." She let go of his shirt and faced the painting again. Her voice evened out. "Now I know that someone else has too. Don't you see? I must find out who painted this because they have seen him, and they have been there, there in that circle. They know where it is, and maybe, just maybe, they know something about Lance."

Daniel had known Lucy for a long time. He moved from Chicago with his mother to the little town of Lacota when he was thirteen. He found work doing odd jobs on farms around the area. Her dad hired him that summer to pick blueberries and took a liking to him. Soon he was spending more time at their house than at his own. He became like a big brother to the twins. He hated that she was bringing up Lance again. He thought that whole mess was behind her. In his opinion, Lance, whether real or perceived, had been the cause of Lucy's isolation from her family and friends. "Look, Lucy, I'm getting a little concerned here. This Lance thing, how long has it been anyway since he disappeared?"

Lucy felt like she'd been punched in the solar plexus. "Oh," she gasped. Tears spilled from her eyes. "It's been seven years, Danny."

He felt terrible for making her sad, but he really didn't know how to handle all this. "Maybe you should sit down a minute, sissy." He hadn't called her that for years. It was what the twins used to call each other and he picked it up from them.

She wiped her cheeks on the back of her hand and went back to surveying the canvas, still trying to find a name on it. She reasoned aloud, "It looks like this frame was handmade. I bet it's concealing at least two or three inches of canvas behind these carved edges. Maybe the name is behind the frame. I need to get it out. Danny, help me." She didn't wait for him. She grabbed hold of the sides and started to pull it from the wall. As the wire on the back slipped from the wall mounts, the full weight of the painting fell upon her. She hadn't realized how heavy it was and started to collapse under the weight.

Daniel caught hold of it, saving both her and the painting from sure disaster. "Whoa there, wait just a minute, Lucy." They shared the weight of the painting now. "You can't do that. You can't just take this down and take it apart. It's not yours, and it wouldn't be right."

Just at that moment, their supervisor Bertha walked into the room. "Hey, you two, what's going on here? There are two floors left to clean and we're a body short tonight." As soon as she realized what they were holding, she bellowed even louder: "What the hell are you doing? Did you knock that down?"

"I did," said Daniel, "dusting it. Lucy is helping me hang it back up."

"Well, hurry up with it. You aren't getting paid to admire the artwork, and be more careful," she scowled. She noticed Lucy looked a little off color and was just about to question her when her radio squawked. She took it from her belt and barked into it. "What is it?"

A staticky voice came back saying, "I'm up on twenty three. The belt to my vacuum just broke."

"Oh, for Pete sakes," Bertha grunted. "I'll be right up." She turned and hurried out of the room, yelling to them to "get a move on it" as she left.

Daniel snatched the painting away from Lucy and rehung it. "Come on," he said, "you'll have to come back in daylight and do this thing right. If we don't get a hustle on, Bertha will give us both the boot."

"But..." She started to argue then realized he was right. "Okay," she sighed, "I'm sorry. You just can't imagine what seeing this means to me."

"I'm sorry too, but we can't talk about that right now. Bertha has been in a really bad mood lately, and you know I need this job."

"Don't worry, Danny. Bertha would never give you the boot. If she did, she'd have to hire two people just to replace you, and she knows it."

Lucy was so excited she could hardly think straight. She went about her duties that night dusting and wiping desks, but her thoughts remained on the painting. "Who could have painted it?" she asked herself. "Is it really a picture of Angus? It certainly looks like him." She settled it in her mind: "It's Angus, all right; there are just too many similarities, like what he's wearing: the same rusty brown vest, the same dark green pants, the same sand-colored shirt, the red pointed hat with the turned-down peak. It's Angus for sure, right down to the pipe in his teeth." The circle—all of it—was just as she remembered.

A smile came to her face. She never thought she'd be happy to see Angus again. "But why now?" she asked herself. Maybe it was because their Fairytale was growing dim. After seven years, she was losing her will to fight for their truth, giving in to the temptation to accept her family's—and just about everyone else's—opinion of her. It was just easier than trying to convince people that things can and do occur beyond their comprehension. This painting proved she was not crazy, had not just made him up. It proved that someone else had known Angus and traveled into the same stone circle that she now so vividly recalled.

"Lance, where are we going?" she called to him. He was running through the woods a little way ahead of her, following a rabbit.

"Keep up, Lucy. I don't want to lose sight of him. He promised to take us somewhere very special."

"Where?" she asked breathlessly as she pushed herself harder to keep pace with him. Lance came to a standstill. She stopped beside him, breathless, as they watched the rabbit hop into the center of a stone circle. When he did, an amazing transformation took place. He turned into a little man. "Is that Angus?" she panted.

"The one and only."

"He is amazing. I have never seen anything like him."

"Aye, he has a different tale to tell than most." Lance said. "Take my hand, Lucy. We'll step in together."

As the two stepped over the circle of stones, it was as if the ground gave way and they were falling through it. Lucy squeezed Lance's hand harder. Soon the falling sensation ended, and they were standing on solid ground. The land looked very different, more vibrant somehow. She noticed the landscape outside the circle was as a winter scene: ice on the trees, snow on the ground. Yet there in the circle, all was mid-spring, just as it had been when they entered it. Lance sat down on a blanket of moss and pulled her down beside him. "Are you going to slay her?" Angus cackled wickedly.

"Keep your tongue and get lost for a while," Lance ordered. Angus jumped out of the circle and a rabbit took off running.

"What did he mean by 'Are you going to slay her'? Does he think you are going to kill me?"

"Lucy, the word *slay* has a whole different meaning to a creature such as he. He is asking if I am going to lay with you and plant my child in you. If I do, you would no longer be who you are now. You would be different. Life would be forming inside of you, and your every cell would change."

"Are you? Are you going to *slay* me, Lance?" She moved close to him and initiated a kiss. It was a kiss of tender passion, a kiss surrendering everything she had unto him.

He whispered to her as he tenderly unbuttoned her blouse. "It is not our time, Lucy, not for that. It will come, I promise you, but you must be patient. Today we will lose ourselves in each other, in our passion and desire. We will traverse to the heights of ecstasy and return as who we are."

He was right; they came completely separated from themselves, lost in sensitivity and sensuality. They built and released and built and released until total exhaustion covered them with sleep.

When they awoke, Angus was back. He had built up a fire and roasted some type of meat. Lucy tasted it and remarked how good it was and what an unusual flavor it had. "What? She's never eaten newts before?" Angus asked Lance, as if not wanting to talk directly to her.

She answered him anyway: "No, I don't believe I have. They are very tasty. Thank you for preparing them for me."

"I prepared them for him; he gave them to you," Angus said with a scowl on his wrinkled old face.

Lance told her this stone circle was one of many that opened doors into other dimensions. Angus had shown him others. "There are many such places all over the earth; some can be accessed only by a Guardian, such as Angus, others require rituals to be performed. Then there are those that can only be entered at special times, like solstices or other stellar alignments. I'm looking for the portal that will take me—take us—back to Elysium."

"Did you find it, my darling?" she whispered into a spot on a desk she had buffed for much longer than necessary.

As her shift dragged on, she pondered the incredible painting and how it had given her back the hope that had been slowly waning from her heart the past few years. She wondered where this revelation would lead her and just what she should do with this new piece of the puzzle. Her mind was settled on one thing: she must come back to this building in the morning and somehow get into that office. She needed to convince whoever was there to let her have a better look at the canvas. She would offer to buy it if she had to, though she had no idea how she would come up with the money.

When her work for the evening was finished, Daniel was waiting for her in the service room downstairs. "Hey, are you doing okay?" he asked as she hurried past him to the time clock.

"I'm just fine, thanks," she said, noticing how quickly he turned away. As he drove her home, he hardly spoke. Usually he was very talkative, detailing the latest antics of his three-year-old son and five-year-old daughter, or telling her about a theory that had been discussed in his psych class. He was working toward a bachelor's degree in engineering, but because of his family responsibilities, he had to do it one class at a time.

Like so many other poor, young farm boys, Daniel had served a tour of duty in Vietnam so he could get college money from the government. He wasn't the same person when he returned from the war. He seemed more serious, more closed-minded than before. She wished she could help him. She felt the awkwardness between them now and it hurt her.

After riding in silence for what seemed ages, Daniel finally said, though a little gingerly, "Have you thought any more about the odd little man in that painting?"

"Actually, that is all I've thought about all night," Lucy replied.

"This is kind of like a *Twilight Zone* episode," he laughed.

"Yeah, my life the *Twilight Zone* episode," she said glumly.

"Hey, I'm sorry. I didn't mean it like that. You have to admit, it's more than a little strange."

"Look," she snapped, "I really don't want to discuss it. I don't expect you to believe me."

They rode again in silence. As Daniel pulled up to the curb, he said, "Lucy, I'm worried about you. Maybe you should see someone."

"See someone?" she repeated through her clenched teeth. "Yes, Danny, that's exactly what I plan to do. I plan to see the person who painted that picture." She hopped out of the car and gave the door a good slam.

"Lucy," he called after her, "I'll pray for you."

Turning around, she stuck her face through the open window. "How about right now?"

"What?"

"Well, if you're going to pray for me, please do it now so I can hear what you're going to ask God to do on my behalf."

She had dealt with religious people in the past who seemed to use prayer as a way to condemn her for her perceived instability. They used their prayer as proof to her of their own righteousness, like the man Jesus encountered in the temple who said, "Lord, thank you that I am not a sinner like this man," referring to another who knelt at the altar repenting aloud of his wrongdoings.

She enjoyed going to church, singing praise songs, hearing sermons, and learning about the Lord. But when it came to fellowship, she found no love or tolerance for her unusual experiences. If she did confide in someone, more times as not she would end up being prayed for by a group of elders who stood around her commanding the demons to come out. She finally stopped attending church altogether because she couldn't cope with people hurting her with their self-proclaimed holiness.

"Well, come on, Danny," she said curtly. "If you're going to pray for me, please get on with it; it's getting late."

Daniel took hold of her hand, closed his eyes, bowed his head, and said, "Lord, You are so good, so amazing. You always know just what we need, and you always provide for us. Lord, please help Lucy. I have no understanding of just what she is going through, but You do. Lord, give her what she needs. Surround her with people who will understand and not judge her. Help her to forgive me, Father, if I have hurt her, and help me to understand what she needs. Amen."

Lucy looked at him with a tear in her eye. "Hey, Danny," she said, "I know this whole thing is weird. But that was really cool how you covered my behind with Bertha tonight. And that prayer just now... well, it means a lot to me. Thanks."

He looked embarrassed, "No problem. I want to help if I can. I hope you know that."

"Sure, I know that, Danny."

"Look, I'm sorry that Donna and I haven't spent much time with you lately, but with me working and going to school and her with the kids, it's just hard. Please call either one of us any time you need something, okay?"

"Thanks, Danny; that's sweet. I'll see you tomorrow night." She slapped the top of the car then backed away from the curb. As he pulled off, she prayed silently, "Thank You Lord for the dear people You have placed in my life. Please watch over and protect Danny and his family." Seconds later there came the screeching of brakes. A big black car had run the red light just up the street. Daniel stomped his brakes and was able to stop just in time to avoid being hit.

Lucy hardly slept at all that night. Anticipation of finally meeting someone who could verify what she knew to be true kept her awake. Her thoughts kept going to the painting. She had to find out who painted it. Whoever it was had seen the same little man, had been to the same stone circle in the woods. These thoughts kept racing around in her mind. She realized the hope that underlay all this was that maybe whoever painted it knew Lance. So many times she had doubted herself, thinking maybe she *had* invented a fantasy world and *was* living in it. But now there was this. It was too much of a coincidence that every detail in that painting was just as she remembered.

By eight a.m. she was waiting at the curb for the bus to take her back to the building. She wanted to be there before it got busy for the day. The bus dropped her off in front of the thirty-two-story office building called Prudential Town Center. The office she wanted was on the nineteenth floor. She normally used the service elevator in the back of the building, but this morning she walked through the main lobby, found the right bank of elevators, and went up. She had dressed in business attire: a basic grey skirt and a black silk blouse dotted with small grey flowers with olive green centers. Over this she wore a fitted waist jacket of charcoal grey with broken, vertical stripes of light grey and olive green. Though her clothes were a few years old, they were classic, and she fit right in with the office workers now converging into the building. She alighted from the elevator on the nineteenth floor, where things looked familiar, and entered the lobby of suite 1900, Donegan and Donegan Celtic Importers. She walked up to the front desk. As the receptionist looked up and greeted her, she realized she hadn't given much thought to this part of her plan.

"May I help you?" the girl asked.

"Why yes, thank you, my name is Lucy Cavanagh, and I would like to see… umm…" She stumbled. She didn't know who it was she wanted to see. She began again awkwardly, "To see the person whose office is down the hall there, on the right." She motioned toward the office with her hand as she spoke.

The girl gave her a puzzled expression. "Excuse me?"

"I need to speak with the person in that office. Could you please tell me who it is?"

The girl, still puzzled, said, "That office belongs to the President, Mr. Donegan. Do you have an appointment?"

"No, I'm sorry, I don't," Lucy replied.

"May I inquire then as to the nature of this visit?"

Lucy was trying to think of a clever story when a still, small voice reminded her to "Tell the Truth." She took a deep breath and began: "You see, I clean these offices at night, and I saw a painting hanging on the wall in there." She pointed again at the office. "I need to talk to the person who owns it."

The girl got a superior look on her face and spoke sternly: "Look—Miss Cavanagh, is it?—Mr. Donegan is a very busy man. If you need to talk with him, you'll have to have an appointment."

"Oh, but this won't take long," Lucy pleaded. "I just need to ask him if he knows who painted the picture of the little man that hangs in his office."

"Look..." the receptionist began, but she was interrupted by a man's voice coming from behind Lucy.

"So you like the little rascal, do you?" Lucy turned with a start. Without waiting for an answer, the man looked at the receptionist and said, "Good Morning, Sara. When is my first appointment?"

"Good morning, Mr. Donegan. It's at 10:30, sir." Sara had returned to using her pleasant voice.

Turning to Lucy, he put out his hand and said, "Okay then, Miss..." He paused.

"Cavanagh," Lucy said, shaking his hand.

"Okay then, Miss Cavanagh, I can give you a few moments this morning. Let's go see what Angus is up to, shall we?

"Angus!" Lucy gasped. Her heart leapt into her throat.

"That's the name my grandfather called the little scoundrel in that painting."

"Angus," Lucy repeated. Her heart was pounding so heavily she thought he could feel it when he placed his hand on her back to direct her down the hall. She took a deep breath to calm herself and thought how fortunate it was for her that this Mr. Donegan showed up when he did. If he hadn't, she was sure Sara would have buzzed security to escort her out. She wouldn't have blamed her.

Opening the door and flipping on the light, Mr. Donegan said, "Good Morning, Angus. You have a visitor." Lucy again stood bewildered before the painting. It mesmerized her just as it had done the night before. Mr. Donegan stood at the credenza by a coffee maker full of fresh brewed coffee. He picked up the pot and motioned to her with it. "Miss Cavanagh, would you like a cup of joe?" he asked. "Sara always makes up a pot when she comes in, unless I've done. Fortunately for us, she's beaten me to it."

Lucy, who couldn't take her eyes off the painting, shook her head no and then managed a "Thank you."

"So, Miss Cavanagh, did I hear you say you work here in the evenings?"

"Yes, that's right," she said, still not removing her eyes from the painting.

"I ofttimes work late, but I don't recall seeing you here before, and I'm quite sure I would remember if I had." He sipped some coffee while looking her over.

"I started a week and a half ago, but last night was my first time on this floor."

"Oh, I see. You just started."

"Yes, my friend Daniel got me the job."

"Daniel Breer?"

"That's right."

"Nice guy, Daniel. We talk from time to time when I'm burning the midnight oil."

"He's as good as they come," Lucy said. Her glance now came to him but returned quickly to the painting.

Mr. Donegan took another sip of coffee as he studied the attractive form that stood before him. "Just exactly what are you looking for?" he asked. "I'm beginning to get jealous of that little fellow."

"I'm looking for my sanity," Lucy murmured half under her breath.

"Oh, and you are going to find it in that painting, are you?"

"You don't know, Mr. Donegan, you couldn't know. And I'm sure if I explained it you'd think I'm cracked. But that is exactly right; I *am* looking for my sanity in this painting, or at least hoping for a clue."

He was intrigued by how seriously she had spoken. "Okay then, look away. I didn't mean to pry." He took another sip from his mug, sat it on the credenza, and walked over to study the picture with her.

Lucy recognized that she had been terribly rude. "I'm sorry," she said. "It was awfully nice of you to allow me in here." It was the same old thing again. She was afraid to tell anyone the truth because of the way she had been hurt in the past. Yet she realized she did owe him an explanation.

Before she could offer one, he said, "Are you sure you want to find it?"

"I beg your pardon?"

"Your sanity," he said with a pleasant smile. "I'm thinking the whole thing is terribly overrated myself." She smiled. He had put her at ease.

He looked her up and down as he said, "Let me see now, you have all your buttons in the right holes, your shoes match, and you managed to talk your way in here, so if you are a little coo-coo for Angus there, it's probably not all that bad."

Lucy turned from the picture and looked directly at him. He had a warm smile and a little twinkle in his eye. She smiled back. "No," she said. "I'm not sure at all if I want to find it. But I have to try. Tell me, Mr. Donegan, if you would be so good, where did you get this painting?"

"Oh, that's easy—please call me Michael—it belonged to my grandfather. It used to hang at his cottage in Saugatuck where I spent my summers as a lad. Old Angus here hung over the fireplace in the den. We were all charmed by him."

Lucy noticed for the first time he spoke with a slight brogue. "Do you know where your grandfather got it, Mr. Donegan?"

"Michael, my first name is Michael, and as a matter of fact I do. My grandfather told me an old farmer that lived near Lake Michigan, somewhere around Glenn, had painted it. Grandfather used to go to his farm in the summer to buy vegetables. They got to be pretty good chums, both being from the old country and all. They would sit swapping tales of the Emerald Isle, taking sips from a jug the farmer kept filled with some pretty potent homemade brew. Dandelion wine, I think Gramps said it was. Anyway, when the old-timer died, Grandfather went to the estate sale and bought this picture, frame and all, and the old clay jug still half full of the golden dream juice."

"So the old farmer was an artist?" Lucy asked.

"Grandfather said this is the only picture he ever painted. The old fellow was a bit of a kook, I guess. Grandfather said he told him he had actually met Angus here, and he had taken him to some magical place. The old guy must have really liked that golden nectar." Michael beamed.

Lucy didn't smile; she felt dizzy all of a sudden and must have gone pale. "Hey there, you better sit down here a moment. Are you feeling ill, lass?" He pushed an office chair up behind her and took her arm as she sat down slowly. He saw tears forming in her eyes. "What's wrong, darlin'?" he asked. "Are my stories that boring?" He was trying to lighten her mood a bit.

"I'm sorry," Lucy said, dabbing her eyes with a tissue she had taken from her purse. "It's just… this is all a little overwhelming, after all these years to hear that someone else has met…" Her sentence dropped off as she realized she had almost let her secret slip. She quickly added, "Mr. Donegan, may I buy this painting?"

"It's Michael. You want to buy Angus?"

"Yes, yes, very much I do. How much?"

"I'm afraid Angus here is like part of the family. I'm certain Grandfather would torment me from his grave if I were to sell him to anyone."

"Please, Mr. Donegan, please reconsider; I must have him."

"Well now, if you want me to reconsider, you'll have to tell me why you want him so badly."

"I'm afraid I can't do that," Lucy said, dabbing her eyes again.

He thought for a moment. This woman intrigued him, not only because he found her amazingly beautiful but also because she had aroused his curiosity and his compassion. "Look, you said, 'someone else had met…' Met who? Angus?"

After an awkward moment she admitted, "Yes, Mr. Donegan, Angus." She glared at him, expecting to be mocked.

"It's Michael, please," he again insisted. "I'm just trying to help you."

This totally disarmed her. "Okay then, Michael. I know how strange this must sound."

"Strange? No. I mean, there have been hundreds of people in this office who have told me the same thing."

"Really?" Lucy asked excitedly as she jumped to her feet.

He felt a little remorseful about teasing her and motioned with his hands for her to sit down again. "I'm sorry, that was a bad joke. I can see you are very serious about this. But really, I couldn't sell Angus no matter what the reason. I'm sorry."

"That's quite all right, Mr. Donegan—Michael. I'm very much used to being teased and made the butt of jokes over this, but the truth is the truth, and I shan't deny it. I have seen him, this very same Angus." Michael studied her face intently. He noticed her beautiful blue-green eyes set under her thick dark lashes. She continued, "I would appreciate anything you could tell me about this painting and the man who painted it. Do you know the name of the farmer and where exactly he lived?"

"His name was Green, I think. I'm going to Saugatuck this weekend; I could check in my grandfather's journals. I'm sure there is a mention or two in there about the old gent and about our pal Angus here."

"Would you? Would you really? That would be great." She became excited again and smiled at him. He liked making her smile, and he liked that she had come right out with her admission, as strange as it was.

"It would be no trouble at all. I'd be happy to do it."

"Mr. Donegan," she started, but remembered before he could correct her. "Michael, do you think—I know this is a lot to ask, you have been so kind already. But do you think we could take the picture out of the frame to see if anything has been written on the edges?"

"Written on it?"

"Yes, maybe on the back or on the sides there behind the frame."

He looked at his watch, then back at her. "I don't see why not, but it'll have to wait for another time. I have a very important client coming in here shortly, and I need to prepare a few things."

"Oh, of course, I understand." She looked disappointed.

"I have an idea. Will you be working here tonight?"

"Yes."

"Well then, why don't you meet me here this evening, and we'll have a go at it. Maybe old Angus will let us in on some secrets."

"That would be wonderful. I can take my break around nine-thirty. Is that too late?"

"Perfect," he said. "Nine-thirty it is, then. That will give me time to go home and pick up a few tools that may help us crack into this old frame."

"That's very kind of you, Mr. Donegan," she said, giving the picture one last glance.

"Michael," he said firmly. "I insist."

"Michael," Lucy giggled. "My name is Lucy. You have been grand. I'll see you here tonight."

"I'm looking forward to it," he said as his phone rang. He answered it as he simultaneously gave her a goodbye wave. As she walked down the hall, she heard him say, "Freddy, you old possum, you were right. Hanging Angus in here did bring me some luck."

7 – Benefit of the Doubt

That evening when Danny picked her up for work, he noticed she was dressed a little nicer than usual and had makeup on, something he hadn't seen her wear in quite a while.

"Hey," he said as she slid into the car, "you feeling any better?"

"Better than what?" she joked. "Yes, Danny, I'm feeling fine, thanks to good people who pray for me." She leaned over and gave him a little peck on the cheek.

"Did you go back to the building and see the painting again?"

"Yes sir, I did, bright and early this morning."

"So what'd you learn about it?"

"I learned that it belonged to Michael Donegan's grandfather and that a farmer named Green painted it. I had a nice long talk with Michael this morning."

"Michael, huh?" Danny murmured.

"He's very nice."

"Oh yeah, we've talked a few times. He seems nice enough."

"He said good things about you too, Danny. I'm going to meet him in his office tonight, and we're going to crack the frame off Angus and see if anything is written on the back of the painting itself."

"Angus?" Danny asked.

"The little man in the painting. He has a name; it's Angus."

"And you know this how?"

"Danny, I told you I've seen him before, with Lance. Lance told me his name. And Michael confirmed what I suspected: it *is* a picture of Angus."

"Oh, so Michael has seen the little guy too, I mean, up close and personal?"

"No, Michael's grandfather knew the man who painted the picture. He is the one who knew Angus and traveled with him to that stone circle."

"Whoa," Danny exclaimed, "this just keeps getting stranger." He had a look of concern on his face. "I'm not sure you should go any farther with all this."

"What?" she squealed. "Are you kidding me? I have to. Danny, I told you, I've seen this same little man. Lance knew him, and now I have proof that at least one other person has seen him too. How could I just leave that alone?"

"I know what you told me, Lucy. But sometimes the enemy tempts us with things just to take our focus off the Lord."

"Danny, don't go getting religious on me. You know I love the Lord."

"It's just a painting of a make-believe creature. All it proves is that someone had a vivid imagination, and the Bible says we are to cast down vain imaginations."

She was becoming upset. "It's not just in my imagination. Can't you please give me the benefit of the doubt?"

"That's just it. I don't have a doubt. I mean, come on, Lucy. A little man?" He paused as if picking a way to say it. "I believe you may think you have seen him, and that scares me."

"Okay, Danny, let's just drop it." She was angry now, and hurt, and it was showing in her voice. "You know, I was treated better by Michael about all this, a complete stranger."

"Ah well, there is that too. Just be careful with that Michael. I've heard he has an eye for the ladies, and, well, he isn't a bad looking guy."

"What?" she said indignantly.

"Don't tell me you didn't notice. He has you wearing eye shadow, doesn't he?"

Her anger spilled out now, and she snapped back, "So what if I find him attractive." She was surprised to hear this come from her lips.

"So nothing," Danny said sharply. "It's just that we've been friends since grade school, for Pete's sake. I worry about you. I just don't want to see you go off the deep end again. How good a friend would I be if I didn't give you a heads up when I sense trouble?"

"Trouble?"

"You know what I think? I think that painting somehow stirred up old feelings that you had for that Lance guy. Am I right? Is that what this is about?"

At the mention of Lance, Lucy felt sick inside. Tears formed in her eyes. She was tired of fighting the same battle whenever she let anyone in on her private truths. But tired or not, she was resigned. "Yes, Danny, it is about Lance. Angus was his companion. He believed Angus to be a Guardian of secret places of power, like that stone circle in the painting."

"Oh God, I don't doubt that, Lucy. From what you've told me, Lance believed a lot of things. He went chasing all over the world on his mission, his quest. But just what did that get him? He's been gone for how long now?"

A tear spilled down her cheek. He'd never spoken to her like this before. "Seven years," she whispered.

"Seven years," Danny repeated, "that's a long time." He paused and came back in a softer voice. "Lucy, maybe it is time you set your sights on another man and accept the fact that Lance isn't coming back." He reached out and took her hand. "But this Donegan guy, I just don't know about him."

Lucy pulled her hand away. "Danny, you can be a big ass sometimes. I haven't set my sights on Michael, and you don't know anything about Lance."

"Lucy, look, please don't take this wrong, but does anyone know anything about Lance? Really?"

"Yes, Danny. I do."

"Oh, all right then, where is he?"

Through quivering lips, she said softly, "God, I wish I knew."

"I'm sorry, kid. That was uncalled for. This whole thing has me creeped out." They rode the rest of the way in silence. After pulling into his usual spot in the parking garage, he turned to Lucy and said, "Look, I'm sorry I was harsh. I just want you to be careful, that's all."

"We are to cast our cares on the Lord, for he cares for us," Lucy replied. Danny put his hands up in surrender.

After punching in, they rode the service elevator together. Danny got off on the nineteenth floor. They normally took their breaks together, but Lucy had other plans for her break that evening. "See you after work," she said, and flashed him the peace sign as the doors slid shut. She continued up to twenty-three.

She was anxious to get started with her chores. They didn't require much thought, so it gave her time to think about other things and remember. This night she thought about all the times Lance had left her not knowing when or if she would see him again. She thought about their first summer when she visited his folks' farm.

"Hello."

"Your voice in my ear gladdens my heart like a meadowlark's song."

"Lance! Is it really you?"

"The last time someone addressed me by name that is the name they used."

"And who was it that called you by that name?"

"It was mum."

"Well, she should know."

"Better than most, I'd say."

"I bet she was happy to hear from you."

"Aye. I'm here with my family now; that's why I'm calling you. I am hoping that you will bring the train down to meet them and spend a few days with us. What do you say?"

"You want me to come down to Ohio to your folks' farm?"

"I'm hoping that you will."

"When?"

"As soon as you can make it would not be soon enough for me. Will you come?"

"Yes, yes of course. But..."

"There are no *buts* to a determined heart."

"My heart *is* determined."

"That's my girl. There is a ticket in your name for tomorrow's train waiting at the station in Bangor. My brother Paul will pick you up here. So it is settled."

"It is settled. I can't wait."

"Good. You're going to love the McKellen clan, Lucy, and they you."

It was after Labor Day and the busy time at the Butler was over. Ashley was more than happy to write her off the schedule for a week, and he even offered to drive her to the train.

That summer seemed like a dream now as she flitted around the offices, doing her nightly tasks.

The farm had been in the McKellen family for three generations and would be Lance's brother Paul's some day. Paul had never moved from the farm. He had married right after high school and brought his new bride, Littlefeather, home to live with his family. She claimed her Native American ancestry from the Hopewell people—known as the "mound-builders"—who had lived in that area for as long as history could tell. They adopted the Algonquin language from tribes that migrated from the North. She told Paul's family when she came to live with them, "This farm may be yours, but the land it is on belongs to my people."

Paul picked Lucy up at the station in Lance's Quicksilver. He told her they would collect him along the way. "He has a lot of people he checks on around here whenever he's home," Paul said.

She asked him how he had recognized her at the station, so he related Lance's description: "She is as a fairy; her hair is long and the color of chestnuts, her eyes are blue like a mountain's pool, and when she walks it is like she is dancing to the music in her soul." Lucy blushed and Paul said, "He sure paints good pictures in people's minds, you got to admit that."

"Yes, he certainly does." She laughed, for she recognized Paul right away from Lance's description of him: he looks like Lil' Abner from the comic strip, with a big grin on his face.

It wasn't long before the truck pulled off the road near a trail that led over a wooden footbridge across a small ravine. A figure was crossing the bridge and in his hand he carried a bouquet of wild mountain lupine in pink, purple and white. She recognized him right away by the leather outback hat he always wore. He walked up to the truck, took off his hat, and handed her the flowers. "Lucy girl," he said.

She couldn't help but beam. "Lance," she whispered as he leaned forward and gave her a tender kiss.

"Did you enjoy the train ride?" he asked.

"Yes, I did, especially the last hour. This is beautiful country."

"Aye, I'm hoping to take you to its heart while you are here." He opened the door and nudged her to scoot over. He hopped in next to her and wrapped his arm around her neck. He gave her another kiss, and this time they lost themselves in it.

"Breathe, Brother," Paul mocked. Lance slapped him on the back of the head, and they all laughed.

"Mom is cooking up a storm, so I hope you are hungry."

"Mom always cooks up a storm when Lance is home," Paul interjected. "You know, the prodigal son returns. I had to kill the fatted calf."

"That's because you already ate the cow," Lance jested as he put his hat back on. He left his arm around her neck. "This is perfect," he said as he squeezed her close to him. She laughed and put the flowers under his nose. He buried his face in them, inhaling deeply and uttering on the exhale, "Thank you for this time of serenity, Lord." As they rode along in happy chatter, he would pull her close and smell her hair. He would stroke the side of her face with the back of his hand and softly touch her ear. Everything did seem perfect.

Lucy liked Mr. and Mrs. McKellen very much. She didn't know what to expect at first or how they would feel about her, but they seemed warm and friendly from the very first moment. She better understood Lance's charm after meeting them. They were simple people with nothing to hide, or so she thought.

She learned later from Lance's mom that he had never brought a girl there before. He introduced her simply by saying, "Mum, Dad, this is my Lucy." She *was* his, of that she had no doubt.

Paul was taller and heavier than Lance, much more like their father. He was also a big kid compared to his more serious older brother. Yet whenever Lance was around him, they reverted to boyhood. Whenever one egged the other on with a jab or poke, they'd wrestle around the living room or kitchen or wherever they happened to be. It was a happy time.

Littlefeather didn't say a word when Lucy was introduced; she just nodded and went about fixing dinner. Nor did she speak at all during the meal. Her eyes danced from Paul to Lance as they joked and teased one another. She listened intently, as they all did, when Lance spoke about where he had been and what he had been doing since the last time he was home. The love for him was intense, and Lucy knew that they all shared in her pain whenever he left them.

Lance's old room was hers that week, and he slept on a foldout couch in the den. The next morning when she came down for breakfast, she found the menfolk had eaten and were off. Lance and Paul had taken the pickup and gone to the feed store in Peebles while Mr. McKellen harvested hay in one of their many paddocks. Mrs. McKellen fixed Lucy ham, eggs and toast and sat sipping coffee and chatting while she ate them. She talked mostly of Lance and things he had done as a child. Lucy loved listening to these stories as much as Mrs. McKellen loved telling them.

Littlefeather came to the kitchen door and motioned for Lucy to follow her. "Littlefeather has a surprise for you," Mrs. McKellen said. Lucy stood up, cleared her dishes and carried them to the sink. "I'll do those up; you run along. It's a beautiful day." She hesitated a moment until Mrs. McKellen reaffirmed her offer. "You go on now. Don't keep her waiting."

Lucy found Littlefeather around the side of the house holding the leads of two saddled horses. One—a magnificent, shiny, coal black stallion—was a powerful-looking animal. She walked toward him, stopped, and slowly reached out her hand to stroke his forehead and then his muzzle. "Hey boy," she whispered softly, "I'm pleased to meet you." He pushed his head into her chest and gave a soft snort. The other horse, a paint, was mostly white with beautiful black and brown markings smattered about his coat. Lucy reached over and patted its neck.

"My horse is called Warlock. That is Takota. He is Lance's horse. Lance and I are the only ones who can ride him." She handed Lucy the reins. "You try."

Lucy looked the horse in the eyes while she continued stroking his muzzle. "How about it, Takota?" she whispered softly to him. "May I have a ride?"

Takota pushed his head into Lucy's shoulder. "Okay then, I'll take that as a yes." She took hold of the saddle horn, put her left foot into the stirrup, and flung her right leg up and over the giant horse. She tried to mount gracefully, but it had been a few years since she rode. She had never owned a horse, but as a child she often rode her cousin's horse Champion or sat bareback on King, her Uncle's old plow horse. Over the years she had rented many different animals from various stables for trail rides, but this horse was like a god compared to any other she had ever mounted. He was tall, powerful, and full of energy. As soon as her weight settled in the saddle, he bolted off. Littlefeather flung herself up on Warlock and raced behind.

Lucy leaned forward and hung on. She patted Takota's powerful neck and said, "Okay, boy. I'm just along for the ride." She was surprised how good he felt under her; it was like she had been riding him for years. His gait was rhythmic and smooth, and he ran with ease and purpose. She let him have his head and just take her.

There was a trail from the barn through the backfields of the farm. Eventually it wound its way alongside the river and then into the woods. Lucy saw that Littlefeather and Warlock were quite a ways behind, so she tugged the reins gently and said, "Come on, Takota. Let them catch up a bit." His pace slowed immediately, and soon the two horses were nearly side by side. Warlock kept a head or two behind Takota's and never challenged him for the lead.

They slowed the pace even more as they ascended the path into the woods. They rode on for some time through dales filled with wild flowers and over small hills. They rode past an old, weathered, and abandoned log cabin. Littlefeather pointed out that it was there she had been born and where she lived for many years with her family. Lucy tried to picture what that must have been like, living so far off the beaten track.

The riders turned off the trail at a point where it wound back toward the river. Riding into a small clearing near the edge of a babbling brook, they dismounted and tied the horses to a nearby bush so they could graze on the tall grass that grew in the partial shade next to the bank. The girls waded for a while in the cold water and then plunked down under an elm tree and watched as the sunlight danced atop the ripples of the little stream.

Lucy liked Littlefeather. Though she didn't speak often, her voice was deep and rich and beautiful. Her English was very good, but Lucy loved to hear her speak in her native tongue. As they sat, Lucy asked her the words for the plants, shrubs and trees that grew nearby then slowly repeated the phonetic sounds of each.

Lucy asked her how she had met Paul, and Littlefeather related the story in simple, non-flowery phrases. She told of how she had known Lance her whole life, and that he used to visit her family in the little cabin as a boy. He'd bring them food or blankets or some other necessity to make their life a little easier. After her father died, she went with her mother to live at her grandfather's house some distance away. But Lance still visited as often as he could. Then one day he brought Paul to meet her. Paul later told Lucy his version: he was smitten at their first meeting and told Lance then and there that he wanted to marry Littlefeather someday. To that Lance replied, "Little Brother, I have known for years that she was to be my sister. I've just been waiting for you to grow up and ask her into our family."

Littlefeather told Lucy that her mother and father used to call Lance *Kackawan Qisus*, meaning "son of the mist." Lucy repeated, "cosh-ka-wan kwee-sus." She was about to ask why they called him that when Takota neighed loudly, bucked wildly, and broke free from the bush where he was tied. He raced over to where Lucy sat and reared high in the air over her. His powerful hoofs came down only inches from her leg. She screamed and crawled backwards away from him as he reared up again and again. Littlefeather jumped to her feet and put her arms in the air, yelling a command in her native tongue. Just then Lance came out of the woods, whistled loudly, and Takota ran over to him. He touched the mighty animal's neck as he hurried over to Lucy, still sprawled on the ground.

"What happened?" he asked.

"What happened is your horse just tried to kill me," she cried, feeling betrayed by Takota's treachery.

"Are you all right?" he asked softly as he bent to help her up.

"I'm fine, just a little shaken. I... I don't understand; we had such a good ride," she stammered.

He left her side and walked over to Takota, who was prancing back and forth a few feet from them. He stretched out his hand and Takota ran up to put his muzzle in it. Lance spoke softly into his ear, calming the big horse. He retrieved the reins and led him to the bush where he had been tethered. As he walked back to Lucy, he stopped and looked down. He picked up a long stick and dug into the tall grass. Raising the stick, he displayed a dead water moccasin that had been pummeled by the mighty horse's hoofs. "I think Takota was trying to kill someone all right, but it was not you." He held the stick out toward her. Lucy looked at the dead snake and then at Takota. He whinnied and shook his head.

"Oh, Takota," Lucy said running to him. She flung her arms around his neck. "You saved my life. I'm sorry I doubted you."

"Lucy," Lance said, "he would never hurt you, and neither would I. You need to trust us."

Warlock had also broken free in the commotion. Soon after Lance appeared, Littlefeather ran off to collect him. She rode back to them moments later, spoke something to Lance, then rode off in the direction of the farm. Lucy noticed the two of them never spoke English to one another.

"Where is Littlefeather off to?"

"She's going back to the farm to help Paul with some chores."

"Shouldn't we ride back with her?" Lucy asked, though she was happy to have this time alone with Lance. She found it difficult to sleep last night, feeling his presence in the room beneath her.

"I'll take you back now if you really want to go, but I was hoping you would stay here in the woods with me tonight."

Lucy's heart soared. "Here?"

"Well, no, not exactly here. We'll ride for a bit. I want to show you something. We'll stay at the old cabin tonight, if that suits you."

"It suits me," she said. "It suits me just fine."

"Good," he said, taking her in his arms. "God knows I've missed you."

"And I you, Lance." He captured her lips, and they fell into the cool grass by the little stream with the mighty horse Takota standing guard nearby.

Lucy had become so lost in this memory that she found herself standing over a wastebasket in the office she was cleaning. She glanced at the clock on the wall and was happy to see the time had moved quickly.

Back in her thoughts of that summer, she recalled that Lance hadn't gone with her to the train station when her wonderful week at the McKellen farm was over. It was Paul who drove her back. He told her Lance had gotten up early, saddled Takota, and rode off. Lucy was hurt but tried not to show her disappointment as she said goodbye to the rest of his family. She half expected to see him waiting for them somewhere along the road. But when he was not, a deep sadness filled her.

After the train pulled away from the station, it wound its way through the foothills and at one point came back by the fields behind the McKellen farm. As Lucy sat quietly gazing out the coach car window, she saw a horse with rider racing along a hilltop beside the train. It was Lance and Takota! They raced to the top of a ridge where the mighty horse reared up, dancing around on his hind legs while his front hoofs pawed the air. Lance took off his hat and waved it high over his head. As the train made its way around the next turn, the sun moved behind the horse and its rider. In the bright light of the sun, Lance was gone. She closed her eyes and held the image in her mind until it was engraved there forever.

That was the image she conjured this night as she dusted the tall bookshelves and moved through the rest of her nightly routine. She was surprised when her thoughts brought up another image. It was Michael. She found herself looking forward to seeing him again, and not just to pry secrets from Angus.

Nevertheless, as her break time approached, she began to feel nervous.

At 9:30 p.m. she took the regular elevator to the nineteenth floor and made her way down the hall to Michael's office. His door was opened halfway, and as she approached, she saw him leaned back in his big, leather chair with his feet propped atop his desk. His head rested on his left hand while his right hand held a grouping of papers that he perused intently. She noticed he had changed from the suit and tie he was wearing that morning. He now had on jeans and a tight-fitting knit sweater that showed off his strong shoulders and well-developed chest. His hair was almost jet black, thick and wavy. He was the classic dark Irishman.

She stopped in the doorway and knocked softly. Looking up and seeing her, he smiled. "Hey, hello," he said, throwing the papers onto his desk and putting his feet down. He stood up and offered her his hand as she walked in.

She smiled, taking it. "Hi."

"So you have returned. I was hoping you would." He held onto her hand longer than convention dictated.

Her heart was racing but not her mind, and there was an awkward silence. Finally she said, "I'm sorry. Am I keeping you from your work? I saw you reading something."

He threw his head back and laughed. "Yes, you are. Thank God. Please don't apologize. I welcome the break."

She noted his "thank God" and wondered if it was just a meaningless expression to him. She liked his laugh and again noticed the twinkle in his deep, dark eyes.

"You're on your break, right?" She nodded yes. "Did you eat anything yet? I ordered pizza. The delivery guy just left so it should still be warm." He motioned to a box on the credenza.

"No, I haven't, save for an apple just before work. I'm starving."

He walked over and opened the box. "Then please join me. It's vegetarian. Hope you like it," he said, handing her a paper plate and motioning for her to help herself.

"Yummy, my favorite," she said as she selected a slice piled high with mushrooms, peppers, and olives.

"Really? I guessed right?"

She nodded again as she bit into the warm pie. She was silently thanking God for always providing for her needs. A piece of the melted cheese dripped from the slice and slammed into her chin.

"There's beer, soft drinks, and juice in that little fridge under the credenza. Help yourself. Oh, and here's the fine linen," he joked, handing her a paper napkin to deal with the sauce the cheese left on her face.

"Such good treatment, the fine linen." She smiled, taking the napkin and wiping her chin.

He stood watching her with a big smile on his face. "Please, take a seat on the couch. You'll be more comfortable."

She selected a can of lemonade from the fridge and set it on a coaster on the coffee table in front of her. When she finished her slice of pizza, he tempted her with another, and she accepted. "I like a woman who isn't afraid to eat something," he said, grabbing another slice for himself. He swirled his desk chair around to sit opposite her at the table. While they ate, they chatted about the best places to get pizza around town.

She finally looked up to see Angus grinning slyly at her. *Wow, she thought, I came here to investigate Angus, but this is the first time I've thought about him since I walked in the room.*

Michael, noticing she had begun to fixate on the painting, said, "Oh, him. I was enjoying the company so much I forgot you came to visit with Angus there."

"Thanks for dinner; that was very thoughtful of you, but I *am* on a mission and on a schedule."

"It was my pleasure," he said, smiling as he looked into her eyes. Feeling awkward, she turned her head away from his gaze and onto the picture. "So should we give a go at freeing Angus there from that old prison of his?"

"That's why I'm here," she said and then regretted the way it sounded.

"Of course," he replied. "Okay then, let's do the surgery." He pulled Angus off the wall with ease and laid him face down on the table before them. He pushed his chair out of the way and grabbed a small bag of tools from under his desk that he had brought from his apartment for this very purpose. He knelt on the carpet beside the table, and Lucy did the same.

A thin layer of old brown paper glued to the frame covered the back of the painting. Michael picked up his letter opener and pushed it under the paper in one corner, separating it from the glue that had held it tight. He slowly slid the opener down one side, across the bottom, and half way up the other side until his reach was strained. He handed the opener to Lucy to finish the job, and she, in like manner, moved it slowly along the edges until it came around to where Michael had started it. He grabbed the top corners of the old paper and laid it aside, revealing the back of the canvas. To Lucy's disappointment, there was nothing written there.

"Sorry, no secrets here," Michael confirmed as he looked up from the canvas and back into her eyes.

Lucy offered a shy little smile then pulled out of his gaze once again. "Would you mind if we take it out of the frame to see if anything is written on the front in the hidden corners?"

"Sure, we can do that," he said, then playfully added, "Nurse, screwdriver please." He held his hand open before her.

"Certainly, doctor." She played along and slapped a small Philips head driver into his hand.

On the back of the frame small metal pieces, spanning each corner, kept the canvas in place. They were secured on each adjacent side by a small screw. Michael removed the eight screws and the four metal plates they held down. As he did, he handed the hardware to Lucy who carefully placed it in an empty ashtray. He picked up the frame so he could get one hand on the front of the canvas and push it up. It started making creaky-crackly sounds that made Lucy wince.

"Oh," she groaned, "I hope this won't hurt him."

"He'll be fine; he's just been stuck in this old frame for a good lot of time." He grabbed hold the canvas and pulled it up and out, laying the frame on the floor beside him. He held the painting upright from each side and set it down on its bottom edge in front of him. Lucy scooted around the table and sat on the carpet next to him to get a good look.

"There," Lucy exclaimed.

"Where?" Michael asked, shifting his glance.

"Right there," Lucy said, pointing at the lower right hand corner. He moved his head down next to hers so he could get a good look. She felt his warm breath on her neck. There, on the canvas under the sprawled signature of I.M. Green, was an odd marking.

"It's some sort of symbol," he said.

"Yes, and I've seen it before," she replied.

He stared at it then grunted, "Huh." He looked over at her and added, "You know, I think I've seen it before too."

"You have?" she asked in amazement, turning her head toward his. "Where?" Their faces were very close, and he again caught her eyes. This time she didn't turn away.

"I... er... I... don't know," he murmured softly. "I can't recall where just now... I'll have to think about it." All the time he was speaking, he slowly moved his lips toward hers.

She jerked her head back when she realized just what he was doing and stuttered, "Oh, I... um... where have you seen it?" Composed, she added, "This is important; please try to remember."

Still hovering closely, he smiled and said softly, "It will come to me." Lucy knew where she had seen it; it was in a letter from Lance. But she couldn't imagine where Michael might have seen it. She was certainly interested to find out.

A noise from the door altered their attention. They looked up to see Bertha standing there with a scowl on her face. "Oh hi, Bertha," Lucy said nervously, becoming aware of how close she was sitting to Michael and how it must look.

Sensing a bad situation for Lucy, Michael belted out, "Hey, Bertha, how are things going?"

"Just fine, Mr. Donegan. I was looking for Lucy there."

"Oh, sorry," he said, "I asked your new girl here to give me a hand with this project. I hope you don't mind."

"Well, Mr. Donegan," Bertha replied curtly, "she is supposed to be working for me right now on some projects up on twenty-three, so I hope you can spare her soon."

"Oh, sure thing, Bertha, just another moment or two," he said, laying Angus down and standing to his feet. Lucy hopped up too. "Say, would you like to take the rest of this pizza?" he asked, making it a sort of peace offering. You could tell by looking at her that Bertha didn't refuse food very often.

"Don't mind if I do, Mr. Donegan. Thank you," she said in a slightly softer tone. She accepted the box from him and backed out the door, shooting a glare toward Lucy.

As soon as she was gone, Michael said, "Bertha looked a little miffed."

"I really need to get back to work," she said, noticing the clock and realizing her break had already run over by ten minutes. "Let me help get Angus back together before I leave."

"No, you run along. I can take care of this."

"Are you sure?"

"It's no problem."

"Gee, thanks. You have been just great." She turned and headed for the door. She felt like she wanted to say more, but she didn't know what.

"I hope you found something that will help you," he said.

"Just more questions, I'm afraid." She turned back toward him. "Michael, please try to remember where you,ve seen that symbol before."

"I will," he said softly. "You better leave me your phone number so when it comes to me I can give you a call." He offered her a pad of paper and pen from his desk.

As she wrote down her number, she asked, "You said the farm Angus came from was around Glenn, right?"

"Yes, that's right."

"Do you happen to know the address?"

"No, but I could find it. My grandfather took me there once or twice to pick up some apples. Hey, I have an idea," he interjected excitedly. "Like I told you this morning, I'm planning on going to the cottage this weekend. Would you like to keep me company on the drive? You could see Grandfather's journals first hand and glean any secrets he may have penned concerning Angus here."

"Really?" Lucy was put off her game and didn't know what to say.

"Sure, I could try to find that farm and take you by there if you'd like."

Lucy stood quietly surveying him, trying to find the right words. She found the offer intriguing but recalled Danny's warning. Sensing her hesitation, he interjected, "Come on, Myra loves to meet new people."

"Myra?" Lucy quizzed.

"My dear sweet Myra, she lives at the cottage. She loves for me to bring home guests."

Lucy was surprised at the way she felt when he mentioned this woman. She had noticed he wasn't wearing a wedding band, but she hadn't stopped to think that he might have a live-in girlfriend.

"Come on," he coaxed. "We could leave tonight when you finish work. I could drive you home to pack a few things, and you could get some sleep on the way down. It's about a four-hour drive. What do you say? I could sure use the company. We'd be back Sunday evening, if that fits your schedule."

Lucy still didn't know what to say. The thought of looking through the journals and possibly visiting the Green farm seemed awfully tempting.

"Hey, lassie." He slipped into a thicker brogue. "I do believe you owe me a favor now. Favor me with your company on this journey."

His charm put her to ease, and she played back to him: "Well now, kind sir, you are right in that thinking. I do owe you a favor or two, one for helping me interrogate Angus there and another for rescuing me from Bertha's wrath."

"Then it's set. You'll go along."

"Be happy to," she replied.

"That's great. What time will you finish work?"

"Around 2:30."

"Perfect. I'll wait for you in the parking structure by the service elevator." He sported a big smile.

"Thanks again. I really have to go now. I'll see you later." She ran out the door and down the hall.

"My pleasure," he called after her. He stood in the doorway, watching her as she ran. He turned and faced the mess in his office. "Thank you, Angus, my friend," he said aloud.

At 2:30 a.m. she went down to the housekeeping office to punch out and found Danny waiting for her by the time clock. "Hey, Lucy, I ran into your buddy Michael when I went in to clean his office. I helped him hang your little friend back on the wall. He sure was talkative tonight. He asked me all sorts of questions about you."

"He did, huh?" she said, not wanting to seem too interested.

"He asked how long I've known you and if you were seeing anyone special."

"Really? What did you say?"

"What do you mean *what did I say*? I told him I'd known you for far too long and that you *should be* seeing someone special—a special doctor." He chuckled.

"Oh, that's nice, Danny. Thank you." She wasn't amused but gave him a playful shove.

"Do you know what he told me?"

"No idea. What?"

His voice got serious: "He told me you were going away with him for the weekend. Is that true?"

"What?" she said indignantly. "He said it like *that*: I am going away with him for the weekend?"

"Well, no, not just like that. He said you had agreed to accompany him to his cottage in Saugatuck."

"And that I have."

"Oh, I see." He put his head down, let out a disgruntled sigh, and turned away.

"Danny, Michael has offered me the opportunity to look over his grandfather's journals. They may contain a clue about Angus. I can't pass that up."

"Yeah, right, the little man," Danny smirked. "Look, Lucy, you don't have to explain anything to me. Like you said today, Lance has been gone for seven years. You're a big girl. Just be careful. Call me; I'll drive down there and pick you up if you need me to."

"Thanks, Danny. I don't think that will be necessary, but it's good to know you have my back."

"You know I do, kiddo. I mean it, Lucy. Michael seems like a nice enough guy, but he's different from us. He's rich and powerful. And they play by a whole different set of rules. Just be careful, that's all."

"I'll be fine. He's waiting for me outside. See you Monday." She hurried out the door to find Michael sitting in a black Trans Am.

He pulled up to her and pushed open the passenger's door. "Where to, lassie?" he said as she hopped in. She gave him her address and explained how the entrance to the expressway was just a couple blocks further up her street. "That's great," he said. "I think there's an all-night petrol station near there. Am I right?"

"It's right on my corner," she replied.

"Okay then, here's the plan: I'll be dropping you off to get your things together while I go get a fill up for McGreedy here then come back to fetch you. How's that sound?"

"I'll be ready when you get back," she promised. She noted that he called his car McGreedy and thought of Lance because he'd named his old truck Quicksilver.

"Be sure to pack your swim suit. We're right along Lake Michigan. Myra will insist you walk on the beach with her."

He let her out in front of her apartment building and sped off. She rushed up the stairs. Finding her keys in her pocket, she unlocked her door. Freea was waiting for her there as always. "Hey, my kitty," she said, picking up the old cat in one hand and kissing her on top the head. "I'm afraid you won't see much of me this weekend. I have a date." She felt embarrassed as soon as she said it. She wondered why she had. She knew this wasn't a date. She knew why she was making this trip, and she knew now that Michael had a girlfriend.

She set Freea down, grabbed her backpack from the hook by the door, and scurried to her room. She snatched up a few items of undergarments, a pair of shorts with a matching tee top, her swim suit, a beach towel, and a spaghetti-strap navy blue dress in case they went to dinner. She left her jeans on but changed her top, putting on a long-sleeve denim blouse instead. She decided to take a wrap-around khaki skirt and a pink cotton blouse with tiny blue roses in case they went to church. Then she ran to the bathroom and picked up her overnight cosmetic bag along with her toothpaste and brush. She stuffed all the items in the pack and set it by the front door.

She walked to a back room off the kitchen where Freea's litter box sat. She was surprised to see the window above it opened slightly, she didn't remember opening it. She shut it, scooped out the box, added fresh litter, and went to the kitchen to wash her hands. She filled Freea's bowls with fresh food and water. Again she picked up the old cat, patted its head, kissed and snuggled it before setting her down in front of the food dish.

She jumped as she heard a loud crashing sound coming from the living room. She rushed in to find Lance's picture had fallen from the shelf where it had sat since she moved in. Her heart pounded. She bent down to pick up the broken glass, and a shard entered her hand. Blood streamed out and fell onto his picture. It ran down his face like a teardrop. Lucy sat frozen for a moment. Her heart felt the old pain. "Lance," she said out loud.

A strange noise came from the back room. She turned to see Freea running into it. By the time she got there, Freea was pacing back and forth, looking up at the window. It was open. "That's odd," she thought. She wrapped her hand in a paper towel, cleaned up the glass, and laid the frame with Lance's picture on the table. She picked up her backpack, grabbed her denim jacket, and hurried out the door. Michael was just pulling up to the curb as she bounded down the front stairs.

"Great timing," he remarked as she got in. They hopped on the expressway and were soon out of the city heading across the state. He had selected a cassette of Irish tunes played on traditional instruments. "Do you mind?" he asked, showing it to her before he engaged the player.

"Mind? No, I love this music." They rode along listening to the beautiful ballads, some sung in the old Gaelic tongue.

He had picked up two cups of coffee at the gas station. He drank his and now reached for the one Lucy had declined. "Let me help you with that," she said as she picked up the cup to pop open the sip spout in the lid. He noticed the towel.

"What happened to your hand?" he asked.

"Angus," she replied. "It's fine, just a small cut, and hopefully it will stop bleeding soon."

"I hope so," he said. "We wouldn't want to attract any vampires; there is a full moon, you know." Lucy hadn't noticed before, but as he said that the big white-yellow orb came bursting from behind a dark cloud. She broke into song:

> *I see the moon and the moon sees me*
> *Down through the leaves of the willow tree.*
> *God bless the moon and God bless me*
> *And shine on the one that I love.*

"I know that song. My mother used to sing it to me," Michael said, smiling over at her.

"Mine too." She returned his smile. She felt sleepy and yawned. Michael suggested she put her seat back and get some shuteye. "Will you be all right?" she asked.

"I'll be fine. This is my second cup of Joe, and besides, after Dan and I hung Angus back up, I took a catnap on my office couch while I was waiting for you to finish up work."

"Well, then it's my turn to catch forty winks, so I'm going to take you up on your suggestion."

Michael reached around her to lift the lever to tilt back her seat. "Sweet dreams, lassie," he whispered. She settled back and closed her eyes.

She had a dream, but it was bittersweet. She dreamed Angus had climbed in the back window of her apartment and handed her a smooth, black stone. When she looked into it, she saw Lance. He was in the midst of a battle with strange creatures the likes of which she had never seen before. He stopped fighting for a moment and looked up at her. As he did, one of the creatures came up behind him and was about to smash his head with a large battle axe. She jerked and was awake.

She wasn't sure how long she had slept. The car was stopped and pulled over to the side of a dirt road in the country. Michael wasn't in the car, but it was running and the keys were in the ignition. Night was lifting and a misty haze was over the land. There were woods on both sides of the road. She peered out through the mist but could not see any house lights. She was startled by a howling coming from the woods. Just then Michael came bounding out from behind a large tree alongside the road in front of the car. He opened the door and got back in. "Hey," he said. "Sorry if I woke you. I had to answer a call from nature. You doing okay?"

"I'm fine now that you're back," she said. "What on earth was that howling?"

"Beats me, but I wasn't going to hang around out there to find out. It was probably just a coyote, but this whole scene is right out of an old Bela Lugosi movie, isn't it? I mean, the dark and the mist and the howling."

"It's spooky all right; now add to that waking up to find your traveling companion missing."

"Okay," he laughed, "you topped me with that one." He pulled the Trans Am back onto the road and put in another tape. This one was *The Orchestral Tubular Bells* composed by Mike Oldfield and performed by the Royal Philharmonic Orchestra. "I certainly like your taste in music, Mr. Donegan," Lucy chimed in.

"I'm certainly happy it pleases you, Miss Cavanagh," he rang back.

Michael reached into the back seat and presented her with a beautiful red apple. "Yummy," she said as she accepted his gift. He reached back again and came up with one for himself. As he bit into it, he gave her a little wink.

She lifted her apple as if to toast and said, "God is good."

He looked at her with a big grin and said, "He most assuredly is."

They rode along munching the luscious fruit, listening to the beautiful music and watching as the world awakened.

8 – Glen Eden

Around seven a.m. Michael pulled into the Glenwood, an all-night diner attached to a small motel. This was a favorite resting spot for truckers driving up and down the Lake Michigan shoreline picking up loads from, or making deliveries to, the little towns that dotted the lakefront. The rooms were clean and the food was good. There were several big rigs pulled into a large parking lot designated for them at the north side of the building. Michael parked in front along with the locals who frequented for a big breakfast at a reasonable price. "I hope you don't mind taking our morning meal here. The place has great coffee and a large menu." He turned off the engine and turned toward her in his seat awaiting her answer. He wasn't in a hurry to get out; now that she was awake, he looked forward to talking with her.

"I don't mind at all. I know this place well, though I haven't been here in a few years."

"Is that so, and just how is it that you know it so well?" He gave her a hard look with a devilish grin. He moved one arm to rest on the back of her seat.

She realized that the motel had a reputation of being a "no-tell" sort of place and figured she'd better explain. "When I worked at the Butler in Saugatuck, the gang from there and the crew from the Coral Gables would meet up here for an early breakfast. It was the only place around still open when we finished work. It doesn't look like it's changed much, though I think the door used to be red."

"Surely it was, a time ago. When was it you worked at the Butler?"

"Oh golly, let me think… Wow, that was over eight years ago."

"Lucky for you I was going to school in Ireland back then. I've been known to cause a fair disturbance in that establishment." He threw his head back and laughed. She liked the sound of his laughter. "That was back in my heavy drinking days."

She sat watching him talk, listening to his laugh and thinking, *Michael Donegan, you sure are one good-looking man.*

As if he read her thoughts, he smiled and winked at her. His voice softened, "Maybe we'll take dinner there tonight. How's that sound?" He touched a lock of her hair as he spoke. She wasn't sure she was ready to step back into her past. The Butler held a lot of memories for her, but she acquiesced with a little nod and a smile. "Myra enjoys going in there to chat it up with the locals, so she'll not give us an argument."

At the mention of Myra, Lucy's conscience was pricked. She had forgotten about Michael's girlfriend. She became aware now of his nearness, of the way he hovered over her, playing with her hair. She was upset with herself for being in this position. "I could really use a good cup of coffee," she said to break the spell he was casting.

"Then you shall have it, fair maiden." He hopped out of the car and ran around to her side, offering her his hand as she stepped out. As they walked through the front door, Michael stopped to buy the morning paper from a machine in the foyer.

The restaurant looked pretty much the same as Lucy remembered. It was a seat-yourself place. The menus were in holders behind the napkin containers on each table. The old counter had been replaced and extended and new stools were put in, the kind that bolt to the floor and spin. The tables looked the same. After a quick glance at the menu, she gave Michael her order and made off to the restroom. She noticed those also had been recently remodeled. As she washed up, brushed her hair, and reapplied her make-up, she thought about the last time she had been there. It was with Lance. She closed her eyes for a moment and tried to remember it clearly, but the images just wouldn't stay in her head.

She sighed deeply, gathered her purse, and marched back to the table. By the time she reached it, Michael was already drinking coffee and reading his paper. He folded it down as she approached, flashed his million-dollar smile, stood up, and touched the back of her chair. She didn't smile back. She was thinking about what a cad he was.

She sat quietly sipping her coffee and waiting for her omelet to arrive. She watched him as he scanned the paper. She remembered what Daniel had said about him having a reputation with the ladies. She could certainly understand why. He was uncommonly handsome and had charm to spare. She thought of how he had leaned toward her in his office last night—possibly anticipating a kiss—how he had hovered over her in the car caressing her hair. *It's probably why he stopped at this place*, she thought, *to see if I'd succumb to his charms. He probably has a room on hold here for his trysts, and all the while he has Myra waiting for him in their little love cottage.* She felt a bad attitude creeping all over her, and it must have shown on her face.

He lowered his paper and looked at her. "What is it?" he asked. "Is the coffee too strong?"

"Well, I do have a bad taste in my mouth, but it's not the coffee."

"Myra will have an extra toothbrush at the cottage. She's well prepared for guests," he said, clueless to the fact that he was the bad taste she was talking about. "We are only about ten minutes from there, but I wanted to give her a chance to wake up before we come tramping in. Tomorrow she'll fix us breakfast. I didn't think it fair to wake her this morning and have her fuss in the kitchen since she doesn't know we're coming."

"What?" Lucy gasped. "You didn't call her and tell her you were bringing along a guest?"

"Absolutely not," Michael said. "I told you, she likes surprises. She doesn't even know I'm coming." He chuckled and his eyes twinkled.

Lucy had to calm herself before she could nonchalantly say, "So, tell me a little about Myra."

"No, I don't think that would be fair."

"Fair? What do you mean?"

"Well now, she doesn't know anything about you, does she? For that matter, neither do I, except, that is, for the obvious facts: you have beautiful blue eyes, gorgeous auburn hair, a great figure, a killer smile when you care to give it, and a fascination with our little buddy Angus." Lucy felt her cheeks grow hot. "So I'll not start you off ahead of her. You can size each other up soon enough by your own measures when I introduce you one to another."

Lucy wondered what kind of game this guy was playing and how she fit into it. She needed to stay focused on the reason she had accepted this invitation: to get a look at his grandfather's journals and hopefully visit the Green farm.

When the waitress—a tall, slender, strawberry blond in her late teens—brought the food and sat it before them, she barely glanced at Lucy; her eyes were fixed on Michael. "I asked big Bob to put extra cheese and mushrooms on your omelet, just the way you like it."

"Well now, aren't you my little sweetheart," Michael said, smiling up at her.

"Yes, I am," she said, giving Lucy a sideways glance. Lucy felt disgusted with him. Michael started to say something else to the pretty waitress, but just then a crash came from across the room. A trucker had dropped his coffee cup onto his plate of food, so she dashed off to clean up the mess.

Michael folded his paper and put it on a vacant chair next to him. He watched as Lucy bowed her head. She was thanking God for the food and asking Him for a calm, discerning spirit. When she looked up, Michael was staring at her.

"You *are* a good girl, aren't you Lucy?" he said. He then bowed his head as he signed the cross.

"Oh brother," Lucy thought, judging it to be an empty gesture. It added to her disdain toward him. They paid full attention to their plates and didn't speak for a while. Finally, Lucy asked, "Have you recalled yet just where you saw the symbol?"

"The symbol," Michael repeated, picking up his coffee cup. He looked around to get the attention of the waitress. He held his cup in the air, and when the waitress looked over, he winked. She winked back and headed straight for the pot. "I have thought a lot about that symbol. It seems very familiar to me. I think it's an ancient rune of some type. I must have seen it in one of Grandfather's books. I haven't remembered which one yet. Maybe when I'm in the study it will come to me. He had quite the collection of old books and manuscripts on all sorts of unusual subjects. He would have me help him with research on whatever project he was working on when I'd come home on holidays. After he died, I left Myra to dispose of his personal things. But as for the study and his books, I've kept everything pretty much just as he left them."

"How long has it been since your grandfather passed on?"

He hadn't expected her to ask. He liked it that she had. It was the first personal thing she'd asked him, and it raised his hopes that she might be showing some interest in him after all. "It was four years ago on the first Sunday of last month. The church in Douglas offers a Mass for him every year, so it helps me remember the date."

Lucy was pleased with herself for asking, for now she knew that Myra had been in his life for at least four years and wasn't just his latest fling. *Poor woman,* she thought. *I wonder how many others he's had in those four years.*

"What about you?" he asked. "Just where is it that you have seen that mark before? Maybe if you tell me, it'll help jog my memory."

"It's sort of a long story" was all she offered. She felt like she had already exposed too much of herself to this man.

"Well, we have a few minutes now. I want to give Myra a wee bit more time to put her face on and get on with her morning routine." Lucy remained silent. "I'd also like to hear more about just how it is you know our little friend."

Lucy was judging his words through her anger now. The way he had said "put her face on" stirred up her distaste even more. She felt sorry for this woman who obviously thought enough of Michael to stay at his place, not knowing when he'd be showing up. "Poor, low-self-esteemed woman, sitting there waiting for her man. And now he would be showing up with another woman in tow." Lucy pitied her for being in love with a louse like this. She certainly knew what it was like to wait for a man. After all, that's what she had been doing for Lance. But with Lance it was different. He wasn't a womanizing rogue like this guy. She was beginning to think this whole trip was a bad idea. Danny may have been right after all.

She was saved from having to answer when the waitress brought a fresh pot of coffee around for refills. Lucy noticed that she gave Michael a folded piece of paper. He took it quietly, giving her that maddening wink of his, and slipped it into his pocket. She refilled Lucy's cup and picked up her empty plate. "Is there anything else I can get for you?" she asked.

"No thank you," said Lucy politely.

"What about you, Michael? Have you had your fill?"

"Aye, I have now. Thanks for looking after me with big Bob there."

"You know I like to take care of you." She smiled beguilingly as she laid the bill on the table.

Oh brother, Lucy thought again as she reached for the bill.

Michael protested, "Hey, no. Don't do that, Lucy. Really, it would be my pleasure."

Lucy cut him off coldly. "No, it's quite all right. I'd like to repay your kindness in this small way for bringing me along to see your grandfather's journals. I insist."

"Well, sure then, darlin'," he said. "If you insist, I must humbly accept."

Lucy could have kicked herself. She lived on a limited income and had already spent her miscellaneous money for the month. Now she was robbing from her food budget. "Oh well," she thought, "at least I won't have to feel beholden to this guy." She excused herself and headed for the restroom again. Once inside the stall with the world locked out, she had a moment to think about what she was feeling. *This is so odd,* she thought. *I feel such a strong attraction to Michael, and I know I shouldn't. My emotions are all over the place. I actually felt jealous that he winked at that waitress. Why should I? Then there's poor Myra.* She mulled this over in her mind. She was tired and confused. When she washed her hands, the water stung the cut and brought Lance flooding back to her. She looked at the wound and started to cry. "God," she whispered, "please give me a sound mind and a rightfully discerning heart. Help me to hold on to hope." The words of a poem she had written long ago came back to her:

> *My tears wash away reality*
> *And from the blurred pain of it all*
> *I think I recall*
> *That you do not exist.*
> *Is it only in my journey to find you that you live?*
> *Condemned then to travel on I go into the void of longing...*

She splashed cold water on her face to snap herself out of it, patted dry with a paper towel, and went back to the table. Michael was involved in his paper, but when she approached, he again stood and touched the back of her chair.

"Are you okay?" he asked. "I didn't mean to upset you. My questions can wait."

"I am feeling pretty tired," she admitted, glad he wasn't pressing her.

"Of course you are. You will have a chance to nap before lunch. We should finish our coffee and get on the road."

"Sure," she said, picking up her cup and taking one last sip. Keeping her promise, she carried the bill to the register and paid it. When she turned back toward the table, she saw Michael hand a $50 bill to the waitress. He leaned down, whispered something in her ear, and gave her a little kiss on the cheek. "Men!" Lucy screamed so loud in her mind she wondered if she'd said it aloud.

They left the main highway two miles south of the Glenwood and turned west toward the lake then north onto a dirt road that wound its way around sand dunes and pine knolls and from time to time offered breathtaking views of Lake Michigan. Along the way, they passed several old manor houses tucked down long drives. Lucy had never realized this community existed, though she grew up less than thirty miles away.

They turned up a long, graveled drive lined on both sides with lilac hedges. The sun was higher now and bobbed in and out behind tall pine trees and atop the hedge on the right side of the drive. At the end of the hedge the cottage came into sight. It was much larger than Lucy expected. What she had envisioned was nowhere near this grand. The two storied, ell-shaped manor sat majestically against the backdrop of the Lake Michigan shoreline. With its Tudor style exterior of large fieldstones and giant dark-stained wooden beams, it conjured an old-world aristocratic eloquence.

There was a wooden balcony leading from leaded glass doors on the second floor. Two mortared fieldstone pillars supported it and framed the main double-door entrance below. The balcony's underside offered a shelter over the main entrance. Between each stone pillar and the house were short stone walls with cushions strewn atop them. Michael drove around the north ell-wing and parked the Trans Am under a carport extending from the side of a small stable constructed in the same style as the main cottage.

"Well, how do you like Grandfather's place?" Michael asked. Though it actually belonged to him since his grandfather's death, he still referred to it as his grandfather's, and always would.

Awestruck, Lucy answered, "It's winsome. Are we still in Michigan, or have you transported me to another time and place altogether?" Lucy wasn't kidding.

"I have indeed transported you to another place, lassie. Welcome to Glen Eden. The time here is the same as it has always been. Glen Eden is a piece of Ireland. Grandfather had all the stones that she's built with brought from County Sligo." Michael jumped from the car and ran to Lucy's door. He opened it and took her by the arm. "Come on now, it's time for you to meet Myra."

A cobblestone patio was laid in the back between the two wings. About it sat a variety of many potted plants, a wooden table, and various wooden benches and chairs. A garden lay at the end of the patio. Michael led Lucy down a pathway into the garden through an arbor trellis covered in morning glories. The sun-warmed flowers gave off a heavenly scent.

They entered a rose garden filled with blooming bushes of all sizes and colors. In the center of the garden was a magnificent fountain carved with figures of naked mermaids being tended by small fairies that brushed and braided their hair. At the end of the garden tall pine trees stood, and through them the deep blue of the lake could be seen. At the base of one of the trees standing with her back toward them was a petite, slender woman with long hair that hung in braids past her waist. She was gracefully moving in and out of body positions.

"Uh oh," Michael whispered, "we've caught her doing her morning exercises."

"She is doing yoga," Lucy whispered back. "Those positions are called 'The Salute to the Sun.'" Seeing this woman stirred up a new surge of jealousy in her and she struggled to take command over the feeling.

"Well now, I'm impressed that you know that. I'll wager the two of you will get on quite well."

They stood quietly as the woman finished and turned toward them. Her face was serene with a far-off look. It took a moment for her to return from her meditative state and recognize that she had visitors. When she did, she smiled widely and came rushing toward Michael. "Michael, Michael my darling," she said as she embraced him. "What a wonderful surprise." She cupped her hands around his face, and he bent down so she could kiss him tenderly on the cheek. He returned the kiss.

Lucy stood waiting to meet her, full of shame and embarrassment. *This woman must be in her sixties,* she thought. Later she learned Myra was actually about to turn seventy-five.

Myra turned from Michael and faced Lucy. "Oh lovie, how wonderful! You have brought a guest."

"Yes, Myra, this is my new friend Lucy. You will be impressed to know she knew the name of the yoga positions you were just doing."

She took both Lucy's hands. "Lucy, let's see... oh yes... Lucy: your name means *bringer of light*. So you know yoga. But of course you do; look at you. You are beautiful." She looked intently into Lucy's eyes and said, "And troubled." Without giving Lucy a second to respond, she went on, "Welcome, my dear. This place is magical, maybe just what you need to sort it all out. I'm so glad Michael has found you and brought you here. I'll go fix us some nice tea and bring it out here to the garden. We can chat and get to know one another. How will that be?"

"Lovely. Thank you," Lucy replied. She was a little put off by Myra's pronouncement that she was troubled. How would she... how could she know? She wasn't looking forward to the chat, though she would like to know more about both of them.

Myra turned and hurried toward the house, calling back to them, "Michael love, take Lucy into the gazebo. I'll join you with the tea."

The gazebo was at the northwest side of the garden and sat atop the ridge of a massive sand dune that led down to the water's edge. Logs had been laid in the sand down the side of it, making a winding stairway to the lake. Lucy was overwhelmed by the beauty of it all. She breathed deeply and filled her lungs with the fresh lake breeze scented by pine trees, roses, and many other intoxicating scents given off by the flora surrounding them. Michael beamed as he led her through the arch to sit inside the magnificent wooden structure. "Myra loves this gazebo. Grandfather built it for her. They used to sit here together and have tea, enjoy a good book, or just meditate on the nature round about."

"It's very beautiful." Lucy breathed deeply again the wonderfully scented air. She looked at Michael beaming from ear to ear and couldn't help but smile herself. "So Myra is your grandmother."

"As close to it as I have. My grandmother died right after my father was born. I never knew her. My grandfather and she had what is called a marriage of convenience. When my father went off to boarding school, Grandfather traveled back to Ireland and found Myra. They had known each other as teenagers in Ballyshannon and fallen in love before he came to America. He promised he'd come back for her one day. She never married and never stopped hoping he would return."

"That's a wonderful story," Lucy gushed. "So after all those years, they were married."

"Well, no. They never did marry, not officially. I don't think either one saw the need for it. They knew they loved each other."

"So she lived here as his mistress?" Lucy felt bad right away for having said that.

"Well, I guess some would put that label on it. Grandfather loved her very much, but my grandmother's family would have been very displeased had he married her. It was one of those silly, age-old clan disputes. They would have tried to ruin him and take away much of what it had taken him years to build."

"So your grandfather wouldn't marry her after she'd waited for him all those years?" Lucy didn't know why that angered her, but it did and she knew Michael could detect it in her voice.

He looked at her thoughtfully and as if trying to make her understand said, "It was actually Myra who would not marry him. She said she would not have something as beautiful as their love causing hate or discontent. She just didn't see the need for a legal document. She told him that if people wanted to think of her as his mistress, then let them. She never has been one to care about what other people think. My grandfather did a lot of good for a lot of people, and she couldn't allow him to be ruined for a selfish need. She only cared that they were together, convention be damned. Of course that meant she was not entitled to anything Grandfather had when he died. He knew if his estate were to fall into the hands of my cousins, she would be put out to dry. So he left it all to me, his youngest grandson, everything he owned. He said he trusted that I would take care of Myra and let her live here as long as she wanted."

"Wow, that's some love story."

"Aye, and what about you, Lucy? Have you found that one person you would wait a lifetime for? Is that what this search for Angus is all about?"

She looked hard at him. Did he know something, or was he just fishing? She was formulating an answer when Myra's voice came from the garden behind them. "Here we go, dears. I brought some tea biscuits and blackberry jam. I'm afraid that's all I have in just now."

"Just the tea for me, Myra," Michael said. "I am still stuffed from the big breakfast Lucy bought me at the Glenwood this morning."

"Thank you, but I'll just have tea too," Lucy said, still thinking about Michael's question.

"Glenwood? Did you see Megan then?" Myra asked.

"Yes, I did, Myra. She sends her love. Oh, here's a note she asked me to give you." Michael pulled the folded piece of paper from his pocket. Myra set the tray down on the round table in the center of the gazebo and took the note.

"Darling girl, Megan," she said as she unfolded and read it. "Oh good, this is the recipe for the dandelion dressing that Mrs. Inch makes." As she handed a cup of tea to Lucy, she said, "So you bought this big lug breakfast, did you?"

"I did. It was the least I could do for his kind offer to bring me along." She felt awkward saying this. She was remembering the kiss Michael had given the waitress. Could she be this Megan, and the note she slipped Michael was just a recipe for Myra? Had she been wrong about him all along? After all, she had thought Myra was his mistress, when in reality she was his grandfather's.

"Well, I'm sure by the way this guy is smiling, he would have been happy to have your company, feed him or not. Am I right, dear?" she asked, handing a cup to Michael.

"Right you are as always, Myra my love. But, you see, Lucy only has eyes for another." Lucy wondered if Danny had told him about Lance. Michael continued, "You remember Grandfather's little pal Angus?" Myra seemed to become a little flushed when she heard that name. She took a cup of tea for herself and sat down next to Lucy.

"Michael, whatever are you talking about, dear?"

"Angus, Grandfather's little friend in the painting. You insisted I take him out of here, so I hung him in my office. Lucy took one look at him and, well, I'm afraid I don't have a chance now. 'Tis the fate of a Guardian." His eyes danced.

"Is it true, Lucy? Do you have an interest in finding out about Angus? My William did a lot of research on the little creature. I must say, I never liked that painting. No good can come from getting involved with the fairies. I told William as much, but his mind was captured. He was quite taken by stories a farmer around here told him. It was the farmer who painted the picture. Michael, you should take Lucy into the study to see your grandfather's notes on the rascal."

"I'm way ahead of you on that one, Myra. I'm afraid you thought incorrectly that Lucy came here to get to know me. In truth, I lured her out here with the promise of looking at Grandfather's papers."

"Well, for whatever reason you chose to let my darling Michael think you accompanied him here, I'm very glad that you did, my dear. I am sure we will all make wonderful discoveries about each other this weekend."

"Thank you very much, Myra. I am happy to be in this beautiful garden enjoying this wonderful tea in the presence of two such charming people." Lucy smiled and raised her cup to the both of them.

"Oh Michael," Myra laughed, "she's kissed the Blarney stone, this one. Have you not, my girl?"

"I am guilty as charged, and you have discovered one of my secrets already."

They all laughed. They drank the tea, and Lucy listened as Myra caught Michael up on some of the local goings on. She could tell the two had a mutual fondness for each other. Myra finally turned her attention back on Lucy. "So now dear, let's hear about you and learn why the fates have brought you to Glen Eden."

Michael could tell Lucy felt uncomfortable when the focus turned to her, so he did his best to rescue her. "Myra, Lucy is tired from the long drive. Maybe it would do her well to freshen up and take a rest now. You can grill her at lunch, and after we can dig through Grandfather's books."

"Oh Michael, get on with you now. I wasn't going to grill her. It's not me you have to protect her from. It's that little rascal Angus. Besides, Lucy is a big girl. She knows how to move off the coals if her seat gets too hot. Don't you, dear?"

Lucy wasn't quite sure how to answer that. So she took the escape route Michael had offered. "A nap does sound awfully good. It's this wonderful country air, I guess."

"Yes, of course, the air. It can be intoxicating. We'll have plenty of time to get to know one another. I'd be happy to show you to your room now, if you like."

"I would like that, thank you."

"You are a dear, Myra," Michael said. "I'll bring our bags in from the car. I've brought you some beads Shannon and I picked up at the Ann Arbor Art Fair. Oh, and your parcel of material came from Ireland. I'll fetch it in as well."

"Wonderful, Michael. How you spoil me. You are just like my William, you are. How is Shannon, and when are you bringing her back for a visit?"

"She was set to come with me this weekend, but then something came up. She sends her love."

"Shannon?" Lucy wondered, but Myra's voice shook away the questions that were about to form.

"Come along, Lucy. I'll show you to your room, and later Michael can show you around the house."

They walked back through the garden—stopping to admire a rose here and there—and back through the arbor and trellis covered with yet more morning glories that had burst open in the light of the full sun beating down on them. They crossed the cobblestone patio and came to the back door of the main section of the house. They walked down a long hall past the kitchen and dining room and into a great room where Lucy noticed the large fireplace made of fieldstone that stood on the outer wall. There were wonderfully colored wool carpets laid about the hardwood floor before it. The staircase up to the second floor had balusters ornately carved with little fairies peeking out from behind flowers and leaves, which held up the smooth, highly polished dark wooden hand railings. They crossed over to the north wing, passing three closed doors. Myra stopped at the fourth, turned a key in the knob, and pushed it open. She handed the key to Lucy. "Here you go, love."

The room was very pleasant. It had a full-size canopy bed with a floral bedcover matching the drapes that hung in the double window with a lovely view of the lake. Myra threw the curtains back and opened both windows to catch the cool lake breeze. "The bathroom is right across the hall. I hope you will be comfortable. Rest now and we'll have a lovely chat at lunchtime. I'll send someone to knock on your door at twelve thirty, if that will be all right for you?"

"Thank you very much, Myra. That will be just fine."

As Myra stepped out of the room she came face to face with Michael. He turned an ashen color as he looked into the room. It was almost as if he didn't see Lucy standing there.

"You are putting her here, Myra?" he asked.

"I am, and it's time this room saw use again, don't you think, my boy?" She didn't expect an answer. She patted his face softly before she turned and walked away.

Michael looked slowly around the room as if remembering some far off time. Lucy thought it was strange that he didn't look at her when he said, "Here's your backpack. Will you be needing anything else?"

"Thanks. I'm fine. This is a lovely room." She took her bag and sat it on a chest at the foot of the bed. He stood solemnly; the sparkle had gone from his eyes, and they looked as though they might be tearing.

"Hey, are you okay?" she asked.

"Me? Sure," he sniffed, "Musty old house. My allergies are kicking in, that's all." He retreated hurriedly from the room.

Lucy shut the door but did not lock it. She laid the key on the bed stand, kicked off her shoes, and lay atop the bedcover. She felt very comfortable and lay thinking about the events of the day. She thought about Michael, how handsome he was and what a striking smile he had. She thought about how relieved she had been to find out that Myra was not Michael's girlfriend. She wondered again about the waitress at the Glenwood. The name Shannon sprang forth with new questions. She slipped from the bed, got on her knees, and prayed to be forgiven for her weak and suspicious nature. Crawling back onto the bed as sleep was claiming her, she touched the cut on her hand and hoped Lance would meet her in her dreams.

She was roused from afar by a soft rapping. She sat up and recognized the room at Michael's grandfather's cottage. Again rapping came on her door.

"Hello," a voice said. "Hello, Miss. Are you awake?"

"Yes, I am. Please come in," Lucy replied as she sat up. She was surprised when the waitress from the restaurant entered.

"Hello, Miss, Myra wanted me to wake you for lunch."

"You're the waitress from the Glenwood," Lucy found herself saying as she chased the tail of sleep away from her mind.

"Aye," the girl said, "I'm Megan. I waited on you and Michael this morning, though I didn't know he was bringing you home with him. He never does that, brings his girls here, I mean."

Lucy was annoyed at being lumped in with *Michael's girls* but tried not to let it show. "Yes, I remember you," Lucy said, again thinking about the wink and kiss. "I'm Lucy Cavanagh." Lucy offered her hand.

Making no effort to take it, the girl replied, "I know. Myra told me. Michael asked me this morning if I could come by after my shift and give Myra a hand today. I usually come by two or three times a week, whenever Miss Myra needs help with something, or whenever Michael comes home."

"That's very kind of you," Lucy said.

"Well, actually, it's very kind of them. They know I'm saving up money to start college this fall. They always pay me handsomely for any little task."

"I'm sure you are a big help and some company for Myra."

"Actually, it was Michael's idea. He has been wonderful to me," she said with what seemed to Lucy to be a dreamy sort of look in her eyes. "He set up a trust fund to pay for my tuition and board at school, as long as I maintain my grades. I work at the restaurant to get spending money for clothes and extras."

"That's great. Michael seems to be a very generous person."

"He's quality," Megan said, then asked, "So how long will you be staying? I was surprised to see you were in Kathleen's room."

"I'm just here for the weekend," Lucy replied. "Who is Kathleen?"

"Oh, I'm sorry," said Megan a little coyly. "I assumed you knew about Kathleen and Michael. I probably opened my big mouth where I shouldn't have. Forgive me. I have to run along now and fill a grocery list for Myra. They're waiting lunch on you. Just go down the stairs when you're ready. The dining room is down the hallway on the right." She turned and hurried out the door.

Lucy called after her. "Thank you. I hope to see you again." She stood up and walked to the basin. She poured water from a matching porcelain pitcher that stood by its side. She splashed a little on her face then patted it dry with a small towel that lay by the bowl. She opened her bag and brought out her brush. She stood gazing in the mirror brushing her long hair, watching it fall smoothly from the brush. As she did, she thought she saw the reflection of a girl in the room behind her. She turned to look, but there was no one there. "Megan," she called, thinking maybe she had come back. But no answer came. She finished brushing her hair and headed on down the staircase to the dining room.

Michael was sitting at the table talking with Myra. In the center a large china soup tureen sat upon a crocheted flower hot pad. Matching salad bowls full of summer greens, tomatoes, nuts, and blueberries sat on a plate before each of them with one on a plate in front a vacant chair. As she entered, Michael stood up and smiled at her. She smiled back, thinking again what a great smile he has. "Feeling better?" he asked.

"I feel wonderful," she said. "I was somewhere else entirely when Megan rapped on the door. I was surprised to see her."

"Isn't she a lovely girl?" Myra asked. "I hope she didn't stretch her claws out at you. She has the biggest crush on our Michael, she has, since she was eleven and he used to do his magic tricks for her. I'm afraid she was a little jealous when she saw you with him this morning."

Michael motioned Lucy to the chair on the opposite side of the table, and as she walked over to it, he circled around Myra to pull it out for her.

"Thank you," she said, looking up at him as she sat down. *God, he has beautiful eyes,* she thought. "I'll try not to make any of your girlfriends uncomfortable while I'm here."

"Would you now? Well, thank you for that courtesy, darlin'," he said with a smile and a wink.

Myra swatted at him with her napkin. "You stop teasing that girl. *His girlfriends,*" Myra laughed. "Someone as handsome as this bloke could have a plenty; heaven knows there are a few chasing after him."

"Now Myra," Michael broke in. But that did not discourage her and she went on.

"But he is too busy with his work, he is, to stop and let any of them catch him. Why, you are the first girl that he's brought here since Kathleen."

"Myra!" Michael said sternly this time then added with a lighter voice, "Let the girl eat her lunch. Lucy has not come here with her eye on me. I told you, it is Angus she is courting, and I've promised her a look at Grandfather's journals after lunch."

"Michael my love, you do not give your charm any credit. There is a spark for you, and I can see it. You would do well to kindle it, in my estimation." Lucy looked down into her salad. She felt blood flowing to her cheeks. She couldn't believe how frank this woman was.

"Myra," Michael piped in again, "stop your shenanigans. Lucy and I just met yesterday. I told you, she is not here to get to know me, only to learn about Angus. Stop trying to push me at her or you'll have her running out the door."

"Okay, Michael Donegan, have it your way. But how long you've known her is not a point with me. Your grandfather and I felt the spark the very first time we laid eyes on each other, and it was enough to keep the hope alive for all the years we were apart. Your Myra knows a thing or two about love." She looked over at Lucy, who was still looking intensely at her salad. "I'm sorry dear if I have put the rose on your cheeks. But the older one becomes, the more one realizes the preciousness of time and the foolishness of wasting it. Let's get to know each other, shall we? Is there a special man in your life, Lucy dear? Besides Angus, I mean."

"Yes," Lucy blurted out, looking up into Myra's intense eyes. Then with tears welling in her own, she added in a quiet whisper, almost like she didn't want to hear herself say it, "Though he went missing seven years ago."

"Oh, my dear," Myra said, reaching over to pat her hand as she spoke. "I am so sorry. I thought I could see sadness deep within you, much like what Michael carries. I want to hear all about your young man. Don't you, Michael?"

"If Lucy wants to tell us, and if it will not be difficult for her."

"What is his name, dear?" Myra asked softly.

"Lance."

"Lance!" Myra exclaimed rather loudly, giving a sideways glance at Michael.

"Yes, that's right," Lucy said, finding Myra's response a bit odd.

Myra changed the surprised look on her face back to one of concern and said, "You go ahead, Lucy. Tell us about your young man."

Lucy took her napkin and dabbed at her eyes. The next ten minutes she spent telling them about Lance: how they had met in the meadow not far from Glen Eden; how they had shared a wonderful summer; and how she'd moved to California to be close to him while he learned the secrets of ancient places of power from the Native Americans there. She had returned to Michigan when he went overseas to investigate Celtic stone circles, megaliths and menhirs. She was planning on joining him there, but during an expedition to a portal dolmen in Cornwall he went missing. "It will be seven years to the very day tomorrow," she said as she came back from her journey into the past. She didn't share the deep secrets of him, only the story of their love and of his strange disappearance.

They sat quietly and intently listening to her. When she paused, Michael asked, "Does Angus have something to do with Lance?"

"Yes," Lucy said, and hesitatingly added, "Lance knew Angus. He told me many tales of him. They were traveling together."

Myra shot a curious glance at Michael and was about to say something when he raised his hand to stop her. "And the symbol on the painting, what has that to do with this?"

"The symbol we found on the painting was the same symbol that Lance drew on the bottom of his last letter to me. Someone had given him a stone that had that symbol etched on it. He told Lance he'd found it in a stone circle in the Findhorn area of Scotland. I later heard from one of Lance's traveling companions that the same symbol was etched near the bottom of one of the base stones in Chûn Quoit, the portal dolmen in Cornwall where Lance disappeared." Her voice squeaked on her last word, and Myra squeezed her hand.

"But why did you suspect the symbol would be on the painting?" Michael asked.

"I didn't," Lucy replied. I was just looking for some sort of clue, just grasping at straws. It has been so long since I've had any hope at all." She swallowed hard to choke back tears, but it didn't work. She put her head down as they spilled from her eyes. She regained control of her voice and said, "Look, I'm sorry. I know how strange this all must sound."

Michael raised his hand to stop her. "Lucy, it doesn't seem strange to me or to Myra. I wasn't completely honest with you about why Grandfather wanted this painting after farmer Green died. It was because Grandfather said he had also seen that little fellow."

Myra chimed in now: "I never saw him, but sure I am that he exists. I'm sure he has been in this house many times. That is why I insisted that Michael take his picture out of here. I think he would sneak in just to admire himself. Strange things were going on while it was hanging here. Windows would open up or close by themselves. Lights would go on and off, and sometimes when I was upstairs I would hear the fairy music coming from William's study where that painting hung."

They were all silent for a moment. Lucy was amazed by what she was hearing, amazed by the fact that she had actually told her story to someone who didn't judge her as crazy for telling it.

Finally Myra said, "We best eat our lunch now so the two of you can be off on your adventures. I understand now, Lucy, about your quest. It is to find Lance. And I think there is a reason that Michael has been chosen to help you. So strange is this thing called fate. I believe it has also been seven years now since we lost Kathleen. Am I right, Michael?"

"Tomorrow," Michael said, closing his eyes and swallowing hard.

"Maybe later, dear, you will share your Kathleen with Lucy. I'm sure bringing her to life in memory again would be good for you, just as sharing her Lance with us was good for Lucy. What do you think, lovie?" she asked as she took hold of Michael's arm.

"I think there is a hungry man at this table who is spoiling for want of your soup and some soda bread. So if you ladies don't mind, I'll offer a blessing and pick up a spoon."

Michael's blessing was simple and sweet: "Dear Lord, all praise is due you and we offer our thanks for this meal you've set before us, for the ones that so lovingly prepared it, and for the one who's come now to share it with us. Thank you for the memories of our loved ones, Lord. Bless the food into our bodies and strengthen our hearts. Amen."

"Amen," repeated Myra, signing the cross.

"Amen," Lucy said. She did feel much better now that she had shared Lance with them. He wasn't just hidden in her past now. He was there with her.

9 – Secrets in the Study

Before they had finished at the table, Megan returned carrying a bag of groceries. Myra called out to her, "Just set those things down in the kitchen, get yourself a setting, and come have a bite with us, dear." She obliged, and when she entered the dining room, she chose the chair next to Michael. She hugged his arm and kissed his cheek.

"So, Megs, what have you been up to this summer?" Michael asked as he ladled some of Myra's potato leek soup into her bowl.

"I'll tell you what she's been up to," Myra chimed in. "She's been driving that Nelson boy crazy, wearing that next-to-nothing swimsuit she has, strutting around on the beach down here on the point. I sit out in the gazebo watching her, and I can see him drooling all the way up here."

Megan looked at Michael like a kid who just got caught eating a forbidden cookie. "I don't strut around for Charlie Nelson," she protested. "He just shows up down there sometimes, that's all. I mean, I can't throw him off a public beach, now can I?"

"No, you can't be doing that," Michael said. Most of the beach front property along the lake was posted as private, but Glen Eden's beach was open to all who knew about it. There was no public access sign to announce it, but William had made a trail from the road through the woods on the north end of the property so locals could gain access to the beach. "But you can't go giving him ideas either," Michael continued. "That Charlie's a wild one, especially when he lets the brew do his thinking for him. I've seen him tossed out of the Butler for putting his hands on one of the waitresses. When he gets something in his mind, you'd be hard put to change it."

"Michael," she said, pouting out her lips and blinking her eyes, "you wouldn't be jealous, now would you?"

"Megs, I'm just saying, you need to be careful. You know how I'd feel if something happened to you."

"Yes, I do know, Michael," she said, turning her eyes on Lucy, "and I'd feel the same way if *you* fell into the wrong hands."

"You don't have to worry about Michael," Myra interjected. "His foolishness days are long passed. Yours are on the horizon, and if you aren't careful, they will gobble up your future."

Still glaring at Lucy and ignoring Myra's comment, Megan said, "So, Lucy, what is it you do in the big city?"

"I work for a company called DME. It's a maintenance service."

"A maintenance service? You mean like janitors and house-keeps?"

"Yes, that's right. I clean offices."

Megan laughed, "So you met Michael cleaning his office?"

Lucy felt like she had to defend herself. "I met Michael when I went to his office to ask him if I could buy a painting I had seen there."

"Oh, I see," said Megan coyly. "So you are an art collector on a cleaning woman's salary, and you've come here to check out his other works of art," she snickered mockingly.

"Megan," Michael said sternly. "What Lucy does or why she is here is none of your business. She is my guest, and I will not have you speaking rudely to her."

"Oh, of course not, Michael. I didn't mean to be rude. I was just interested. I'm sorry if she's touchy about what she does."

"Megan!" he said again sharply.

"Michael, please," Lucy interrupted. "It's fine." Then to Megan she said, "I know Michael surprised you all by bringing me here. I don't want to cause any trouble for him or you. He has been very kind to me and so has Myra, and I am grateful to them both."

Leaning toward Lucy, Myra said under her breath, "Didn't I say she'd stretch out her claws." She sat back up and said aloud, "Michael, you and Lucy run along into the study. I'll keep Megan company while she finishes her soup."

"Thank you, Myra," Michael said as he stood up and placed his napkin on the table. "Lucy, are you ready to do some detective work?"

"Yes, I am, and anxious." Turning to Myra as she rose from her seat, she said, "Thank you for the wonderful lunch, Myra; the soup was delicious. And thank you for listening to my tale. I do feel so much better having shared it." She bent down and kissed Myra on the forehead.

"Oh brother," Megan blurted out. "Isn't that just so sweet."

"Megan, that's enough." Michael snapped.

"Yes, it is. It's too much," Megan fired back as she jumped up and ran from the table.

"Megan," Michael shouted, "come back here right now. What on earth has gotten into you?"

"The green-eyed monster, I'd wager," Myra said, standing and taking hold of his arm. "Michael, let her go now before she says more she has to take back later. Let her run off and think about things a while. I'll call her when she has had some time to cool down."

"Lucy, I'm sorry," Michael said apologetically.

"Michael, please. I'm fine. Don't be hard on her. She's young."

"Lucy is right," Myra said. "She is young, and she is hot headed and stubborn like her father. I'm afraid she views Lucy as her competition."

"Her competition?" he said with a puzzled look on his face.

"Michael, you can be so oblivious at times, dear. Now, go on with you. Take Lucy into the study and discover what secrets you may. A lot of things are going to be stirred up this weekend. It's started already."

"Myra, let me help you clear the dishes and clean up before we rush off," Lucy offered.

"Sure, Myra, we'll give you a hand. You did yourself proud on that soup."

"Well, I never refuse help from good company."

The three of them cleared the table and carried the things down to the kitchen. Lucy was surprised to see how apt Michael was with the chores. As Lucy washed, Michael dried. He began to sing an old Irish ballad. Myra put the food and dishes away as she jigged around the kitchen to the tune he sang. Lucy worked quietly listening to Michael's beautiful voice.

A lady fair in a garden walkin'
When a well-dressed gentleman came ridin' by.
He stepped up to her, all for to view her
And said, "Fair lady, would you fancy I?"
"I am no lady but a poor maiden
And a poor girl of low degree.
Therefore, young man, seek another sweetheart;
I am only fitting your serving maid be.

And oh, kind sir, I have a lover,
Tho' 'tis seven long years since I did him see.
And seven years more I will wait upon him,
For if he's living he'll return to me."
"Perhaps your lover is dead or drownded
Or maybe sailing all over the sea.
Or maybe he is another's husband
And ne'er return to marry thee."

"O, if he's married, I wish him happy,
And if he's dead, sure, I wish him rest.
No other young man will e'er enjoy me,
For he's the one that I love the best."
He put his hand into his bosom
His lily white fingers they were long and small;
He took out the ring that was broke between them
And when she saw it she down did fall.

He took her up all in his arms,
He gave her kisses most tenderly;
Saying "You're my jewel and I'm your single sailor
And now at last I've won home to thee.
I am your true love and single sailor
You thought was drownded all in the sea.
But I've passed o'er all my toil and trouble
And I've come home, love, to wed with thee."

Come all young maidens, now heed my story
Don't slight your true love and he on the sea;
And he'll come home and make you his own,
And he'll take you on over to Americany

"Oh Michael, how full you make this house with your singing. Your grandfather and I always loved it when you would sing."

"That's because it would scare the mice out of the pantry." He laughed, shaking out his towel and putting it on a hook.

"That's not true. You have a wonderful voice," Lucy said, "and a remarkable ability to select a song for every occasion, may I add."

Michael chuckled. "How about you, Lucy, do you sing?"

"Well, I haven't in a long time, other than in the pew, I mean." Lucy untied the apron Myra had given her from around her waist and placed it on the hook next to Michael's towel. "There used to be a pub in Grand Rapids called the Green Dragon. I don't know if it's still there. It was owned by an acquaintance of Lance. We went there once and I was persuaded, after a pint or two of Murphy's, to put air to my pipes. She chuckled, then sobered and added, "Lance didn't sing; he whistled. He whistled like his breath was an instrument. He whistled while I sang. Sometimes we would whistle together." She felt as if mentioning Lance just now had changed the whole mood of the kitchen.

"William and I used to sing together," Myra said in a low, soft voice. Then louder, "Many were the winter nights when I would get down the dulcimer and Will his squeeze box and we'd have at a tune. Remember, Michael?"

"Aye, of course I do, Myra. Those were grand evenings."

"And Kathleen... Oh now, she had the voice of an angel, she did. She could take a ballad and bring you to tears." Myra's voice was again soft and dreamlike. The three stood silent a moment, each remembering a different melody and a different time. Myra broke the silence: "You kids go on now to the study. I'm going upstairs to read for a spell. Then I'll phone Megan. What time will you be wanting dinner this evening so I can make the plans?"

"I was hoping to take Lucy to the Butler tonight, if she'd favor me with her company, that is." Michael turned his glance on Lucy as he said this.

Caught in the comfortableness of the moment, she said, "I'd be happy to."

He then turned and put his arm around the older woman. "Myra, I'd love to escort two beautiful women to dinner tonight. What do you say?"

"Oh, no thank you, dear. You will be eating much too late for me. I'm at the age where I have to swallow my last bite of the day long before the sun goes down or I won't sleep a wink. I have plenty to keep myself entertained this evening with all those new beads you brought. Get on with you now to the study, and don't mind the dust. I don't have much occasion to go into that part of the house, and it's been a while since I gave those old books a brush off." She stretched on her tiptoes and kissed his cheek as he bent toward her. Then giving Lucy's hand a squeeze, she left the kitchen.

"Come along now, Lucy. Let's see if we can unlock the mystery behind your friend Angus and that symbol we found." He put his hand gently on her back and guided her down the hall toward his grandfather's study. Even this nonchalant touch excited him.

It was a large room spanning the rear of the lower east wing of the cottage. There was a large window with a seat on the west wall that overlooked the garden, gazebo and, further on, the lake. On the south wall was a large stone fireplace with a highly polished oak mantel. On the mantel stood many old photographs, all in wonderfully carved wooden frames—the Donegan ancestry, Michael told her. Bookshelves and wooden filing cabinets covered much of the rest of the walls. In the center of the room at an angle to accommodate the view from the window—and the heat and glow of the fireplace—stood a large, ornately carved, wooden desk. Drawn to it, Lucy said, "This desk is fantastic."

"Aye, it is that. It has been passed down from generations of Donegans to my grandfather's father. When he died unexpectedly, no one knew just who the desk should pass to. All his sons wanted it; there were seven. They settled it as Irish gentlemen would, in a contest. They got drunk and started fightin'. The winner of the desk was to be the least bloodied after a twenty-minute brawl. Grandfather was the youngest and smallest and not much into scrappin', so on the first punch from his brother Sean, he went light in the head and staggered out of the reach and thoughts of the other six brothers, who were busy pounding the hell out of each other. Grandfather's Aunt Bridie was the judge who kept the time and helped clean the boys after the fight." He pointed at various photographs as he mentioned names. "There were broken noses, swollen eyes, split lips, and missing teeth. They were all fairly bloodied except for young William, who, besides having a buzzing in his ears that lasted a good week, was unscathed. Grandfather insisted that avoiding the fight was not his intention, but his brothers thought he had been playing sly. They called him 'William the Fox' after that. His brothers hired a chap to carve this scene before the desk was crated up and shipped to America." Michael pointed to the upper right corner of the left side panel of the desk. In an impressively detailed forest scene, a fox sat atop a large boulder while six hounds sat baying around its base.

"My goodness, that's a colorful tale."

"Each scene on this desk shows something of the men who've owned it. They either commissioned an artist themselves, or loved ones had it done after they passed."

Lucy spent several minutes studying the other carvings. One showed a man on horseback holding a sword high in the air. Another was of a captain standing on the deck of a schooner with sails full. Yet another showed a pious looking man holding an open book. "So who owns the desk now?" she asked.

"Well, it was to be passed to my Uncle Bub. But my grandfather outlived both his sons. The cottage and everything in it was left to me. Myra said Grandfather told her I was the one with traits most like him, and that's why he willed to me the things he loved the best. It sure took me out of favor with my cousins, though my grandfather was generous with them all."

"So you're a sly fox like your grandfather?" Lucy teased.

"I'm not sure that was the trait Grandfather was referring to," he said defensively.

"Have you thought about what scene you'll have carved on it?"

Michael glanced away from her. He turned and faced the window. After a pause he walked to one of the wooden filing cabinets and pulled out a scroll tied with a brown ribbon. He handed it to Lucy. She untied the ribbon, unrolled it, and stared down at a penciled sketch. The background of the scene she recognized right away as the tall pines atop the dune cliff behind the cottage. It depicted a man—Michael, she thought—standing by a beautiful young woman in a flowing dress seated sidesaddle on a powerful-looking horse whose front leg was raised as in prance. The horse had flowers braided into its mane and tail.

"Michael, is this you and Kathleen?"

"Aye," he said softly, looking down upon the sketch. He stretched out his hand and with the back of his finger brushed the pencil strokes of the young woman. "I had this drawn up and would have had it etched just here after our wedding." As he spoke, he placed his hand on the upper left side panel just opposite his grandfather's fox scene. "I guess I tempted fate by having it drawn up too early." After an awkward pause, he added, "So it's not to be." He took the sketch from her and rolled it up.

"Michael, what happened? Why didn't you marry her?"

He gave her a blank stare, and as if forcing himself to speak, he simply said, "She died." He turned and put the sketch back into the cabinet.

Lucy could feel his sadness. She reached out and softly touched his arm. "I'm so sorry," she said. He gave her a nod. "Want to know what I think?" she asked but didn't wait for his response. "I think you should go ahead and have it carved here."

He turned back and gave her a puzzled look. "You do?"

"Yes, I do," she said firmly.

"But you see, Lucy, I haven't given up the hope that someday I may marry. I do want children. Then, if any woman would have me, what would she think about the carving there of an old love."

"Well, if she truly loves you, then she'd know that Kathleen's story is part of who you are."

He stood silent again, staring into her. Then his grave face gave way to a grin. "Lucy, you are so refreshing. I can't tell you how much I've enjoyed the short time I've been with you." As he said this, he moved closer to her.

She held his gaze a moment and then stepped back nervously as she murmured, "Michael, Lance isn't dead."

"Aye, Lance," he whispered, closing his eyes. Then he too stepped back. His voice strengthened. "And you are here to find him." He put his hands squarely on her shoulders and declared, "I'll make you this promise, Miss Lucy Cavanagh: I will do everything in my power to help you learn the truth and find your Lance, if you will allow it."

"Oh Michael, you don't know how much that means to me. I've felt so alone and powerless. You have given me back to hope."

"Okay then, let's have at it." He turned to grab hold of one of the antique high back chairs that stood scattered about the room and placed it in front of the desk. "There now, have a seat and I'll get the journals. We will begin our hunt."

Obediently, she sat while Michael walked to the filing cabinet again and pulled out three large, leather-bound books, each one about two inches thick. He flopped them down on the desk in front of her.

"The first two tell of Grandfather's coming to America and starting up his business, of meeting my grandmother, making his fortune, and yearning for Myra. It's the third book that will be of most use in our quest. Grandfather had the pleasure in later life to let his business run on the efforts of others so he could pursue his interest in mystical and ancient secrets involving alchemy and various elements of the Fairy faith. Though I've never taken the time to read them all through, I'm pretty sure it is in the third journal that Angus will have his mentions." He placed that book in front of Lucy. "While you look through it, I will try to find where it is I've seen that symbol."

Lucy nodded and opened the cover of the big book before her. It was written with pen and ink in William Donegan's strong, intelligible hand. For the next two hours she became lost in its contents as she skimmed over some entries and lingered on others. She was fairly oblivious to Michael, who sat poring over various books of ancient runes and symbols.

Lucy learned that the Fairy faith had been passed down to William from his grandmother's side of the family, who claimed to have been visited in each generation by a type of fairy known as a Gentry, a good spirited man-sized sort that watched after the family and made sure there was no lack. It also made sure other races of fairies that were more prankish in nature did not bother them. These were fairies that would snatch babies and leave others in their places, ones that would carry off to other realms someone who had wandered too close to an enchanted hill or stepped unknowingly into the midst of a fairy circle. Those poor souls most often never returned. The ones that did manage to find a way back were never quite the same; daft or touched they were called.

According to William, the families known to be of the Dragon bloodline were especially empowered by having the ability to see into other dimensions. One born into this ancient, pure bloodline—through his mother Mary—was

Jesus Christ. It was for the reason of this bloodline that the Holy Spirit chose her to bear the Son of God.

This was not the first time Lucy had heard of the Dragon bloodline. Lance had mentioned it once to her as one of his interests. He told her that certain people from this bloodline were thought to have been the builders and guardians of the sacred sites. They were the placers of the megaliths, menhirs, dolmens, pyramids and ancient stone circles, some of which were used as portals to pass from this dimension to another.

She was totally engrossed in reading when she heard Myra's voice from behind her. "Hello, lovies, I thought you might like a nice cup of tea while you work here." She placed the tray she carried on a small round table that stood between two highbacks near the door. "And Michael, dear, I'll have a word with you if you will spare me a moment."

"Thank you for the tea, Myra, but I am in Lucy's service now. So I'll have to be asking her permission to leave our task. Lucy?"

"Of course, Michael. Don't be silly," Lucy said.

"I am not being silly," he said earnestly. "I was serious when I gave you my word, and I would not break it until you release me from it."

He seemed to her just now to be so much like Lance that she was momentarily taken back. She smiled and bowed her head, giving him the permission he sought. He walked over to the table, picked up a cup of tea, and handed it to her before he retreated from the room with Myra. Lucy took a sip then poured herself back into the journal.

After a while, she thought she heard voices coming from the garden. She walked over and saw Michael standing with his back to the window. Megan stood close to him in what Lucy decided was the "next-to-nothing swim suit" Myra had talked about. She certainly did have a great body. She was sure Michael could not help but notice. It looked to Lucy like Megan had been crying and that Michael was trying to comfort her. After a few more words, which Lucy tried to make out but couldn't, Megan jumped up and flung her arms around Michael's neck and her legs around his waist. Her mouth fell upon his. Lucy fell back away from the window holding her breath. She returned to her seat and tried to concentrate on what she was reading. She tried to pull her thoughts together.

Why should she care what relationship Michael had with Megan, or anyone else for that matter. He was just a friend. Isn't that what she wanted? She had to be honest with herself: she did feel an attraction to him. Not since Lance had her body stirred at the mere presence of a man. His looks, his voice, his smell, they were becoming intoxicating to her. "Lance," she whispered under her breath as if invoking a spirit that would clear her thoughts.

It worked. She sighed deeply and focused on the manuscript in front of her. When Michael returned some time later, she did not even look up at him. He sat down quietly and began perusing again the old books he had taken from the shelf earlier and piled atop the desk.

The two souls sat separately in their purpose to learn the fate of another who would soon turn both their worlds upside down.

As the sunlight faded, Michael walked around the room turning on old lamps that were placed here and there. He returned to his seat and opened yet another book.

Lucy gasped.

Looking up, he saw the color drain from her face. "Lucy, what is it?" he asked.

"Lance," she said.

"What?"

"Lance. It's Lance. I've found him."

"What are you saying?" He arose and walked to the back of her chair. "Where?"

"Here," she said. She was shaking. She pointed with a quivering finger to a passage. "He was here."

Michael read aloud:

Date: May 26th 1966

A young man visited me today. Lance McKellen he gave as his name. He said Angus asked him to come see me. Angus had indeed foretold of his visit. His interest, as mine, has been investigating places of power, as possible portals to other dimensions. Though he did not confide his origin or bloodline, so intense, noble and likable a fellow is he that it is my belief he may indeed be a Gentry, or of some other noble blood. His strange appearing to a family in Ohio when he was approximately two years of age from a dimension he has called Elysium would support my belief that he was snatched and placed here by the Guardians so as not to fall into the wrong hands and meet an untimely fate. Here he could grow to manhood and come into his full power before returning to his own dimension. Angus has hinted that he may be in the bloodline of the kings of that realm, if Angus is to be trusted. I sometimes wonder whether his manipulations are for good or ill. Nevertheless, I must suffer him if I am to help this young man. The fate of Lance's bloodline is somehow tied to my own. On any account, the young man has gained my complete trust. I have no doubt in his sincerity and his competence. I have this day set up an account to finance him in his endeavor to find a portal back to his dimension. The success or failure I believe may be the very hinge on which the door to our humanity will swing. He, in turn, will keep me totally informed as to his investigations and findings. I shall henceforth keep record of his reports in The Green Book of Esoteric Knowledge. I have given him complete access to all the rare and sacred documents I have collected over the years and have promised to introduce him to the other Keepers.

Michael stopped reading and placed his hand on his head. He was too stunned by what he had just read to comment. Lucy's quivering hand was now on her lips as tears streamed from the corners of her eyes.

"Wow" was all he could say.

"Michael," she sobbed, "your grandfather financed Lance."

"So it seems," he said. Seeing her distress and wanting to comfort her, he gave her a command: "Lucy, come on now, stand up here. Look at me."

Lucy rose and turned her head up toward him. She felt sick and weak. After all this time, a mention of Lance. Lance had been here, here in this very room, perhaps sitting at this very desk. Her head was spinning. Michael's grandfather was the Keeper Lance had told her about. She could hardly breathe.

"Come with me now. We need some air." Michael took her hand and led her out of the study, down the hall, past the staircase, into the foyer, and out the front door. As he did, he grabbed one of Myra's shawls from the coat stand. "Here," he said, "let's put this around you so you don't catch a chill." He wrapped her like a little child and led her to the stone half-wall under the balcony with the pillows strewn upon it. There they sat quietly trying to sort their thoughts and contemplate the implications of what they had just learned.

The early-summer sky was darkening, but there was still purple and orange streaks left in the clouds over the lake where the sun sank. Lucy saw a small twinkle on the western horizon in the distant night sky. "My star," she murmured under her breath.

Michael looked up from out of his own thoughts and saw her gazing at the heavens. Her head was tipped up in such a way that the dim and fading last light of the day danced across her face. For a fleeting moment it was Kathleen whom Michael beheld, and he whispered her name.

"What?" Lucy asked. Michael didn't reply. He just stared at her. "You just said 'Kathleen,' Michael. You whispered her name."

"Aye, I did. I'm sorry. It was just the way the light came across your face just then. It reminded me…"

"I remind you of Kathleen? Michael, do I look like her?"

"There is a favor. It's not so much a physical one."

"I don't understand."

"Never mind me, Lucy. I get melancholy on a summer night. We used to sit here in the evenings listening to the lake and the night sounds. The light on your face just now it… It was just a memory, that's all. A memory of the way I used to feel."

"Michael, tell me about her. Tell me about your Kathleen."

An owl hooted from out of the rafters atop the stable. He looked in that direction and sat silent. After a moment or two, he began: "I was in college in Dublin when we met. She was the sister of a buddy of mine. He had taken me home with him to Ardrahan for a weekend with his family. Kathleen was just out of high school and waiting to see if she'd been accepted to The Royal Irish Academy of Music. I loved her the moment I saw her. She played the harp and sang for us that evening. She captured my soul with her voice. It was the voice of an angel she had. I couldn't get it out of my head.

"When we went back to school, I wrote her almost every day, and she wrote back. Come that fall, she was accepted at the Academy and moved to Dublin. She got a small flat with her brother James, my buddy. We saw each other as often as we could. We were both busy with our college schedules and her with rehearsals and concerts on top of that. We became engaged the day I graduated. She still had two years left at the Academy, and I had been given a position with my grandfather's company here in America. I didn't want to leave her, and I knew I could not ask her to leave her music.

"Not long after I came back to America I got a call from James telling me that Kathleen had collapsed right in the middle of a performance. He said she had been feeling poorly, not eating well and run down. Everyone thought it was because I had left and she was just lovesick, or something foolish like that. She became frailer and soon left school too weak to continue with her schedule. The doctor in Ardrahan thought she had a flu virus and prescribed bed rest. But when she didn't improve, he ordered blood tests. That's when they found she had leukemia.

"Now there are some fine hospitals in Ireland, but Grandfather helped me persuade Kathleen's folks she should be here where she could get the best treatment. Grandfather arranged a corporate jet to bring her and her parents over here. We placed her in the cancer treatment center at the University of Michigan hospital in Ann Arbor. And well she did there. After only two months of treatment, she went into remission. When she got out of the hospital, she came here to Glen Eden and her parents went back to Ireland.

"We spent a wonderful spring together. Kathleen loved to ride. Her favorite horse was Shashad, and he loved her as well, or he would not have put up with all that woman did to him. One day she rode him right down that dune into the water and gave him a good scrubbing." He nodded in the direction of the lake with his head and stared into the night as if watching it happen all over again. "Then she brought him up here and braided flowers into his mane and tail. Peter Nelson, a friend of Grandfather's, was here that day and sketched us out back in the garden. That was the sketch I showed you in the library."

"Yes, it's wonderful."

"We walked the beach nearly every day," he went on, "when the weather was warm enough for her. In the evenings we would sit just here, she wrapped in a shawl, in my arms. We'd look at the moon and the stars and make plans for our future. Our first son was to be Michael Jr." He breathed in and out in a long sigh. He swallowed hard and began again. But his voice changed; it betrayed the grief he still carried. "We had planned a solstice wedding in Ardrahan. It was to be in the church on the hilltop overlooking the village, and the party following would be on her parents' farm.

"The day came when she was to fly home. Myra had made her wedding dress and went back with her to help with the final wedding arrangements. Grandfather and I were to fly over as soon as we had some business tied up here. I drove them to Chicago to catch a plane. I worried because she was looking pale again. She insisted she was just a little tired and had some nerves about flying and leaving me. A week later we got a call from Myra that they had taken her to the hospital in Dublin. She had relapsed. When the doctors could give us no hope, she asked to go home to the farm to die. We were all with her, her mum and dad, James, Myra and me. She was holding my hand, and I was trying to be strong. But she saw into me. I leaned close and she said, 'I'm sorry I cannot be your wife, Michael Donegan, but I'll be helping God to send you another love. And she'll have my blessing on her. She'll love you like you deserve to be loved. And maybe as a favor to me, so Myra's wonderful work will not be wasted, she could wear my beautiful dress.'

"Three days later was the solstice, but instead of our wedding, we had her funeral." He put his face into his hands, rubbed his eyes, took a long, deep breath and let it out slowly. "So there you have it," he said, regaining himself. "I'm sorry, Lucy. I have not talked about this with anyone before."

"No, Michael, you've no cause to be sorry. I can tell you loved her very much. I'm glad you shared her with me. It's I who am sorry for your loss." She reached out to him and put her hand on his arm.

"And I for yours," he said. "But then, you still have your hope, my girl, and I meant what I said: I will help you find your Lance."

"Michael, I don't know what to say."

"Well, I know what you can say. You can say you'll be getting yourself ready for dinner. We have a date at the Butler tonight, remember?"

"I'll be running upstairs to change then. Now that you mention it, I'm starving. Just give me twenty minutes."

"That's my good girl," he said.

Lucy thought, but did not say it, *No, Michael, I am Lance's girl.*

10 – The Butler

Upstairs Lucy quickly showered, taking care not to get her long hair wet. She promised Michael she'd be ready in twenty minutes, and she wanted to hold to her word. Sitting in front of the vanity mirror, she brushed out her hair, gathered it behind her head, and wound it to form a neat little twist that lay at the nape of her neck. She secured it with two large hairpins that sported blue rhinestone heads. She applied makeup lightly, highlighting her eyes with a dark blue liner and applying just a touch of mascara. She used a soft pink lipstick and brushed on a hint of blush.

She had pushed open the window adjacent to the bed when she entered the room earlier, and felt a cool breeze drifting in. She could hear music now. It was the sound of a woman's voice lamenting to the strums of a harp. The words sounded to Lucy to be in the Gaelic language. She thought Myra must be playing the old Victrola she had seen in the sitting room downstairs. The music was hypnotic. She closed her eyes and saw Michael dressed handsomely and dancing with a woman in a long white dress. The music stopped, and Lucy opened her eyes to behold herself in the vanity mirror. Again she thought she saw the image of a woman standing behind her. She turned quickly but no one was there.

An atomizer sat on the vanity and Lucy, having not brought any fragrance of her own, picked it up and whiffed it. "Gardenia," she thought. She decided to use just a wisp. She slipped into the navy blue spaghetti-strapped dress that she was happy she thought to pack and gazed at herself. It had been a while since she had gotten "gussied up" as Danny would have put it. She wished Lance could see her. "Can you? Can you see me?" she asked into the mirror. Realizing her time was nearly up, she slipped on her sandals, picked up her handbag, and hurried out the door.

Myra was standing in the hallway. "Well now, don't you look lovely. I'm so happy you are here and spending some time with Michael. I know it did him a world of good to speak to you of Kathleen. He told me he did and that you had found mention of your Lance in one of William's journals. I'll be looking forward to hearing all about it in the morning, but hurry on now because that big Irishman is hungry. I'm off to my bed now with a book." She added without hesitation, "Will you be going to Mass with us in the morning, dear?"

"Thank you, Myra. Yes, I would like that very much."

"Wonderful. Run on now and good night to you."

"Good night, Myra. Sweet Dreams."

"Yes, yes. Oh my, yes. And also to you."

Michael was standing by the door at the foot of the stairs. He had changed his clothes as well and sported a kelly green, three-button golf shirt with a blue and green plaid blazer. He turned when he heard her on the stairs. "Wow," he said. Lucy threw her head back and laughed. "Miss Cavanagh, you honor me with your presence." He took her hand and kissed it. She looked away and blushed. The grin was still affixed to her face. It was almost as large as his.

He had already pulled the Trans Am into the drive in front. He hurried ahead of her and opened the car door. The drive to the Butler took only about ten minutes. On the way there, they drove by her old apartment. She pointed it out to Michael.

"Did you know Mrs. Garrett, then?" he asked.

"Yes. Yes, I did, quite well."

"She was Megan's grandmother. We must tell Meg; maybe she'll be nicer to you knowing that you knew her granny."

Lucy thought now of the picture of the little blond girl that had set upon an occasional table in the old woman's apartment. She remembered Mrs. Garrett showing it off to her. How small the world seemed sometimes, and how big and lonesome at others. She pictured Lance standing at her door, backpack slung over his shoulder, waiting for her to come back from delivering the medicine they had picked up as a favor for Mrs. Garrett.

They drove on past the Blue Nile, still doing business, and Lucy wondered if Asad still worked there.

There was the usual Saturday night summer crowd at the Butler, college kids who converged on Saugatuck to party and hang out on the beach; they came to hear the band that would start after the dinner crowd left. The dinner clientele was by and large made up of Chicago people off their yachts. They would cross Lake Michigan and pull into one of the many quays that lined the river to the west between the village and the sand dunes.

Lucy wondered as they drove up whether any of the old gang would still be working there. Michael told her on the drive that the Whites still owned the Butler. The three-story, cracker-box-looking building, a landmark for the area, was one of the oldest structures in Saugatuck, having been built in 1892 and maintained as a steam powered grist mill before becoming a hotel. The upstairs had been closed for several years now, and only the bar and restaurant located on the ground level were being utilized.

A small crowd sat around waiting for tables in the beautifully preserved lobby where dozens of old photos hung, showing the establishment in bygone days. The Butler didn't take reservations; they were too busy in the summer for that. It was a first come, first served basis.

They were met at the door by a hostess who seemed very pleased to see Michael. A friendly kiss on the cheek, to divert attention from the folded bill being slipped into her hand, got them seated right away. It was a cozy little table in the far corner on the bar-side of the building. Lucy recalled that pool tables used to occupy this area. They had been removed to cater to a larger dinner crowd, she guessed. They would probably be hauled back in once the summer crowds dwindled to entice the full-time residents to come in for a friendly game, beer, and the famous Butler burger. Several people came up to say hello to Michael, shake his hand, or pat his shoulder as they walked by. They strained to get a look at the girl he escorted through the crowd.

The waitresses serving dinner were all dressed the same, in short black skirts and white blouses with little black bowties. Lucy recalled wearing the same attire when she worked there. The hostess left them with little cards announcing the dinner selections for the evening. By the time the waitress arrived at their table, they had decided on the catch of the day. It came with a baked potato and sweet peas with pearl onions. Lucy granted Michael the permission he sought to order a bottle of wine from the extensive list that had been handed him.

They sat chatting over their salads, which were brought out immediately, while waiting for their entrées to arrive. Lucy told Michael how she had earned extra money as a seamstress while working at the Butler. She had made matching outfits for one of the house rock-and-roll bands. Mr. White insisted that his bands look "sharp" by having matching attire, so she volunteered to make the cash-strapped musicians bell-bottom pants with reversible vests so they could please the boss and still maintain their hip personas. One side of the vest was a psychedelic paisley design in brocaded satin, like the pants, and the other a midnight blue in crushed velvet. After seeing her workmanship, Mr. White contracted her to make outfits for his weekend night waitresses. The girls were happy to toss off their black and whites once the dinner rush was done and don the white laced go-go outfits Lucy had designed herself. She enjoyed sharing these stories with Michael; he was easy for her to talk to, and he seemed to enjoy listening.

He was about to share one of his own past adventures there at the Butler when a man walked up to the table. "Had any luck at the track lately, Donegan?" he asked, setting a drink from his hand on the edge of their table so he could shake Michael's hand. His other hand held a cigarette and was politely extended away from them.

"Last weekend Strider finished in the top three in all his efforts. I came away with enough cash to pay for this meal and buy you a cold beer to boot." They both laughed, still shaking hands.

"I see your luck with the ladies has gotten better. And just who is this ravishing creature?" Before Michael could answer, the man blurted out, "Well, bless my stars, if it isn't Lucy Number One."

"Hello, Ash," Lucy said, extending her hand. He took it, kissed it, and held on to it.

"I see no introductions are needed then," Michael conceded.

"No sir, Lucy stole my heart when we worked here together. But she ran off to California with an old acquaintance of mine. What have you done, Lucy, traded in one Irishman for another?" Michael wondered how Lucy would handle this remark.

"Ashley Randall, you know perfectly well it was I who was smitten with you. But the line I had to stand in before my number would be called was much too long."

Ashley chuckled, "Haven't you heard of saving the best till last?"

"Yes, Ash, I have. I just didn't think I would be at my best when I turned 80." They all laughed.

Michael liked the way she was playing. This was a different side than he'd seen before. So far he liked them all. But what he didn't like was how Ashley was still holding her hand.

The waitress appeared with their meals. Ashley stepped back so she could set the plates on the table and said, "Oh good, you have Babs tonight; she's by far the finest waitress this place has ever seen, present company excluded of course." He winked at Lucy. "Babs, did you know Lucy used to work here with me? How long ago was that, eight, nine years?"

"Eight," Lucy said.

"Then you know what I have to put up with every night," Babs said, rolling her eyes at Ashley.

"You see, she's in love with me too—aren't you, cutie pie?"

"Yes, Ashley, deeply, madly."

Lucy didn't doubt that. It wasn't that he was so good looking; Ashley just oozed charisma. All the girls eventually ended up on his arm if they stuck around long enough. The funny thing was that no one was ever jealous of the other. With Ashley you knew right away what you were getting. He was fun loving and always had a smile on his face and a twinkle in his eye. He never had a bad word about anyone. He never really made a date ahead of time because he couldn't trust himself to keep it. If he was free and you were there, you might get asked to keep him company for dinner or to go to a party he'd heard about that evening. She recalled a little black book he kept in his wallet. Each page represented a city—Chicago, L.A., San Francisco. He was a player and everyone knew it. But he was so likable no one cared.

"You two go ahead and chow down. When you finish, come on down to the Hacksaw room. You can buy me that cold beer, Michael, and Lucy here can fill me in on what she's been up to. You do remember where the Hacksaw room is, don't you Lucy?"

"Yes, Ash, I do." She was surprised he was asking them down there. The way she remembered it, it was just a room in the cellar with a couple of old couches and an old desk with a bottle of Scotch in the drawer. Mr. White used to go down and catch naps in the afternoon. There were rumors of card games that transpired between Mr. White, Ashley and some local businessmen on winter nights when the bar wasn't busy. It was also rumored a bartender could escort a girl down there to get to know her better after the bar closed up. No woman was allowed in the Hacksaw room if not escorted by one of the favored few men, not even Mrs. White.

One evening Lucy and a bartender named Gary had closed up. Everyone else had left. Gary turned to her. Dangling the key in her face, he said, "Say, Lucy, have you ever seen the Hacksaw room?"

"No, I haven't. But I sure am curious."

"Want to have a look?" he asked. Gary was a local guy. He had married too young, had four kids and another on the way. He worked a full time factory job and tended bar on the weekends to make ends meet. He didn't talk about his family much. Lucy thought that was because he liked to think of himself as single when he tended bar so he could flirt with the girls. But he always left alone, and she never heard any rumors that he cheated on his wife.

A lot of stories had crawled to the surface out of the Hacksaw room, and Lucy was curious about what it looked like. So she followed him down the old stairwell. She was surprised when she saw it. It was not grandiose at all. It smelled of smoke and was dimly lit. Gary shut the door behind them. Lucy squinted through the dark, and then having seen what she could, turned around to leave. Gary stood in her path. "So this is the famous Hacksaw room, eh? I guess I haven't missed much."

"I'll show you what you've been missing," Gary said as he pushed her up against a supporting beam. His body pressed against her while his hands tried lifting her skirt. "Hey, cut it out, Gary," she said, trying to push him off. He would not retreat. "Stop it. Stop it!" she yelled, becoming frightened that no one could hear her.

"Come on, baby, you want this."

"Gary, stop!" she pleaded. "Leave me alone. You're drunk." Her voice was panicked. "Stop it right now!"

"Oh, you little tease. You know you don't mean that."

"Yeah, Gary, I think she does," came a voice from under a blanket on a couch in the back of the room.

Gary stopped and stepped back from her. "Oh hey, Ashley, I thought you went home. Lucy and I just came down her to have a little fun. You know what I mean."

"Yeah, I know what you mean, Gary ol' buddy. Trouble is I don't think Lucy here is having fun."

"Why don't you just keep your nose out of it," Gary shot back.

Ashley was up on his feet now, standing in front of Gary in his skivvies. "I've got an idea, Gary. Why don't you just get your sorry ass off home to your wife and kids. Maybe if you can muster up an apology to Lucy here before you leave, this whole thing can just stay between us and no wind of it will ever have to blow from the Hacksaw room."

Gary stood quiet a minute, clenching his teeth. Finally, he laughed, "Yeah, what the hell. I don't want to waste my marriage over some tramp waitress."

Ashley had enough; he grabbed Gary by the collar and shoved him against the wall. "That didn't sound like an apology to me."

His arm was cocked back ready to bloody a nose when Lucy yelled, "Just stop it. Please just stop."

"Come on, Ash. I didn't mean anything by it."

"Then apologize to her and get the hell out of here."

"Okay, okay," Gary said, putting his hands up in surrender.

Acquiescing to Lucy's request, Ashley released him. Gary turned to Lucy and mumbled, "Sorry, hon'. Can't blame a guy for trying."

"Go home, Gary" was all she could say to him.

He bolted up the stairs, slamming the door on his way out. Ashley turned to Lucy and scolded, "What the hell did you come down here with that jerk for?"

"Because he asked me if I'd ever seen the Hacksaw room. I was curious, that's all. I didn't know he would try..." She stopped mid-sentence and looked at her admonisher with tears in her eyes.

"Well, here it is," Ashley said in a voice still sounding a little miffed as he spread out his arms and turned around. He stopped turning right in front of her. Suddenly, he dropped his head to view his naked legs and boxers. All the excitement had gotten his blood up and his manhood was evident through the thin, cotton covering. "Oops," he said, dropping his hands to cover himself. "I better get some pants on."

They heard the door open and someone bounding down the stairs. It was Mark the weekend bouncer. When he saw Ashley standing in his boxers and Lucy looking disheveled, he assumed something was going on, so he backed up the stairs saying, "Oh, excuse me. Sorry. I'll get my lighter later on."

"Mark," Ashley called after him. He grabbed the lighter from the desk and tossed it up the stairs. Mark caught it and said, "Thanks, pally. Good work there. Carry on." He was out the door before Lucy or Ashley could say a word. They looked at each other and both started to laugh.

"I'm going to get dressed and drive you home before anyone else gets in on this little drama."

"No, Ash, you don't have to do that. You've already done enough. I'll walk."

"No, you won't. What if your buddy Gary is still out there sulking? Besides, owing to Mark's imagination and his propensity for gossip, tomorrow you will have the reputation of being the future Mrs. Ashley Randall. I hope you know I treat my ladies better than making them walk home." He smiled and pinched her cheek.

For the next few weeks, their "affair" was the buzz of the Butler, of all Saugatuck for that matter. Mark was somewhat of a town crier. Being single at the age of thirty-two and still abiding with his mother, he lived vicariously through the lives of others. Lucy and Ashley both got a kick out of being the center of the gossip mill. Though they denied the rumors, they purposely did it in a way that made people disbelieve them. Ashley would blow kisses at her from across the bar when he knew Mark or another staff member was watching. Lucy played along. Having the reputation of being Ashley's woman made the local creeps who were always hitting on her back off. This made her job a little more pleasant. Once, when she took a round of beer to a table full of dockworkers, one of them hit on her in a drunken sailor sort of way. Another man at the table said, "Hey, brother, leave her alone. That's Ashley's woman." She was surprised at how far their little non-secret had spread.

Michael lifted his wine glass as Ashley slipped back into the crowded room. "Lucy, let me offer our thanks, will you?"

"Of course, Michael." She bowed her head.

"Thank you, Lord, for this food, your grace, and this time we have to share. Amen. I mean it, Lucy. I am thankful Angus brought us together. For what this is worth to you, I really enjoy being in your company." She wanted to say she enjoyed his company too, but the memory of Megan kissing him in the garden came into her head. So she remained silent.

While they ate, they talked of different things. She asked him about Strider and learned he was Michael's race horse in its third season at the sulky tracks. She knew of the tracks in Hazel Park and Northville, though she had never been. "The next time Strider is making a run, I'll let you know, and maybe you'll go with me to watch him."

"Sounds like fun," she said, neither confirming nor denying in her own mind that she would go.

"He is really a handsome animal. He was sired by Shashad. I was thinking maybe tomorrow after Mass we could saddle up the horses and take a ride over to the old Green farm. You said you wanted to see it. Myra reminded me it's at the end of one of the trails that connects to the main path along the lakeside. Should be a nice ride, if you're up for it."

"That would be nice, Michael. I would very much like to do that."

"Good," he said. "Now, if I may ask, what's with Ashley calling you Lucy Number One? Not that I disagree with that; I'm just curious."

She explained that the Butler got its seasonal help by hiring college kids on their summer breaks. There was always a big turn over because Saugatuck was a party town, and work cut into party time for some of the girls. So it was easier for the bartenders and kitchen personnel just to call the waitresses by their section numbers. Lucy, who was year-round help, had earned the best station where the most tips could be made, so she was tagged "Lucy Number One."

"Oh, that's all it is? Well, I'm thankful for that," Michael said. She wondered what he meant by that, but before she could ask, Babs walked up to take their plates and offer dessert, which they both declined.

The band started to play and people were moving to the dance floor. It was hard to carry on a conversation over the music, so Michael suggested they find Ashley so he could buy him the beer. As they pushed through the crowd, Lucy grabbed hold of Michael's hand to lead him to the Hacksaw room. They walked through the lobby, now empty, to the base of the stairs. Lucy tried letting go of Michael's hand, but he just squeezed hers tighter. She tugged slightly, and he let loose his grip.

On the back side of the stairwell, the outline of an unmarked door could be seen in the paneling. There was no handle, just a key hole; the only people that could use this room were those with a key. Lucy knocked, and shortly a burly man with a crew cut pushed open the door. "How's it going, Lucy?" the man asked. "Ash told me you were here and would be down."

"Oh hey, Mark, this is a surprise. It's good seeing you again." She gave the man a kiss on the cheek, and he returned it in kind while keeping his eyes on Michael.

"Mark, this is Michael Don…" Lucy began, but he cut her off.

"I know who he is. I have a cap on my front tooth courtesy of his knuckles."

"Hello, Mark. Are you bearing me a grudge, then?"

"Well, no. Hell, we both know I deserved it. I was way out of line with your missy. I'm not getting sloshed like that anymore; saves on the dental work." He laughed and held out his hand to Michael. "Come on down, both of ya." Lucy wondered what "missy" Mark referred to.

They descended the stairwell that Lucy recalled having rough hewn planks and being open on both sides. But it was now enclosed and the steps carpeted. The Michigan block walls had been wood paneled halfway with attractively painted wallboard on the upper half. Soft lighting had also been installed along with exhaust fans to carry enough cigar smoke up and out to make the room suitable for the few women who were invited down.

Ashley stood leaning over with his elbows resting on a small bar. Supporting his face in his hands, he talked to a shapely blond sitting opposite him. "Well, howdy, folks," he said as they approached. "Pull up a stool. Sit down. You both know Skipper." The blond turned around to show a face looking as much like her twin brother's as was possible for someone of the opposite sex. It was eerie to see them together. Ashley was the senior by only thirteen minutes, though he had always seemed like a much older brother.

"Lucy, how are you?" Skipper asked as the two girls embraced.

"I'm good, thanks Skip. You look fantastic as ever."

"Well, you are so sweet to say that."

"I'm saying it too," Michael piped up.

"Well, looky here who you've snared in your net, Lucy girl. Saugatuck's most eligible. Hello, handsome."

"Skipper," Michael said, leaning in to kiss the cheek she offered.

"Lucy, just how do you do it? First you steal my brother's heart. Then you run off with Sir Lancelot. Now you come back with this gorgeous hunk. Chickiepoo, I want to know your secret?"

Lucy could tell her lips had been loosened by the golden liquid that sat in the half empty glass before her, and she wondered how many others she had had before that one. Lucy liked Skipper. She had the charm of Ashley but displayed a certain vulnerability Lucy had never seen in him.

"Okay, Sis, I don't mind you baring your own soul, but leave what's left of mine alone, will you?" He moved the glass from in front of her and threw its contents in the sink.

"Hey, give me my drink. I'm only telling the truth. I can't help it if you let her run off with that Lance guy before you confessed your love. Just ask Mom, Lucy. He told us if he was ever to marry anyone, it would be you."

"Hey, zip it up," Ashley ordered. She paid no attention.

"Go ahead and ask Mom about the funk he was in after you left. Now you come back, and before he even gets wind of it, you snatch up Michael here. You've missed your chance again, Ash. It's likely Lucy will hold on to this big fish."

"Shut up, Skipper. You're crocked." Ashley grabbed on to her hand, but she pulled it back.

She turned her attention to Michael now. "I was wondering, Michael, why you hadn't called me for another roll in the hay."

"Ashley, you better get some black coffee down her before everyone's soul lays bare." Lucy just stood there taking it all in. She wondered how much was truth and how much was the booze.

Skipper slid off the stool and fell flat. Michael scooped her up and carried her over to an unoccupied couch on the rear wall. Ashley and Lucy followed behind him. "For Christ's sake, Ashley, why do you let her get so drunk?" Michael snapped.

Ashley shot back, "Better here with me than out somewhere else where there would be no one to watch after her. I guess you didn't care how drunk she was one night, did you, Donegan?"

"Ashley, I was even more drunk than she was, and we have already had that fight." Actually, it wasn't a fight. Ashley had walked up to Michael the morning after—when Michael was still in the throes of a massive hangover—and sucker punched him. Michael hit the floor with a bloodied lip but then got up and let Ashley hit him again. He hadn't even raised his hands. He knew if he were Ashley he'd be doing the same thing. "I would not want her hurt for anything. We both made a mistake, and we both know it. I apologize for being out of line just now. I know you do everything you can for her. You're a good brother. I just hate to see her like this."

"She always did like to drink, but since Jay got killed she doesn't seem to know when to stop."

"What?" Lucy whispered, "Jay killed?"

"Four years ago in a car accident," Ash whispered back.

Lucy wondered if anyone was ever happy for long. Skipper married Jay, a drummer in one of the Butler's house bands, just before Lucy met Lance. Skipper and Jay seemed made for each other. The wedding had been on the lawn at the Butler. Lucy had received an invitation and intended to go alone, but Ashley called her the night before and asked if she would accompany him. They sat at the family table and this of course fueled the fire of the rumor that they were an item.

Ashley left and returned with a cup of coffee for Skipper. But by the time he got back, she was passed out on Michael's arm. "Shall we wake her, or let her sleep it off?" Michael asked.

"No, let her sleep. I'll wake her when I close up and drive her home." Michael slipped his arm out from around her and propped her head up on a cushion. "Are you buying me that beer now, Donegan?" Ashley seemed less pissed now.

"Sure thing," Michael replied, "unless you'd rather a Dewar's at this hour."

"A Dewar's it is, then. And what for you?"

"I'll have the same"

"Miss Lucy, what can I get for you?"

"Nothing, thanks." She had had the wine with dinner, and she wanted to keep her wits about her. Michael was just too appealing for her to let down her guard.

"I know, let me make you a grasshopper. Do you still like them?"

She was surprised he remembered. "I haven't had one since the last one you made for me. I'd love one if it wouldn't be too much trouble."

"For you, trouble is a pleasure, my dear. I'll be right back." Ashley hurried away toward the bar. Michael took a throw that was folded on the end of the couch and put it over Skipper. Then he brushed the hair away that had fallen across her face. Lucy watched this and appreciated the tenderness he showed.

He looked up at her and smiled. "You see, we have more in common than either of us knew. We share some mutual friends."

"We do," Lucy smiled back.

"And they both knew Lance, I take it?"

The smile left Lucy's face. She felt that familiar sick feeling crawl over her. "They both know Lance," she corrected. "They know him. He is not dead."

"Of course not, of course not. I'm sorry. It was just a slip of the tongue." Michael stood and put his arms around her.

She buried her face in her hands and leaned against him. "It's such a nightmare," she whispered. She was tired of this sick feeling.

"Shhh now, I know, I know, and I promise it will not go on much longer. We will find your Lance. We will learn the truth." Even as he said this, his body stirred. She felt so good in his arms and she smelled wonderful—like Kathleen, he thought. He was tired of the sick feeling too, of the heartache of missing love. Yes, he had known women since Kathleen. But he had not known love.

"Here we go, folks," Ashley said, walking up with a tray. Michael released his arms from around Lucy, and they both turned toward Ashley as he approached. He could see something serious had come up. "Lucy, are you all right?"

Michael did not give her time to answer. "She is missing her love, Ashley, as I am missing mine. We came here for dinner in friendship to fight off loneliness for one more night. I think assumptions have been made by seeing us together. I would not have her feel like she has betrayed Lance, only that she has blessed me by sharing a table and some time." He took a tumbler off the tray. Lucy just stared at him. He had snuffed out the sick feeling once again.

Ashley handed her the Grasshopper he had painstakingly made, took his glass from the tray, and raised it: "To love and friendship then shall be the toast."

"To love and friendship," Michael repeated, raising his glass and staring back at Lucy.

Lucy raised her stemmed glass filled with a frothy green liquid to Michael. "To love and friendship," she said softly. Then, turning her eyes on Ashley, she repeated the same line. The memory of his old heartbreak returned to Ashley at that second, and he quickly took a slug from his old comforter.

They moved back to the small bar and sat down. Ashley assumed his stool behind it across from his companions. "So Lucy, do you want to fill in your old fiancé here on just what's been going on with you?"

"Old fiancé?" Michael sputtered, almost choking on his drink. Ashley and Lucy both laughed. They took turns relating how the rumor of their involvement grew that summer.

"Here's something you didn't know, Lucy. Remember when Mr. White took me to the track in Chicago after the summer season was over that year? Well, he did it because you brought Lance in here and everyone could see you were totally gaga over him. He thought I was nursing a broken heart, and he wanted me to forget about you. He was mad as hell at you for slighting me, his favored son, and wanted to fire you."

"Oh brother," Lucy moaned.

"I told him," Ashley continued, "you had caught me with Norma, your old roommate, and just couldn't forgive me for it. So, you see, I got you off the hook and set up Lance as your rebound guy. We all came out of it with our dignity."

"Except poor Norma," Lucy laughed.

"Well, okay. We came out of it with our jobs, though you didn't stay long after that."

"Ashley, you are something else," Lucy said, shaking her head.

"I know. Hold your applause. Now let's hear where you ran off to." Lucy spent the next quarter of an hour telling Ashley of her life with, and then without, Lance. Visibly shaken after her story, she excused herself for the restroom.

Michael, who just sat there sipping his drink, watching, and listening to the two old friends catch up, leaned into Ashley and asked, "So you knew this McKellen guy?"

Ashley was surprised by his voice. He had been gazing after Lucy, watching her as she walked away, secretly wanting her all over again. "What? Ah Lance... yeah, I know him."

"So what kind of a guy was, I mean, is he?" Michael corrected himself.

"Quality," Ashley replied, then added, "The kind of a guy a woman like that deserves."

"That's what I was afraid of, but I had to ask."

"I understand, man, more than you know. He would not just have left her. There was something about the two of them together. It affected everyone that saw them. It was like... you know, like a fairytale. Like the kind of love mortals can only dream about."

"Okay, I get it," Michael said, picking up his glass and sucking the last drop of gold from the melted ice.

Ashley brought up the bottle of Dewar's, but Michael covered his glass. "I need to keep a clear head if I'm going to be around that one."

"Glad to hear you say that."

"Ashley, about Skipper: there's a hospital in Chicago that she'd do well to spend some time in."

"Yeah, I know it. Jay didn't exactly leave her set. I'm saving up for it. Maybe after Christmas if my horses come in."

"I want to pay for it, Ash. I can call and make all the arrangements if you can get her there, the sooner the better."

"Sure, I'll get her there. Are you kidding me? That's great. Hey man, why are you doing this? Are you feeling guilty? Because you shouldn't. Hell, I know how she can be."

"No, Ash, I'm not feeling guilty. I like her. I want to see her doing well. She got dealt a bad hand. Hell, so did I. Maybe I just understand her. She knows better than anyone that needs are different than wants. Oh yeah, and one other thing: I would appreciate it if she doesn't know I'm involved. Just tell her your horse came in, okay?"

"You got it, Michael."

"What does he have?" Lucy asked, suddenly appearing at the bar side.

"He has my promise to come up and see his pony show," Ashley spoke up.

"Better for him to win or place," Michael played along, "but showing will help pay down his feed bill."

"Well, when that takes place, be sure to let me know about it. I'd love to see you two wheeler-dealers in action."

"If he doesn't call you, I will," Ashley replied. "Maybe you could be my lucky charm."

"I don't think I can be anyone's lucky charm, but I would very much like to go along."

"Are you ready to head back now, Lucy?" Michael asked.

"Yes, Michael. Ashley, please give Skipper my love. I will pray for her. It was wonderful seeing you both again."

"You too, Number One." He took her hand and kissed it. He held his breath as she withdrew it, and he felt her slip away.

He watched her walk off, took a deep breath and let it out in a loud sigh. He picked up the bottle of scotch, held it up and made a whispered toast: "Be happy." He took a big swig and felt the warm liquid flow down his neck hoping it would soon numb the corners of his aching heart.

11 – Time Times Seven

Sunday morning Lucy awoke to the sound of a rooster crowing. She sat up and gazed out the open window. As was her habit, she offered thanks to God for waking her into a new day. She felt refreshed and strangely happy. Then she recalled the dream she had had.

She and Lance had climbed the face of a tall mountain. He left her sitting on a narrow ledge where she was to wait for him. It seemed in her dream she had been there a long time. She was cold, hungry, and frightened, wondering if something had happened to him. The sky turned black and storm clouds moved in around her. The ledge began to shrink; it became smaller and smaller, and then the earth crumbled under her feet as terror and darkness enveloped her. Suddenly, at seemingly the last moment, a hand gripped her shoulder just as the final bit of ground fell from beneath her toes. She clutched it and was pulled to the safety of a higher place. She clung to her savior thinking it to be Lance, but when the storm subsided and the light returned, the man in her arms was Michael. He was dressed in warrior's garb, complete with chain mail and a sword. He bowed to her and explained that he had been sent by Lance to rescue her.

"Oh Lance," she whispered now into the morning. "Why haven't you come for me? *Have* you sent Michael?"

A wonderful breeze from the open window reached her, and once again Lucy heard music carried upon it. It was the same lovely voice she had heard the past evening accompanied by the strains of a harp. But there was no lament this time. The music conjured a happy feeling that sent Lucy bouncing out of bed, dancing around the room as she dressed for breakfast. She must remember to ask Myra what music she was playing on the old Victrola downstairs. She was excited to begin the day, excited to have another session in the study. The shock of finding Lance there had been replaced with enthusiasm to learn more about his research. She would cherish any mention she could find of him. But, for now, she would have to suppress this desire as she had promised Myra she'd accompany them to Mass.

Myra and Michael were already at the table when she entered the dining room. "Good morning," she chirped. Michael rose quickly and offered her that wonderful smile of his. His eyes glistened. She could do nothing else but smile back. He hurried over to her chair and pulled it out.

"Top of the morning to you, lass. Did you dream well?"

"Yes, thank you. And you?"

"Of gallant deeds on a mountaintop, if I recall correctly." She wanted to press him about that remark, but Myra took over the conversation.

"I hope you don't mind, love, we've started breakfast without you. Michael thought it better to let you sleep after the exciting day you had. He got up early and cooked up these hotcakes for us. Some Irish Catholics won't eat breakfast before Mass, but I've always felt it was better for the menfolk to listen to what the father has to say than to the rumblings of their stomachs. You are still joining us for Mass this morn, aren't you, dear?"

"Yes, Myra" is all she had time to say.

"Oh, wonderful, wonderful. Go ahead, eat now." Myra handed her a warming plate stacked with golden pancakes. "Try some of this huckleberry syrup on them. Ashley's mum Winnie made it from the wild blueberries on back her farm." She offered a small crystal pitcher filled with the dark blue compote. "Winnie is a very dear friend of mine. We meet regularly in the winter along with some other ladies and do quilting. We usually get a couple done before bazaar time and auction them off. The money goes to provide meals to the less fortunate at the holidays."

"That's wonderful," Lucy said, taking the hot syrup and pouring it generously over the cakes on her plate.

"Myra does lovely work," Michael said. He had finished his breakfast but sat drinking coffee, waiting on the women. "You'll have to come by my room and take a look at the quilt she made for me. It is a work of art."

"Oh, look at how the honey drips from your mouth, you rascal. Kathleen and William both helped on cutting the pieces for it so I'd have it done in time."

"And all behind my back. It was a Christmas present, and I've had none finer."

"I'd love to see it," Lucy said, enjoying the loving feeling generated between them. She bowed her head and thanked God not only for the food but for that feeling and for her new friends.

"Poor Winnie," Myra went on, "she does worry over that daughter of hers. It was a terrible thing her losing her husband. Those two were made for each other." She shook her head and took a sip of tea before going on. "I'm afraid she's gone over the edge with her drinking now."

"Myra," Michael corrected, "it's not like you to gossip."

"Oh now, Michael, the whole town knows that girl has a problem. I think Lucy saw it firsthand last night, so it's not really gossip if one simply states a fact. Is it, Lucy?" Lucy was glad Myra didn't wait for a response. "Skipper turned to Michael for a time after Jay died, for comfort. Isn't that right, Michael?"

He didn't answer, and Myra's tone led Lucy to believe this had been some sort of sore spot between them. "Winnie was hoping that the two of them would connect, you know, in a more permanent way." Michael sat staring into his coffee cup. He wasn't smiling now.

Myra went on, "Well now, we know God's plan is always better than those we cook up. We need to have patience and use it wisely. It's just sad to see young people alone." She took a sip of tea before moving on to a new subject.

"I was so curious about what the two of you discovered in William's journals yesterday. I simply could not wait for you to join us, Lucy, so I coaxed Michael into filling me in. I hope you don't mind. It's all so amazing, all so wonderful. I mean, your Lance right here with my William. This is a thing of hope, my dear."

Lucy smiled but didn't respond. She was not quite sure she'd have enough time, and she wouldn't have; Myra was on to something else. "Michael, did you happen to run into Megan last evening? I'm beginning to worry. She never did return my calls. That isn't like her."

"No, Myra, we didn't see her." He was relieved she was on a new topic. "But she'll likely be at Mass this morning."

"I hope so. She is so headstrong, that one. Just like her father." She paused, and Lucy used the opportunity to get a word in.

"Myra, I was wondering about that beautiful music you were playing last evening and this morning."

"What music, dear?"

"The music from the Victrola, I think. My window was open and I could hear it."

"No, dear, you are mistaken. The Victrola is broken. Michael has promised to carry it back to the city to find someone to work on it. We simply cannot find anyone here who will do it. It's very old, you know."

"Yes, I saw it. It's beautiful. But if you weren't playing it, you must have had a radio on. It was such lovely music. I was hoping to hear more of it."

"Lovely music, was it?" Michael popped in jovially. "Well then, you must have heard me singing in the shower."

"No, Michael, I did not, though you have a fine voice and I am hoping to hear more of it." A spark danced between their eyes. Lucy looked down and went on, "It was a woman's voice I heard, singing in Gaelic, I believe, and accompanied by a harp."

Myra's water glass slipped from her hand. "Jesus, Mary and Joseph," she said, signing the cross on her chest and turning whiter than the linen tablecloth. "It's Kathleen."

"What?" Lucy gasped.

Michael jumped up and went to Myra's side, bending down to pick up the broken water glass. "Now, Myra, calm yourself a bit. Lucy probably heard a radio playing on the beach."

"Michael, you don't believe that any more than I do. A woman's voice singing in Gaelic accompanied by a harp, come on with you now. I hear what the kids play on their radios down on the beach these days, if music you can call it, and Gaelic certainly is not on the top 40. No, Michael, it was Kathleen and you know it."

"I know no such thing, and that is enough talk on the subject. You're going to upset Lucy with this gibberish. She has enough on her mind with what she's learned here about Lance."

Myra cut him short. "Lucy is stronger than you give her credit for, my boy. She is strong and sensitive, sensitive to things most people could never understand. You know that about her. It is part of the attraction, is it not? Now she has heard your Kathleen; who knows what else her presence here will reveal. I think it is wonderful. Don't you think so, Michael?"

"What I think is that we best be getting along to Mass now." Michael put the broken glass on the table and took Myra's arm to help her up. "Are you ready, Lucy?" he asked without looking at her as he ushered Myra from the room.

He was quiet on the ride to church. Myra sat chatting, pointing out places of interest, gardens, and houses along with the relationship of the homeowner to herself, William, or Michael—whether quilting bee lady, poker buddy, or old girlfriend.

Saint Peter's Church in Douglas, Michigan was a fairly modern Catholic church. It was set on a quiet street in the center of the little village. Its congregation was drawn from Saugatuck, Douglas, and from the surrounding farming communities of Ganges and Glenn. Michael and Myra knew almost everyone there, and Lucy was introduced to a number of people by name, with the explanation that she was a house guest for the weekend. She caught a lot of sideways glances and knew immediately that she was being thought of as the new woman in Michael Donegan's life. She tried not to let that bother her. They sat in the pew with Myra between them. She spotted a few men she had seen bellied up to the bar the prior evening, now sitting with wives and children and trying to look awake and interested.

"Oh God," she prayed silently, "open hearts and minds to your will and your ways. Help me to draw ever closer to your purpose for me in this life. Thank you for Michael and Myra and bless them with comfort in their hearts for the loss of their loved ones." Then the voice in her head switched to the language of the angels, because when she would pray for Lance that is how she would pray. She didn't know what his needs were nor did she understand the words she used, but she believed beyond a doubt that God knew. "Amen."

She enjoyed the service, especially the singing. She tuned her ear to Michael's voice and let all the other voices, including her own, just fill in the air around it. He had managed not to look at her since breakfast; she wasn't sure if it was intentional, but at any rate, she missed his smile.

After, she was anxious to get back to Glen Eden to resume her hunt in the study. But since Megan had not been at church, Myra persuaded Michael to stop by her apartment on the way home. Lucy was secretly happy when no one answered the door, which meant they could go back without further delay.

Michael dropped the women off at the front door and then parked the car under a carport at the stable end of the drive. Lucy raced up the stairs to change her clothes. As she emerged from her room a few minutes later, she heard voices coming from Michael's room. When she walked up to his door, she heard him say, "This has got to stop." She knocked and he opened the door right away, but only enough to put his head through the opening.

"Lucy." He seemed surprised.

"Hey, Michael, I thought this might be a good time to get a peek at your quilt."

"My quilt?"

"Yeah, you know, the one Myra made you. You said I should pop by and have a peek at it. May I?"

"Well, actually, Lucy, this is not a good time. I need to tidy up in here a bit." He seemed nervous. "I thought you were anxious to get into the study." She heard a noise come from behind the door. Was someone else in the room with him?

"Yes, I am. I'll see you down there."

"Sure, I'll be down in a bit." He closed the door almost before the words left his mouth.

"What on earth is that all about," she thought, hastening down the stairs and into the hallway leading to the study. Stopping before the door, she suddenly felt hesitant to go in. She closed her eyes a moment to gather strength and pictured Lance standing just inside. She took a deep breath and flung wide the double doors. Sunlight filled the room and made it look more cheerful than she remembered from the night before. The books were still piled atop the desk with the exception of the journal containing the mention of Lance. She wondered if Michael had come in and put it away, or Myra perhaps. She walked over to the filing cabinet from where Michael had taken it, but it was locked. She grew anxious, almost panicky.

She ran out of the study, back up the stairs, and pounded on Michael's door. He didn't answer. But as she knocked, the door swung open. "Hello?" she asked, questioning if anyone was there. When no answer came, she knocked again, pushing the door open a little further. "Hello? Michael?" The door was open enough now for her to peer into the room. She noticed it was very neat; everything looked in place. The bed was made, and lying across it was a beautifully colored quilt sewn with all fashions of velvet and brocades, lovely yet very masculine. Where had Michael gone? He was there just minutes before. "He certainly tidies things up in a hurry," she thought. She wondered if she *had* heard someone else in his room and, if so, was that why he didn't permit her in.

She ran back down the stairs and searched through the house. She suspected Myra would be in the kitchen cleaning up from breakfast as she had said she'd do when they got home. She had insisted on doing it alone so Lucy and Michael could get on with their work in the study. But there was no sign of her either, and the dishes were still in the sink.

Lucy ran into the garden, but it was void of any human life as well. Then once again she heard the music. It swirled around her in a dizzying, dancing frenzy and Lucy was caught up in it. Like a dervish she whirled and danced. The music had taken hold of her and she could not fight it. An invisible hand grabbed hers and yanked hard. A woman's voice whispered in her ear, "Lucy, this way, run this way." She ran and leaped and danced for a length of time she could not even guess. The music stopped and released her in a clearing. She bent to catch her breath, and as she stood she spotted someone standing at the far end. It was Lance!

A blue flash of light whizzed by her head. "Run, Lucy girl, run," he shouted. He didn't have to tell her that, for the moment she knew it was him she ran as on the wind. "It was Lance! Lance! Her heart pounded as the distance between them shortened. A red blaze struck the ground just before her, causing her to stumble and fall. Lance charged toward her. More flashes of light whirred and whizzed around him. He grabbed hold of her hand, pulled her to her feet, and took off running. She was with Lance, and they were running for their lives. A blue flash whooshed by them and Lance changed their direction. "Come on, Lucy, it's not much further. Run hard! Run!" She didn't know where the strength came from, but she did as he commanded. Her head was pounding and her heart felt as if it would beat from her chest.

A green blaze hit Lance and he went down. Struggling to stand, he said, "Help me. We must get into the circle." His shoulder was bleeding where green shards of light still pierced it. Just ahead of them in the clearing was a stone circle. She gave him a shove and they fell into it. She lay atop him, trying to catch her breath. His eyes were closed and he felt very hot.

"Lance! Lance!" she cried, showering his face with kisses.

He opened his eyes, gave a weak smile, and whispered, "Hello, darlin'. Now that was a close one."

"Oh God, Oh God, are you all right?" Lucy panted.

"We are safe in here." His voice sounded labored. Lucy looked up and saw balls of colored light smashing into the air above them; they were in an invisible bubble.

"Where are we?" Lucy asked.

"In a moment, darlin'; let me catch my breath. Would you get the flask from my belt and help me with a sip?"

"Sure, Sure." Lucy fumbled to pull a leather pouch from his belt. She loosed the cap and held it to his lips. Something oozed from the flask the color of the blueberry syrup she had eaten that morning. The moment he swallowed it the green shards that were piercing his shoulder stopped glowing. They turned to puffs of smoke then dissipated.

"There now, be a good girl and rub some of it on my shoulder, will you?"

"Yes, yes, my love." She poured the dark, sticky substance onto her hand and carefully rubbed it on his wound. He grimaced. Sweat beaded on his face.

"I'm sorry, I'm sorry," Lucy said, beginning to cry. "I'm hurting you."

"No, No," he whispered. "Your touch is healing me. Just lie here with me a moment. I think it was in time." She lay snuggled against him, praying silently for God's mighty healing to find him. She felt his temperature dropping and saw color return to his face. He was breathing easier now.

A voice came from just beyond where their heads lay in the circle. "So was it worth it then, laddie?" She looked up to see Angus. He was sitting on the ground leaning against one of the rocks, his little legs stretched out in front of him. He was just as he had been in the picture, except now there sat a large book on his lap. It looked suspiciously like William Donegan's journal, the one that went missing.

Lance laughed, raised up on one arm, and looked into Lucy's tearful eyes. He touched her face, wiping her tears with his thumb. He cupped her face in his hand and brought it toward him. They kissed. The years and fears melted away from her heart. The terrible pain that had become part of who she was fell to the ground with a heavy thud. She was alive again, every molecule of her. "Lance," she moaned. She nestled her face in his hair and breathed in his scent. Flowers burst into bloom around them and birds sang from the trees above.

"Okay then, I have my answer by the fool you are," Angus chirped.

"Fool maybe, but this is what I am fighting for, Angus, a man's right to be with the woman he loves for even a moment of happiness."

"Lance, what is going on? Where have you been? Why have you been gone so long?" Lucy's questions came in a barrage.

"Yes, Lance," Angus mocked, "where have you been, and what have you been doing? Your love awaits an answer."

"Be silent, Angus, and leave us alone for a moment."

"Whose moment, yours or hers?" Lance grabbed the hilt of his sword, Angus disappeared, and a rabbit hopped from behind the stone where he'd been sitting.

Lance closed his eyes tightly, breathing out a heavy sigh. The sting of his wound was still fresh but healing fast as he lay in Lucy's arms. She saw the grimace on his face and asked, "Lance, are you all right?"

"Yes, love, I am now, here with you. But I am afraid I don't have long, and there is a lot I need to say."

"Lance, what do you mean? Please don't tell me you are leaving me again. Please, Lance, don't say that."

"I'm sorry, darlin'. I must say it, though the words are like poison in my throat."

"No, Lance, you can't leave me again; I won't let you."

"My darling, there is no choice. You must understand there is more at stake than us: the whole human race, mankind as we know it…"

"I don't care. I don't care, Lance. You can't leave me again. I won't survive. I don't want to."

"No, don't say that, Lucy." Lance leaned forward and clutched his shoulder. "Please, just listen to me; this is hard enough. I need to make you understand."

Lucy saw the pain on his face. She grabbed him tighter and showered more kisses on his face as she whispered, "I'm sorry. I'm so sorry. I'll listen. I'm listening now."

"That's my good girl," he said, relaxing into her arms. "There is a war going on Lucy. It is raging in the dimension beyond. Every dimension is affected by every other dimension. If evil is allowed to prevail in one then all others will suffer because of it. There is a day coming—and not far off—when the veil between the dimensions will lift. If hearts and minds are not prepared, humanity as we know it may be lost."

"Lance, I don't understand. What has this to do with you, with us?"

"I never knew my real family, Lucy. They placed me in the care of the Gentries when I was a baby to hide me from the evil that would destroy my bloodline. I was sent here to grow and become strong so I could go back one day and fight the dark powers. The war rages on, Lucy, and I must not delay my return. The dark and evil ones that would overthrow our people in the dimension of Elysium would then be able to gain access into this dimension. Believe me, the people here are not ready for that. They would surely destroy themselves as they have done in the past, as in the days of Lemuria and Atlantis."

"Lance, I don't understand. I…"

"Darling, my time here is growing short; please just listen now. A prophecy has foretold that the evil cannot win as long as one of my bloodline exists. That is why I was hidden here. That is why you are hidden here too, Lucy." He stopped talking and looked hard into her face. He touched a little line that he noticed by her eye. Then he asked hesitatingly, "Lucy, how long is it that I have been gone?"

"What?" she asked.

"How long has it been since you last saw me?"

"Don't you know, Lance?"

"Please, Lucy, there is no time. I need to know. How long has it been?"

"Seven years," Lucy said softly.

It was like she had slapped him. His eyes widened and anger came upon his face. "What? It cannot be?"

"Seven years, Lance," she repeated. "Believe me, I've felt every tick of the clock for all of them."

"Oh my darling, my precious darling, seven years," he whispered, squinting his eyes as if deciphering a puzzle. He struggled to his feet and yelled at the top of his lungs. "Angus!" He yelled again even louder, "Angus!"

"Stop screaming; I can hear you." The little man suddenly appeared again in the same place he was before, without the book this time but with a long pipe clutched between his teeth.

"Why didn't you tell me?"

"Tell you what?"

"Tell me about time," Lance screamed in his face.

"Oh that. Well, for one thing, you never asked me, and for another, what possible difference would it have made? Could you have come into this circle even one second sooner? It was just another burden you would have to carry for this love of yours."

"Angus, is there anything that can be done? Anything?"

"Lance," Lucy jumped in, "what on earth are you two talking about?"

"Time, Lucy. Time, my darling. I have been away the length of only one year in Elysium. Yet I have been away from you, here, for seven. When I leave you now, I may be gone even longer. Lucy, I may come back too late, too late for…" His voice dropped off, and he stared into her eyes.

"Then take me with you, Lance. Take me with you now."

"Oh darling, how I wish that were possible. But this is not where you can enter, and this is not the time. You must trust me on that."

"Then what can we do? You can't stay and I can't go. Lance, I would rather go with you now and die than stay here and live without you for even one day longer. Please do not ask that of me, Lance."

"And yet I must ask it." Lance turned away and looked directly at Angus. "There must be a way. There must."

"Well, maybe," Angus said, taking a puff from his pipe.

"Angus, tell me now and make it quick. I have been away from the battle far too long as time on this plane is measured, and I must get back soon ere it bode foul for my men." Angus held up his hand and crooked a finger, beckoning Lance to bend down. Angus whispered into his ear all the while his beady eyes glared at Lucy. "You old scut. I'd like to hew you in two for what you've put her through. But if you are sure that is the only way, then you must tell Michael."

"Michael?" Lucy repeated loudly.

"Yes, I'm here." She heard a voice call, Michael's voice. She turned to see him riding up on horseback holding the lead of a riderless horse. When she looked back, Lance and Angus were gone.

"No!" she screamed.

12 – Facing the Truth

Lucy fell to her knees with the heaviness of despair. Michael jumped from the saddle and hurried to stand beside her in the circle. "Lucy, what is it?" She didn't respond. She knelt staring at the space Lance had just occupied, trying to will him back. "Lucy, what's wrong? What are you doing out here? Talk to me." He reached out to touch her but she jerked away, jumping to her feet.

"No, Michael," she shouted, "what are *you* doing here, and where is Lance?"

Michael looked confused. "Lance?"

"Yes, Michael, Lance. He was here, right here, just a moment ago. He and your little buddy Angus." Lucy was pacing around the circle. Her barrette had fallen out, and her hair hung mussed about her shoulders, full of sticks and weeds. Her eyes were wild and wide.

He was concerned by the way she looked and how she was acting. "Lucy, I don't know what to say. I… I didn't see anyone. You were just staring into space when I rode up. Then you called my name."

"You're lying," she screamed. She came at him in a fury, her arms flailing. He grabbed one of her hands, but the other eluded him and she began pounding on his chest. "You're lying. Lying!" she screamed. "Lance was here. He was right here. You had to see him. You had to. Why are you lying?"

"Stop it! Stop it, Lucy!" he commanded. But she kept pounding him, screaming in his face.

"I'm sorry, Lucy. Forgive me for this," he said, and then slapped her. She stopped railing and put her hand to her face. She looked frightened and took off running.

"Lucy, stop," he yelled. "Come back here." He ran after her, leaped, and tackled her to the ground, pulling himself on top of her. He rolled her over and pinned her arms. As she struggled under his weight, something came over him.

"No, No, let me go," she cried. "Let me go."

He felt her body twisting and writhing under his. It was too much. He opened his mouth and came down on hers. She stopped struggling and lay perfectly still, as if he had just killed her.

As the guilt of what he had done washed over him, he rolled off her and raised himself to his knees. "Oh God, Lucy, I'm so sorry. I'm sorry. I don't know what came over me." She rolled over and began weeping uncontrollably. "Please, Lucy, don't cry. Forgive me." He felt helpless as she lay sobbing before him. He wanted to comfort her, to take her in his arms, but he feared his touch would repulse her.

Spent, she finally stopped crying. She lay with her face buried in her hands, trying to put her mind back together. At last she sat up and rubbed the tears and snot from her face onto the sleeves of her shirt. Michael was kneeling before her. She saw the look of remorse on his face and a tear on his cheek. The anger left her, and she felt sorry for him. "Michael, forgive me. I had no right to come at you like that." Her voice broke. "To scream at you." She wiped another tear on her already dampened sleeve.

"I'm a fool Lucy. I..." He wanted to explain his despicable behavior but couldn't find words.

"No, Michael, I took out my anger at losing Lance again on you. You didn't deserve that. My mind is twisted, Michael, twisted so tight I can hardly breathe. I don't know why this is happening. It's so strange I can barely believe it myself. Sometimes I think I'm crazy. But crazy or not, I can't give up."

"No, of course you can't, Lucy." He found an out: "Is crazy catching?"

She knelt now facing him, and a slight smile came to her lips. "Thank you, Michael," she whispered softly.

She could not have said anything to shame him more. "Can you tell me what happened?" he asked gingerly.

Lucy told him everything, looking deeply into his eyes. As she spoke she saw it all play out in her mind as if she were watching a movie. He sat quietly listening to her, feeling her pain and his shame. She told of how the journal was missing from the study, so she went to ask him about it. "I went to your room, but you were gone. Where were you, Michael?"

"There was something I had to take care of," he said, not wanting to mention that the something was Megan, who was waiting in his room when they returned from church.

Lucy told him of how she had been taken by the music when she went into the garden to look for Myra, of the woman's voice that whispered in her ear and how the music led her to Lance. She told him of the attack and how Lance had been wounded. Remembering the blue substance, she looked at her hand with hope that some trace of it remained to verify what she was saying. He saw her angst at finding nothing there and offered her an explanation: "It probably wiped off while you were crawling around in the tall grass." She looked at him with gratitude in her eyes and continued. She told him how Angus appeared with what she thought was the journal, and how Lance reacted when he learned he had been away for seven years. She told him that Lance was discussing what to do about it all with Angus when they mentioned his name, and that was the moment he rode up.

"My name?" Michael questioned.

"Yes, it was clear as a bell. Lance told Angus, 'You'll have to tell Michael.'"

"You don't suppose they could be talkin' about another Michael, now do you?"

"Nice try, Donegan," she said. "Like it or not, you are in this up to your neck now."

"Only my neck? Well then, that leaves me some breathing room." He offered her his smile again. It was the first one since breakfast, and it lightened her.

It was his turn now. He told her how he had tidied his room, talked with Myra a moment about an errand she was going off on, and then came down to the study. (He didn't look into her eyes and he didn't mention that the mess in his room was actually Megan. She was in a snit over Lucy being there, and that's why he could not allow her into his room when she showed up at his door asking to see the quilt. He ushered Megan out the back door and sent Myra to have a talk with her.) "When I reached the study, you were gone. I noticed the journal was missing and assumed you had taken it with you. When Myra returned, she told me she had seen you dancing in the garden, and that you had run off down the trail into the woods, so I saddled up the horses and went looking for you." As he spoke, he pulled twigs and debris from her hair, trying to avoid her glance. "I spotted you standing in the circle. When I approached, you said my name." He paused. "The rest we shared, and I hope you can forget how deplorably I behaved."

"Never," Lucy whispered, touching her reddened cheek then brushing her fingers across her lips.

Michael wondered how she meant it but was afraid to ask. "We best be getting back to Glen Eden. Can you ride now?" She nodded, and he helped her to her feet.

They rode back in silence along a path Lucy did not remember. She tried to recall just how she had come to the circle, but nothing looked familiar. Michael told her it had been approximately three and a half hours from the time she came to his door to see the quilt to the time he found her standing in the circle. Yet to her mind, that time seemed to be only about half an hour. She did some quick math in her head and found that it was a 7 to 1 ratio. Could it be that she had been on Lance's time for that while?

Michael studied her form as she rode in front of him. She sat easy in the saddle and rode comfortably. He liked the way she had introduced herself to Sazi, the Arab mare he had brought for her to ride, and how she had asked the animal's permission before she mounted. "You are a beautiful and intriguing woman, Lucy Cavanagh, and I am a fool of a man." He said this to himself while thinking about the kiss he had stolen as she struggled beneath him.

Then he thought of something else, something that troubled him more than just a little. This beautiful creature he was falling in love with could quite possibly be insane. He didn't want to think about that. He wanted to push it far from his brain. But for her sake and his, he had to face it. After all, what would have happened to her if he hadn't found her when he did? She didn't even remember how she had gotten out there. Then there was the way she acted. She had certainly been out of her head; she had violently attacked him. She even admitted her mind was twisted. "God, what am I to do."

He remembered vividly that when Kathleen died, he thought he would go insane. But he came out of it. After all, he was falling in love again. But how terrible it must be for someone like Lucy not to know what's happened to her love, to wake up each day with the hope that some word may come only to have it dashed by the setting of the sun. Every knock on the door, every ring of the phone must be torture. He could see how a situation like that could push anyone over the edge. He decided the help she needed was way beyond what he could give her.

Back in his study, Michael searched his conscience as he pondered what he should do about Lucy. He was sickened by his behavior. What was he thinking? He wasn't. He'd lost control and let animal nature overcome him. Now he had to make amends. He had to gain Lucy's trust for her own sake. He prayed, "Father, I'm a fine one behaving that way to Lucy. I'm asking that you'll forgive me. You who know my heart will surely understand—even better than I—how sorry I am. I know you'll forgive me, Lord, because your Word is true and your forgiveness in this mess is the easy part. But Good Lord, help me to forgive myself for being such an oaf. Please help me to find a way to help Lucy. In the name of Jesus and His Blessed Mother, Amen."

Now that he had talked to his savior, he talked to his love: "My darling Kathleen, I'm such a lummox. How is it that one as wonderful as you could ever have loved me? I miss you so, my darling. I've felt so lost in this world without you." He was trying hard to remember Kathleen—the way she felt, the way she smelled. But all he could conjure in his mind was the two-dimensional, twenty-five by thirty-six-inch painting of her in the den.

He sat with his face in his hands and his elbows on his desk as he continued: "Since Lucy's come into my life, I've felt alive again. She's a good girl. You would have liked her. She is so lost and alone and afraid, like I was. She is trying so hard to hold on to her love that it is breaking her mind. I want to help her, but I've made such a mess of it. I've acted a fool."

A voice took him from these thoughts. "Michael, I'm sorry to bother you." It was Lucy. "I was hoping to have a little more time in here before we have to head back to the city. What time will we be leaving?"

Michael raised his face and looked at her. She was so beautiful, so alive and vibrant even with the sadness that lay just below the surface. Her skin shone with an aura of brightness as she walked toward him in the dim light of the study. They had hardly talked at all on the ride back from the circle, nor while they unsaddled and brushed the horses. Lucy was lost in her thoughts of Lance, and Michael was hiding from her attention in the shame of what he had done. Once back in the house, Michael retreated to the study and Lucy went to her room to clean up.

"So you're not afraid to be alone in the same room with me?" he asked.

"Don't be silly, Michael. The door is open and Myra is right down the hall," she said with a sly grin on her face, toying with him. But when she saw his hurt look, she quickly added, "You have apologized and I have accepted. It is I who feel ashamed, ashamed of the way I screamed at you, the way I accused you. It was just such a shock to see Lance again and then to have him vanish like that. But that is no excuse for the way I behaved toward you. I was out of my head. Please, forgive me."

"We could blame it on our ancestors."

"What?"

"You know, the Irish tempers—hot blood and hard heads." He smiled up at her sheepishly.

"Say now, there's an idea," she laughed. He had done it again, made her smile even after her whole world had turned upside down.

"So with the ancestors to blame, are we friends again?" He held his hand out to her.

"Friends," she said, but the touch of his hand hinted at a desire for more. She took a deep breath to clear her head. "So what time will we be leaving tonight? I was hoping to have a chance to look for that journal before we go."

Her question set a plan formulating in his head. "I was just pondering that very same thing. You see, there's a bit of a problem that's come up, and I was wondering if maybe you could help me with it."

"I can't imagine how I could be of any service to you, but I'll surely do whatever I can."

"Well, you see, my problem is with Myra." He lied, but she took the bait.

"Myra? Is there something wrong with her?" she asked with genuine concern.

"Wrong? Oh no. It's just that since she's as stubborn as the day is long, she won't admit to needing any help around here. I will be off to the U.K. soon on a business trip, and I just wouldn't feel right leaving her here on her own. My business might keep me over there a while. I had thought Megan would be around to look in on her, but it seems I can't count on that now."

Lucy really didn't think of Myra as someone who needed help. She was in wonderful shape for her age and had amazing vitality. "I don't quite understand, Michael. Just what is it you want me to do?"

She asked him the right question. He felt a little guilty using Myra as his ploy. She probably would have boxed his ears if she heard this exchange. But he needed to keep Lucy there if he was to get her the help he felt she needed, and this was all he could come up with on the spur of the moment. "You see, I was counting on Megan to be around through the summer, you know, to look in on Myra and help her out with some of the chores around here. After that, Myra's cousin Rose is coming from Ireland. She's accepted my invitation to stay here through the winter. She's a widow now herself, and she and Myra get on splendidly. They will be great company for each other. But she won't be arriving until summer's end." He hesitated to make it seem hard for him to ask. "So, you see, I was wondering if you could help us out." He paused again. She was waiting. "I'd like you to stay until Rose can come. I don't know what your job pays, but I would be happy to match it and put some on top to boot. I know Tom Fegan, the owner of DME, Bertha's boss. He owes me a favor. I helped him get the cleaning contract for that whole complex. I could ask that he arrange for you to have a leave of absence, if you like, until you finish here. Though I'm sure Bertha will take it poorly, you would be doing me a great favor."

Lucy said nothing, so Michael quickly added, "You would be free to come and go as you please and would have access to all my grandfather's books and journals. Myra is fond of you, and she would not be much of a chore. What do you say, can you help us out?"

Lucy's heart quickened. The chance to be here in this study where Lance had spent time with Michael's grandfather and to read all the journal entries that might shed light on just what he had been doing before he disappeared—this offer was too good to be true. She hesitated before answering trying not to let her excitement show. "Spending time here with Myra would be a pleasure not a chore."

"Oh, God bless you, that is what I hoped you would say. You'll do it then?"

"Not so fast, Michael. I said it would be a pleasure, but I have another consideration besides my job. I have Freea."

"Freea?"

"Yes, she's my cat. She is a very good kitty and not messy at all. I couldn't possibly board her or leave her with someone else for so long."

"Of course you couldn't. Myra and I love cats. Boomer is buried in the back garden just under the big pussy willow bush. He was Grandfather's cat. He died just this past winter at the fine old cat age of twenty."

"Twenty. Wow, that's good. Freea just turned eight. She was a gift from Lance before he left."

"Your Freea is welcome here."

"Well then, Mr. Donegan, I am honored to be in your employ." She held out her hand for another shake to seal the deal.

He stood up and took it. He felt the excitement rise in his blood again. "Thank you, Lucy. You can take my car into the city tomorrow, if you like, to pick up your Freea and gather what you need of your things." Michael was pleased at how well his plan was working. Now that he had Lucy pledging to stay for a while, he could ask his old friend Fred Loch to come for a weekend to evaluate her. Maybe there *was* a tad of his grandfather "The Fox" in him after all.

Lucy's eye caught sight of a book lying on the floor just under the desk. "Michael, is that the journal, the one I thought was missing? Where did you find it?"

He was just as surprised as she was. "Now how on earth did that get there? I could swear it wasn't there when I looked for it earlier. Maybe Myra found it and brought it in."

"Found what?" came Myra's voice from behind them.

"Grandfather's journal. Did you bring it back in here?"

"Heaven's no, I haven't been in here all day. I have been cooking our dinner since Megan left. I couldn't talk any sense into her."

"Megan was here? I'm sorry I missed her," Lucy said.

"Well, don't be. She is so green with jealousy there's no telling what she would have done. Michael found her here after we returned from church. Didn't you tell Lucy, Michael?"

"No, Myra, I hadn't mentioned it. Lucy and I have been busy discussing other matters." His voice betrayed his irritation.

Lucy knew now who Michael was talking to in his room and why he had acted so nervously when she came to his door. She wondered now if it had been a good idea for her to accept his offer to stay. *I was right about him in the first place*, she thought. *His grandfather may have been a fox, but he is more of a wolf.* She scolded herself immediately for that thought. *And just why should you care what he is? You have an opportunity to stay here and learn more about Lance from the journals. Just concentrate on that and accept Michael for the cad he is.*

"Cod," Myra declared.

"What?" Lucy said, feeling like her thoughts had been read.

"I have prepared cod. Will you help me get it to the table so we can take a meal together before the two of you have to leave? I have something exciting to share with you both over dinner."

"Myra, Lucy and I were just discussing something. How would you like to have house guests for the summer?"

"Michael, what are you talking about? For heaven's sake, spit it out; the cod is getting cold."

"I have invited Lucy to stay for a while so she can study Grandfather's journals. She has accepted and will take my car back to the city tomorrow to pick up her kitty, Freea, whom I have also invited to be our summer guest."

"Nice going, young man. This is just what the doctor ordered for you." This wasn't quite the response he wanted from Myra, especially in front of Lucy. But he had to admit to himself that she was right. It was as much for his benefit as hers that he wanted her to stay.

Myra went on, "And Lucy, I look forward to spending time with you and your dear kitty. I'm sure you will benefit from access to my William's journals. This is all so exciting. Now can we please go get the cod to the table?"

Myra had prepared a wonderful meal of baked cod in lemon sauce, pease porridge with rice, steamed greens, and freshly baked soda biscuits. The three worked together getting the table set and the hot food carried to it. Michael offered Grace, and Sunday dinner occurred.

Myra began the meal's conversation by relating to them her talk with Megan. All the while Michael sat squirming in his chair. "Megan is convinced, Lucy, that you are a gold digger here to play Michael for his money. She is also convinced that Michael had begun to look at her like a real woman, until you showed up, that is."

"What?" Michael gulped, choking on his peas.

"Are you all right, dear? Drink some water." Myra leaned over and gave him a good smack on the back. "I told her that I know my Michael. He loves to look at a thing of beauty. But he is not one to have the wool pulled over his eyes. I told her that even people who dig gold sometimes fall in love with the field it is in. Did you fall off your horse, dear? I saw the two of you ride up a while ago, and judging from the shape your hair and clothes were in, Sazi was a bad girl."

"No, Myra," Lucy said slowly, still trying to analyze the gold digging comment. "Sazi gave me a wonderful ride. The ground did rise up to meet me, more than once. But that was not Sazi's fault but my own."

"And mine," Michael admitted.

"Good heavens, you play rough, Michael," Myra scolded, and he felt his shame all over again. She had an uncanny way of knowing things.

"Of course this is your business, Lucy, but I think you should tell Myra what happened this afternoon."

"You do, Michael?"

"Yes, I think it would do good to get Myra's perspective." He wanted to see how she would relate the events in the circle.

Myra spoke up before she had a chance: "Lucy, before you begin, there is something I want to share with you and Michael. It might make it easier for you to tell me your tale. When Megan left today, I walked her to the end of the drive. As I was returning, I saw you dancing in the garden, and I am certain I heard Kathleen's music." Michael put his elbows on the table and dropped his head to his hands. "It was particularly haunting, spirited, fast, almost desperate."

"Yes, Myra, I heard it too. It took hold of me and led me to a clearing on the old Green farm." She paused as if afraid to go on then took a breath and blurted out, "Lance was there waiting for me."

"Saints have mercy! Are you listening to this, Michael? It was your Kathleen that led Lucy to her Lance."

Michael was so annoyed he wanted to shout, "Why is it the two of you can hear Kathleen and I cannot?" But he didn't. Instead he said, "Myra, stop interrupting Lucy so she can tell us her story."

"Oh, so you do not believe her? You think she is making up a story?"

"Oh, for the love of God woman, I didn't say that. Will you please just let her talk."

"Certainly, dear. Eat your peas. Go ahead, Lucy."

Lucy continued to recount every detail just as she remembered it. Myra did not interrupt, and Michael stared at her all the while she spoke. He watched her every expression and hung on her every word, trying to detect any variation in the story or telling body movement that would give her away.

When Lucy finished, Myra sat silently eating her meal. She looked over at Michael. He was convinced now that she believed everything she recounted no matter how incredible it seemed to him. Much to his relief, Lucy had stopped at the point where he rode up.

"Well, there you have it, Myra," Michael said. What do you think?"

Myra chewed her last bite of fish, picked up her water glass, took a sip, dabbed her mouth with her napkin, and said, "What?"

"Myra, weren't you listening? Lucy said she saw Lance."

"Yes, I heard that."

"Well, what do you think of it?" His voice was showing signs of his annoyance with her.

"What do you mean 'What do I think of it'? I think it is wonderful she saw her love. Don't you?" Michael didn't answer. He was ready to explode. This wasn't going at all like he intended. "Or do you mean 'Do I think she is lying'?"

"Myra, of course I don't mean that."

"Then just what are you asking, Michael?"

Lucy watched this exchange and felt somehow that Myra was on her side. There was nothing anyone could think or say. She saw what she saw. She saw Lance; she had kissed him and touched him. Those were the facts, and they were as real to her as the cod on her plate.

Michael glared at Myra but didn't speak. She ended the awkward silence by asking, "Is anyone ready for the bread pudding?"

"I'll get it," he said, taking up his plate and gathering Myra's and Lucy's as well.

He walked out toward the kitchen, and when he was out of earshot, Myra asked Lucy how she was holding up. "It must have been a terrible shock for you when he disappeared."

Lucy lowered her head and bit her bottom lip, trying not to cry. She nodded yes.

Myra took hold of her hand and squeezed it. "There, there, little one, it will be better soon. Michael is going to help you. Lance even said so, did he not? Trust him, Lucy. Trust both of them."

Lucy dabbed her eyes and said, "Thanks, Myra."

"This is going to be a very interesting summer, Lucy. I'm so glad you will be staying for a while."

"Me too."

Michael returned carrying a pan of warm bread pudding in one hand and three dishes in the other on top of which balanced a bowl of chilled whipped cream. "Can you give me a hand here, ladies?" he asked. Almost as if they had talked it over, the two women started to applaud. The room brightened as the three of them broke into laughter.

After they finished with dessert, Michael volunteered to help Myra clean up. He told Lucy to go on to the study and promised to meet her there later. Lucy insisted on helping them, but Michael put up a stronger argument, reminding her she needed to get an early start for the city in the morning. "So if you want to do any reading before you leave, you should do it now." She relented and went on her way down the hall to the study. This gave Michael a chance to talk to Myra alone as they did the kitchen chores.

"So, Myra, tell me what it is you think of Lucy?"

"I think she is charming, absolutely charming, same as you."

"Aye, she is that. But I mean, just what is it you think about her meeting Lance in the meadow?"

"I think she believes it with all her heart."

"Aye, so do I, and that's what worries me."

"Why, Michael? Why should that worry you?"

"Why? Because she's delusional."

"And why is it you say that?"

"Myra, she was alone in the circle when I rode up. She was staring into space."

"Just because you didn't see him doesn't mean he wasn't there, Michael. You didn't hear Kathleen's music."

It was like she slapped him. "That's right. I didn't, and why is that, Myra? Just why didn't I?"

"I don't know. All I know is I heard it. Maybe I'm delusional too. Or maybe Kathleen is here because Lucy is here."

"And what is that supposed to mean?"

"I'm not sure, lovie. Sometimes answers take a while." She stood on tiptoes and kissed his cheek. Softened, he confided in her how he had talked Lucy into staying and about his plan to have Fred Loch come for a visit to meet and evaluate her. "Oh, Michael, that was very sly, young man. I see William's influence shining right through you." She hugged his arm and started humming. Michael soon took up the song.

Lucy felt Michael's presence before she saw him. When she looked up from the passage she was reading, he was standing by the fire holding a load of wood in his arms. "Hey," she said, smiling gently at him.

"Hey yourself. I'm sorry to disturb you. I thought I'd get a fire started in here before the sun vanishes completely and a chill comes in."

"That was thoughtful, thank you. Where is Myra?"

"She's taken her tea and gone out to the gazebo. She goes out there most evenings to watch the sunset and talk with Grandfather. I think she has a lot to tell him tonight." He smiled and gave her a wink. "Shall I bring you in some tea?"

"Oh, no thank you, Michael. That's awfully sweet of you."

"Well, I'm an awfully sweet kind of guy, if you haven't noticed, when I'm not taking advantage of a damsel in distress, that is."

"I've noticed both Michael Donegans," Lucy said, returning her gaze to the book before her.

He built up the fire and then sat a moment watching her read in its flickering glow. When he got up to leave, he walked over to her chair. He wanted to reach out and touch her hair, to kiss her softly, to inhale her. "I'll be leaving you now. I have some phone calls to make regarding my new employee and some errands to run. Don't be staying up too late; you should get an early start in the morning. I've left a few planks for you to throw on the fire when it goes down, if need be."

"Good night, Michael. Thank you for everything." He nodded and left her.

His first call was to Tom Fegan regarding her job. Thom was more than happy to repay in some small way the favor Michael had done for him. He didn't have an easy time telling Bertha she would be a body short until he could hire a new employee. When he told her the request for Lucy's leave had come directly from Mr. Donegan, she blurted out, "I thought there was something funny going on with those two the night I walked in on them in his office."

"Now, Bertha, that's none of our business, and don't go starting any rumors."

"Oh, no sir," Bertha promised. But before the end of the following day all Lucy's co-workers were aware that she was "having an affair" with Mr. Donegan. Danny was the only one who defended her. He told Bertha in front of four others that she must have gotten the story wrong. She was not happy with his interference in her sport and made him pay by ordering him to stay an extra two hours to help catch up on the work Lucy was to have done.

Michael's next call was to The Stonehouse. It was a small, exclusive, alcohol and drug rehabilitation clinic in Chicago. The director, Leon Scott, had been a very close friend of Michael's grandfather, who had been an early benefactor of the clinic.

"Good to hear from you, Michael. How are you? How is Myra?"

"We are both well, thank you, Dr. Scott." Michael got right to the point. "I'm calling to see if you have space available for a friend of mine. She has had a rough time of it since her husband died four years ago. She needs to dry out and maybe get some grief counseling. Do you have room?"

"We'll make room, Michael."

"Good. Her name is Leslie Hopkins. Her brother, Ashley Randall, will be bringing her in a day or so."

"I'll personally make all the arrangements."

"Thank you, sir. I will be taking care of all the expenses but would like to remain anonymous. She thinks it's her brother paying the tab, and that's just fine with me. Understand?"

"Sure, of course, my boy."

"Good. Just call and let me know if there is anything she needs."

"I certainly will, Michael. We'll get her back on the right path."

"I'm counting on you for that. Thank you."

Michael's third call was to his old college chum and soccer buddy Fred Loch. Fred had a private practice in L.A. where he was well known for a book he had published based on several patients he had treated who believed they had been abducted by aliens. The phone rang three times and then the answering service picked up. Michael left a message for Fred to call as soon as possible. He then found Myra to tell her he was going out and asked if there was anything she might need.

"Orange juice for the morning. That's all I can think of."

"Orange juice it is then, Myra. Good night to you." He kissed her atop the head and started to walk away.

She called to him, "Michael, do be careful. You are in a state that might make you vulnerable to certain influences."

"Myra, what's this about? I'll be fine."

"Of course you will. Just be careful dear."

He grabbed his car keys and jacket and bounded out of the house. He bought the orange juice and filled the car with gas for Lucy's trip in the morning. He couldn't stop thinking about her, about how much he wanted her. He needed a drink.

He walked into the Butler, and as he hoped, Ashley was working. He nodded, and Ash slid a beer down the bar in his direction.

"Hey, Michael, where's Lucy? Is she tired of you already?"

"Not too, I guess, since she has agreed to spend the summer with Myra while I come and go."

"Really? Well, hey, that's good news. So where is she?"

"She's back at the cottage, in the study. It seems that she found a mention of Lance in one of Grandfather's journals."

"Is that right?"

"Yeah, she's back searching through them for other mentions, hoping to find out what happened to him."

"Well, it must have been pretty bad for him not to come back to her. You know, legally, after someone is missing for seven years, you can have them declared dead."

"Well, I don't think I'll be bringing that up to her any time soon."

"Why not? Maybe you'd have a shot if she thought Lance wouldn't be back."

"Look, Ash, let's drop it. I've come to tell you everything's set for Skipper at The Stonehouse."

"That's great."

"I told them you'd be checking her in in a day or two. And Ash, remember our deal."

"Sure thing, Michael. I don't know what to say."

"Don't say anything. Just draw me another beer."

"You got it."

Michael stayed till almost closing, drinking maybe more than he should have. As he was walking out he ran into Skipper, who had spent the evening at the Coral Gables' Rathskeller just up the street. She walked over to get a ride home from her brother, but now she had a better idea. "Hey, Michael, where's your girlfriend?"

"Skipper, Lucy is just a friend. She is still in love with Lance. She has no interest in me."

"Well, now, that's a shame." She smiled provocatively. "Say, big guy, will you give me a lift home so I don't have to wait for Ash to lock up?"

"It's sure I will, Skip. Come on." As they walked toward his car, she tried to snuggle under his jacket to keep warm. He took it off and put it around her shoulders.

"You are such a gentleman," she said.

She was staying with her mom in the family home near Glenn about ten miles from the Butler. As he drove, Skipper nestled up to him.

"So, Michael, you're telling me Lucy isn't taking care of your needs?"

"Come on, Skipper. Don't go there."

"No, I mean, she gets your blood up; I can tell." She put her hand on his leg and slowly moved it up.

"Skipper, what are you doing?"

"You know, Michael. You know very well. You can have me, Michael. You can have me tonight, no strings attached."

"Skipper, stop it. You're drunk."

"I'm not that drunk, Michael. I know what I want. I need a man, Michael, and you need a woman; I can tell. Lucy won't let you have any, but I will. You can pretend I'm her if you like. I don't care."

"Skipper…"

She put her finger over his lips. "Come on, remember last time?" she whispered. He felt her hot breath on his neck. She ran her tongue around his ear. She took hold of him. There was an abandoned farm just ahead. He pulled into the drive and parked behind the barn.

13 – Waste Not Beauty

Lucy had fallen asleep in the study in one of the overstuffed chairs by the fireplace with William Donegan's journal on her lap. She was roused by the sound of the front door closing. The fire Michael had built before he left, and that she had stoked with the extra logs, was now only glowing embers. He had given her the key to the filing cabinet so she could lock the journal away when she was through with it. She was sure that Angus had taken it before because she saw it on his lap in the circle. Just what he was doing with it she had no idea, but until she had a chance to read it all, she didn't want him running off with it again. After placing it in the cabinet, she tugged on the drawer to make sure the lock was secure before she left the study.

She walked down the hall to find Michael just hanging up the phone, and she wondered whom he was calling at that hour. He removed his jacket to hang on the hall tree and jumped when he heard her behind him.

"Jesus, Lucy! What are you doing up?"

"I'm sorry if I startled you. I fell asleep in the study. What time is it anyway?"

He looked at his watch. "It's three ten." He ran his hand through his hair to straighten it. He felt himself grow nervous in her presence. "Here, take the car keys now." He held them out for her. "It's all gassed up and ready to go. I won't be seeing you in the morning; I'll be sleeping in."

"Sleeping it off is more like it," she thought, after getting a whiff of his breath. She picked up another scent from him. It was perfume, familiar perfume. She remembered it from last night; it was Skipper's.

"So where'd you go?" she asked coyly.

"I ran some errands and stopped into the Butler to see Ashley. He asked about you. I hope you don't mind that I told him you'd be staying here this summer… to look out for Myra."

"No, that's fine. I look forward to seeing him and Skipper again. Was she in the Butler as well?"

"No," he answered quickly, telling himself it wasn't a lie because technically she wasn't in the bar; he'd met her outside. But he felt uncomfortable and changed the subject. "Did you find any other mention of Lance in the journals?"

"I did. I was hoping to talk to you about them."

"Sure." He felt badly that he hadn't been there for her.

"There were several entries, just dates really, saying your grandfather had received some type of reports from him and that he was keeping them in something he called *The Green Book Esotery*. Do you have any idea where I can find that book? I've hunted on all the shelves in the study."

Michael was drunk and drained from his session with Skipper, but the closer she got to him the more awake his body became. "I recall Grandfather making mention of it. But I'm sorry; I don't know where he kept it." She made a sigh and looked disappointed, so he quickly added, "I'll search for it tomorrow while you're away. Did Myra fix you up with an alarm clock?"

"She's promised to wake me herself at 7:00 a.m. sharp."

"Bless her heart, she'll do it." As he turned to switch off the hall light, Lucy noticed the lipstick smear on his collar. She felt suddenly angry and had to remind herself she had no reason to be.

They walked up the stairs together, she just a step or two in front. He couldn't take his eyes off her as she moved before him. He paused a moment at her door. "I want to thank you again, Lucy, for agreeing to stay here this summer and put my mind at ease about Myra."

"No, Michael, thank you for the offer and for everything else. If you hadn't invited me here, I wouldn't have seen Lance. I have real hope again, thanks to you." He was standing so close to her now that she could feel the heat from his skin. "Good night, Michael," she said quickly, slipping into her room and closing the door.

He stood for a moment with his head resting against the jamb then turned away and made for his room. He slumped across his bed still thinking about her, remembering how she felt twisting beneath him, remembering how she tasted when he forced his tongue into her mouth. He got up, took a cold shower, and fell back in bed.

Lucy undressed quickly, slipped into her gown, and slid under the covers. She lay thinking about the events of the last two days, especially about seeing Lance. She went over every detail of him: the feel of his skin, the light in his hair, the taste of his lips on hers. Her body ached for him. *What is it you mean to do, Lance? What is it you want me to do?* She thought about the way he looked when he realized he had been away for seven years. Whatever plan he and Angus had discussed, she was certain Michael was somehow to be a part of it.

She thought about Michael now, of how he had slapped her, forced his kiss upon her, and how he had felt laying on top of her—so strong, so powerful. She stopped herself. "What am I doing? Why am I thinking about him?" She remembered the perfume, the lipstick. She rolled over and socked her pillow. "I'll not be enchanted by you, Michael Donegan. God help me, I won't!" She fell to sleep in prayer.

If she had dreams, she didn't remember them. A gentle knock on her door roused her. It was Myra, her alarm clock. "It's a new day, dear. Come see what it holds."

"Coming, Myra. Thank you." She sat up and stretched. She thanked God for waking her then hopped up. She showered, dressed, made up her bed, and bounded down the stairs. She found Myra in the kitchen stirring eggs, onions, and tomatoes in a large skillet atop the stove. "That smells yummy," she said.

"I hope you don't mind if we eat here in the kitchen, since Michael won't be joining us." She pointed to a small white table with two chairs against the far wall.

"It's fine with me," Lucy said, pouring herself a cup of coffee and moving to the toaster to butter the hot browned bread that came popping up.

"Michael and I usually take our breakfast in here when it is just the two of us, just as William and I used to do when Michael was away."

"I like it here," Lucy said. "It's cozy." They fixed their plates and carried them to the little table. Myra took a jar of black currant jelly off a pantry shelf and handed it to Lucy to open.

"It's Michael's favorite. He always has some when he comes home. He brings me a jar or two whenever he goes over the pond. I can't find it anywhere around here. I think he has a trip planned soon. I hope so; that's the last jar."

"It's very good," Lucy said, taking another bite of the toast she had smeared it on. The phone rang.

"Good heavens. Who is phoning this early? Someone looking for Michael, I'll wager. Or maybe Megan has come to her senses. I better get it." Lucy ate her breakfast while listening to a one-sided conversation.

"Hello." ... "Oh hello, Winnie. How are you?" ... "Michael? Yes, he's here. He's sleeping." ... "No, Winnie, I won't be waking him. Just calm down. I can't understand you, dear." ... "What?" ... "Oh no, Winnie. I am so sorry. Is she going to be all right?" ... "Yes, I'll tell him, Winnie. Try to get some rest, dear. Goodbye." Myra came back to the table with a worried look on her face.

"Is everything all right, Myra?"

"That was Winnie, Skipper's mum. She said Skipper came home around three o'clock last night. She was drunk and upset, something about Michael. They had words and she went off to her room. Ashley came by and went up to check on her. He found an empty bottle of sleeping pills by the bed and rushed her off to the hospital in Holland. Winnie was just getting home now. She felt Michael should know about it."

"That's just awful," Lucy said. She was horrified. She thought about what time Michael had gotten home and knew Skipper's house was only about ten minutes away. She thought about the lipstick on his collar, about the perfume she was sure was Skipper's. Had he gotten her drunk and had his way with her? *The bastard, taking advantage of a poor troubled drunk,"* Lucy thought. *What's wrong with him? Does he think he can do whatever he wants?* She was so angry she wanted to march up stairs, pull him out of bed and give him a good kick. She thought about his kiss again and this time it sickened her.

"Lucy, what's wrong?" Myra noticed she wasn't eating and that her thoughts had carried her off. "Is there something wrong with your eggs?"

"No, Myra, they're fine. I'm just not as hungry as I thought I was. I better get going."

"Certainly. I'll clean up here; you go ahead. Can we expect you back for dinner?"

"No, I'll grab a bite before I leave the city. I won't be returning until late, midnight maybe."

"Well, you run along and be careful. I'll let Michael know so he won't worry."

"You do that, Myra," she said coldly.

Lucy turned on the car, and as she sat there making adjustments to the seat, the mirrors, and the radio, she caught another whiff of Skipper's perfume. She saw something on the floor and bent over to examine it. It was a bra. "Good God, Michael Donegan, you are a bastard." She stuffed it in the glove box so she wouldn't have to look at it. She gunned the engine and tossed dirt up as she left.

She was just about to the main road when a motorcycle turned into the drive right in front of her. She slammed on the brakes as the motorcycle dodged around the front fender and slid on its side into the brush along the drive. The rider jumped up and pulled off his helmet. It was Ashley. "Hey there, girl, where are you going in such a hurry?"

Lucy jumped out of the car and put her arms around his neck. "Ash, oh Ash, I'm so sorry. Are you hurt?"

"Nah, I'm fine."

She was clinging to him and he liked it. She was shaking. "I'm sorry. I was driving too fast. I could have killed you."

"Shhh now. It takes more than a slide in the dirt to do me in. I've had worse spills from hitting a bug. Remember?"

Lucy did remember. The first summer they worked together he sold his car and bought what she thought was the very same bike lying in the ditch before them, a Harley Sprint. At that time he wore an old German army helmet that his father had brought home from the war. It was the only thing he had of his father's, who died when he and Skipper were small. Though it looked really cool and satisfied the helmet law, it afforded little protection. One night on his way to work, his forehead met a June bug going sixty miles an hour. His head jerked to the side, taking his shoulders, arms, and hands—still clutching the handles—with it. The front wheel hit the curb at an angle causing bike and rider to become airborne before landing in a wet, marshy area. It was a blessing really, for had he come down on hard ground or pavement, his mention in this story would be nil. As it was, he walked away with just a large welt on his forehead. He came into work that night covered in marsh grass and mud, with a bulbous bruise between his eyes. After that, he wore a regulation helmet with a full-face shield.

Lucy let go of him and stepped back. They both smiled. "Ash, what are you doing here so early?"

"Maybe I couldn't wait to see you again."

"Or maybe you've come over to pop Michael Donegan in the eye."

"Now why is it I would be doing that?"

"Your mom called Myra this morning and told her about Skipper. Ashley, I'm pretty sure she was with Michael last night."

"She was, and good thing too. I was just coming over to thank him."

"Thank him?" Lucy gasped.

"Yeah, that Michael is quite a guy. I didn't always think so, but my opinion of him has done a one-eighty of late." Lucy was confused, and it must have shown because Ashley explained: "He stopped by the Butler to see me last night and ran into Skipper on his way to the car. She was stumbling drunk so he took her home. I guess she came on to him pretty hot and heavy. When he refused her, she went a little nuts. She told him she didn't want to live anymore. He calmed her down and got her home, but he was worried enough to call me about her. I was crashing in the Hacksaw room. When I got his call, I went right over there. And it's a good thing I did. I got her to the hospital in the nick of time. I don't know what would have happened if someone other than Michael would have come across her."

Lucy was speechless. She had done it again: judged Michael entirely wrong. Why did she keep doing that? Did she want him to be a cad because he would be just too appealing if he were not? These were the things she thought about on her way to the city.

She reached her apartment just before noon. She barely noticed the three and a half hour drive. Freea was waiting for her right inside the door. "Hello, my kitty. Did you miss me?" Freea answered with a "meow." "I'll be taking you with me when I go back. You're going to love it at Glen Eden, plenty of places for you to explore." She went through Saturday's mail then wrote a note to the mailman telling him to hold her mail at the post office until further notice. She grabbed her big suitcase from the back of the closet and set it open upon the bed. She then put her cowboy boots by the front door so she wouldn't forget to take them. She was looking forward to doing a lot of riding over the summer. Though the circumstances had not been ideal, she liked riding Sazi.

She was pretty much all packed within an hour and set about straightening her apartment. She put fresh sheets on the bed and gathered the towels and other laundry items to carry downstairs. She wanted to have everything clean in case Lance would be coming with her when she returned.

She moved to the kitchen and made a tuna sandwich that she shared with Freea. When she sat down at the table, she saw the frame she laid there when she left. She thought about the cut she had gotten from the broken glass and looked down at her hand. It was completely healed. "Wow, that healed fast," she thought. "It must have been the blue gunk I put on Lance's shoulder." She picked up the frame expecting to see Lance's picture, but it wasn't there. She didn't remember taking it out of the frame, but she must have. The phone rang. She walked to the living room still trying to think of what she had done with Lance's picture. It was the only one she had of him.

"Hello."

"Lucy, it's Michael."

"Hello, Michael, what's up?" She was surprised he called.

"I was just checking that you made it there all right. Ashley told me you nearly wiped him out at the end of the drive this morning and that you were pretty shaken up by it."

"Only because I missed the blabber mouth," she chuckled, then added, "I'm fine, Michael, and your car is in one piece too, if you were wondering."

"Well, that's good news." There was an awkward silence, which he broke by saying, "So, I'll let you get on with it then. Come back safe."

"That is my plan, Michael, the Good Lord willing."

"Of course it is." There was more silence. "So, see you this evening. Goodbye now." He hung up feeling like a fool. He had just wanted to hear her voice. He mocked himself: "Come back safe." What was he, back in high school? "God, I'm an idiot."

She searched around the apartment, trying to remember just what she had done with Lance's picture. Had she packed it to take with her when she left with Michael? She *had* packed in a hurry. She would have sworn she left it in the frame, but she must have taken it. It must be in her backpack at Michael's. She'd looked everywhere else. She put it from her mind and made a list of things she needed to do before she left.

There were several calls she wanted to make. The first one was to Paul and Littlefeather to let them know where she could be reached in case they heard from Lance.

"We're sorry. The number you have dialed has been changed or disconnected. Please check the listing and try again."

"I must have dialed wrong," she thought. So she tried again. She got the very same recording. She called the operator and was told there was no listing for McKellen in the Peebles area. She added a note to her list: *Write to P & L.*

Next, she called Peggy at work.

"Peg Roch, can I help you?"

"Hey, Peg, it's Lucy."

"Where have you been? I tried calling all weekend." When Lucy told her she had gone to Saugatuck with Michael Donegan and that she would be staying there for the summer, Peggy was beside herself. "You're kidding me! Michael Donegan? *The* Michael Donegan? Rich, handsome Michael Donegan? *Metro Scene's* most eligible bachelor Michael Donegan?

"Okay, all right already. I guess that's him. He *is* rich and pretty good-looking. I don't know about all that other stuff."

"Girlfriend, I'm coming over there right after work and I want the low down."

"I was calling to ask you to stop by. Think you can pick up a pizza on your way. I'll treat? Big Daddy's Vegetarian. Okay?"

"Sure, and I'll let you pay for the whole thing yourself now that you are into the big bucks."

Her final call was to Danny. She thought he would be up by this time.

"Hello."

"Hi, Danny. It's Lucy."

"Lucy, just what the heck is going on? Bertha called a little while ago and asked if I could come in a little early for the next couple of days until they can hire someone, seeing as how you are on an extended leave of absence, at the request of Michael Donegan no less. Is that right?"

"Well, yes, that's right. I am."

"Lucy, are you involved with that guy?"

"Danny, hold on a minute. I've agreed to work for him for the summer, that's all. I'll be back to DME in September."

"Yeah, right. Just what kind of work are you doing for him?"

"He's hired me to look after his grandmother while he goes on some business trips." That explanation was easier than trying to explain Myra's real relationship to Michael and how Megan had run off.

"Bertha made it sound like you're having an affair with the guy. Your reputation is shot."

"Danny, I have an amazing opportunity to find out what happed to Lance. I really don't care what people think." She meant it when she said it, but a moment later she would prove herself wrong.

"So have you found the little man you were looking for?"

"I have found mention of him in Michael's grandfather's journals." It bothered her that she did not say she'd seen Angus for real in the stone circle, nor did she mention she had seen Lance. She told herself it was because Danny wouldn't understand and would probably think she'd gone over the deep end; she didn't want him to worry. She'd tell him the whole story someday when she had more time, but just not now.

"This whole thing is a little fishy, if you ask me. I don't trust that Donegan guy. Be careful."

"Danny, Michael is really very nice." She was surprised to hear herself say it. "Don't hate him just because he's rich."

"Just remember what I said, Lucy. They don't play by the same rules."

"Yes, Danny, I'll remember. How are Donna and the kids?" She changed the subject on purpose. Her mind was tired, tired of trying to skirt the truth. She loved hearing about the little ones, about their carefree moments of childhood, the funny things they would say or do.

Danny and Donna were wonderful parents. They didn't have much money and Danny worked a lot, but when he was at home he was there for them. He was always willing to get down on the floor and play or read them a story. He was an old fashioned family man, secure in his role as the disciplinarian. His kids listened to him and behaved themselves. Donna was a stay-at-home mom and considered her job the most important thing she could possibly do. They were very much like her own parents.

"I'll be by to see you all a little later."

"Good," he said. "We'll lay hands on you and pray that you'll have God's protection."

"Great. See you later." She hung up the phone and lay back on the couch. She felt melancholy all of a sudden.

She thought about how wonderful it would be to be married to Lance and have his children. She thought about what a wonderful father he would be. She closed her eyes and in her daydream she watched as he played in the yard with their son. She watched them hunting and fishing and swimming. He was teaching his son how to dive. He jumped from a large rock into a beautiful clear blue lake. But then he didn't come up. The boy stood by, watching the water, waiting for his father to re-emerge. Suddenly, the surface broke and a man stood up. But it wasn't Lance; it was Michael. She jumped with a start.

"No, no, that's all wrong," she thought. Why was this happening? Why was Michael invading her musing? She was mad at him all over again, as if somehow he'd made that thought happen.

She busied herself so she didn't have to think. She took the laundry downstairs to the common room in the basement where the washing machine and dryer were. She was in luck; no one was using them and there was no *Out of Order* sign for a change. She started her laundry and returned to her apartment.

She put on her favorite cleaning music—The Youngbloods—and sang to all the songs just to keep her mind free of any thoughts of Michael. She vacuumed to side one, from "Grizzely Bear" through "Get Together." She dusted to "One Note Man" and scrubbed the bathroom from "The Other Side of Life" to "Tears Are Falling." She moved into the kitchen and cleaned out the fridge and pantry while listening to the rest of side two. She put anything that would not keep over the summer in a bag to give to Danny and Donna.

As she was folding the last item from her laundry basket, a knock came on the door. She thought it was Peggy, but when she opened it a deliveryman was standing before her holding a bouquet of roses. She thought he must have the wrong apartment. "Lucy Cavanagh?" he asked.

"Yes."

"Sign here."

"There must be some mistake."

He looked at his clipboard. "You're Lucy Cavanagh and this is apartment seven. They're for you all right." He pushed the clipboard at her to sign.

"But I don't know who could have sent them."

"Look, lady, just sign here and read the card. I have a truck full of deliveries. Flowers wilt you know."

After she signed, he handed her the bouquet, turned, and hurried down the stairs, nearly colliding with Peggy on her way up carrying a large pizza box and a two-liter bottle of soda.

"Ooo la la, flowers from Greenlady's," Peggy said. "I bet I know who sent them."

Lucy paid no attention to her, letting her squeeze through the door with her parcels while she tried to get the card from the little envelope. It simply said, "Have a Good Day. Michael."

"That jerk," Lucy said out loud.

"Who's a jerk?" Peggy asked, setting the food on the table.

"Michael Donegan, that's who."

"Lover's spat already?"

"Cut it out, Peggy. That's not funny."

"Ouch. What's gotten you so riled up?"

"These, that's what." She tossed the roses on the table where Peggy had just set the pizza.

"The roses? They're beautiful."

"Read the card."

Peggy took it, held it at arm's length and read aloud: "Have a good day. Michael." Not understanding the problem, she looked at Lucy and asked, "So?"

"So?!" Lucy repeated, then stammered, "The nerve of that guy."

"Lucy, I'm lost here. Help me out, will you? You're pissed because he sent you flowers wishing you a good day?"

"Yes," she answered definitively.

"Wow, that guy is a real bastard," Peggy said sarcastically. "Just who does he think he is, wishing you a good day?"

"Peggy, you don't understand."

"You got that right. Clue me in, will you, because so far this isn't making a lot of sense to me."

"Why, Peg? Why would he send me flowers?"

"Taking a wild guess here, Lucy: maybe he likes you?"

"What? How can you say a thing like that?"

"Ah, well, let's see, maybe because he asked you to his cottage for the weekend, and now he's asked you to spend the summer. He's letting you drive that adorable sports car, and he sent you flowers. Correct me if I'm misstating the facts here." Lucy let out an exasperated sigh. "Just what is your problem? Wasn't the bouquet big enough? Should he have signed it 'Love, Michael'?"

"No! God no, Peggy. That's not it at all."

"Well, excuse me if I don't get what you are so upset about."

"Peggy, I told you I accepted his invitation because I wanted to see his grandfather's journals."

Peggy interrupted her: "Yeah, Yeah, the little man, blah blah Lance the mysterious missing lover yada yada. Lucy, *you* are missing *my* point: he just might like you, cute little unpretentious, unassuming you."

"Peggy, wait." Lucy started shaking her head.

"No, you wait. Damn it, Lucy, what's the matter with you? On one hand you have a guy named Lance, who, by the way, you haven't seen nor heard from in years, not a letter, not a phone call. You stopped living your life to sit and wait for a guy who, frankly, I'm not even sure exists. On the other hand, you have a guy who sends you flowers the very day you leave him just to say 'have a nice day.'"

"Peggy," Lucy said more harshly.

"No, shut up and listen to me. You aren't getting any younger you know. Just what do you have for all your waiting? You are a wonderful person, Lucy. Maybe that's what Michael sees. Heck, I don't know. Maybe he likes you because he thinks he can't have you. Men like him get that way, you know. He's probably used to having beautiful women throw themselves at him, more for his money and his lifestyle than for who he is. Now you come along and pay no attention to him at all because you're looking for soul boy. He probably finds that pretty damn refreshing."

"May I speak now, Peggy?" Lucy asked resignedly.

"Only if you admit what I said might not be too far from the truth." Lucy sat quietly pushing a mushroom around on the top of her slice of pizza. "Lucy, come on, be honest. Hasn't he given you any hint that he might be at least a little bit interested in you?"

"Well, he did try to kiss me."

"Good God, you are an idiot," Peggy shouted. "I rest my case." She jumped from her chair and ran to her purse in the living room. She returned thumbing through a copy of *Metro Scene* magazine. "Here, I just want to get something straight. Are we talking about this Michael Donegan?" She turned to an article titled "Most Eligible" and laid the magazine down in front of Lucy. There, occupying the whole page, was a color photo of Michael in a tuxedo surrounded by four beautiful women in scant, sparkly evening dresses.

Lucy grabbed the magazine. "Oh God, Michael, what are you doing?" she thought. She actually felt sorry for him as she read his bio:

> *Number one on Detroit's most eligible list is Michael Donegan, President and CEO of Donegan & Donegan Celtic Importers whose head office is in Southfield. This Irish born hunk stands at 6' 2". He has thick, dark, wavy hair and dark, brooding eyes.*

Lucy turned the page where there were two smaller pictures of Michael, one of him in a swimsuit running on the beach and the other of him riding Shashad. She continued reading:

> *This reporter spent a weekend at his Saugatuck get away where he disclosed that some of his favorite things to do are running on the beach and taking long rides on his favorite horse. Any woman would be thrilled to be serenaded by his rich Irish tenor voice. This shamrock may just be your four-leaf clover, girls. He has it all, and he is looking to share it with the right woman.*

Lucy slammed the magazine closed. "God, that's terrible," she said. "It's like a Michael advertisement."

"Yeah," Peggy said. "So that's the jerk who's sending you flowers?"

"Yep," Lucy said, "that's him."

"Poor baby, must be tough to be you." They both laughed. Peggy, dear Peggy, could always bring her spirits up. They had been roommates for a brief time in San Francisco. They had met in a dance class and hit it off right away. One night the door bell rang and Lucy found Peg standing on her porch with a black eye. The guy she had been living with was drinking and doing drugs and she was frightened for her life. Lucy was the only person she knew that didn't know him. Besides, she was too embarrassed to go to any of her other friends.

"Hey Luce, I have an idea. If you decide you want hunk man here off your case, just invite me down for a weekend. I'll play hard to get and you can go chase Lancelot around Camelot. Shoot, I haven't gotten any flowers in years. The last guy I dated made me pay half the dinner check."

"Maybe I'll just do that," Lucy said, but she wasn't thinking of Michael when she said it; she was thinking about Ashley. "They would make a perfect couple," she thought. Peggy left about seven and Lucy finished straightening up the apartment. She carried her bags down and then came up to get Freea. "Come on, kitty," she said. "Let's go see what you think of Myra and Michael."

Lucy made a quick stop at Danny's to take him the groceries. She read *Hop on Pop* to the kids and helped carry them off to bed. Danny and Donna insisted on laying hands on her and praying before she left. She was happy for it. She needed all the prayer she could get to return to Glen Eden—for protection, discernment, and a sound mind.

The drive back to Saugatuck seemed twice as long as the drive to the city, but it gave her time to think about Lance and Michael. She loved Lance, of that she had no doubt. It was her physical attraction to Michael that confused her. But she realized she had to stop blaming him for it.

She pulled up to the front of the cottage just before midnight. She noticed the ruts she put in the driveway when she left that morning and felt ashamed. Michael came bounding out the door as if he had been waiting for her. "Here, let me help you with your things," he said. He pulled the big suitcase from the back seat and grabbed hold of her boots. She managed a smaller bag and the bouquet of roses.

"Where is your kitty?" he asked.

She pulled open her jacket to reveal Freea's backside. "She always rides with her head buried in my chest. I guess she feels safe that way."

"I would," he said, with a devilish twinkle.

They stood a moment quietly looking at each other. She had the roses under her nose, breathing in their intoxicating scent.

Freea started to wiggle under her jacket and Michael noticed. "Let's get your kitty inside. I fixed her a litter box off the pantry by the back door, if you'd like to show her. I'll take these things up to your room. Maybe you'll join me in the kitchen for a cup of tea. I have it steeping now."

"I'd love one." She set her bag and the roses by the foot of the stairs as he went on up with the other things. She carried Freea to the litter box and set her down. She made use of it straight off then hopped out to begin exploring. Lucy went into the kitchen, washed her hands, hung her jacket over the back of one of the chairs, and poured out two cups of tea. The kitchen smelled wonderful. Myra had been baking, she could tell. Michael came in and cut a slice from a freshly baked loaf. "Will you be having one?" he asked.

"No, not now, thanks." He walked into the pantry and came back with the black currant jam and heaped it on his bread. "So you like a little bread with your jam?" she joked. He nodded his head because his mouth was already full. They sat chatting comfortably and when they were done, she washed the cups and saucers and he dried.

They again walked the stairs together. She carried the roses and he carried the bag she'd left at the foot of the stairs. He set it down in her room where she directed. She waved the roses under his nose. "These were thoughtful. Thank you. I brought them along because I didn't want their beauty to go to waste."

"Beauty should never be wasted," he said, staring once again into her eyes. "That's my philosophy." He bade her good night. She started to shut her door, but then remembering Freea, left it slightly ajar.

Michael again lay upon his bed thinking about the woman he so desperately wanted who lay just down the hall. He had only known her for four days, and yet ever since he first saw her he was unable to think of anything else. He also knew her love was saved for another. He was glad he was leaving tomorrow. He needed to get away to clear his head.

14 – From Magic Garden to Stonehouse

She slept wonderfully, better than she had in a long time. She didn't recall a dream. Freea had found her way to Lucy's bed and slept as she always did, above Lucy's head on the pillow. "Hey, my kitty," she said. "You found me." Freea stretched out a paw and opened her mouth in a wide yawn. Lucy had no idea what time it was; no one had awakened her. Through the open window, it looked like a beautiful morning. The sun had been up for a while taking the chill off the air and warming the soft breeze.

She dressed in a simple white sundress and let her hair hang loose down her back. She made up the bed and walked down the stairs carrying her kitty. She wandered into the kitchen, but no one was there. She strolled to the back door and looked out over the garden. She felt like she had woken up in a fairytale. The colors of the flowers were brilliant. The morning glories around the arched trellis were beyond any blue she could describe. Bumblebees were busy visiting each blossom, blending their buzz with the calls of the birds into the harmony of the morning. Monarchs and Bluetails were flitting about, adding their colors to the tapestry she beheld. "Myra was right: this is a magical place," she thought.

"A beautiful morning made even more beautiful," came Michael's voice from behind her. She turned and smiled at him. He had reading glasses balanced on the end of his nose and was dressed in a well tailored business suit and tie. He strolled to her side and leaned against the jamb. They stood for a moment just looking at morning in the garden. He had a coffee cup in his hand and took a sip. "I was wondering if I'd see you before I left."

"Oh, you're leaving?" She was surprised he hadn't mentioned it the night before.

"I am," he said. He thought she looked like an angel standing there in the doorway with the sunlight and colors of the garden framing her. "You're looking grand this morning." She blushed and looked down, so he added, "Well rested."

"Thank you," she said, returning her glance to him, "and you are looking very CEOish."

"Is that good?" he asked.

"Someone has to do it," she replied.

"Aye, and as long as I'm dressed the part…"

"There you go," she said.

He raised his cup to her then took a drink. *God, she is beautiful,* he thought. "Where's Myra?"

"She's about—walking on the beach, I think. She'll likely be back soon." He removed his glasses and tucked them inside his jacket. She still held Freea cradled in her arms. He reached out and lifted the cat's face. "Good morning, Miss Freea," he spoke right to her. "Let's have a look at you, now. You are a pretty little thing, aren't you? Shiny silver gray coat, and what a pretty white vest you're wearing. I hope you're finding things to your liking here." She purred loudly as he rubbed her chin and cheek with his finger.

"Well now, Mr. Donegan, it seems you have charmed my cat."

"Quite the opposite. It is she who has charmed me." He winked and walked over to the coffee pot to get a refill.

"How long will you be gone?"

"I'll be back on Friday. Will you be missing me?" He didn't wait for an answer. "I'm leaving my car here for you and Myra. Do try not to kill any of the locals, will you."

"Oh, that's funny," she chuckled.

"Ashley will be picking me up anytime now. We have some business to attend to in Chicago today." He took a sip of his coffee, keeping his eyes on her as he did.

"Well, then that's one local I can't kill." She smiled. He liked it when she did.

"I have Strider entered in a race there tonight. We'll take that in and I'll fly out of O'Hare to Los Angeles on the morrow. My schedule is on the calendar in the study if ever you have need of me." He took another sip of coffee thinking how much he'd like to kiss her. "When I return, I'll have a friend with me. He'll be spending the weekend, and maybe longer. While he is here, I'd like you to stick around… to help Myra with meals and things." He said that so she'd have no idea that Fred Loch was actually coming to evaluate her. "Is that good with you?"

"Sure, Michael, that's fine."

"Normally when I'm here with Myra, you'll be free to go off as you like."

"Michael, since I am in your employ now, I'd like to discuss just what it is you expect of me."

"Just what you have been doing: give Myra a little check on from time to time and help her out with some of the chores around here. We have a hired man who comes around for a few hours every day. He's a good lad, Scottie Brown. He takes care of the horses and does some of the heavier groundwork, at Myra's direction. She enjoys doing the lighter gardening herself. She'll let you know if she needs something."

"That's it?" Lucy quizzed.

"That's it," he said with a devilish grin on his face because he was thinking, *Unless you'd like to take off your clothes and let me have you right here, right now.*

"I'm not sure I'm qualified to do all that," she said, making a crooked smile and rolling her eyes.

"Not qualified for what, dear?" Myra asked walking up to them. They were both glad she didn't wait for an answer. "Because I think a person can do whatever it is she sets her heart on doing. If she can't do it, it's just because she didn't want to bad enough."

"I totally agree with you on that, Myra," she said, looking at Michael and winking her eye.

He smiled widely back at her. The sound of a car horn came from the front drive and pulled him from her spell. "That'll be for me," he said, raising his cup and throwing down the last of his coffee. He walked quickly to the sink to rinse it then over to Myra. He kissed her gently on the forehead as he reached out a hand to stroke Freea, who was still in Lucy's arms. "You girls have fun, the three of you." He turned and rushed down the hall picking up a valise that waited for him by the door.

"Goodbye, lovie," Myra called after him. "Take care."

"Good luck to Strider," Lucy said, putting her hand up in a little wave. He looked back at her, smiled, then hurried out. Through the open door Lucy saw a black, four-door sedan. A man, Ashley, sat in the driver's seat, and there were two women in back. The one sitting behind the passenger seat she thought might be Skipper. The one sitting behind the driver's seat she didn't get a good look at. *Just what on earth are you up to now, Michael Donegan?* she thought.

"No good!" Myra declared.

"Excuse me?" Lucy asked.

Myra was standing in the back door looking outward. "The bulbs I bought last fall were just no good. Only half of them came up. Look there." She pointed to an area alongside the back wall where irises and jonquils were sparsely growing. Lucy walked over to see just what Myra was fussing about. "Do you like to garden, Lucy?"

"I've never really had one myself. I've always lived in an apartment since I left Twin Willows."

"Twin Willows?"

"That's what my mom calls their small blueberry farm near South Haven. She and Dad both have the green thumbs."

"Oh, so you are from South Haven?"

"That area—the farm is actually in Casco."

"Are your parents still living there?"

"Yes, ma'am."

"Do you see them often?"

"No, not really." Lucy looked down and Myra could tell she had struck a nerve.

"Good heavens, why not?"

Lucy was sorry now she had mentioned them. With her voice filled with emotion, she said, "It's just better for them if I stay away."

"But why?"

"It's a long story, Myra."

"Yes, I'm sure it is, and well it should be. I, nevertheless, would like to hear it." She saw the pained look on Lucy's face and added, "Sometime, when you are ready to tell me."

"Myra, if you don't mind, I'd like to go unpack my things now." She bent down and let Freea out of her arms.

"Yes, of course, go on. I'll sit here and visit with your kitty for a time. She is very regal looking." Freea sat upright, busily cleaning herself. The sunlight danced off her shiny silver coat.

Lucy hurried up to her room. She lay across the bed and hugged her pillow. She didn't like to think of the past. "This isn't going to work," she thought. "I forgot about living with people. They always end up wanting to know about you." She sighed and said quietly, "Lance, please come back for me. Come quickly." She closed her eyes to conjure him into her thoughts, but it was Michael who came to her, Michael riding up on horseback like he'd done on Sunday at the circle. Michael calling to her, "Yes, I'm here." Michael pulling himself on top of her, forcing his tongue into her mouth. "No," she shouted as she sat up. "It's all wrong."

She slid from the bed and fell to her knees. "Father, forgive me. I want to be in your will. Give me a sound mind, dear God." Then she slipped into the tongue of the angels. She knew not what to pray beyond what she had done, but she trusted that God loved her and knew exactly what she needed. So she let go of her thoughts, of her doubts, of her past, and gave it all to Him.

Though Michael wasn't looking forward to this trip, he was relieved to be on it. Being so close to Lucy was driving him mad. She was so alluring to him that all he could think about was having her. To hold that desire at bay was something he wasn't used to. After a hello shake from Ashley, a little kiss from Skipper, and a rather chilly "Michael" from their mom, he sat back in his seat and tried to push her out of his thoughts.

"So how's your house guest doing?" Ashley had to ask.

"She's fine. Settling in, I guess. She's brought her cat."

"Her cat Frieda?"

"Freea," Michael corrected.

"Freea, yeah that's it. She still has Freea, huh?"

"Is Myra's cousin here, Michael?" Winnie asked.

"No ma'am, she's not coming till September."

"Oh, that's right." She was fishing, but he didn't go for the bait. "So who is this house guest of yours? Myra hasn't mentioned a house guest."

"It's Lucy, Mom." Skipper piped up, giving the back of Michael's seat a little nudge with her foot. "You remember Lucy from the Butler."

"Lucy? You mean Ashley's Lucy?" Ashley sunk a little in his seat and gave a sideways glance at Michael.

"Yep," Skipper said. "She's back and living with Michael."

"Well, that certainly explains a lot." She reached out her hand and patted her daughter's to console her.

"She's not living with me," Michael said defensively. "She is staying for the summer to look after Myra."

"Myra? Is there something wrong with Myra?" Winnie asked.

"No, she's fine." He didn't like where this might go. "I just don't feel right leaving her alone way out here when I'm off on business."

"Well, that's very thoughtful of you, Michael, but where is Megan?"

God, will the questions never end. "Oh, she's around, just busy with her job at the Glenwood and her preparations for school."

Skipper enjoyed watching him squirm. Megan had already given her her gold-digger uptake on Lucy.

"I see," Winnie said patronizingly. She remained quiet the rest of the trip.

Michael and Ashley decided, after the little stunt Skipper pulled with the sleeping pills, that they needed to get her help right away. Together they phoned Dr. Scott just yesterday morning to make the arrangements at The Stonehouse. Ashley asked Michael to go along because he thought he might have trouble convincing her to stay once he got her there. He had talked with her several times about going somewhere to "dry out," but she insisted she didn't need to do it and didn't want him wasting his money on her. He told her the trip today was about visiting their mother's first cousin while he and Michael went to the track. Actually, that was the plan (*after* they had her safely locked away).

Dr. Scott had assured them that once they got her physically inside the building, there wouldn't be a problem. Her mother, being next of kin, could sign the papers admitting her, and she would be sequestered for the duration of her treatment. Getting her inside would be up to them.

After Lucy prayed, she felt at peace again, like she felt when she awoke that morning. So she set about making this room—this room that had been Kathleen's—her own. She filled the drawers and closet with her things, spread her brushes and combs on the vanity along with her own fragrance, and pushed her emptied suitcase under the bed. She searched through her backpack for the picture of Lance, but it wasn't there. Now she wondered if someone could have taken it. Angus came to mind.

She went downstairs and found Myra on her knees pulling weeds in the garden. "It's such a lovely day out. Shall I fix lunch and bring it to the Gazebo?" Lucy asked.

"Oh my, yes. What a lovely idea."

Lucy went to the kitchen and opened the fridge. She pulled out the bowl of leftover potato-leek soup and poured it into a pot. It would be just enough for the two of them. While it warmed, she sliced Myra's homemade honey bread and spread mayo on it. On that she arranged slices of cucumber, tomato, and watercress. "Voila!" She cut the sandwiches into fourths, put them on small plates, poured the soup into bowls, and set them on a tray. She found glasses for the iced tea and long spoons to stir in the sugar cubes and lemon slices.

"Here it is," she called to Myra as she carried the tray through the garden. "Go on in, wash up and join me."

Myra hurried to do as she was told. Soon the two of them were chatting away, enjoying their fare and each other. When they were done, Lucy gathered all the dishes upon the tray to carry back in the house. "I'll do these up; you go on with your gardening. I'd like to get back into the study, if you don't mind."

"Of course you would. You go right ahead. Thank you for the lovely lunch and the delightful company. And Lucy, I'm sorry about upsetting you earlier with my prying. Michael is always warning me against it. The trouble is I don't really think about it much. I ramble on and before I know, I've put my foot right in it. Please forgive me. Just know that I'll be here for you, to listen, dear, whenever you like."

"Thank you, Myra," she said earnestly.

"Lucy, I have a wonderful idea. What say I treat us to dinner tonight? If you wouldn't mind driving us in to Fennville, that is. The Hotel has liver and onions on Tuesday nights. Winnie was going to take me, but now she's gone off to Chicago with Skipper and the boys. What do you say to it? If you don't like liver, they have fish or chicken. Their food is quite good."

"Sure, Myra. It sounds like fun. What time would you want to go?"

"Oh, I'd say we leave here by five-thirty."

"Five-thirty it is then." Myra went back to pulling weeds and Lucy washed and put up the dishes before heading down to the study.

She unlocked the file drawer and once again held William Donegan's journal. For the first time she felt apprehensive about what she might learn from reading it.

So far she found out that William Donegan was "the Keeper" whom Lance had visited many times over the summer when they first met. She learned that William called Lance "the Searcher" and had financed him to find what he called "power points" on the earth. These points, he believed, as did Lance, were known by native peoples and regarded as very sacred sites. Temples or stone monuments were built on them, rites and rituals were held there, and burial mounds, tombs, or kerns were usually found nearby. At some of these places miracles of healing would happen, power and wisdom could be gained, or divine inspiration would occur. Many, if not all of them, were believed to be portals to or from ancient worlds, other times, or other dimensions, such as the fairy realm. This seemed to be William's chief curiosity. He recorded many stories connected with the Fairy faith, stories that had been passed down through his family or that he had obtained from others.

In particular, he'd mentioned tales that were collected by a Robert Kirk, who had been the Minister of Aberfoyle in the late 1600's. Lucy found an old edition among the books in the study entitled *The Secret Common-Wealth of Elves, Fauns, & Fairies*. The text by Robert Kirk contained an 1893 commentary by Andrew Lang. Besides that book, she found an old manuscript kept locked away in a cedar box in one of the filing cabinets. It was handwritten with a title page that read

THE SECRET COMMON-WEALTH
OR
THE CHIEF CURIOSITIES
AMONG THE PEOPLE OF
SCOTLAND AS THEY
ARE IN USE TO THIS DAY

This document carried the date 1692. Lucy read in the commentary that the original manuscript by Robert Kirk went missing soon after the 1893 publication, and she wondered if the "Old Fox" had somehow gotten his hands on it.

William's journal cited other texts, many of which she had also found on the shelves. She pictured Lance sitting in this very room poring over these ancient books. She felt close to him here. She knew he had traveled to many of the sacred locations mentioned. There he had interviewed shamans, holy men, and elders to learn the stories and legends of those sites passed down through the ages.

Though William would briefly mention when he had received a report from the Searcher, he didn't disclose what it said; instead, he noted GB next to the entry. Lucy took that to mean he was keeping all of Lance's reports in *The Green Book*.

She found a passage which read, "The Searcher's report confirms much of what I have long suspected. Because of the danger of such knowledge falling into the wrong hands his reports will be kept in *The Green Book Esotery* under my close watch behind the rock. Furthermore, the spot will be doggedly guarded by six jealous brothers." She put a bookmark on the page so she could show Michael. Lucy desperately wanted to get her hands on *The Green Book*. It would contain reports in Lance's own hand. She had searched the shelves of the study Sunday night while waiting for Michael to return but had not found it. Michael had promised he'd look for it while she was away yesterday. She wished she had thought to ask him about it before he left. "I'll have to wait until Friday, I guess."

She wondered if he would call. She wondered what he was doing with Ashley, or more mindfully, with Skipper. She wondered what his true feelings for her were. She recalled the way he had tenderly brushed the lock of hair from

Skipper's face when he carried her to the couch in the Hacksaw room. "Stop it," she shouted to her brain. "Stop thinking about him!" She looked at the clock. It was 4:45 p.m. She locked up the journal and rushed upstairs to get ready for dinner.

The Stonehouse sat in a lovely suburb of Chicago. It was a large, unassuming building originally built in the 1800's as a hotel. It was eventually abandoned and then purchased in the 1940's by a group of businessmen to house this private clinic. It was staffed with the finest psychiatrists of the time. Its purpose was to be a secret place where the wealthy could go—or send wives, mistresses, sons or daughters—to dry out or kick a drug habit so as not to cause public scandal. Michael knew while he was away attending secondary school in Ireland his own father had received treatment there for his alcoholism. The marker outside simply declared THE STONEHOUSE, giving no hint as to what it was. Many of the residents of the same street didn't even know.

"What is this place?" Skipper asked when Ashley pulled up to the curb.

"A pub," he said.

At the same time Michael declared, "It's a restaurant." Trying to clear up the confusion, he spat out, "A pub with a very fine restaurant."

The four alighted from the car, and Ashley took his mother's arm to help her negotiate the front steps. That left Michael to escort Skipper. She thought he was clutching her arm rather tightly, and she noticed the uneasy look on her mother's face. The door opened into a plush lobby, and just as she was about to step over the threshold, the elevator door at the rear of the room slid open to reveal a man in a wheelchair escorted by two orderlies dressed all in white. That was all it took. She kicked Michael squarely in the shin, causing him to lose his grip, and bolted down the stairs.

"Ouch!" he hollered, hopping on one foot.

"Grab her, Donegan," Ashley shouted.

She ran wildly into the street with Michael now right on her heels. A yellow cab came to a screeching stop, almost clipping the frenzied pair. "What the hell, dumbasses!" The cab driver yelled, laying on the horn.

Michael couldn't bother with a reply, though he wanted to punch the guy. He reached out and caught her by the shoulder. This time she secured her freedom by bopping him in the face with her purse. "Goddamn it, Skipper, cut it out." He was done playing with her. He reached out again and grabbed her by the hair, yanking her back into his arms so he could pick her up and throw her over his shoulder like a sack of potatoes. Ashley caught up to them and Michael barked a command: "Grab her hands! She's pounding a hole in my back."

Ashley secured her hands and she spat on him. "Bastard!" she yelled. "You're both bastards!" She fought all the way back, but Michael didn't let loose of her until they were ushered through the lobby into a small, private admitting room and the door was tightly shut.

Dr. Scott came in along with a male orderly to help secure her as Michael put her down. They restrained her by strapping her in a chair. "So Michael, you decided to come yourself," Dr. Scott said, almost letting the cat out of the bag.

"Oh no, I'm not here to check myself in, doctor." He winked. "I've just come along with a friend of mine."

"Oh, I see," the doctor said, remembering Michael's wish to remain anonymous. Michael introduced him around the room.

After seeing how roughly her daughter had been treated, Winnie balked at signing the papers. Ashley had to talk her into it all over again. This wasn't an easy task since she had to listen to Skipper's pleas and promises. Finally, Dr. Scott escorted them down the hall to his private office, away from Skipper's influence. This left Michael alone in the room with Skipper and the big orderly.

"So this is your idea of a pub with a nice restaurant?" Skipper said sarcastically, squirming against her restraints.

"Well, as I understand, the food is excellent here." He reached out and touched the end of her nose.

"Michael Donegan, if I find out this was your idea, your balls are mine." She was staring daggers at him.

"I'm afraid it's Ashley's balls your foot will have to target. I just came along at his request to act, it would seem, as his shin protector." He hiked his pant to display a big red-blue bump on his leg.

With her hands and feet secured he felt safe enough to get close to her. He got down on one knee beside her. "This is for the best, darlin'. They can help you here to get yourself better," he whispered as he brushed her disheveled hair from her face and then kissed her tenderly on the cheek. "I know Jay would not want you hurting yourself and neither do I." He felt badly that he had been brutal with her.

Skipper's mom looked done in as the three battle-worn companions made their way back to the car. Michael slid into the back seat so she could sit next to her son. Ashley kept reassuring her that Skipper would be fine. "She never would have gotten this bad if a certain man hadn't taken advantage of her grieving." Michael knew whom she meant, and he prayed that wasn't true.

The restaurant in the hotel in Fennville had changed since Lucy's last visit. It was restyled to have the ambiance of an old train depot, which it had also been in bygone days. There were pictures on the walls of those earlier years, along with railroad memorabilia displayed here and there. The old bar had been replaced with a highly polished model, and new padded bar stools stood before it. Some of these were occupied with customers waiting for tables. There were three large ceiling fans, so it was not as smoky as Lucy feared it would be.

The meal was very good, and Lucy enjoyed listening to Myra's stories. She reminisced about the old days with William before he left for America. Lucy could tell she enjoyed having someone new to tell these tales to.

She excused herself to go to the ladies room, and when she returned Myra exclaimed that she had ordered them an after dinner cocktail. "Baileys on the rocks," Myra said mischievously. Lucy was surprised when the bartender delivered the drinks himself. He looked familiar. *Oh no, it's Gary, the old bartender from the Butler.* She tried not to look directly at him so he wouldn't recognize her. But to her dismay, Myra decided an introduction was in order.

"Gary, meet my new friend, Lucy Cavanagh. Lucy, this is Gary Teesdell."

"Lucy Cavanagh, for crying out loud, it is you."

"Hello, Gary," she said.

"Oh my, you two know each other."

"We sure do. Lucy and I go way back. We worked together at the Butler, back when she was engaged to Ashley."

"What? Lucy, you were engaged to Ashley?"

"She sure was. It was the talk of the town. Only woman he ever came close to marrying."

"Really? What happened, dear?" Myra asked.

Lucy certainly didn't want to go into that now since the rumor had started after Gary's inappropriate behavior toward her in the Hacksaw room. A waitress called to him from her station at the bar: "Gary, are you gonna mix this order or do I have to do it myself?"

"Keep your shirt on, Charleen, I'll be right there," Gary blurted out, then answered Myra's question as he set down her drink: "She ran off with some other guy, that's what happened." He set Lucy's drink in front of her and, before heading back to the bar, said "I'll say this, Lucy, you're still a real looker."

"Thanks, Gary" was all that she could think of saying, though she felt somewhat insulted.

Myra was amazed. "Well, well, this is all so interesting. You are a bundle of surprises. Engaged to Ashley. Why, you must know Winnie then. Of course you do. I can't get over this. You, engaged to Ashley. Does Michael know? Not that it is any of his business, or mine really. I just find it so interesting."

Lucy sat quietly sipping her drink, letting Myra ramble. She didn't know if an answer was expected, and she didn't really want to give one anyway.

"What a small world this is," Myra went on. "Let's drink to old loves, shall we?" She picked up her glass, and Lucy did the same. "To old loves," she said, but just before their glasses touched, she added, "and new."

Michael called about 10 p.m. Lucy was back in the study and heard the phone ring. She was hoping it might be him. Myra answered it in the hall, so Lucy heard her side of the conversation.

Michael was hoping that Lucy would answer, but it was Myra's voice that said, "Hello."

"Myra, I haven't gotten you up, have I?"

"No dear, I was just going up to bed now. Michael, where are you? There is a lot of noise?"

"Sorry, Myra, I'm at the track with Ashley. I wanted to call you before it got too late. How are things going there?"

"Lovely, dear. Lucy drove us to the Hotel in Fennville. You know, they have the liver and onions I'm so fond of on Tuesday nights."

"So you had a good dinner?"

"Yes, dear, lovely."

"Did Lucy enjoy herself?"

"Oh yes, dear. Lucy bumped into an old friend she used to work with. Did you know that she used to be engaged to Ashley?"

Michael recalled the tale as Lucy and Ashley had told it at the Butler on Saturday. He laughed to himself thinking about what Lucy must have gone through when Myra got wind of it. "Is that right" was all he said, to the disappointment of Myra, who thought he would find it much more interesting than his response suggested. Maybe she had misjudged his interest in Lucy.

"Would you like to talk with her?"

Lucy stood up, waiting to run to the phone when her name was called. He wanted to talk to her, to hear her voice, but he said, "No, Myra. Strider is just about in the gate, so I'll just say good night."

"Oh good night, lovie. Thank you for calling." Lucy slumped back into the chair when she heard Myra hang up the phone.

In reading William's journals, Lucy felt she was coming to know Michael a little better. His grandfather had great love and respect for him, and mentions of Michael were peppered throughout the pages. Lucy wondered if Myra or Michael had ever read these journals, for if they had she felt honored that they would let her share in their family secrets. Besides being full of research on sacred and powerful places, as well as fairies and the belief in them, William had included snapshots of his own life. Perhaps, she thought, at the times of those notations, he had been under the influence of a liquid spirit, for his entries would suddenly turn more personal and a little melancholy. For instance, she found this passage:

> *Michael has left to go back to school. He turned twelve this summer. He is big for his age. He grows more and more to look like Irene every day, hauntingly so. Perhaps that is why his father couldn't bear to have him around. Beautiful, beautiful Irene, why is it you chose to leave your young son? He is such a fine, brave lad. I can understand your leaving Aidan; he is a disappointment even to himself. I can only imagine the pain he put you through. I don't think it was his intention to hurt you, though hurt you he did. It was because he is weak. In his weakness he could not overcome the desires of his flesh. Being away from you as much as he was, and being a man living in a world full of temptation,*

he stumbled. We all had to bear the consequence for that weakness. Is that weakness his fault or mine? Did I not train him up right? Heaven knows there was no example for him of how to love a woman. Yet I was faithful to his mother with my flesh, if not my heart. Could you not love him the more for that weakness? Could you not have been his strength? I fear in trying to make it right I have condemned us all. I pray Michael will not have to pay the price for our sin.

Lucy wondered what sin he might be talking about. In another journal, written nearly four years after that entry, she read this:

Michael left this morning to return to school. He is taller than I am now. What a fine, brave lad he has become. I was concerned when he did not cry at Aidan's funeral. I think perhaps he was trying to stay strong for me. Is it more terrible for an old man to lose his son, or for a young lad to lose his father? I suppose maybe I did have the greater loss. After all, how well did Michael even know Aidan? He's barely seen him these past few years, since Irene died. I guess Michael grew to realize that when he lost his mother the man he knew as his father was also lost to him. His grief at losing them both is somewhere in the past, while mine is fresh. I never gave up hope my son would someday come back from the depths to which his hate, guilt and despair had taken him.

Michael, upon his leaving, embraced me. It was the first time that he was holding me and not the other way round. He whispered in my ear, "Grandfather, it will be okay now, for him. All will be forgiven. He can rest and we can love him." My dear Michael is an amazing lad. It is my prayer God will leave me on this earth long enough to see him become the fine man I believe he will be.

"Did he, William? Did he become a fine man?" Lucy could not yet answer that question in her own mind. Despite her attraction to him, or perhaps because of it, she couldn't trust herself to judge his character.

15 – Dreams in a Midsummer's Night

   Lucy had been in the study since coming home from Fennville with Myra. It was almost two a.m. and her eyes were tired from reading, yet she didn't feel ready for bed. She guessed her body was still on the sleep schedule she had had to maintain for work. She would just be getting done with her shift and heading downstairs to punch out. Usually, by the time she got home, wound down, and ready for bed, the clock on her nightstand read four a.m. or after.

She decided a nice walk in the moonlight might be in order. It was a wonderfully warm evening. The moon was waning but still almost full, and the sky was blanketed with stars. She walked down the path that led past the stable to a small meadow on a little rise where the grass was green and tall. Lucy enjoyed being in nature where her senses came alive, and though she was totally alone she felt connected to it all. A gentle, summer breeze came dancing off the lake. She loved to feel the elements on her skin, so she took off her dress and stood naked in the night. She closed her eyes, stretched her arms, twirled around and breathed deeply the fresh warm air. Here on this little hill alone in the moonlight she felt at peace, free of the burden she carried. As the wind encompassed her, she thought of Lance. He was there in the wind. He was there in the stars of this summer night. He was even there in her thoughts of Michael. "Lance," she sighed as she fell into the cool, tall grass and let his essence fill her.

Strider placed in his first two races and won his third that night, making both Ashley and Michael a little richer. Michael attributed Strider's success to the fact that a new driver had been hired for him at the beginning of the season. The kid, just over from Ireland, had been handpicked for the job by Uncle Mickey.

Mickey Mullin and William Donegan had grown up together in Ireland and in later life became partners in the horse racing business. William put up the money and Mickey looked after the horses. He managed their care and training and arranged for all the races. He was the hands-on guy. When William died, his partnership in the horses went to Michael. Michael had known Uncle Mickey since he was a tot and deferred, as his grandfather had done, to his judgment on all matters concerning the horses.

After Strider's last race, Michael left Ashley in the company of a couple of racetrack honeys and made his way to the stables. Uncle Mickey was right where Michael expected him to be, in the stall with Strider. He was rubbing the horse with ointment and talking to Jonny, the red haired, freckle-faced lad who was Strider's driver.

They both greeted Michael with hugs. The three men genuinely respected each other and the contribution each had made toward the goal they would celebrate this night. The bond they all shared with Strider made the victory all the more sweet. Michael took off his jacket and rolled up his sleeves so he could help rub down their champion. With Michael on one side and Jonny and Uncle Mickey on the other, they massaged the mighty animal while discussing every aspect of each race: the track, the competition, and Jonny's choices of just when to give Strider free rein and when to hold him back. They came to the conclusion, much to Jonny's delight, that he had made near-perfect decisions.

When they had Strider well taken care of, they shared a cab to the hotel where they hoisted ale, joked, and sang till the bar closed. Michael made them promise to join him for breakfast, and they said good night in the lobby.

Michael had given his mind a much needed break from thinking about Lucy. But as soon as he closed the door and faced his empty room, thoughts of her came flooding over him again. As he unbuttoned his shirt, he envisioned her standing in the doorway that morning looking out over the garden. He smiled, picturing her in that cute little sundress holding Freea. "God, woman, you are driving me mad," he thought.

He was glad he had reports to read for the board meeting in LA tomorrow. He had planned to read them on the plane but decided this might be a better time since he wouldn't be able to sleep for a while because of what the thoughts of her had done to him.

When he did sleep, he dreamed of her. She was standing naked in the moonlight. Her hair hung long and free and the breeze blew it gently around her. He went to her and took her in his arms. "Lance," she sighed. He didn't care what she called him; he just knew he wanted her. He carried her to a place where the grass was green and tall, and he lay with her.

16 – What's Love Got to Do with It?

Lucy woke in the meadow with dew on her skin and a chill about her. She dressed quickly and went inside to find Myra busy in the kitchen sectioning grapefruit for their breakfast.

"My goodness, you are up early, dear. Did you sleep well?"

"Fantastic," Lucy said. After they ate the light fare, she joined Myra—as she often did in the morning while at Glen Eden—for yoga in the garden. It was a wonderful way to start the day. After, they took a stroll on the beach and chatted happily about this and that. Myra learned Lucy had been a seamstress and suggested a sewing project they might do together.

"I want to make formals—fancy gowns—to give to girls who can't afford them."

Lucy thought that a wonderful idea and after lunch drove them to a material shop Myra knew of in Holland. They bought reams of taffeta, chiffon, brocade and other materials with interesting textures and colors. This day would set the pattern for the rest of their summer.

Lucy still had plenty of time to do her own things. She spent five to six hours a day in the study. After she finished reading William's journals, she pored over the rare books he had mentioned in them. She found most of them on his shelves or locked away in a filing cabinet. She felt close to Lance when she was reading that material. She could tell his own beliefs and philosophy had been influenced by some of these very same books, for she recalled several conversations they had had where he had used quotes from the literature she was just discovering.

On this the second evening Michael was away, Lucy found herself again hoping he would call. But when he had not, by the time Myra came to say good night, she asked, "Did William ever mention *The Green Book* to you?"

"*The Green Book*? No, I don't recall it."

"It's mentioned in one of his journals as the place where he kept Lance's reports. I wasn't able to locate it, and Michael promised to look for it on Monday when I went off to get my things from the city. I forgot to ask him about it yesterday morning before he left, and he didn't mention it."

"Well, dear, why don't we give him a call? I don't think he'll mind. He's probably had his dinner and is back in his hotel room by now." Lucy was hoping she'd say that. She found the hotel number on his planner and dialed it for Myra.

He answered a soft rapping on the door.

"Hey, handsome, you didn't call me. Are you alone?" she asked, peeking around him into the room.

"Yes, I am. I've been busy, and I'm a little tired." He lied. Truth was, he had wanted to call her. He had expected he would. He actually picked up the phone once, but his mind was so bothered by thoughts of Lucy that he couldn't go through with it.

"Well, that's good to hear," she said, pushing her way past him. "I thought maybe you had gone and fallen in love and brought her along this time. I've been expecting that to happen one day. Men like you don't stay on the market forever."

"Well, I haven't," he said.

She grabbed him by the tie, pulled him to her, and kissed him. Noticing that his kiss was unusually reserved, she asked, "Haven't what, fallen in love or brought her along?"

"Look, Maureen, I told you I've been busy, and I'm a little worn out."

"Well, then I have just the medicine the doctor ordered." She pulled a bottle of massage oil from her pocket, letting her topcoat slide from her shoulders. She stood before him in a revealing black negligee.

Wow, he thought and then voiced, "Maybe you're right. Maybe I could use a dose of doctor feel good." Turning to secure the lock, he said, "Why don't you call room service and have them send up a bottle of champagne, some oysters, and some of those chocolate-dipped strawberries you fancy. I'll hop in the shower and join you when I'm done."

"That's my handsome Irishman," she said, coming to him for another kiss. This one was much more enthusiastic.

Maureen worked as concierge at the Beverly Bel Air Hotel, where he had a standing reservation every fiscal quarter for the two nights he spent in L.A. for board meetings. They met three years ago when she first took the job. They had enjoyed dinner and drinks, and later, sex in his room. Since then, she kept her schedule free for the times he would be in town. Though she never expected anything from him other than a good time in bed, he would usually bring her some little trinket, jewelry, or perfume. They never spoiled what they had by talking about anything personal. She had learned all she needed to know about him the first night: he was witty, handsome, and they found each other mutually desirable. Michael wasn't the only man she enjoyed these trysts with. She also had a German and an Italian. They were both married. She didn't mind. She told herself she was doing their wives a favor. If she didn't satisfy them while they were out of town, they might hook up with a gold digger wanting to make trouble for them at home.

She wasn't looking for love or money. She had already found her one true love. His name was Ty Gordon. They dated all through high school and had intended to marry when he returned from Vietnam. He was an artist now, a mouth painter after coming back from war a quadriplegic. They would never marry but platonically shared a life. There was only one thing he couldn't give her, and she planned on getting that tonight from Michael.

The phone rang.

Over Maureen's protest, and thinking it was someone from the board who had promised to call him with projection numbers, he said to her, "Hold on, darlin'; I need to take this call. It will just take a minute. Here, have a strawberry and be a good girl; we have all night." He picked up the phone. "Hello."

"Michael?"

He was surprised to hear Myra's voice. She usually didn't call him when he was away. He gestured at the phone and to Maureen and mouthed, "My Granny."

Maureen was used to being interrupted by the German guy's wife, and once in a while the Italian's. She usually made them suffer for it by performing some little trick that made it extremely difficult for them to concentrate on the conversation at hand. This had never happened to her with Michael before.

"Myra, is everything all right?"

"Oh yes, Michael. Lucy and I had a wonderful day."

"That's g… g… good," Michael stuttered. Maureen had started an attention-grabbing act.

"Lucy was wondering if you found something called *The Green Book*."

"*The*… grr… *Green Book*?" Michael replied. Upon hearing Lucy's name, he tried to get Maureen to stop her mischief.

"Michael, are you all right, dear?" Myra asked.

His attacker relented for a moment. "I'm fine, just busy," he answered with a perturbed voice.

"Then I won't keep you, dear. Here, talk to Lucy."

"What? No, no, I can't right now." It was too late. Myra didn't wait for his response. She had already handed the phone over.

Lucy wasn't expecting her to do that. "Hey, Michael."

Michael certainly wasn't expecting to talk to Lucy, especially not right now. "Lucy, what is it?" he asked, and her name brought on another onslaught of shenanigans from Maureen.

"Sorry to bother you, but I was wondering if you had had a chance to look for *The Green Book* while I was away. I found other mentions of it in the journals."

"I… I… uh… looked. But… but… didn't find it." Maureen had launched a strong attack. "Stop that," Michael commanded, trying to conceal the loud whisper by putting his hand over the phone. But it was too late; Lucy heard it.

"Oh, you're with someone." She was embarrassed. "Sorry to bother you. Good night." She hung up.

"Good night," he said to the dead line. He hung up feeling like a heel. Why? Why should he feel that way? She had no feelings for him. She was trying to find Lance and using him to do it, that's all. Why should he care if she knew that he was with someone? He shouldn't. But he did.

Maureen could tell the call had bothered him. "I'm sorry, baby," she said. "I didn't know you had someone you cared about."

"I don't. I don't have her. She isn't mine, and that's that."

"Come here, baby," Maureen said. "I'm yours, for tonight anyway. Let's forget about this unfair world for a little while."

17 – A Straw of Hope

Myra went up to bed, and Lucy took Freea out to sit on the stone half-wall in front of the cottage to enjoy the warm, summer night. Suddenly, Freea stiffened then hissed. Lucy looked down and there stood Angus.

"Don't let go of that beast," he said in a terrified voice. "I hate cats!"

"Angus!" she gasped, not believing her eyes. "It's you."

"Yes, your Highness, I am me," he cackled and lit his pipe.

"Is Lance all right?" she blurted out.

"That is what he sent me to find out about you. I told him I see you every day. You look the same. But he says to me that I must talk to you now. My days of just watching are over." He took another puff of his pipe and blew a smoke ring that surrounded Freea's head. She reached out a paw and swatted it. It broke up and disappeared. He cackled again.

"Angus, please tell me how he is. How is Lance?"

"You know, he is brave and he is strong and he is smart and he is silly and he is…"

"Yes, Angus, I know he is all that. But is he okay?"

"Okay? He's okay with me. What about you?"

She was becoming exasperated and was afraid he would vanish again before she could get anything out of him. "Angus, what does Lance want you to talk to me about?"

"Oh, that. He wanted me to tell you… let's see… What was it now?… Ah yes, he wanted me to tell you to watch this." He took a long draw from his pipe and blew another smoke ring. This one grew larger as it floated up before Lucy's face. At first, she could look right through it, but then a blue haze appeared, filling the ring. Out of the blue, there was Lance.

"Lance," Lucy gasped as she reached for him. Her hand went right through the image.

"Shush," Angus commanded. "You can only listen."

The image of Lance looked right at her as it spoke. "Lucy, it was wonderful seeing you again, my darling. I have never stopped thinking about you. I'm so very sorry for all the years that have passed for you. I didn't realize. Forgive me. Time can be a friend or an enemy, depending on your purpose. You looked beautiful, more beautiful than even I remembered. I'm afraid I can only offer you a straw of hope. There are many things I must learn yet, many things I must do. I am encouraged by the fact that you have found your way to William's. He was a seventh son. His place is one where magic can happen. You must try to find *The Green Book*; it will tell you much. It contains the legend we may be in. William told me he kept it hidden to keep it safe. If that book falls into the wrong hands, it could be used to generate more evil, and then I fear all would be lost. Michael is William's son. Noble blood runs through his veins. He is an honorable man and he will remember it. He will take care of you. He doesn't know it yet, but he may have a very big part to play in our tale before it ends. Lucy, it may be that you will have to forget me for a while so that everything can take its course. But I promise you, my darling, you will not have to forget forever." He put his hand on his heart, bowed his head to her, then he was gone.

"No," she said, stretching out her hand again. "No, I will not forget you. Angus, you tell him that. I won't forget him," she cried. But Angus was no longer there.

She hadn't noticed Myra standing on the balcony just above her. She had stepped out to get a breath of air and heard everything Lucy said. "Oh dear, Michael," she thought. "You will need to be strong for her if she is dealing with that little demon Angus."

Lucy fell to her knees before the spot where Lance had appeared. Whenever she didn't know what to do, she prayed. "Father, Creator of all life, have mercy on me. Give me the strength to become the person you would have me to be. Father, be with Lance. Protect and watch over him and keep him safe in your light." Lucy didn't know it, but her prayers had shielded Lance from countless harms.

She sat back upon the wall hoping against hope that Lance would again appear. Her thoughts took her back to the last time she had been with him.

"Hello, Lucy. It's Paul."

"Paul! Hi. It's good to hear your voice. How are you?" Even as she said this she had a quivering in her stomach. Why was Lance's brother calling her? He never called. She would talk every now and again to his mom; whenever either one got a letter from Lance, they would call the other and share what news it held.

Her heart sunk as he replied in a soft tone—very uncharacteristic for the big man with a usually booming, jolly voice, "Things aren't so good here. Have you heard from Lance, or do you know where he is?"

"I haven't heard from him for over three weeks. The last letter I got was from Scotland, the Findhorn area. He said they were breaking camp and heading out. He gave the letter to a friend, who wasn't going on with them, to mail. Why, Paul? What's happened?"

"It's Dad, Lucy. He's passed. The service is day after tomorrow, and we were hoping Lance could get home."

"Oh, Paul, not Dad. I'm so sorry. But how?"

"He didn't come up for lunch after Mom rang the lunch bell, so she sent Littlefeather to fetch him. Littlefeather saw him sitting under the tree, you know, by the grave."

Lucy knew the exact spot. She had come across it one day while riding Takota. She turned the horse onto a trail she had not been down before. It went up and down over smaller hills with cornfields on each side and ended atop the largest hill on the farm, at a spot where a big weeping willow stood. A large boulder sat under the tree and grass grew around the base of it. On the opposite side of the tree stood a small cross bearing the name Windson. Lucy never asked about it, thinking it possibly to be the grave of a favorite pet.

Paul went on, "When Littlefeather got close enough, she could tell his spirit was gone. Doc Fowler said it was probably a massive heart attack. But Mom said no to an autopsy, so we can't be sure."

"How is Mom, Paul?"

"Well, she's doing okay, I guess. I know she'd love to have Lance home. We all would."

"Paul, I want to be there. Would it be all right if I come?"

"You know it would, Lucy. I didn't want to ask, but I know Mom would love it, and Littlefeather would too. Please do come. Stay at the house with us, Lucy. It would mean a lot to us all."

"I'll be there, Paul. I'm going to call and check on trains right after we hang up."

"There's only one into town from your direction. It will get here at four p.m. tomorrow. I'll be there to pick you up. Having you here will be almost like Lance is home."

Lucy's voice was starting to break from the sorrow that rose to her throat. "Okay, Paul, I'll see you then, and please give Mom and Littlefeather my love."

"Will do. See you tomorrow."

She hung up the phone, took Lance's picture off the shelf, and sat down on the couch. Freea jumped on her lap and nestled into her neck. Lucy cried like she hadn't cried in years. It wasn't entirely over Lance's father; it was for Lance and for herself as well. She cried herself to sleep. Freea slept too, on her chest beside the picture. In Lucy's dream a man stood in the bow of a ship. He was surrounded by mist. A foghorn sounded in the background. She realized the man was Lance. Tears rolled down his face as he intoned a lament. He looked up and said, as if he could see her, "I know."

When Lucy woke she called Amtrak and, like Paul had told her, there was only one train into Peebles from her direction. In order to catch it she needed to leave her apartment by 7:15 a.m. She would have to make a connection in Cincinnati. She made the reservation and phoned her friend Peg for a lift to the station.

"Sure thing, kiddo," Peggy replied. "Lance's dad, huh? That's rough. Do you think Lance will be there?"

"I don't know. I'm not sure where he is or if anyone can reach him."

"Yeah, well, what's with that?"

"Please, Peg, don't start. Not now."

"Sure, okay, too bad is all. But it is good of you to go."

Peggy had often tried to set her up with a guy. She thought Lucy was wasting her time waiting for Lance to stop his wandering. She didn't understand how Lucy could wait around for someone who had made no promises. Lucy loved Peggy like a sister, but it was annoying when she'd start in on how Lucy should find herself someone in the real world. Peggy had never met Lance, so Lucy knew she'd never understand.

In a small suitcase she packed a navy blue lace dress for the funeral service and a cardigan in the same hue in case the weather turned chilly. She took her jeans and cowboy boots, hoping to have a chance to ride Takota. She laid out brown slacks, a beige blouse with little blue forget-me-nots embroidered on it, and a tailored brown jacket for the train ride.

She showered early so her long hair could dry before she went to bed. She had a habit of turning on the cold water after taking a long, hot shower. She had read somewhere that this was good for the skin, and that it would actually help you get to sleep. She rinsed the conditioner from her hair and changed the water from hot to cold. It always took her breath for a moment. As the cold water beat against her back, she recalled one of the times Lance had taken her camping near his family's home.

They rode Takota into the mountains and slept under a sky so big and full of stars Lucy could hardly believe it was real. In the morning they walked along the mountain stream to a majestic waterfall. Lance fished while Lucy explored the nearby meadow filled with flowers and wild berries. By noon the sun was high and beating down on them. Lance called her to follow him as he climbed to a ledge jutting out from a cliff just behind the falls. Lance removed his clothes and Lucy did the same. They stood for a moment beneath the cold, cascading water. He took her hand and they leaped into the mountain pool below.

The phone rang and Lucy quickly turned off the water and grabbed for her towel. She reached the phone by the fifth ring and heard a fuzzy voice on the other end. She could barely make out what was being said because of the static: "Lu zickkkkk this zick Lan zickkk crackle zickkkk…"

"Lance, your dad. Do you know?" Lucy yelled into the receiver. "Lance, I'll be there. Are you coming?"

"Zickkk crackle last night snap zickkk I can't crackle crackle zickkk crackle time crackle." Then nothing. The line went dead.

"Hello… Hello," she shouted.

She hung up quickly hoping he would call back. She held her breath and stared at the phone, waiting for it to ring. But it didn't. "It was Lance," her mind cried. "Did he know, or was it a coincidence?" She struggled to piece together the broken words: "He said, 'I can't.' Can't what? Can't believe it? Can't come home? Can't hear? What can't you do, Lance? What about 'last night,' what were you trying to tell me?" She didn't know where he was calling from or how to call him back, so she sat mulling over his broken words.

She decided not to go to bed but to sleep on the couch beside the phone so she'd be sure to hear it. She fell asleep listening to silence. In the morning, when the phone did ring, she had just gone into the bathroom where she was giving her hair a final brush. She raced through the kitchen into the living room and dove for it.

"Hello, Hello! Lance!" she shouted into it.

"Lance? No, this is Peggy. Are you ready? I'm just about to leave."

"Oh, Peg," she said, "Lance called."

"He did? Where is he?"

"I don't know."

"You don't know? Does he know about his dad?"

"I think so."

"You think so? What on earth did you two talk about?"

"That's just it; I don't know much of anything. The connection was so bad I couldn't really hear him. It was just a bunch of static, and then we were disconnected. He hasn't called back."

"Always the man of mystery," Peggy replied. "Listen, you better be ready; I'll pick you up in ten. You wouldn't want to miss your train, especially now that you know Lance might—or might not—be there."

"Okay, smarty pants, I'll be ready. Maybe he'll call before you get here."

"I hope so, kid. See you in ten. Bye."

Lucy's hopes were dashed when Peg pulled up in front and honked the horn. She slipped on her jacket, kissed Freea—who was sitting on the shelf next to Lance's picture—picked up her suitcase and purse, and walked out the door. She locked her apartment and tucked the keys safely into the bottom of her purse. She was halfway down the stairs to the lobby when she heard a faint ringing. She stopped dead in her tracks and listened. There it was again. It was a phone, her phone. She dropped the suitcase, turned around, and bolted up the stairs. The phone rang again and then again. She fumbled to get her keys from the bottom of her purse. Again the phone rang. She dropped the keys. Another ring. *Was that six or seven?* She flung the door open and bounded for the phone as it rang one last time.

"Hello, Hello!" she shouted. A dial tone was her answer. As Lucy put the phone down she heard Peggy's horn honk again.

"Okay, okay, I'm coming," she shouted to no one.

She boarded the train at eight a.m. for the five-hour ride to Cincinnati. There she waited an hour and a half before catching the eastbound train to Peebles. She wandered around the station and decided to buy a sandwich to eat on the train. Once aboard, she settled back in her seat and watched as the world rolled by the window. The train made several stops in small towns. It was at one of these depots that an old Indian woman boarded and chose the seat directly across from her. The old woman stared intently at her. Lucy smiled and nodded hello but began to feel uncomfortable.

"I'm Lucy," she said at last, extending her hand.

"I know who you are. You are going to Peebles for the Christian service for Mr. McKellen."

Lucy was shocked. "Yes, that's right. But how do you know that?"

"Daughter of my daughter is Littlefeather. She told me you belong to Kackawan Qisus and you would be on this train."

Lucy fumbled her words, but she managed to say, "Kwe-kwe, how do you do?" She added awkwardly, "I like Littlefeather very much."

"Unh," grunted the old woman. "She has the gift from me. I too will attend the Christian ceremony of Mr. McKellen. He has been very good to my family, my people. Many will miss him. He goes now to rest and collect the rewards for his kindness."

"Do you know Lance?" Lucy asked.

"Since they found him. I was at my daughter's when her husband brought him in."

"Found him? Brought him in?" Lucy questioned.

"From the mountain."

"I don't understand."

"He was two years, maybe three. Not a stitch of clothes. My daughter wanted to keep him, but her husband said no. He was for the McKellens."

Lucy's thoughts were swimming. Lance was adopted? "Where did your daughter's husband find him?"

"In the great meadow beside the waterfall, on the mountain behind the McKellen farm. It was the time when the leaves fall. There had been a storm the night before and a great ball of lightning rested on the mountain. My daughter's husband thought it was a sign from the Great Spirit that the hunting would be good. He went out early in the morning and came back a few hours later with the boy. The child was naked, wearing only a necklace." Lucy had seen this necklace many times. Lance never took it off.

The old woman went on, "My daughter's husband said his bow was bent with aim at a great buck when it jumped behind big bushes. When Talking Bear crept closer to the bushes, he saw the child standing in a clearing surrounded by mist. That is why we call him Kackawan Qisus, son of the mist."

Lucy couldn't believe what she was hearing. "So your daughter's husband took him to the McKellens."

"Yes, that same day. I made for him a robe from a feed sack. Mr. McKellen was in the field visiting his son's grave when Talking Bear and the child approached. When Mr. McKellen looked at him, the boy leaped into his arms.

Mr. McKellen took the child home and gave him to his wife. She was sick with sorrow since their baby died two summers before."

"Did they ever find out who left him in the field?"

"Girl, you did not listen to me. He came from the mist out of the Great Spirit's light on the mountain. You know what I say is true. You are his."

At these words, a tear formed in Lucy's eye. She put her head down in an attempt to hide it and fumbled in her purse for a tissue. She spotted the sandwich and offered half to the old woman. She accepted it, grinning widely. "You are kind like Kackawan Qisus. Are you strong like him too?" Lucy did not know what to say. "He would not have chosen you if he did not know that to be true."

They ate the sandwich and rode along in silence, watching as the sprawling land gave way to small hills, which eventually grew bigger, turning into foothills and then mountains.

Paul and Littlefeather were standing side by side on the platform when the train arrived at the station. Lucy and Littlefeather's grandmother alighted together. They sat in the front seat of Quicksilver—Lance's truck—with Paul, and Littlefeather rode with the suitcases in the bed. They first stopped at Littlefeather's grandfather's farm and left Grandmother off. Littlefeather joined them in the front seat for the rest of the ride. They wound up the mountain on the same dirt road Lucy had traveled two summers before the first time she visited the farm.

Lance's mom lay down to rest when Paul and Littlefeather left for the station. She made them promise to bring Lucy straight up to her room as soon as they returned. "Lucy dear," she said, half rising when Lucy entered the bedroom. "Come over here, dear, and let me look at you. You are as pretty as ever I remember you. Dad is well pleased that you have come."

"Oh, Mom," Lucy said, sinking to her knees at the bedside. "I'm so very sorry. I…"

"Hush, child. We would all have him back if we could, but this was his time to let the sorrows of this life pass. We must thank God he'll be receiving his peace and time of rest." Lucy rested her head on the bed near Mrs. McKellen's chest and let her tears gently fall. As Lance's mom stroked and patted her head, she began to hum the old Irish tune "Tura Lura Lural." Lucy had heard Mr. McKellen whistle it on countless occasions as he worked around the barns or in the fields. She stopped and whispered, "Lucy, I don't want to stay here without him."

"I know, Mom." Lucy felt bad. She wanted to comfort Lance's mom but she could think of nothing more to say.

Paul walked through the door. "Mom, I'm sorry to be disturbing you, but Father Greeley is here to talk to you about the service tomorrow. He said he would come back later if you aren't up for it just now."

"Oh heavens, I'll never be up for it. But he's taken his time to drive out here, so I won't be sending him off till it's done. Tell him to come on up here. You take Lucy downstairs and give her a cup of tea. Have Littlefeather bring up a tray for the Father and me."

"Sure thing, Ma."

"And Paul, put a shot of the Irish in the pot for the Father would you, just the way he'd be having it if Dad were here. And put some of those little biscuits on the tray, the ones that your dad so loved. The Father shared his fondness for the sweet of them. Lucy, you go get some rest so you will be at your best when Lance comes tomorrow."

Paul took Lucy's hand to help her up. He said, "Mom, we couldn't reach Lance. He doesn't know."

"Of course he knows, dear. Lance knows. He'll be here. Lance always comes when he is needed. Dad doesn't need him now, but we do. Don't we, Lucy? He'll come. You'll see; he'll be here."

Lucy felt the warm tears run down her face. "Of course he will, Mom," she made herself say as she turned and walked from the room.

At the foot of the stairs stood a small, elderly man with silver hair. His face was worn and squinted, but his eyes were clear and twinkling. He was dressed in the old style: long, black priest's garb with a white cord belt tied around the middle. A big chain with a crucifix hung from his neck around the starched white collar.

"Father Greeley, this is Miss Lucy Cavanagh. Lucy, this is Father Greeley."

"Lucy, yes of course, Lance's fiancée. How are you, my dear?" the Father asked as he extended his hand.

Lucy didn't know what to say. The word *fiancée* surprised her. She held out her hand, but the old priest pulled her close and embraced her as he kissed her lightly on both sides of her face. "How I love your intended," the Father said. "Now, there is a man handpicked by Jesus himself to do His work. I have known him since..." He paused and looked thoughtfully a moment then went on. "...Since he was a wee lad. Is he here yet?" Lucy shook her head. "Did he tell you that I had my eye on him to go to seminary? Seeing you now, I have no doubt what changed his mind."

"Now, Father," Paul broke in. "It's not fair you putting that on Lucy. Lance made up his mind on that before they met."

"He did now, did he?" the father said thoughtfully, still holding Lucy in his gaze. "Well, whenever he decided, I'm sure after meeting this one I'd be hard put to change his mind." Lucy felt a little like she had just been disparaged.

Paul rescued her from the old priest's glare. "You go on up to Ma now, Father. Littlefeather will be bringing up some tea in a while."

"Of course, my boy. How is your mother?"

"Strangely calm, I think," Paul answered.

"Oh, that's the shock of it all. I've seen it a hundred times. The grief will arrive soon enough. After the planting, in the quiet of the evening, that is when it will come upon her. That is when she'll be needing you all close by."

"Yes, Father," Paul murmured.

The old man slowly walked up the stairs to attend to his duty while Paul and Lucy went into the kitchen. Littlefeather was like a bee flitting around gathering cups and saucers and spoons, preparing the serving tray. Paul put his arms around her from behind. She stood still a moment while he held her.

Lucy looked lovingly at this odd couple: he, a tall lumbering white man with sandy red hair and she, a small Native American with long, thick, dark braids. Lucy locked her arms in front of herself imagining an embrace like that from Lance.

"Put some Irish in the pot for the Father," Paul instructed as he released her, "and some biscuits on the tray." Littlefeather had already done all that, but she made no comment. She poured a cup from the steaming pot for Lucy. Lucy thanked her, but as was her custom Lillefeather did not respond. She picked up the tray and carried it out of the room.

"Well, I'm off to do the evening chores," Paul said as he put on his old ball cap. "I have to start earlier without Dad." He looked away. "I've carried your bag to Lance's old room, Lucy, where you stayed before. Just make yourself at home." He opened the door and started to leave then he turned and said, "I'm glad you're here."

"Thanks, Paul," Lucy said to his back as he hurried from the house.

She sat alone now in the kitchen, thinking about how the father had used the word *fiancée*. Marriage was a word that had never been spoken between them, but she wondered if Lance had told others that he intended to marry her. She had thought of no other man since their first kiss in the garden the night they met. She truly believed that after Lance finished his research they would be together. Maybe they'd get a small farm nearby or live right here with Mom, Paul, and Littlefeather. She closed her eyes and felt happily lost in this daydream.

When she opened her eyes again, Littlefeather was sitting quietly at the table. "Oh, Littlefeather," Lucy said, "I didn't hear you."

"Tomorrow night after the Christian service, my people will have a celebration for Powpow." Powpow is what Littlefeather always called Lance's dad. Lucy didn't know why. "You will come with me. Paul will stay with his mother." This declaration was Littlefeather's way of asking.

"Sure, I'd be happy to," Lucy said.

"Good." Littlefeather nodded her head much like her grandmother had. Lucy could see the resemblance now in her face.

Lucy finished her tea and went up to her room to change. She came down wearing jeans and carrying her cowboy boots. Littlefeather was not to be found, so she walked out on to the porch, sat down in the old rocker, and pulled on her boots. Maxwell, the big old basset hound who always lay sleeping on the porch, popped up his head to look her over. "Hey, Max," she said. Recognizing no threat, he opened his mouth in a wide yawn. He put his head back down on his paws and gave forth a whine. "Oh Max, you miss Dad, don't you?" He rolled on his back, exposing his stomach. Lucy took it as an invitation and bent over him to massage his underside. She remembered how in the evenings, after dinner, Lance's dad would sit on the very same chair with Max at his feet. He would smoke his pipe and rub Max's tummy with a socked foot.

She headed out toward the animal barn where she heard someone rambling around. It was Paul. He was shoveling a stall and talking to himself. "You have to be the man now, you numby. Dad is gone and it's likely Lance will never be back, to stay anyway. So you need to step up to the plate. Grow up, Pauly. Stop the sniveling and grow up."

Lucy took a few paces back and started whistling to signal her approach. "Hey, Paul, can I help?" she asked as she came up behind him.

"Sure, Lucy." He sniffed and wiped his nose on his sleeve. "Why don't you put out the oats and fill the water buckets. Lock the stall gates open so the horses can get in if it storms tonight."

"You got it," Lucy said. "What about the chickens? Did you feed them yet?"

"No, I haven't gotten to it. You can do that too, if you will, while I tend the cows."

"Sounds like a plan." Lucy fell back into the old routine she had learned from Lance two years ago. She loved the farm, the animals, this way of life. She wondered if she would ever have it as her own.

The dark had closed in and encased the farmhouse by the time they finished in the barn and went walking back to it. "Thanks for the help, Lucy," Paul said. "We all better get some sleep if we can. We have a rough time ahead of us tomorrow."

Though she didn't think she would, Lucy fell asleep almost immediately after sinking under the covers in Lance's old bed. She felt comfortable, like she was home. She dreamed she was lying in the grass under the old willow next to the small grave. Lance was there, talking with his dad. Dad began to whistle and then Lance joined in. They soon locked arms and started dancing. A wind swirled around and swooped them into the sky. Lucy hopped up and tried to grab hold of them, but they were gone. Takota ran up to her and she jumped upon his bare back. She felt arms lock around her from behind. It was Lance. They were flying on Takota over the farm. Lance's mom and dad were dancing now next to the tiny grave below. As they danced they grew younger and soon a little blond boy danced with them.

The alarm rang and her eyes sprang open. She dressed quickly and went down to help Littlefeather in the kitchen. The service was to be at ten followed by the interment. After that, there would be a luncheon in the basement, hosted by the women's Martha and Mary Society, who would do all the cooking, serving and cleaning up as was the custom in the small church.

Paul was sitting at the table having a cup of coffee. Lucy poured a cup and sat with him. "Where's Mom and Littlefeather?" she asked.

"In Mom's room. Littlefeather is helping her get dressed. I'm worried about Mom, Lucy; she's talking weird. She said Lance was here with Dad last night."

"What?" Lucy exclaimed.

"Why don't you go on up and talk to her." Lucy didn't have to be asked. She had already bolted from the table. She rushed back up the stairs into Mrs. McKellen's bedroom.

Mrs. McKellen sat at the vanity. Littlefeather stood behind her brushing her hair. "Oh, good morning, child. How did you sleep?" She had a strange smile on her face.

"Well. I slept well." Lucy was surprised to see she was wearing the same dress she had worn in her dream. "How about you?"

"I took that pill Dr. Fowler gave me and I was out pretty fast. I was sleeping just fine when Dad and Lance came in to wake me."

"Dad and Lance!" Lucy exclaimed.

"Oh Lucy, I have wonderful news. They told me I don't have to stay. I don't have to stay here without him. Did you see Lance last night, Lucy? Did you?"

"Yes, Mom, I saw him. We rode Takota."

"Oh, that's right. Dad and I saw you. You looked so happy riding together. It's going to be all right, isn't it, Lucy?"

Lucy thought this talk was a combination of shock and grief and the sedative the doctor had given her. "Yes, Mom, it's going to be just fine."

Littlefeather started to pin her mother-in-law's hair up in the way she had worn it for years, but Mrs. McKellen stopped her. "No, dear, leave it down. Dad likes it down." Littlefeather did as she was told with no argument.

"Lucy dear, please bring me my blue pumps from the closet, will you? They were Dad's favorites. He bought them for me as an anniversary gift to wear when we'd go dancing." Now she turned toward the mirror and looked beyond what the others could see. "Oh, that man loves to dance."

Lucy brought the pumps from the back of the closet and knelt down to help Mrs. McKellen get them on. Her feet were so swollen it took several tries. Lucy pleaded with her after a couple failed attempts to wear a more comfortable pair, but Lance's mom wouldn't hear of it; she was determined. Finally, with the help of an old shoehorn, she was pried into them. Her feet bulged over the tops.

"They must be terribly uncomfortable," Lucy said. "Mom, why don't you wear your slippers? No one will mind."

"Oh no, dear. Dad likes these. It'll be okay. I won't be in them long. Come on now, help me up. We must be on our way." The two girls—each on a side—helped Mrs. McKellen down the stairs and into the kitchen. "Where is Pauly?" she asked as they paused at the big empty table.

"He's bringing the truck up to the door," Littlefeather replied.

"Oh good, and where has Lance gotten off to?"

Lucy felt her heart sink. *Oh God, Miracle of Miracles, please bring Lance home to be with his family,* she prayed in silence while tears slid down her cheeks.

Littlefeather spoke now: "He has taken Takota for a ride."

"What did you say?"

"Takota is not in the field. Lance must have come and taken him for a ride."

"He will probably meet us at the church then," Mrs. McKellen added. "Let's get on now. Are you all right, Lucy?"

Lucy was puzzled. Was Littlefeather just trying to placate her mother-in-law, or had she really seen Lance? She didn't know what to say. But she didn't want to dash Mrs. McKellen's hopes. "Sure, I'm fine. We better get going." The two girls walked out the door together as Mrs. McKellen turned for a last look around the kitchen.

"Psst… Littlefeather, did you really see Lance?" Lucy whispered to the Indian girl as they waited for the widow.

"Not with my eyes," she whispered back.

Paul hopped out of the truck and opened the passenger door for his mother to slide in. Lucy slid in beside her, and Littlefeather climbed into the back of the truck as she had done with the luggage on the way from the train station. Paul had placed a heavy blanket atop a crate in the bed to help her ride easier.

The church's parking lot was full of old cars, trucks, buggies and wagons with a tractor or two and an occasional horse tethered here and there. Paul stopped the truck at the front doors and Lucy slid out. He lifted his wife from the truck bed and came around to help his mother. A horse and rider that came racing up from behind the church caught Lucy's eye. In one smooth motion as the mighty horse halted, the rider jumped from its back. He took off his hat in midair, and by the time his feet were on the ground Lucy was at his side. They embraced and kissed.

"My darling, I'm so glad you're here. It means a lot to my family and to me."

"Lance! I'm sorry about your father."

"Thank you, my love." He kissed her hands. "Dad is fine now."

"Yes, I know. But I'm very worried about your mother."

Mrs. McKellen stood quietly waiting for the lovers. Lance turned to her and held her in an embrace. Paul was next. As the brothers shook hands, Lance pulled him close for a hug. Paul started sobbing. "Lance, Dad's gone. He's gone, Lance. What am I gonna do now?"

"You are going to become the man Dad raised you to be, Pauly." Paul sniffed hard, wiped his eyes, lifted his head, and nodded. "That's it, brother. Dad is proud of you, and so am I."

Littlefeather stood quietly, as she always did, waiting for her chance to greet her brother. Lance took her by each shoulder and softly kissed her forehead. Leaning in close, he whispered something to her in her native tongue. Littlefeather nodded her head.

The bells on the church peeled a ten-o'clock call to service and people began hurrying inside. As soon as the bells stopped, music playing within drifted out the doors to meet them. Lance put one arm around his mother and the other around Lucy. Paul was on the other side of his mom supporting her by the arm and holding the hand of his wife. The little band walked up the whitewashed stairs of the little country church into the dark mouth of the open doors.

Father Greely stood in his funeral vestments with an altar boy at each side. One was a Native American boy called Rush, short for Rushing Water, and the other a red-headed, freckle-faced kid named Jimmy McCrackin. The two had been best buds for years. Lucy and Lance ran into them once when they were riding Takota. The boys had been fishing the stream that ran through the back of the McKellen's farm and proudly showed Lance their catch. They got taller in the time that had separated them all from that summer, but their eyes still lit up to see Lance. Lance greeted the Father with a hug then reached out to both boys, putting a hand on each one's shoulder.

"Are we ready then?" the Father asked.

Lance looked to his mother for the answer. "Yes, Father. Let's get started," she replied.

The casket stood open at the front of the church. Mr. McKellen's body lay with its hair slicked back and lips positioned in a half smile. He had on his Sunday suit jacket with a blue shirt that matched the color of his wife's dress. Lucy again thought of her dream and vividly recalled that these were the very same clothes she had seen them dancing in.

The family started its ascent up the aisle past a group of twenty or more Native Americans that lined the walls at the back of the church, past friends and neighbors and distant family members who now inhabited the pews along both sides of the aisle. They approached the casket, and then silently took in the form that lay before them. Mrs. McKellen turned slowly toward Paul and Littlefeather. She took their hands, kissed Paul on the cheek and said, "God bless you both. You are the man of the house now, Pauly." She turned to Lance and, taking his hand, she put it on Lucy's and held them together. "You are free to fulfill your destiny now, my boy. God could not have given us a better son." She kissed his cheek lovingly and turned back toward her husband. With a smile on her face, she climbed atop the little bench used for kneeling in front of the casket. She bent over his body and whispered softly. She kissed his cold head tenderly, straightened up, and took a backwards step off the platform.

Her arms went straight to her sides. Her purse slipped off her arm and hit the floor. Her body followed, falling stiffly backwards to land on the floor between her two sons. There were gasps and screams from around the room. Lance bent down and took one of his mother's hands, placing his fingers under her neck to find a pulse. He looked up at Paul and shook his head. Someone in a pew whispered loudly, "She's dead," and the echo spread through the church.

Paul dropped to his knees on the other side of his mother, and Littlefeather moved in close to him, her hands on his back. She looked over at Lucy, making a motion with her eyes for her to look at something. Lucy, who had fallen on her knees next to Lance, looked to where Littlefeather indicated. There on the floor in the middle of the aisle, about three feet from where Mrs. McKellen lay, were the blue pumps Lucy had pried onto her feet. They were standing upright side by side. It was as if Mrs. McKellen had risen up out of them and fallen over dead.

Lance took charge to quell the disquieted gathering. He first made sure his family was okay, then he went to the old priest who stood frozen, repeating over and over again, "Oh dear, oh dear, oh dear…"

Taking the holy man by his shoulders and giving him a gentle shake, Lance instructed, "Father Greely, please ask everyone to sit down and remain calm." He turned to the altar boys and sent Rush for the sheriff and Jimmy to fetch Dr. Fowler. He walked over to the distraught organ player, took her hand, and asked if she would play something to soothe the tension. "Maybe you could lead the congregation in song while we determine what to do next. Would you do that for me please, Mrs. Lundy?" She was a woman in her mid-eighties and had been a widower since she was forty. She was a fixture in the church, playing organ and teaching Sunday school faithfully. Over the many years she never missed a Sunday or a chance to serve the Lord. She loved Lance like a grandson.

"Of course I will, my boy," she said. They embraced, offering each other the strength that comes from the comfort of a loving touch.

The music began and softly rolled over the congregation like a calming wave. With the doctor and the sheriff standing by, Lance and Paul picked up the body of their mother and carried it to a small room off the rear of the vestibule. Littlefeather picked up her beloved mother-in-law's purse and Lucy once again carried the blue pumps to Lance's mom. As the congregation sang "Peace in the Valley," Father Greeley took his leave to join the small group in the back room.

After ten minutes the old priest came back and stood by the casket. The family came in next, moving to the front row pew while the doctor and sheriff rejoined their family members who sat among the waiting congregation. Lance addressed the crowd.

"Thank you everyone for coming out to honor my family in this beautiful way. As you may have already surmised, my mother has decided to join my father today. Though it is good and right that we mourn their passing, we must remember that the light that they carried can never be extinguished and will go on to live within us all if we will allow it. The spirits that inhabited these bodies have left and traveled beyond the place where sadness, pain, or sickness can reach them. For that reason, even though we mourn their deaths, we must also celebrate their life-force and the liberation it has now found. We have asked Father Greely to go ahead with the planned sacraments for my father and to extend them now for my mother as well." With that Lance took his place between Paul and Lucy in the pew.

"Lance, I'm so sorry," Lucy whispered as she hugged his arm.

"It's part of the cycle, Lucy. It is as it should be. Mother has been blessed and will not have to suffer loneliness as you do." He looked deeply into her eyes. "For that, my love, it is I who am sorry."

After the service, several of the Native American men helped Paul and Lance load two pinewood caskets into the back of Quicksilver. Lucy rode with Lance on Takota and they followed the truck back to the farm. Under the tree where Littlefeather had found Mr. McKellen, two graves had been dug next to the little cross bearing the name Windson.

Lucy wondered how a second grave could have been prepared so soon. Two men stood with shovels off to the side. Lance dismounted and then helped Lucy down from Takota's back. He approached the men speaking only in Algonquin. Paul backed the truck as near to the site as possible and the four men lowered the caskets from the truck bed into their earth beds. This done, the two men departed, leaving the family to be together a last time. Paul and Lance shoveled the dirt to cover their parents while Littlefeather chanted a lament, and Lucy voiced the 23rd psalm as her contribution to the moment. The four stood together in silence. Finally, Lance reminded them they should go back to the church for the luncheon the ladies had prepared.

Lucy couldn't remember much about the luncheon, only that Lance was kept busy greeting and accepting condolences from church members and friends of the family. Lucy did recall vividly the celebration that evening around a bonfire at the foot of the hill where three graves now stood. Littlefeather's grandmother was there along with all the Native Americans Lucy had seen standing in the back of the church, and many others as well. She remembered watching Lance dance with the men—stripped to the waist, barefoot, stomping, jumping, circling the fire, shouting, howling, exorcizing his grief. Then later he enfolded her in his arms and watched as Littlefeather danced with the women, tears glistening from the fire light as they ran down her cheeks. They all slept there on blankets under the stars.

Returning from her memories to the heartbreak she now owned, she slipped into her prayer language and let the angels take charge over her.

She was at peace in the morning when she woke and joined Myra for their morning yoga session. They ate breakfast and then walked on the beach. She laughed often, listening to Myra's funny little tales of things Michael had done while growing up.

"Then there was the time, let's see, Michael was about six. We were sitting in our pew at St. Peter's. Michael, all dressed up in a cute little suit, was sitting between William and me like a precious little angel. I looked down and saw the pocket on his jacket moving. 'Michael Donegan,' says I, 'just what is it you have in that pocket?' 'Fred,' his precious little face says back to me. 'And just who is Fred?' I say to him. 'He is my frog, Granny Myra. See.' He pulled out a large, slimy creature and put it right in my face. I screamed and swatted it away with my hand. It flew up and landed on Mrs. Inch's bosom. She hollered and the poor frog leaped right onto Mr. Logan's bald head. Well, the whole place was in an uproar. Michael couldn't stand it that Fred was being swatted here and there and went to his rescue. So of course Father Percy, a penguin of a man he was, stopped the service and everyone was in a dither. Michael grabbed Fred and William grabbed Michael and escorted them both outside. I thought the poor boy would be gettin' a good lickin' for sure. But when I found the two of them, they were sitting under a tree just as happy as larks, and Fred was back inside Michael's pocket.

"'William, just what is it that you said to the boy,' I asked him later.

"'Well,' he says, 'I asked him, 'Why did you do it? Whatever possessed you to bring that frog to church?'

"'You did, Grandpa,' he says.

"'I did?' William asked.

"'Yes, Grandpa. You told me that Jesus said the Gospel should be preached to every creature. So I thought Fred should hear it so he could tell his family, and they could all go to heaven someday.'

"Of course William couldn't give Michael a lickin' for that." Finished with her tale, Myra sat down on the sand and picked up a stone that had been warmed by the sun.

"Of course not," Lucy chuckled and plunked down next to her.

Myra moved the stone from hand to hand then handed it to Lucy to inspect. "Aye, he has a good heart in him, that lad. But it has had its share of breakin', what with his mother and then Kathleen."

"His mother?" Lucy questioned.

"Oh, there I go again. Sorry, dear. That is not a tale for me to tell." She snatched the stone from Lucy's hand and put it in her pocket. "I just couldn't bear to see him hurt again, my Michael." She stood and headed back up the beach toward Glen Eden.

Lucy had no doubt of the genuine affection Myra felt for Michael, and somehow, after listening to the tales about her "precious little lad," Michael didn't seem to be quite the arrogant brute her mind had made him. Lance had told her Michael was an honorable man of noble blood, but Lance also said that he was William's son. She was sure he had been wrong on that point.

18 – Fred, Chants, and Charms

"Fred, it's so nice to see you again."

"Myra, dear Myra, you look younger every time I lay my eyes on you."

"Now, Freddy, you'll be getting a pimple on your tongue for lying."

"I certainly hope not. I want to enjoy that wonderful dinner I smell." They both laughed as they fondly embraced.

"Miss Lucy Cavanagh, this is Fred Loch," Michael said, looking at her for the first time since he'd walked in the door. After their last phone conversation, while he was bedding Maureen, he was glad he didn't have to face her alone. He didn't know why he should, but he felt ashamed. Nevertheless, her smile was pleasant, and he was happy to see it again.

"Hello, Mr. Loch," Lucy said.

"Fred, please," he said, taking her hand to his lips. "I am charmed. May I call you Lucy?"

"Certainly, Fred."

"Just call him blockhead," Michael said, giving Fred a shove away from her with one hand while loosening his tie with the other. Fred shoved back, so Michael gave him a little slap on the back of his head.

"Oh goodness," Myra said, "you boys never grow up. Lucy, I swear, every time they are together they revert back to their school days. Now go along the both of you; get changed and wash up for your dinner. Lucy and I will get the table ready, so hurry along."

"Yes, ma'am," Fred said. Picking up his bag he bounded up the stairs like he knew exactly where he was going.

Michael unzipped a pocket in the front of his bag and pulled out a small package. He handed it to Lucy and said, "Please see she has this to use for her dinner." He gave Myra a kiss on the forehead and then launched up the stairs after Fred.

Lucy tore back the tissue exposing a small white, ceramic bowl. It was adorned with tiny purple violets and had the name FREEA written in large gold letters across the front. On the bottom of the bowl was stamped "Thank you for supporting Handicapped Artists of America. Mouth painted by Ty Gordon."

"Michael," she called up the stairs after him, "this was very thoughtful of you. It's lovely."

He turned and smiled, making a little gesture with his hand. Lucy was glad Michael was back at home again. She was looking forward to telling him about the vision of Lance she'd had via Angus's smoke ring. After all, she thought, he'd handled the incident in the stone circle pretty well. At least he hadn't treated her like she was stark raving mad. She had no idea that the real purpose of Fred's visit was to evaluate her sanity. She was hoping Michael would find some time to search for *The Green Book*. She was sure he'd look in earnest once she told him what Lance had said about it. But all that would have to wait for now; she couldn't expect him to desert his guest tonight.

Myra and Lucy busied themselves in the kitchen. They had worked that afternoon preparing a feast and now wanted to get it hot to the table. Lucy carried in the dishes of food while Myra took a batch of soda biscuits from the oven. "Oh boy, roast mutton and colcannon," Fred said as the two men entered the dining room. They had shed their suits and ties and sported polo shirts with casual slacks.

"Freddy, you sit there next to Lucy," Myra directed, walking in with a basket of biscuits in her hands.

"My pleasure, Myra dear," Fred replied.

"And Michael, you come sit next to me across from Fred." Michael and Fred pulled back the chairs of their lady tablemates and stood until they were seated. Then Michael offered Grace. It was a happy reunion. Lucy sat mostly silent as the two old buddies bantered back and forth. She couldn't help laughing along with them as they related old stories from their school days. She gathered from what they said that Fred had been to Glen Eden a number of times in the past and that he had known Kathleen well.

Fred was going on with a long-winded story about a soccer game they had played in while Michael sat watching Lucy. It was hard for him to take his eyes off her. He watched as her lips touched her water glass and her head tilted back when she swallowed, exposing her neck and throat. She was hypnotic to him.

"Isn't that right, Michael? Michael?" Fred repeated.

Michael had heard nary a word of Fred's discourse because he was so captivated by his thoughts of Lucy, and now he was asked to verify some point of it. "Right you are, Freddy boy," he said, though he didn't have a clue as to what had just been said. "Here, have some more mutton." He shoved the platter toward Fred and made a vow to himself to pay closer attention to his old friend for the rest of the meal.

"I always knew it was you, Michael, and now after all these years you admit to it."

Michael wondered just what it was he had admitted to, so he thought fast and recovered. "The only thing I'm admitting, Fred, is that you're an idiot." Actually, Fred had related a prank that was pulled on their soccer coach. Someone had filled his car with frogs. Michael was caught green handed, so to speak, but claimed he was innocent and that he was only trying to get the frogs out of the car. Since no one came forward to vouch for his story, he received the blame and was benched for the next three games. Michael knew full well who it was that had put the frogs in the car, but he wouldn't give him up. It was Kathleen's brother James, his old roommate.

When they were finished with the meal, Fred excused himself to go outside for a smoke and invited Michael. "You go along, Freddy. I'll help the girls with the dishes and then I'll join you."

"Michael, I swear you are more Scot than Irish, too cheap you are to buy Myra a dishwasher."

"He tried, Freddy, but I refused the contraption when it was delivered. I'll not have a thing like that around here. I'm perfectly fine to do up a dish or two."

Lucy stood, cleared the plates, and carried them to the kitchen. Myra started to follow her with a load, but Michael stopped her. "Here, Myra, let me take those. You go on out and keep Fred company. I'll help Lucy wash these up. I want a chance to talk with her about something."

"That's fine, dear. And Michael, I think it is a good idea that you've asked Freddy here. I'm afraid Lucy may need more help than we can give her."

"Why do you say that? Has something happened?"

"Well, last night I couldn't fall off to sleep, so I went out on the balcony to get some air. I heard Lucy talking to someone on the front steps. I looked down but there wasn't anyone there, save her kitty."

"Maybe she was just talking to Freea, Myra. Heaven knows, you and Grandfather used to talk to Boomer like he was your very own child."

"Sure, Michael, we did, but it was not her kitty Lucy was talking to; it was Angus. It was a very still night. I could hear her plainly. She was talking to Angus, asking him about Lance."

"I see."

"There is something else, Michael. I think that Lucy has been troubled for some time. Do you know anything about her family?"

"No, Myra, I don't," he admitted.

"Well, perhaps she'll confide in you, dear. I want you to help her if you can. I've grown fond of her in this short time. She is very special."

"I think so too, Myra. Run along now and see to Freddy." He carried his assortment of dishes to the kitchen and found Lucy already busy at the sink. Freea was sitting by her feet licking her paws. She looked up and meowed when he entered. "Hello, Miss Freea. You are looking well." He set the dishes down beside Lucy and bent to rub his finger under Freea's chin. She meowed again. "Well, you're welcome," he said, peeking around the corner to see that the bowl he brought for her had been licked clean. He washed his hands and picked up a towel for drying.

"No, Michael, you go on now and be with your friend. I'm more than happy to do these up myself." She was hoping he would stay.

"That was a fine meal you and Myra prepared, and I'm happy to do my share." He dried a platter and took it to its place on the shelf. "Myra tells me she's grown very fond of you. I hope she's given you some time to yourself."

"I've grown fond of her as well, and I've enjoyed being here. How could I not? Did she tell you we started a sewing project together?"

"You have now? No, she hasn't mentioned it. And what is it you'll be sewing?"

"I drove her to Holland and she bought reams of gorgeous material to make fancy dresses for girls who can't afford to buy one."

"Well, that's a grand idea."

"We already have one designed and the material cut for it. Maybe we'll have it done to show you before you leave again."

"I'm looking forward to it. Will you be modeling it for me?"

Lucy laughed. "Sure, if you like. I'll feel like Cinderella."

He saw an opening to get her to talk about her past. "Did you go to your high school prom, Lucy?"

"What? My prom? Oh… I…" She stopped washing the dishes and closed her eyes. "I did. I did go. My older sister helped me make my dress. I didn't have money to buy one, so we used the curtains from her apartment. She was an excellent seamstress. It was by necessity, really. She has six children. Her husband is in the army, so they've never had much money. I learned to sew helping her." She opened her eyes and started scrubbing away at the dishes. She hadn't shared her family with anyone since Lance.

Michael was leaning on the counter watching her. She stopped scrubbing and looked at him. "What?" she asked.

"Oh, nothing. I was just enjoying that little trip into your past. I hope you will take me there more often."

"Well, that's kind of you," Lucy chuckled, "because I've enjoyed a trip or two into your past via Myra's memory of her darling little Michael."

"Oh no, now just what stories has she been telling? No wait, maybe I don't want to know. Just tell me this: did they leave me with any dignity in your eyes?"

"Of course, Michael. But it seems that you have a history of making trouble with frogs. Like the time you had all of Saint Peter's in an uproar because you took one to church."

"Oh that," he said, putting his head down and shaking it.

"Well, I think it was very sweet of you to be concerned about the salvation of your little friend."

"I'm afraid I was not thought of kindly by many in the congregation after that. I still get weird stares from some of the older members. They thought I was a demonic child. Did Myra tell you that after my mom died some of them had me to blame for it. They told my grandfather he should be having me exorcised."

"What? Oh my God, that is the cruelest thing I have ever heard of."

"Aye, Grandfather was fit to be tied. He didn't want to go back there after that, but dear Myra said that God in His grace forgives us our ignorance, and he expects us to forgive others theirs. She's right, of course."

"Michael, how did your mother die?" After she saw the look on his face, she regretted asking. "Oh, I'm sorry. That's none of my business really."

"No, it's just that I've never told it to anyone before. She took her own life. I was almost seven. Something happened between her and my father, something they couldn't get past. They never fought in front of me, but one night I heard my father screaming at her. I got up out of my bed, tiptoed down the stairs, and peeked at them. My mum was on her knees begging my father to forgive her. She said she had done it for them, and the result was so wonderful, how could he hate her so. He sat like a stone and wouldn't look at her. She was crying and he wouldn't comfort her. I wanted to go to her but I was afraid, so I crept back to my bed. That's the last look I had of my beautiful mother." He fell silent.

"Michael, I'm sorry," Lucy said softly.

He looked up at her from a far off place deep inside the plate he had been drying. He turned, put it on the shelf, picked up another to dry and continued: "Grandfather woke me in the morning and told me to get dressed because he was taking me fishing. There were strange people going in and out of my mother's room. My father wasn't around. Grandfather said he'd tell me about it when we got to the lake. We were sitting in this little rowboat that Grandfather kept to the ready on a small inland lake near here where he fished for bluegills. He said to me, 'Michael, this is a beautiful day, is it not?'

"'Yes, Grandfather,' I said.

"'This is a beautiful lake, don't you agree?'

"'It is, Grandfather,' I said.

"'God makes beautiful things and beautiful places, but none as grand as he's made His heaven. You believe that, don't you, Michael?'

"'Yes, I do, Grandfather,' I said.

"'Your mother believes that too, so she's asked the angels to take her there to have a look.'

"'Is she going to come back, Grandfather?' I asked.

"'No Michael. It is much too beautiful there. She would not be happy to come back here again. You do want her to be happy, don't you, Michael?'

"'Yes Grandfather, I do. But I want to go with her. Can I go there too, Grandfather? Can I go be with her?'

"'Sure, sure you can, my boy,' he said. 'But not today. Today we have fish to catch.' Grandfather and I never pulled so many fish from that lake as we did that day. I never went back to our home again. I stayed here with Myra and Grandfather. I didn't see my father for months. He didn't go to Mother's funeral. Grandfather told me it was because he had his own way of grieving. Whenever I'd start missing my mum, Grandfather would assign me some task to complete. He said things are easier when you take one day at a time and do the task at hand the very best you can."

Lucy wanted to reach out and hold the child that was conjured in her mind. Her heart broke for him as he related this painful tale, and she now knew what Myra had meant about his twice-broken heart.

"It was my father's decision to send me to boarding school in Ireland. I think so he wouldn't have to see me or feel guilty about not seeing me. It was Grandfather and Myra who would send for me on summer breaks and holidays; I only saw my father once a year after that. He'd show up here for an afternoon and we'd go for a swim or kick a ball around. We wouldn't talk about anything really. He'd ask about my studies or what sports I was playing. He never mentioned my mother to me, nor me to him. He had a problem with the drink and didn't make much of his life after she died. He was killed in an accident when his car didn't make dead man's curve and slammed into a tree, just up the way there on Blue Star Highway." He motioned with his head southward. "I was sixteen and had been expecting him here all summer. On the last weekend before I was to return to school, he phoned and said he had something important to tell me, something he said it was high time I knew about. He was on his way here when the accident happened. Whatever it was he wanted to tell me, he took it to his grave."

He finished drying the last dish and laid it atop the stack. The back door opened and Fred yelled in, "Hey, you two are missing a beautiful evening. Let's take a walk on the beach. What do you say?"

"Keep your shirt on, Freddy boy, I'll be right out," Michael hollered back. He was mad at himself for spending the time he had with Lucy talking about his own past when he really wanted to find out about hers. "Will you join us, Lucy?"

"I'd like that Michael. Let me grab a wrap. I'll meet you in the garden."

Michael strolled out the back door to meet Fred. Lucy walked the opposite way down the hall to pick up her shawl and decided to go out the front way and circle around the side of the house. As she walked down the steps, someone called to her. "Over here, Lucy," came a voice she thought was Fred's. She saw a figure standing in the shadows by the woods down the path that led by the stables.

"I thought you wanted to walk on the beach, Fred," she called out as she scampered off to meet him. "Michael's gone out back."

Meanwhile Fred and Michael stood in the garden near the back door waiting for her. "Did you hear that?" Michael asked.

"Hear what?"

"I thought I heard Lucy's voice from out front."

"Where is she anyway?"

"I don't know. She said she was going to grab a wrap and meet us."

"Women. She probably went upstairs to put on some lipstick," Fred scoffed.

"No, Lucy's not like that." He was worried about her. "Fred, you go through the house and see if she's there. I'm going to walk around front. I'll meet up with you in the drive."

Fred did as he was told, calling for Lucy as he walked through the house. Myra came out of the sitting room where she had retreated after returning from her stroll with him. "I'm looking for Lucy; have you seen her?"

"She was in the kitchen talking to Michael when I came in. I didn't want to disturb them, so I came in here. I haven't seen either one of them since. But I did hear someone go out the front door a few moments ago."

Fred moved out of the house onto the steps, and as he did he saw Michael running at full speed down the path to the woods. "Hey, Michael, what's up?" he called.

"It's Lucy," Michael yelled as he disappeared into the trees.

Fred dashed off at a dead run and caught up with Michael down the trail a bit. Lucy stood several yards in front of them murmuring in a strange tongue. She appeared to be in some sort of trance. Michael approached her slowly, speaking her name. When she didn't respond, he took her by the shoulders and shook her.

"Stop that," Fred ordered. "Let's get her back to the house."

Michael picked her up and carried her back down the trail with Fred bringing up the rear. He carried her into the sitting room and laid her on the couch. Her eyes were open and she was softly uttering words they couldn't understand. Her mind seemed far away from them.

"Good heavens, Michael. What's happened?" Myra asked as she rushed over to join the men standing over Lucy.

"Myra, go get her a blanket, will you?" Michael urged. She hurried off. While Michael covered her the best he could with her shawl, Fred bent down, checked her pulse, and proclaimed it normal.

Myra returned with an afghan, laid it over Lucy and took her hand. "She does feel cold." She tucked the afghan more tightly around her. "Michael, what on earth has happened to her?"

"I don't know really. I walked around the front of the house and saw her at the edge of the woods. I called to her and she turned toward me." He paused and looked first at Myra and then at Fred, trying to find words to explain just what he had seen. "It was as if something, or someone, jerked her into the shadows. I ran as fast as I could, and when I broke into the trees, she was just standing there, speaking in that strange language. I went up to her, but she looked right through me. What's happening to her Fred?" His voice was panicked.

"I don't know, old man. I'm not quite sure what we are dealing with here. Perhaps you better tell me everything you know about her, Michael. Start from the beginning. I believe you told me you met her when she came to you to ask about the painting of Angus."

Michael had already told Fred almost everything he knew about her on the plane trip from L.A., including what happened in the stone circle on Farmer Green's, that she had some sort of hallucination in which she saw her lost lover,

Lance. But he again recounted the events: how she had shown up at his office one morning wanting to buy the painting of Angus, and that she seemed to be upset by it; how she had returned to his office later that evening so they could pry off the frame; how she had gotten excited when they found the symbol hidden in a corner of the painting. "She said she'd seen it before but hasn't told me where. What's strange is that it looked familiar to me too. I think *I* may have seen it before in one of Grandfather's books, though I haven't been able to find it yet."

"What sort of symbol?" Fred asked.

"It's like an elongated cursive M turning into a C. In the center of the C there's an oval, and in the center of that is a sort of arrow pointing down with the shaft split into three parts that point up and out."

"Michael, you must try to remember where you have seen it. It could be key to what is going on here. When you have a moment, draw it for me will you, as closely as you can. Please continue."

"I felt sorry for her. She looked so desperate to learn more about Angus I invited her here to have a look through Grandfather's journals. You do recall, Fred, where Grandpa William got the painting?"

"Yes, Michael, I do. A farmer named Green painted it. I had many long discussions with your grandfather about it. I once offered to buy it from him."

"No kidding?"

"That's right, but if I am going to help Lucy, you must be one-hundred-percent honest with me."

"I am."

"Oh really, because I don't think your feeling sorry for Lucy had anything to do with why you invited her here."

"What do you mean by that?"

"He means, Michael, that you are attracted to her," Myra interjected.

"Myra," Michael snapped.

Fred jumped to her defense. "For Christ's sake, Michael, just admit it. Myra and I aren't dummies. You can't take your eyes off her."

"All right, so I admit she's a beautiful woman, and there is some attraction. But what does that have to do with anything?"

"Maybe nothing, maybe a lot. But Michael, I must reiterate: if you want me to help her, I must know everything." Michael glared at him and then began again, recounting all he knew. He related how Lucy had found mention of Lance in Grandfather William's journal, and that they learned his grandfather was funding the expedition from which Lance went missing. Fred took a notepad from his pocket and jotted down notes. "So Lucy didn't know of Lance's connection with your grandfather until she read it in the journal?"

"That's what she claims, Fred, and I believe her," Michael responded.

Now Fred's eyes shifted to Lucy. He studied her very closely as he asked loudly, "And why is it you believe her? After all, Michael, she could just be playing on your sympathies to get you to fall for her, which it appears you have." If Lucy could hear what was being said, she certainly didn't make any reaction that Fred could tell. But Michael did.

"What the hell, Fred, you don't know her to judge her that way. I tell you, she has shown no interest in me. It's Lance she's here for."

"I'm not judging her, Michael. I'm just trying to get to the bottom of what is going on. It is possible that a clever woman, especially one as beautiful as this, could play you for a fool." Fred studied Lucy very closely but again spotted no reaction.

Myra chimed in: "Michael, tell him about how she heard Kathleen's music."

Michael was annoyed. "Myra, first off, we don't know it was Kathleen's music."

"Don't be silly, of course it was. Freddy, Lucy told us she heard harp music accompanied by a woman's voice when none was being played anywhere in the house. She heard it again the day she saw her Lance. She said it was the music that led her to that clearing."

Fred, still studying Lucy's reactions, said, "Myra, she probably learned Kathleen played the harp and sang and was just making that up as part of her ploy."

"Nonsense, Freddy. I heard it too."

"Whoa, wait a minute, Myra, you heard it too?"

"Yes, I did, Freddy, and it was Kathleen. I'd swear it."

"What about you, Michael? Did you hear it as well?"

"No, Fred, I did not." Michael hated admitting that. He wanted to hear Kathleen's voice again—he longed for it. Why hadn't he heard it?

"Interesting." Fred made more notes. "Michael, please go on."

"Sunday when we returned from church, we went to our rooms to change. I had invited Lucy to my room to see my quilt."

"See your quilt?" Fred interrupted with a sarcastic tone.

"Yes, to see my quilt, the one Myra made for me. We had talked about it at breakfast. But when she came to my door, I couldn't let her in to see it because Megan was there."

Fred interrupted again, "In your room? Michael, she is a child." Shaking his head, he scribbled something on his pad.

"Get your mind out of the toilet, Fred. Shall I continue?"

"Go ahead."

"Myra said she'd seen Lucy run off through the garden, so I saddled the horses and went to look for her."

"What made you look on Green's farm?"

"We were planning to take a ride over there together. Lucy wanted to see if we could find the stone circle in the painting of Angus. Myra told us at the table that the path to the old farm intersected with the one that led along the top of the dunes. I thought maybe Lucy got anxious to go there. I found what I thought were her footprints in the sand at the edge of the yard, so I followed them. I rode up and saw her standing in a stone circle. Her back was to me, but she said my name rather loudly. I called in response, dismounted, and went to her side. She told me Lance had been there. When I said I hadn't seen him, she called me a liar and came at me. I restrained her, but she was acting so wildly I slapped her."

"Michael Donegan," Myra scolded.

"I didn't know what else to do. She was out of her head—wild, I tell you. She ran from me and I tackled her. She fought me again and I..." He turned away from them to finish. "I kissed her."

Myra gasped and Fred admonished, "Good God, Michael, that may not have been so wise."

"I don't know what came over me. I... I just lost control."

"Never mind. What happened next?"

"Well, she stopped fighting me and just lay there. I rolled off her and... and I apologized. I was humiliated, of course." He paused a moment then turned back toward them and continued. When he finished relaying to them Lucy's tale of what had happened in the circle, he said, "I realized that she was going through more than what I could help her with, so I concocted a story to keep her here. When she agreed to stay, I called and left a message for you."

"That was good thinking, chum. Is there anything else you can tell me?"

"I left her in the study Sunday night; I had to go run errands. But I saw her around 3 a.m. when I got home. She'd been in the study the whole time and told me she'd found other mentions of Lance in the journal. We walked upstairs together and said good night. I didn't see her the next morning. She took my car to go back to Detroit to pick up her things and get Freea, her cat. She left before I woke up. I saw her again briefly that evening when she returned and briefly the next morning before I left. She seemed to be fine."

"Her cat, where is it?" Fred asked.

"She'll not be far off. She was in the kitchen with us when we were doing up the dishes," Michael said.

"Good. Go find her, Michael, and bring her here. Cats sometimes have psychic connections with their owners. It may help to snap her out of this. Meanwhile, Myra can tell me what she's learned about Lucy while you were away."

Michael left the room to hunt for Freea. He looked first in the kitchen, but she wasn't there. So he took a walk through the study and then went upstairs. He pushed open the door to Lucy's room and stepped in. "Lucy's room," he thought. It was no longer Kathleen's room to him, a room to be avoided because of the hurt it caused his heart. It was now Lucy's room, and he felt the difference right away. He saw her clothes hanging in the closet and her hairbrush and combs on the vanity. He saw the roses he had sent her in a vase on the nightstand.

Something brushed against his pant leg. It was Freea. She must have come in behind him. She jumped up on the bed and meowed. He reached for her, and she let him pick her up. "Come on, old girl. Lucy needs our help." He cradled her in his arms and carried her back downstairs.

In the meantime, Myra told Fred what she had learned in her time with Lucy. (Fred had to keep redirecting her back to just the facts.) As Michael walked into the room with Freea, Myra proclaimed, "She was engaged to Ashley. You know Ashley, don't you, Fred?" In true Myra fashion, she didn't wait for his answer. "Why, of course you do; anyway, she broke his heart running off with this Lance."

"Is that right," Fred said, scribbling more notes. "I shall want to talk to him."

"No, that's not exactly right," Michael proclaimed. "It was sort of a joke engagement. I'll tell you about it later. Here is the Lady Freea." Freea leaped from his arms to the floor, ran over to the couch, and jumped up on Lucy's chest. She pounded her face into Lucy's chin and meowed. When Lucy didn't respond, she pumped Lucy's chest with her paws, finally giving up and lying down upon it as if on guard.

Michael kneeled alongside Lucy, who was still murmuring softly. He tried to make out what she was saying. "Myra," he said, "listen closely to her. Do you recognize that language?"

Myra bent down closer to her. "It sounds like she's speaking Old Gaelic," she said.

"Aye, that's what I thought." Michael recognized some of the words because Kathleen used to sing ballads in the native tongue. He jumped up, ran into the study, and came back with a tape recorder. He set it on the table nearest to her head. Freea stood up and meowed in disapproval, but Michael reassured her: "I would not hurt her, Freea. You know that about me, don't you, kitty?" Freea lay back down and licked Michael's hand.

Michael looked at Fred, who was poring over his notes. "Fred, is there anything we can do for her?"

"I think it best that we just leave her alone and wait for a while. She may be in some sort of trance or self-induced hypnosis. If she hasn't snapped out of it by the morning, we should transfer her to a hospital where she can be monitored. Meantime, she shouldn't be left alone tonight. We can take shifts sitting by her."

"Whatever you say, Fred. I'll stay with her now. You and Myra run off to bed. I'll wake you to take over if I need you."

Myra said good night by giving Michael a big hug. "She'll be all right, lovie. I'll pray. Call me if you need me."

"I will, Myra. Good night."

Fred bent and took Lucy's pulse again. "Seems to be fine," he said, turning to Michael. "Speaking as a doctor, I think it best if you try to leave this girl alone. Don't play with her, Michael. We don't know what her psyche can handle."

"So now you are convinced that she needs to be wary of me," Michael said sarcastically, "and not the other way around."

"I'm not sure of anything yet, Michael. I don't know just what we are dealing with. In order to determine that, I need to investigate this from all angles. Remember, you asked for my help."

"Sorry, Fred. I appreciate it. It's just… I care about her, Fred. I want to help her not hurt her."

"And I don't want either of you hurt. Just give her some room. Call me if there is any change or if you need me to sit with her." He gave Michael a slap on the shoulder and headed out of the room.

"Sure, Freddy. Good night."

Michael pulled one of the big armchairs over close to his sleeping princess. He watched her as her eyes stared toward a far off place, and he listened as she spoke beautiful words, words that he did not understand, words that touched his heart.

He closed his eyes and listened. His mother came to him. She kissed her child's head as he lay sleeping in his bed. He saw her gently wipe a tear from her eye as she stood over him. She took a cross that hung from a silver chain around her neck and hung it on the post at the head of his bed. It was a cross carved from a crystal, cut to catch every color the light would bring to it.

"My dear little one," his mother whispered over her child, "may God protect and watch over you always. You have a destiny now that I shall no longer be part of. Please forgive me, for I am not brave enough for this world and the pain it holds."

"Mom," Michael called out as she backed away. His eyes opened and he beheld Lucy. She was sitting on the couch in front of him. Her hand reached out and touched his. He stared at her but didn't say a word. She was so beautiful he thought she must be an angel.

"Michael," Lucy said. "You were dreaming."

"Who are you?" he asked.

"Shh… listen. Can you hear it?"

Michael closed his eyes as the music from Kathleen's harp filled his mind. "Yes, I can hear it now."

Kathleen sat on a red velvet chair atop a far green hill. She played a beautiful melody on the harp while her voice blended with it in perfect harmony. Michael walked up the hill toward her. But when he got to where she was sitting, the music stopped and she disappeared. His grandfather walked to his side and pointed to a boat that floated on a small lake beyond them. In the boat sat his mother. A man also sat in the boat facing her. As Michael watched, the man turned toward him. It was his father. He was smiling. He pointed to something floating in the water. It was shining. Michael ran to the edge of the lake and peered in. His grandfather walked to his side. "You must save her, my boy," he said. In the center of the shimmering water, he saw a girl floating face up. It was Lucy. He reached out for her but something pulled her under.

"No!" he shouted as his eyes sprung open again. Lucy sat on the couch watching him.

"Michael?"

"Yes."

"Are you all right?"

"I'm fine. I had a dream." He rubbed his eyes then ran his hands through his hair.

"Where are Fred and Myra?"

"They've gone off to bed."

"That's good."

"Lucy, why didn't you come out back by us this evening?"

"I started to, but Fred called to me from the path by the stable."

"No, Lucy, Fred was in the back waiting for you with me."

"Oh," she paused a while. "I remember I picked up my shawl and walked out the door. I thought it was Fred's voice that called me to the woods. I didn't see him. I thought you must be down there too, so I started off in that direction. I don't remember anything else. The next thing I know, I'm sitting here with you. But I don't remember how I got here."

"I carried you, Lucy. I found you in the woods staring into space again, talking in a language I couldn't understand." Now he paused and then said rather sternly, "Lucy, I want to know what's going on."

"I told you all I can remember, Michael."

"Look, I want to help you, but I can't if you won't tell me everything," he said sternly.

Lucy jumped to her feet. She felt hurt by his tone. Was he accusing her of lying? "I'm sorry if you don't believe me. I have told you everything I can remember. Now, if you will excuse me, I've caused you enough trouble for one night." She was trying to fight back tears, but they spilled from her eyes as she turned away.

Michael jumped up, grabbed her by the shoulders, and spun her around toward him. "Look, Lucy," he said, "I'm not talking about just tonight. I'm talking about Angus, about Lance, about everything."

He was interrupted by Fred's voice: "So our sleeping beauty has awakened." Michael released her and she turned from him.

"Fred, I'm sorry if I've disrupted your time here with Michael and Myra. I'm embarrassed. Forgive me." She wiped her eyes.

"Nonsense," Fred said. "If anything, you have made it more interesting."

"That's kind of you, Fred."

"I just came down to see if Michael here needed a rest. He insisted on sitting with you."

She turned to look at Michael as she said, "He has been very kind to me. I'm afraid I have put him through a lot. In light of what has just happened, I don't think he can trust me to stay here to look after Myra."

"Then we will just have to look after each other," Myra said as she came into the room. She walked up to Lucy and put her arm around her.

"Myra, Fred, sorry if I woke you," Michael said, realizing it was his shout that had brought them both downstairs.

"No problem, chum, but as long as I'm up, I think I will pop off into the kitchen and get a slice of Myra's apple pie, if that's all right with you, Myra."

"Of course, Freddy, I made it especially for you. I'll come along and put on the kettle. Will you two be joining us?"

"No thank you, Myra; nothing for me," Lucy said. "I feel exhausted. I'll just say good night to all of you now."

"Wait, Lucy," Michael commanded. "I'd like to have a few words with you in private." To Myra and Fred he said, "You two run along to the kitchen. I'll join you in a bit." Michael's voice sounded stern and authoritative.

"All right, Freddy, let's go get you that pie." Myra locked arms with him and led him from the room.

Lucy turned to look at Michael, who gestured for her to sit back down. He had thought of another plan to get her to open up to him. He would use her own words to find out what he could.

He looked at her severely, rubbing his hands together. "Lucy, you brought up a good point. I do need someone I can trust to be here for Myra while I am away."

"I'll understand, Michael, if you want to reconsider having me stay."

"I don't want to reconsider, Lucy. But that's just it. I need to understand what just happened. I thought you had agreed to let me help you, but I can't if you won't confide in me."

She didn't want to have to leave before the summer was up, before she had a chance to find out more about Lance and his mission. She enjoyed being at Glen Eden; she had grown fond of Myra and of Michael. But she had offered explanations to others in the past, to people she cared about, for events such as what had just occurred, the little periods of missing time that she couldn't explain. She dreaded having to do it once again. She knew she owed him an explanation, and she also knew too well how strange it was going to sound. She swallowed hard and began: "All right, Michael, I'll tell you everything."

"Lucy," Myra called out, walking back into the room. "Here you go, lovie. I thought you could use these." She handed her a handkerchief and a glass of water.

"Thank you, Myra," Lucy said, taking the hanky and making use of it. She drank some of the water and sat down.

"Michael, can I get you anything?" Myra asked.

"No, Myra, I would just like some privacy, if you don't mind."

"Well, I'll just say good night to the both of you then." She stroked Lucy's hair as she whispered in her ear, "He means well." She walked out of the room and slid the door only partially closed.

Michael sat quietly, waiting.

Lucy took a deep breath and began: "These things have happened all my life, not so anyone would notice at first. I mean, my mom would find me sitting in the hall, staring into an old mirror, and 'talking gibberish,' as she would put it. She'd carry me off and put me in bed, thinking I was just sleepwalking. They finally took down the mirror. After that, they found me in the back of a closet. I had been missing for hours and they thought I was hiding on them, but I wasn't. I couldn't remember even going into the closet. I guess there were a lot of little moments like that when I was young, but then it stopped for a while.

"It started happening again when I was in high school. I was walking to the school bus stop one morning. I was alone because my sister had stayed overnight with a girlfriend. The next thing I remember, I found myself in a field behind an apple orchard on a farm that neighbored my father's. I didn't know how I had gotten there. I found my way to the road and saw my sister coming down it. She had just gotten off the school bus and wanted to know where I had been and why I wasn't in school. I told her what happened, and she said I shouldn't tell our parents because they wouldn't believe me and I would get in big trouble for skipping school. My attendance record had been good up to that point, so when my sister faked my mom's signature on a note to excuse me for the absence, the school didn't question it.

"It happened again three weeks later. This time I found myself on a riverbank behind my uncle's farm. I was gone about the same amount of time as before.

"I tried not to walk to the school bus stop alone after that, but one morning about two months later my sister forgot her math book and ran back home to get it. She missed the bus and assumed I had caught it, but I hadn't. I ended up on the big stone on the corner near the bus stop. I found myself there just as the bus was pulling up, bringing the kids home from school. It was like whatever was happening, who or whatever was responsible, they made sure I would be back so as not to alert my parents to what was going on."

"They?" Michael questioned.

"They… it… whatever…" She sighed. "May I go on?"

"Of course, please continue."

"Like I said, I tried not to walk to the bus alone since it was only happening to me on that one stretch of road when I was by myself. But just before school let out that year, I was walking only ten feet or so behind my sister. I was reading notes for a test I was to take that day. Again I found myself on the big stone on the corner just as my sister was getting off the bus. She told me she turned around that morning and I just wasn't there. She thought I was playing a trick on her and hiding in the weeds. She was upset with me. She didn't want to miss the bus because of finals, so she stopped trying to find me and ran off to catch it.

"I wanted to tell my parents, but my sister convinced me I shouldn't. She said I would upset them. 'Just quit it,' she said to me. She's my twin, the closest person in the world to me, and she didn't believe me. She said she wouldn't write any more notes for me after that one."

"You have a twin, Lucy?"

"Yes, Michael, we're identical. I'd like to continue; this is hard for me."

"Go on."

"It happened two more times over the summer break. Once, when I was riding my bike to a girlfriend's house—she only lived about a mile away—I lost seven hours and found myself in a ditch just up the road from her house. The next time, I was picking blueberries on our farm. My sister would start at one end of a row and I would start at the other and we would pick toward each other. When she didn't see me, she assumed I had just jumped onto a different row because the berries were bigger or something. I only lost four hours that day. She thought I'd fallen asleep under a bush, but she gave me half the berries she picked anyway so I wouldn't get in trouble with our folks.

"In my senior year, it happened four more times. At that point, I finally told my folks about it. But as my sister had warned, they didn't believe me."

She stopped, bit her lower lip, and sniffed. He watched her intently but said nothing. She took another sip of water and continued: "They accused me of sneaking around to see a boy. The next time it happened, my mom took me to the doctor to see if I was pregnant." She took the hanky, wiped her eyes and blew into it. "I finally did start to lie to them just because it was easier. I told them I *had* skipped school to see a boy; that's what they believed anyway. They were able to deal with the lie better than they could handle the truth.

"After high school, my sister and I scored high enough on our tests to join the Air Force. We wanted to get money for college, so we signed up together and were supposed to stay together. We were doing fine, but after six months, I didn't show up for my assigned duty one day. As they put it, I went AWOL. When they questioned me about where I had been, I told them the truth: that I didn't know. I was relieved of duty and placed on medical leave. I was given a battery of physical and psychological tests, which all showed negative results. I confided in a psychiatrist about the other episodes of missing times. His diagnosis was paranoid schizophrenia, and I was medically discharged.

"I went back home, but it was hard to see the disappointment in my mom and dad's eyes. I married my high school boyfriend for all the wrong reasons. It was a big disaster. After six months I moved back home." A tear rolled down each cheek. She wiped them with the hanky and took another sip of water. Michael wanted to reach out and comfort her, but he dare not. She was finally opening up to him and he didn't want to stop her.

"I started seeing a Christian psychiatrist who told me I was feeling guilty about something and manifesting punishment on myself. I had no idea what he was talking about. On our nineteenth birthday, my sister took leave and was coming home. My mom planned a big party for us. She baked and cooked for two days. My aunts, uncles, and cousins that lived nearby were coming along with some of our close friends. I left home to go to the train station in Bangor to pick up my sister, but three days later I found myself sitting on a rock by Hutchins Lake near Fennville. I didn't even know where the car was. I walked to a nearby house and called home. My mom answered and started crying. My father took the phone and told me about all the trouble I had caused. They even had the police looking for me. My sister had found the car at the train station with the keys in it. It was after that incident that my father told me it would be better if I found somewhere else to live because I was causing my mother too much pain, and he was worried about what all this nonsense was doing to her health."

Tears were rolling freely down her face now. She dabbed at them with the hanky. Michael couldn't stand to see her like this. He leaned forward and took her hands. "I'm sorry this is so hard for you."

"I moved to Saugatuck and started working at the Butler when it happened again. One morning I woke up, dressed, and ate a slice of toast. I was looking forward to having two days off in a row. I saw something out the window and stepped outside to see what it was. Two days later I found myself in a meadow on the wildlife reserve not far from here. That's the day I met Lance. He saw me sitting alone and called to me. He could see I was confused. I don't know why, but I told him I didn't know how I had gotten there. He offered to drive me home. He knew that it wasn't the first time things like that had happened to me. He said Angus had told him about it."

She let out a big sigh. "So welcome to my nightmare," she whispered. She had only glanced at him a few times while relating her story. Now she looked right into his eyes. "I'm sorry, Michael. I thought I was done with all this. I'll understand if you want me to leave."

Michael tightened his grip on her hands. "That's not what I want, Lucy. I want to help you. We'll figure this out." He found himself lost in her eyes. She was looking into his soul, asking him for help. He saw the image he had dreamed of, her face floating in the lake. He looked away. "I want you to hear something."

He reached over to the tape recorder and hit the rewind button. While it was rewinding, he said, "When I found you in the woods tonight, you seemed to be in a trance. You were murmuring something. I've recorded part of it." He hit the play button.

She listened intently and finally said, "Michael, I'm sorry. I don't know what it is I'm saying."

"Myra and I believe it may be Old Gaelic."

"But I don't know that language," she insisted.

"Lucy, do you mind if I give this tape to someone who may be able to interpret it."

"Of course not, Michael. I don't mind at all. God knows how much I want to get to the bottom of all this."

A knock came on the partially opened door; it was Fred. "Michael, I don't want to butt in here, pally, but it's quite late. Don't you think Lucy should be getting some rest?"

Michael looked at his watch. It was twenty past two. "Right you are, Freddy. I didn't realize it was so late. I'm sorry to have kept you up, Lucy. How are you feeling?"

"I'm all-in."

"Right, of course you are. So we should get on off to bed then."

"Michael, are we still getting up at seven for a run and a swim?" Fred questioned.

"Sure we are, Fred, if you can handle it."

"Don't worry about me, mate. Lucy, may I escort you up the stairs." Fred offered his arm. Michael set about switching lamps off in the room while Fred and Lucy ascended.

"Fred, I'm sorry again for this evening. I was looking forward to a walk on the beach with you boys."

"Then you'll just have to give us a rain check on it."

"Sure, Fred, happy to."

They stopped at the top of the stairs and Michael joined them. Fred walked to his room, bidding them both a good night. Michael and Lucy moved on toward their end of the hall. Once again, Michael stopped by her door.

"I apologize for being hard on you tonight, Lucy."

"Michael, you have every right to want to know what's going on with a guest in your house. To be honest, I feel much better now having told you."

"Really?"

"Yes, and as a matter of fact, I'm hoping to have a chance to talk with you again soon. There is more I'd like to share, something Lance told me."

"I take Fred to the airport Sunday afternoon, so Sunday evening I can be all yours."

"I look forward to it. You have been wonderful to me. Thank you." She leaned forward and softly kissed his cheek. "Good night."

Freea bumped his leg and meowed loudly. He bent down and picked her up. Patting her head gently, he placed her in Lucy's arms. "Watch over her, Freea," he said softly in the old cat's ear.

Michael lay on his bed thinking about the dreams he had while sitting with Lucy. What did they mean? Had his mother really come to him as a child the night she killed herself? What about the cross she placed on the bedpost? He remembered it now: sitting on her lap as a wee lad he would play with it, moving it this way and that to catch the light and capture the different colors. It hadn't been brought to his mind for years.

He thought of Lucy again, how she sat before him shining like an angel. He thought about the kiss she'd placed on his cheek, and he thought about his dream of her floating in the water. He would tell Fred everything in the morning so they could work on a plan for how to help her. But for right now he would go to his Father.

"Lord Father God, thank you for your grace, your tender mercies and your goodness toward us who believe. Help me Father to have the wisdom I need to help Lucy. Father, you know what it is she needs. Please grant it. Amen."

It was hard for him to pray that, for in his own mind he thought what she needed most was Lance.

19 – The Knowing Ledge

Lucy was exhausted from drudging up her past and presenting it to Michael. "What must he think of me?" His concern seemed genuine, and she didn't blame him for the rough way he had questioned her. After all, she put him through a lot in the short time she'd known him. He had asked her to tell him everything, but she had only told him about the episodes of missing time. Fred saved her from getting into the Fairytale, as Lance called it.

Though Lance had told her many things, she knew he had not told her everything. She wondered now if his promise of someday would be kept. She knew he had been investigating sacred sites, looking for portals into other dimensions, and that the dolmen from which he went missing was thought by the locals to be an entrance into the fairy realm. Had he willingly exited this world, or had he been taken by the wee folk—Angus's kin—as legend suggested they would do if one got too close to their gates?

What he was planning to do now, she did not know. From the brief reunion they had had in the stone circle and from his words to her in the smoke ring, she gathered he had somehow found his way to this other dimension and that a war was going on there. What his role was in it, she dare not guess. She hoped to find some of the answers in William's journals. She was certain *The Green Book* contained valuable information that could answer many of her questions, if it were found, and that Michael was somehow the key to finding it. From William's written words she knew he considered Lance's work important and his reports very valuable, so much so that he kept them hidden from everyone. Lucy knew now that Michael was the one person his grandfather had trusted above anyone else, even Myra.

She was glad Michael hadn't asked her to leave. He had assured her that he would help her, and she desperately wanted to believe him. He promised her Sunday evening as a time they could talk alone. She was resolved now to tell him everything. "Would he believe it?" she wondered. Sometimes she didn't believe it herself. When a shadow of reason would come upon her, she wondered if Lance really existed at all, or if he were just a dream she had invented to keep herself searching for joy in a world where she felt foreign and alone. She wrestled with her mind at those times to hold on to that dream. She closed her eyes and remembered the kiss in the garden the night Lance found her, the kiss that had carried her to the green and golden lands that felt like her home. Then she remembered how Mrs. Garrett's window opened and he vanished.

She searched for his picture among her things at Michael's, but it wasn't there. She was certain she had thoroughly scoured her apartment for it. Had someone taken it, had it just disappeared, or had it never really existed at all? She explored her memory, as she often did in the late hours of night, trying to remember moments with him. Now she tried to recall just when it was he had given it to her.

⚜

She left her job at the Butler and moved to San Francisco in the fall of 1968. Lance had gone out there a couple of months earlier. They had discussed her plans to move before he left. He told her that once she was there and settled, she should post a message for him at the Haight-Ashbury Switchboard.

Young people in droves were moving to the bay area at that time. Kids from across the nation were converging on San Francisco to experience what they called "a new vibration." The devastating war in Vietnam was dividing the nation. As more and more young people disagreed with the policies of their elders, a movement took root. The generation gap widened as the free-thinking young people began to question all aspects of society, from the government, to the church, to corporate America. Spurred on by so-called enlightened leaders advocating the use of LSD and other mind-altering drugs—like Timothy Leary, who encouraged them to "turn on, tune in, and drop out"—and invigorated by the anti-war, anti-establishment, pro-drug lyrics of rock and roll music, the movement grew. They would call themselves the "Peace and Love Generation." But many who came to the area looking for Peace and Love only experienced drugs and sex.

The Switchboard was created as a place where the wandering youth could get messages from their families and friends who would otherwise have no way to contact them. It was run by volunteers in an old store front on Haight Street. Whoever happened to be manning the phone would jot down the message and post it on one of the giant bulletin boards, or just tape it to the wall. People would wander in and out at all hours to look for a message, or post one.

Lance taught her rune symbols to use for the message she would post. "It is the Guardian Code," he told her. "There are only a few now who can read it, and they'll know how to find me."

She rented an apartment in a house owned by a girl she had met the summer before in Saugatuck. Syboney was a beautiful French woman with curly, ebony hair and dark eyes. She was ten years Lucy's senior and had traveled extensively all over the world. She had come into the Butler one night in the company of a man she'd only known for a short time. They had an argument, and she refused to leave with him. Lucy, who had been their waitress that night, witnessed the incident. When Syboney inquired of her how to obtain a taxi to fare her back to Grand Rapids where she was staying, Lucy asked if she'd like to spend the night with her. A taxi would have to come from either South Haven or Holland, and either way it would be very expensive and dangerous, Lucy thought, for someone in Syboney's alcohol-induced state. Syboney seemed both relieved and grateful. She waited patiently, sipping coffee until Lucy finished her shift.

They acquainted themselves on the short walk to Lucy's apartment and over a cup of hot tea chatted into the wee hours. The next day they sunned together at the Oval, and the two became fast friends. Lucy knew that Ashley had the day off, so she phoned him to ask if he'd give them a ride to Grand Rapids. He was more than happy to do it, remembering, as he put it, "the bombshell" from the bar the night before.

Several years earlier, Syboney had inherited a house on Miramar Street in South San Francisco from her grandmother. She converted the top floor into an apartment to let, to help with the expense of maintaining the large old Victorian. She didn't have a job but lived carefully off an inheritance doled out in monthly stipends from a trust fund her grandmother had arranged. When Syboney learned of Lucy's strained relationship with her family, she invited her to give San Francisco a go. Lucy kept this invitation in the back of her mind. The following summer, when Lance suddenly left for the west coast, she phoned her old friend and learned the apartment was available.

Lucy knew the only way she had to find Lance was for him to find her through the coded message she had hung, per his instructions, with a silver thumbtack at the Switchboard on Haight Street. She posted it there the very first day she arrived in San Francisco at the end of October. But it was Christmas Eve now, and she still had not heard from him.

She was feeling lost and homesick. It was the first Christmas she had been away from her family. She had gotten a Christmas package from them in the mail a few days earlier. Her folks had sent her a very sensible, if not fashionable, winter jacket in lumberjack plaid of red, black, and yellow. Also in the package, wrapped in a page from the Lakeshore Flashes, was a small, decorated evergreen branch from a blue spruce. Lucy guessed it was probably from one of the two thousand trees she had helped her father plant a dozen or so years previous on the back of their farm. The idea was to sell them as Christmas trees when they were big enough, but her dad ended up giving them away to anyone who wanted to hike through the snowdrifts to cut one down and drag it back to the road. A note was tucked in with this parcel, written in her mom's hand: "From our Christmas tree at home. We miss you and send our Love and Prayers as always, Mom and Dad. P.S. Your father picked out the jacket for you himself. Hope you like it." Lucy never knew her dad to go shopping for clothes, not even for his own. She took the gesture to mean that he cared about her and was sorry for the way things were between them.

At ten o'clock that evening, she sat before this little symbol of home, lost in memories of happy Christmases past while Freea sat watching the front door. When a knock came on it, Lucy thought it was probably Syboney since she didn't know anyone else who would be visiting. She opened the door without question. There before her, as if in a dream, stood Lance. He put his right hand on his heart and bowed. "My queen," he said, "you stand as a vision almost too beautiful to behold."

She stood frozen as her heart filled with joy, and no words found their way from her mouth.

"May I enter?" he finally asked. She stepped back from the door, and as he walked past her she breathed deeply, filling herself with his scent. He turned back to look at her and saw a tear rolling from the corner of her eye. He cupped her face in his hand, brushing the tear away with his thumb. "What is this?" he asked.

"It is joy," she said.

"Ah, then I have given you the gift I had intended."

"The gift I was hoping for."

He took her in his arms. The light was so bright between them they had to close their eyes. Their lips touched and they became lost in each other.

When the kiss ended and they again stood in her apartment, he whispered softly in her ear, "There is a very special place I'd like to take you tonight. Will you come with me?"

"I will," she replied.

"Good. Then let's be off."

She grabbed her new jacket and zipped it up. "A Christmas present from my mom and dad," she said as she spun around for his inspection.

"It's a fine, sensible coat, and you can be no warmer than wrapped in love."

Freea called for his attention while she rubbed her head on his leg. He bent down and scooped her up. "Freea, so we meet again. You have taken very good care of our lady and she of you, I see. For this, I am grateful." He rubbed his finger under her chin. She purred loudly, begging for more. He had rescued her from the middle of the Blue Star Highway just south of Ganges late one night in a rainstorm, a lost, soaked, and frightened little kitten. He took her to Lucy, whose maternal instincts had already been awakened by him.

While he was distracted with Freea, Lucy slipped a small tissue-wrapped package into her pocket. "I'm ready for our adventure," she said.

"Then that is just what we shall have." He pulled her close once again to capture her mouth with his.

He opened the driver's door of Quicksilver and she slid in. She sat close to him on the blanket-covered bench seat. His arm was around her, and every now and then he kissed her head tenderly. She told him all about her move and how she found a job working in a toy store on Sutter Street.

He told her that since he arrived in California, he'd been living in a forest in a remote part of Humboldt County. There he had come upon a tribe of strange yet wonderful creatures. "They have existed in that forest since before the Native Americans arrived. They have learned how to avoid human attention, thriving in nature, keeping their existence a secret, for the most part, save from the Guardians. Even so, there are a few scattered reports of the Yeti."

"The Yeti!" Lucy exclaimed. "You mean like Bigfoot?"

Lance laughed. "Yes, they have fairly large feet, but not disproportional to their size. Most full-grown males stand between ten and twelve feet tall. I have met one pushing fourteen."

"Lance, you have been living with these wild creatures?"

"Oh, they are not wild, Lucy. They are very civilized. More so than humans, I'd say. They are not interested in killing or conquering. They are content to live in their communities and have never harmed man nor beast, that I have heard. They live in harmony with nature and are very sensitive to the vibrations of this planet."

Lucy always marveled at the strange and wonderful things he told her. From anyone else she may not have believed a word, but from Lance, it was gospel to her.

He didn't talk about where they were going, and Lucy didn't ask. She didn't care; as long as she was with him, it didn't really matter. This would be her first of many times on Mt. Tamalpais. It was considered a sacred place, especially to those on a spiritual quest. Yet the site they would visit this night, she was never able to find again.

Lance pulled Quicksilver off the main road and they hiked for a while through the mighty redwoods, their way lit only by beams from the moon and stars that broke in here and there through the thick canopy of the majestic trees. Lance seemed to know exactly where he was going and held her hand firmly. They climbed upwards through a rocky pass and came out onto a large stone ledge that overlooked the city far below. She felt like she'd stepped into a fairy tale.

Several Native American men and women were gathered around a campfire. Some were chanting, some were beating drums, and others were dancing. Three men sat in a semi-circle smoking a long pipe. They nodded to Lance as he walked past. He led Lucy to a blanket spread on the ground near the far side of the ledge. She recognized it as the one he had covered her with the first time she rode in Quicksilver, the day they met. Lucy sat down while he took a small fruitcake, a bag of nuts, a round of cheese, and a bottle from his pack and set them on another blanket near the fire, where other food offerings were laying. He knelt behind with his legs straddling her and enfolded her in his arms. "Merry Christmas," he said quietly in her ear.

"Lance, it's beautiful here. It's like being in a different world." They sat quietly, absorbing the sights and sounds that encompassed them.

After some time, she pulled the small tissue-wrapped package from her jacket and handed it to him. "Merry Christmas," she said. He smiled widely as he unwrapped it. It was a small, handcrafted buckskin pouch, which she had carefully burnished with his initials and her representation of a crescent moon and a star. Inside the pouch was a thin, leather-covered tube with a tightly fitted cork stopper. Inside the tube were several small, rolled-up sheets of paper and a pencil.

"I have never been presented with a finer gift," he said, taking her hand and bringing it to his lips. "When I am alone in the wild, thinking of you, I will write your name and leave it under a rock to prove you were there with me."

A small stream fell from the high ground above them into a shallow pool on the ledge just to their right, before spilling from it to run down and join the river that rushed below. The stars that blanketed the sky were mirrored in the small black pool. It was as if they sat between two worlds.

At midnight a man with a painted face walked up to them and bowed. He bent on one knee and thrust forward a silver chalice. He spoke in soft, melodic tones, using no words Lucy could recognize. Lance took the cup and bowed his head as the man backed away.

He gazed at her and said, "This place is called the Knowing Ledge. This cup contains the water of life that runs from this mountain. In it has been mixed a bitter herb called *kalahanameya*, which means 'the substance of knowledge.' I will drink of it this night. Will you drink it with me? Before you answer, you must understand that knowledge can be both beautiful and terrible. Things that become known cannot be unknown, though they may be forgotten and veiled in time. They will forever exist as part of who we are. If we drink this together, we will know each other. Nothing will be hidden; nothing can be held back. Do you understand?"

"Yes, Lance, I do."

"Do you want to know me, Lucy? Do you want to see who I really am, and are you willing for me to know you beyond what eye and heart reveal?"

Without hesitation she said, "Yes."

"Then let us drink on this special day that celebrates when the light of truth came back into this world. Let us drink and know the truth of us." He handed her the cup and she put it to her lips. She gazed into his eyes as she let the bitter liquid flow over her tongue. She handed it to him and he drank an equal portion. The sound of the drums began to fade, and the others on the ledge withdrew into shadow.

The air around them became full of color and light. It danced and swirled around their heads and turned into tiny beings both strange and beautiful. Little winged creatures whizzed by her head. She saw them darting here and there, jumping from stone to stone, holding on to a drop of water and falling into the pool.

The light from the moon and stars settled in around them, illuminating all she beheld in a silver glow. All of her senses were heightened, and she became acutely aware of the life force in everything. The very rock they sat upon seemed to be alive and breathing. She lay her face down upon its surface and felt the warmth it had stored from the sun. She breathed in its earthy, mineral scent and listened to its groaning vibrations. She felt as if she were becoming part of it.

"Lucy," a soft voice spoke, "look at your hands."

She withdrew her mind from the rock and stared at her hands. How strange they seemed. Their flesh tone was really a mixture of many colors, moving, vibrating, connected by her life force. She rubbed them together, felt the heat that was generated, and saw the glow of the charged air around them. She moved them to her face and closed her eyes. She was seeing herself just by touch now, the way a person blind from birth might see her. She felt the flesh over her bones, tight across her forehead and around her eyes then squishy on her cheeks. Her fingers followed her jawbone from her cheeks downward to the fleshy padding of her chin then upward to her lips. The sensual feeling increased as she touched them, as she ran her fingers back and forth across them. She moved from her mouth back down to her chin then tilted her head back to feel her neck and Adam's apple.

She touched something that seemed foreign and lifeless. It was the collar of her new jacket. It now seemed heavy and confining. She slipped it off her shoulders only to find more confining lifeless material. She pulled off her shirt and felt the cool night air against her skin. It almost took her breath away. She jumped to her feet and loosed herself of the rest of her clothing. It was if she was just being born, coming into a new world from the confinement of the womb. She spread her arms and lifted her hands and head high toward the star-filled night sky. She felt free and liberated. She sensed the sphere she was standing on hurtling through the universe. The stars were streaking by her head as she roamed further and further away from herself.

"Lucy," the soft voice spoke again, "close your eyes. I am going to touch you." She obeyed as the voice, godlike in her new world, resonated in her brain. Soft hands, attached to a warm presence she felt behind her, touched her gently.

The hands were on her waist and she moved her hands to cover them. They roamed slowly up her body to her breasts. She groaned as they came across her nipples. Experiencing new levels of excitement, she leaned back against the strong warmth behind her. The hands continued to slowly explore the contours of her form. The touch was so light and so electric that she felt every molecule of her body vibrate under it. The hands left no area unsearched as they roamed freely across the flesh that made up her face, her lips, her ears, her neck, her shoulders, her torso, and now back again to her breasts, exploding her senses. Lucy stared at Lance as if she was seeing him for the very first time. His hair was the color of spun gold. His skin was bronze shining with a light from within. His eyes were beyond green and full of life and wisdom. She felt she belonged to his gaze.

The drums began to beat loudly again, bringing Lucy back to herself. She realized she was naked and became afraid. Lance quickly wrapped her in the blanket. "Lucy, there are others near. I sense there will be trouble."

Her peace was shattered by a rough, ugly voice, "Well now, looky what we have here: a hippie and his old lady."

Lance stepped in front of Lucy to confront two men who had stumbled upon the ledge. "Peace be unto you, brothers," he said.

"Well, hell yes brother," the bigger man grunted as the other man guffawed maliciously, "but it's spelled P I E C E, which is what we want for Christmas from your old lady there."

Lance pushed Lucy back while he stepped closer to the men. "We want no trouble here," Lance said in a calm yet stern voice. Lucy stared wide-eyed, like she was watching a movie she was not part of.

"No, I don't suppose you do. But let's face it, brother. There are two of us. So if you don't want anyone to get hurt, just give us our Christmas present and we'll move along. Your old lady there looks higher than a kite. Hell, she'll probably enjoy what we want to give her." They laughed wickedly, and as they did their faces changed in Lucy's sight. Instead of men, she saw demons: big, black, slimy creatures slathering at their mouths. Her knees felt weak as she realized she was the present they were talking about.

"It's not going to happen that way, boys, so just move along off this ledge," Lance commanded.

"The only one moving off this ledge is you," said the larger man as he lunged forward.

Lance stepped aside at the last moment and the man fell hard on the ground. The second man launched toward Lance, and the same thing happened to him. They both lay cursing in a heap. They struggled to get up. The bigger one pulled a knife. Lucy gasped in horror.

"Cast away fear, Lucy, and trust me," Lance reassured as he moved further away from her. The two men separated so as to come at Lance from different directions. Lance made one final plea: "Okay fellas, this has gone far enough. You don't have to give in to the darkness."

"I don't know who you are, mister, but it's you who will be seeing darkness when I stick this here poker in your heart." He nodded his head to the other, and both men rushed at Lance. A bright light suddenly surrounded him and he was gone. The two men collided into each other. The knife intended for Lance's heart was now lodged in the shoulder of the shorter bully. "What the hell! Where'd he go?" the bigger man shouted.

"I'm right here, friend, and I think there has been enough foolishness. Now take your buddy there and get him to a hospital. Be thankful that there has been a Christmas miracle and mercy has been shown to you." Lance walked over to help them up. The countenance of the men changed as the demons screamed in anguish and left them. Their stature shrank, and they were sobbing. Lance spoke to them softly about forgiving the ones who had hurt them when they were young. "Go hence and do no evil." He escorted them into the woods to the path that led off the cliff, and they walked away. The fire grew up and the others appeared again, dancing and chanting as if nothing had occurred.

Lucy started to speak, but Lance put his finger to her lips. She heard his voice but did not see his lips move. "There are no words for what I want to show you. For I want you to know me without words. I want you to know me with your whole being, as I want to know you. He smiled, and she was once again filled with joy. He touched her cheek and her breath failed. He picked her up in his arms and carried her down a path that led to a tepee. The man with the painted face was standing in front of it. As they approached, he pulled back a leather flap, letting Lance walk in with his precious bundle. He placed her gently upon soft pelts. The blanket fell from around her and she lay naked upon them.

The top of the structure was open to the sky, letting out the smoke from the lit fire and letting in the starlight. Lying on her back against the tiny sphere soaring through the universe, Lucy peered into the heavens. Darting here and there from star to star above her head were the little winged creatures. She could hear the sounds of the earth groaning and the water singing.

Lance lay down beside her now and with his mouth explored where his hands had roamed before. She melted into a pool of sensations. He stopped only long enough to remove his own clothing. She felt the heat radiate from his chest, and she turned her head to bury it in his warmth and scent. Her lips and hands now moved over him. He groaned as she moved her tongue down his taught abdomen. She became lost in him as their two bodies melded.

She watched from atop the mountain as the lovers below moved upon each other. They made love as tenderly as a bee pollinates a flower, and then as savage and raw as wild beasts. She fell back into the body that was writhing and jerking as every molecule was stimulated to its peak and exploding with sensations that could never be described.

They spent themselves on each other over and over again, until the soft light of morning crowded out the darkness.

She didn't remember leaving the ledge or how she had gotten home. She woke Christmas day in the early afternoon, lying on her couch before the small evergreen branch from home. She felt full and empty at the same time. She could still smell his scent on her. For the first time, she knew the man she loved was no ordinary man.

After that night, he would show up from time to time, always unannounced though always expected. She lived every moment anticipating his return. He would take her camping, hiking, or climbing, stay for a day or two, and then be off again. Their nights were spent in passion, enjoying sensual pleasures bestowed mutually upon each other. The more he had her, the more she wanted him. She never asked when he'd be back. She had asked him once where he called home since he left his parents' farm in Ohio, and he replied, "You are my home, Lucy. The space we share when we are together, no matter where that is—on mountain ledge, by riverside, in this apartment or in my truck—if you are there, then I am home."

He came to her apartment late one night and told her he was leaving in the morning for South America with an old Mayan Shaman he met on Mt. Tamalpais. "Lance, why are you leaving me?" she asked, and then felt bad that she did.

"I'm not leaving you, Lucy; wherever I go, I carry you here." He placed his hand on his heart. "You cannot walk where I do, at least not now. There are things I must learn. Yapaka knows the path of the Starwalkers and has promised to teach me. I must go, my love."

"How long will you be gone?" she asked, then again felt bad.

"Only as long as it takes." He softly grasped her face and looked into her eyes. "Lucy, are you afraid you will forget me?"

"No!" she protested.

"Because the only way I'll ever leave you is if you do. As long as you keep me clearly in your heart, I'll always return." He kissed her. "Here," he said, handing her a sheet of paper.

She looked at it and turned it over. It was blank. "What's this?"

"It's to help you remember me." He kissed her again and she suckled his tongue as if it were feeding her soul. When he withdrew his mouth from hers, her breath came only slowly back. She looked down again at the paper she held. There was his image smiling back at her.

"How did you do that?" she asked. But when she looked up, he was gone.

He had bought a silver frame with a crescent moon in the upper left corner and a star in the bottom right. She saw him purchase it at the flea market in Marin City just that past weekend when they were returning from a hike on Mount Tam. Lucy loved to go to this open air bazaar—a mixture of arts, crafts, antiques, and music—because there was always such a festive atmosphere. It was set atop a barren hill overlooking the bay. She always came away with some little treasure to adorn herself or her apartment, but Lance usually only invested in a used book or two, which after he read he promptly gave away. He tucked the frame into his pack while she was at a neighboring booth selecting a handmade turquoise barrette as a birthday gift for Syboney.

She now understood who the frame was for. It was for her and the picture she held in her hand. She walked into her bedroom and there on the nightstand, right where she knew it would be, was the frame. She plunked down on the bed and opened the back of it. The picture fit perfectly, of course. She cradled it to her chest and fell asleep.

Now the picture was gone, and Lucy couldn't help but think about Lance's words: "I'll never leave you, Lucy, as long as you keep me clearly in your heart." Lucy wondered if the picture had vanished because she had unintentionally let another cloud her heart.

She prayed as she always did, in the spirit, for Lance, and tried to fall asleep remembering him. But it was thoughts of Michael that finally brought her rest.

20 – The Great Serpent Mound

Michael rolled out of bed at 6:45, slipped into his swimming trunks, tiptoed past Lucy's room, and was just about to reach for the bathroom knob when the door swung open and Lucy walked out. Not expecting anyone to be there, she ran right into him and almost fell over. She gave a startled little gasp as he caught her in his arms.

"Oh, Michael, I… I didn't see you." Her arms were on his bare chest.

"Sorry for the start," he said, still holding her. Her hair was all tossed from sleeping and her thin cotton nightgown didn't leave much to the imagination. Michael was delighted over this turn of events and stood with a big grin on his face.

Freddy came out of his room at that moment and saw what he perceived was an embrace. "Oops!" he said, "Sorry, just off to have a cup."

"Top of the morning to you, Freddy," Michael beamed.

"Good morning, Fred," Lucy sleepily added as she turned her head toward the man hurriedly heading for the stairway.

Fred didn't turn around but just raised a hand and said, "Lucy." She suddenly realized what this early morning collision must have looked like to him. She felt her face getting hot and bolted for her room. Michael used the restroom then went down to the kitchen.

Fred sat at the table with a cup of coffee in front of him. He was just about to have a swig when Michael walked in. "God, Michael, you don't listen to me for one moment, do you? I don't know why you even bother to ask for my advice if you aren't willing to use it."

"Freddy, look…" Michael tried to explain, but Fred kept talking.

"I'm very serious about this. I told you not to play with this girl. It's very obvious to me that she has suffered some type of emotional trauma which her psyche is trying to deal with by manifesting some very odd behavior. You could push her over the edge if you aren't careful, Michael, and I'll not let that happen."

"Freddy, cool down…" Michael again began.

"Christ, Michael, get a grip on yourself. Didn't you just visit your little tart out in L.A.? What, one woman at a time isn't good enough for you anymore?"

Michael's ire was raised now. "Look, Fred ol' boy, you are way off the mark on this. So maybe you should just keep your trap shut."

Fred jumped to his feet. "Yeah, well maybe you should just keep your pants zipped."

Michael postured himself close to Fred and clenched his fist. "You know, for a PhD you're sure a blockhead sometimes. In the first place, Maureen is not a tart, and I should push your teeth back in your head for saying so. In the second place, what you saw upstairs this morning isn't what you think: Lucy merely ran into me coming out of the loo. I have already told you that she is not interested in me; she is mad for her Lance. And in case I need remind you, Freddy, I know what it is like to lose someone you love so completely that the world is never the same after." His tone softened. "So I know how awful it must be for her not knowing just what has happened to him. I'm not playing with her. I'm trying to help her."

Fred held his hands up and backed against the counter. "Michael, let me explain to you what it is my PhD stands for: that would be Perfectly Huge Dumbass."

Michael unclenched his fist and put his hand on Fred's shoulder. "That's exactly what I thought. Come on now, chum. Let's run off some of this frustration."

They stretched in the garden, and Michael took the lead as they ran down the winding path to the lakeshore. Michael loved to run this time of morning and be in his own thoughts. This morning the sky still carried some of the orange and pink from the sunrise, and the water, he thought, was the deep blue of Lucy's eyes. As his strides pounded the wet sand left by the retreating waves, he brought to his thoughts the crystal cross he had seen in the dream of his mother. He was convinced it was real and that he had played with it as a child. He wondered what had happened to it and decided to ask Myra when he saw her.

Michael would normally run eight to ten miles. But he noticed Fred beginning to lag further and further behind, so he decided to cut it to six and walk some so the two of them could talk. He was anxious to tell the PhD what he had learned about Lucy's past. Fred was pleased when Michael slowed and turned toward him. They jogged for a while then slowed to a fast walk then to a normal stride.

Michael told Fred everything Lucy had confided in him the evening before but left out mention of the dreams he had had. They planned what to do next. The tape would have to be translated; if it weren't just gibberish, it might give them some sort of clue as to just what was going on. Fred suggested Michael have a private investigator look into Lance McKellen to see if they could discover what had happened to him.

"I'm way ahead of you on that, Freddy. I called Shannon right after we found mention of him in Grandfather's journal. She has our agency working on it."

"Good. We also need to know just what that symbol has to do with all this. I'll carry the drawing you made to a symbologist friend of mine at Berkeley; if anyone can dig up what it means, he can. Meantime, let's not mention I'm a psychologist. Since she'll be staying here all summer, I'd like to see if she'll confide in you a little more before we tell her that. I'll come back in a couple of weeks and we'll put together what we've been able to learn. If any more episodes like last night occur, then we better rethink all this. You can of course call me anytime. I'll consult some colleagues who have a little more experience with the paranormal than I have."

"The paranormal?" Michael came to a full stop.

"Of course, Michael. Both Lucy and Myra have heard Kathleen's music. I think that qualifies for paranormal activity, don't you?" Michael stood silent. "I'm not sure just what Lucy has to do with it, but it would seem there is some link between her and Kathleen since no one heard the music before she arrived. Isn't that right?"

Michael was flummoxed. "So you don't think it's just in her mind? You think Kathleen is…?" The expression on his face was intense and pained.

"I hesitate to make any guesses, ol' boy." He reached out and put his hand on Michael's shoulder. "Let's take this a step at a time. Right now I'd like to step into the lake to cool off. What do you say?"

"Sounds good to me, Freddy. To the buoy and back. Then we'll go up and see what kind of magic Myra is working in the kitchen."

When the two buddies walked back through the garden, the smell of frying bacon came wafting out of the kitchen to meet them. Dripping through the back door, they heard it snapping and popping on the griddle. They rushed the kitchen like schoolboys. But it wasn't Myra working magic; it was Lucy.

"Hey guys, ready for breakfast?" she asked, swatting Michael's hand away from the bacon plate with a spatula.

"Boy, are we," Freddy replied. She dumped a fry pan of potatoes O'Brien onto a metal platter. There was a bowl of eggs, also scrambled with onions and peppers, ready to pour in the pan and garlic and goat cheese simmering in a pot. "It smells great. I'm starving. I'll run up and dress. Be down in a few." He grabbed a slice of crisp bacon as he scurried by her.

"Do you need a hand with anything?" Michael asked.

"No, I have it under control; maybe just reach that jar of black currant jam so I can carry it to the table. You'll be wanting it for your toast, right?"

"Woman, you've won my heart," he said as he obeyed her order and handed down the jar. *Little does she know,* he thought, *that I'm not kidding.* She handed him a bacon slice as his reward.

The guys quickly showered off, dressed, and came bounding down the stairs as Lucy carried the final dish to the table. Michael walked over to pull out her chair. But before he could, Fred gave him a playful shove and pulled it out himself. "My lady," he said with a sweeping bow. Lucy smiled widely, enjoying all the boyish attention.

"Shall we be waiting on Myra, then?" Freddy asked.

"Oh, I'm sorry. I thought you knew. She got a call from Winnie early this morning. They left about an hour ago for Chicago to visit with Skipper."

"Skipper? Is she all right?" Michael inquired.

"I assume so. Myra didn't hint otherwise. I guess she's decided to stay there with a cousin or something. I thought you'd know about it." He shrugged his shoulders and raised his eyebrows, playing dumb. "Anyway, Myra said she'd be gone all day and asked me to apologize to Freddy."

"Go ahead, Michael, offer the blessing before it all goes cold," Fred requested. Michael obliged and the three sat eating and talking as if the strange events of the past night hadn't happened at all.

After breakfast they all did a part in the cleanup, with Michael and Fred singing some of their old school fight songs as they tossed the dishes around. Lucy's heart was light and happy. She felt comfortable with Michael, even after she had shared her most damning secrets. As they finished up in the kitchen, Michael announced that he had some work to do for a few hours in the study and asked Lucy if she would mind keeping Fred occupied.

"I would be delighted," she replied. "Now just what is it you would like to do this fine day, sir?" she asked Fred with a little curtsy.

This was working right into their plan. Fred wanted to get her back to the stone circle to observe how she would behave. "I think I would like to go horseback riding, if you're up for it, that is."

"Sounds lovely. I'll go up and put my jeans on and meet you in the stable."

While Lucy went to change, Michael told Fred of the path that left Glen Eden from behind the stables and went on through the woods to meet up with the path that led to Farmer Green's. "You'll come to the clearing just beyond where the stone circle stands. If you approach from that direction, you'll have her there before she realizes where it is you're going."

"Well, this seems to be working out well. You're a fox Michael, just like Grandpa Will."

Michael had been told that before, and he always hated it. "Just be careful Freddy that nothing happens to her."

Fred let out a sarcastic chuckle. "Don't worry, mate. I won't knock her down and force myself on her, if that's what you're worried about." Michael didn't chuckle; he didn't even smile. He gave Fred a shove and headed into the study.

Later, as Michael tried to concentrate on his work, he found he couldn't get Lucy out of his thoughts. He felt badly about deceiving her and had to remind himself once again it was for her own good. His own work done, he decided to look through some of his grandfather's books for the symbol Farmer Green had put in the corner of his painting of Angus.

He thumbed through two books of symbols but didn't find anything even close to the mark. He replaced the books back on the shelf, and as he did so he thought he heard someone call to him. He turned quickly but saw no one, so he walked to the door of the study to get a view of the hallway. There was no one there. He shrugged his shoulders and returned to his desk. He was just about to sit down when his eyes fell on a book sitting open on the chair by the fire.

"Lucy must have left it out," he thought, though he didn't recall seeing it earlier. He picked it up, turned it over, and recognized immediately the picture displayed on the left page. At least he recognized the shape of it. The book was entitled *The Atlas of Sacred and Mystical Sites* by David Douglas. The picture he was staring at was a drawing of the Serpent Mound in Adams County, Ohio. It was the shape he'd been searching for. Michael read the four paragraphs describing the mound: its size, age, and physical characteristics. He read the theories presented by different groups about who built it and why; it was still pretty much a mystery. "Lucy must have wanted to show this to me," he thought, so he replaced the book on the chair where he had found it. He was anxious to see her again.

The phone rang. "Michael, it's Shannon. I'm calling to check on something with you."

"Shannon, darlin', what is it you need?"

"Well, the agency investigating Lance McKellen has come up empty-handed: no birth certificate, no school records, no anything. Are you sure he was from Ohio?"

"That's what I understand. Tell them to keep checking, will you? I'll see if I can find out any more on this end."

"Okay, Michael, it's your dime. Who is this guy anyway, and just why are you so hot to find him?"

"He was… er… is the fiancé of a friend of mine. He sort of dropped off the face of the earth seven years ago."

"I see, and would this friend be a Miss Lucy Cavanagh who is staying out there with you and Myra?"

"Yes, that's right love, and just how do you know about that?"

"Michael, darling, it's me Shannon. Just what is it you think you're paying me to do here? I watch your back, that's what."

"And you think my back needs watching, do you?"

"Well, according to Bertha, who stopped in to see me last Monday."

"Bertha?"

"Yes, that's right. She asked if I was surprised by the affair you're having with one of her girls. Just what is going on with you and that cleaning girl anyway?"

"Oh, so now I'm paying you to listen to office gossip?" Michael was annoyed by her question. It put Lucy in a bad light, and he didn't like it.

"Michael, your wellbeing as CEO of this company is the concern of all of us here."

"Look, Shannon, do me a favor and be less concerned over idle talk and rumors and more concerned about digging up the information I've requested. Call me when you have something on McKellen." He hung up the phone.

He buried his head in his hands. He felt like he was losing control and regretted that he had been harsh with his old friend. When the phone rang again right away, he thought she was calling him back. "Shannon, I'm sorry I got a little prickly with you."

"Michael, this is Myra. Why are you prickly?"

"Oh hello, Myra. I'm not anymore. I'll explain later. How is Skipper?"

"That's why I'm calling, Michael. She is having a rough time of it. She's going through something they call BB's."

"DT's, Myra."

"Yes, well, whatever they are, she is having a rough time. Winnie wants to bring her home."

"No! Myra, don't let her do that. Skipper needs to be right where she is. I knew it was too soon for Winnie to visit."

"Winnie is Skipper's mother, and she hates to see her child suffer."

"I know that, Myra, but you have to make her understand. It's important that she goes through with this if she ever wants Skipper to have a normal life. Tell her, Myra. Make her understand."

"I'll try, lovie."

"I'm counting on you." He was about to hang up when he remembered what it was he had wanted to ask her. "Say, Myra, now that I have you on the phone, I was wondering if you knew anything about a crystal cross that my mother used to wear."

"Certainly, dear. William gave it to her when she became pregnant with you. Why are you asking about that?"

"It just came into my mind the other day. I was wondering just what became of it. Do you know?"

"William had it. He said he was keeping it to give Kathleen if she were to become pregnant with your child."

"And where is it now?"

"I'm not sure, dear. I haven't seen it in years."

"Oh, I see," he said with some disappointment.

"I'll search for it, Michael. I can't imagine your grandfather giving it up to anyone."

"Will you, Myra? I'd appreciate it."

"Surely, Michael. I need to go calm Winnie down now, dear. I'll be back after dinnertime, so don't wait on me."

"Be safe, Myra."

"Thank you, dear. My love to Fred and Lucy. Bye now."

He hung up the phone and walked to the kitchen for a cup of coffee. He was eager to see Lucy again. He wondered what was going on and whether she would see Lance again in the stone circle. He took his cup into the garden, and as he strolled toward the gazebo he heard the thunder of horses' hoofs. He turned to see Lucy astride Sazi and Fred on Shashad racing up the drive. They were laughing, and for an instant he was jealous. They dismounted as he walked up.

"Have a good ride, you two?"

"Excellent," she replied beaming.

"Meat and Potatoes, old chum" was Fred's reply.

"Speaking of meat and potatoes, why don't you two go on in and change while I put the horses up. I'll drive us over to Whatnot Inn for burgers and a cold beer. Sound good?"

"Excellent plan," Fred replied.

"What about you, Lucy? Are you in on it?"

"Sure, but I'll put up Sazi, if you don't mind. She gave me a wonderful ride."

He handed Fred his cup and took the reins of Shashad. He led Strider's sire down the path to the stable, with Lucy and Sazi following close behind. Once in the stalls, the horses were unsaddled and brushed down. Michael, in Shashad's stall, had a clear view of Lucy as she worked lovingly on the sleek Arab mare. He watched as she bent, stretched, and rubbed against the lucky beast. His desire for her was almost more than he could control. She looked up and smiled at him and he dropped his brush. It went sailing out of his hand and landed at her feet. She picked it up and walked into Shashad's stall.

"Thanks," he said, taking it from her and looking quickly away. He thought if he looked at her, she would be able to read what he was thinking.

"You're very quiet, Michael. Is anything wrong?"

"Wrong? No, just hungry I guess." She took that to mean for lunch, but he meant for her.

She turned on the hose and filled the horses' buckets with fresh water. "Let's go clean up and be off to get you that burger. Race you to the house." She took off running the second it left her mouth, giving her a clear lead. He caught up with her easily, but as he went to pass she grabbed his arm, slowing him down. She took hold of his shoulders then jumped up and straddled his back.

"So you haven't had enough horseback, eh?" He looped her legs with his arms and quickened his pace. He ran into the house and up the stairs, putting her down in front of her door. He was panting and laughing at the same time.

"There you go, lassie," he said. "Now may I expect the same treatment you gave Sazi?"

"Sure thing, Michael," she said, patting his nose.

She showered upstairs while he washed up in the kitchen. Fred was sitting at the table with a cup of tea.

"So how did our plan go, Freddy?" He was anxious to know.

"You mean the plan where I was to follow your directions and wind up in a non-existent stone circle?"

"What are you talking about?"

"I'm talking about the fact we rode all over that meadow and there was no stone circle."

"Did you turn right where the path from the stable tees?"

"Of course I did. And the meadow was right where you said it would be. But there was no stone circle."

"You're kidding me."

"No, Michael, I'm not."

"What did Lucy say about it?"

"She said nothing about it. She just rode around like Calamity Jane or Annie Oakley or somebody like that. I don't think she had any idea she was in the same meadow." They heard Lucy on the stairs and changed their conversation.

"Ready to go, are you, horsewoman?" Michael asked when she walked in. She had on the little sundress she had been wearing the day he left on his trip.

"Yes, I am, and I could eat a horse."

"Me too!" said Fred.

"Well, I best get us on the road then if only to keep my animals safe." Fred hopped in the back seat, letting Lucy ride in front.

"Michael, I was wondering if you had any time to look for *The Green Book*," she questioned.

"No, sorry, Lucy, I haven't. But I did find the book that you left for me on the chair in the study."

"I didn't leave any book in the study for you. I always put back the ones I use."

"I'm talking about the book you left on the chair by the fire, the one opened to the page of the Serpent Mound. The drawing of it is the same shape as the symbol we found on Angus."

"Michael, I didn't leave a book there." She paused and a look of bewilderment came on her face. Half under her breath she said, "The Serpent Mound, of course. Why didn't I make that connection before?"

"Lucy, let's talk about this a moment. You never did tell me where you saw the symbol before."

"It was on the bottom of the last letter I received from Lance. He copied it from an etching on a stone someone had given him. He told me he thought it was key to finding what he was looking for."

"Just what was he looking for?" Freddy asked.

"I'm not sure. I'm hoping *The Green Book* will shed light on that. But I think he was looking for a way home."

"A way home?" Fred and Michael asked at the same time.

"Yes." Lucy didn't offer more, and Michael could see that the questions were making her uncomfortable, so he changed the subject and shot Fred a glance to drop it.

"Well, here we are, my hungry mates," he said as he pulled the car into the parking lot of the little bar.

It was very evident to the men, especially Michael, that Lucy's mood had changed. She excused herself to the rest room right away, leaving her order with Michael —a cheeseburger with just pickles and mayo. When she returned, Michael was sure she had been crying, so he didn't press her for conversation as they sat through lunch.

Lucy seemed to be lost in thought as she sat, barely touching the burger he'd ordered for her. And indeed she was. She rebuked herself for even coming on this little outing. *I should be back at Glen Eden looking for clues to find Lance.* She was certain Angus had left the book out for Michael to find. *I'm getting way too comfortable with Michael, and it's not right.*

She became aware of how close they were sitting in the booth and moved over. Noticing, Michael asked, "Lucy, is everything all right?"

"Everything is fine, why?"

"Because you've hardly touched that burger."

"I didn't wolf it down like you boys, if that's what you mean. But I'm working on it." She picked it up and forced another tiny bite.

"Freddy and I are going to order another beer, if you don't mind. Would you care for one?"

"No thanks; you go ahead." Michael ordered the beers and Fred excused himself for the loo.

Michael was worried about Lucy. Since he mentioned finding the book in the study, her countenance had changed. He berated himself for opening his big mouth. He liked seeing her smile and play. He felt close to her when they were horsing around at the cottage. Now she had distanced herself from him again, retreating inward where he knew she felt only loneliness and pain.

Fred returned and issued a challenge to them: "Hey, you two, they have a new Sky Riders pinball game in back. It can accommodate four players; want to give it a go?

"I'm in," Michael said. "How about it, Lucy? Want to try your luck against the experts?"

"No, I think I'll just sit, watch, and learn from 'the experts'." She rolled her eyes and a slight smile returned.

"Let's make it interesting, Fred ol' boy. Loser buys dinner at the Tara tonight."

"You're on, mate." The three moved to a table near the pinball machine in the back and Fred and Michael squared off.

While Lucy sat watching the shiny balls as they danced, spun, and bounced off the bumpers, causing explosions of lights and sounds of whirring and bells, her thoughts wandered back, back to a time with Lance, back to the Serpent Mound.

Lance unsaddled Takota and stashed the saddle on the limb of an elm tree. He helped Lucy mount the bare back of the magnificent animal and then slung himself up behind her. She never felt so happy. It was as if she were in a dream world. With Takota under her and Lance behind her, they moved through the world as one.

The surefooted Takota carried them back and forth across the stream that snaked its way around the hills of southern Ohio. The mighty horse moved as if he knew the mind of his master. Lucy imagined herself an Indian maiden riding with her warrior through the sacred grounds of their people. They rode for two hours without seeing any sign of a house or road or any trace of civilization. As they rode, Lucy leaned back against her brave and he shared the history and legends of the land they rode through and talked of the place he was taking her.

"The Great Serpent Mound is very sacred to the Native Americans of this area. It lies in a bluff overlooking Bush Creek, which is the larger end of this stream we have been crisscrossing. It is a thirteen-hundred-foot-long mound shaped like a great snake. One end, the tail, spirals around, while the other, its head, is in the shape of an open mouth. There is a separate oval mound just outside the open mouth, which some archaeologists describe as an egg about to be eaten. Many scholars think it was constructed as a burial mound by the Adena or Hopewell peoples about two thousand years ago, even though excavations there have never revealed any bones or artifacts. Geologists have found that it is built over a very unique site. There is probably not another such site in the entire United States. But I learned from the Keeper there are others in different parts of the world, all containing some sort of sacred marker, be it megalith, dolmen, mound or temple. Under it, there is a condensed area of faults, compacted and localized. The term is *crypto-volcanic* because geologists cannot be sure just what caused them; they surmise either a volcanic disturbance or maybe a meteor impact."

"If it wasn't used for a burial mound, then what *was* its purpose?"

"Same as it is now, to my mind. And that, my love, is what I am hoping to discover. It is a place of power, to be sure. Legend among Littlefeather's people tell it as a place where the Great Spirit Gods come from the Heavens to bless the planting and the harvest of crops.

"As a boy, I used to be visited by an old Shaman named Shapato. He told me many times that he had seen orbs of light either rising from or descending into the egg-shaped mound. Shapato was a very kind soul. He taught me many ways of the shaman. He is the one that first told me my life was to be a quest for the Truth."

"Everyone's life should be a quest for the Truth."

"Right you are, my girl. 'Ye shall know the truth and the truth shall set you free.'"

"Amen."

"Yes indeed. Amen. But you know as well as I do, Lucy, many people are afraid of the Truth."

"Why is that, Lance?"

"It is the pervasive spirit of this world they live in. Satan was given reign over it, and he keeps things pretty confused. We'll cross the river here."

They came once again upon Bush Creek, but here it was wider and faster than where they had crossed it before. Lance hopped off Takota and then helped Lucy down. He led the big horse down into the water, and the three of them waded across the icy stream. On the other side, the bank rose sharply and turned into the side of a fairly large hill where birch, elm, maple and evergreens grew, with a buckeye here and there to add local flavor. The three companions wound back and forth up the hill until they broke the top and stood about thirty feet from the egg-shaped earthwork at the head of the Great Serpent.

The trees had all been cut back to clear the mound to open view and the grounds over and around it were groomed for a park-like setting. Lance tied Takota in the shade and took Lucy's hand. He led her to the edge of the egg and whispered in her ear, "Do you feel it?"

Lucy didn't know what he meant at first, but then a slight vibration coursed through her. "The earth is humming," she said.

"Yes!" he shouted triumphantly. "I knew you would feel it too. Not everyone can. Sometimes it is much stronger, on nights of the full moon or on a solstice. I used to come here as often as I could at those times. The vibration does something to me, Lucy. It expands my mind, opens my chakras, and strengthens me. I'm sure that's why the Indians found this place to be sacred. They are much more in tune with Nature and the Earth than people in this modern-day world. It is a place of power."

"But, Lance, how would these ancient Indian people know how to build a thing like this?"

"You ask wonderful questions, darling. Let us lie here against the mound, clear our minds of all things, and see what the earth has to tell us." He took her hands and fell to his knees, bringing her down with him. He turned his back to the raised earth and lay against it. She did the same. It felt good to Lucy to lay against the warm earth in the bright sunlight. She had gotten chilled from crossing the stream and standing atop the hill in wet clothes in the midday breeze. Now, lying quietly beside Lance, she looked upon the wonderfully blue sky as billowy white tufts of cloud floated here and there, creating an ever changing canvas above her.

She took a deep breath and let it out. She exhaled all her thoughts and brought in clear, pure air. She felt the oxygen mix with her blood and open her vibrating mind. When she exhaled this time, she followed her breath out and up. She floated above herself in the blue. She turned to behold two earthly forms lying side by side on the egg near the serpent. In the center of the egg stood Lance, also outside his body. He was a glowing, glittering form. A very small man stood next to him dressed all in earth tones except for a bright red cap, and the two faced a tall being of pure white light. Sensing Lucy's gaze, the light-being pointed at her hovering spirit, and instantly she fell back into her body.

When she opened her eyes, the sky she beheld was not the blue sky she had watched before but a dark violet color. Gone were the gently floating puffs of cloud, and in their place were long grey fingers. She raised up on an elbow and realized she was alone; Lance was not lying beside her. Slowly she got to her feet and looked around. Takota was gone too. "Where would Lance have gone," she wondered. She walked slowly the length of the mound, and as she approached the spiraling tail, she saw that the little man who had been standing next to Lance was sitting on its very tip, smoking a long pipe.

Lucy had never seen a creature such as this. "Hello," she said.

He looked at her with disdain and blew out a smoke ring that was bigger than he was. "Hello yourself," he replied.

"I am very sorry to disturb you, but I was wondering..."

He interrupted her: "You're not sorry to disturb me. You are pleased to do so. You have a question you want to ask and you mean to ask it, disturb me or not."

Lucy was flustered. "Well, yes, I do have a question. But I was only trying to be polite."

"It would be more polite if you would stop wasting my time and ask your question. Now what is it? And be quick."

"I was wondering if you knew where the man went who you were standing next to a little while ago."

"He didn't go anywhere. Good day." He turned his back on her and took another puff on his pipe.

"Excuse me," Lucy said, feeling a lot like Alice talking to the Cheshire cat. "I need to find him."

"Tell me why you want to find him, and I might tell you where he is."

"I don't really see how that is any of your business. I simply asked if you had seen him." Lucy surprised herself at this rather rude response to the irritating little man.

"No, you didn't. You already know that I saw him. You asked if I knew where he went."

"Well, do you?"

"I already told you."

"No, you did not. You said he didn't go anywhere, but I know he did because he was not by me when I woke up."

"Maybe you weren't by him."

"What are you talking about?"

"Like I already told you, he did not go anywhere."

Lucy was tired of arguing. She decided to walk back to the serpent's head to see if Lance had returned. As she crossed by the spiral to the other side of the mound, the little man blew a gigantic smoke ring that passed right in front of her. She had to step through it to stay on the path. As she did so, the blue sky returned. She hurried along and arrived at the spot to see her body lying just as she had left it. She climbed back inside her sleeping self and opened her eyes. Lance was leaning on one elbow looking into her face.

"And just where have you been, Lucy girl?"

"I was looking for you."

"Oh you were, eh? And just why were you doing that?"

"Because, Lance, I love you."

He smiled at her and then his face turned grave. She had never seen him look that way before. She didn't want to hear what he might tell her, so she kissed him. When they finished, he turned his head away and began talking. She knew it was so that he didn't have to look in her eyes.

"We best be on our way to make the cabin before dark. I snagged two bass earlier and left them in the stream near where we stashed the saddle. We'll stop and pick them up for our dinner."

"Sure, sounds great," she said, trying not to let the fear of the unspoken words creep into her voice.

They inched down the hill to its base where the river ran. Lance lifted her to sit astride Takota for the crossing of it. "I don't want you to get wet again or you'll be cold on the ride back." Lucy didn't argue; her heart was still in her throat. On the other side, Lance again flung himself up on his steed. His lady sat between his legs, but the joy that had infused her on the earlier ride was cloaked now in a veil of sadness.

They rode in silence until finally she found the courage to ask, "Lance, what's wrong?"

"I have made a mistake, Lucy, a grave one. One that I am afraid may hurt you. I let the desires of my heart and flesh take charge of my judgment."

"Lance, please don't say that making love to me was a mistake. You told me right from the start that you couldn't give me much time. I accepted that."

"Yes, I know, darling, but taking you to a place of power as I have just done was very foolish."

"Why?"

"Because, Lucy, it is not your time."

"Please don't talk in riddles."

"I thought that you would follow me, but you did not. You could not. Not now anyway. Maybe never. But still I must go."

"If I can't go with you, then I will wait for you to come back."

"What if I can't?"

"I'm a god!" Michael roared, celebrating his win. His voice brought her back to the side of the pinball machine. In his competitive exuberance, he picked her up and spun her around.

21 – Angel or Devil, or No Good Deed Goes Unpunished

🕊 A surprise awaited them when they returned from the Whatnot: Megan had dropped by with one of her girlfriends.

"Hello, Uncle Freddy," she said, running up to give him a hug.

"Hey, cutie-pie, I was hoping to see you."

"Myra left me a message that you were here." She was dressed in a pastel pink tank top tucked into matching short shorts from which her long tan legs ran down to meet her short pink socks cozied into white tennies. "Michael, Uncle Fred, this is my friend Carly. We'll be roommates at school this fall." She totally ignored Lucy who was standing right there.

Michael cleared his throat and gestured with his head toward Lucy as he reached out to take Carly's hand. "Pleased I am to meet you, Carly."

"Oh yeah, that's Lucy," Megan said, without even a glance in her direction.

"Nice to meet you, Carly," Lucy said.

"Sure, hi" was the response she got from the tall, buxom, twenty-something girl in a short white tennis skirt.

"Michael, Carly is going to school on a tennis scholarship."

"Is that right? Good for you."

"We were wondering if you would take us and Uncle Freddy to your club in Holland to play some."

"Sure, I could do that. What do you say, Freddy?"

"Sounds good to me. Lucy, do you play?"

"Not very well, I'm afraid. But you all go right ahead. I planned on doing more research in the study this afternoon."

"Great," chirped Megan. "Come on, Michael. Let's go."

"Wait a sec, Megan. I don't want to leave Lucy here all alone."

"Please, Michael, I'll be fine. I promise."

"There you go, Michael; she'll be fine. She's a big girl," Megan said, tugging on Michael's arm. He shot a glance at Fred who gave him a nod, so he acquiesced to Megan's pleas.

Lucy walked straightaway to the study and found the book Michael had asked her about still on the chair. She decided to learn all she could about the Serpent Mound. After three hours of searching through books on sacred sites and places of power, she found little mention of it. She was about to give up and go to the kitchen to fix a cup of tea. Before she did, she straightened up some books on a shelf in order to replace one she had been reading. A book slid from its place and slammed to the floor. "Oh no!" she exclaimed, thinking she may have done damage to it. She read the spine as she bent over to pick it up. It was a book on Indian lore and legends. It had fallen open to a page headed "Dream Quest Visions of a Warrior Chief." She hurried back to the desk and began reading.

The story told that as a young brave, Chief Tecumseh visited the Serpent Mound on the night of a winter solstice. There he had a chance encounter with a man he described as "a warrior not of this time." He told of how the serpent spit out the warrior from the egg in its mouth. The warrior told the chief he had traveled to many lands searching for a way home and that the mound was a tunnel through time. Tecumseh described the warrior as light of skin, fair of hair, and with eyes the color of winter moss.

"Lance!" Lucy said aloud.

"It's me, Michael," came a reply from beside her chair.

"Oh, Michael, I didn't hear you come in. I've found a mention of Lance in this book. Look." Michael took the book and read the passages she indicated. He stood silent when he finished and gave her a puzzled look. "Well?"

"Lucy, I know how badly you want to find Lance, to find out what's happened to him. But this is…" He checked himself. "Just because this time traveler has green eyes…"

She saw his doubt and interrupted him. "It's not *just* because of that. It's partly that, but it's about how I found this book. It just jumped off the shelf at my feet. And it's about the way you found the book you thought I'd left out for you when I hadn't. Don't you see, Michael? It's Lance. He has Angus giving us these clues."

He saw her wide-eyed enthusiasm and said as gently as he could, "I know you want to believe that, Lucy, but this is grasping at straws. I just don't want to see you set yourself up for more disappointment."

She turned her head and swallowed hard. "I understand, Michael." She wanted him to encourage her.

"Say, look, Fred is upstairs changing for the dinner he owes us at the Tara. What do you say we go get ready? We'll stop on the way and pick up Megan. I hope you don't mind. I know she's been curt with you, but I had a talk with her about it."

"You didn't have to do that, Michael. But of course I don't mind. It will give us a chance to get to know each other."

"That's what I was hoping you'd say, you sweetheart. Come on now, let's go get ready."

Lucy only had one other dress with her that was suitable for night dining, and it was some years old. She bought it in a designer's resale shop in San Francisco in hopes she could wear it for Lance some night. But the occasion never materialized. It was a black crepe, ankle-length number with off the shoulder lace sleeves. She let her hair hang long and parted it on the side Veronica Lake style, Peggy called it.

Michael was again waiting for her at the bottom of the stairs. He had on a dark burgundy shirt with a black velvet dinner jacket and black pants. This time Fred was waiting by his side. He was wearing the dark gray pinstriped suit he had arrived in, with a conventional white shirt and navy blue tie. Michael's eyes lit up when he saw her. Fred let out a whistle. They both offered an arm and escorted her to the car. Fred jumped in the back seat and grumbled about Michael being too cheap to buy a four-door. Lucy sat in front on the way to Megan's. They parked in front of her apartment house, which was just up the highway from the Tara, and Michael jumped out. He returned with Megan hanging on his arm. As they approached the car, Lucy couldn't imagine the girl's dress being any tighter, any shorter, or any lower cut. It was sparkling silver and she looked absolutely wanton to Lucy's mind. She knew miniskirts were the fad of the day, but it was the idea this type of dress could put in a man's head that bothered her. She felt ancient. When Michael opened the passenger door, Lucy slid out. "Hi, Megan. You look lovely."

Megan offered a chilly "Hello."

"Here, you ride in front. I'll go in back. Do you mind, Fred?" Lucy did it because she couldn't imagine how Megan could climb in the back seat in a dress that short without exposing herself to Fred and whoever else might be watching.

The Tara sat atop a little hill on the corner of Blue Star Highway and Douglas's Center Street. It was located on the site of the old Spencer Farm. The original farmhouse—built in the 1850's—was later turned into a fine dining restaurant and named after the plantation in the movie *Gone with the Wind*.

Both of the young ladies turned a lot of heads as they were ushered to their table. Michael stayed behind because he wanted to say hello to the owner. When he joined them they started their dining experience with a chilled goblet of shrimp cocktail. Next came lobster bisque, with the waiter adding a drizzle of sherry when he set it before them. Then came the Caesar salad and for the entrée, chateaubriand with béarnaise sauce. Michael selected an exquisite bottle of French wine to accompany it.

Lucy had never eaten such fabulous food. She had always wanted to dine at the Tara, but it wasn't a place you'd go to alone. Michael seemed to be right in his element and enjoying himself. She tried to imagine Lance there, but couldn't.

Recorded dinner music had been softly playing in the background while they ate. But soon after their empty plates were collected, a woman took the stage just beyond the dance floor. The stage was barely visible before, given the low light from the candles that sat about on every table. Now the singer on stage was framed by a soft beam from a spotlight. She gave a little wave to Michael and gestured a kiss in his direction. He raised his glass to acknowledge her. Lucy rolled her eyes then hoped no one had seen her. "Stop it," she commanded her mind. She looked hard at the girl and, recognizing her, smiled widely.

A man with long hair, a slight beard and bright brown eyes also made his way to the stage. As he passed their table, he stopped to shake Michael's hand. "Hey man, nice to see you. Thanks for coming," he said. Though he didn't see her, Lucy sat with pleasant wonder on her face.

After he took his place at the piano, the woman made their introduction. "Hi, everyone, we're happy to be here tonight. That's Smith," the piano player raised his hand, "and I'm Gayle. We've come here direct from the City by the Bay—San Francisco—to be with you tonight." As the piano began its intro to the song "Dancin' in the Moonlight," she invited the diners to "come on out to the dance floor."

Megan grabbed Michael's arm. "Come dance with me," she said as she pulled him up.

Lucy sat watching the pair, thinking of what a striking couple they made, despite their age difference, which she doubted anyone who didn't know of it could tell. Megan, dressed the way she was, certainly looked older than her years. "They're dancing awfully close," she heard her thoughts say and commanded them once again to be still. When after the first song ended and they stayed on the dance floor, Fred asked Lucy if she'd like to dance. "Yes, I would very much. Thank you."

Fred wasn't a natural dancer. He was stiff and slightly awkward, sometimes counting steps as he tried maneuvering her to the music. Lucy was relieved when the third song was the Monkee's hit "I'm a believer." Now she would be able to unshackle herself from her partner, and they could dance independently together. Three more fast songs followed. She closed her eyes and danced with abandon.

"We're gonna slow it down now," Smith announced, "with a hit from ol' Blue eyes: 'Strangers in the Night.'"

Lucy was just about to excuse herself from the dance floor when Michael walked up and tapped Fred's shoulder. "Change partners, old man?" Fred bowed slightly and gave Michael Lucy's hand. She felt her body weaken as he took her around the waist and pulled her close. "Are you enjoying yourself, lassie?" he asked softly in her ear.

"I am now," her mind said. "Very much," her lips spoke.

He guided her across the floor effortlessly. They stepped to each note like they had become part of the music. She didn't know if she were dancing or floating. When the last note left the air, she was bent across his extended leg as he leaned over the maiden in his arms. He smiled and brought her up.

"Michael, Michael Donegan, come on up here and treat these people to a song," Gayle invited. Michael breathed deeply as he tore his eyes from Lucy's.

"Thanks, Gayle, but the audience isn't drunk enough yet to enjoy my pipes."

"Don't be silly, Michael. Come up here."

An older patron stood up and loudly requested, "Sing 'Danny Boy', Michael." Others offered encouragement with applause, and Michael gave in.

He walked Lucy back to the table and said, "Will you save me another dance, if they don't throw me out after this?" Lucy smiled and nodded. Her body was still atingle.

Gayle handed him her mike and sat down on the piano bench next to Smith. Lucy sat spellbound as he sang the old ballad. She wasn't alone in that; not a sound was heard from anywhere in the restaurant save his voice. "He surely has done this before," she thought. He finished to thunderous applause and then sang another request, "When Irish Eyes are Smiling." Lucy felt like he was directing this song at her since he barely looked in anyone else's direction while he sang it. When he finished, Gayle made him promise to sing another before the night was over.

He returned to the table and suggested they order coffee and some dessert. The foursome sat enjoying the fare and chatting, with the conversation centered mostly on Megan. Lucy was grateful for that, never liking to be the center of it herself because of the secrets she was forced to conceal. Michael invited Smith and Gayle to come sit at their table on their breaks and picked up the tab for whatever they had to drink. Smith headed right for Lucy and took her hand. "Hello, Lucy. I thought it was you when I saw you dancing."

Lucy stood to greet him and they embraced. "Hi, Smith, you look well."

Michael sat slack jawed over the fact Smith and Lucy knew each other. He had met Smith and Gayle playing at The Playboy Club Lounge in San Francisco. He went there at the request of a business associate and after buying the duo a round of drinks, his associate persuaded them to let Michael sing. The three of them hit it off immediately. Eventually, they confided to Michael they weren't happy playing there. But as Smith put it, "The pay is good, and a gig is a gig when rent has to be paid." Recently, Michael gave the owner of the Tara a tape of one of their sets and secretly agreed to pay their first week's salary if he would give them a chance.

"Gayle, look! It's Lucy," Smith said, and his partner immediately rushed over to give her a hug. Fred ordered a bottle of Champagne, and the mood became light and giddy.

"So just how is it you know my Lucy?" Michael asked. Lucy picked up on the possessive pronoun and shot him a questioning look. Megan also heard it and shot an even harsher look at Lucy. "My friend Lucy," Michael clarified.

"She's my angel," Smith offered then explained: "My wife was suing me for a divorce that I didn't want. So I was forced to get an attorney. Lucy happened to be working part time in his office and we had a nice conversation while I was waiting to be seen. A few weeks later, I stopped into the International House of Pancakes on Lombard Street and there she was again, waiting tables. I offered her a ride home after her shift and invited her to come see me play in this jazz combo the following weekend in Half Moon Bay. I never dreamed she'd show up. But there she was. She came in—in the middle of a set—and I didn't see her at first. Then I noticed a girl dancing all alone in the corner."

"I wasn't dancing alone," Lucy protested.

Smith reached out and put his hand on her head and she swatted it away. He continued: "I was in a really bad place at the time, and during my break we took a walk on the beach. She asked why I was playing so guardedly. I was a little upset with her for saying that since she'd never heard me play before. Then she asked, 'What is it you don't want people to hear?' I told her about my divorce and how angry and hurt I was. I said I knew it was affecting my music. She told me I should pray about it and play the emotions, and then she prayed for me. I cried like a baby. It was the first time I'd cried over my divorce; I had been too angry. I told her I would play it if she would dance to it. The third song of the next set I looked up to see her standing alone in the center of the dance floor."

"I was so jealous of her before we met," Gayle added. "The way Smith talked about her as his angel. Then he took me to meet her, and she became mine as well. You see, I am seventeen years older than Smith, not that anyone can tell." She winked at him. "But Lucy told me she knew I was in love with him. She told me she believed he was in love with me too. We had sung together for years, and I knew there was a platonic connection. We were offered a two-week gig at the Playboy Club in Honolulu, and of course we jumped to take it. Lucy came to see me before we left and brought me a tie-dyed dress of hers that I had admired. She told me she bought it to wear as a wedding dress, but things hadn't worked out." She looked at Lucy and took her hand. "It was *my* wedding dress, Lucy; I wore it in Hawaii when Smith and I were married. I always wanted to tell you that."

Michael lifted his glass of Champagne. "To our angel," he said. The spotlight came up, calling the musicians back to the stage.

As the evening progressed, Megan began to show the effects of the wine. She began clinging to Michael, and she monopolized his time on the dance floor. As promised, Michael sang one more song: "My Wild Irish Rose." He sang it with such emotion that Lucy couldn't help but think he was singing it to Kathleen. After his applause died down, he leaned over and whispered something to Gayle. Two fast songs later, with Lucy paired again with Fred and Michael with Megan, Gayle announced, "We'll slow it down for the last tune of the evening, a request: Stevie Wonder's 'You are the Sunshine of My Life.'"

Michael again tapped Fred's shoulder and handed Megan over to him. He took Lucy's hand and spun her around as Smith's piano spilled forth the first strains of the song. She performed every move he required of her as if she could read his mind. He pulled her close again and felt his desire for her rise. She felt it too. She became totally his for this dance; Lance did not cut in to her thoughts. They were one with the music and Michael hated for it to end. When it did, he wanted to kiss her so badly his tongue was tied. As the other couples left the floor, she stood locked in his arms, holding her breath.

"Once again, we'd like to thank Michael Donegan for treating us to his wonderful voice," Gayle announced, breaking the spell. "This is Smith and Gayle reminding you that Love is all you need."

Lucy inhaled deeply, turned, and walked slowly back to the table. She was afraid to look at him now, afraid she had given too much of herself away. Megan sat glaring at her.

Smith and Gayle stopped by the table to say good night and thanked Michael for getting them the job. Gayle announced that the owner had asked them to stay on for the rest of the summer. Fred called for the check and requested the waiter bring back six glasses of Galliano for a celebratory toast.

While Gayle chatted with Michael, Smith softly spoke to Lucy: "It was good seeing you. Michael is a great guy, and I'm glad he has someone of quality in his life now. You've put a sparkle back in his eyes and it's good to see." Lucy didn't know what to say. She was glad he didn't give her a chance. "You dance so well together, like you were made for each other. It was a pleasure to play for you again."

"Hearing you play is always *my* pleasure," Lucy said.

The Galliano arrived and Fred offered the toast this time: "All you need is Love." They all repeated it as the glasses were raised. As the glass went to Lucy's lips, her eyes fell on Michael. He was looking right at her, and as he put his glass to his lips, a gleam from his heart shot from his eyes. She lowered her head and put her glass down, leaving the golden soother untasted. She was mindful not to look in his eyes again.

In the car on the way home, Megan laid her head on Michael's shoulder. "We'll have you home in a jiffy, Megs. Do come by and look in on Myra. She misses you."

"I'm sorry, Michael, for the way I behaved. Now that I understand the situation and how you and Uncle Fred are just trying to help poor Lucy, I'll be by Monday to give Myra a hand." Michael prayed Lucy didn't hear that. Fred was chattering away in the back seat, and he hoped to God Lucy was listening to him and not to Megan.

Lucy stayed in the back seat after they dropped Megan off and Michael strained to hear what was being said. They hadn't talked to each other since their dance ended. He dropped his passengers off at the front steps and drove the car down to the port at the end of the drive. He parked and rushed to the house, hoping she hadn't gone off to bed and he'd have a chance to talk to her. He wanted to tell her how he felt. He had hope now, since the dance, that she might be receptive to him.

A car pulled up the drive just as he was about to enter the cottage. It was Myra returning from Chicago. "Myra, you're getting back late." He moved back down the stairs to meet her.

"Oh Michael, I don't know what to say to you."

"Well, I know what to say to him," Winnie said, jumping from behind the wheel of the car. "You are a no good scoundrel, Michael Donegan, and I curse the day you were born."

Michael had no idea what this was about. Lucy and Fred heard the car drive up and came to stand in the open doorway. Winnie looked at Lucy, pointed her finger, and, filled with even more wrath, screamed, "That girl is the devil's sister, if you ask me. First, she breaks my son's heart, and now she's causing anguish to my girl."

"Winnie, what in heaven's name are you cackling about? Lucy hasn't hurt Skipper." He didn't mind her calling him names, but calling Lucy the devil's sister got under his skin.

"Now, now, Winnie, that's enough. You aren't doin' any good behaving this way," Myra said, trying to calm her friend down.

"Myra, will you please explain to me what's going on?" Michael requested.

"What's going on, Michael, is that Skipper told Winnie…" She looked up at Lucy and finished her sentence guardedly. "Well… she told Winnie about… you know what."

"No, I don't know what, Myra, and I'd be happy if you told me."

"Oh Michael, Skipper told Winnie about the baby."

"What baby?"

"Your baby."

"My baby!? Michael gasped.

"Skipper is having your baby, Michael. She told us you know about it, and that's why you talked Ashley into putting her in that place."

Lucy turned and ran up the stairs. She could hear no more of this.

"What!?"

"Skipper told Winnie she needs to get out of that place because she's afraid they will hurt the baby."

"I'm going to wring her neck," Michael exclaimed.

"Now, now, Michael, that's no way to talk about the woman who's having your baby," Myra admonished.

"She is not going to have my baby."

"Oh Michael! You'll not ask her to have an abortion, will you?" Myra was truly shocked.

Winnie came after him now with her purse. "Devil! Devil! Devil!" she screamed. Fred ran down the stairs to help Michael restrain her. Fred picked her up from behind and backed her away from Michael.

"Can you all please just calm down so we can get to the bottom of this?" Fred asked, holding tightly the flailing woman. "Michael, what do you have to say for yourself?"

"If Skipper is pregnant, it's not mine."

"And how can you be sure of that?" Fred kept up the interrogation. "You are aware that protection fails sometimes, aren't you?"

"Yes, of course, Fred. I'm not an idiot."

"Well, that remains to be seen. How can you be sure the baby isn't yours?"

"Fred, I wouldn't hit a woman, but I'll knock you across this drive."

"How far along is she, Winnie?" Fred inquired, ignoring the threat.

"She didn't tell me. But she did tell me it had to be Michael's because…" The woman gasped for breath. "… because he took advantage of her one night when she had too much to drink."

"Winnie, I swear to you it only happened once, and I didn't take advantage of her. We were both drunk and we… we…" He stopped trying to explain; after all, this was her mother.

"It only takes once," the old woman cried.

"Well, there's no way to settle this tonight then," Fred interjected. "We all better just give it up this evening and get some rest. We can hash it out with cooler heads tomorrow. Winnie, I'll drive you home. Michael, you follow us and bring me back." Everyone followed Fred's instructions and no one uttered another word.

Lucy heard the whole sordid business from her open window. She rebuked herself for giving in to the charms of such a rogue—she had given herself to him with that dance. She blamed it partially on the fact her senses had been dulled by drink. She would keep her distance from now on and not make that mistake again. She also had to admit there was a desire in her flesh that was not his fault alone. She spent time in prayer asking her Father's forgiveness. She asked for comfort for Winnie and help and healing for Skipper. She also prayed for Michael that he would accept the love of his savior and turn from his wicked ways. A soft knock came on her door. "Yes?"

"Lucy, it's Michael. I didn't wake you, did I?"

"No, Michael. What do you want?"

"I'd like to talk with you a moment. May I come in?"

"No, I'm in bed. Is there something you need?"

"Something I need…" He wanted to say, *Yes, I need you!* But he detected the coldness in her voice. "I wanted to talk to you about what happened downstairs."

"It's none of my business, Michael."

"No, of course it isn't. I just wanted to make sure you're all right."

"I'm fine."

"Okay then." He stood with his head leaning against her door.

When she didn't hear him move away, she said, "Michael, will you still have time to talk to me about what I've learned of Lance after you take Fred to the plane tomorrow?"

"Sure, Lucy. I look forward to it."

"Good. Good night then."

"Good night."

He staggered to his room. Removing his jacket and tossing it on a chair, he fell onto his bed. His mind was moving in ten directions at once, but his body was stuck on an overwhelming desire for Lucy. He found it impossible to think straight, so he climbed once again into the shower and shocked himself with a good blast of cold water.

When Lucy came downstairs the next morning, she found the house empty and Myra in the garden. "The boys have left for Chicago. Fred changed his flight to leave from O'Hare and Michael has gone to visit Skipper. I think they mentioned picking up Ashley. Anyway, there is a big pot of hot porridge on the stove. Eat some and come do yoga with me. It's an exciting new day."

"I could do with a little less excitement, if you know what I mean."

"I suppose I do, dear, but that's what makes the quiet times so enjoyable." Lucy had to laugh about the optimistic way Myra looked at things.

After a cup of coffee, a bowl of steel-cut oats smothered in butter, and forty-five minutes of yoga postures in the fresh air, Lucy felt somewhat normal again. She took a long walk on the beach and waded awhile in the cold wave-ends as they washed up and back on the shore. She took a stick and, without really thinking, wrote *Lance* in the sand. She read it aloud just before the last surge of a wave washed it away. She looked at the barren sand and said, "This is what I am."

Myra hadn't wanted to walk with her because she was expecting a call from Michael. When Lucy returned, Myra was on the phone. So she carried a tray of hot tea to the gazebo and waited for her to finish.

"That was Michael on the phone," Myra said when she came out to join her. "He wanted me to tell you that he would be back around three and that he will be all yours after that." She sipped her tea and then looked hard at Lucy. "I'd like to ask you not to encourage him until after he's sorted this Skipper thing out."

"Encourage him?"

"Well, you know, dear. He has his eyes on you. And, well, maybe he shouldn't, I mean, until after he figures out whether what Skipper says is true. I know my Michael; if she is pregnant with his child, he will do right by her."

"Myra, I assure you, I have no interest in Michael. I am desperate to find Lance, and Michael has promised to help. That's all."

"I know that's what you think, dear. But what if you can't find Lance, Lucy? Then what?

She was already in the study when Michael returned. He looked exhausted. "Hello, Michael."

"Lucy."

They both sat quietly. Then at the same moment they both spoke. He said, "I have no idea what you must think of me." And she said, "I know you have a lot on your mind right now."

They paused another awkward moment, and she began, "It's really good of you to give me time like this. I know you're dealing with a lot right now. I'd completely understand if you want to put this off."

He raised his hands. "No, Lucy, that's not what I want to do. I want to help you find Lance, to get to the bottom of it. But before we start, I want to explain what happened last night with Winnie."

"Michael, please, that is not necessary."

"Well, I think it is, for me anyway. So please listen." She nodded. "Ashley and I visited Skipper this morning after we dropped Fred off for his flight."

"How is she?"

"That's what I'm trying to get at. She's confused. She is fighting to get the demons to let go her mind. Alcoholism is a terrible thing. To go without drink after it has consumed you is horrible. We saw the demon spirit in her." He closed his eyes and ran his hand through his hair. "It breaks my heart to see what it's done to her. None of us realized it had gotten this bad."

"Oh Michael, I'm sorry."

"We're all sorry, Lucy, sorry and sad and sick."

"Won't all this hurt the baby?"

"The baby… There is no baby, Lucy. She was pregnant when Jay died, but she lost it. She can't have children now." He stood up and walked over to the window. "I'll never understand why God gives some people so much to bear."

"He's not the one who gives it to them. He's the one that helps them bear it."

"Of course you're right, Lucy. I'm sorry." He put his hands to his face and Lucy could tell he was wiping his eyes. "Skipper told her mom she was pregnant because she thought Winnie would sign her out. Thank God Myra was with her and talked her out of it."

"What's going to happen to her?"

"She's in the best place she can be. Dr. Scott, the director, said he has seen worse cases turn around."

"Well, that's some hope to cling to. Michael, let's pray for Skipper right now. Do you want to?"

He turned and looked at her then dropped to his knees. She walked over and knelt next to him. "Lord, our Father, whose love never fails, forgive us that we have failed You. Strengthen us against the attacks of the wicked one. Help us to know and do Your will. Be with our sister Skipper. You who created her can put her back together and make her body whole and her mind sound. Grant it, dear God, in the name of the One who is Love. Amen."

"Amen," Michael echoed. He offered a little smile and mouthed "Thanks," as he helped her to her feet. "Now let's find Lance."

As they walked back to the desk, hope welled in her again. She told him about all she'd learned in her studies. Then she told him about seeing Angus and of the smoke ring which carried Lance's image and of the message Lance gave her: "Lance said there are many things he must learn and do. But he was encouraged by the fact that I'm here. He said William was a seventh son and that magic can happen here. He said we need to find *The Green Book* because it will help us understand. William told him he hid it to keep it safe. Lance said as William's son noble blood runs through your veins, Michael, and you have a big part to play in our story." Lucy left out the part where Lance told her she may have to forget him because she knew she would never do that.

The two sat together once again united in their quest to find the man that held the key to their fates. They refused Myra's proposal for dinner, so she brought them in sandwiches.

Lucy studied other material on time travel and legends of people who had done it while Michael perused his grandfather's journal, the one Lucy had read. Something Lance said of him to Lucy struck a chord: "That as William's son, noble blood runs in his veins." Was that just an archaic way of saying grandson, or did Lance mean William was actually his father? The more he read the journal, the more he wondered. Could that be the horrible truth that led his mother to take her own life? Is that what his father was coming to tell him the day he was killed, that he in fact was not his father but the man he called Grandfather was?

Lucy saw the expression on his face and asked, "Michael, what is it?"

"It's confusion, Lucy. The more I seek the truth, the more confused I become."

"You know who authors confusion."

"Aye, 'tis the devil, and he won't leave me alone."

"He only hunts those that have a good heart. He already has the rest."

Michael told her his suspicions then walked to the door and summoned Myra. "Myra, come in here, please. I'd like to talk with you." Lucy asked if he'd like her to leave. "No, please, I'd like you to stay."

"What is it, Michael? Would you like some tea?"

"No, Myra, I'd like the truth."

"Oh dear," she said. "Well, I knew it would come to this someday. If you must know… Yes, I have had relations with Mr. Kendal. But Michael, they in no way diminish the feelings I had for your grandfather. It's purely physical, that's all. You know I loved William."

"Myra, Myra, hold on. This has nothing to do with… Wait a minute. You're having an affair with Old Nick Kendal?"

"He's not so old. He's a very good looking man for his age." Lucy put her hand to her mouth so as not to show her snicker at this turn of events. "If you want me to leave, Michael, I will." She started to cry.

Michael shook his head to clear his thoughts and said, "Myra, I don't want you to leave." He went over and took her hands. "I love you, don't you know that?"

"Oh, Michael, I love you like you were my own, and I always have."

"Then tell me the truth, Myra. Was William my father?"

"Saints have mercy! But he swore me to secrecy."

"Then I have my answer." He stood up and went back to the desk. "Curse him." He picked up the journal and threw it across the room.

"No, Michael, please, no. You need to understand. Aidan had contracted syphilis because of his philandering, and it left him sterile. He was the last hope for the bloodline to continue."

"The bloodline? Curse the bloodline, if it's not already," Michael shouted.

"Michael, your mother wanted a child very badly, and her husband could not give her one. She thought if she were to become pregnant, and if Aidan could believe by some miracle it was his, they would find the love they once had for each other. William loved them both; do not judge your father unless you've stood in his shoes."

"So I was the reason my mother took her life." His voice cracked. Myra came to him and put her arms around him.

"Heavens no, Michael. She contracted the disease from Aidan. It drove her mad. Aidan could never forgive himself for it. That's why he could not be around any of us. Michael, they were flawed people, like we all are. But son, never forget your mother and your father loved you very much."

Lucy left them alone in the study and made a pot of tea. She carried in the tray and found them sitting at peace, Myra in a chair reading the journal Michael had thrown and Michael at his desk reading a book on bloodlines. They both thanked Lucy. Somehow this drama made her feel like she was part of a family once again. She loved these people and shared their pain.

Myra soon excused herself and went off to bed, stopping to kiss Michael's head and whisper an "I love you."

"Lucy, what you must think of us," Michael said with his head down.

"What I must think of you? Oh, let me see… Well, I think you are the most interesting people I've ever met, and I thank God that I met you." He smiled. "I also think you need to get some rest. You look a little worse for the wear, Donegan."

"Oh, is that right? Well, I think you're in need of a little rest yourself. What say we both call it a day?"

"A very interesting day."

22 – Brutal Honesty

The garden at Glen Eden was in its full glory now. With the warmer days of July on them, new flowers burst forth every day. It was an ever-changing tapestry that Lucy never tired of seeing. Michael left for the city early on Monday mornings and set his schedule to return early on Friday evenings. He had postponed his trip to Europe; Lucy didn't know why.

The women settled into a routine: yoga after breakfast, a walk on the beach if weather permitted, housework in the early afternoons, and sewing after that. After an early dinner, they went in different directions: Lucy to the study and Myra increasingly absent. Lucy had her suspicion that old Nick Kendal had something to do with it.

Lucy focused her efforts on searching through old manuscripts and texts to learn of the places she knew Lance had been. Though Michael didn't agree, she was certain the "warrior out of time" was Lance. She thought more and more about visiting the Serpent Mound again herself. She set it in her mind that she would go there on the winter solstice if Lance hadn't returned by then. Michael was unsuccessful in locating *The Green Book*, and she began to wonder if it would ever be found. She made it a point to sit on the porch every evening in the hope that Angus would bring her another message from Lance. But those efforts had thus far been in vain.

Megan dropped by nearly every day after her shift at the Glenwood. Although she still didn't seem to be warming to the idea of Lucy being there, she was at least cordial. She often brought groceries from a list Myra would give her the day before, or she would take Myra herself to the grocery. This is what she intended to do on Thursday when Lucy strolled into the kitchen just as the two of them were about to leave. "Say, Lucy," Myra said, "why don't you go to the market with Megan today? I want to snap off the old petunias on the lee side of the garden."

"I'd be happy to, if it's okay with you, Megan?" She really didn't want to leave Glen Eden; she felt safe there. But she wanted to make an effort at a better relationship with Megan. She knew it would make Michael and Myra happy.

Though the expression on her face indicated otherwise, Megan said, "Sure, Lucy, I'd like that."

As soon as they were in the car, Megan lit a cigarette. She offered one to Lucy, who declined. "Don't you dare tell Myra or Michael about this. I'd never hear the end of it."

"I won't. But really, Megan, smoking isn't good for your health. You ought to think about quitting." Megan gave her a disgusted look and blew out the sickening smoke in her direction. Lucy coughed and put her window down. "Look, I'd like us to get along this summer. I know that would make Michael and Myra happy."

"Oh, so now you're an expert on what makes Michael happy?"

"I didn't say that."

"Look, Lucy, you may have the two of them snowed—they always look for the good in people. But that 'poor little Lucy with the missing lover' act doesn't work with me. I saw the way you danced with Michael, and I know what you're up to: you're trying to drive a wedge between us."

Lucy couldn't defend the dance. *It was stupid of me,* she thought. She also thought of how good it had felt to be in Michael's strong arms, to just let go for a few moments and trust him completely. She tried putting that from her mind. "You're wrong about me, Megan. I only agreed to stay because Michael didn't think you would be coming around to look in on Myra."

"Well, I'm back and you're still here. So feed that line to someone else."

Lucy couldn't argue that point either. She knew why she was staying. Lance had been there. She'd have to explain way too much to make Megan understand, so she didn't try. "I'm sorry you feel that way. Maybe you should try to talk to Michael about how you feel."

"What Michael and I say to each other is none of your business." She turned up the radio so she could totally ignore her.

Grocery shopping done, Lucy offered to buy them a soft serve at the Dairy Queen, but Megan responded, "No way! I want to end this little outing as soon as possible."

Lucy felt sympathetic toward this young girl. She was obviously in love with someone who couldn't see it. *Or maybe he does see it and it strokes his ego in some weird way.* Lucy had to admit Michael was still an enigma to her.

Peggy had called earlier that day to ask for a weekend invitation. Lucy told her she'd have to check with Michael and Myra and give her a call back. "Let me know what the Lord and Lady have to say. I really need to get out of this city for a while, and I'm just dying to see what's up in Shangri-La."

Myra was excited by the idea. "Of course dear, of course your friend is welcome. It's wonderful to have young people coming and going again."

When Michael called that evening, she passed the idea by him. "Lucy, I want you to think of Glen Eden as your home while you are there. You needn't ask to have friends in." Then he offered a suggestion that pleased her: "Say, why don't we have a barbeque Saturday afternoon. We could ask Smith and Gayle to come by, if you like."

"Great, what about Ashley, can we invite him too?" Lucy asked with a little too much enthusiasm for Michael's liking. It made him wonder if there had been more than just a pretend relationship in the past between the two of them. Winnie and Skipper certainly thought so. But in fact, Lucy was thinking about hooking Ashley up with Peggy.

"Ashley? Sure. I'll give him a call. Let me talk to Myra to get things set with her."

"She's not here right now."

"Where did she go?"

"I'm not sure. She didn't say."

"That doesn't sound like her. Is something going on?"

"Well, I do have an idea where she might be."

"You do? Where?"

"Come on, Michael, use your imagination… old Nick Kendal."

He laughed. "You may be right. Say, maybe we should invite him to the barbeque. He's really a very interesting chap."

"Well, I am curious to meet him," Lucy said.

"Good. Let Myra know of the plan, and I'll call the others. I'll tell them to come by around two. How's that sound?"

"It sounds perfect."

"So what have you learned of Lance?" He couldn't believe he was using Lance to keep her on the phone. He had established his life in the city after Kathleen passed. His apartment was totally free from attachment to any painful memories. It was the cottage that gave him lonely pauses. But now, since he'd met Lucy, his apartment seemed empty. It lacked light and color. The light he wanted to be in was at Glen Eden now, and he couldn't wait to get back into it.

"I haven't learned anything, really. I've just been gaining insight on some places he visited."

"Well, I'll let you get on with it. See you on the morrow. Good night."

"Good night, Michael," she replied, then without really thinking about it added, "Sweet dreams."

He listened for the disconnect sound with the phone still at his ear. "Sweet Dreams," his mind repeated. "If I have them they'll be of you."

She hung up his call then dialed Peggy's number. Peggy was super-excited. "I'm taking my packed bag to work with me and ducking out at two; that should put me there between 6:00 and 6:30, depending on traffic." Lucy gave her turn-by-turn directions but said she'd be waiting at the end of the drive for her because it was easy to miss.

Friday the women's routine was as usual except they did extra fussing with the house chores knowing guests would be coming. For Peggy, they made up the room Freddy had stayed in, putting freshly ironed linens on the bed and bringing in the down pillows and comforter they'd hung outside to freshen in the warm breeze and sunshine. Lucy was looking forward to Peg's arrival, but she was also thinking about seeing Michael again.

He arrived home around 5:30 with an armful of roses. He handed Myra and Lucy each a bouquet with no explanation. He was heartened by Lucy's smile when he first saw her. She quickly ran off to get vases for the flowers, dividing her bunch into two bouquets and placing one on Peg's nightstand and one on her own. She set the table before walking to the end of the drive.

She only waited about five minutes before spotting Peg's little green Vega coming along. The introductions were made and Lucy showed Peggy upstairs to her room. "Oh my God, Lucy, you have fallen off the end of the world and landed in my dream cottage with Prince Charming and a fairy godmother."

Lucy laughed. "Well, yes, I guess I have." The girls chatted and giggled while Peggy washed up and changed. Michael had promised to take them to the Butler to hear some music after dinner, so they dressed accordingly. Lucy thought the idea excellent because it would give Ashley a chance to meet Peg before the barbeque.

Peggy was her usual vivacious self and the dinner conversation was lively and enjoyable. Michael carried to the table the Shepherd's Pie Myra had baked, while Myra brought in a basket of biscuits and a big bowl of fresh greens tossed with carrots, beets and raisins. When the meal was at an end, Michael suggested Lucy take Peggy into the garden while he and Myra saw to the dishes. Lucy protested but he insisted. "Oh my God, he does dishes too?" Peggy snickered in Lucy's ear as they walked out the back door. She took her friend's arm and they strolled away from the porch light into the candle-lit gazebo. "So come on, Lucy, before he comes out here. Fill me in on what's going on."

"There is nothing going on."

"Yeah, right, I saw the way he looks at you."

"Peggy, don't let your imagination run wild. Michael and I are just friends. He's helping me to find Lance, end of story."

"Oh, don't be a big fat idiot. I know that guy has feelings for you. If you blow this, you might not get a second chance."

"Peg, stop it! I don't want a second chance. I don't want a first chance. I just want to find Lance, and with Michael's help I have hope that I can do that now."

"Methinks she protests too much."

"Fine. Think what you want."

The Daze End, a local rock and roll band, was the entertainment at the Butler that night. The two girls took turns dancing with Michael, and Lucy was glad the band didn't play a lot of slow songs. When they did, she made up an excuse to sit out, or she deferred to Peggy. Ashley, as they had hoped, was working the bar, so they sat at it instead of a table. He accepted the invitation to the barbeque and spent as much time as he could, for a busy Friday night, talking with them. He made Lucy a grasshopper, which she nursed for most of the evening, not wanting a repeat of what happened at the Tara. When the band started playing their rendition of "Nights in White Satin"—a song Lucy loved—Michael grabbed her hand at the same time Peggy grabbed Michael around the waist and pulled him toward the dance floor. Lucy's hand slipped slowly from his as he backed away with his eyes still fixed on her and shivers ran up her spine. As she watched the pair enfold within the music, she noticed Peg lay her head on Michael's shoulder. Ashley noticed too and commented, "Looks like Michael has scored a hit with your friend there."

"What woman doesn't he score a hit with?"

"You," Ashley replied as he refreshed her drink.

Back at Glen Eden, Michael offered the girls a nightcap by the fireplace. Lucy declined and said good night. She was annoyed when Peggy accepted and plunked herself down next to him on the big leather couch.

Lucy lay in her bed waiting to hear them come up. She thought she heard two sets of footsteps on the stairs, but then she only heard one door open and close. "That's Michael's room," she thought. She knew Peggy was not above casual sexual encounters. She lay there thinking about the two of them making love right down the hall. She rolled out of bed and got on her knees to repent. She spoke in her prayer language and it led her to thoughts of Lance. And with those firmly in place she crawled back under the covers and found sleep.

She was having toast and tea in the kitchen with Myra the next morning when Peg found them. "Would you like me to fix you some eggs and rashers?" Myra asked.

"No, just coffee for me. Michael was such a good host last evening that I have a slight hangover." But Myra insisted she eat something and sat a glass of orange juice and a plate of toast before her. Peggy looked at Lucy and said, "I could get real used to the treatment around here."

"I bet you could," Lucy said under her breath.

"Where's Michael? Is he still sleeping?" Peg asked.

"Don't you know?" Lucy replied.

Her question was answered when he came in wet with perspiration from his run.

"Ladies," he said. He noticed Lucy didn't smile or look at him.

"Hey, handsome," Peggy said, perking up.

"I'm going to shower and run into the Mayflower Market to pick up the steaks for the barbeque. Does anyone want anything?"

"I do," Peggy was quick to answer. Then she winked at Lucy and said, "Oh, never mind." Lucy kicked her under the table.

Smith and Gayle arrived around two, just after Ashley got there. Michael was the perfect host, making sure everyone had a beverage. He had dragged out lawn chairs and set them here and there about the patio. He'd also set up a badminton net and a croquet course. The guys, spurred on by Ashley, challenged the ladies to a croquet test. Shots were added together and in the end, thanks to Smith's ineptness with a mallet, the ladies won by one stroke.

Lucy couldn't remember having such a good time in years. Jokes and laughter were abundant, and with different sets of partners making constant challenges, the badminton court stayed busy all day. Nick Kendal arrived around three. Myra met him at his car and brought him into the back. She introduced him to the other guests and then brought him over to Lucy. "Pleased to meet you," she said.

"But we've met before," he replied. "I used to play baseball for Douglas against your dad on the Casco team. You and your sister were yea high back then." He touched his leg just above his knee. "No one could tell you two apart. Your folks were so proud. How are they doin', anyway?"

"They're fine," she said, then swallowed hard. She missed them, especially when reminded of the early years before all the strangeness began. Michael took notice of what was being said and went to stand by her side.

"So you know Lucy's father, Mr. Kendal?" Michael asked.

"Oh, haven't seen him in years. He was on the old Casco baseball team. Baseball used to be a big deal back then. All the small towns and communities had a team. Sundays were the days we'd square off on the diamond. Vern, Lucy's dad, had a bunch of brothers that played on the team with him." He put his hand on his chin and looked off as if trying to see into a time past. "Let's see, Vern used to pitch. Gene and Clint played outfield, Seth was the catcher and… let me think… there was another brother."

"Claude," Lucy said.

"Yep, that's right, Claude, first baseman. Darn fine ballplayers, all of 'em. We were hard pressed to beat that team. Don't recall that we ever did. Guess they're all gone now, except for Vern. He was the youngest, right?" Lucy nodded. "Guess you don't remember much of those games, do you?"

"I was pretty little."

"Yes, you were. Cute little things, you were, came up to here." He motioned again to the spot on his leg.

"Lucy, Nick is a very fine artist. He chisels wildlife statues out of stone," Myra said. Maybe when the party's over, Michael will drive you over to have a look at his work."

"Happy to, love to see it myself," Michael voiced.

"I'd like that," Lucy said.

Michael grilled the steaks to perfection. Earlier that day, Myra and Peggy had made a large bowl of potato salad while Lucy made a blueberry cobbler and whipped up fresh cream to top it.

Smith and Gayle were the first to leave because they had to get ready for their gig at the Tara. Ashley asked Peggy if she'd like to go with him to the Mouse Trap club in Grand Rapids where he was going to check on a new band to hire for the Butler. She gladly accepted and Lucy was pleased her plan to get the two of them together seemed to be working. She hoped her suspicions of the night before had just been the workings of her overactive imagination.

Nick and Myra sat chatting in the gazebo while Lucy and Michael straightened up the yard. They took down the croquet set, but before pulling up the badminton net Michael challenged her to a game. He loved watching her competitive nature. She would dive head long—slamming into the ground to make the shot—then hop back up to get set for the next one. After the match, which he won but not as easily as he thought he might, he suggested they go for a swim to cool off.

The water in Lake Michigan was the warmest she'd felt it yet that summer. She stayed close to the shore while he swam out so far she couldn't see him above the waves. For one terrible moment she thought he was gone. She held her breath and shaded her eyes as she scanned the horizon. She sighed long and hard when she saw the speck of him returning. They toweled off and slowly walked back, talking about the events of the day. They both agreed the barbeque had been a great success and that they should do it again soon.

After changing out of their swimsuits, Michael drove her to have a look at Nick's art. He lived in a cottage on the lake side of Ganges—the small town had been split in half when the highway came through. Sitting about his yard were statues of rabbits, dogs, squirrels, beavers, and a bear. Lucy was impressed with his work, and he was pleased to show it off to them. They made their way down a path to the woods that was his backyard when Lucy's knees went weak. There on a stump sat Angus, or his stone clone as it were. She shot a quick glance at Michael who stood in awe as well.

"Nick, where did you get the idea for this one?" he asked.

"Oh, I don't know. It just came to me. Do you like it?"

"I do," Lucy said. She had gone over to it and knelt down to inspect it closely. The detail was incredible.

"Lucy, let me buy it for you," Michael said.

"Michael, I couldn't."

"Sure you could. You wanted the painting, which I can't really part with. But I'd be happy to get this for you. What do you say?"

"I'd love it, but I don't have a place to put it. No yard. It would look out of place sitting in my apartment."

"You can set it in the garden at Glen Eden until you have a garden for it yourself. How's that sound?"

"Say yes, Miss Lucy," Nick chimed in. "I could really use a sale this summer."

Nick helped Michael carry the stone Angus to the car and set it carefully in the trunk. Lucy thought about it on the way back and declared, "Michael, I want to pay you back for the statue. How about this: keep half my wages until the cost is covered."

"No, I'll not do that. It's a gift, Lucy, just accept it."

She thought a moment then relented. "It's very nice of you. Thanks."

Back at Glen Eden, Michael used a wheelbarrow to haul the heavy piece into the backyard. Myra picked a spot for it at the very end of the garden facing the lake where she wouldn't have to feel like it was watching her. She wasn't happy to have the likeness of Angus back at Glen Eden and complained that he'd probably trample down her flowers trying to get a good look at himself.

It was just the three of them for dinner, and Lucy thought how pleasant it was. Later, when she and Michael were back in the study, she said enthusiastically, "Maybe Angus *will* come back to admire his likeness in the garden, and I can ask him to take a message to Lance."

"That'd be nice," Michael said, not wanting to burst her bubble. "Oh, by the way, when I stopped at the post office to get the mail today, this was in the box for you." He took from his desk drawer an envelope and handed it to her. It was the letter she had written to Paul and Littlefeather to let them know where she'd be staying for the summer in case they heard from Lance. It had been stamped by the post office No Such Address. Addressee Unknown.

Lucy stared at it and said aloud, "This is the right address, I know it."

Michael saw her bewildered expression. "Look, maybe the post office got it wrong. Check the address and post it again." He wanted to get her mind away from it. He was sorry he'd given it to her just now because he sensed a sadness come upon her. "I think I'll take a walk on the beach. Would you like to come along?"

"No, I'll wait here for Peggy. She's leaving in the morning, so I won't be going to Mass with you and Myra."

"Of course. Tell her for me she's welcome here anytime."

Lucy sat alone now in the study thinking about what a wonderful day she had had. It was so nice to be with friends, laughing, having fun, and enjoying each other's company. Michael was certainly a people person. He made everyone feel important, feel special, like Lance did. She thought of the person she had become these last seven years: sitting, waiting, alone, and lonely. What if Lance couldn't come back to her? She closed her eyes and thought about Michael, about the dance they had shared, about his smile, about the way the water ran down the muscles of his tanned chest after he came from the water that afternoon.

She heard a noise at the window like someone had tossed a pebble at it. Going to it and looking out she saw no one at first but then thought she saw movement in the flowers heading toward the statue of Angus. Her eyes searched the yard, and there in the dim light from the candles in the gazebo she saw Michael. He was holding Megan in his arms. She was naked. "Oh Michael," she sighed, falling back from the window. She ran upstairs and started to pack.

She left in the morning with Peggy while Myra and Michael were in church. She laid a note on the kitchen table:

Myra

*Something has come up and I need to leave Glen Eden.
I will never forget your kindness.*

Love, Lucy

She sat on her couch petting Freea and reading the classified section of the newspaper. She had to find a job and soon. She estimated her savings would hold out for two months living as meagerly as possible and barring any unforeseen expenses. She didn't want to go back to DME and have to answer the rumors that were going around about her and Michael, and she certainly didn't want to take a chance of running into him. A knock came on the door that startled her; she wasn't expecting anyone.

"Hello," she called through the door. "Who is it?"

"It's Michael. May I come in?"

Michael. Her heart all but stopped. She didn't want to see him. "I'm sorry, Michael, this isn't a good time."

"Lucy, please let me in. I just want to talk to you. It won't take long, I promise." Reluctantly, she opened the door but did not ask him in. She backed only a few steps from the threshold, and he stood in the jamb looking as strikingly handsome as ever. "Lucy, why did you run off like that?"

"I had to get back here to get on with my life. I troubled you long enough."

"Cut the crap, Lucy. Something happened to make you run off the way you did, and I think I deserve an honest answer."

"You're right, Michael," she said coldly. "You do deserve an honest answer, and I am trying to give you one if you will listen."

"I'm all ears. Go right ahead."

"You and Myra were very good to me. I grew fond of you both and got comfortable being there with you. It was very selfish of me. When I saw you with Megan, I realized that maybe I was keeping you from getting on with your own life."

"Saw me with Megan?" he interrupted.

"Michael, you're not listening. I know she has feelings for you. She made that very plain, and it's obvious that you have some type of feeling for her. My being there was just complicating things for you both."

"Yes, I have feelings for Megan, but not the way you think. She's my goddaughter. She's like my niece or something. I can't help it if she has some schoolgirl crush on me, can I?"

"Michael, I saw you with her. She was naked."

"Oh God, is that what this is about? You completely misunderstood the situation."

"It's pretty hard to misunderstand something like that. I saw you holding her, and she was naked. You don't owe me an explanation." She stepped back to close the door, but he grabbed it.

"Shut up, woman, and listen to me. Megan was on the beach with that Charlie Nelson creep. He was as drunk as the skunk he is. He got her drinking and the situation turned real bad. He ripped off her suit and tried to rape her. I had gone for a walk on the beach after our little talk, and I heard her screams. Thank God I got to her in time. I half killed that little twit, but not before he got some licks on me." He pulled up his shirt to reveal a large, swollen, reddened area on his left rib cage. "The little bastard hit me with a piece of driftwood."

She stepped closer to him, touching his bruise tenderly. "Oh Michael, that looks awful. Have you seen a doctor?"

He pulled his shirt down gingerly. "Myra laid some kind of poultice on me last night, but never mind about that. I still want to know why you left, Lucy."

"Haven't you been listening to me, Michael?"

"You told me some crap about not wanting to complicate things for Megan and me, but I'm not buying it. I don't believe that's the whole truth."

"Of course it is. Why would I lie?"

"You aren't lying, Lucy. I think you're just afraid to admit the truth. You're afraid that admitting it will diminish Lance in some way."

"What on earth are you talking about?"

"The truth, Lucy. Isn't that what you're searching for?"

"You're talking in riddles, Michael. Please just get to the point."

"Okay, maybe I'm a fool. No, there's no maybe about it. I *am* a fool, but here it goes anyway: I think the reason you left doesn't have as much to do with thinking you were complicating things between Megan and me as much as it does…" He paused. "Is it possible that when you saw Megan and me together that you were…well, that you were jealous?"

"What? Oh my God! You think a lot of yourself, Michael Donegan."

"Aye, and I'm hoping that you think a lot of me to. At least more than you are willing to admit."

Lucy was so mad she felt her face grow hot. Who does this guy think he is? She glared at him. She was clenching her teeth. He stood silent before her like a little boy waiting to be scolded. "The nerve, the absolute gall," her mind declared. She took a deep breath.

He stood his ground, waiting. He half turned his body to protect his sore rib cage in case she was going to hit him.

"You…" is all she managed to get out. She was still trying to formulate how to answer him. "You…" She thought hard about what to say. She thought about how terribly she had misjudged him, first with Myra, then with Skipper and Megan. She thought about the talks they'd had about Kathleen and Lance, how good it was to be able to talk to someone. How kind he had been to her. She knew he was developing an attraction to her. She was flattered by it, and she certainly had felt an attraction to him. But how dare he put it in words. Now he had come to her wanting the truth. What else could she do? "You might be right," she murmured.

"I might be right," he repeated timidly. "Oh thank you, Lord. I might be right." He clenched his fists and shook them in jubilation before his face then grimaced a little because he had jarred his sore ribs.

She couldn't help but smile. "Michael, just because I felt jealous doesn't mean I had the right to, or that I think there could ever be anything for us. I'm sorry I left the way I did. You've been wonderful to me, and I have enjoyed the times we've spent together."

He put his hand up to stop her. "I'm not asking you for anything but the truth. So now that you have given it to me, I want to clear something up."

"What do you mean?"

"May I come in and sit down? My ribs are killing me." He held his side.

"You stubborn Irishman, you need to see a doctor. You need to get x-rays."

"I know, but I had to find you first to see that you were all right. I didn't know what had happened to you."

"Okay, so now you know. So will you please go to an emergency room?"

"I will if you'll come with me."

"Michael, I think it would be better if we don't see each other."

"That's where you're wrong, Lucy. I vowed to help you find Lance, and I'll not go back on that. I have something to show you. He pulled out a small brown book from his back pocket.

"What is this?" she asked.

"It's a bank book. I found it last night. Look at it."

Lucy opened it slowly. Three names appeared as the account holders:

Lance McKellen

William A. Donegan

Michael A. Donegan

She gasped and backed away from the door, letting Michael come in. He leaned against the foyer wall as she shut the door and turned toward him. "So let me get this straight. You knew? You knew Lance all along and have been lying to me."

"No, no, God no, I never met him."

"But Michael, your name is on this account with his."

"I know, but Lucy you have to understand this: my grandfather and I were partners in the business. He would draw up papers, I would draw up papers, and we would have each other sign. We trusted each other, Lucy. Half the time I didn't even read what I was signing. Grandfather would just come in and say, 'Here, be a good lad and sign this,' and I would. He'd do the same for me. Sometimes we discussed it; other times we did not. Remember Lucy, he was 'The Fox'."

"Yes, and his grandson has inherited some of that trait, I believe."

"I know you didn't mean it as such, but I will take that as a compliment. My grandfather…er father… was a very good man, Lucy. It appears that your Lance thought so too. I wish you would have known him."

"I would hope you inherited a small bit of that trait as well," she quipped.

"Believe it or not, I do try."

"Oh, Michael, I'm sorry. I have no reason to believe that you lied to me."

"Well, that is what I have come to tell you. I have."

"You have?"

"Darlin', do you think I could sit a moment." He walked past her into the kitchen and slumped uneasily onto a chair. As soon as he settled, Freea jumped up on his lap and started to rub against his chest. He grimaced again but spoke softly to her while stroking her head. "Hello there, Freea. I'm pleased someone is happy to see me." Freea usually didn't bother with people. The only other person Lucy recalled her jumping up on was Lance.

The teapot whistled and Lucy jumped. She forgot she had put it on before sitting down with the paper. "So will you be showing me the hospitality of a cup, then?" he asked sheepishly. He coughed and grabbed his side.

"I will if you promise to drink it in a hurry and get yourself to the nearest hospital."

Lucy poured the tea while Michael sat with Freea, who was curled in a ball upon his lap and purring loudly. When she turned back around to deliver the cups, she noticed that he looked pale and had begun to sweat.

He sat with his forehead resting on his hand. When she set the tea before him, he looked up and smiled at her and gave her that little wink of his. "God, he is cute when he does that," she thought, softening toward him for a moment. Her second thought stiffened her up again: "And he knows it."

He nodded a thank you and tried to remove his jacket. Sweat was pouring from his head and he set his jaw.

"Here, let me help you with that," she said, coming up behind him and reaching around his neck to grab the jacket and pull it down over his shoulders. She felt his warmth, breathed in his scent, and softened all over again. She put her hand on his forehead. "Michael, you're burning up," she said. "I insist you go to an emergency room right away."

"And I have made that promise, have I not? After we have had a wee chat." He coughed and gripped his ribs. "For the time being, would you happen to have any Irish to add to this cup? I could use the *uisce beatha* about now." She walked to the cabinet over the sink and produced a bottle of Inishowen and placed it on the table before him.

"Oh, you sweetheart, you've conjured a bit of the land of my ancestors. You know, this is the only peated malt Irish blend in the world. It's from the county Donegal in northwest Ireland." He poured a healthy portion in his cup and without asking splashed some of the poteen in her tea as well. He raised his cup to her before downing some of the hot brew. He coughed again, clutching his side tightly. "Now sit quiet and let me get this matter off my chest. Then you may escort me to the house of healing, if you see fit."

"Well, that remains to be seen," she said, sitting down at the little table. "Just what is it you have to tell me?"

He took another gulp from his cup, replaced it in the saucer, and looked her in the eyes. "Fred Loch isn't just an old college chum that happened to visit. I called him, Lucy. I called him because I was worried about you."

"Go on."

"He is a clinical psychologist who has long studied the paranormal and written books on it."

"Fred?"

"You must admit, all the stuff you told me was a bit strange: about hearing the music that led you into the woods; about Lance and Angus in the stone circle, not to mention how they disappeared the moment I rode up and how wildly you acted. I didn't know what to do."

"Oh, I get it. So you never really believed me, did you? You think I'm just crazy, don't you? Remember, Michael, I'm not the only one who acted wildly that day."

Her words stung him. "No, Lucy, not crazy... just hurt and confused... and obsessed by hope maybe."

"Obsessed by hope? You're right, Michael. I am obsessed by hope, especially now since I've seen Lance, since I know about the time difference, and since I know he and Angus are working on a plan that, like it or not, has something to do with you."

"And there now is another thing. Just what does it have to do with me? I never met Lance, and I certainly have never seen Angus."

"All I know is what I heard Lance say. But I can't expect you to believe that since you don't believe I saw him." Her voice betrayed her emotions and her tone displayed her disappointment. Tears welled in her eyes.

He reached for her hand and she withdrew it. He grabbed it and held tight. "Lucy, let me talk. I'm in love with you, damn it. Since the first time I saw you. I don't expect you to love me back, not the way you love Lance, because I can't love you the way I did Kathleen. Kathleen is gone, and I've accepted that. There may still be a chance for you and Lance. If there is, I have vowed to help you find him. But Lucy, it has been seven years."

"It has only been a year to Lance."

"Wait, listen to me, Lucy; I'm not through. I didn't know what to do, so I pretended I needed someone to stay to keep an eye on Myra. When you agreed, I called Fred."

"Oh my God, the two of you must have had a field day, talking about your crazy house guest, especially after you found me in the woods in that trance. Michael, I confided in you that night about my past. I trusted you."

"I know, Lucy. I know how hard that was for you. Please believe me. I'm only trying to help."

"Then how about being honest with me, Michael?"

"That's what I've come here to do, if you'll let me talk."

"It may be a little late for that. I've probably provided your buddy Fred with enough material to write a new book."

"That's not fair, Lucy. Fred is a good man and a good friend. If I would have told you he was a doctor, would you have stayed?"

"I don't know the answer to that, Michael. Maybe I would have."

"Well, I couldn't risk it, Lucy. I couldn't risk you just running off, out of my life. Look, I told you I'm in love with you. I want you to be happy. Please believe that. I know you can't feel the same about me because of Lance. I accept that. You can't blame me though for holding out the hope that someday you will be free from this obsession and be able to return my feelings."

"You're right, Michael. I do know that you have feelings for me. I don't know if it is love. I can certainly feel the physical attraction we have one for another. I would be lying to say differently."

"Oh for God's sake, woman, it's more than that. I'm crazy about you. I can't eat, sleep, or think straight anymore."

"Then maybe it is you who should be talking to your old friend Fred about *your* obsession." She looked away from him.

"Lucy, there's something else. I found *The Green Book*. It's in the car. I found it last night in a secret compartment in Grandfather's desk along with the bankbook I showed you."

"You found it?!"

"Wait, let me finish. Lance was looking for a portal. He believed he had found it. A portal to Ely…"

"Elysium," she helped.

"Yes, to Elysium. His last report had him at a site in Cornwall, at the portal dolmen of Chûn Quoit. He was planning to enter the chamber on the night of the solstice, the very same night it was reported he disappeared.

"Oh Michael."

"Look, Lucy, to be honest, I don't know if I believe all this stuff. I do know that two of the people I have loved most in this world do: you and my grandfather. There *is* something to it, and I mean to find out what.

"Michael, I…"

"Wait." He raised his hand to silence her. "There's one more thing: I went to the bank this morning. I took Grandfather's death certificate so I could change the account. I had myself removed as well." He handed her a new bankbook. She opened it to find the account owners listed as Lance McKellen and Lucy Cavanagh.

"Michael, what is this?"

"All you have to do to activate it is go to the bank and sign a signature card. I don't want you to accept my invitation because you have no other means of finding Lance. There is enough money in that account for you to investigate all this by yourself, if you want no part of me."

"Michael, I can't accept this money."

"Lucy, it belonged to Lance. He would want you to have it."

"I don't know what to say."

"Then don't say anything right now. Think on it. Pray on it. I've made my feelings known. I would be honored to accompany you on this quest. But for now I am hoping you will accompany me to the hospital. You can read Lance's reports while they are taking x-rays and taping me up. What do you say?"

"Yes, Michael, I'll go with you to the hospital, and I will think about what you have said and I will pray about it." She stood up and walked again behind his chair to help him on with his jacket. After pulling it up, she put her hands on his shoulders and bent to gently kiss his cheek. "You are a good man, Michael Donegan," she whispered. "I'm sorry for ever doubting that. You have helped me so very much, and yes, I do have feelings for you."

He crossed his body with his right arm and laid his hand atop hers. "Lord, help us," he said.

"Yes, Lord," Lucy prayed in agreement. They stayed that way a moment, neither one saying a word.

Freea jumped from his lap to the table and nudged her head into his face. Lucy grabbed her and scolded, "Bad kitty, you know you shouldn't get up on the table."

"It's okay, Freea," Michael defended. "Don't mind her. She's just acting a little jealous again." Lucy playfully slapped his shoulder and he winced. "Hey now, don't be beating on an injured man."

"Oh, I'm sorry."

"Well, if you're really sorry, then give me another sip of the water of life to shore me up for this trip to the hospital." Lucy obliged and pushed the bottle of Inishowen toward him. He didn't bother pouring it in his cup this time but poured it straight down his throat. "There now, let's be off while I can still make it under my own steam." Lucy ran for her jacket and purse and came back quickly to help him up. He didn't know if it was the pain, the brew, or the letting out of all the things he had held in his heart that made him lightheaded, but whatever it was he was glad he had her to lean on.

At Providence Hospital the emergency room was fairly empty. After filling out the paper work, they took him to an examination room. She sat in a corner of the waiting room poring over Lance's reports, getting lost in his handwriting, unaware of anyone or anything else around. Two hours slipped by when she heard a man call out, "Mrs. Donegan, Mrs. Michael Donegan." Lucy looked up and the man noticed her. He walked straight for her and said, "Are you Lucy Donegan?"

"No, I'm Lucy Cavanagh. I am Mr. Donegan's friend."

"Oh, I'm sorry. I just assumed. Forgive me."

"That's quite all right, doctor." She was more annoyed by being drawn away from her reading than by the mistake made of her name.

"Mr. Donegan is asking to see you. Will you follow me, please?"

"Certainly," Lucy said, gathering her jacket and purse. "How is he?"

"Well, his fever is extremely high. The x-rays show two badly fractured ribs. His left lung was nearly punctured and some infection has set in. We have decided to admit him for a few days. He is extremely lucky you brought him in when you did. We've given him something for the pain. That coupled with whatever he's been drinking has him pretty out of it."

When Michael saw her enter the room, a big grin came on his face. "Hey doc, you found Lucy," he boomed. "Isn't she beautiful?"

"Michael!" she scolded, her face turning bright red.

"You're very lucky she talked you into coming in to be seen, Mr. Donegan. Jason here has come to take you to your room. Get some rest and I'll see you first thing in the morning."

"Right you have it, doctor. Shanks again."

The young, black orderly gathered Michael's jacket and clothes and put them on the bed. Michael insisted on shaking his hand and introducing him to Lucy. Jason asked Lucy to push Michael's IV stand while he negotiated the hospital bed, and the three were soon off winding down the hallway and riding the elevator to the fourth floor. Michael was put into a semi-private room with a man about his own age who had been in a car accident. His ankle was broken and his tibia had been snapped. He had undergone two surgeries to have pins placed in his leg. He was a self-employed auto mechanic with two children who were staying with their grandparents so his pregnant wife could be with him. The introductions were made and then the curtain was drawn so Michael, who was now nodding in and out of consciousness, could get some sleep. Lucy guessed he had been put on morphine but couldn't be sure.

Michael insisted Lucy take his car home and asked her to give Myra a call. She promised she would as soon as she got back to her apartment. He took her hand to say goodbye, put it to his lips, and kissed it. He pulled her down close so he could whisper. "Lucy, I've told you how I feel about you. I shall not say it again. If ever you feel we can be more than friends, it is you who will have to tell me. Is that a deal?"

"Yes, Michael, it's a deal. Now you get some sleep. I'll be back in the morning." He nodded off again, still holding her hand. When she slid it from his to leave, she heard him murmur, "Come, Kathleen, play me a song."

Lucy found a parking place for Michael's car in front of her apartment and hurried up the stairs. The car was full of his scent, and she couldn't help but think of him and of everything he had said to her. But Lance was on the pages of the book, and she was anxious to get back to it, back into his presence. Before she could do that, she had to give Myra a call as she had promised. She hung up her jacket and laid *The Green Book* next to her purse on the couch.

When she sat down, Freea jumped onto her lap. Freea had been Lance's cat, but now she knew Michael. Lucy was beginning to feel like everything was different. Even the feeling in her apartment was changed since Michael had been there.

"Hello, Myra, this is Lucy."

"Oh Lucy, thank goodness. Michael and I were worried about you. Are you all right, dear?"

"Yes, Myra, I'm fine. I'm sorry I left so abruptly."

"You needn't explain a thing to me, dear. But Michael has been terribly worried; have you heard from him?"

"Yes, Myra, I have. He was here this morning. I talked him into going to the emergency room at Providence Hospital in Southfield to have his ribs looked at. Two of them are fractured and he was running a high fever. They've admitted him and want to keep him there a few days."

"Oh good heavens, that man is as stubborn as William was. I told him he should go see a doctor, but he wanted to make sure you were all right first. He gets something in his head and there is no changing his mind. Look after him, will you, dear? I don't know what I'd do if something were to happen to him."

"I will, Myra. I'm sure he'll call you himself tomorrow. They have him pretty drugged up right now."

"Did the two of you get a chance to talk? It's really none of my business… But Lucy, I must tell you, he is head over heels for you. It is both good and bad for me to see him that way. I mean, he grieved so long for Kathleen, and now he finds you, and, well, you aren't exactly free, are you, dear?"

"No, Myra, I'm not."

"No, of course. Your young man Lance. How long has it been again since you've seen him?"

"Seven years," Lucy heard herself answer. But wait, it was just a couple of weeks ago that she saw him in the circle, wasn't it? *Let's see, when exactly was that?* she thought. She was annoyed now that Myra had asked.

"Seven years," Myra repeated. "Oh, that's right. You told me that. I'm sorry, dear. Time just has a way of slipping away from me, from all of us. Lucy dear, Michael is really a good man. You could have a future with someone who would treat you like a queen. Please don't hurt him by holding on to ghosts. That's all I'll say on that subject."

Lucy felt herself grow angry. A ghost? Is that what Myra thought of Lance? Her heart sank to her stomach. "Myra, it would never be my intention to hurt Michael."

"No, of course not, dear. It would never be your intention. Hold on a moment; there is someone here who wants to talk to you."

"Hello, Lucy, it's Megan."

"Oh, Megan, are you okay?"

"I'm fine now, thanks to Michael. Lucy, I'm sorry I was acting like such a brat. We had a long talk like you suggested. I hope I haven't ruined things for the two of you. It's very plain how he feels about you, and I hope I didn't do anything to make you doubt him."

Lucy was so annoyed she wanted to hang up the phone. How in the world had things gotten so complicated? "Megan, things between Michael and me are fine. I value his friendship very much. I have to run now. I'm glad you weren't hurt."

"Thanks, Lucy. Maybe we can get to know each other a little better when you come back. I'd really like that."

"I'd like that too." Lucy hung up the phone. Her head was pounding. She remembered the way she felt the day Lance found her. It was like she had a big knot in her brain and couldn't think straight. Now she couldn't stop thinking about what Myra said. Was she holding on to a ghost?

23 – Roller Coaster

Michael was in the hospital for over a week, and Lucy visited him every day. She worried at first that it would be awkward to be around him because of what he had confessed to her. But true to his promise, he did not mention his feelings for her again, and their relationship returned to the easiness she had felt before she saw him with Megan that night. Lucy resolved that his confession had been the result of his fever and the alcohol content of his blood. He was always happy to see her, and they would take walks together in the courtyard where she would report what she had learned the evening before from reading *The Green Book*.

One day when she came late from a dentist appointment, he was not in his room. She asked one of the nursing nuns where he was, and that's when she learned he was no stranger to Providence.

"He's in the leukemia ward," came Sister Anne's reply.

"What?" Lucy gasped. A look of horror came upon her face.

"Oh no, my child, I'm sorry if I startled you. He is there reading to the children. He has done so faithfully for the past several years. He sometimes sings to them too. The other sisters and I love it when he sings; he has such a beautiful voice. He is quite a good man, that Michael of yours." Lucy didn't bother to correct the end of the sister's statement. "Come now, I'll take you to him."

When they got to the ward, Lucy didn't go in but peeked through the window in the door. Michael sat in a rocking chair between two of the beds. A frail blond girl sat slumped on his lap with her head resting against his chest. She offered a faint smile as Michael read, changing his voice to become a silly little chicken proclaiming the sky was about to fall. Lucy smiled too then backed away from the door and found her way into the chapel. She felt selfish and cold and needed to repent for focusing on her own sorrows for so long.

When later she returned to Michael's room, she found he had a visitor. A fairly attractive woman with flaming red hair stood beside his bed holding his hand. Lucy recognized her as one of the women who surrounded him in the photo in the *Metro Scene* magazine Peggy had showed her. Michael's other hand held his ribcage as he laughed out loud. He looked up, saw Lucy, and motioned for her to come in, but only after he pulled his hand from the other woman's. "Lucy Cavanagh, this is Shannon O'Connor. Shannon, this is Lucy."

"Oh yes, Lucy," the woman said. "I've heard about you from Freddy."

"Hi," Lucy said nervously, wondering just what she had heard.

"He tells me you are Myra's companion for the summer. That's wonderful. Michael does worry about her being alone at the cottage. He has to spend much too much time out there when he should be here, paying more attention to the business."

"Now Shannon, don't be an old hen, darlin'; I pay enough attention to the business. I have you to worry after the rest."

She puckered her lips and blew him a kiss. "Yes, you do, my love. Hurry and get well so I won't have to work so hard."

"It's sure I will," he chuckled, taking her hand again and kissing it.

"I've heard of you too," Lucy spoke up.

"Oh?" Shannon said, turning to look at her with a cool glance.

"Yes; that is, if you are the same Shannon from the cheer squad when Michael and Freddy were in college together."

"She is," Michael said, laughing out loud. He enjoyed seeing Shannon squirm for once. Usually it was she who was the cause of it in others.

"Good God, Lucy, don't believe a word from either of them when they start gibbering on about their soccer days." She gave Michael a scowl.

"Well now, darlin', I guess if you want to set the record straight with Lucy here you'll have to drive out to Glen Eden some weekend." He winked at her.

Lucy suddenly felt flushed and thought how she hated it when he winked at anyone else. She forced a smile and said pleasantly, "Please do come. Myra so loves to have visitors."

"Yes, well, I have been meaning to get out there to see just what is going on; Michael has been so secretive and elusive these past weeks. Are you turning his world upside down, Miss Cavanagh?"

Michael spat out a sip of water he had just taken. "I'm still in the room," he sputtered.

"Yes, you are, Michael, and please remember just how you got to be in this room. Trying to save a damsel in distress, wasn't it? The prettier the damsel, the more danger, I suspect."

"I'm still here too," Lucy said, meeting her icy stare.

"So you are, and I'm just wondering why."

"Shannon," Michael said loudly, rising up on one elbow. "Behave yourself. Don't you have an appointment to keep somewhere?"

"It's okay, Michael. I really should be going," Lucy said.

"No, Lucy, please stay. Shannon was just leaving. She has to be getting back to the office now, don't you, Shannon?"

"Yes, Michael, I suppose I do. Please take a moment to look over those files I brought you. I think you'll find them very interesting. I'll come by tomorrow with some papers for you to sign, if that's okay with you, Lucy," She added cattily.

"I'm afraid you misunderstand," Lucy began, but Michael talked over her.

"Shannon, when I'm feeling better I'm going to take you down and paddle your behind for being such a brat. Now get out of here before I try it now and hurt myself." He tugged on her arm and she leaned down and kissed his cheek.

"I'm off then." She picked up her briefcase that was lying at the foot of his bed and headed toward the door. "I apologize, Lucy, if I seemed rough on you, but you are a big girl; I'm sure you can handle it."

"Big enough," Lucy said as the red head brushed by her. Michael viewed this exchange with a big grin on his face.

"Shannon is my corporate lawyer and an old friend, as you already know, since college days." He reached for the files she had laid on his bed and turned them upside down as Lucy approached. "So how was your dentist appointment?" he asked to change the subject.

"God, I hate dentists," she moaned. "I have such a phobia. I don't know why. I arrived right on time but sat in the car for five minutes trying to muster enough nerve to go in."

"Weren't you just having your teeth cleaned?" he asked.

"Yes," she snapped. "But I hate dentists."

"Doctor Sylvan is a great guy. I'm sure he wouldn't hurt you."

"But he did."

"He did?"

"Yes, when he touched a tender spot under my gum line with his pick. I started crying. He apologized and said he couldn't see a reason for it to hurt. Later, when he looked at my x-rays, he said they showed something, a dark spot in the center of that tooth, like a metallic rod. He asked if I knew how it got there, but I don't have a clue."

"That's weird."

"He said as long as it isn't bothering me, we should leave it alone. He made a note in my chart not to pick on that tooth the next time. He is going to send a copy of the x-ray off to a colleague to see if he knows what it might be."

"That's good then. I told you he'd take care of you."

"He said to tell you hello, and he thanks you for the referral. I don't really think he meant it though. Dentists don't like crybabies any more than I like dentists. Oh, and his receptionist Nancy told me to say hi. I wish I could bat my eyes the way she did when she said it so you could get the full effect."

Michael smiled. "Did she send me a grape sucker? She always gives me a grape sucker."

"No, no she didn't. I guess you'll have to spank her bottom too when you're feeling better."

"I guess I will," Michael said, and they both laughed. He wanted to pull her down close and kiss her. He ached to do so. *Please God, honor my patience with a perfect work*, he silently prayed.

"Hey, where is your mechanic friend?" Lucy asked, noticing that the bed next to his was empty and made up.

"Oh, they transferred him this morning to a private rehabilitation facility where he can get the physical therapy he needs for his leg."

"How on earth are they going to afford something like that?"

"Don't know," he said, purposely ignoring her glance while trying to adjust his position in the bed. She leaned over to help him and noticed a homemade thank-you card tossed on his nightstand. She picked it up and read it out loud:

Michael,

There are no words that can thank you for the kindness you have shown to our family. Russell and I will forever be in your debt. You have displayed to us the love of Christ and we will remember you always in our prayers.

With highest regards,

Russell, Evelyn, George, and Carol Ann

"Aww, that's so nice. And just what would they be thanking you for?" She already knew the answer.

"Oh, I let her have my lunch tray yesterday. I wasn't hungry."

"Yeah, right."

"I did."

"Oh, I don't doubt that," Lucy said, laying the card back where she found it. He picked it up and threw it in the trash. *Knowing you, Michael Donegan, is like being on an emotional rollercoaster ride,* she thought.

"I was happy when I heard you second my invitation for Shannon to visit at Glen Eden. I was worried that you wouldn't be returning with me."

"Michael, are you sure you will be needing me? When I called Myra like you asked, Megan was there. They've patched things up, and I think she will be around for Myra this summer."

"Lucy, I want you there… I mean… we have this whole Lance thing to sort out, don't we? Unless, that is, you don't want my help anymore."

"Of course I want your help, and I need access to your grandfather's library. But it wouldn't be fair to continue in your employ. Megan will be there for Myra."

"Okay, fair enough," he said. "You're fired."

"No, I'm not fired. I just quit."

"Nope, I fired you."

"Not before I quit."

"How about laid off, will that work for you?"

"Well, since I do recall being laid on," Lucy raised her eyebrows and batted her lashes, "I guess I can accept being laid off."

"Ouch," Michael said. His eyes locked on hers. She felt as if she were being pulled into him. A cough caused him to turn his head and grab hold of his side. He grimaced as his chest heaved and shook. One of the files Shannon left slid from the bed and hit the floor. Lucy bent down to pick it up and noticed the folder contained her name.

"What's this?" she said as she thumbed through the papers.

"Lucy, don't," he managed through his coughs.

"Michael, what *is* this?" she asked again indignantly, though she now knew well what it was. It was a portfolio of her life.

His face tensed. "Lucy, I didn't ask for that. Shannon did. I haven't even looked at it."

"No, but you were going to."

"Lucy, look, I'm a very rich man. I have people in my life that watch out for me. I need them. Anyone in my position needs people around them they can trust. It's just the way it works. It's nothing personal. Honest, Lucy, they investigate everyone who gets close to me. It's their job. It's what they do."

"Then by all means, Michael, read it. Go ahead. I'm sure it has provided Shannon with hours of amusement. God, Danny was right about you. You play by a whole different set of rules."

"Lucy, please try to..."

She didn't let him finish. "No, Michael, I don't want to play your games. I don't really know who you are either, but I was willing to find out in my own stupid little way—by trying to get to know you, figuring out with my head and heart just who you are. Do you know what I just found out? I found out that I know quite enough already." She threw the file at him, turned on her heel, and marched out of the room.

"Lucy, stop," he shouted, bringing on another coughing fit. He was trying to get out of bed to go after her when Sister Anne, hearing the commotion, rushed into the room.

"Michael, what on earth is going on? You get back into that bed. Here, let me help you." Michael was coughing uncontrollably now.

"Sister, please go after her. Tell her to come back," he wheezed between coughs.

"Oh, I see, you have a live one on the hook, now do you? Well, I think all that can wait until you're better. I'm going to give you a little something to calm you down so you can get that cough under control."

Lucy marched down the hall heading for the exit. She stopped suddenly when she remembered she had Michael's car and his keys. She stamped her foot and let out an exasperated sigh. Her first thought was to go back to his room and throw the keys at him; she'd take a cab home. But if she did that she would have to see him again. "I'll leave the keys along with the parking space number in a note at the nursing station. I'm sure Shannon would be more than happy to move it for him," she thought. With this plan in mind, she turned heel again and started back toward his room.

The walls of the beautiful Catholic hospital were lined with art portraying scenes from the Bible. She had been admiring them on her daily visits, but now as she walked past them they seemed to convict her for her anger. She found herself in front of the chapel where she had been less than an hour ago. "My God," she thought, "I *am* on a roller coaster. I need you Lord to help me get off." She walked back into the small room, fell on her knees, and came into the presence of her God. She stayed there until peace once again filled her. With a cool head, she walked back into Michael's room. As she entered, she overhead him talking to Sister Ann. The good sister had given him a shot to calm his cough and help him rest.

"She keeps getting mad at me, Sister. All I've tried to do is help her. It's like she wants to believe the absolute worst about me."

"Well, there you have it. Maybe she does."

"But why?"

"A woman who has been deeply hurt will try to guard her heart, Michael, with all that is within her, to keep it from happening again. Maybe she's afraid to see the good in you because it would make you too appealing." She put her hand on his head and patted it like he was a little child.

"But I'd never hurt her, Sister."

"Then why did you fire me," Lucy asked, walking over to the bed and taking his hand.

His wonderful smile lit the room once again. "I didn't fire you. You quit, remember?"

Sister Anne gathered up her tray and gave Lucy's arm a little squeeze. She leaned close and said, "When I passed by the chapel, I saw you having a chat with my boss. I'm glad to see you know where to go when you need help with something."

"Yes, Sister, I do."

"Do what?" Michael asked, annoyed at being left out of the conversation.

"She knows a bullheaded Irishman when she sees one," Sister Anne laughed as she rustled out of the room.

"Lucy, I'm sorry you were upset. I completely understand. I would have reacted the same way if I were you. Here, take the file. Burn it if you want. I don't have to see it. I trust you, Lucy."

"No, Michael, please keep it. As a matter of fact, let's look at it together. I'd like to see just how the world views me. Not that I don't have a pretty good idea already. But at least I could explain or defend myself, if need be."

"I'm serious, Lucy. I don't have to see it."

"Come on now, someone went to a lot of trouble and spent a lot of your money digging this stuff up, so let's have a look. You wouldn't want to disappoint Shannon, now would you?"

"Lucy, I want you to believe me; I didn't ask for it."

"I believe you, Michael, and I believe that Shannon only had your best interest in mind. You are very fortunate to have friends like her and Fred. Come on, scoot over and let's have a look at my life." Michael slid over to the side of the small bed. Lucy kicked off her shoes and climbed up beside him, placing the file on her lap. "Michael, before we begin do you think you could do something for me?"

"Sure. Name it."

"Will you pray with me? We need a spirit of discernment to help get us through this, okay?"

"It's more than okay, Lucy." Michael remembered how she had knelt and prayed with him for Skipper in the study. His heart felt broken as she first thanked God for His many blessings: for the opportunity they had to meet and become friends, for his healing, for Myra, and for Megan. She asked for a calm spirit of discernment as old wounds were about to be exposed. She asked for the wisdom they would need to make sense out of the reports in *The Green Book*. Lastly, she prayed for Lance, that wherever he was God's angels were protecting him.

The file was very comprehensive. It contained copies of her birth certificate, baptismal record, elementary and high school transcripts, her Air Force records and psychological evaluations, discharge papers, marriage license, divorce decree, and transcripts from Grand Rapids Community College in Michigan and The College of Marin in Kentfield, California. There was a written report listing all the places she had lived and all the jobs she'd had. The compiling agency had even talked with some of her past employers and some of the people she had worked with. There was a list of churches she'd attended and interviews with pastors and lay people that knew her. As they shuffled through the reports, Lucy gave Michael her side of the accounts she thought were unfairly biased against her. She almost came to tears when she read Rayme's account of their failed marriage. To her surprise he accepted the full blame, admitting he had been an alcoholic at the time and physically abusive to her. She was glad to find out he was remarried and regularly attending a church.

She had read the psych reports before and didn't want to go over them again. She told Michael to read them later and that he could show them to Freddy if he wanted. They described her as being schizophrenic and suggested she was suffering from a psychological disorder that involved a process of dissociation, or a splitting of conscious awareness, and of lacunar amnesia for previous events or memories, including fugue states in which she wakes up in a strange place and has no knowledge of how she got there. These episodes, the reports concluded, may have been brought on by a severe traumatic event. Such an event, however, was denied by the patient and her parents.

"What's this?" he quizzed, producing a copy of an arrest report from the Grand Rapids Police Department.

"Oh my God!" she exclaimed, pulling it from his hand. "How on earth did they find this?"

"Let me see that please," he said, gently taking it back from her and studying it intently. The report detailed her arrest for the charge of "hindering and obstructing an officer trying to perform his duty." There was a newspaper clipping attached to the report. Michael read the headline aloud: "Woman Claiming to Be the Mother of Jesus Arrested for Inciting a Riot on Northwest Side." Lucy laughed out loud when Michael read it. She laughed even louder visualizing Shannon reading it. Michael read the rest of the article silently. His brow furrowed, and he looked at her with a puzzled expression that made her start giggling again. "Lucy, I don't understand what's so funny. Did you really tell the police you were the mother of Jesus?"

"No," she said, "that was a mistake made by the officer who wrote up the report. He asked for my name and I told him Mary Magdalene. He didn't know his Bible, I guess, because he thought Mary Magdalene was the mother of Jesus." She giggled again, but Michael remained silent.

"Did you think you were Mary Magdalene?" he asked solemnly.

Lucy sobered up and looked at him innocently. "Sorry, Michael, I realize that you think you are dealing with a nut case, and this certainly adds fuel to that theory. But I can explain."

"Then please do," he said sternly, "and I would also appreciate it if you would stop telling me what it is I think. As I recall, I have laid my cards out on the table for you, have I not?" His voice sounded a little angry.

Lucy saw hurt in his eyes and felt a strong desire to kiss him. In the comfort she felt with him as they were reading through the reports, their bodies had slid next to each other on the bed. Now hers stiffened, and she shifted away so as not to touch him. She was determined to fight the attraction she felt, for his sake and for hers. She couldn't risk getting tangled up with him any deeper than she already was. She had to keep her head and heart clear to maintain the hope of finding Lance.

"Again, I apologize. It was just funny remembering what happened that day."

Michael noticed she moved away from him and regretted the way he had talked to her. "Then please share it with me so I can laugh too."

She began the story: "I was working at the International House of Pancakes on 28th Street. I was head waitress at the time, so if another waitress didn't show, I had to cover her shift as well as my own. I was working an insane schedule of six evenings a week, ten or twelve hours a day, trying to save money to go back to school.

"On this particular day, my roommate Stacy borrowed my car to go see her boyfriend Greg who was home on leave from Vietnam. When she brought the car back, she parked it on the side of the street that becomes a traffic lane between the hours of four and six: rush hour. That wouldn't have been a problem because I normally left for work at 3:45. The problem was that she walked up the street to visit a friend with the keys still in her pocket. I didn't know that till I got ready to leave and they weren't on the hook. I called work to let them know I'd be a little late, and I called Stacy's friend's house to tell her to come home with the keys. Then I went next door to ask the guys who lived there if they would help me push the car around the corner to keep it from getting ticketed. They were stoned as usual and their apartment was a mixed cloud of marijuana and incense smoke.

"By the time I got back outside, a policeman had stopped and was writing me up. Get this picture: there I was in my official IHOP uniform. It was bright orange with white cuffs and a crisp white apron. On my head was a little starched white cap."

"I remember those uniforms," Michael interjected. "In my heavy drinking days I used to frequent the IHOP on Woodward Avenue in Royal Oak. It was the place to go after the bars all closed because it was open 24 hours. I bet you were cute in that get up." Lucy smiled, glad for this little interruption. Michael usually didn't make small talk, and the fact that he just did put her at ease.

"I explained to the police officer what had happened. I told him that Stacy should be back any moment with the keys and in the meantime my friends were here to help me push the car around the corner. He took one look at the guys—shirtless, shoeless, with long hair—and his demeanor changed. He said he didn't think the "girls" could handle it, and that he had already called for a tow truck. Stacy showed up with the keys at the same time the tow truck got there. I went to the driver of the truck and told him I would write him a check for his services right then and there if he would please not tow my car away. He said that'd be fine with him, but the cop got irate. He shouted at the guy to back up the truck and tow the car away. He told me to stop interfering, that once the tow truck showed up the car was officially impounded, and I would have to go downtown to pay the parking violation, the towing and storage charges, and an impound fee."

"That seems harsh," Michael said sympathetically.

"That's what the crowd of local hippie types who had gathered around thought too. They started calling the policeman names and giving him the business for harassing 'the little pancake girl'. Well, he got nervous and called for backup, and two more squad cars came screaming up.

"I just couldn't believe how unreasonable he was being, but I decided to make one last appeal to him. I stepped behind the tow truck and said, 'Look, sir, if you take my car, I can't get to work. If I can't get to work, I won't have the money to pay all those fines you just mentioned. So please just let me take my car and go to work. Besides, if you're really concerned about blocking traffic, I have the keys now and can move it faster than the tow truck guy can hook it up to haul it away.'

"The crowd liked that plan, but the cop wouldn't have it. The suggestion made him even more irritated. 'Look lady,' he shouted, 'I've had it with you. You are under arrest.' I couldn't believe my ears. 'Under arrest!? For what?' I asked. He didn't answer. He grabbed hold of me and jerked me from behind the truck.

"Now I was acting as irrationally as he was. I wrapped myself around the tow truck chain. Other policemen moved in, and it took five of them to get me in cuffs and in the back of the squad car. I thought seeing red was just an expression before that day." Michael was smiling now.

"This happened during the time my father was in intensive care at Borgess Hospital in Kalamazoo. He had just gone through open heart surgery, and I'd been driving to Kalamazoo every morning to see him. I was stressed and exhausted, surviving on three to four hours of sleep a night, not that that is an excuse for my behavior, but it was certainly a contributing factor."

"No doubt," Lance said.

Lance? No, wait. Lance didn't say that; it was Michael. Michael said that. Why did I write Lance? Lance never heard that story. He never heard any of my stories. Oh well, I'll go on.

"Now the crowd was throwing beer cans at the cops and nightsticks were wielded. More squad cars pulled up while they were driving me away. The crowd was yelling 'Police Brutality!' and 'F-ing Pigs!'"

"All over a parking violation?" Michael shook his head.

"Anyway, in the commotion I never went back into my apartment to get my purse, so I didn't have any ID on me. I was so upset at the station that when the booking officer asked for my name, I didn't want to give it. I was thinking of how this was going to hurt my mom and dad if they found out. So I gave my name as Mary Magdalene. The officer responded, 'So you're the mother of Jesus, huh?' I didn't think I was in any position to give him a 'Who's Who in the Bible' lesson, so I didn't say anything."

Michael, his eyes getting heavy, lay smiling at her. "Then what happened?" he asked.

"Well, Stacy got Greg to drive her out to the Pancake House to tell my boss, the owner, what had happened. He was a very influential, well-connected man in Grand Rapids. He arranged my bail and picked me up so I could go to work that night. He later phoned one of his golf buddies who happened to be judge of the district court. When I appeared before him a couple days later, he threw the whole thing out and gave the officer a lecture about how it might do well for the image of the department if he would show a little understanding and compassion in certain situations."

Michael was still grinning when she finished, but she could tell he was fighting to stay awake from the shot the sister had given him. "If there is such a thing as reincarnation, I can see where you may have been Mary Magdalene."

He reached up and brushed her hair back from her face and once again fought back the urge to kiss her.

"Thanks, I think," she said, sliding out of the bed and handing the folder to him. "I should leave now and let you get some rest."

"The doctor said I could possibly go home day after tomorrow. I'm hoping you'll be returning to Glen Eden with me. We can study Lance's reports and plan out what to do next. What do you say?"

"I say hurry and get well. I look forward to being there again."

"Myra will be happy to hear that. She misses you. She's asked about you every day." He was using Myra as an excuse. He wanted her to come back, not just because he was crazy in love with her but also because Fred called and told him he had discussed her case with some of his colleagues. They decided the best course to follow was hypnotherapy, if she would agree to it. Under hypnosis she might be able to recall what went on during those periods of missing time.

There was something else Michael needed to tell her, and it wouldn't be easy. The other file that Shannon left for him bore the name of Lance McKellen. He managed to hide it in his bedstand before Lucy came back to the room. He had asked for this investigation himself, but the file was full of deadends. The detective agency Shannon hired was unable to learn anything about a Lance McKellen. There were no birth, education, or employment records. No social security number or military registration. Records from the county seat showed there hadn't been anyone by the name of McKellen living in or near Peebles, Ohio for well over fifty years. Their conclusion was that he either had given her a fictitious name or that he did not exist.

24 – Look into My Eyes

Michael was discharged on Tuesday, and Lucy was there to pick him up. This time she drove while Michael slept. Freea sat on his lap with her head buried in his jacket. Lucy's bags were in the trunk and *The Green Book* was safely tucked inside her purse.

Myra and Megan had a wonderful dinner prepared for Michael's homecoming. Lucy felt at home too, and everyone got along well and chattered happily. Michael still needed to take it easy. His ribs were taped and he was on antibiotics and cough suppressants. He enjoyed all the female attention, and after dinner he and Myra retired to the sitting room while Megan and Lucy tackled the kitchen chores.

Freddy phoned and said he would be arriving first thing in the morning, so Myra and Megan set off to prepare his room. Lucy wanted to help, but Michael asked her to sit with him so they could talk. He needed to tell her about Fred's idea to question her under hypnosis. He was surprised at how well she took it.

"Will you and Myra stay with me when Freddy puts me under?"

"Of course we will, Lucy, if that's what you want."

"I do. I'm more than a little frightened. But I'm also anxious to get to the bottom of it all." She sat curled on the couch next to him with Freea on her lap. He put his arm around her and she laid her head on his shoulder. He couldn't muster the courage to tell her about Lance's file.

Fred arrived mid morning and after the lunch chores were accomplished, they convened in the parlor. Lucy sat in the big chair Michael had occupied the night he watched over her while she was in the trance. Fred sat in an identical chair across from her while Michael and Myra sat quietly on the couch.

Fred began by having Lucy do some breathing exercises to relax. When he felt she was ready, he asked her to focus on a gold watch hanging from a chain that he swung slowly back and forth in front of her. He softly counted backwards from 100, telling her every third number or so that her eyelids were getting heavy and that she was getting sleepier. At the number 87 her eyes closed and her head nodded forward.

"Lucy, can you hear me?"

"Yes."

"How do you feel?"

"I feel light."

"Good. I want you to think back to a time when you were very young. Will you do that for me?"

"Yes."

"Good. I want you to go back to the day when you were first missing for a time. Can you do that?"

"Oh…"

"Just relax. Stay light. Go back in your memory to that day, okay?"

Big sigh. "Well… yes… yes… okay."

"Where are you?"

"I'm in the woods behind our house."

"Is anyone with you?"

"Yes, sissy is here."

"What are you doing?"

"We're picking wild flowers and putting them in a big basket."

"Why are you doing that?"

"Because it's May Day and we're going to make little bouquets and hang them on doors for Aunt Lill, Mrs. Skodak, Elsie Beatty and the Dopp sisters."

"Is anyone else there besides sissy?"

"No… well… yes… but they're only watching."

"Who, Lucy? Who is watching?"

"The little ones."

"The little ones?"

"Yes."

"Have you seen them before?"

"Yes, many times."

"Where?"

"In the woods… Oh, and… in the big willow tree at home where we swing, and I've seen them in the bridal wreath hedge too."

"Does your sister see them?"

"Yes… I think so… No, wait… I'm not sure now. I don't know now." She begins to fidget. "Maybe."

"Okay. It's not important. You see them, right?"

"Oh yes."

"What do they look like?"

"Like… Oh…" She pauses.

"Lucy, can you describe them to me?"

"Yes, but they are different."

"Different? What do you mean?"

"They are not all the same."

"So there are different kinds of little people?"

"No, not like people… Well… some are sort of like people. They're all mixed up."

"What do you mean by mixed up?"

"Some are like butterflies… some like dragonflies or birds… They have different parts."

"Lucy, look at just one. Do you see it?"
"Yes."
"Okay, tell me what that one looks like."
"It's beautiful… It has butterfly wings and the face and body of a lady with shiny lavender skin. She doesn't have hair but pretty feathers, like the blue color of a pheasant. You know, that pretty blue."
"Yes, I know. Now look at another one. Can you see it?"
"Yes."
"Okay, describe it to me."
"It has black, shiny wings with a dark red-brown, bony man's body. Its head is shaped like a man's only with big, black bug eyes and no mouth or nose; it has a beak instead and long grasshopper-like legs and long bony arms. It only has three long fingers on each hand and a claw-like nail on each finger."
"Can you talk to them?"
"I tried, but they don't talk like I do."
"They don't speak the same language?"
"No… They make sounds."
"Sounds? Like what?"
"Like bells and hums and whistles, but not exactly. I can't say exactly."
"That's okay. Let's move on. You're in the woods picking flowers with your sister and the little ones are watching you. What happens next?"
"They're watching me, and they start to make sounds and fly around me… They change into little balls of different colored light… They take me up… I'm floating in the center of them."
"Where do they take you?"
"To school."
"Your elementary school?"
"No, the other school with the tall, white teachers."
"Where is this school, Lucy?"
"I don't know. They take me there in a sparkling."
"A sparkling? What is that?"
"The light is sparkling. I can't see anything because it's so bright and full of flashing colors."
"Are you afraid?"
"No."
"Tell me what's happening, can you?"
"They put me down at a desk… my desk."
"Tell me what you see."
"I'm in a room, but… there are no walls. Just like wavy air. There are desks and books… big books."
"There are desks?"
"Yes."

"More than one?"

"Oh yes, more."

"Are there other people at the desks?"

"Some are people."

"Not all of them?"

"No, there are others."

"You mean, not all of them are like you?"

"Some are, some aren't."

"What are they?"

"Oh... they're different... Oh." She cowers down in her chair.

"Don't be afraid; they can't hurt you. You're only remembering." She sits back up. "Now, tell me what they look like?"

"Some are like... oh... big insects, like a praying mantis. Some are like reptiles, like big lizards, only dressed in clothes like uniforms maybe."

"Are they like the little ones?"

"No, no, not like that. They are not small and they are not mixed up. Some are like insects and some are like lizards. That's all. They're not in my class. I'm not supposed to look at them."

"Are there others in your class?"

"Yes."

"How many?"

"Three. Yes, three right now."

"Are they like you?"

"Yes. They are children too."

"Tell me about them."

"There is a girl with long dark hair and darker skin. She talks in a different language. The teacher calls her Princess Amira. There is a boy with curly blond hair and deep green eyes. He smiled at me. He told me not to be afraid." She paused and smiled as if remembering something pleasant.

"Is there anyone else?"

"Yes, there's another boy. He has dark hair and he's taller. *U nada dey ambalana.*"

"Lucy, what did you say?"

"He has the crystal cross. He showed it to me... Oh, now there is trouble... Oh no..." She becomes agitated and cries out, "Don't take it. Stop it!" At the mention of the crystal cross Michael leaned forward. He turned to look at Myra who seemed like she was just about to say something. He put his finger to his lips.

"Lucy it's all right, calm down, you're only watching. Tell us what is going on."

"The teacher took the cross from the boy and the boy is trying to get it back. He said it was his mother's and that she is dead. The teacher says it is not his to keep. Oh no! The blue ones are coming." She cowered again. "They are taking him away. They are going to hurt him. 'Don't hurt him!'"

"Lucy, just relax, you don't have to be afraid or sad. You are just remembering. Take yourself out of the emotion and just tell me what you see."

"The shorter blue ones, they took the boy and they are hurting him. The blond boy grabbed the cross from the teacher. He shows her his book. She says, 'Yes, that is right. It was a test.' She tells the blue ones to let the other boy go. She tells him that the cross is not his, that it is a key only the true king can use to ignite the crystal skulls once they are all found. The blond boy puts the cross in his pocket."

"The blond boy has the cross now?"

"Yes, he has it."

"Go on."

"The bigger boy is really sad. The teacher goes to him and opens the book on his desk. She shows him a page. He is smiling now and… Oh!"

"What just happened, Lucy?"

"He… he winked at me."

"Do you see the book she showed him?"

"Yes."

"What does it say?"

"It doesn't say anything… The pages are blank."

"They're blank?"

"Yes. We each have our own book. We can't see the pages in the others' books, only if they show us. The teacher says not to show our books to others because it will tie their story to ours and maybe that won't be good."

"Do you see your book, Lucy?"

"Yes."

"Can you tell me what you see in it?"

"I see this." She motions with her hands, making big circles all around her.

"See what?"

"This." She motions again.

"I don't understand, Lucy?"

"Now that's on the page."

Fred looked over at Michael and indicated he'd like to end the session. Michael agreed and Fred guided Lucy back with a few words of instruction. He told her she would be able to remember what the session had revealed if she liked. But her first question to them when she opened her eyes was "Did it work?" Michael had recorded the whole thing. He rewound the tape and played it back for her to hear. Myra was unusually quiet, for which he was grateful.

Lucy was excited by what she heard. "The blond boy, that must be Lance. And the taller boy is you, Michael. You were there too."

"Lucy, don't jump to conclusions. I have no episodes of lost time and certainly no memories of anything remotely like this." Myra cleared her throat loudly when he said it, and he shot a stern look in her direction.

"I'll go put the kettle on, if you will excuse me," the older woman said, matching Michael's stern look. "Michael, be a good lad and give me a hand in the kitchen." It was more a command than a request.

"Sure thing, Myra. I'll be right along."

Lucy asked if she could hear the tape again and he hit the rewind button. "I know about the crystal skulls," she said. "Lance wrote a report on them in *The Green Book Esotery*. He said there are thirteen, and all but four had been found at the time he wrote it. I'll show it to you." Michael nodded and hit the play button.

Now it was Fred who shot a look at Michael. Michael excused himself and Fred followed him out of the room. "So what do you think, Freddy?"

"Sorry to say this, ol' boy, but since you're asking me for my opinion at this time, I'd have to say she is delusional. Her subconscious is recalling bits and pieces of information she has read in that book or Grandpa Will's journals and then filling in the spaces of her lost memories. There is simply nothing there that is credible. Like you said, you have no episodes of lost time and no memories to corroborate what she says."

Michael said nothing. He patted Fred's shoulder as he turned to make his way to the kitchen where Myra was waiting for him. Fred went back into the study by Lucy.

"Okay, Myra, I'm here, so let me have it."

"Michael, why on earth didn't you tell Lucy about your mother and the crystal cross?"

"I have my reasons. You'll just have to trust me on this. Lucy has enough to think about right now without me throwing more sticks on the fire."

"Michael, you know as well as I do that the Truth is what sets us free. I don't see how withholding the fact that you are the tall boy in that school she was talking about can possibly hurt her."

"Myra, Lucy is confused. Fred thinks she's delusional and her mind is just piecing together things she's read to fill in the blanks in her memory."

"Have it your way, Michael, but at least we know now that Lance has your mother's cross."

"Good God, Myra, weren't you listening to me? There was no school. It's just a figment of her imagination. I was never there, so it stands to reason that Lance wasn't either. He doesn't have the cross, I do." He reached in his pocket and pulled out a small velvet bag. He untied it and dumped the contents into his hand. Attached to a gold chain was a multi-faceted crystal cut in the shape of a cross. "I found it along with *The Green Book* in a secret compartment in Grandfather's desk."

"Saints have mercy on us. I thought I'd never see it again." She reached for it but Michael hurriedly put it back in the little velvet bag and slid it into his pocket. "William gave it to your mother to wear the night you were conceived. Now you listen to me, Michael: He believed Aidan had taken it after she died. I distinctly remember they had a terrible row about it. Maybe it was Lance that gave it back to William because he took it from the teacher who took it from you."

"Myra, that's enough. I can only deal with one delusional woman at a time." He was sorry the minute he said it.

"Michael Donegan, maybe you are the one who is delusional. You have diluted your mind to think that you are trying to help Lucy find Lance when in truth you don't want her to find him at all."

"That's not true, Myra."

"No? Well then let's find out the truth. Have Freddy put you under and maybe then we'll get to the bottom of this."

Just then Fred walked in. "Say, what's taking so long with the tea? Are you waiting for the leaves to dry?" he chuckled.

"No, Fred, we are not. We are having a discussion about…"

Michael cut Myra off mid-sentence. "About what to do next for Lucy." Myra slammed the teapot down and walked out of the room.

"What's up with Myra?" Fred asked. "Did I upset her with my comment about the tea?"

"Well, she does get touchy about such things," Michael said. "Here, let me pour you a cup."

"That's fine, chum. I'll go apologize to Myra."

"That won't be necessary; best to leave it drop."

"Sure, if you think it best." He took a sip from his cup and looked hard at Michael. "Lucy is asking if I'll put her under again. She wants to learn more about what's been happening to her. She keeps listening to that tape. She says she doesn't remember any of it even though I told her before I brought her out that she could remember it if she wanted to."

"So what are you going to do?"

"Well, we could try it again later this evening if you're in agreement." Michael nodded. "I think I'll go up to my room and read those psychological reports that you gave me. Say, did you ever get a translation on that tape we made of Lucy in the trance?"

"I had it sent off to Ireland to an old priest very learned in the ancient Gaelic dialects. I'm told he's had some success with it. Shannon phoned this morning to say she'd received his report. I told her you would be here and asked her to drive it down. She's on her way now." He looked at his watch. "She should be pulling up within the hour."

"Shannon is coming? Great, I look forward to seeing her, and maybe that report will offer some clue as to what direction to steer Lucy." Fred went upstairs and Michael carried a cup of tea into the parlor where Lucy sat on the couch, deep in thought, staring at the tape recorder on the end table. She jumped a little when he walked up. He could see the track of tear on her cheek.

"How are you doing?" Michael asked softly. She looked up, blinked, and gave him a smile "Sorry this took so long." He set the tea down in front of her and himself next to her. "I wanted to let you know that Shannon is on her way here. She's bringing a transcript of the recording I made of you in the trance."

"Oh."

"She wanted to see Freddy anyway, but if she'll make you uncomfortable, I can ask her to leave."

"No, Michael, don't do that. I know she's a close friend of yours and Fred's."

"Aye, but if it will make this more difficult for you…" She interrupted him.

"Michael, it'll be fine." She shivered and crossed her arms in front of her. He picked up a lap robe and put it around her shoulders. He wanted to take her in his arms. He wanted to tell her everything would be fine, but he was beginning to doubt that himself.

"Fred said you asked to be hypnotized again." She nodded slightly and looked to him like a frightened child. He put his arm around her and drew her close. She rested her head once again on his shoulder. She closed her eyes and fell into a dream. Lance stood before her dressed in the same warrior's garb he'd been wearing when she saw him in the circle.

"Lance," she cried, running to him and leaping into his arms. His body enfolded hers and the kiss they made exploded through her body. He picked her up into his arms and carried her to a soft, mossy spot under the shade of a weeping willow. As he laid her gently down, she saw a look of sadness on his face. "Lance, what is it?"

He hesitated for a moment and then began: "Lucy, the path you have begun holds many dangers. I wish I had more time to explain, but the war still rages and while I am on a dream visit, my mind and spirit are fully with you. My body lies vulnerable, guarded by a trusted friend whose life is put in peril." She started to say something but he put his fingers to her lips. "Listen, my darling. There are many memories in your mind; some are false, some are so fantastic that you may perceive them as false, and still others are hidden deep, with safeguards that will not allow you access to them until the time is deemed right."

She pulled his hand from her lips. "Lance, they are my memories. Who has the right other than me to control them?"

"Lucy, none of us belong totally to ourselves. You know this. Long ago we were given freewill. Every moment of every hour of every day we make decisions who we allow ourselves to become. We decide who to give the power to. We are molded and shaped into the minds of others. Some perceive us as angels, still others as demons. Everyone we meet along our life's path will influence us. We give and take of each other. We are, after all, at the very core energy. We attract both positive and negative influences. There are psychic vampires who come into our lives so full of negative energy that they suck the positive from us and fill us with negative pictures and images and thoughts about ourselves and others. They would steal our light and enslave us to the darkness that rules them. The battle I fight is against an army of such creatures. Once they were innocent but allowed the darkness to have control. Now they are lost to the power who hates all light." He paused and looked deeply into her. "Love generates light." He took her head into his hands and moved his lips close to hers. When his tongue touched her lips her body went limp. Her breath failed when his tongue entered her mouth to dance with her own. She was naked now, lying in the bosom of the earth. His hand moved over the wet clay and pulled her up, his fingers forming every line, every point, every chasm of her body, his tongue smoothing her flesh over her bones, waking up every cell and nerve ending until she pulsated with the warmth of his being. He kissed her eyes and they opened to behold his nakedness. He was raw nature, animal nature, and she wanted him. She breathed deeply the breath he exhaled and it filled her. He took her breath now and all of her with it. She not only felt her sensations but his. They exploded together back into time, back to their clothed bodies lying in the cool moss under the willow.

She swallowed hard, trying to keep from asking the questions that would have answers she did not want to hear. "Lucy, it doesn't matter what others think. I am real to you and you are real to me. I will keep you so through time. The pages in our books are blank until we fill them. But our story was written long ago, and this is not the first telling." He stood, placed his hand on his chest over his heart, and then extended it toward her. He turned and walked off. She watched as his form disappeared into the forest.

She woke on the couch in the parlor with the lap robe over her. Michael must have laid her there. She heard voices, so she rose and stole down the hall to the great room. Michael was there with Freddy and Shannon. "I'm telling you, Michael, this Lance guy doesn't exist," Shannon proclaimed. "He never did. People may disappear without a trace, but they always leave at least a hint that they were among the living."

Lucy crept back into the parlor and lay back down on the couch, waiting for her host to join her. It wasn't long before she heard footsteps enter the room. She sat up and saw Michael's grave face. She knew what he had come to tell her. "I'm sorry I dozed off on you. That session took a lot out of me." She sat up and patted the couch next to her. "So what is it you've come to say?"

He accepted her invitation and sat next to her. He sighed deeply as he ran a hand across his mouth then up his face and through his hair. A dark lock fell across his forehead and Lucy brushed it back with her hand. As he felt her warmth he closed his eyes. How could he possibly tell her? "Michael, it's okay," she said softly. "What is it?"

He felt totally vulnerable to her. "It's me, Lucy. I don't know who I am anymore. I used to consider myself a fairly decent man, a man of my word, but when I look at you I see how truly pathetic I am."

"Michael, stop. You are a good man."

He lowered his head and shook it. She moved her hand through his hair. He caught it and held it. "Lucy, I'm sorry. I've been lying to you through omission. Shannon brought me two files in the hospital that day, one was yours and the other was Lance's." Her glance narrowed and he hung his head again.

"Go on, Michael, get this off your chest. You'll feel better."

No, I won't. How could I possibly feel better making you feel worse, he thought. "I'm sorry, Lucy," he began. "Shannon had our best agency on this. There is no evidence that Lance McKellen ever existed. They have exhausted all the leads I could give them. I even gave them Lance's brother's address, which I took from the letter you wrote to him. No one anywhere in that area has ever heard of Lance McKellen."

A breathy "oh" was her only response.

"The detective talked to residents of that area, both Native American and white, but they came up empty."

"I see," she said. Lance had already prepared her for this in her dream.

Michael couldn't stand destroying her hope, so he declared resolutely, "I've instructed Shannon to order the agency to put another man on it, double their efforts."

"Michael, please, that's not necessary. If Lance doesn't want a trace to be found, none will be. If you continue to search, it is for your own interest, not mine. You must understand: I don't care what a detective agency has to say. But I can understand that you do. You needn't advise me of what they have to report because it matters not."

"Lucy, I want so badly to help you, but I don't know how I can."

He looked sad. *Poor, dear Michael*, she thought and stroked his head. "But you already have."

He was about to tell her about the crystal cross when Myra entered the room. "There's my beautiful girl. Are you hungry?"

"Yes, ma'am, I am."

"Good, come along then. Freddy and Shannon are already at the table."

Lucy jumped up and headed for the stairs. "I'll wash up and be at the table in five minutes."

"What about you, Michael, are you ready to eat?" Myra asked. Her heart broke for the lost look on his face. It was the same look she'd seen so often after Kathleen died.

He stood up and put his arm around her shoulder. "How could I not be hungry with the delicious smells you've sent through the house? You've cast your spell on me yet again."

"I'm not the only one who has you under a spell, now am I? Come along, my boy, let's eat. Everything will turn out the way God intends, you'll see."

"Sure it will, Myra," he said, trying to muster the faith to believe it.

Lucy walked into the dining room with all eyes on her. Michael and Fred stood up, and Michael slid back the chair next to him. Shannon remained seated and nodded a hello. Myra gestured with her hand for Lucy to come in and take her place. And there it was. Lucy recognized it the second she'd entered the room. Like a lover whose presence doesn't have to be announced because it can be felt, it waited for her. Pity was at the table. She didn't want it, it changed everything, and she'd been through it countless times in the past. Pity would change to resolution, resolution to dissolution, dissolution to discontent. She didn't want that to happen.

She tried her best to pretend she couldn't feel the pity. She smiled through insignificant chitchat and tried to swallow the food she'd put upon her plate. Every time she looked at the others at the table, their eyes left her as if they were trying to hide what they were thinking. Michael was the only one who wanted to hold her gaze, but she couldn't bear to see him being eaten up with remorse for being unable to save her. Finally, the meal was finished. She rose and started gathering plates.

Myra knew Fred and Shannon would be going outside for a smoke, so she hurried them off and sent Michael along with them. "Lucy and I will take care of all this. We'll meet you in the parlor with a pot of tea at half past the hour." With everyone in agreement, Lucy and Myra made several trips to and from the kitchen until the table was clear and the dishwashing could commence. Myra had been unusually quiet and the din of it weighed heavy on Lucy's heart. "What is it you plan to do next?" Myra finally asked halfway through the stack of dirty dishes.

"You mean after the dishes are done?" Lucy tried not to guess what Myra meant.

"No, I mean after the day is done and you have gleaned from the hypnosis session whatever secrets are locked in your mind."

"I guess I'll have to wait and see what clues are there to help me find Lance."

"Yet you already know where he is, don't you?"

"What?" Lucy felt sick to her stomach.

"Come on, Lucy. He has been missing for seven years and you can only see him in visions in stone circles and fairy smoke rings. I know you are desperate to bring him here, to have him exist here where you are, yet you already know that he cannot."

Lucy felt like she'd been punched. "No, Myra, you're wrong. Lance *does* exist."

"But not here, Lucy, not now. Michael does, and you're destroying him." Lucy looked down and shut her eyes, and Myra felt slightly remorseful. "I haven't told Michael this, but Nick took me to visit your mother and father. While he and your dad sat chatting about their old baseball days, your mom and I sat out under your willow tree. She is a lovely person, Lucy, and very concerned for you. I told her you've been staying at Glen Eden and that Michael is trying to help you.

"She confided something to me, Lucy, something she'd never told anyone. She told me she had twins in her bed there at Twin Willows, and that one of them died. I know they never told you. Your father took the baby's body to the funeral home, yet when he returned two babies were in the cradle. I'm guessing someone put you there, someone who stole you from your real parents, Lucy. I'm willing to bet that someone was Angus."

"Myra, I don't know what you're talking about. I have a twin sister. We look just alike. We even won loving cups for it at the state fair." Lucy's head felt as if it were about to explode. She sank to her knees.

Michael walked into the kitchen as she fell. "Myra, what's happened?" He rushed to Lucy, taking her up in his arms.

"The truth has happened, Michael."

"Whose truth?" he demanded. He thought Myra had told her about the cross.

"I'd like to lie down. My head is pounding. I'll let Myra fill you in, Michael, but it seems that neither one of us is who we thought we were."

He carried Lucy back to the parlor and laid her upon the couch. Myra came in with an aspirin and a glass of water. She looked sheepishly at Michael and then told him what she had done behind his back. He started to reprimand her for meddling, but Lucy stopped him. "Myra was only doing what she thought was best. Maybe things will be better between me and my folks now that this dark secret has seen the light of day."

"That's what your mother is hoping too, dear."

Fred and Shannon came in the back door and headed for the parlor as planned, but Myra cut them off and escorted them to the kitchen so Michael and Lucy could have a minute.

"Lucy, I'm sorry about all this. You don't have to go through with another session if you aren't up to it." He coughed and his hand went to his side.

"I want to go ahead with it, now more than ever." She noticed he was gripping his ribs again. "You shouldn't have carried me in here. You've hurt your sore ribs."

"No, no I haven't. Actually, I felt better with you in my arms." He looked longingly into her eyes. She looked away quickly, and he was sorry he said it even though it was the truth.

25 – Tuatha De Danaan

While Lucy rested, Michael joined Fred and Shannon, who were in need of a nicotine fix, in the gazebo. While the two smokers satisfied their urge, Michael read aloud the report Shannon had brought with her. It was from Father Wentworth, the Catholic celebrant from Ballygall parish in Ireland, where Michael sent the tape recording he made of Lucy the night they found her in the trance. According to the old priest, the dialect she was speaking was indeed Old Irish. Father Wentworth conceded that, though he could not interpret every word she uttered, he was amazed at her command of this ancient tongue—one of the oldest forms of Goidelic languages, similar in morphology and inflection to Gaulish, Latin, Classical Greek, and Sanskrit.

From what the good father could make out, Lucy gave an account of the children of the goddess Danu, known in Irish myth as the Tuatha De Danaan. He went on to say he had established his knowledge of the Danaan from studying a collection of Celtic manuscripts called the Wurzburg Codex dating from around A.D. 700—specifically, The Book of Leinster and The Book of Ballymote. He also said that references to the origins of the Danaan were included in the History of Heroditus, the writings of Homer, and had been found in hieroglyphs on the walls of the Temple of Rameses III.

The Danaan were a wandering people who left Ireland and went to the Northern Isles of the world where they learned wisdom and wizardry. No one is sure just where these Isles were, but many believe them to be what was called the "Other World" or realm of the Fae. Having mastered magic, music, poetry, and all forms of stone, metal and wood crafting, they returned to Ireland as a mist. They were like unto mortals, yet not. Aging very slowly, they lived well beyond the ephemeral lives of men. Being invisible to the physical world, it was said the only way to know them was to feel them. "Like fresh air being drawn into one's lungs." No words a mortal could utter would adequately describe them. After an age they melded with the Aos Sí—the spirits of woods, hills and mounds—and were called the "People of Peace." And when allowing themselves to be seen, they appeared as a pale, comely race with emerald eyes and long, curly yellow hair.

Their wisdom, kindness and love of the natural world made them enemies of the Firbolgs, a race of giants living in the land, lovers of war ruled by greedy kings. They would nonetheless band with these beings in an attempt to defeat the Milesians, who came from Brigantia on mighty ships to claim Ireland as their own. These were the Gaelic people. To stave off a bloody battle a bargain was struck between the Milesians and the Danaan: the Milesians would take their ships and leave Ireland a distance of nine waves. They would then attempt another landing. If the Danaan could keep all the ships from making shore, the Milesians would never return. But if they failed, then they would be banished forever into the hills and mounds. Owing to the unholy union the Danaan had made with the Firbolgs, their magic was diminished. So when they attempted to conjure a great storm to turn back the Milesian ships, two made it through.

Father Wentworth was familiar with most of the myths surrounding the Tuatha De Danaan but was surprised by Lucy's account. She spoke of a select few who left the earthly realm of the Emerald Isle via a dimensional portal at New Grange, which opened only on the twelfth year of every century at the exact time of the winter solstice. With this noble band, known forever after as the Guardians, were sent the sacred treasures of this gallant race, namely the Stone of Destiny, The Spear of Victory, the Sword of Lugh and the Cauldron of the Gods. Because they feared these artifacts might fall into the hands of the mortals who would be corrupted by their power and use them for all manner of evil.

Lucy's version foretold that in a far distant time, when the whole world had been fouled by greed, the crystallized skulls of the old kings would be gathered together and ignited by a key passed down for generations in the bloodline of the dragon. That with the turning of this key a portal to the kingdom of the blessed would be opened. The one foretold to do this was the true king of Elysium who would possess a ring cast from the melted, condensed metals of the sacred artifacts of the Danaan and set with the stone of destiny.

Father Wentworth concluded by saying he would be very interested to learn from where Lucy's legendarium had come.

"Wouldn't we all," Fred murmured, taking a last drag off his cigarette and then tossing the butt aside in the garden.

Annoyed, Michael bent down, picked it up and handed it to him. "What's with you smokers? Do you think the world is your ashtray? Myra works hard and takes pride in her garden, and you just toss your stinking cancer stick down with no regard for the beauty of it."

"My, my, aren't we getting testy?" Shannon mocked, bristling Michael further.

"Sorry, Michael, that was a little careless of me." Fred put the butt in his pocket.

"Just be happy I saw it instead of Myra. It's likely she'd have boxed your ears."

"Let's forget about my little faux pas, shall we, and concentrate on how I'm to handle the next session with Lucy. I'm thinking now that I'll have her revisit her time in the woods where we found her in that trance since that's what's fresh in our minds after reading that report. We'll see how it goes, and then if all's well I can ask her to concentrate on the episodes which took place during her high school years, the ones she told you about."

"You're the expert, Fred ol' boy." Michael was wondering if he should come clean with what he knew of the crystal cross before the session started but decided to wait and see if Lucy mentioned it again.

<hr />

"Michael, start the tape recorder, please. Let this record show the following people are present in the room: Michael Donegan; Myra O'Flannery; Shannon O'Connor; Lucy Cavanagh, the subject; and myself, Fredrick Loch, PhD, licensed hypnotherapist." He took her into the trance using the same technique he'd used before, but this time she was under at the count of 92.

"Lucy, do you feel relaxed?"

"Yes."

"Good. Now I want you to remember the time about three weeks ago when I came here to Glen Eden, the first time I met you. Do you remember that day?"

"Yes." She smiled widely.

"Good. Can you tell me what you're recalling?"

"Michael brought a gift for Freea, a ceramic bowl with her name on it. It was very sweet of him." Michael smiled at this.

"Good. Now do you remember that after dinner I went out to the garden to have a smoke and that Myra joined me, leaving you and Michael to do the kitchen work? Do you remember that?"

"Yes, Michael asked if I'd gone to my prom. I told him how my older sister made my dress. He said he'd like to hear more about my past. I felt uncomfortable and wanted to change the subject, so I brought up things from his past that Myra had told me about. Then I asked him what happened to his mother; Myra wouldn't tell me. She said it was his story to tell."

"Did he tell you?" Fred looked at Michael and he nodded his head.

"Yes. I was sorry I brought it up. I don't like to see him sad."

"Okay, Lucy, let's move along. I want you to think about what happened after I came in to invite you both to go for a walk on the beach."

"Michael went out the back door. I walked down the hall toward the front to get my wrap from the hall tree and decided to go out the front door. When I walked out on the porch, I heard you call to me from down by the stable. I saw shadows in the woods and thought you were both there, but you weren't. They were."

"Who are 'they,' Lucy?"

"The Watchers."

"The Watchers? Can you tell me about them?"

"I don't know much, only that they watch over the chosen people."

"Are you one of the chosen people, Lucy?"

"Yes."
"Who chose you?"
"God."
"God chose you? For what?"
"To do His will."
"Hasn't he chosen us all for that?"
"No, not all. Only the ones that chose Him."
"Okay, so you are in the woods and the Watchers are there. Can you tell me how many there are?"
"I don't know. There are a lot."
"Look around, Lucy. Take a guess: five, ten, more?"
"I don't know. I can't tell." She turned her head from side to side.
"That's okay, Lucy. We don't have to know how many. Can you tell us what they look like?"
"Like mist and like shadow."
"What is it they want with you?"
"They put something in my mouth."
"What is it?"
"I don't know. Something they said I need to carry with me."
"What does it look like?"
"I didn't see it."
"Can you tell me anything about it?"
"It tastes like popcorn."
"It tastes like popcorn?"
"Yes, and it stuck in my tooth." Lucy opened her mouth and pointed at one of her incisors.

Fred looked at Michael, who motioned to him then leaned over and whispered in his ear: "She just went to the dentist. She told me that an x-ray showed a metal object in one of her teeth. The dentist didn't know what it was."

"Lucy, do you remember anything else the Watchers said to you?"
"They said, 'thank you.'"
"Why did they say that?"
"For coming to them, I guess. They said, 'Many are called but few answer.'"
"Have you encountered them before, Lucy, before that evening when they put something in your mouth?"

She remained silent for a few moments, closing her eyes more tightly, furrowing and unfurrowing her brow as if trying to think. Her head jerked and she said loudly, as if suddenly it came to her, "Yes!"

"When? When did you see them before?"
"Long ago. In the mound at the Boyne."

"How long ago?"

"Maybe centuries."

Fred gave a puzzled look at Michael, wondering what he should ask her next. Michael leaned in and whispered, "Ask if she remembers anything else from that night in the woods."

"Lucy, come back to the woods at Glen Eden. You are there with the Watchers, they put something in your mouth, it tastes like popcorn and sticks in your tooth, is that right?"

"Yes."

"Do you remember anything else about that night?"

"I remember Michael leaned over the water and reached for me." Michael dropped the pen he'd been holding, recalling the dream he had that night while sitting in the chair as he watched over her.

Fred thought he had confused her in some way because he knew there was no pond or stream in the woods where they found her. "Lucy, you are in the woods at Glen Eden down the path by the stable. Do you remember talking in a language other than English?"

"What? Oh, you mean on the tape?"

"Yes. Michael made a recording of the language you were speaking. You listened to it."

"I remember listening to the tape."

"Do you remember what you said?" She let out a big sigh and started speaking in Old Irish. "Lucy, please speak in English."

"I am."

"No, you are speaking in Old Irish, I think."

"I don't know that language."

"Okay, let's move on. Let me ask you this: do you remember how you got back to the cottage?"

"Michael said he carried me."

"Do you remember it?"

"No… no, I don't… He reached for me in the water, but they pulled me under."

"Who pulled you under?"

"The Watchers."

Fred looked totally confused, and Michael knew he'd have to explain his dream before he could go further with questions about that night. So he leaned into Fred and whispered, "Forget it and go on to another time."

Fred studied the notes he had made from what Michael told him of that night. "Okay, let's move on. I want you to go back in your memory to a time when you were sixteen. Your sister had stayed with a friend and you were walking by yourself on your way to the bus stop. Something happened and you didn't make it to school. What happened?"

"A twinkling."

"A twinkling, like you told us about before?"

"Yes, the little ones, they fly all around me and become orbs and they take me up."

"Where did they take you, Lucy?"

"They took me to... I don't know where I am. I'm in a big room. There are rows and rows of glass chambers."

"Can you see what's in them?"

"There's a mist inside."

"Mist? Is that all? Look at one carefully, Lucy. Do you see anything else inside?"

"Oh... there is something. It's so small... It's a light."

"A light? What kind of light?"

"Ah... it's like how a firefly looks on a dark night. Like a spark."

"Do you know what they are?"

"I asked the teacher. She said they are soul seeds waiting to be accepted so they can have bodies."

"Do you know what she means by that?"

"I think so. It was one of our lessons. Soul seeds are tiny sparks of life waiting to be born, or maybe born again if there is still something they need to do or learn before they can earn a beaming cloak."

"What is that Lucy, a beaming cloak?"

"It's a garment, like Jesus had. A light body."

"How do they earn one?"

"Like any of us. You earn one by living an upright life. If you don't have one you can't go through the stargate. You can't go before the throne. You'll have to wait to come back here and start all over again. If there is still time." Fred was trying to form his next question when she let out a sigh. "Ohh... She says these two are mine."

"What did she say?"

"She said the two in front of me are to be my children. She told me to look in my book. Now I'm at school again. I don't know how I got here. My book is on the desk in front of me. On the page is a picture of me. I look a lot older. I have on a beautiful dark blue dress with little white flowers on it. It has lace around the neckline and bodice, and pretty puffy white sleeves. I'm wearing a necklace—*U nada dey ambalana*—a beautiful crystal cross. I'm sitting in a meadow next to a wooden fence." She falls silent, but before Fred can ask her another question she says, "Oh, he's so cute."

"Who is cute?"

"The little boy standing behind me with his hands on my shoulder. Now there is a littler boy sitting on my lap. What a sweet face. The teacher says they are waiting in the chambers to be my children. They have been waiting for a long time, longer even than I have been alive. She says they will be the last chance for our people, so I must never give up. I tell her I don't understand. She picks up another book and shows me a picture of a baby asleep in a little pink blanket. My mother is holding her. The teacher says, 'This was her book. I can show you because your lives are already tied. She volunteered to be a sacrifice to prepare a way for you to come here, a place to hide until the time is right. She was able to move on because of what she did.' Oh no, Mommy is crying. Don't cry, Mommy! Please, Mommy, don't cry!" Lucy is crying now herself, so Fred decides the session should end.

"It's okay, Lucy, don't cry. It's just a memory. Relax, take a deep breath. I'm going to count now, and when I reach five you are going to wake up. You will be refreshed and able to remember everything you've just told us, if you like. Okay?"

Lucy sniffs and says, "Okay."

"1… 2… 3… 4… 5."

Lucy opened her eyes, covered her mouth, yawned then stretched. "Did I go under? I feel exhausted. Did you learn anything about Lance?"

"You don't remember?" Fred asked.

"No. Can I listen to the tape?" Michael had already pressed the rewind button. Myra left the room to make tea. But the others stayed with Lucy, watching her reaction as she listened to the tape.

When she was done listening, Michael showed her the report from Father Wentworth. She read it with a blank expression on her face. "Lucy, do you understand any of this?"

"I'm not sure. I'm so tired." She put her head in her hands. "My thoughts are all jumbled." She raised her head and looked around the room. "I know you're all trying to help me, and I appreciate it very much. But I'm so very sleepy. I don't think I can stay awake." With that, she put her head down and was out.

Fred checked her pulse and said he had heard of this type of reaction before. "It occurs when a person has had to use a lot of personal strength to dig deeply into the subconscious." He assured Michael she would be fine after she woke up naturally. Michael carried her up to her room and laid her on her bed. He covered her with an afghan that Myra had made for Kathleen. But he didn't think of that; he only thought of Lucy. He wanted to hold her, to kiss her, to tell her it would be all right, only he wasn't sure it would be. He knelt beside the bed and offered a prayer for God's protection of her heart, mind and soul.

Freea hopped up on the bed and went straight to the spot above Lucy's head, pacing in a circle before settling down and curling into a ball. "Good girl, watch over her now."

Shannon and Fred headed for the fresh air so they could fill their lungs with smoke again. "What do you think of Lucy?" Fred asked when they were out of Michael's earshot.

"She is either the best liar I've ever seen, or she really believes all that stuff and is a certifiable crazy." Shannon sat on a patio chair and took a long drag on her cigarette. Blowing it out and watching as the smoke disappeared in the background of the roses. "Either way, it's plain to see Michael is deeply taken with her. The question is, Fred, what do *you* think about her? You're the expert."

"Well, I don't think she's lying. I think this stuff is coming from her subconscious. Just how it got there I've yet to determine."

Myra, who had been waiting for Michael in the kitchen, came at him with her question: "Did you tell her about the cross?"

"No, I did not. She fell asleep. She needs rest."

"Are you going to tell her? She needs to know it's your baby she'll be havin'."

"It wasn't but a few weeks ago you were sure Skipper was with my child. Now you have it being Lucy. Do you want a grandbaby so bad that you'll be content wherever the seed falls?"

"Come now, Michael, she said she's wearing the crystal cross in the picture she talked of. You have it, do you not? There *is* the legend behind it."

"And just what would that legend be?"

"Still asleep, are you? Well, you'll wake up soon enough. At least that is the hope I have."

"Woman, what are you going on about?"

"About the legend. One of the purposes of the *U nada dey ambalana* is to protect the woman wearing it and to mark her to receive a promised child of noble spirit."

"Oh yes, a noble soul. Well, I don't hold much faith in that old legend. Wasn't it the crystal cross my own dear mother was wearing when she committed adultery with my grandfather to conceive me?"

"Shame on you, Michael Donegan. Is your soul blind? It *is* faith that you are lacking, and until you find it you will not be doing yourself or Lucy any good."

"Faith in what, an old superstition about a necklace?"

"There is nothing new under the sun. God thought of it all. It's in his plan." With that, Myra picked up her teacup and marched off toward the sink, leaving him to mull over what she had said.

Maybe he did lack faith, faith in himself. He usually felt self-assured and confident in his decisions, but he had to admit since he'd met Lucy all bets were off. He didn't have a clue what he was doing. His confidence was shaken to its core. Or was it even deeper than that? Was it faith in God he lacked? After all, hadn't he believed with all his heart that God would heal Kathleen? How could a God who supposedly loved him take away everyone he'd held dear? He had a good head for business, a knack for making money, but it wasn't enough.

Everything else in his life seemed to fall apart. His thoughts were getting darker. Maybe he was cursed by the very act that gave him life.

He reached in his pocket and pulled out the little velvet bag. He opened it and spilled the contents in his hand. He held up the wonderfully carved crystal to catch a ray of light that came peeping in the kitchen window. It not only caught it but magnified the little beam into a brilliance that exploded in his eye. A rainbow of colors danced about him, pulling his mother's face from a childhood memory and projecting it in the magnificence of the light. She smiled at her child as if saying, "There, there, Michael, take heart. All is well." He clutched the cross and kissed it. When he let it loose it burst again with color. This time the picture didn't come from his memory but from Lucy's. He saw her sitting in the meadow in the blue dress she described. A young boy stood behind her and a toddler straddled her lap. The older boy looked just like a picture of himself about that age which sat on a nightstand in Myra's room. "That must be my son!" he let his mind exclaim as joy erupted in his heart. The younger boy looked nothing like him. "He must favor his mother's people," he thought.

He heard the back door open and quickly replaced the cross in its little velvet pouch and slipped it back into his pocket. It was Fred and Shannon come to invite him for a swim. "Let's do it, and after I'll drive us into South Haven for a steak at Fiddleman's. Sound good?"

"I'm all for that," Fred said.

"Me three," Shannon voted.

Before changing into his swimsuit, Michael sought out Myra to let her know the plans and ask if she'd like to go along.

"I'll go if Lucy is awake by then; otherwise, I'll stay here and fix us a cozy dinner."

"Myra, you're the best. He put his arms around her for a hug. "Sorry for my rant earlier."

"I know you are dealing with some hard issues, Michael, and maybe your heart has your head a little confused. I have faith in you, my boy. Have you decided to tell Lucy about the cross?"

"I will tell her someday, Myra, but not just now. She must first learn to accept the truth of Lance. That he isn't coming back. Until she does that, I don't think I'll stand a chance, crystal cross or not."

"I suppose you're right, dear. But how will you convince her of that?"

"It won't be me that convinces her."

Lucy hadn't awakened by the time they were ready to leave. A consensus was reached that it would probably do her good just to sleep. Myra checked on her from time to time as she waited for the three old chums to return.

Lucy woke up refreshed the next morning but lay in bed for a time trying to discern reality from her dream. In it, she had been with Lance. They were in an underground cave. They made love and after he showed her a ring. "This ring is what is left of the enchantment and treasures of our people. The Guardians have kept it safe. I will give it to my son one day. It will identify him as the true king of Elysium."

She lay now wondering if the boys in the picture she described in her last session were Lance's sons. She wished she could remember it, but she was just giving herself a headache trying. She noticed the time and hurried to dress so she could honor her promise to accompany Myra to Mass. Michael and his house guests were sleeping in and wouldn't be accompanying them, having stayed for last call at the resort last night.

Returning to Glen Eden after church, Myra and Lucy found a note from Michael telling them he'd picked up Megan and the four of them were off for some tennis. He told Myra not to fuss with lunch, as he'd bring home something to throw on the grill. Lucy, on one hand, felt she was being avoided, and on the other enjoyed giving her mind a rest from questions that didn't have any answers, or whose answers were even more confusing than the questions themselves.

The foursome returned from the court and it wasn't long before Nick showed up. Michael grilled freshly caught Lake Michigan Trout, sweet corn and red peppers. For dessert there was a blueberry pie still warm from Myra's oven. There was no talk of the hypnosis sessions or about the report Shannon had brought. It was a pleasant day and Lucy was grateful for the escape. She truly liked all these people. They were treating her as if she belonged there.

Fred left with Shannon around seven. She would be dropping him off at Detroit Metro Airport for his redeye flight back to L.A. Shortly after that, Nick and Myra drove Megan home on their way to play cards with Winnie. Myra tried to visit with her often since Skipper was away. This left Michael and Lucy alone.

Michael felt awkward around her now. He couldn't keep a smile off his face when he looked at her. Kathleen no longer haunted him. It was awkward for Lucy too. She couldn't help but notice his smile and feel his attraction. She did her best to avoid looking in his eyes because when she did the gleam that surged forth pricked her heart.

She saw something on his face now that she'd not noticed before. It was vulnerability. Had she done that to him? She remembered Myra's words: "You're destroying Michael." She certainly didn't want to hurt him. Maybe there was more to his confession of love than just words to frame his fever and lust.

She recalled something he'd said to her. It was her first evening at Glen Eden while they were sitting on the half-wall after she'd found mention of Lance in William's journal. He'd looked at her and murmured Kathleen's name. When she asked him if she resembled Kathleen, he said the light on her face had evoked a memory, a memory of the way he used to feel when he sat there with her. She understood what he meant by it now, because she had begun to feel the same way around him. She knew Michael was holding on to the hope that she would someday forget about Lance. He had that hope, she supposed, partly because he could feel her attraction to him. She couldn't help it. She tried not to feel it but failed. And worse yet, it was getting stronger. It was beginning to confuse her. She knew that if she were ever going to find Lance, she could not allow herself to be distracted. She also knew she was not being fair to Michael. "Dear Michael, he's been so good to me." She needed to make plans, plans that did not include him. She needed to leave Glen Eden and soon to search for Lance on her own. Now that she had the money in Lance's account, she could do that.

She had already decided that half of the funds should go to Paul and Littlefeather, if she could find them. Beyond that, she had earmarked a sum she believed would cover Danny's tuition, books, and a living stipend to be given to him anonymously in monthly payments. Michael helped her make the arrangements with the bank to handle that part of it.

She wanted to learn more about the Tuatha De Danaan, even if that meant a face to face with Father Wentworth, because she now had the suspicion these were Lance's people and possibly her own. She had seen him work magic on the ledge in California when the two men came at him. She remembered the toast to the Guardians in the Blue Nile, and the Guardian Code he had taught her for her note at the switchboard on Haight Street. She remembered how he had escaped from the sheriff and caught the killer in Saugatuck, all without the use of violence. His stories of the bird that came back to life in his hand when he was younger and of how he had lived with the Yeti all pointed to the fact that he was an extraordinary being. Certainly he was a Guardian. But she still wasn't sure where Angus fit in.

She knew Michael had put off a business trip to the U.K. to deal with her problems and that he now rescheduled it. She would bide her time until he left. Then she would make the break. It would be easier to leave if he were not around, easier on both of them.

26 – Confronting Demons

It had been six weeks since Lucy left Glen Eden. Michael tried phoning her apartment nearly every day, but there was never an answer. He had even gone by her apartment at least three times, but no lights were on and there was no answer to his knocking. He got Peggy's number from Ashley and phoned her to see if she'd heard anything from her friend. Peggy expressed her own concern because she was watching Freea, and it wasn't like Lucy not to call and check on how things were going. The only thing she could tell him was that Lucy said she was going to visit Lance's brother in Ohio and would possibly be gone a couple of weeks. Peggy had driven her to the train station. "That was over a month ago. I went to the police to file a missing person's on her, but they wouldn't take it seriously because I'm not next of kin. I had to admit to them that there were times in the past when I hadn't seen or heard from her for longer than this. I wish I would have pressed her for an address when she left."

"Well, if you do hear from her, please let me know."

"No problem, Michael, and you do the same. To be honest, I was very surprised when she left Glen Eden. I thought when she went back there with you after you got out of the hospital that she had decided to stay. What happened, Michael, if you don't mind me asking?"

"I wish I knew. I had a business trip planned for parts of the U.K. I wanted her to go with me to maybe visit some of the sites there that Lance had written about. She said she wasn't ready for that yet, so I left it alone. While I was gone she told Myra she'd be leaving to investigate a lead she'd found. Myra tried to talk her into staying at least till I returned, but she said it was something she had to do right away and on her own."

"A lead, huh? It was probably something to do with finding Lance. Sometimes I wish that guy would drop off the face of this earth. If he hasn't already."

"Be careful what you wish for, Peg. I'm afraid if he did that, she might try to follow him. Let's just do what she would want us to do and pray. Pray for them both."

He didn't tell her but he already had a detective agency working on it. So far all they were able to tell Michael was that Lucy had paid six months' rent on her apartment and bought a train ticket to Peebles, Ohio. From there she hitched a ride from a farmer who claimed he dropped her off at the entrance to the Serpent Mound. The detective then talked to the park ranger at the site who told him a girl fitting Lucy's description had been seen talking to a local shaman on the eve of the autumnal equinox. From there the trail went cold.

Michael hadn't gone back to Glen Eden since he returned from his trip. He couldn't bear thinking of being there now since Lucy left. The same emptiness that filled the rooms when Kathleen died would surely have returned. But Myra repeatedly asked him to come for a visit, so he resolved he would have to face the new emptiness, if only because he knew Myra felt it too. He thought he could handle it for her sake, but after being back for only a few hours he headed for the Butler to get what people mistakenly call fortified.

Ashley could tell the minute he walked in that something was up. He had the dazed look in his eye he'd carried after Kathleen's death. Though they never talked about it, Ashley knew Michael had fallen for Lucy. *Now she had up and left him too, poor guy.* "Hey, Michael, good to see you. Where've you been hiding yourself?"

"Not hiding, Ash, just busy. Over the pond for a while."

"Yeah, Myra told me. She told me that Lucy took off again." Michael nodded, looked down, then shook his head. "So what can I get you? Want a cold one?"

"No, that won't do it. Better get down the Dewars."

Ashley the bartender did what his customer ordered. But Ashley the friend hated to see him hit the hard stuff so early and alone. "I talked with Dr. Scott today. He said Skipper is making good headway."

"Glad to hear that, Ash. Have you been to see her lately?"

"I was there this past weekend. She had the flowers you sent in her room, and she showed me your postcards." Michael raised his glass, stared into the elixir for a moment, then poured it down his throat. "I went by the track and picked up a little change on Strider. I half thought I'd see you there."

"How'd he look?"

"Like a champion. He's so damn tight on those turns. That red haired kid sure knows how to drive him."

This was exactly what Michael needed. He needed to get his thoughts off Lucy. By closing time the Dewar's bottle was dry and Michael tottered for the door. Seeing this, Ashley asked one of the other bartenders to close up so he could drive him home.

Ashley listened to Michael singing the whole of "Tura Lura Lural" on the drive. He didn't mind. He enjoyed it. He even joined in on the chorus:

> *Over In Killarney,*
> *Many years ago,*
> *Me mither sang a song to me*
> *In tones so sweet and low,*
> *Just a simple little ditty,*
> *In her good ould Irish way,*
> *And I'd give the world if she could sing*
> *That song to me this day.*

Too-ra-loo-ra-loo-ral, Too-ra-loo-ra-li,
Too-ra-loo-ra-loo-ral, Hush now don't you cry.
Too-ra-loo-ra-loo-ral, Too-ra-loo-ra-li,
Too-ra-loo-ra-loo-ral, That's an Irish lullaby.

Michael got out of the car singing the second chorus.

Oft, in dreams I wander
To that cot again,
I feel her arms a-hugging me
As when she held me then.
And I hear her voice a hummin'
To me as in days of yore,
When she used to rock me fast asleep
Outside the cabin door.

Ashley told him he'd come by with his car in the morning. He drove off leaving Michael standing in the drive by the front steps. He waved goodbye to Ashley and turned to go in. He looked at the wide balustrade where he and Lucy sat the night he told her about Kathleen. He stood frozen in the memory of it. The sadness broke into his heart again like a wave crashing over a breakwater. He stumbled to the back of the cottage and along the path through the garden until he came to the statue of Angus. "Angus," he shouted. "Angus, you foul-hearted demon, you tell me where she is." The only reply Michael heard came from the crickets. "Angus, you vile wretch, you better show yourself or I'm going to smash this carving to pieces and line the horse lane with the bits of it."

"Oh now, Michael Donegan, why would you be wreckin' such a fine piece of art?" Michael turned to see the shadowy figure of a little man standing atop the dune near the walk down to the beach.

"So there you are, you little vermin."

"Now what sort of way is that for you to talk to someone you'd be wantin' a favor from?"

Michael staggered a few steps closer to the object of his incantation. He tried to get his eyes to focus. "Angus, is that you?"

"Sure it be now, Michael Donegan, and it's taken you long enough to request the honor of my presence. To what desire do you owe summoning me forth? Would it be a lady that's driven you to this madness, or would it be madness that's driven you toward the lady?"

Michael's head was spinning and he was in no mood to play games with the likes of this fae. "Shut up and answer my question. Do you know where Lucy is?"

"Just like your father, you are. Or are you still calling him Grampa?" Angus cackled a wicked laugh. "He used to say to me the same foolishness. 'Shut up and answer my question.' Now just how can I answer anything if I'm to shut up? Tell me that."

"Answer my question, Angus, or I swear I'll pick up this statue and toss it to the bottom of Lake Michigan. Do you know where Lucy is?"

"Calm down, Michael, now that I know what it is you want me to do, I'll do it. I'll answer your question now that I understand you don't really want me to shut up. The answer is yes."

"Yes what?"

"Yes, I know where Lucy is."

"Tell me where."

"She is here but not now, and she is there now and again."

Michael was standing still and whirling at the same time. "What on earth are you talking about?"

"I'm answering your silly questions. She is here sometimes and she isn't at others. She is tumbling, tumbling, tumbling." He was skipping around in a circle when he said it. "It's her own fault. She wouldn't wait, like Lance told her to, here with you. She had to go running off to find him. He told her she couldn't go where he is. Not now. Not yet. She wouldn't listen. It's her own fault. Why did she leave here, I wonder? He told her to stay, here with you, where she would be safe. Maybe she didn't feel too safe. Maybe you forced her away? Did you say something that made her think she couldn't stay? Well, no matter. She's done it, and now she is tumbling, tumbling, tumbling." He skipped in a circle again. "He's trying to find her. Maybe he can. Maybe he can't. Her true love, he is. Not a drunken, selfish, arrogant Irishman. No, he is a gentleman, a king. Her heart is true. Is that why she had to leave, because you would not let her be? You knew her heart was true. That's what you loved about her. But you went and chased her away, couldn't leave her alone when she is not yours. Not yet. Afraid, she was, she'd be hurting you if she stayed. Now she is tumbling, tumbling, tumbling."

Angus jumped aside as Michael lunged at him. "I ought to ring your little neck, you sawed off... Wait a minute, what did you mean by 'Not yet?'" The patio light went on and Myra's voice broke into the night.

"Michael, is that you? Who are you talking to?"

Michael turned to see Myra walking toward him. When he turned back, Angus was gone and a rabbit jumped under a honeysuckle bush near the stone statue.

"Michael, what on earth are you doing out here at this hour?"

"I was talking to Angus." Michael said, turning back around and falling flat on his face.

"Oh Michael, you've had a bit much, haven't you?" She bent to help him up, but his legs were like noodles. She knew he was in no shape to walk and that he was way too heavy for her to carry, so she scurried to the cottage and brought back a blanket to put over him and a pillow for under his head. By the time she returned, he was already out.

"There, there, my boy. Just sleep it off here under the stars." She looked around and then said very loudly, "You leave him alone, Angus, or you'll deal with me." The rabbit under the honeysuckle scurried off toward the woods.

When Michael again opened his eyes, he was staring into the face of a Brown-eyed Susan. A visiting bumblebee took flight for another bloom and the drone of its buzz drove a spike into Michael's brain. He rolled over on his side then up on all fours, then he slowly stood on his two feet, letting the pounding between his eyes settle before heading for the cottage. Myra was standing at the door with a mug of hot coffee ready to hand him.

"Here you go, lovie, hot and strong."

"Thanks, Myra, and thanks for the bedding. I'd appreciate it if you would hold off on any lectures till my head settles."

"You'll not get a lecture from me, Michael. I think you're old enough to know when you are acting a fool. It's not any of my words that can mend what ails you. If I thought they could, I'd talk until your ears fell right off." She fumbled getting the lid off the aspirin bottle then poured out two into her hand. "Here, take these, have another cup of coffee and go on up and take a cold shower. Ashley called and said he'd come by with your car around eleven. He'll need you to drive him to work."

The previous evening was coming back to Michael. He wondered how much of what happened in the garden had been just a dream. Had he really conjured up Angus? He stood braced against the shower wall letting the cold water rush over him, trying to sort out the reality of the past evening. The aspirin kicked in to ease his headache but offered no relief for the ache in his heart.

In the city, he had some success fending off the way he missed her. He kept his schedule full and buried himself in either his work or fundraising efforts for Kathleen's foundation. But here at Glen Eden there was no way to avoid the emptiness her leaving had revived or to abate his longing.

He decided he'd go riding later on and threw on an old pair of jeans and a sweatshirt. He pulled on socks and slipped into his deck shoes. He'd change to his boots in the stable later. The frost had visited the area a couple times now since she left, and the newly turned leaves painted the landscape in yellows, oranges and reds. He thought of how he'd like to share the beauty of it with her and wondered if she were somewhere where she could enjoy it.

Ashley pulled up in Michael's car just as he strolled out the front door. He got into the passenger seat, nodded a hello, then thanked Ashley for getting him home last night. "I hope all that fine Scotch didn't go to waste, and you at least got one good hallucination from it. I danced stark naked with an angel on top Mt. Baldhead one night after consuming less than what you did last night." He threw his head back and laughed.

"I didn't dance naked with an angel, but I did conjure up a little demon out back in Myra's garden. She found me out there where I kissed the ground and laid a cover over me so I wouldn't freeze to death, bless her soul." Now they both laughed. "How stupid are we to do that to our bodies for a couple hours of what—suspended reality?"

"I don't know, but it was a damn fine dance," Ashley chuckled. He pulled around to the back door of the Butler and got out. "Want to come in for a little hair of the dog?"

"Not on a bet."

"How about I have Tweedy rustle up a couple of Butler burgers?"

"That's more like it." Michael got out and followed him in.

"Good morning, Tweedy," Ashley said a little too loudly, causing Michael to grab his forehead. "Throw on a couple of Butler burgers for us, will ya?"

Tweedy stood at the grill, a little old man quite possibly in his late eighties, no one knew for sure. He had been a fixture at the Butler for years, since long before his body could no longer do the work of a longshoreman. He quite possibly was the oldest living patron of the bar as well. When his days of living hard, working hard, and drinking hard were over, he became the lunchtime fry cook and overall handy man around the Butler. Verse let him live rent-free in a room on the third floor of the old hotel. It was his kitchen now, and the intrusion of this young upstart ruffled him, barking orders without so much as a *permission to board, captain*. "Put them on yourself, you lazy little bastard. I'm cooking for the paying customers."

Ashley's eyes sparkled and a big smile came to his face. He loved sparring with the old guy. "I was hoping you'd say that. I want to make sure they're cooked right for me and my buddy here." He walked over and took two raw beef patties from a plate and tossed them on the hot grill.

"Get the hell out of here, you young yahoo. I could outcook you with one hand tied behind my back." He swatted at Ashley with the hot spatula. His eyes danced and he smiled a toothless smile. "You want the works on them and fries?"

"You bet, Gramps."

"Don't *Gramps* me, you syphilis-ridden man whore."

"And you don't be stingy with the ham."

"Stop grabbing my balls, girly. Go on out and buy your girlfriend a beer. I'll send the plates out with one of the waitresses."

"Thanks, Pops."

"Thank me I don't cut off your crank and feed it to the seagulls. At least some creature would get some use out of it." Michael realized this harsh talk was a form of endearment between the two of them. "By the way, I saw you last night with number one over by the ferry dock. What the hell was a good-looking broad like Lucy doing with a scurvy dog like you?"

"You're delusional, old man. I wasn't with Lucy last night. She's left town," Ashley said.

"Don't tell me what I saw or didn't, you snot-nosed pantywaist. You were all dressed up in a monkey suit with a rose pinned to your chest, and she had on a long blue dress with a big floppy brimmed hat. She was a vision, she was, and you were a toad waiting for a kiss."

The smile on Ashley's face straightened to one of nervousness as he ushered Michael out the kitchen door into the bar. "What was that about Lucy?" Michael asked.

"I don't know. I think maybe Tweedy is slipping over the edge. He's remembering the night of Skipper's wedding. Lucy was my 'fiancée' at the time, remember? She went with me to the reception, and after we walked down to the ferry landing. We saw Tweedy drunk on his ass sitting under the old willow tree. You know what's funny about this? I thought of that evening last night too. After I dropped you home, I came back here to help lock up. I took a walk down that way. I thought of that night and of how beautiful…" He caught himself and said, "Hey, I'll go grab us a couple of drafts, is that good with you?"

"Sure." Michael wondered whether Tweedy's vision—at seemingly the exact time Ashley was thinking about the same past event—had anything to do with what Angus said about Lucy tumbling. "Maybe she's tumbling through time." Michael surprised himself by that thought. Tumbling through time. Christ, was he going nuts now?

The burger was great, a half pounder piled high with grilled ham. It had melted cheese, tomato and lettuce with Thousand Island dressing smeared on the grilled bun. The fries were the fat kind he liked, crispy on the outside and soft in the middle.

He felt better after eating, and when he got home he went straight to the stable to saddle Shashad. They took the path from the stable north through the woods following the directions he had given Fred the day he went riding with Lucy, the directions that were supposed to bring them to the stone circle. He found the meadow and rode the circumference of it. Fred was right: there was no stone circle. Michael rode beyond the meadow and then decided to turn back and enter it from the way he had gone the day he found Lucy there. The wind picked up and shook loose the dryer leaves, carrying them dancing past the horse and rider. Something else was carried on the wind, and Michael reined Shashad to a halt when he heard it. He was sure it was a woman's voice. It called his name.

Now Michael was the wind as he raced toward the voice. A hurling leaf hit Shashad in the face and he reared up, throwing Michael to the ground. He landed hard near a boulder that he was sure had not been there before. Soon more boulders appeared, forming a circle around him. "Michael, what are you doing here?" It was Lucy.

"I was looking for you."

"Where is Lance?"

"I don't know."

"He was right here. You had to have seen him."

"Lucy, I'm sorry… I didn't."

"You're lying. Why are you lying?" Her hair was mussed and her eyes were wild. She came at him, pounding him with her fists. He apologized then slapped her. She took off running, but he easily caught her and tackled her to the ground. As she struggled beneath him, he couldn't fight his desire for her. He kissed her. She returned this kiss and wrapped her arms and legs tightly around him.

"Lucy, I love you. I want you. I can't live without you."

"I love you too, Michael," she whispered in a voice so beautiful it brought tears to his eyes. Then came a harsh, cackling voice, disturbing his ears.

"Isn't that sweet," the voice mocked. "'I love you too, Michael.' But it isn't time. Not yet. No, not yet." They both jumped to their feet to face Angus.

"Get out of here, you demon," Michael commanded, stepping in front of Lucy to protect her from his nemesis.

"You can't have her. No, not yet. It's not your time."

"Shut up." Michael lunged at him just as he disappeared. He slammed hard into the ground where Angus had been, shook his head, and rolled over. Lucy was gone too, and so was the stone circle. Shashad stood nuzzling him gently.

27 – Time and Again

Lucy stood in the center of the large, uncultivated field that lay at the foot of the woods across the road from Twin Willows. Breathing deeply the cool, crisp, mid-autumn air, she gazed at the horizon as the last light of day withdrew from around her. She came back in her thoughts from some distant memory and realized she must now be somewhere in her future. Wherever she was, she had lingered too long and must now find her way over uneven ground in the dark.

Realizing that she was not dressed adequately to be out after the warmth of the sun faded, she pulled her jacket collar up around her neck and stuffed her hands in her pockets. That's why she went face first into the ground when minutes later she tripped on a clump of dirt piled around a woodchuck hole. As she rubbed the dirt from her face she noticed blood on her hand. It was her own blood from a nasty gash on her chin.

As soon as she realized she was bleeding, a long strange howl came from behind her. She struggled to her feet and hurried even faster in the direction she thought was her home. A heavy mist had settled upon the field, and she wasn't quite sure which way she should be going. There was an orangeish glow on the horizon in front of her that she took as the last hint of the sun settling in the west, toward her home. There was that howl again. This time it seemed to be coming from in front of her. It made goose bumps rise on her skin. Another fifty feet on she stopped in her tracks. Squinting in the dark through the mist, she could make out large dark shapes. She thought she must have gotten turned around and was heading into the woods again. Then something grabbed at her shoulder. She turned in fright to see absolutely nothing. She started to run but the howls seemed to get louder, as if she were running toward them even though she had turned and was now running in the opposite direction from before. Was she surrounded? But by what? Her heart beat more rapidly, her mouth was dry, and her breathing uneven. Still she ran through the darkness.

She stumbled again and fell to the ground. Her shoe had gotten wedged in a rut and was pulled off. Her terror was so great that she didn't even try to retrieve it. She jumped up and ran on without it. Again and again she fell, until finally she didn't have the strength to get up. She lay listening, but her own breath was heavy in her ears. Scripture came to her mind: "We wrestle not against flesh and blood but against principalities and powers of darkness in high places." She knew that all fear is perverted faith and that faith without works is dead, so she exercised faith. She said as loudly as her winded breath would allow, "There is none higher than you, oh my Lord. Give your angels charge over me and lead me safely home. I pray in the name above all names, the most high Jesus." The world spun under her as her fear fell away and she drifted into thoughtlessness.

When her eyes opened again, she was on the front porch at Twin Willows. A mother wren called from a nest in the eaves above her head. She heard a tractor and looked up to see her dad turning over last year's cabbage field. Her mom came to stand in the doorway. "Where on earth have you been? We were worried sick about you. Sissy came back from the woods with the flowers and said she couldn't find you. Were you hiding on her? How did you hurt your chin? Come on in and get cleaned up. Look at what a mess you are. Where is your other shoe?"

Lucy was too confounded to say anything. It was another time jump. Judging from how young her mom looked, she must be about eleven or twelve. She must have made this jump from a time in the future because in it her body felt achy and stiff, and though she wasn't in it long enough to see herself in a mirror, she remembered that her hands looked old.

Her mom helped her clean up, put a band-aid on her chin, and sent her to her room to change clothes. It was strange for her to realize that no matter what age she was physically, she always felt the same inside. She'd have to look in a mirror or at a calendar to determine at what age she was being perceived.

She glanced around the room she had shared growing up with her twin. There were their bunk beds. Hers was the lower one with the autographed baseball card of Rocky Colavito taped to the headboard. Sue always had the top bunk, and today her stuffed toy tiger was guarding it. Lucy's bunkmate was a stuffed toy leopard. They had won their plush friends at the county fair the previous September by tossing balls into a basket.

She walked over to the little portable record player that was sitting on the corner of the desk to see what 45 rpm disc was on it: Ricky Nelson's "Never Be Anyone Else But You." She turned it on and put the needle in the groove. She remembered the words and started singing with him. Sue stomped into the room and turned it off. "That wasn't very nice of you, running off on me like that. Why did you do it? I had to make all the May baskets myself and take them around. Ma said she's gonna make you do the dishes all by yourself for a week."

"I'm sorry, sissy," Lucy said, giving her sister a hug. "I couldn't help it."

"Just don't ever do it again. I was scared."

Lucy remembered now how close they had been at this age. Being born twins and living in the country, they had naturally become each other's best friend. "Do you want to go outside and play before dinner?"

"Sure, but I choose the game."

"One... Two... Three... Four," her sister shouted with her head buried in her arms and her eyes shut tight. She was leaning against the trunk of one of the three tall sugar maples that grew in their backyard. That trunk was now the goal in their game of hide and seek, and Lucy must get as far away from it as possible before the count reached fifty.

She raced off toward the south yard and the hedge of bridal wreath bushes, giggling aloud on purpose so her sister could hear her. She let her footsteps pound the ground heavily to be sure Sue could tell what direction she was headed in. When she thought she had gotten far enough away, she quietly doubled back toward the old barn that sat crumbling to the northwest of the tree goal. Alongside the old barn that now housed the family's small flock of chickens sat an old, green Nash Rambler her dad would one day resurrect to use as his work car. But for now, it sat with tires flat and clutch needing repair. She picked up her speed and dashed wildly toward the back of it as she heard the count fill the air behind her: "47... 48... 49..." She dove head first behind the car as "50" rang out, followed by "Here I come, ready or not."

She crawled behind the rear wheel and sat still as a stone until her heart stopped pounding. Carefully, slowly, quietly she lowered herself to the ground to peek under the steel fortress. There was Sue heading into the sideyard just as she hoped she'd do. She would sit in the warm sun and wait until her sister passed behind the hedges. Then she would make her move and sneak back to the goal and be safe. Oh what a wonderful plan she'd made, and it was working just as she hoped. She sat gloating, thinking just how clever she was. She watched a big, white hen scratching in the dirt nearby.

"Okay," she thought, "enough time has passed and Sissy should be out of sight behind the hedges by now." Carefully, slowly, quietly, she crawled upon her belly to peer again under the old car. Her heart stopped as she looked into the face of a girl stooping down on the other side of the car and looking right at her. "I see you," the girl giggled as Lucy sprang to her feet and madly rushed back toward the goal. She looked over her shoulder to see how close her pursuer was and to her surprise no one followed her. Looking toward the goal again, she saw her sister racing in from the sideyard. Reaching the goal before her, Sue counted aloud, "One, two, three, you're it!"

Lucy couldn't believe what just happened. She thought it was her sister on the other side of the car when she jumped from her hiding place and started racing toward the goal. Yet now she stood at the goal having come from the opposite direction. That's when it struck her. She raced up and clutched at her sister. "Sissy, Sissy, I saw her, I saw her," she cried breathlessly, trying to get the attention of one silly with winning pride.

"I got you. I got you," Sue sang as Lucy tried once again to get her to listen.

"Sissy, please. Please listen to me. I saw her. I saw her."

"Who?"

"That girl, that girl that looks like us, the one that stands at the foot of my bed sometimes. She was over there by the car. I thought she was you come to find me."

"Don't be silly. You're just mad that I counted you out."

"I'm not, come with me quick. Let's find her." Clutching her sister's hand and half dragging her, the twins ran back to the old car.

"I don't know what you're talking about. I didn't see anyone. I heard you running toward the tree and I beat you there but good."

"I was gonna sneak back when you were behind the hedges, but when I peeked under the car, there she was. I thought she was you, so I tried to beat you back to the goal. Only when I started running, I saw you come from the sideyard. I know she's hiding here somewhere. Please help me find her."

Still holding hands, the girls walked around the car. They looked under it, behind it, and in it, but found no one. Finally, they walked into the dark barn where the chickens made their nests in wooden apple crates their dad had set on their sides upon a high shelf so the fox couldn't get to their eggs. "Lucy, there's no one here," Sue said, tiring of the hunt.

"I saw her, I tell you. I saw her. She must be here somewhere." Lucy continued to look around and jerked on her sister's hand to follow.

"Lucy, Mom said we shouldn't play these games."

"What games?"

"You know, the make-believe games like we see little people and fairies."

"But that's not pretend. You've seen the fairies too. I know you have. You told me you saw them."

"Well, maybe I was just pretending with you."

"I wasn't pretending, and you saw them too and I know it." She felt betrayed.

"Mom says there are no such things and it isn't good to play like that. I never saw that girl, the one you say looks like us."

"Oh but she does, Sissy. She looks just like us. Do you think she could be Verene?" Verene was their younger sister who died when the twins were three.

"Why would you say something like that?"

"Well, it's just that she looks like us, and, and…" She hesitated. "Well, maybe where she is she misses us and so she comes to see us now and then."

"You mean like her ghost?" Sue asked.

"Yeah, I guess."

"Don't say stuff like that, and don't you let Mommy hear you say that either. It would make her start crying all over again. Do you want that?"

"No, I don't want Momma to cry. But Sissy, if it *is* her, don't you think Mom and Dad would want to see her too? To know she's all right? To know she comes here to visit us?"

"No, I don't think they would want to know that. I think they want to forget about her because it hurts them to remember. So don't you go making them feel bad, and stop playing all this pretend stuff."

"But Sissy, I see…"

"No," Sue screamed, "I said just stop it. I don't want to play with you anymore." With that, Sue turned and ran for the house leaving Lucy to stand alone in the old barn.

"I'm sorry," she sniffed as if someone other than the chickens were listening. "I can't play with you. It would hurt Mommy and Daddy, and they cried for a long time. I guess you know that." She paused a moment, rubbing her nose. "And it will make Sissy mad at me, and, well, I guess it isn't natural for you to come here." She sniffed a couple more times. "So... so I guess I can't see you anymore. I'm sorry, truly I am." With tears falling off her cheeks, she ran outside and around the old barn, falling in the tall, cool grass that grew behind it. There she lay sobbing until the old barn cat came up and crawled atop her, purring. "Hello, Pepper, you good old kitty. You saw her too, didn't you?" Pepper pressed her nose against Lucy's chin and purred all the more loudly.

After a little while she heard her mom calling, "Lucy, come in now for dinner." She jumped up and ran to the house. She didn't want her mom to cry, so she said nothing of the girl she had seen.

While she was doing the dishes that night, all by herself, something touched her shoulder. This time when she turned she was back in her room again. The bunk beds were gone, replaced by two twin beds. The pictures on the wall had changed too. Instead of the baseball cards, pinned there were pictures cut from *Teen* Magazine of popular movie and TV stars of the day: George Maharis, Clint Eastwood, James Garner, Troy Donahue, Ed Burns, and others. She hurried over to the mirror. There was no gash or cut on her chin, just an old healed scar. She was now in her early twenties. She slipped her feet into the flip-flops that sat under her bed. Pulling her house jacket around her, she scuffed off toward the kitchen. No one was at home. The phone rang. She hesitated before answering, trying to determine just what time she was in now. "Hello"

"Hi, I'm leaving my house now, and I'll pick you up in, oh say, twenty minutes. I have to stop to get gas. So be ready."

"Ready for what?"

"Oh man, you didn't forget did you?"

"Forget?"

"The fair. We're going to the fair today. This is the only day I can go. You said you'd go with me. You are going, aren't you?"

"Oh yeah. Yeah, sure."

"Did you just wake up?"

"Ah... yeah."

"Did your mom and dad leave already?"

"I think so. They aren't here."

"Okay, see you in twenty. Get ready. Bye." Twenty-eight minutes later a dark blue Mustang convertible pulled into the front drive and Lucy watched as a young woman with long, dark, curly hair, sprang from the driver's seat. Lucy went to the screen door, holding it open as the girl came rushing in. "Oh man, I gotta pee. Are you ready?"

"Yeah. Just need to brush my hair."

"You look great. I love that tie-dye top."

"Thanks."

Tossing her purse on the hall tree bench as she rushed by, Lynn said, "Sue and Irene are picking up Jane, so we'll meet them there."

"Okay."

"You'll never guess who was at the gas station."

"Who?"

"No, you have to guess, but wait a minute 'cause I really have to go." She ran off toward the bathroom. Lynn had spent a lot of time in this house when the two of them were in high school and nothing had changed much, neither in the house, nor with her old friend. Lucy caught a whiff of Heaven Sent when Lynn hurried by, a perfume Lynn had worn since the 8th grade.

As Lucy waited, she looked out the front window, brushing her long, auburn hair. Across the road beyond the big field just before the woods, a movement caught her eye and she peered hard trying to make it out. "That's odd," she thought.

"Okay, let's hit it," Lynn said, then noticed Lucy watching something out the window. She stopped and peered out too. "What is it?" she asked. When she got no response, she asked again, "What are you looking at?"

"Someone was there."

"Where?"

"Just at the end of the path by the woods."

"I don't see anyone."

"No, they're gone now."

"Maybe it was a hunter? Isn't this the season for killing some poor, dumb animal? Come on, let's go. Bring a tie for your hair. I'm going to leave the top down." Lynn, who was always in motion, was already out the door when Lucy turned from the window.

She knew this day was from her past: they would go to the fair and meet her parents. Her sister would be there too with Irene and Jane; they were all friends. It would be a good day. Yet what she had just witnessed didn't belong to this memory. What she thought she saw for just a brief moment was a man dressed in armor engaged in battle with a tall figure in a long, black, hooded robe. She shook her head to stop thinking about it.

It was a perfect late summer day. Big fluffy white clouds floated across the blue sky, allowing the sun to play peek-a-boo on the world below. They drove down the dusty country road past farms of relatives and neighbors headed toward the highway with radio blaring and ponytails streaming, two friends off for some fun. "Then I saw her face. Now I'm a believer..." Lynn sang, bouncing to the music of a Monkee's hit tune as she clutched the steering wheel, her head bobbing rhythmically back and forth.

Lucy thought how beautifully happy Lynn looked, then her heart broke remembering what soon would befall her friend. She had been trapped in these events for so long that she knew there was no use in trying to change anything. She must simply live for the moment and enjoy the seconds as they soon passed, once again. "Hey, you didn't tell me who you saw at the gas station?"

"Oh," Lynn squealed, reaching to turn down the radio. "Guess. You have to guess."

"Come on."

"No. Guess."

"I don't know. Give me some sort of a hint."

"Okay… Dreamy! Dreamy! Dreamy!"

"Dreamy, huh? I got it," Lucy said with a chuckle. "George Maharis"

"Come on, be serious. Real life dreamy."

"Oh, that's some hint. Do better."

"Okay, let's see: quiet, mysterious, soul deep green eyes and long sandy hair."

Oh my God! She saw Lance, Lucy thought. This was certainly a new event. Lance had never met Lynn or any of her old friends. "Come on, tell me, please," she begged.

"It was Lance."

Lucy's heart nearly stopped. "And guess what was the very first thing he asked me—after we hugged and he told me how gorgeous I look, of course."

"I don't know, Lynn, just tell me. Tell me everything."

"You silly, he asked me if anyone had heard from you."

"What did you say?"

"I told him you were in some prison in Mexico, clipped for trying to smuggle weed across the border."

"Oh you shit, you did not. Stop teasing me and tell me."

"Why should I? It's not like you tell me anything. I don't even know what happened between the two of you."

"Lynn, I swear if you don't tell me everything right now, when we get back I'm going to phone up Ricky Thorngate and tell him that you have a mad crush on him."

"Oh my God, this is black mail," she giggled. "Now who's a shit? If you do that, he will stalk me for another three years." She threw her head back and laughed out loud.

"Come on, Lynn, tell me what Lance said, please."

"All right. Let's see, he said he's just back from a place in Romania—Bran, I think. He said he didn't know how long he could stay here. You know, I never really understood just what it is he does. I thought once he might work for the CIA or FBI or something like that; he's always so mysterious."

"Is that all he said?"

"I told him I was on my way to pick you up and that we were going to the fair. This is where it turned strange. He asked me to tell you he was trying to find a portal. And if he did, you'd have a sign you could not ignore. He made me promise to tell you that. Do you have any idea what he's talking about?"

"Sort of." Lucy thought of the battle she had glimpsed earlier. The warrior must have been Lance. Maybe he was there to rescue her and bring her back… or forward… or… she didn't care really, as long as she would be with him. "Is that it? Is that all he said?"

"Yeah, strange, huh? I'm not sure what happened to you guys in California, but I thought you made a good pair. How come you left him and came back here anyway?"

"I didn't leave him. He left me. I mean, he went away."

"Sorry," Lynn offered meekly, but she only paused a moment before asking, "Why did he go away?"

"I'd really rather not talk about this right now."

"Okay, Miss Tell-Me-Everything. I'd just like to know, Is he a spy or something? Just what's the big mystery?"

"Look, Lynn, I'm looking forward to having a fun day and not thinking about the past. Let's just enjoy ourselves, okay?"

"Okay, all right already, I'm sorry. It's really good having you back, and I'm looking forward to some fun too. Just promise someday you'll let me in on the big mystery."

Lucy just smiled. She reached over and turned up the radio. "Johnny Angel" was playing and the two friends harmonized along.

> *Johnny Angel, 'cause I love him*
> *And I know that someday he'll love me*
> *And together we will see how lovely heaven will be.*

Lucy sat staring at the road ahead, playing with a medallion that hung from a silver chain around her neck. Her thoughts went to a summer day not so unlike this one. She was lying on a hill full of wild daises and sweet clover. The bees were humming as they skipped from blossom to blossom. Lance was there beside her. He was raised up on one elbow to block the sun from her eyes. The sunlight encased him, giving him a golden aura. He brushed her lips with his fingers and bent to kiss her. He found her hand and placed the medallion in it. The memory of this made her feel happy and sad all at the same time. She brushed a tear that came sliding down her cheek and checked to see if Lynn had seen it. Lynn was adjusting the radio and didn't notice her friend's moment.

It was noon by the time they reached the county seat and the fairgrounds. Lucy had been coming to this fair for years. It was always in or near her birthday week. She and Sue would save up the money they earned working during the summer, picking berries on their father's farm, or cherries and peaches on their uncles'. They would spend most of it shopping for school clothes but always kept enough for a good time at the fair.

In the small Midwestern farming communities like the one Lucy grew up in the fair was the social event of the year. Just about everyone would go at least once during the week it was on. Mothers would buy little tee shirts for their babies proclaiming *My First Fair*. Grandmas and grandpas would be helped from exhibit barn to exhibit barn to see the newfangled inventions the big city salesmen brought to demonstrate. Moms entered competitions for knitted, crocheted, or home-sewn items, home-canned goods or baked-from-scratch cakes and pies. Dads would look over the latest and greatest farm equipment on display. Parents and grandparents alike would watch with pride as one of their brood exhibited a calf, pig, sheep, chicken or other farm animal they'd raised, hoping for a blue ribbon. There'd be something for everyone to get excited about: pie-eating contests, pony rides, a chance to dunk the county sheriff in a tank of cold water. Then there was the midway with its games, rides, freak shows, and all varieties of fried foods, hotdogs, cotton candy, ice cream and popcorn.

They pulled up to a man wearing an orange striped vest. Lynn handed him a ten dollar bill and said, "Hey Jeff, how are things going?"

"Pretty fine, Miss Lynn, thank you," he replied while making change from a roll of bills in his hand.

"Good to see you, Jeff," Lucy called out.

"Well, look who's here? Hey cuz, heard you were home. Your sister went in about ten minutes ago. She asked for the hill. Your mom and dad went up early in their motor home to get the spot near the edge where they can look down over the racetrack. I told 'em all I'd be on the lookout for you to tell you where they parked."

"Oh yeah, as if I wouldn't know. Daddy tries for that same spot every year since they opened up the hill."

"Yeah, it's a good one. Gives a view of the whole grounds. You tell Auntie Irene I'll be by on my break to get some of her blueberry cobbler."

"I will, Jeff. See you up there." Lynn pulled slowly away and followed the line of other cars snaking up the hill.

Lucy was living in the moment and remembering it at the same time. She had been lost in what she guessed was some type of time-space continuum since she'd visited the Serpent Mound a couple weeks after leaving Glen Eden. She had no idea how long ago that was. She had gone there at the time of the autumnal equinox hoping to enter the time tunnel, which she was sure was there, to find Lance. She confided this notion to the Native American park ranger who watched over the sacred spot. Once she mentioned Lance by his Indian name, he was more than willing to help her. He told her exactly where to stand and what time to stand there. The air in front of her became charged with energy as an opaque, oval-shaped hole opened before her. She stepped into it as quickly as she could and immediately started tumbling. She soon realized she had no control over where she would end up.

She landed in a hammock tied between a willow tree and a pole in the front yard of Twin Willows. She must have been about three years old. She never knew just how long she was going to stay in a particular time. She'd be old one minute and experiencing things she wasn't sure would even be part of her future. Then she'd slip back to a time in her past where events would happen again pretty much just as she remembered, like rereading a favorite book. There were those things you'd recall before you read them again and things you couldn't remember having read before.

The time event she found herself in now was an exception. Though she remembered the day and going to the fair, she was sure Lance had not been there in the past. Since he had found his way into this time, then it must be because he was looking for her. If that were true, then the message he gave Lynn about trying to find a portal must mean a way for them to escape and be together. Maybe he'd find a way to get them out and back to the time between her past and her future, a time that she couldn't really call her present because ever since she had entered the time slip, her past and her future were her present. It was too confusing to think about.

As she sat atop the hill above the fairgrounds on a blanket her sister spread out next to her folks' motor home, she tried to recall how many time events she'd experienced. She recalled a time picking blackberries with her grandmother when she was very small; she got stung on the thumb by a black wasp when she mistook it for a big berry. Then there was the time she'd come home from work early and walked in on Rayme having sex with their landlord's wife. The time she and Sue switched classes in high school to see if anyone would notice—and no one did. The time, again when she was very small, she was with her dad in Bob Wood's hardware store in Lacota; she saw a little creature peeking out at her from one of the large nail bins. She briefly visited the time when she first got her driver's license and drove her grandmother to Junior Wood's grocery, also in Lacota, and watched as he cut roasts from a beef shank at his butcher's table in the back of the store.

What else? Oh yes, there was the time she accompanied Ashley to his sister's wedding, and after they walked down to the ferry landing in Saugatuck. She had a feeling he might try to kiss her, but just when she thought he would, Tweedy, who was drunk and sitting under the big willow tree, started singing a seafaring song. There were other times from what she guessed might be her future. These weren't as easy for her to recall, maybe because she didn't want them to be her future; Lance hadn't been there and neither had Michael. But Lance was here now—somewhere—in this time, and it seemed as if she could feel him watching her.

She spent a wonderful day at the fair encountering many old friends and family. She enjoyed watching the sulky races with her dad. As she did, she thought about Strider and whether he was winning any races for Michael in a future time. She wondered if she'd ever see him again.

She half expected to see Lance at the fair to give her the sign he told Lynn about. But near midnight, with the midway closing down, they left. They drove M-89 from Allegan to Fennville where they dropped off Jane at her apartment. She had stayed with them when Sue and Irene left early to visit their boyfriends in Pullman. Jane, Lynn and Lucy palled around a lot together before Lucy moved to California, mostly going to local dances, drag races, or the roller rink in Plainwell. Lucy visited Jane's grave with Lynn during one of her jumps forward in time. She tried not to think of that. But when they dropped Jane off, Lucy got out of the car to give her a hug and tell her she loved her. That was something else she was sure had not happened in the past.

They continued through Fennville on M-89 till it junctioned with Blue Star Highway, old US-131, and turned south. Lucy, glancing out the passenger's window, commented on how big and orange the moon was. "Lucy, the moon is over here," Lynn replied, pointing through the driver's window to the small, whitish crescent.

"Then what is that?" Lucy rolled down her window to get a better look and pointed to a yellow-orange orb growing bigger and brighter as it silently descended the sky. "Turn left down that gravel road," Lucy instructed. Now they were heading straight for it.

They drove slowly around a curve and pulled over to the side of the road, coming to a stop at a point as close as they could get to where the object appeared to have settled to the ground behind a grove of pine trees. "What the hell is that? Lynn asked, becoming wary. "I think we should get out of here."

"No, Lynn, don't you see. That's my sign," Lucy said, opening her door and stepping out. "The one Lance said I wouldn't be able to ignore."

"Lucy, this is crazy. Get back in the car."

"No, I have to go now, Lynn. See you again in the future." She ran as fast as she could through the sandy soil, dodging outgrowths of fescue and wild raspberry bushes. She ran straight toward the glowing oval. The closer she got the less brilliant it seemed. She could see distortions inside the circle that looked something like a heat wave. She stopped in front of it, feeling unsure of what to do. Someone grabbed her arm. It was the same feeling she had before each time change had occurred. She turned and Lance stood before her. She leaped into him, locking her arms about his neck and showering his face with kisses.

"Lucy, stop!" he said sternly, unlocking her arms from around him. "We don't have time. What you did was very foolish. It may have cost us dearly. You must trust me and never try this again."

"But, Lance."

"No, Lucy, there is no time. You must go back." He shoved her backwards through the glowing access way. She fell to the damp ground in the center of the Great Serpent Mound's egg. She stumbled to find her way in the pitch dark. Twenty minutes later, a park ranger making his rounds came upon her. He told her she wasn't allowed in the park after dark and escorted her to the front gate. He was going to call the local sheriff to check her out and give her a lift into town, but when they reached the gate a small Native American woman jumped from the passenger seat of an odd-looking silver truck and embraced her. Lucy told the ranger her family had found her, so he didn't make the call.

Lucy's questions started as soon as the truck's door was shut. "Littlefeather, Paul, what are you doing here? I'm so glad to see you, but how did you know? Lance told you, didn't he? Is he here, or at the farm? I tried to write you, but my letter came back. And when I tried calling, the phone operator said there was no such number."

Littlefeather placed her finger on her lips. "Let Paul explain."

"Oh man, Lucy," he began, "this is going to be tough. Lance told me how it is and I thought he was joking. Now he wants me to explain it to you. I hope I don't mess it up. You see, it's like this: Lance said you are to stay at the farm with us tonight, and tomorrow we'll take you to the train in Peebles."

"Paul I'd really like to stay with you and Littlefeather a while, if I could."

"Well, that's just it, Lucy. You can't. I mean, we'd love to have you, but, well, you can't because, well, because you aren't… Oh, I know I'm messing this up."

"Paul, just tell me what Lance said."

"Gosh, Lucy," he said. "You're from a dimension in a future time. The only way you got to the farm before was in Quicksilver. The same way we got here tonight. You see, we're from the past… not your past. Well, I guess we are now, but… Golly, I'm messing this up."

"Please, Paul, go on."

"You see, I guess you normally live in a future distant to us. When you came to the farm before, we always picked you up in Quicksilver because it's able to pass some dimensional divide. I didn't know of it myself until just tonight when Lance came and had us drive him here. He told us all about it on the way. He said to wait until the sun came up. If you came out and found us, we should tell you all this. If you weren't here before the sunrise, then he had failed. That's it. That's all I know."

Littlefeather squeezed his arm and said, "Tell her."

He took a deep breath and wetted his lips. "Lance wanted me to tell you never to try that again."

"He already told me that, Paul"

"He said I should tell you... Oh man." He swallowed hard. "That I should tell you that he will never stop thinking of you and that he loves you. I know that's true, Lucy. I never saw my brother with tears in his eyes, not even when Dad and Mom died. But he had them tonight when he said your time together may all be in the past."

"No, Paul."

"He said that looking for you he lost the opportunity he had to return to your future. He's not sure now if he can, and it isn't fair to you to wait for him."

"I will wait, Paul."

"He doesn't want you to, Lucy."

"Lance told us you must take a different path," Littlefeather said. "He will dreamwalk with you again, and you must trust in what he shows you. He gave me feathers and asked me to make you this." Littlefeather handed her a dreamcatcher made with feathers unlike any she'd ever seen. She slept with it pinned to the bedpost above her head that night in Lance's old room at the farm, but he did not find her.

She awoke early and rode Takota to the graves on the hill, and then she rode on to the waterfall where she had held Lance's hand and leaped into the pool. She was trying to remember, but instead she felt as if she were saying goodbye.

28 – Shalala

Lucy took a train from San Francisco to Portland and from there began hiking up the Oregon coast. She was on a quest to find peace again. Having returned to her life in the present, she found her memories of Lance fading. She had not seen Michael, though she had managed to keep in touch with Myra. She even visited Glen Eden a couple of times through the winter, but only when she knew Michael was away. Myra respected her wishes and did not ask where she had been. Lucy loved being at the cottage because she could picture Lance there more clearly than anywhere else now. She would always go there with the hope he would come to her again, if only in dream. But he did not, and Michael's presence, even when he was away, was too much for her to ignore.

Freea loved being at the cottage too, so when Lucy decided on this journey, she phoned Myra to ask if she would look after her. She couldn't ask Peggy to watch her again after what had happened last time. Lucy was relieved when Myra happily agreed. Myra's cousin Rose, who had come to stay over the winter, left to return to Ireland. So Freea would be good company for Myra and vice versa.

Peggy was happy to drive the pair to Saugatuck. She and Ashley had become a long-distance item, and since he worked weekends she was the one who normally made the drive to keep their romance alive. Peggy brought along a section from Sunday's *Detroit Free Press* to show Lucy on the way. There was a photo of Michael dancing with Shannon and a caption that read

> *Most handsome pair at the Spring Fling gala, a fundraising benefit for the Kathleen Mullin Foundation for Leukemia Research, was the hunky Irish president of its governing board, Michael Donegan, accompanied by his long time love interest, corporate attorney and Irish lass Shannon O'Conner. Is the emerald and diamond ring worn on her hand a promise of soon-to-come wedding bells?*

She breathed deep, sighed, and silently prayed for his happiness.

Lucy came upon a roadside vegetable stand displaying beautiful red, ripe tomatoes, fresh golden yellow sweet corn, and a variety of other fruits and vegetables grown locally. Everything looked good to her. At the sight of such bounty her hunger flared, making her mindful of the empty feeling in her stomach. Before leaving San Francisco, she had stopped by a health food store and purchased a coconut and a large bag of the store's special trail mix: raw almonds, walnuts, philberts, dried fruits, and a variety of seeds such as sesame and chia. She judged these to be the most sensible things to take on her adventure since she had just gone through a ten-day fast and purification; she wanted only raw, natural food to sustain her. This assortment was easy for her to carry as she was not sure what accommodations she would find. She planned on doing a lot of roadside camping. The fresh bounty she now looked over seemed a welcome change.

For the afternoon's fare she decided on a wonderfully formed, brilliantly colored, mouth watering tomato—to be consumed immediately—and two large ears of sweet corn—to be carried with her and eaten raw as she walked. After making her purchase, she sat down on a large boulder shaded by a massive redwood growing by its side. She wiped the tomato carefully on her shirt. She licked a small spot on which she sprinkled a pinch of sea salt that she carried in an envelope in her pack. She held the luscious fruit up to the sun and offered praise for it to the Creator and Mother Earth. Sinking her teeth into the large red orb, Lucy felt its juices spray over her taste buds. "This is the best tomato I've ever eaten," she thought.

She sat feeling the warm breeze on her skin while looking over the landscape. She finally felt at peace. She was totally in the moment, not allowing the past—with its heartaches—bother her. She noticed a chipmunk nibbling at an ear of corn on the ground, trying to coerce it to a more secluded spot but having difficulty doing so because the ear was bigger than he was.

When she looked back to the vegetable stand, she saw a beautiful girl with long, reddish-blond hair that hung in ringlets past her waist. The girl was bartering with the vendor. She presented him with a large box of freshly gathered salmon berries and in exchange picked out a melon and a tomato. When the girl took the tomato in her hand, she looked suddenly at Lucy, beamed a big smile, blinked, and nodded. Lucy smiled and nodded back, calling out, "These tomatoes are wonderful." She held up her own red, bitten ball as testimony.

The girl laughed a strange sort of laugh, like a little child's, and said, "Oh, and so they are." She wore a long, full length, earth tone skirt with a matching tunic over the top. It was tied at the waist with a belt made out of what Lucy thought to be braided meadow grass. She put her barter into a leather bag slung across her body and walked toward Lucy. "I'm Shalala," she said, more singing it than speaking it.

Lucy jumped up and held out her hand for a shake. "I'm Lucy," she said, "I'm glad to meet you."

"Lucy," the girl repeated in a singsong way. She reached out her hand, but instead of shaking Lucy's she stroked the back of it three times. Lucy tingled as she touched her. They struck up a conversation about the tomatoes and before long were chatting about auras and earth harmonics. Lucy felt immediately drawn to this girl, and when she received an invitation to go home with her for a rest from the journey, she accepted gladly. She tucked the ears of corn she had purchased into her backpack and nodded to her new friend that she was ready to go.

"Okay then, follow me," Shalala said. They left the main road around a curve just a short distance from the veggie stand yet out of view from anyone who may have stopped there. Lucy could not make out a path in the forest floor and puzzled over it.

Shalala sang a beautiful melody as she walked. She looked back once in a while to smile at Lucy and see how she was doing as the walk became a climb. Shalala paused at the top of a rise and perched on a big boulder while she waited for Lucy to catch up. Lucy was amazed to see how the sunlight danced off this girl, how golden she looked sitting there in the sunlight. When Lucy made the top, a beautiful view awaited her: the ocean. You could hear the sound of its waves roaring to the shore, carried on the wind up this side of the mountain. As she beheld it, she let out a breathless "Oh my." This made Shalala laugh. She threw back her head and let out a sound somewhere between the whinnying of a young colt and the tinkling of bells.

The sight and the sound brought immediate joy to Lucy's heart, something she had not felt in a while. "Would you like to rest here for a spell?" Shalala asked. Then she added, "It's really not far now."

"No, I'm fine. We can go or stay; you're the hostess."

Shalala laughed again. "Okay," she said. "Here we go. Keep up now." She took off on a dead run like a child who just tagged Lucy "it" in a game of hide and seek.

"Hey," Lucy yelled, "come back here."

"Catch me, catch me, catch me," Shalala called as she disappeared into the dark forest.

Lucy took off running at full stride, laughing as she ran. She felt young and light again. *This girl is quick*, Lucy thought as she glimpsed Shalala's back in the distance. She could see Shalala up ahead dodging here and there in between big Sequoia trees, Red Pines, Oaks, and boulders. Lucy splashed across a small stream as she tried to keep pace. The water was cold and her shoes were soaked. "Hey, slow down," she yelled. As the other girl's lead increased, Lucy began to get winded and slowed down. She hadn't caught a glimpse of Shalala in a few minutes but knew she was running in the direction where she last spotted her. Soon she came to a stop and tried to catch her breath. She hadn't run like this for years. When her breath came back, she called, "Shalala." She was surprised when "Shalala" came back at her in an echo. *We must have run into a canyon*, Lucy thought.

She heard the girl's faint laugh on the breeze but couldn't tell where it was coming from. It did not fill her with joy this time; it frightened her. It sounded light a naughty child's laugh.

"Hey, come on," Lucy shouted.

"On," the forest replied.

"Where are you?" Lucy pleaded.

"Are you," the trees echoed.

Lucy turned in a circle but didn't remember from which direction she had entered. "Shalala, don't lose me," she called.

"Lose me," the canyon mocked.

Then came a distant hushed reply: "You can only lose yourself. Come on. Come on, Lucy, you can find me. You must look. Look now. Look now!"

Off in the distance Lucy saw a twinkle in the trees. She started running again but soon found it was getting darker and the forest was getting thicker, with big trees crowding each other for the earth below. Lucy began to feel despair. She hadn't seen her friend in quite some time. *If that's what she is*, Lucy thought. She knew when the sun went down it would get plenty cold there, and she became frightened. *Are there bears here, or other predators, mountain lions maybe?* She no sooner had that thought than she heard a blood curdling big cat cry. She couldn't tell which direction it came from. She was surprised that this cry did not have an echo. "Shalala, if you're playing with me, I am not having fun," she said in a loud angry voice.

"Fun" returned faintly, and then an even more fainter "Why not?"

How could I be so stupid to follow a complete stranger into the woods? Again she saw a flicker. This time, as Lucy ran toward it, she realized there were more and more flickers all around her. *Fireflies*, she thought. She always loved seeing fireflies, but realizing these flickers were not a signal from her friend, she began to despair all over again. She sat down on a nearby log to think. She really didn't know what direction she should go in, and since the dark was closing fast, she needed to plan what to do for the night and the coming cold. If her friend was planning on abandoning her here, she needed to prepare, and soon.

She took stock. She had a sleeping bag and some matches, some water, the corn, and the trail mix. *Okay, I have the necessities to survive for a while, if I don't become dinner for a forest creature. I need to find a sheltered area and build a fire.* She got up and walked on, picking up dry sticks as she went. *I never pictured myself being lost all alone in the Oregon woods. I wouldn't be frightened if Lance were here, or Michael.* The old knot squeezed her brain. But the big cat's cry made her forget about it, and she concentrated on her survival.

A chill ran down her spine and she dropped the pile of sticks. She peered around and made out some big stones not far from her. She thought maybe she could camp among them. She picked up the sticks and walked toward the stones. She saw they were all about three to four feet high, some wider at the base than others. But what was odd was that they seemed to come out of the ground in a perfect circle. She walked to the middle of it and found that some other poor soul had built a fire there some time ago, the remains of it lay charred and black before her. A small pile of sticks stacked Indian fashion had been left in its center. This was something she had seen Lance do for the next visitor in the night when he left a campsite. This was even the way he had taught her to stack the wood. She dropped her load of sticks and knelt beside them, hunting through her pack for the matches. She put some small dried twigs mixed with a few dried leaves under the stack in the center of the blackened circle and lit a match. It went out immediately.

"Oh shoot!" she said aloud.

"Oot!" the forest replied.

She struck another match and sheltered it with her hand this time. She put it under a crisp, brown leaf until it started to smoke and then flame. She put another leaf on that and some dried moss and soon the flame was strong and licking at the pile of sticks. When the fire looked strong enough, she left it and walked the circumference of the circle, picking up a few logs and more sticks until she thought she had enough to last her through the night. She went back to the fire, added a few larger logs, piled the rest nearby, and spread out her sleeping bag. She sat down on it and removed her soggy shoes, propping them up on sticks near the fire to dry. She did the same with her socks then put on a spare pair. She decided to sleep with her sandals on just in case she had to get up and run or fight. She sat with her feet toward the fire as they were the coldest part of her body. She layered on an additional sweatshirt and a flannel shirt, preparing for the night when sleep might take her away from tending the fire. She took out the piece of sweet corn, peeled away the husk, gave thanks for it, and bit into its sweet kernels. This ear tasted especially good, perhaps because she had worked up such an appetite.

She felt better now that she was warm and her tummy had something in it. She started thinking about Shalala: *What kind of person would lead someone into a forest and lose them?* She got up and selected one of the longer logs to use as a club if she needed it. She laid it near her sleeping bag and sat back down. She was watching the flickers of fire dance above the flames when she heard something approaching on the other side of the stone circle. She reached for the club and moved it to her lap. Her heart was beating faster and she could taste the fear in her mouth. Beyond the flames to the other side of the circle something leaped over the stones. There before her stood a large mountain lion. It stayed its ground eyeing her, their gazes locked in the glow of the flaming logs. She sat frozen, holding her breath and clinching the log, her only weapon for defense. The big cat started to crouch, and Lucy feared it was getting ready to spring. But instead of lunging, it lay down then turned its head to watch as something else entered the circle. It was Shalala.

"There you are, Lucy. I told you you can find me. And so you have. Looks like you're doing very well."

Lucy rose slowly, still looking at the big cat. She managed to say in a very squeaky voice just above a whisper, "Shalala, where have you been?"

"When I saw you enter the circle, I walked down to the stream where I keep my melons cold. I brought you some." She held out a slice of honeydew like it was a peace offering.

"I was scared to death," Lucy said.

Shalala laughed her child's laugh again and said, "Not to death, silly. I did sense your fear. But death was not there. You have handled the fear very well. You did not let it make you do something foolish. What do you think of Arro?" She reached out and stroked the head of the magnificent cat.

Lucy, her fear gone, beheld the majesty of the magnificent animal. "He's beautiful," she said.

"He really is, Lucy." Shalala laughed again and buried her face in his neck.

"Is he your pet?" Lucy asked.

Shalala laughed again. "Friend, like you," she said. "I found him here wounded by a hunter's arrow. He was afraid of me at first, and me of him. But we share a good friendship now. We depend on each other. Can we depend on you, Lucy?"

"Depend on me for what?" Lucy asked.

"To trust us, of course. Isn't that what friendship is based on?"

"You can trust me not to lose you in a forest" was Lucy's sarcastic reply.

"Well, I think you've already done that once, have you not?" Shalala laughed.

"Yeah, right," Lucy said. She saw the girl's eyes twinkle like the flickering of the fire and she laughed too. Joy had found its way back into her heart. They sat by the fire, ate the melon, and watched as the stars blanketed the night sky. Shalala asked Lucy why she had come on this journey, and Lucy told her the details of the past. Every once in a while Shalala would laugh out loud when Lucy used words like *heartache* and *pain*. "Why are you laughing?" Lucy finally asked.

"Your heart did not break, silly. You conjured pain to blame someone else for your disappointment that they hadn't followed your own plan for them."

"What?" Lucy said indignantly. "What do you know of my life or my pain?"

Again Shalala laughed. "Okay, okay, have pain if you want it so bad. This is exactly why I don't live among you humans. You all want to hurt or be hurt instead of just being happy to be."

"You humans?" Lucy asked in surprise. Then jokingly added, "What are you, some sort of alien?"

"No more than you," came Shalala's reply.

"You are an odd one, my friend," Lucy said.

"Oh, yes I am, and very pleased to be so," Shalala laughed.

"Hey, you said you were taking me to your place. Where do you live?"

"Right there," Shalala said, pointing to the top of a tall tree nearby.

"What? No way!" Lucy exclaimed.

"Way!" The forest called back.

Lucy peered up into the branches of the tall tree and saw what appeared to be a small house silhouetted against the star-ladened sky. "Do you want to sleep here with Arro or come up in the branches with me?" Shalala asked.

"Well, no offense to Arro, but I would like to see your place, if you don't mind?"

"Okay then, climb the rope and make yourself comfortable. I'll be up sooner or later. I have some errands to run."

Lucy was surprised to see a long rope with large knots spaced about two feet apart. She hadn't noticed it before. When she looked back toward Shalala, she was gone. The mighty Arro lay just a few feet from her. He opened his mouth in a wide yawn and Lucy saw his enormous fangs, but she was not afraid of him now. He settled his head on his paws and looked into the darkness. She gathered her sleeping bag and pack, kicked dirt on the fire, and started the climb up to the top of the tree. The rope was easier to climb than she thought it would be. It went right into a round hole in the bottom of the little dwelling. Once inside, Lucy was surprised at how warm it was. Lanterns were lit and hung here and there on each side of the little house. There was a small table on one side of the hole, and on the other was a pile of blankets and fur pelts. Lucy took off her pack, pulled from it the dreamcatcher Littlefeather made for her, and lay back on the pelts. She fell immediately into a deep sleep.

She awoke a couple of times somewhere in the night, each time to beautiful singing. She couldn't make out the words, but the melodies were peaceful and soothing. She soon fell back to sleep and had another wonderful dream. She dreamed about being little and playing with her sister in the woods behind her father's farm. She dreamed about picking blackberries with her grandmother. And she dreamed about being with Lance, about riding with him on Takota, and about swimming naked with him in a lake under a beautiful waterfall in a land where the colors were vibrant and alive.

When she awoke in the morning, she had a smile on her face. Shalala was sitting on a stool near the table watching her. On the table sat a bowl of wild berries, a plate of nuts, and a pitcher of clear, cold water. Lucy stood up, stretched, and said, "Good morning, my friend. I slept better than I have in years. And I had such wonderful dreams."

At this Shalala threw her head back and laughed delightedly. "Come see what the forest has given us for breakfast today." She took a plate and cup off the shelf above the table and set them down in front of Lucy. Lucy noticed that there were many sizes of plates and cups on the shelf. Some were very small. She pointed at them and asked, "Just who are these for?"

Shalala laughed as usual and said, "Lucy, do you think you are my only friend? I have lived in this forest for a very long time. I have many different visitors. They sleep safely here and have good dreams, and they leave me gifts when they continue on their journeys. They all promise to return; some do some don't. That is not for Shalala to decide. See, here are some of my gifts." She opened up an ornately hand-carved wooden box. It contained a wonderful collection of beautiful things. There was a brilliant red feather, a blue gemstone, a pearl button, a cat's eye marble, a very tiny gold bell, a smooth white stone, and a shiny, silver whistle. There were all sorts of odd but beautiful items. As Lucy moved her fingers through them, her heart nearly stopped. She couldn't believe her eyes. There among the treasures in the little chest was a ring. Lucy knew this ring. It was Lance's, the one he had told her would be his son's one day. She picked it up, but as soon as she did Shalala snatched it from her hand.

"Please," Lucy begged, "let me see it."

"You saw it," Shalala said.

"But where did you get it?" Lucy asked.

"You know," Shalala said.

"But how? When?"

"He comes here to rest, to have good dreams. He gave it to me when last he was here."

"No, he wouldn't have. That ring is for his son."

"Shalala has it now." Lucy felt an odd feeling come upon her that she didn't like. Shalala jumped to her feet and drew a knife. Lucy leaped up and faced her. "Lucy, you have to leave now."

"No, not until you tell me why Lance gave you that ring."

"Lucy, you're sick. Look at your hands; they're turning green." Lucy looked at her hands and felt ashamed. She dove for the hole in the floor and slid down the rope until she landed hard on the ground below. Arro stood up and growled, loud and fierce. Lucy felt sick and heavy.

"Oh God! What have I done?" she cried out loud. Shalala came down the rope with almost no effort and alighted softly on the ground beside her.

"Lucy, I know what it is you must do: cut your flesh to let the poison drain, go to the stream and stand under the falls to let the water cleanse you."

"What? You *are* crazy," Lucy cried. "This is a dream, a bad dream." As she said that, Shalala began to age before her eyes.

"Please, Lucy, you must do this now, for the both of us. You must go. Leave the circle, go to the stream, cut yourself, and stand naked in the waterfall. Hurry, before it's too late. Poison has reached your heart, and it is killing me." She fell on the ground. "Lucy, go. You must go now; trust us."

Lucy watched as this strange creature withered on the ground beside her. She started to drag herself across the circle, but she waited too long. She wouldn't make it. Her head sunk and she started to lose consciousness. Arro sprang forward and bit into her. His teeth pierced her skin and cold, green blood ran out. He dragged her like an old Raggedy Ann doll to the river and jumped in. He paddled upstream, carrying her in his mouth until he reached the waterfall. The icy water revived her and she tore at her clothes. Naked in the cold mountain stream, she stood beneath the fall, screaming from the depths of her soul, "Oh God! Forgive me!"

She stayed there until the blood streaming from her side turned red and her skin was once again the color of her flesh before the poison of jealously had tainted it. She fell back into the water and let it carry her to the bank, where she crawled out and collapsed.

She awoke that evening dressed in her old clothes and wrapped in her sleeping bag. She was again in the stone circle and next to her the fire was blazing high. But there was sadness in the woods. A song of mourning was being sung by the breeze. She saw Shalala sitting over the body of the magnificent cat. "Shalala," Lucy cried. "Arro?"

"Arro gave himself to save us," Shalala said. "He now sleeps in the valley of his ancestors and has found his way to the den of his mate who hunters took three summers ago. He will be happy there. He has left for me his pelt. He has given you his tooth." She handed Lucy a long, white fang. Lucy clutched it in her hand and put it to her heart.

"Shalala, are you okay?"

"We are both okay," Shalala said. "Thanks to our friend." Lucy's sadness spilled from her eyes as the forest lamented.

"Lance loves us, Lucy. He comes here to be safe and to dream, dream of you, just as you came here to dream of him. We can only own the moments we are with him. We must not sicken ourselves with selfish desires. He is son of the mist. He is here for a greater purpose than belonging just to us. Our love makes him who he is. Your purpose in his life was set before these boulders were born. You are right, Lucy. That ring will one day belong to Lance's son. It will identify him as the true king returning to claim the throne in a time when all hope has been lost. But that time is not now, and Lucy, you could not keep it safe. That is why Lance gave it to me. I keep it among all the charms of goodwill that have been given me in love and friendship. Evil cannot find its way into that box, Lucy."

"I understand now. I am only sorry that Arro had to die because of my selfishness." Her grief fell splashing on the ground.

"Arro did not die because of your selfishness. He chose to love us and to become what he was created to be. You were always part of his destiny, just as you are part of Lance's and he of yours."

Shalala changed now right before her eyes. Lucy saw beautiful wings of gossamer shining from her back. Her earth tone clothes were gone and her body was a prism of soft light contained in clear skin. Her hair became golden ringlets and her voice soft and soothing.

"Shalala, I want you to have this." From around her neck Lucy took the medallion that Lance had given her. Shalala laughed with childlike delight as she took the gift from Lucy's hand. She flitted up into the night sky and disappeared among the starlight.

In the morning, Lucy rolled up her sleeping bag, packed up her backpack, and stacked firewood in the way Lance taught her on the darkened circle of all the fires from the past. There was no sign of Arro's body or of Shalala. The tree, with its secret house high in its limbs, was gone. As she leaned against one of the large boulders in the circle, wondering which way she should go, she kicked a small rock at her foot. It rolled over and she saw something under it. A small piece of paper folded in half was lying in the dirt. She bent down and picked it up, but she knew in her heart before she opened it what she would find. Written in Lance's hand was her name.

She put the paper in her pocket and clutched Arro's fang in her hand. She closed her eyes for a moment and envisioned once again the magnificent animal. She felt the sun on her face and a cool breeze on her skin. When she opened her eyes, she was sitting on the stone by the roadside stand. Nearby a chipmunk struggled to carry an ear of corn to a more secluded spot. She reached to touch the medallion Lance had given her, but it was gone. She tucked the smooth white object she clutched in her hand into her pants pocket next to a piece of paper. The breeze picked up and carried to her ears the sound of childlike laughter off in the distance. She picked up her pack and walked off down the highway.

29 – Serendipity

"Hello, Myra, it's Lucy"

"Hello, dear, where are you?"

"I'm at my apartment. I just got back last night. How's my Freea doing?"

"She's fine. She misses you. I may have spoiled her a bit. She follows me out to the hill every morning and waits while I do yoga. The minute I'm done, she starts meowing until I go in and warm her a plate of milk."

"Thanks for taking such good care of her."

"She's been good company. When Michael was here last weekend, every time he'd sit down she'd jump in his lap and demand a good petting."

Lucy was pleased to hear that Michael had just been there because she knew he didn't go there often anymore, and since he'd just been to Glen Eden it wasn't likely he'd be going back anytime soon. "Would it be all right if I come get her this weekend?"

"Sure it would, but only if you promise you can stay a couple of days. We have so much catching up to do."

"I will, Myra, but please don't tell Michael I'm coming."

"Heavens, no! I do have some big news to share with you as far as he is concerned, but I won't do it on the phone." Lucy thought she already knew what this big news was, remembering the emerald and diamond ring pictured on Shannon's hand in the news article Peggy had shown her.

"I'll bring the bus down tomorrow. Ashley said he'd pick me up at the station. He asked if I'd have dinner with him, so I'll be over after that, before dark for sure."

"I'm looking forward to your visit, dear. It's been lonely since Rose left and Nick went away."

"Nick went away? Where did he go?"

"Michael found him work in Brittany. He's carving stone animals for a forest walk in Brocéliande. He'll make quite a bit of money."

"Wow, France! That's great for him."

"Oh yes, he was very excited. He asked if I'd go with him, but I couldn't. I have a lot to do here before Michael's big… I have a lot to do here. Oh Lucy, we need to talk."

"Sure, Myra. See you tomorrow night."

Michael pulled into Glen Eden a little after sunset. The sky over the lake was still tinted with an orangey hue. He ran around to the passenger's side and opened the door. "Thank you, darling," Shannon said, taking his hand for a help out. As soon as her feet hit the ground, she stretched her arms over her head and then bent this way and that, de-kinking her back from the near four-hour drive. "I don't see how you can make that drive as often as you do. It's positively grueling."

"Come on, love, be a trooper. The drive's not that bad. I do it for Myra. She seemed a little down to me when I was here last weekend, so I thought I'd surprise her with a visit from you."

"The drive may not be bad for you, but I think my backside has fallen asleep."

"Really? Well, let me see what I can do to wake it up. I bet a good spank will get the blood flowing."

"Michael, don't you dare," she said, backing away from him then breaking into a run for the porch. She made the first step, but on the second her foot slipped and down she went. "Ohh," she moaned, grabbing her ankle and rocking back and forth.

"Let me see that," Michael said, coming to her side. She let him take hold of her foot and turn it slowly from side to side.

"Ouch!" she complained.

"Here, grab hold of my neck. I'll carry you in and get an ice bag for your ankle."

"You just love playing the part of the big, strong hero, don't you?"

"It's big, strong, handsome hero, thank you," he chuckled as he hoisted her up in his arms.

He turned the knob with his hand and then pushed the door hard with his foot. As the door swung open, it framed the figure of a woman standing midway down the hall.

"Lucy!" he said aloud. He let Shannon fall from his arms and land on her good foot.

"Michael!" she said, with as much surprise in her voice as he had in his.

"Oh, so you're back," Shannon injected into the silence that followed and menaced the room.

"Hello, Shannon. Yes, I got back last evening and brought the bus down today to collect Freea. Myra has been caring for her while I was away."

"Yeah, yeah, your cat. Well, what a surprise. Isn't it, Michael?"

"Unh, yeah. I didn't know. I mean, Myra didn't tell me. Because Myra didn't know I was coming, so she didn't have a chance to tell me." Again the awkward silence fell heavy in the room.

Lucy's eyes fell on the glimmering ring displayed on Shannon's left hand, and her mind once again recalled the article Peggy had shown her. It suddenly hit her like a dart to the heart: Michael was engaged to Shannon. Even though her mind knew of this possibility, it hadn't really affected her until now. Maybe it was seeing the two of them together. "Shannon of all people," she thought. She knew they had been friends since their college days, but Lucy would never have guessed there could be anything beyond that. She liked Shannon well enough but found her to be somewhat cold and off-putting, not at all like the warm and caring person she had come to know Michael as.

"Oh, what a surprise! Michael, you've come. And you have brought Shannon!" Myra exclaimed, rushing in from the parlor. Michael's eyes stayed fixed on Lucy.

"Hello, Myra," Shannon said while hopping on one foot. She grabbed Michael's arm to steady herself. "He should have called you to let you know we were coming. He's all into surprises."

"That's because he knows how much I like them. Don't you, dear? She stretched on tiptoe to kiss his cheek, and seeing how fixed his gaze was on Lucy, gave his other cheek a good pinch with a little slap to break the spell. He looked slowly away from Lucy and scooped Shannon up again. "Good grief, what has happened to you?" Myra asked.

"I tripped on the step trying to avoid a spanking from our big, strong, 'handsome' hero here."

"Actually, Myra, I think she may have tripped on her tongue," Michael said. "You know how she loves to wag it." Shannon punched him playfully in the shoulder. He carried her to the parlor and set her down on the couch, grabbing a pillow to put under her injured foot. "Myra, would you kindly bring an ice bag for her?"

"Certainly, dear. And I'll put on the kettle."

Lucy found her voice: "Let me help, Myra."

Myra took Lucy's arm and turned her toward the kitchen. She whispered softly, "Are you all right, dear? You're shaking. Come along." Once in the kitchen, Myra declared, "I know it was a shock for you to see Michael again. And judging from the way he was stammering, he was put back as well. I swear, Lucy, I didn't have any idea he would be out this weekend. It's serendipitous, don't you think?"

Lucy took a deep breath, trying to center herself. "Myra, I think it would be best if I leave as soon as possible. I'll call Ashley. Maybe he'll drive me back."

"Oh for heaven's sake, Lucy, you can't leave until you tell us what you have been up to these past six months. I want to hear all about your adventures. You have been promising to tell me, and I'm sure Michael will be interested as well. So no more talk of leaving until we have had a chance to chat. Promise?" Lucy put on a smile and nodded her head. "You're among people who care for you very much, dear. You do know that, don't you?"

Lucy put her head down and a tear escaped from her eye. Myra put her arm around Lucy's shoulder and squeezed her tightly. As she kissed her head she whispered, "It's going to be all right, Lucy. God has written our destiny. Trust in Him." In a louder voice she directed, "Now get some tea brewing while I run this ice bag to Shannon."

"Sure, Myra." Lucy felt as if she were home in this kitchen. She filled the big kettle with fresh water and set it atop a lit burner. Then she went about setting teacups on saucers and placing them on a large serving tray. She poured some milk into a small pitcher and set it, along with the sugar bowl, on the tray as well, remembering from last summer what Shannon liked in her cup. The kettle whistled and she moved to it to drop in the tea ball. As she replaced the lid, she felt a presence in the room. She knew immediately it was Michael. He had come to stand just behind her. She held her breath and slowly turned around.

He smiled and nodded. "Lucy," he said softly. "It's good to see you."

"It's good to see you too, Michael." She lied. It was awful. Her knees felt weak and her breath came hard. The old attraction she felt for him was stronger than ever.

He moved closer and she nervously backed against the stove. "Myra said she talked you into staying this weekend. I'm glad. If you like, you can ride back to the city with Shannon and me on Sunday."

"Thank you, but I have a ride with Peg. She's coming down tomorrow to see Ashley." Her body was like a magnet to him. He moved closer, and as he did she pressed herself into the stove. "I… ah… I heard about you and Shannon," she stammered. "I mean, I read about it… you… at the Spring Fling. You're engaged. Congratulations."

"Oh, you did now." His eyes were fixed on her lips.

"Yes, I did. I… think it's great. I'm happy for the both of you."

He took a step back and sighed, pulling his eyes from her. He folded his arms across his chest, leaned against the counter, and recited into the kitchen space what he had been telling himself: "I care deeply for her. We have been friends for a long time. I lost my true soulmate, my dear Kathleen." He hesitated, not saying aloud that he had also accepted the fact the woman he now truly loved would never be his. "I'm not getting any younger, and I want children. I want a wife to come home to, not just an empty apartment and a string of women who can only satisfy a physical need. Someone to be there, to share things with, a confidant, someone to sit on the porch and gaze at the moon with." He looked in her eyes once again. "Understand?" She didn't answer, so he made his case with resolve. "Shannon is a good person. She wants pretty much the same things I do. So it makes sense."

"Sure." Lucy swallowed hard to get her heart out of her throat. She turned her back to him and said, trying her best to sound aloof, "I should get the tea carried in."

"Here, let me take that." He stepped up to her taking hold of the tray, and as he did he kissed the top of her head. "It's really good seeing you again." He lied. It was awful. He felt like his mind had been blown apart. He thought he had his life back on a viable course, but the minute he saw her again he began to doubt everything.

He carried the tray to the sitting room and placed it on the table between the two high back armchairs. Myra was seated in one and Lucy sat in the other.

Michael sat on the couch next to Shannon, who immediately cozied into him. "Well, here we all are," she said, raising her cup. "So, Lucy, are you going to let us in on your exploits? These two can't wait, I'm sure."

"Shannon, Lucy doesn't have to tell us anything if she doesn't want to," Michael said.

"Oh sure, protect poor Lucy from the big bad bully," Shannon pouted.

"Don't be a brat. It's not 'poor Lucy.' If the two of you ever square off, my money would be on her. I've been on the receiving end of some of her punches." Michael stroked Shannon's head while he looked into Lucy's eyes.

Lucy felt like she should say something, so she declared a little stiffly, "Shannon, I'd like to congratulate you on your engagement to Michael. I think it's great."

"Do you? How sweet. See, Michael, she thinks it's great that you've been awarded a consolation prize."

"Do you have to do this, Shannon?"

"No, love, I don't have to. I'm just having fun."

"Are you? Because I'm pretty sure you're the only one? What do you think, Myra? Are you having fun?"

"Oh my, yes!" Myra exclaimed. She said it with so much enthusiasm they all had to laugh.

"I've got an idea," Shannon said. "Why don't I let Lucy go ahead and mesmerize the two of you with her otherworldly tales while I go take a hot soak? What do you say, Michael, will you be my big, strong, *handsome* hero one last time and carry me up those stairs?"

"My pleasure, love." He stood and picked her up.

"I'll say good night then, and Lucy, believe it or not, I'm glad you're safe." Michael carried her off. You could hear them talking and laughing up the stairs.

"Shannon is a genuine soul. She says what she thinks and there's no holding her back," Myra said. "She makes Michael smile and maybe that's all one can hope for. What do you think, Lucy? I mean, really think?"

"I think smiling is a very good thing. I like to see him smile."

"He told me that same thing about you once." She took a sip of her tea, looking over the edge of the cup to see how Lucy received her comment. "So how is Ashley?"

"He's good. I'll let you in on a secret. He took me to dinner to show me the ring he's giving Peg. He's going to ask her to marry him."

"Oh, that's no secret. Winnie already told me. He was going to ask her two weeks ago but lost his nerve. She also told me that he bought that ring over eight years ago for someone else but never got the chance to ask her." Lucy was very surprised by this new revelation and wondered just who it could have been. "Maybe that's what life is all about. Settling, I mean."

"You didn't settle, Myra. You waited for William."

"Well, I'm not sure I waited really. I just was never able to find anyone I loved as much as I did William, so I guess you could say I didn't settle for a lesser love. But I used to dream about children. I settled for a life without them." She sipped her tea and reflected. "Well, I have Michael. He is like my own son and grandson," she chuckled. "I'd like to see him do more than settle. I'd like to see him achieve the desire of his heart."

"How's Megan?" Lucy thought a subject change was in order.

"Well, hold your hat for this one." Myra's eyes danced. "She is dating Charlie Nelson."

"What!? Are you kidding? The guy who tried to rape her and broke Michael's ribs?"

"The very same. She said he's sworn off the bottle and he's been going to Mass with her at St. Peter's. She's talked him into taking art classes. He can draw quite well. Takes after his father Peter on that, I guess." She took a sip of tea and started anew: "Michael was fit to be tied over the whole thing. He calmed down a bit when I reminded him of the grace *he's* received over the years. Why, it was only last fall I found him out back in the garden hollering at Angus. So drunk he was he passed out right in my Brown-eyed Susans. I couldn't get him up, so I left him lay right there and threw a cover over him. I was terribly worried for a spell. He was awfully depressed when you left, Lucy. Shannon pulled him through it, bless her heart. I'd certainly hate to see him go through that again." Again she looked hard at Lucy.

"I'm sorry for that too, Myra. I truly wish him to be happy. I'd do anything to see that happen."

"Well, that's good because maybe you'll have to." Lucy was prevented from asking her what she meant by that when Michael strolled back into the room cradling Freea in his arms. He gave her over to Lucy.

"Well, ladies, did I leave you alone long enough to catch up on all the local gossip?"

"There's my kitty. Where have you been?"

"She was up lying on my bed."

"Oh, I'm sorry."

"No, it's okay. She slept there with me last weekend. The only reason I had to move her now is because Shannon is sleeping there tonight and she doesn't see personality through fur."

"How's Shannon's ankle?"

"It's fine. There's a little swelling."

At that Myra jumped to her feet. "You two catch up. I'll go make her a poultice." She was out of the room before either one could come up with an excuse for her to stay. Freea jumped from Lucy's lap and followed her to the kitchen.

Michael broke the silence. "Lucy, I don't want it to be awkward between us. If I've said or done anything in the past to make you feel uncomfortable, I'm sorry. I have my life set on a course now, and I mean to follow it." He walked over to the couch and sat down on the edge of it, leaning toward her, his elbows resting on his knees. He looked in her eyes and smiled. "I'm dying to know where you got off to. I was worried. Peggy was at the point of calling the police to put out a missing persons on you."

"I know. She read me the riot act. I'm sorry I worried you. I did something really foolish and now I'll have to pay for it." She put her head down and he saw the sadness come upon her face.

"Hey, what is it? Please tell me. Maybe I can help."

"You're very kind, Michael, but you can't help, no one can. I really blew it this time. I went to find Lance on my own when he told me I should wait here. Something happened, and I may have ruined his chance of coming back"

"It was my fault you left, Lucy. I let my feelings for you scare you away. Angus told me that."

"You talked to Angus?"

"Hell, I don't know if I talked to him or if the Dewar's just gave me hallucinations. I was pretty messed up. Angus, real or imagined, told me I drove you away with my arrogant stupidity. He said you were tumbling through time and that Lance was trying to find you."

Lucy fell to her knees in front of him, taking hold of his hands. "My God, Michael, that's exactly what happened."

"What? Wait? Come here?" He helped her up and sat her next to him. "What are you saying?"

"I went to the Serpent Mound on the autumnal equinox. I thought there might be some type of vortex there that would open a door in time so I could find Lance. I was right; only when I stepped through it I had no control over where I would be. I kept tumbling through different times in my life, times in my past and times in what I suspect might be my future. I didn't think I'd ever be able to escape. I was being tossed from one episode to another. I was always me, the me I am now—with all my memories of my family, Lance, you, and Myra—only I'd be a little girl one minute and an old lady the next." The more she talked the more emotional she became. Tears tumbled from her eyes.

"You poor kid, come here." He put his arms around her.

"Only I blew it. I blew it. Lance was upset with me. He said I cost us our chance. I should have waited here like he said." She was sobbing with her whole body.

"Shhh, Shhh," he stroked her head. "We'll figure it out, I promise. You saw Lance, then?"

"He came for me. He found me somehow and made a way for me to come back. I was with my girlfriend Lynn. We had been at the fair. She told me she saw

Lance, only I couldn't remember him being in that event before. So I knew he must be looking for me." She caught her breath. "There was this big orange orb in the sky. I'd never seen anything like it before. I thought it must be a sign from him, so I ran toward it and there he was. I wanted to stay with him, but he said I couldn't and that since he had had to search for me, he'd lost his opportunity to return back here like he'd planned. Oh God, Michael, I blew it."

"Calm down, Lucy, please. We'll find a way." He paused. "I was sure I'd never see you again. After you left here, I had a detective agency looking for you. They traced you to the Serpent Mound but lost track of you there. I was certain you had found Lance and stayed with him. They kept the case open, and by chance an agent went back just after Christmas and showed the rangers your picture again. One of them remembered seeing you the night of the winter solstice. He said he escorted you to the front gate and that you got in a silver truck with a Native American girl."

"That was Littlefeather. Lance sent her and Paul to pick me up."

"Lucy, the detective agency said they've never been able to find a bit of evidence that any McKellen has ever lived in that area."

"I know, Michael. That's because they live in a parallel dimension. Oh God, I can't believe I'm telling you this. You must think I'm really mad." She put her hand to her face, realizing what a mess she was.

He stood up and went for the Kleenex box. She took one, wiped her eyes, and blew her nose. "I don't think you are any more mad than I am. Tell me about Paul and Littlefeather."

"They told me the only reason they could pick me up was because they were in Quicksilver. That's Lance's truck. It's not a truck really. It just looks like one. It's some sort of vehicle that can travel into different dimensions. That's why I was able to go to the farm the times I did because Paul always picked me up at the train station in Quicksilver. They said they hadn't known any of this until Lance told them about it that night. They were as shocked as I was. To them, *I'm* someone from a different dimension. Littlefeather handled it better than Paul. Her culture has always believed in Wind Walkers. They let me stay at the farm that night and drove me to the train station the next day.

"When I came back, I didn't know what to do. It was like Lance was fading from my mind. His picture was gone, I had no way of contacting Paul and Littlefeather again, and I couldn't even..." She put her head down and began sobbing. He rubbed her back, not knowing how to help her. "I couldn't even dream about him. I read the Bible and meditated. I fasted and prayed, and then I went on a journey. I thought if I went out to San Francisco and visited the places where we had been together and happy, I could somehow reconnect with him. I went to Lands End, Half Moon Bay, to the top of Mt. Tamalpais, places where we'd camped, talked, and made love. But they only made me realize how alone I am." She wiped her eyes and sniffed. "Then I remembered that Lance told me about a place once where the Guardians would go to rest, have peace, and dream of home and loved ones. I knew it was in the forest somewhere north of Portland, so I took a train from San Francisco. I started walking north up the coast highway, making camp at night near the ocean."

He sat listening intently as she told him how she had chanced upon Shalala at the produce stand and gotten lost in the woods. She told him of stumbling upon the stone circle and of coming face to face with Arro, about finding Lance in her dreams that night in the treehouse, and of finding his ring in Shalala's treasure box. She told how she'd turned green and made Shalala sick, of how Arro had bitten her and dragged her to the river. She told him of the mighty cat's death. Fumbling in her pocket, she produced Arro's fang. "He gave his life to save us," she said.

Michael took the tooth and clasped it in his hand. She indeed lived in a fantastic world. "You are the bravest woman I have ever met."

She looked down and dabbed her eyes. "I am the stupidest woman. I have lost everything because I wouldn't wait like I was told. I even cost that magnificent animal his life."

"Hey, stop that. Shalala told you it was his destiny. You dreamed of Lance, so that was a good sign. And you found his ring."

"I found this too." She reached in her pocket again and took out the folded piece of paper with her name on it. "It was under a rock in the stone circle. It's Lance's handwriting. I gave him notepaper for a Christmas present once, and he said he would use it to write my name and hide it in the places where he would camp and dream of me." She held the little scrap of paper in her hand like it was a precious jewel. With his hand, Michael closed hers around the keepsake.

"Lucy there is yet hope."

"I cannot see it. My folly has ruined the chance we had."

"Don't let go of hope, Lucy, not now. I have an idea. I'll ask Angus to take Lance a message from me. I conjured the little bugger one time, and I'll do it again."

"Michael, that may be dangerous. Lance told me he didn't altogether trust Angus."

"I don't trust him either. But if there is one thing I've learned about him, it's that he's vain. I'll use that weakness to trap him. You said Peg is coming down tomorrow, right?"

"Yes, she is, but…"

"Good. I need you to call her and ask a favor, and I need your friend Danny to help her. Let's go make some phone calls." He stood up and then helped her. He took her hand and led her to the study.

"Michael, where is your desk?"

"I've taken your suggestion. I'm having Peter Nelson's sketch of Kathleen and me engraved on it. I told Shannon what you said and she agreed with you."

"I'm glad, Michael." She thought better of Shannon now.

"Hello, Danny, it's Lucy. I didn't wake you, did I?"

"Hey, kiddo. No, I was studying. I was so blessed to receive that scholarship that I want to make the best of it. Where are you?"

"I'm at Glen Eden with Michael."

"Whoa girl, you're with Michael? That's a shocker. I thought you were through with that guy."

"Danny, please, just listen. We need you to do us a favor."

"*Us*, huh? Well, well, well, this is very interesting."

"Oh shut up, Danny. Just listen, will you? Michael said he'd pay you fifty bucks to meet my friend Peggy at his office in the morning to help her load the picture of Angus in her car. Will you do it?"

"Fifty beans? Sure, I'll do it. I'd have done it for nothing to keep from having to look at that little guy again. He gives me the creeps."

"Thanks, Danny. I'll have Peg call you to set a time."

Lucy hung up and gave Michael a thumbs-up. "Okay, good," he said. "Now get Peggy on the horn. I'll sleep better knowing the first stage of the plan is all set up."

Lucy tried several times to call Peggy, but each time the phone was busy. "Bet she's talking to Ashley."

"That's a sucker's bet you won't be getting me to take," he laughed.

They sat alone in the study waiting for Peggy's line to clear. Lucy sat staring at the phone and Michael sat staring at her. Myra came in and said she wrapped Shannon's ankle with a slippery-elm-root poultice and that Shannon asked for Michael to come up. He went up, leaving Lucy instructions to keep trying Peggy. If she was successful, she was to find out what time in the morning she would be meeting Danny at his office so he could clear the removal of the painting with building security. Lucy loved how he would take charge, make a plan, and set it in action. She felt hope returning.

"Say, beautiful, how's the ankle?" he asked, flopping down on the bed beside Shannon.

"Oh, it's just great. Myra covered it in some smelly slime, and now I have to lay here wishing I had a clothespin on my nose."

"You don't have to wish. I'll be happy to run down and find you one." He grabbed her nose and pinched it, and she swatted his hand away.

"So are you all caught up on Lucy's comings and goings, or are you going down to hold her hand some more?"

"Shannon, just what is it you're worried about?"

"Michael, I'm not an idiot. When you asked me to agree to this happy-ever-after plan of yours, I'm sure you thought Lucy was out of the picture for good."

"She is out of the picture, Shannon. Lucy is and has always been in love with Lance."

"Michael, Lucy is in love with the idea of Lance. She hasn't been with him in years, except for dreams and visions. If he were to come back tomorrow, she'd see how he doesn't stack up to the man she's been inventing in her mind all these years." She took his hand and squeezed. "She's in love with you too, Michael. The air is so charged between the two of you, everyone else around you gets zapped. She's almost ready to let go of the fantasy that keeps her sleeping alone. I can tell. I think if I shove this ring back in your face in front of her and let her think she's the reason I did it, it just might give her the excuse she needs to let go of her fantasy world."

"Or it just might send her running off again. I don't want that, Shannon. I want to help her. Please understand that, darling. Come back out of *your* fantasy world. I need you to keep me tethered to this earth." He kissed her hand and went back downstairs to see how his plan was progressing.

Lucy sat by the fire chatting with Myra. Freea was curled on her lap. "Well?" he asked. He knew if his plan worked, she would have Lance back and he would lose all hope of having her forever. Yet the only thing that mattered to him now was her happiness.

"I'm happy to report the kidnapping of Angus has been successfully arranged." She smiled widely at him. He had thrown a buoy of hope into her ocean of despair.

His reward was her smile.

30 – Resolutions

Peggy arrived at Glen Eden just shy of noon. She was greeted by two anxious conspirators. Michael promptly retrieved the covered painting of Angus from the back seat of her car and carried it straightway to the study.

Lucy led Peg through the house to the patio out back where Myra was sitting with Shannon while she puffed on only her second cigarette of the day. She had promised Michael she'd stop smoking by their wedding day, which was probably why a date had not yet been set. Sometime in September was all she would say when asked. Michael was leaving it all up to her.

Myra greeted Peggy warmly and introduced Shannon to her as Michael's fiancée. Peggy's eyes widened when she heard this piece of news, and she wondered why Lucy hadn't told her of it. The two exchanged pleasantries and before long were engaged in conversation about wedding customs, fashions, and planning. Lucy envied Peggy's ability to talk with people; she always had something interesting to say.

Myra disappeared and returned with a pitcher of iced tea and several tall glasses. Michael followed her carrying a bowl of lemon wedges and a sugar shaker. "Well, well, the cock has come to join the hen party," Shannon said playfully.

Michael replied with theatrics: "Cock a doodle doo." This made all the women giggle. He pulled up a chair next to Shannon.

"Darling, Peggy has the most creative ideas about floral arrangements and wedding staging," Shannon said, laying her hand on Michael's. He groaned and winced.

"Look, Shannon, you have my financial backing; just give me the date and I'll show up with bells on, if that's what you want me to wear. Other than that, it's your show, darlin'. I'd rather not be involved with the details." He could see by the looks on the faces of the hens that the rooster had made a misstep, so he added, "You have such wonderful tastes. I'm sure whatever you decide will be fantastic." He saw approving smiles on the flock and decided to quit while ahead.

"Shannon, I'd be interested to know just how Michael proposed to you," Peg said. "I bet it was terribly romantic."

Shannon burst out laughing. "Should I tell them, darling?"

"Since when do you need my permission to flap your jaw?" Michael said lightheartedly.

"Okay then, Mr. Romantic, your myth is about to be tarnished."

"What, you didn't think my proposal was romantic?"

"Well, there were no violins playing or rose petals strewn about, but I guess if paper cuts are romantic then so was his proposal."

"Do you want me to take it back and do it again? Write me a script this time; it's the only way I could get it right." He flicked her nose and she kissed him.

"No, darling, it was perfect the first time. I was just having fun. Besides, if you take it back you may not ask me again." He just smiled. "Let's let Peggy be the judge of how romantic it was. I'll even give Lucy a vote." Michael looked at Lucy and winked. "You see, girls, Michael and I have worked together since school. William hired me right after graduation to be Michael's assistant. We've spent many hours in and out of the office together through tough personal times and grand times of celebration, like landing big contracts for the company. He has always complained that I nag him too much, and he started referring to me as his 'office wife.' I would from time to time accompany him to some business or social function, or serve as his last-minute date when an occasion popped up that he didn't have one for. When we went to the Spring Fling in April, he gave me this ring to wear. He said it was his mother's, which he would someday give to the woman he intended to marry. I assumed he meant Lu… someone else.

"I had for some time been thinking about moving to the West coast. I don't care for the weather here in Michigan, especially the winters. I felt it was time to move on. A dear friend of ours told me of a position opening up in a law firm in L.A., so I applied. When I heard back that they were interested in me, I told Michael that I may be moving out there. He took me totally off guard by saying I couldn't leave because I was wearing his ring. I said, 'I don't understand,' and he said, 'Don't you remember? I told you it was my mum's ring, and I would give it to the woman I intended to marry.' I asked him if that was his way of proposing marriage to me, and he said he didn't want to lose me.

"So there you have it. Pathetic or Romantic? You be the judge."

Michael took her hand and kissed it. "I don't want to lose you."

"I think it was sweet," Peggy said. "Don't you, Lucy?"

"Very sweet."

"Peggy, will you be staying for lunch?" Myra asked. "Lucy and I made chicken vegetable pies this morning."

"Sounds delish, but I'm taking Winnie and Skipper to Bill Knapp's in Holland for lunch today, so I really should get rolling."

"How is Skipper doing?" Michael asked.

"She's taking it a day at a time. But she looks great. She has a new man in her life. Get this: he's a Mormon missionary."

"That's good," Lucy said. "Mormons don't believe in drinking or smoking, so she should be pretty safe seeing him."

"Better hide from those evil smokers," Shannon snapped, taking out and lighting cigarette number three.

Michael spoke up, "Lucy didn't mean anything by that, Shannon. It's just easier to be around people who don't tempt you when you're trying to quit a nasty habit."

"There you go, defending her again. Lucy, don't you get sick of Michael jumping in front of the sword for you all the time."

Everyone looked at Lucy. She reflected for a moment and then said, "I guess I didn't realize that's what he was doing. Why would he have to jump in front of your sword, Shannon? Are you trying to hurt me?"

Now all glances turned to Shannon. She applauded. "Bravo, Lucy. You've jumped in the game and scored a point. I knew you could do it. See, Michael, she can take care of herself. Actually, it was I who felt attacked. Wrongfully, I guess. Quitting these damn things isn't easy?" She crushed the cigarette she just lit and threw it down in the ashtray. "It makes you sort of bitchy even under the best of circumstances."

Peggy stood and said her goodbyes and Lucy walked her to her car. "Well, kid, I guess Michael Donegan is officially off your options list. This Lance guy must really be something. I hope for your sake he decides to come back someday, or you'll be kicking yourself in the backside for letting Michael get away."

"Please don't start."

"I'm just saying, everyone can see the spark he still carries for you. I don't blame Shannon for not wanting to have it in her face."

"Peg, look, I came down this weekend to pick up Freea. I didn't even know they were going to be here. Do you think I like causing contention between them?"

"Maybe you do."

"Oh, stop."

"Well, it's got to be hard for Shannon having you here. If Ashley ever took to looking at anyone the way Michael looks at you, I'm not sure how I'd handle it, and we aren't even engaged." *Not yet,* Lucy thought. "If you ask me, I think Shannon is showing a lot of class."

"If Shannon is anything, it's classy."

"Meow," Peg said, sliding behind the wheel and turning on the engine. Lucy watched her to the end of the drive and was about to go inside when another car appeared. She didn't recognize it or the man in a hat with sunglasses who was driving. He stopped the engine, stepped out of the car, and pulled off his glasses.

"Freddie!" Lucy exclaimed, running up to him. They embraced. "Michael didn't tell me you were coming."

"Michael didn't know. Myra called me last night and said I'd better get down here. So I got on a red eye to Chicago and drove from there. What's going on?"

"Myra called you?"

"She said it was urgent and that I should come immediately but wouldn't explain why. Are you doing okay?"

"I'm good."

"You were AWOL for quite some time. You had us all worried."

"I'm sorry, Freddy."

"Well, you're back now, and I'm delighted to see you again."

"Thanks. I don't know what Myra has up her sleeve, but I'm pretty sure I'm not the focus of it."

"There must be something going on with Michael then. I haven't talked with him in a couple of weeks. I bet he's pleased you're back."

"Oh, so you don't know the big news?"

"Big news?"

"Come on, let's go in. We were just about to take lunch. I better not spill the beans."

Michael and Shannon were shocked when Lucy walked into the dining room with Fred in tow. They had noticed the extra place setting on the table but thought Myra set it before she knew Peg wouldn't be staying. Shannon ran to him and gave him a big hug. You could barely notice the limp she'd been exaggerating all morning. Michael shook his hand, and gave his back a good slap. Myra waited her turn to give him a hug and then instructed him to go wash up for lunch.

When everyone was back at the table and seated, Myra stood up and declared, "My darlings, it is so wonderful to have you all here under this roof. She smiled and looked at each of them. "It is time for some Illumination. I think there is something Michael and Shannon need to share with you, Freddy."

"Oh, and what is that?"

Neither Michael nor Shannon volunteered a word. They looked at each other and then at Fred, each waiting for the other to speak.

Finally, Myra said, "Good heavens, the cat has gotten to their tongues. I'll be very happy to share your news, if that's all right."

"Well, someone tell me before I die of curiosity."

"I'll tell him, Myra," Shannon declared. "Fred, I… we didn't know we'd be seeing you this weekend. We had talked about flying out to L.A. together and arranging a dinner with you to tell you. But since you're here…" She took Michael's hand and squeezed it. "Michael has asked me to marry him." Fred's eyes widened. He sat like a man frozen. After a moment Shannon added, "And I have accepted his proposal." She stretched out her hand and flashed the ring. Still there was no reaction from their stunned friend.

"Well, what do you think, old man?" Michael asked.

"I think you're out of your minds. I can't believe it. Shannon, I thought you had more sense than this."

"Well, clearly I don't have as much sense as you've given me credit for," Shannon said, "because I'm going to marry Michael."

"Thank you, darling, I think," Michael said. "Look, Fred, we thought you would be happy for us."

"Happy that my two dearest friends are about to ruin their lives? Hardly."

"Well, I guess asking you to be best man is out of the question then." Michael smiled as if he were getting some kind of enjoyment ruffling Fred. Lucy sat taking it all in, surprised at the way Fred was reacting. To see two of his oldest and dearest friends about to commit to a life together should have made him happy. But he clearly was not. Then there was Myra; she sat strangely quiet, gloating like the cat that ate the canary.

"God, Michael, you make me sick. I know you're ready to jump on anything that moves, but Shannon?" Isn't even friendship sacred to you?"

"Now wait just a minute, Fred. We aren't still in school. It's marriage I've proposed," Michael said, trying to defend himself. But Fred wasn't appeased.

"What happened, Michael? Did you run out of floozies to diddle?" Michael jumped to his feet and Fred leaped up to face him. It was a good thing a wide table separated them.

"Fred, you forget yourself," Michael admonished. "You are in the presence of ladies."

The two stood in a stare down. Finally, Fred recanted. "Myra, Lucy, Shannon, forgive me for speaking frankly, and I apologize that I spoke so crudely in front of you, but I do not take it back." He set his jaw and glared at Michael. "Let's take this outside."

"Take this outside? Why? Do you want to fight me?" Michael laughed. "Do you think I'm just going to stand there and let you take a swing? You better think hard on what you're asking, pal."

"Will the two of you please stop! Take the macho vibrato down a notch," Shannon reprimanded. "Freddy, what on earth has gotten into you? Where is all this coming from?"

"Don't you know, Shannon?" Myra asked.

"The only thing I know is that these two are acting like idiots."

"Freddy, why don't you explain it to her. This may be your last chance." Myra seemed to have grown in stature as she presided over the barney.

Lucy noticed a look come across Michael's face. It was a knowing sort of half smile, a proud-of-himself look. She'd seen it on his face before whenever he thought he was being clever. Fred glanced away from Michael toward Shannon. He looked like he was trying to figure things out. He returned his gaze to Michael and said in a smaller voice, full of emotion, "Have you slept with her?"

Shannon gasped, "How dare you."

"Michael?"

"No, Fred, I have not. This is Shannon we're talking about. I respect her. We're waiting for our wedding night. Just what business is that of yours?"

"It's my business because…" He put his head down and closed his eyes. "…because I love her."

"What?" Shannon gasped, falling back into her chair.

Fred hurried around the table and fell to his knees at Shannon's side. "I love you. I've loved you since school."

"Freddy, dear, sweet Freddy, why didn't you ever say anything?"

"Because I was afraid if I did, and you didn't feel the same way, it would ruin our friendship. And I've cherished it. Besides, I didn't think I'd stand a chance. I thought perhaps once you moved to L.A., away from Michael's influence, and we had a chance to be around each other for a while, maybe you could, I mean, that you would… You're so beautiful, so perfect. I just can't stand by and let you marry Michael—or anyone for that matter—without a word."

"Freddy, I don't know what to say."

"Tell me I'm the biggest fool in the world, and I'll walk out that door."

"You are a big fool, but only for not telling me sooner. Please don't walk out the door, because I love you too." They fell into each other's arms as if no one in the room existed. Michael walked to the other side of the table and sat in the chair that had been vacated by his best friend, leaving the chair next to his fiancée free for Fred.

When the two love birds returned their focus to the dining room, they both stared at Michael. "I'm sorry, Michael," Shannon whispered. She slipped the ring off her finger and slid it over to him. He left it lie. "So you knew about this, Myra? That's why you asked Fred here?"

"I saw the look in Freddie's eye last summer when the two of you were here. I'm quite good at recognizing that look, you know. I see it quite often." Michael scowled at her. "Oh Michael, you aren't mad at me, are you? You'll see it's for the best."

"Cut me a piece of that pie, will you?" He handed her his plate. "Are you guys ready for some pie over there?" He pushed one of the pie dishes across the table toward Fred and Shannon.

"Michael, we need to talk—in private, I mean," Shannon said.

He picked up the ring and rolled it around in his hand before putting it in his pocket. "If you like. But for the life of me, Shannon, I can't think of anything you could say now that we all can't hear."

"All right, Michael. Tell me, will you, was this your plan all along to shake Fred into action? I mean, is that why you asked me to marry you?"

He looked at her with that half smile and winked. "You figured me out, you clever little minx." Lucy didn't know if that were true, or if Shannon said it just to provide Michael a way to save face. After all, she'd been watching his back for years.

They ate in relative silence. Michael asked for a second slice of pie and offered kudos to the cooks. The phone rang and he excused himself to answer it. He came back in the room with a bottle of Champagne. He set it on the table and walked to the crystal cabinet for five wine glasses. He looked different in a way that Lucy couldn't put her finger on.

He popped the cork and poured the bubbly. When everyone had a glass, he made a toast: "To Fred and Shannon, my two best friends, may together they find the happiness they deserve, the happiness we are all searching for." They clinked then drank the special wine. "I promise to do better at your wedding, if I'm asked to be the best man, that is."

"Of course you'll be the best man, and you don't have to do better because that was perfect," Fred said, reaching across the table to shake his hand.

Shannon clung to Freddy's arm, looking radiant. Lucy was happy and sad. She remembered what Myra had said to her about how Shannon made Michael smile. He wasn't smiling now. He had a steely reserve about him and he looked tired. "If you'll all excuse me, I could use a run on the beach." He didn't wait for permission. He walked out of the room.

"Come on, Freddy, let's have a smoke," Shannon said. The new couple excused themselves and headed for the garden.

"Myra, let me take care of this," Lucy said, standing and gathering the dishes.

"We'll do it together, love." By the time Michael came back, Lucy and Myra were done with the kitchen work and sitting in the garden. Fred and Shannon had gone for a walk.

"Ladies," he said as he hurried by them. Lucy had forgotten what a magnificent body he had, tanned and wonderfully toned. She rebuked herself for wanting to reach out and touch him.

"Myra, do you think he'll be okay, I mean about Shannon and Fred?"

"He will be, dear. After all, she was not the love of his life, though I've no doubt that he loves her. They have shared a lot over the years, working closely like they do. I don't think he would have asked her to marry him if he didn't think he could make it work. Now he's back to being alone again, isn't he?"

"Yes, I suppose so." Lucy knew now what that look was, the look Michael had walked back into the dining room with. It was the look of loneliness.

"I'm glad you're here, Lucy. He really wants to help you, you know? It will take his mind off his own troubles. Maybe you can help each other." She patted Lucy's hand and stood. "I best get busy. I need to go start a roast for dinner tonight, and I want to open up the small room at the end of the hall upstairs for Freddy." Lucy volunteered to help her and carried fresh linen upstairs. She was making up the bed when Michael came out of his room and saw her.

"Hey, just what are you doing? You don't work for me anymore, remember?" He grabbed a corner of the sheet she was putting on the bed and tucked it in. They finished the chore together. "I was just on my way to the study to have a little talk with Angus."

Lucy's heart skipped. "Do you want me to come with you?"

"No, I think it better if I deal with him myself. Maybe you could provide me with some prayer cover for the task. I'd hate for that little demon, if that's what he is, to best me."

"I will, Michael," she said breathlessly. "Please be careful." She kissed his cheek, went straight to her room, and fell on her knees.

Michael walked down to the study wondering if his plan would work or if he was just giving Lucy false hope again. Before he entered, he took the crystal cross from his pocket, put it around his neck, and tucked it into his shirt collar. Once in, he locked the door behind him. He walked over to the painting, hanging now in its original spot above the mantle, and said, "Okay, Angus, it's time we had another little chat."

Michael jumped when from behind him came the scratchy voice of the little elf: "What, no threats of how you're going to burn my likeness or smash my statue?" Angus sat on the corner of the desk. He reached over the edge and struck a match on the head of Michael's newly carved likeness.

"So you've taken to reading my mind now?" Michael had actually thought of using those threats again if necessary to get the attention of the little imp. Now that he had it, and in the sober light of day, he wondered if he were up for this task.

"Don't flatter yourself, Michael Donegan, and don't waste my time. You want something, or more to the point, someone." He hooted and then cackled.

"I want to talk to Lance. Can you make that happen?"

"Maybe," he said. He tilted his head back and took a long drag from his pipe. "And just what would be in it for me?"

"That's simple. Haven't you figured it out? I won't burn your likeness or smash your statue."

"Devil!" Angus shouted. He kicked his heels into the desk.

"Now, now, there's no need for name calling. We're just negotiating here. Can you comply with my request or not?"

"Your father, rest his soul, was much more skilled in the gentlemanly art of caviling. So much more courteous was he. I never once appeared to his summons that he failed to offer me a cordial taste or two."

"You're right, Angus. I did forget my manners; I apologize. May I offer you a spot of whiskey?"

"That's more like it, Michael Donegan. I will have a wee bit of the homeland spirit." Michael went to the liquor cabinet and pulled down a bottle of fine Irish blend. He poured some in the cap and handed it to Angus. "Won't you be joining me?"

"I better not. I need to keep my wits about me to deal with such a skilled negotiator."

"So you do, Michael Donegan, so you do." He laughed and hooted some more. "Now where were we?"

"I asked you if you could arrange for me to talk with Lance."

"Oh, that's right. So you did." He put his hand on his chin and tapped his face with his fingers. "Might I have just a wee spot more of that fine grain to help me think of a way to make that happen?" Michael complied and filled the cap once again. "Such a fine gentleman you are, sir." Michael knew he was being toyed with but felt he still held the upper hand, having the ability to destroy the objects of his little foe's vanity. Angus rolled on his back, crossing one leg over the other. He started to hum and cackle.

Michael, tired of the wait, asked, "Well, Angus, have you thought of a way?"

"A way for what?"

"A way for me to talk with Lance."

"Oh, yes, that's right. I'm very sorry, Michael Donegan. There is no way." He hooted and rolled on his stomach, slapping his hands against the desk.

Michael lit a candle and carried it over to the painting. "Such a shame to destroy Farmer Green's fine work."

"Hold on, Michael Donegan. I wouldn't be doing that if I were you; unless, of course, you don't want to be seeing the note I have for you in my hat."

Michael lowered the candle. "You have a note for me?"

"Yes, yes, that's right."

"From whom?"

"Oh ho ho," Angus guffawed. "From whom? From whom?" He pounded the desk some more, laughing in his irritating way.

"Angus, you are trying my patience. Am I right to assume you have a note in your hat for me from Lance?"

"Yes! Yes! Yes! That's right. For you from Lance." He stood up, put his hands on his hips, and started dancing a jig.

"Give it to me, Angus."

"Just another capful, Michael Donegan, and your promise not to destroy either the painting or the statue, and I shall gladly hand it over."

"How do I know you even have a note? And if you do have one, how do I know for sure it's from Lance?"

"Oh, Michael Donegan, you can't be that much of a fool? You have the reports in the king's own hand, do you not? You can compare the script. Now fill this cap and make it quick before I decide not to be so amicable." Michael picked up the bottle and started to pour some into the cap that Angus held out. As he did, he made a grab for the little man's red pointed hat. But Angus was too quick for him. He jumped back, and Michael fell upon the desk, spilling whiskey on his shirt. "Now that wasn't at all nice, was it? And here I thought we were having such a nice, gentlemanly parley."

A knock came on the study door. "Michael, are you all right?" It was Fred. He and Shannon had been strolling past the study when they heard the commotion. "Michael, please open the door. We'd like to have a word with you."

"Angus, give me that note." Michael demanded in a lowered voice.

"Let me first have your word that you will never harm my portrait and that it will never move from the wall where it now hangs."

"You have my word."

"Good. Now give me another cap of whiskey." Michael lunged for the hat once again, and this time when Angus jumped back, he knocked the lamp from the desk. It crashed to the floor, and Angus, thinking this all wonderful sport, hooted ever more noisily.

"Michael, open this door immediately," Fred demanded.

"Knock it down," Shannon urged. "He may be hurting himself. That laugh sounded half mad."

"The note, Angus, and be quick." Angus jumped upon a stack of books, took off his hat, and clutched a piece of paper in his hand. Before handing it to Michael, he elicited one more promise: that Michael would never harm nor move from the garden at Glen Eden his precious statue. Michael agreed and Angus handed over the note. It was at that moment the study door came crashing open and Fred and Shannon rushed in. Angus jumped from the desk and ran under a chair.

"Fred, you kicked in the door!" Michael said in disbelief.

"Sorry, old boy, we were worried about you. Good lord, Michael, how much have you had to drink? You've trashed this place."

Shannon came to his side. "Oh dear, I've hurt you, haven't I? I'm so sorry. I thought you were in love with Lucy and just settling for me. I had no idea you cared so deeply. Please forgive me, darling." She stroked his hair and kissed his cheek.

Fred came over and patted his back. "Forgive us."

"Fred, you are a lucky man," Michael said, going along with their version of things and explaining nothing. He better understood now the dilemmas Lucy had faced her entire life. "If you don't mind, I'd like to be alone for a while. I haven't had that much to drink really. I just spilled the bottle when I hit the desk. I'll be out soon, I promise. Ask Myra to put on some coffee, will you?" He saw the little man run out the door.

"Are you sure you'll be okay, darling?" Shannon asked tenderly.

"I'll be fine, really. I just need some time to gather myself. Please."

"Okay, love. Don't be long." She took the bottle from his hand, capped it and put it away on the shelf.

"I won't." The two guilty lovers walked from the room. Michael closed the door the best he could, with the latch bent and the catch shattered, and began reading the crumpled note he held in his hand.

Michael,

I know you don't remember me, but we did know each other long ago when we were both children and were taken to a secret school. Our destinies were tied way back then to Lucy. The truth of this is hidden in your mind.

She does love you, but her heart is true and was promised to me. Yet I am unable to return to her as I once thought I could, and she would not be safe here. You and I both know how she has suffered for my love. I do not wish that for her. I believe that you love her and will protect her. You can give her the happiness that I cannot. If you will agree to the terms of this message, it is you she shall marry. And to you she will bear her first son.

As long as she holds any memory of me, she will fight this. There is no longer time to waste. That is why it is imperative that all memories of me must be blocked from her mind. I have the ability to do this. Bring her to the stone circle on Green's farm at midnight on the next full moon. Tell her only that I have agreed to meet her. When she leaves that circle, it will be as if I never existed and she will be free to give you her heart.

Nevertheless, she must also bear my son. You must return her to me for one night. When that time is near, Angus will bring you instructions where to deliver her—at a time when the stars have aligned in a favorable way for my son to be conceived. Remember, if you agree to this, you shall have her for a lifetime, I for only one night so the prophecy of our people can one day be fulfilled. She will have no memory of our union, and she must not know the child she will bear is mine. You must promise to raise him as your own, to be the brother of your own son. Give her the crystal cross to wear when she agrees to be your wife. It will protect her and our sons in her womb from those who may seek to harm them.

I shall sign this message in my blood as my bond. I ask you, if you agree, to do the same. No one else must see it. Put it under the statue of Angus in the garden. He will bring it to me, and our fates will be sealed.

My brother, it was for this purpose you were born to this flesh from the mist of our people, in the bloodline of the Dragon, as was I and was Lucy. We serve the same living Lord in different dimensions of his creation.

Peace be unto you,

Lance

Michael read the note over again then jabbed his hand with a letter opener so he could sign with a drop of his blood. Although he didn't have a memory of the school, he knew what Lance said was true. He had, as Myra had suspected, been the boy with the crystal cross in the memory Lucy recalled in her first hypnosis session. He stole out to the Garden, and making sure that no one was watching, he tipped the statue of Angus and placed the note under it.

Myra, Shannon, and Fred stood talking when he walked into the kitchen. "Saints have mercy, Michael. You smell like you did the night I found you passed out in the garden."

"Not quite, that was scotch. This is malt whiskey. I'll go shower. Have you seen Lucy?"

"She was in her room praying earlier. It wouldn't hurt you to do a little of that, Michael."

"You're right, Myra. It wouldn't hurt any of us."

He took his second shower of the day, a quick one to wash away the alcohol smell, then dressed in a hurry. He was anxious to tell Lucy that he had negotiated a way for her to see Lance. But she wasn't in her room. He found her sitting on the beach watching the waves roll in. "There you are."

"Michael, hi. How are you feeling?"

"None the worse for my run in with our little friend."

"You saw him? You saw Angus?"

"Aye."

"Oh Michael!" She jumped to her feet. "When Shannon told me you'd gotten drunk and smashed up the study, I didn't think… I mean, I thought that you didn't… Oh my God! What did he say?"

Michael snickered at the excitement in her voice. "So let me get this straight: you thought that I didn't go through with conjuring Angus because I had gotten drunk over being dumped by Shannon?"

"You don't have to pretend with me, Michael. I know you're happy for your friends, but it has to hurt."

"I am happy for my friends, and yes I did feel hurt… do feel hurt." He had to be careful what he said now and how he acted around her. He sobered his face. "I'm back at square one after thinking my life was finally on course." He didn't want to tip his hand before he had a chance to deliver her to Lance. Since he'd read the note and knew Lucy would soon be his, he was happier than he had been in years. Only he had to be careful that he didn't show that joy to anyone. He had to tell himself over and over to get the smile off his face. "But let's not talk about me. I have some good news for you." Lucy's eyes widened and she held her breath. "Angus is arranging for Lance to meet you in the stone circle on Green's farm the night of the full moon." If she hadn't already been sitting in the sand she would have fallen in it. He knelt before her. "That's in two days, Lucy. You're going to see Lance in two days."

She screamed and threw herself at him. He picked her up and twirled her around and around. Her jubilation was so great she felt weightless, like she was flying. He put her down but still had his arms about her. "Thank you," she whispered. She laid her head on his chest and stood against him. It felt good to be held. But her thoughts were of Lance, and when she realized Michael was holding her she quickly backed away.

"I should go up now," he said. "I've promised Myra a little help with the dinner preparations." Leaving her stand there was torture. He wanted her so badly his body ached. Yet he knew he'd have to avoid her as much as possible for the next couple of days. He suddenly felt sorry for Lance. All this time he had been thinking of him as some kind of jerk who left her alone for his own folly. He understood now the sacrifice Lance was going to make for her happiness. He wondered: if the roles had been reversed, would he have been able to act as gallantly?

That night after dinner, Peggy and Ashley stopped over to tell Lucy and Michael their engagement news. Lucy acted surprised when Peg showed her the ring—per the agreement she'd made with Ashley the night before. When Michael offered his congratulations, Ashley asked him to be the best man. "Second best seems to be the best I can do," Michael joked, offering Ashley a handshake in acceptance.

"Peg told me someone finally managed to tie you down, Michael. I'd sure like to meet her."

"Here she comes," Peggy said, running up to Shannon, who had just entered the great room with Fred. "I've just gotten engaged. Come meet my fiancé." She pulled Shannon by the hand and introduced Ashley as her husband to be. To Ashley she said, "This is Shannon O'Connor, the future Mrs. Michael Donegan."

"Actually, Peggy, a lot has transpired since you left here this morning. Hasn't it, darling?" Both Michael and Fred answered yes, and then broke out in laughter.

Michael introduced Fred as his oldest and dearest friend and invited everyone into the sitting room. "I'll fix a round of drinks while the ex-future Mrs. Michael Donegan explains her new title."

Peggy's mouth dropped open and she shot an accusing glance at Lucy. Lucy put her hands up and shook her head. "I had nothing to do with it, thank you very much."

Soon the parlor was filled with chatter as the two happy couples acquainted themselves with each other. Shannon conveyed her version of what transpired at the lunch table and after, including a short, hushed description—when Michael left the room to get more ice—of how badly he had taken the news. "He is such a wonderful man putting Freddy and my happiness above his own."

"He's even agreed to be best man at our wedding," Fred added.

"I asked him to be best man for me too," Ashley said. Now he understood what Michael meant when he said second best seemed to be the best he could do.

"He is such a dear," Shannon said. Then she looked around the room for Lucy, but she'd gone off to check on Myra. She didn't want her to hear what she was about to say next. "We have to work on a way to get Lucy to forget about that guy she's agog over. Let's face it; I don't think it's any secret that Michael is desperately in love with her. I resolved to marry him despite that fact because I thought she'd run off somewhere for good. I could have made him happy, with her out of the picture." Fred cleared his throat and she added, "I had also resolved long ago that my true love, my darling Fred, would always only think of me as his friend."

"And you are, my darling." They kissed. There was a lot of kissing going on.

Michael returned with the ice and put on some music. Lucy came back into the room with Myra and found a party going on. Michael insisted on dancing with both Shannon and Peggy. Then he asked Myra for a dance. As Lucy stood watching and remembering the dance they shared at the Tara, she was visited by the Michael Donegan fan club. One by one—and sometimes two at a time—they touted the fine qualities of their hopelessly-in-love-with-her friend. Lucy didn't have to be told. She knew of them all and more. She was grateful that this evening, even though she wanted him to, he did not ask her to dance. As a matter of fact, he was doing his best to avoid her. Every now and then he would look over at her and sometimes he'd catch her looking at him. Then he'd offer only a half smile or wink.

That night she lay in bed trying to think of what Lance might say to her. Was he going to take her with him, or tell her she'd have to wait yet longer? Was he going to tell her goodbye? In the middle of all this she thought about how good she felt in Michael's arms. She couldn't sleep, so she stole downstairs to make a cup of hot milk.

Michael tossed and turned in his bed. He wondered if he had done the right thing agreeing to Lance's terms. He wanted Lucy so badly that the idea she might finally be his caused his thoughts to race. He never checked the handwriting on the note. What if it wasn't Lance's? Was it all just a trick by Angus to get Lucy into the circle in order to take her into another time or dimension, maybe do her harm? Michael remembered that William had written in his journals that he was suspicious of Angus and did not think him totally trustworthy. Michael wondered if Angus had gotten the note yet. If he hadn't, he might still have a chance to compare the handwriting. He would feel better about the whole thing if he did. He jumped up, hastily dressed, and went out to the garden.

The note was gone. He didn't know what else to do, so he fell to his knees and prayed, asking God to give him peace that what they were about to do was His will. When he finished praying, he stood staring at the reflection of the moon and stars on the dark blanket that was Lake Michigan. He heard the distant sound of harp strains and then the hauntingly beautiful voice of his beloved Kathleen. As tears streamed from his eyes, peace washed over his being and he knew then all would be well.

Lucy was stirring milk on the stove when she heard the back door open. It unnerved her because of the late hour. She stood as quiet as she could in the dark kitchen. Someone was coming. Michael hurried in not expecting to see anyone. They both let out startled yelps. "Good God, Lucy, you scared my hair straight! What are you doing down here?"

"I couldn't sleep so I was making some hot milk and honey. Only I'm not sure I can drink it now since you scared my stomach into my throat. What were you doing outside at this hour?"

"I couldn't sleep either, so I took a stroll."

"Would you like some hot milk?"

"Does it work?"

"It worked when I was little."

"Sure, I'll try it. Why is it you can't sleep, excited about seeing Lance again?"

"Oh Michael, I'm so worried about what he is going to say. What if he tells me I can't go with him, and he says goodbye forever? Or what if he leaves me here again for who knows how long? I couldn't take it. I want what Peggy and Ashley have. I want what Shannon and Fred…" She stopped herself. "I'm sorry. I'm so selfish. I'm so fixed on… on…" She started to cry and he pulled her to him.

"Shh, there, there, it's going to be all right, I promise."

"I feel so selfish. You're thinking about me when your own life has fallen apart."

"You're wrong, Lucy. My life hasn't fallen apart; to the contrary, I've accepted that it is as it should be. Now tell me something: do you trust Lance? Do you trust him with your happiness?"

"Yes, Michael, I do."

"There, then you see. It's going to be fine." He kissed the top of her head. "Now pour me a glass of your potion."

31 – What Cost Free Will

◈ Michael was up before anyone else. He fried up a pound of bacon and an equal share of sausage. He prepared the griddle and made a batch of buttermilk pancake batter. He brewed the coffee, set the table, and called up the stairs for everyone to "rise and shine." Only then did he start ladling the batter onto the hot griddle. He turned out a platter full of golden cakes.

Lucy was the first one down, followed closely by Myra and then Fred. Shannon had to be summoned yet again so Fred volunteered to go knock on her door. They ate heartily, and at Michael's request agreed to attend Saint Peter's for Mass.

Fred drove the rental car to more easily accommodate the five churchgoers, the fellows in front while the women graced the back seat. Megan was standing in front of the church with Charlie Nelson when the little band arrived. She nervously watched as Michael approached. He walked straight for her and greeted her with a hug. He shook Charlie's hand and introduced him to the others. Myra he already knew. "Say Megs, why don't you bring Charlie by Glen Eden this afternoon and we'll play some badminton? I'll pick up something to throw on the grill." Megan was elated. She'd missed being at Glen Eden with Michael and Myra. She considered them her family. But whenever she found free time to come home from school, it was Charlie she was most interested in seeing. She didn't think he'd be welcome at Glen Eden.

Charlie didn't say much. He still remembered the trouncing he'd received by Michael's hand. He had a permanent kink in his nose because of it. He didn't hold a grudge though, because he knew he'd had it coming. He also knew it would mean a lot to Megan if he and Michael could get past that awful day. So he nodded his head and said, "I'll be there."

Megan embraced Lucy and said, "I'm happy you've come back." Lucy noticed the difference in her right away. She no longer looked like a kid with a crush. She looked like a young woman in love.

Peggy had told Winnie and Skipper of Michael's engagement to Shannon when she took them to lunch at Bill Knapp's. Winnie mentioned it to Mrs. Inch, who then phoned Mrs. White, who then called Mrs. Mullen, and soon pretty much the whole congregation knew of it. People strained to get a look at Michael Donegan's fiancée. Most had seen both Lucy and Shannon with Michael and Myra before, and since neither one had an engagement ring, they were kept guessing on whom he had decided. Michael sent Myra to sit with Winnie so she could explain the details of what transpired between Shannon and Freddy. He figured that would be the quickest way to spread the news of his broken engagement.

Michael, who was intentionally trying to avoid any close contact with Lucy, chose to sit next to Fred, who was sitting next to Shannon, who was sitting next to Lucy. He didn't want to give rise to any new rumors before the old ones had time to rest. If all went according to plan, he had thirty-eight hours before Lucy's scheduled meeting with Lance; he didn't want to screw anything up.

Lucy was disappointed when Michael didn't sit next to her. She didn't know why but she had a weird feeling about going into the stone circle. As much as she longed to see Lance, she was apprehensive about what he might tell her. She felt strangely sad thinking she may never see Michael again. The more she tried not to think of him, the more she found herself doing exactly that.

The sermon that day centered on two Biblical topics, freewill and straddling the fence: the devil did not want God to give people freewill, especially since God had the power to make them worship Him; and the most conflicted people on earth are those who know about God but choose not to commit themselves fully to him. Instead, they sit straddling the fence with half a mind leaning toward the things of God and the other half leaning toward the ways of the world.

As much as he wanted Lucy for his own, Michael was conflicted about what was going to happen. Lance promised in his note that he would make her forget all about him so she would be free then to fall in love with Michael. But was that the right thing to do? He thought it was at first. She wouldn't have to suffer any longer waiting for someone who could not return, and he was certain that if she would give him the chance, he could make her happy. But now he felt oddly guilty about the plan, that by not telling her of what Lance was intending to do, he was deceiving her in some way. Shouldn't she have freewill to choose whether she wanted to forget him or not? He knew how much she loved Lance, and he didn't believe for one minute that she would ever choose to forget him. Yet that's what Lance proposed to make her do. Michael didn't know whether Lance planned on telling her first, or if he planned on tricking her. It bothered Michael that he didn't know. The peace he felt the night before in the garden had left him. It wasn't that he doubted that he loved her—his love for her was the surest thing he knew—it was apprehension over what would transpire in the circle.

Fred and Shannon planned to drive back to Detroit together. His flight for LAX left DTW that evening, and they wanted some time alone before he left. So they prepared to leave Glen Eden soon after returning from the service.

They both felt it necessary to talk with Michael separately before they left. Fred took him aside first. He offered a heartfelt apology for any pain his procrastination in confessing his love for Shannon may have caused. He also asked forgiveness for the despicable way he'd behaved when he first got the news of their engagement. Michael assured him that he was sincerely happy for both of them and that their friendship was in no way in jeopardy.

When it was Shannon's turn she cried and held him close, saying that if it weren't for Fred and Lucy, she was certain they could have had a wonderful life together. "Things won't change between us, will they, darling? Because I couldn't stand it if they did. Not even dear Freddy could make me completely happy if I lost you."

"You don't have to worry about that, love." Michael felt blessed to have her in his life and the only thing that bothered him was that he was pretty certain Fred would convince her to move to L.A., and soon. She'd always been there, at the office, looking out for him. He would miss her sorely in that situation. Shannon had one more meeting before she left Glen Eden, with Lucy.

Lucy was in her room having just changed into her jeans from the dress she'd worn to church when a rap came on her door. She was surprised to see Shannon there. "Fred and I will be leaving in a little while, and I'd like for us to have a private talk before we do. May I come in for a moment?"

"Certainly, Shannon."

Shannon made sure to close the door when she stepped inside. "Lucy, I must admit I had a very inaccurate impression of you when we first met. I thought you were just another one of the beautiful women who thought Michael would be an easy mark. Later, when I learned he had such deep feelings for you, I was even a little jealous."

"Shannon, look, you don't have to say any of this."

"Please, Lucy, let me finish. I agreed to marry Michael after you left because I thought you were out of the picture for good, and it seemed to make perfect sense: we've known, loved, and respected one another for a very long time. After we got here Friday and there you were again, I realized the mistake I almost made. Even if Freddy hadn't confessed his love for me, I would have broken it off with Michael. Because the truth is he's head over heels in love with you. If you don't realize that, you must be blind. And if you do realize it, then you're one of the cruelest people I know."

"Shannon, I..."

"Let me finish, Lucy. I came here to speak my mind and I mean to do it. I don't know anything about this Lance guy. But I do know that Michael Donegan is one of the kindest, nicest men there is. He doesn't have a mean bone in his body. His is generous to a fault. No one knows half of the good he does because he does it out of a sincere compassion for his fellow man, not for recognition."

"Shannon, I know Michael is a wonderful man." Her voice cracked and tears welled in her eyes. "I do have very strong feeling for him, but I promised my life to Lance."

Shannon went to her. "I'm sorry, Lucy, truly I am. I believe you're suffering too. But maybe it's time to let go of that promise and start living a life that could have some real meaning. Promise me that you'll think about it; that's all I ask."

Michael was standing with Fred near the car when Shannon and Lucy walked from the cottage arm in arm. Michael was surprised at Shannon's sudden girlfriend behavior. He'd never known her to have a girlfriend. Shannon declared nonchalantly that she asked Lucy to be her maid of honor. When it came time for her to kiss Michael goodbye, she whispered in his ear, "There you go, darling. I've arranged for her to walk down the aisle with you. I'd say that makes us even."

As Fred's car left the drive, it passed Charlie's car entering. Michael was happy that the distractions kept coming. "Lucy," he said, "be a love, will you? Take my car and run over to the Mayflower Market. Buy seven of the best steaks they have." He took out a roll of bills and handed her a fifty.

"Seven?"

"Oh, I forgot to tell you, Peggy called when you were upstairs. She said she was calling to make arrangements to pick you up later today. I took the opportunity to ask if she and Ashley would like to come by for steaks."

"Great! I'll do it." She took the keys he dangled in front of her.

"Megs, why don't you go with Lucy? Charlie can give me a hand setting up the badminton net and firing up the grill." Megan looked apprehensively at Charlie, but he nodded his head giving her permission to leave. She chatted happily as Lucy drove into town. It was certainly a far cry from the way she'd behaved the last time they went to the store together. Her chatter about school and Charlie was a welcome distraction for Lucy. But then came the question: "So are you and Michael going to give it a go now?"

Lucy knew exactly what she was asking, but her mind and mouth weren't working in sync when she tried to answer. "Michael is… I mean, I am… We're friends."

Megan laughed. "Oh, that's pretty clear. When are you guys gonna get it together and realize you were made for each other?" Megan could tell by the look on Lucy's face that she was struggling with an answer, so she let her off the hook. "I bet you almost died when you came back and found out he was engaged to Shannon. I know I was shocked."

"I was surprised. But not as surprised as I was when I heard you were dating Charlie, especially after what he tried to do to you."

"Yeah, well, that was a really weird time for both of us. I mean, I knew he liked me, but I was totally screwed up in my head thinking I was in love with Michael. God, I was such a dope. Then when you came and I saw Michael getting interested, I threw myself at him. It was awful. He laughed at me and told me I was just a kid. I was so humiliated. I wanted to prove to him that I wasn't just a kid. I got really drunk and went looking for him on the beach; I knew he liked to run in the evenings. But I found Charlie first. He was drunker than I was, and I tried to use him to make Michael jealous, only things went further than I planned. That's when Michael came along and saw us. I was embarrassed, so I screamed rape. Before poor Charlie knew what was going on, Michael was all over him.

"I'm really ashamed about the whole thing. I could have gotten one of them killed. I need to tell Michael and Myra so they won't hold it against Charlie, but I'm too embarrassed." She put her head down, but then a thought came to her. Turning to Lucy, she asked excitedly, "Will you tell Michael, Lucy? Will you, please? He really should know that it wasn't Charlie's fault. Please, Lucy."

"You're right; he does need to know. I'll tell him."

Megan squeezed her arm. "I'm sure glad you're back."

Lucy felt good that Megan had confided in her. She thought of how Shannon had opened up to her too, even asking her to be in her wedding. She felt like she was part of a group of people who cared about one another. She wasn't so alone. Michael had done this. He had given her a family to be part of. Lance had taken hers away. As soon as that thought came into her head, her heart jumped to his defense "That's not true."

It wasn't. Actually, she was estranged from her family by their inability to cope with her periods of missing time. She didn't blame them, but she also didn't want to continue to hurt and disappoint them. They never met Lance, though she had told them about him and of her love for him before she went to California. On the rare occasion when she would talk to them—usually on Christmas or a birthday or other holiday—they never asked if she'd seen or heard from him, and she never volunteered the information that she had not.

She called her mother after Lance shoved her into the orb to bring her back to this time. It was then she learned that Michael had stopped by Twin Willows one Sunday afternoon. It was after she'd disappeared and was still trapped somewhere in time.

"He asked if we'd heard anything from you. I told him we hadn't. He seems like such a nice young man, Lucy, and very good looking."

"I know he is, Mom."

"The hitch broke on Daddy's trailer while he was here, and he walked with your dad to the back of the farm to help him bring it up to the barn. He worked out there with your dad for about two hours getting it fixed. You know how your dad is about rich people; he doesn't trust them. But he told me Michael seemed like a pretty regular guy. That's high praise coming from your father."

"He's anything but regular, Mom."

"Well, you know what Daddy meant. He's not snobbish."

"I know, Mom. Can we talk about something else?"

"Did you let him know that you're back from, well, wherever it was you ran off to?"

"Not yet."

"I promised I'd call him if we heard something. He seemed genuinely concerned."

"I'll call Myra. She'll let him know."

"Oh, okay then. Be sure you do. You know Myra sent us a lovely card at Christmas."

"She did? That was sweet."

"Daddy and I had a nice time when Nick brought her out here."

"I'm glad, Mom. I like Myra very much."

"Well, I'm glad you have such nice people looking out for you." Lucy wanted to tell her how she ached for Lance, how she'd went searching for him and gotten lost tumbling through time, and about how he'd rescued her. But she knew she could not.

As she remembered the heartache of that phone call, she realized that the only person who really knew and understood her love for Lance was Michael. How ironic was that.

By the time the girls returned with the steaks, Peggy and Ashley had arrived. Myra was busy in the kitchen cutting potatoes she'd boiled for potato salad. Lucy went to help. "This won't be as good as I usually make, you know. Potato salad is always better if it has time to sit. I had no idea we'd have all these people here this weekend or I would have prepared something. I suppose Michael is trying to forget about his own life for a few moments by keeping his mind occupied and focused on others."

"It's going to be wonderful, Myra. Don't worry."

"What's going to be wonderful, dear, Michael's life or my potato salad?"

"Both, I hope," Lucy said, with as much resolve as she could muster.

Out of respect for Charlie, Michael didn't offer beer. Instead, he helped Myra make iced tea and lemonade. The weather was sunny and a little cool, just right for playing badminton and enjoying a meal outside. Peggy sat with Lucy on a blanket watching Ashley and Michael smash the shuttlecock back and forth. Charlie sat with a sketchpad doing a charcoal drawing of Myra and Megan, who were sitting still for him in the gazebo.

"Peg, I want you to know that I'm very happy for you and Ash. I think you guys are great together."

"Thanks, girlfriend. You're going to stand up with me, aren't you?"

"I'd love to. But I'm not really sure where I'll be."

"What? Oh my God, Lucy, you aren't planning on leaving again, are you?"

"Maybe."

"But you just got back, and you're here with Michael and he's… unencumbered, shall we say. You need to make your move now. How long do you think he's going to last back on the market?"

"Stop it, Peg. This isn't about Michael."

"I knew it. It's about Lance again, isn't it? God, I hate that guy."

"Peggy!"

"I mean it. Who does he think he is to tie you up like this? He's not just hurting you anymore; he's hurting Michael."

"Peggy…"

"He's hurting all of us who love you and want you to be part of our lives. I know you think he's Mr. Perfect, but let's face it: the guy is selfish."

"Please stop. You don't know what you're saying."

"Look, I don't want to argue with you. You're my best friend. I just wanted you to be part of my special day."

"I want that too. It's just that, well, Michael has arranged for me to see Lance."

"Michael's arranged… What? How did he pull that off?"

"Never mind about that. He has, that's all. And the meeting is tomorrow night. I'm hoping Lance will be able to take me with him this time. Oh Peg, please understand."

"I'm sorry. I've tried to understand. I do know that if the shoe were on my foot… Oh hell, if the shoe was on my foot and I was you, I'd kick it off and run barefoot into Michael's arms."

Lucy looked up to see Michael looking over at her, smiling. He had a towel wrapped around his neck that he'd used to wipe the sweat from his face. He winked and caught himself doing it. He wiped his face again and this time the smile was gone and he looked elsewhere.

Peg and Ashley left first. He had to work at the Butler and she had to drive back to the city alone. She didn't mind, though. She was happy Lucy would be staying. She was hoping Lance would do the right thing and cut her loose.

Lucy found a moment to talk with Michael about Charlie as Megan had asked. "I figured that out when they started dating," he said. "I'm glad she's owned up to her part in it. She's all grown up. I have some hope for them as a couple now. If he can stay off alcohol, they just may have a chance. Did you see the sketch he did of Meg and Myra? It was pretty good. Not up to his dad's level yet, but with training he'll be just as good or even better, I'm thinking." No one knew but he and Shannon that the anonymous scholarship Charlie received for art school had been paid for by a certain Irish businessman.

Michael and Lucy stood together on the patio as the sun rested on the horizon, its cascading colors spread across the lake and sky adding a golden glow to the garden at Glen Eden. They shared the beauty of the moment unspoiled by words though his arms ached to hold her. Megan came up behind them and asked, "Hey, what's going on out here? Is this a private party, or can anyone join?"

"The dues are pretty stiff. Truth is involved," Michael said.

"Oh, I see. Lucy told you. Well, I'm glad. I'm glad it's out in the open, and I'm sorry I was such an awful brat." She put her arms around him and laid her head on his shoulder. "I'm sorry that you were hurt. I've felt terrible about it. Will you forgive me?"

"I will if you can beat me in a game of charades." He knew she loved playing charades. They had played since she was very small, there in the parlor with Grandpa Will, Myra and her Auntie Kathleen.

"You're on," she laughed, giving him a squeeze. Lucy and Megan were up for it but Charlie needed to be coaxed. Myra was the phrase giver, timekeeper, and referee. The teams represented one of the oldest rivalries on the face of the earth: guys against girls. They played till well past 10 o'clock, with everyone seemingly having a good time. Laughs were shared and plenteous. When all was said—or not said—and done, the score was guys 12, girls 21. Michael blamed the bias of the phrase giver for the disparity in the scores, and Charlie agreed with his partner.

Lucy said goodbye to the couple in the house, but Michael walked them to the car. He slipped Megan money for gas and some extras and told her not to be a stranger. He shook hands with Charlie and said, "I guess we've put the past behind us, am I right?"

"Yes sir, I hope so. Sorry about your ribs."

"And I about your nose. If you ever want to get that straightened, I'll foot the bill. I know a doctor in Rochester Hills who makes it his specialty."

"Maybe someday, sir. But for right now looking at it helps me stay off the bottle."

"Glad I could be of service then." Michael threw his head back and laughed. He didn't go back in the house right away. He was afraid of seeing Lucy. He instead walked down to the stables to check on the horses.

Lucy was in bed by the time he went back in. She fell asleep better than she thought she would. She dreamed of Lance in a sort of montage of all the times she'd been with him. It ended in a fairytale setting in an unknown land. She was sitting on a throne and Lance was standing at her side wearing a crown. Standing across the hall was Michael dressed in military finery. On a green velvet chair in the center of the room sat Kathleen strumming a harp while her voice blended with the music floating from the strings.

Lucy felt well rested howbeit very nervous when she awoke. She went downstairs hoping to find Michael but instead found Myra, who told her Michael had left early to run a few errands. "I was hoping to talk with him this morning. Did he say when he'd be back?"

"He said not to wait dinner if that gives you some idea."

Lucy was very disappointed. She wanted to spend some time with him. She wanted to make sure he was going to be all right. "Perhaps it's better if we don't see much of each other," she thought, and decided to spend the day in prayer and fasting. She took a canteen of water and her Bible and walked down to the beach, finding a secluded spot to lay a towel. Here she stayed until the sun went down.

Michael's car was in the drive when she came back to the cottage. She found him sitting at his desk in the study with the Bible in front of him. He looked up when she rapped on the still broken jam. "May I come in," she asked softly.

"Please do."

She moved slowly into the room, like she was being blown by a gentle wind. His eyes followed her as she moved. She was the most beautiful woman he'd ever seen. It would be the easiest thing in the world to keep his mouth shut right now and just let what he knew was going to happen happen. But he could not. He had to tell her. He had to give her the choice. "It won't be long now, Lucy. Soon you will see your Lance." He watched her face as she smiled and took a deep breath. "I'll go out later and saddle up the horses. We'll leave here at eleven."

"Thank you, Michael. Thank you for everything." She reached out and laid her hand on his.

"Lucy, there's something you should know. Something I've been wrestling with." He looked away from her. He was filled with such grief he didn't know if he could go on with it.

"What is it, Michael?"

He cleared his throat and tried his voice. It was weak but there. "I don't think you will be able to go with Lance. He told me that much in a note he gave Angus. And he will not be able to return for a very long time." He watched her shrink.

"So it is as I feared. He has summoned me to say goodbye."

"I'm afraid so, Lucy. I'm so very sorry." She bowed her head and the tears fell. She didn't sob; the pain stayed inside her head. She turned ashen and he could do nothing but watch. He closed his eyes and the sickly helplessness he felt when he lost Kathleen revisited him.

After a while she raised her head and asked in a voice he couldn't even recognize, "You have a note from Lance? May I see it?"

"I'm sorry, Lucy, you can't. I had to sign it in my blood and put it under the statue in the garden for Angus to take back to him so he would know that I agreed to bring you."

"Agreed to bring me? What do you have to agree for? This is between Lance and me. Michael, just what is going on?" Her voice was strong now.

"Lance will explain everything to you. It seems I was the boy in the school with you and Lance just as you thought."

"I knew it was you."

"I still have no memory of it. Lance asked me not to show you the note, Lucy. He will explain everything to you. It is a grand tale."

"I have no doubt of that," she said staunchly. He was surprised at how strong she had become. His heart was still breaking for her. But she was determined not to let this be the last word. She excused herself and went to find Myra; she needed a cup of tea. Myra was in the sitting room and the teapot rested at the ready on the tray before her. Lucy went to the couch and sat down beside her, laying her head on Myra's shoulder.

"There, there, lovie. What is it you've learned?"

"Michael got a note from Lance, and he's to take me to the stone circle on Farmer Green's tonight so that Lance can say goodbye."

"Oh, I see. So that's how it's going to be?"

"I'm going to try to convince him to take me with him. I don't care about the consequences."

"Now, now, dear, we can't just think of ourselves. I'm sure from what I know of your Lance and the love you've shared he would not be doing this unless he felt there was no other way. This will not be easy on him either. Maybe you should continue to trust him like you always have. Trust him that he's going to do the right thing. For all of us." Myra rocked her in her arms, and soon she fell asleep from bearing the heavy weight of her thoughts.

Michael woke her gently at twenty to eleven and told her to dress warmly; he was going to saddle the horses. She arose and did what she was told. As she said goodbye to Myra, she realized how much she had come to love her. "You take care, lovie. It will work out for the best. I'll be praying for you and your young man."

Michael rode up to the front of the cottage at exactly eleven. Lucy rushed out the door and mounted Sazi. Quietly they rode through the night. The bright light from the full moon gave the night woods a magical hue. The air was still warm, but the breeze off the lake chilled them. Lucy was full of anticipation as Sazi strode at her commands over the trail worn in the forest floor.

They reached the meadow early, before the circle appeared. Michael checked his watch. "Seven minutes till midnight," he announced. Lucy rode Sazi to the center of the meadow and dismounted, and Michael followed suit. They stood staring into the shadowy darkness. A sudden howl caused Lucy to jump next to Michael. "That's a coyote, I think," Michael said. "When I was growing up around here, there weren't any. Some people brought pups in from out West to raise as pets. But as they grew they began to eat the other animals the people were keeping as pets, so they let them go off into the wild." He was making small talk to alleviate some of the tension.

One of the few dark clouds in the sky that night moved across the face of the moon, causing the darkness to stretch out and blanket the meadow. The howling started anew and a chill wind picked up. Michael moved closer to Lucy's back to shield her. He stretched his arms over her shoulders and pulled her in close to him. He felt her shiver. They stood this way frozen for a time, peering across the meadow.

As the cloud slowly began to withdraw from the celestial orb, the shroud lifted revealing monoliths standing as before in a circle at the north end of the meadow. Lucy withdrew from Michael's arms and took a step toward the circle. A man now appeared there. He held out one hand and she knew immediately it was Lance. Michael put his hand up as a gesture of greeting but held his ground as Lucy bolted toward the circle. "God protect her. Your will be done," he prayed as he watched her run away from him and into the arms of the waiting man.

She jumped into Lance's arms and they faded into darkness. Michael moved the horses to the far end of the meadow and tied them to a young white birch tree. He removed their saddles and built a small fire to keep the cold and damp off while he waited. He figured he would be there for a bit—possibly all night—and he tried not to imagine the lovers in the circle. He took a small flask from his jacket and tipped it to his lips. A rabbit ran through the meadow and he watched it approach. "Angus, would that be you?" Michael called out into the night.

"And so it is, Michael Donegan, so it is. You've kept your bargain and brought the lady, I see. He will be pleased." The little man walked into the light of the fire and stretched out his hands to warm himself.

"I have only accompanied her. It was her desire to see Lance. She is not my prisoner."

"Oh, so noble of you, Michael Donegan. Just what is it you have there in your jacket pocket?"

Michael laughed. "Sit down here a minute, Angus, and keep me company on this long night." He took the flask once again from his pocket, poured a drip or two into the lid, and handed it to Angus.

"Such a fine gentleman you are, Michael Donegan. I don't mind resting by the fire for a spell." He sat leaning against one of the saddles and stretched his short legs in front of him. "Ah, now this is more like it." He tipped the cap and wiped his mouth with the back of his hand. He stretched out his arm, waved the cap in Michael's direction, and with a pathetic look on his face said, "Please, may I have just a drop or two more of that lovely elixir?"

"Sure, Angus, here you go." Michael stared at the magnificent creature really for the first time. He looked to be very, very old. In the past, Michael had thought this little imp was evil in some way. But now, sitting here just the two of them, he noticed the little guy looked sort of sad, lonely maybe. He was starting to take a liking to him. "Just exactly what is your part in all of this, Angus? Are you just a messenger, one of Lance's minions?"

Angus hooted. "A messenger? A minion, is it? Sure, sure, that's what I be. Same as you, Michael Donegan, same as you." He hooted some more then drained the cap. Michael thought about it and took a hit off the flask himself. Angus was right: this story wasn't about him. He was just doing his part same as Angus. It was about Lance and Lucy. Now they were simply waiting to follow the plan that had already been given them.

He felt a certain kinship to Angus now. He poured his little companion another capful of the liquid that bound them, and Angus's tongue was loosed. "I remember when you were a wee lad, Michael Donegan. It was the night your mother was called home. She hung the cross on your bed and said goodbye. She was brave and beautiful. My favorite Danaan, she was. I took the cross so you wouldn't lose it. William thought Aidan had taken it, and they had a hell of a fight." He laughed wickedly. "I gave it to you to hold once when I brought you to the secret school, but the teacher took it from you and gave it to Lance. That's what tied your fate to his and Lucy's, by the fact that Lucy would be the one to wear it when it was her time to bear you each a son. Lance gave it back to William, who would be able to keep it safe."

"Safe from whom?"

"Safe from the evil ones. Oh, they're here all right. They hide themselves in others who have not guarded their hearts. They are not in total control. Not strong enough yet. But more will come if the war in Elysium goes ill. You have forgotten a lot, Michael Donegan. Lucky you were to be hidden here. It's the Danaan who have always fought against this evil. I brought Lucy here myself when she was just a wee babe. I hid her in the crib of a baby who had died. The mother of the child accepted her as her own and nursed her beside the other baby's twin. They have looked for her, searched day and night, the evil ones have. But we have kept her safe. It is she who will be queen, she who will give birth to the promised one. Say, Michael, my mouth is getting dry."

"Here you go, buddy," Michael said. He filled the cap yet again. "Just where is Elysium?"

"Oh, it's here, here in this world. Just a dimension beyond. If you knew how to tune your frequency, you could go there. But you have forgotten. Your mother is there, and Kathleen."

"What are you saying, Elysium is heaven?"

"Not *the* heaven, no. It was *a* heaven, a paradise, until the fallen came there."

"The fallen?"

"Michael Donegan, haven't you read your Bible? The fallen, the ones who rose up against the Creator until an army led by your namesake caused them to fall. Some fell here, some fell there, some are still falling. Because Elysium was so beautiful and unspoiled and the Danaan so fair a race, they couldn't blend in or hide inside the people. So they've manifested as the hideous creatures they are: orc-like and troll-like, easy to recognize. That is what Lance battles against. Foul creatures they are. They don't just kill, no. They torture for the sport of it. Lance is right not to bring the queen there." Angus stroked his long beard and fell silent, staring into the fire.

Lucy ran straight for the circle as soon as Lance appeared. She leapt into his arms and showered his face with kisses. He found her mouth and lost himself in the delight of the taste of her. The kiss melted away the memory of all the lonely nights they'd spent apart. He was complete again, if only for a little while. When the kiss ended, he let her feet again touch the ground. "Lance, please don't make me live without you."

"It is a memory and a dream of me that you love. I cannot be real to you now, my darling. Michael can. He is a good man, Lucy, and he loves you. You know this is true, and you will love him. You love him already, though you will not allow yourself to think of it. I can lock all your memories of me deep in your mind where they cannot cause you any pain or interfere with that love. You will then be free to give your heart to Michael."

"But Lance, I love you so. And what about our son? You promised me. You said I would have your son. I have seen him, Lance. Don't you remember?"

"Yes, darling, of course I remember, and you shall give birth to our son. Michael has promised to raise him as his own."

"But how? When?"

"When the time comes, Lucy, Angus will let Michael know and he will deliver you to me. You will have no memory of it, or of anything I'm telling you now."

"Please, please, don't make me forget you."

"It will not be forever, my love. I promise. But darling, my humanness is beginning to fade. I cannot long linger here. Give me your finger." Looking longingly into his eyes, she did as he commanded. He took a stone from his pocket. "Look at the marking on this stone, and trace it with your finger. As you do, I will say the words to lock my memory in your mind. This is the way it must be, Lucy. Trust me."

"No, Lance. Please!"

"Michael is a good and noble man. He will protect you, love you. He will give you moments of true joy that I cannot. You will also bear his son. Enjoy this life, my love." He was beginning to glow and his flesh was fading.

"Lance, wait," she whispered. "Please wait."

"I cannot. We will be together, but in another time. Trust me, my darling." He took her finger and traced the marking on the stone as he spoke the spell of forgetfulness. "Michael needs you. You need each other. You are free to love him now." His warmth slipped from her hand and soon even the light faded. She sat staring at the ground.

"Lucy!" a voice called to her. As she drifted back, she saw a man standing in the sunlight. He was tall and strong and handsome. He walked toward her. As he came closer, filling her sight, details of him filled her thoughts and began flowing like a river into her heart. It was Michael, wonderful Michael. He had come for her. He reached out his hand and she took it. She pulled him to her and he fell upon his knees.

He saw himself in her eyes now. The sorrow had left them, and they shown into him for the first time. He wanted to turn his head to keep her from seeing any evil thing that might be there inside of him. She raised his hand to her mouth and she kissed it, still staring into his eyes. Something squeezed his heart and he gasped: his frailty was known to him. All that he was, every fiber of his being, longed for her. For the first time she heard the cry of his soul, and she answered with her own: "I'm here, Michael." He picked her up, and as he carried her she fell asleep listening to the sound of his heart.

She wakened to the smell of clean linen. She heard birds chirping and felt the breath of a summer day coming through an open window. She was back in her room at Glen Eden. Michael sat in a chair close to her bed. His head rested upon one of his outstretched arms that lay on the bed beside her. He was asleep. She stroked his hair and his eyes opened to behold her. "You've chosen to come back to us, then?" he said softly.

"Hello, Michael."

"How are you feeling?"

"I'm feeling like I have something to say."

"Something to say?"

"Yes, to keep a promise I made you."

"And just what promise would that be?"

"You told me once you loved me, and that you would never tell me again unless I asked you too. So, Michael Donegan, I'm asking, do you still love me?"

"Since the moment I saw you, and it has only grown stronger every second I've known you, from that moment to this."

"I'm so very glad you said that, because I love you too, Michael."

"You do?"

"Yes, I think I always have. I don't know why I denied it for so long. I guess it was because I couldn't believe someone like you could really love someone like me." He moved upon her and they kissed for the first time. It was soft and tender, an intimate submission of their hearts' longing.

"Lucy, darling, marry me. Please marry me. Together, we can help each other be better than either of us could possibly be alone."

"Oh Michael, are you sure?"

"I have never been surer of anything."

"Then yes. Yes, my love, I will marry you."

Three weeks later at the time of the summer solstice, standing before friends and family—and the little stone statue—in the garden at Glen Eden, Michael and his Lucy were wed. She wore the dress Myra had made for Kathleen and the ring that had belonged to his mother, the one that had been for a short time on Shannon's hand. As soon as they were pronounced man and wife, Michael presented her with a brilliant crystal cross on a golden chain. She vowed she would never take it off.

32 – The Day Gets Stranger

Tap. Tap. Tap.

Lucy opened her eyes.

Tap. Tap. Tap.

She had been dreaming of the green and golden land. Sitting high on a hilltop, she watched a pleasant little stream as it wound down to a heather-filled meadow in a valley below. It was the kind of dream you don't want to wake up from because everything seems so wonderful and you're at perfect peace. She closed her eyes and turned on her side, trying to go back.

Tap. Tap. Tap.

She stretched in the cozy old cherry-wood bed her father made as a wedding gift for her mother. It had been part of this room since before she was born. It was in this very bed, here at Twin Willows, where she and her sister began life.

Tap, Tap, Tap came the sound again on the window next to the bed.

"Oh, all right, Mr. Cardinal," Lucy shouted, irritated by his persistence. "I'll get up. I should've never started putting feed out for you. It's making you lazy and you're becoming a pest."

As she reached for her housecoat, she threw back the wonderfully colored quilt that her grandmother made. Lucy and her sisters had helped cut out the squares for it. It was a memory quilt, made entirely from swatches of clothing worn, and worn out, by people in her immediate family. These included pieces of house dresses worn by her grandmother, skirts of her mother's, shirts worn by her father, and baby blankets, buntings, and school dresses that had been shared between her and her sisters. It was more than a quilt; it was a comforter, at least in the sense that it was little pieces of childhood memories sewn together with love. It wasn't quite finished when her grandmother died, so Lucy's mom took up the task. That made it even more special. When Lucy's sons were little and not feeling well, they would always ask for Grandma's quilt. It was a magic healing cover to them. She would wrap it tight about them and tell them that sickness and bad things could not stay long in the warmth of such love.

Tap. Tap. Tap.

"You're going to break the glass with your tapping," Lucy yelled. She stood up and hurried to the window to shoo the pesky bird. He always seemed to be satisfied that she was up and on the way to the feeder once the curtains were opened. She reached for their cord and gave it a tug. As the curtains slid back, she expected to see the bright red cardinal that had been waking her up all winter whenever the bird feeder went empty, but she was suddenly taken back.

There was something bright red all right in the drab, bare branches of the tree that grew just outside the window, but it wasn't a bird's feathers. It was a little man's hat.

Lucy stood stone still, her heart racing, all thoughts slipping from her mind. He leaned from the branch and tapped the window again, shaking her from her stupor. He motioned for her to open it. She hesitated only for a moment. She struggled with the latch and then with trying to lift up the stubborn old window in its wooden frame; she hadn't opened it since early October. But when she finally tugged hard enough for it to slide up, a cold blast of winter air added to her rude awakening. She stood facing the little man.

"Hello," she offered. "My name is Lucy. I am certainly happy that you…"

"Hush up!" he commanded. "I don't have all day to be hanging in this tree. I have a message for you."

"For me?" Lucy exclaimed. "From whom?"

"From whom do you think, woman? Have you forgotten him already? Oh, that's right; you have," he cackled impishly.

"Forgotten whom?"

"Will you be quiet for a moment so I can give you the message before I forget what I was sent to say?"

"Yes, yes, I will," she blurted. "I'm sorry. Go right ahead."

"Now that wasn't being quiet, was it?" he snapped. "You've made me forget." His eyes had a devilish twinkle.

Lucy was horrified. "You've forgotten?"

"Well, who could blame me with all your babbling?"

"Oh, please," she pleaded. "Think hard. Try to remember."

He sat crosslegged on top of a limb. The fingers of his right hand stroked his long, straggly gray beard while the fingers of his left hand tapped on his dark green, woolen trousers where they hugged his knee. He rolled his eyes up to the right and then to the left and proclaimed, "I have it!"

"Oh, thank God, you've remembered."

"I didn't say that."

"But you just said you have it."

"Aye, and so I do."

"What? What do you have?"

"I have an idea how I might remember," he cackled again.

Lucy was becoming skeptical of his motives. "And how is that?"

"Well, I think my brain got cold," he said pathetically, "sitting here tapping on the window, waiting for you to open it up."

"Would you like to come in and warm yourself?"

"Oh, no, I don't want to impose on you; besides, I'm not partial to indoor spaces. I thought perhaps if you have a small thimble-full of the mash, it might warm up my remembering."

"The mash?" Lucy asked.

He seemed irritated again. "The mash: wheat, barley, malt," he hollered.

"Oh, whiskey," she blurted. "You want a thimble-full of whiskey?"

His voice became calm and pleasant again. "Well now, it's very kind of you to offer. I do believe a touch might just warm up my recall."

"I'll be right back. Don't go anywhere."

"Oh no, I will sit right here, and I will try to remember what he sent me to say."

"He?" Lucy asked, hoping to catch him off guard. The little man seemed annoyed again and motioned for her to be off. She hurried to the kitchen and found a half-filled bottle of Inishowen. It had been her husband's favorite brand of Irish whiskey. She recalled the night he opened this particular bottle. That was almost four years ago, on the last night they would ever spend together. She twisted off the cap, and as its scent broke into the air, she remembered the smell of it on his breath and the taste of it on his lips.

Searching through the junk drawer in the kitchen, she found a small silver thimble. She filled it to the brim and carried it to the bedroom. The little man sat in the very same position. He looked to her almost like a plastic lawn gnome. When he saw her coming, he jumped up and did a little jig on the branch.

"Thank you, dear lady," he said as he accepted the precious brew. He tilted it up and drained it clean. Then he handed the empty little goblet back to her.

"Well?" she asked.

He stroked his beard. "Yes, yes, I almost have it. Just one more thimble full and I believe it will come to me."

Lucy felt like he was playing with her now, and she plotted what to do about it while she hurried back to refill the tiny cup with his ransom. This time, after she stretched her arm out the window, she withdrew it just as he was about to take hold.

"What are you doing?" His scream was a deep grumble that sounded something like the woeful call of a bullfrog on a hot summer night.

"I'm helping you to remember my message."

He threw his head back and laughed. "A clever gesture worthy of your lineage was that." He squinted his eyes and stared at her for a moment, stroking his beard a few more times. Using his polite voice, he said, "I'm afraid I haven't been able to recall the whole thing yet. I'm sure that tipping that cup will bring it all back." He grinned widely and held his hand out toward his prize. She tipped it just enough to spill a drop in the snow.

"No!" he croaked. "Look what you did, woman!" His bullfrog voice was back.

"I'm trying to help you remember the message. But my hand is getting cold and it's starting to shake, so you better hurry on with it before my tremors cause any more to be wasted."

"She-devil," he spat. Then again he laughed. "I think he may be right about you."

"Who is right about me? Whom are you talking about?"

"The message sender. You do want the message, don't you?"

"Of course I do," Lucy insisted.

"Then give me the thimble and I'll get on with it."

Lucy's hand shook another precious drop onto the snow. "The message and then the thimble," she declared staunchly.

"Oh, you have a wicked heart in you," the little man moaned.

"My heart is not wicked, but my hand is very cold." She started shaking it again.

"No, stop that! Stop that!" he moaned. "The message... I remember it now. He told me to tell you the time is almost right. He will be returning for you as he promised, so you must prepare."

He jumped to the window ledge, snatched his prize, and drank it all down. He shoved the little goblet back at Lucy, tossed his hat high in the air, jumped up, spun around, and clicked his heels together. The hat came down and settled on his head. "I'm off," he said.

"Wait!" she screamed. You didn't say who. Who is returning?" She felt confused and dizzy like she had been imbibing along with him.

"I have given you the message and you heard me, so good day."

"But I... I don't understand," she stammered.

"You will," he cackled, and with that he leaped from the window ledge and landed in a French lilac bush just out of Lucy's sight.

"No, wait. Please wait," she pleaded, leaning as far out the window as she could to catch another glimpse of him. But she couldn't see him and there came no reply.

She raced through the house stopping only long enough to slip on a pair of boots that stood by the back door before she bolted into the garage. She grabbed the freezing metal handle of the big garage door with one hand and yanked on it while pushing up on the massive slab of aluminum with the other. It screeched in its cold, steel tracks as it rolled up. She pushed it just high enough for her 5' 5" frame to pass under. She ran down the drive to a path she had shoveled in the snow leading to the ornamental elm that stood in the yard just outside her bedroom window.

She scanned the snow-covered ground around it and under the lilac bush searching for tracks. There were lots of them made by squirrels and rabbits that had come to collect what the messy birds dropped from the feeder. But try as she did, she saw none made by tiny boots. She turned to retreat back to the house. The picture of the little man's face, the sound of his voice, and what he had said to her were playing over and over in her mind.

A large male cardinal called to her, and she remembered she had to fill the bird feeder. Back in the garage, she picked up a covered bucket containing a variety of seeds and carried it to the feeder. She fumbled as she pried the lid off the can because her hands were so cold. In her haste to see the little man, she had come out in only her nightgown, housecoat, and boots. She hadn't bothered to put gloves on, nor did she have a hat on her head or a scarf around her neck. She was usually very careful to bundle up. Having thrice had pneumonia in the past four years, each time a little more severe than the last, she didn't want to chance getting it again. It was pneumonia that kept her from going on the trip with her husband, the one he had not returned from.

She put a big scoop of the wild bird feed onto the homemade feeder and shouted, "Come and get it" to the cardinal who was hopping from branch to branch atop one of the twin willow trees. A bitter wind stirred, sending shivers running up and down her. She hurried back to the garage, holding the bucket of seeds under one arm. She was just about in when the wind picked up again and caught the heavy aluminum door just so. It came sliding downwards and struck her on top the head. She heard the seed bucket crash to the floor, and then everything went black.

When she opened her eyes, she had an intense headache. She found herself in the breezeway, lying on the couch, wrapped in the afghan that usually lay across its back cushions. There was a man she did not recognize sitting at the table near her. Her head throbbed as she tried to sit up. "Oh," she moaned, giving up the attempt and falling back against the pillow he had placed under her head.

The man turned toward her and smiled. "Don't try to get up yet. You've taken a nasty blow. I didn't find any ice in your fridge, so I packed a plastic bag with icicles from the garage." He positioned it over the lump on her head.

"What happened?" she asked, her thoughts still muddled. Then the crashing of the birdseed bucket came back to her.

"You'll have to tell me," he said. "I saw your boots sticking out from under the bottom of the garage door as I walked by your drive. I called to you, but you were out cold. I found your door unlocked and carried you in so you would not freeze to death. I stoked the fire. Is there someone you would like me to call for you?"

Lucy was still confused. "Call? Well, I live here alone... I mean..." She stopped herself mid-sentence. She noticed this guy had a large hunting knife hanging from his belt. Should she be afraid? She wasn't. If he had wanted to hurt her or rob her, would he have gone to the trouble of making a fire and fixing an icebag for her head? "I'm sorry. I'm a little foggy. How did you happen to find me?"

"I was walking by your drive when I heard a cardinal making a lot of racket. He was hopping from branch to branch, so I stopped to see what had him so riled up. That's when I spotted your boots."

"I'll not complain about Mr. Red waking me ever again," she murmured, her head pounding with every word. "I'm sure glad now that I don't have dainty little feet. I always wondered why God gave me these giant clodhoppers." She wiggled her toes under the blanket.

"It's a sign that you are a woman with a very kind heart," he said, smiling as he rose to stand over her. "God knew exactly what he was doing when he put every lovely strand of hair on your head."

It had been a while since anyone gave her a compliment like that. She saw him plainly now. He had a handsome face and a pleasant smile. She suddenly felt embarrassed about the way she must look. She tried brushing her hair back with one hand, but her head was so sore that she cringed for trying it. "Do you live around here?"

"No, not really around here." She watched him as he unsheathed his knife and picked up a willow stick that he must have carried into the house.

Lucy became a little nervous. "Are you going hunting?"

"No, I'm not hungry right now, though I would like a good cup of tea."

"Oh, of course, where are my manners; let me fix you one." She started to get up, but her head pounded her back down. "Oh!" she groaned.

"Just lay still there. Your manners are fine; they've just been trounced on a bit. I can brew up a pot, if you don't mind?" His voice and smile calmed her.

"No, of course not, go right ahead. Thank you. The kettle is already on the stove, and the tea is in a tin on the shelf just over it. The pot and cups are above the sink." Then she thought, *What a nice guy.* She tried to guess his age but couldn't. He had an ageless face full of wisdom, probably beyond his years. His body was lean and muscular, and his skin was the color of tanned leather, like he spent much of his time outdoors. His hair was long, pulled back, and tied. It once was golden, she could tell, though now gray strands were dispersed through it. He had a mustache and a short, rugged beard. But it was his eyes that enthralled her. They were greener than any she'd ever seen. *Right good looking, he is,* she said to herself.

His voice from the kitchen pulled her away. She thought she heard him say, "You're still using your grandmother's old kettle, I see."

"What?" she asked, wondering how he'd know something like that.

"You use a grand old kettle, I see," he answered.

"It used to belong to my grandmother," she replied.

"Did it now?" he laughed.

Lucy lay there with her head throbbing when her morning, with its strange events, came rushing back to her. "Holy God," she said aloud, remembering the little man.

"No truer statement can be uttered," the stranger said, coming back into the room with two teacups on saucers.

"You know him well then?" She was impressed not only by what he said, but by the fact he had matched the right cups with their saucers.

"Every creature knows him. Problem is, they don't all choose to serve him."

"I've never understood that, really. If they know him and know of his love, mercy, grace, and power, then why wouldn't they?"

"Cupidity, I guess."

Good word, she thought. *He must be a well read man.* As she struggled again to sit up, he came to her side to help. He repositioned the pillow behind her back and adjusted the ice bag to balance on her head. "Thank you. You're being very kind to me."

"Being kind to someone as beautiful as you is my honor." He spoke tenderly. Lucy felt herself blush. The kettle screamed and he turned away to fetch it. In his absence, her thoughts turned again to the little man. She was excited to have seen him again. Her suspicions had been confirmed: he was bringing her a message. But just exactly what had he meant by it? Who would be returning for her? Had he meant her husband? She dared not hope, though his body was never recovered. Or maybe he meant Jesus; was she going to die? A chill came upon her and she shivered.

The stranger returned with the teapot and set it on the small table next to the couch where he had placed the cups. "We'll let it steep a bit longer," he said, turning toward her to pull the afghan up around her shoulders. "I boiled down a bit of willow bark to help you with that headache and threw in a touch of another herb to lift you. It might taste a wee bitter, but if you have some honey for it, it will drink well and help to keep the cold off."

"I do have honey. It's in the pantry next to where you found the cups." Lucy recalled that years ago her Aunt Nellie used to boil down willow bark and keep it in a dark bottle to use as medicine. But who did that in this day and age? And who on earth carried herbs around with them? Her thoughts were making her dizzy again.

He came back with the honey. "You should not be alone today. Is there someone I can call to come stay with you?"

"What time is it?" she asked.

He didn't have a watch on, but he looked out the window and replied, "It is getting on past the eleventh hour."

"My son is driving out from the city today. He'll be here around noon."

"Then you'll not have long to wait. I'll fetch more wood for that fire. You should stay quiet and warm."

"Thanks."

He walked out the door and returned a few moments later with a load of logs in his arms. He piled them in the box next to the hearth and tossed one on the fire. As Lucy watched him, she wondered why she should feel so comfortable in the presence of this stranger. He made her feel younger, more vital, even as she sat there with no make-up, her hair mussed, and a plastic bag on her head. It was a feeling that she missed.

"Now let's have that tea," he said. He poured some of the steaming brew in each of their cups. He was right; it was a little bitter, but Lucy felt better and warmer soon after she took her first sip.

"Which one of your sons is it that's coming today?" he asked.

Lucy was again taken back. "How do you know I have more than one?"

"From the picture on the window ledge in the kitchen," he replied. "It's a lovely picture of you with two handsome young lads on your lap. They look to be two or three years apart. Am I right?"

"Three," she answered, amazed at his powers of observation.

"So which one is coming?"

"The one in the picture with the long blond curls, my youngest. He runs his father's import business in Detroit."

"And the oldest, where is he?

"He and his wife are missionaries living in Romania."

"Ah, so both your sons are about their father's business."

"Yes, they are. They are both wonderful boys. I've been very blessed."

"I have no doubt of that." He raised his teacup toward her then took a sip.

"What about you, Mr.... Oh, I'm sorry. I don't even know your name."

"It's McKellen," he said with a smile.

"I'm Lucy Donegan, and I'm very happy to meet you, Mr. McKellen. Do you have any children?"

He took a sip of his tea, replaced the cup in the saucer, and replied slowly, "Yes, Lucy Donegan, I have a son, though we have never met."

"Oh, I'm sorry. I didn't mean to pry."

"It's quite all right. His mother raised him. She married a fine and honorable man who loved my boy as his own."

"Do you ever hope to meet him?"

"Yes, as a matter of fact, I have high hopes of meeting him very soon."

"That's wonderful. I hope everything goes well."

"I'm sure it will." He smiled again.

Lucy felt lightheaded. She didn't know if it was from the blow she had received, or if it was from being in the presence of this man. He was different from anyone she'd ever known. Maybe she hadn't woken up this morning; maybe she was still dreaming. That would explain both the little man and the handsome stranger who sat comfortably beside her.

"Just what is it that you do?" she asked.

"What do I do?" he repeated. "You mean apart from making a darn fine pot of tea?"

"Yes, I mean apart from that." She laughed and took another sip. She couldn't stop grinning.

"Well, it seems I rescue damsels in distress." His eyes twinkled and locked on hers.

"So you do," she whispered, holding his gaze. A horn honked and they turned to see a car pulling into the drive. "That's my Dustin, right on time."

The minute he pulled in, Dustin knew something wasn't quite right. His mom wasn't sitting in the windowseat as she always did when she knew he was coming. He walked in and was surprised to see her sitting on the couch in her nightclothes next to a curious-looking man that he'd never seen before. "Hey Mema," he said, struggling through the door with two sacks of groceries he'd brought for her. She didn't get up to help him, and then he noticed the plastic bag on her head. He set the groceries on the big table in the middle of the room and moved to her side. "What happened to you? Are you all right?" he asked, eyeing the stranger as he bent to kiss her.

"Hello, lovie," she said, kissing his cheek tenderly. "It seems I had a little accident with the garage door this morning. The wind took it down on my head and knocked me out cold. Mr. McKellen here came along and rescued me."

"Well, I owe you a debt then, sir," Dustin said, putting out his hand to the stranger. He stood and took Dustin's hand, and as he did he put his other hand on Dustin's shoulder. He looked intently into his face.

"I'm just grateful God put me in the right place at the right time, where I could be of help to your mother." Lucy looked at the two men standing face to face. She noticed they were about the same height and had a similar build.

"I meant what I said, sir. I am in your debt. If I can ever aid you in any way, please don't hesitate to call on me." He reached into his jacket pocket. "Here's my card."

Mr. McKellen took it and read it aloud:

"Donegan & Donegan
Celtic Imports
Southfield, Michigan
Dustin L. Donegan, President and CEO."

He slipped the card into a very weathered leather pouch that hung from his belt. The initials LM—which had been engraved on it many years ago—though worn, could still be read. "Donegan and Donegan," he said. "William would be your grandfather then?"

"No sir, William was my great grandfather."

"Was he now?" Mr. McKellen shot a puzzling look at Lucy.

Lucy had never told her sons their father's secret about who William actually was, but she sensed by the look he gave her that this stranger somehow knew it. "Did you know William?" she fished.

"Well enough to know he was a kind and generous man. He passed on before you were born, I guess," he said, looking back at the younger man.

"Yes sir, that's right. Did you ever meet my father?"

"Aye, we met when we were just lads and once again in later life. He did me a favor that goes beyond anything the world could ever repay. You were raised by a great man, son."

"Yes sir, I know."

"I'm proud of you. You've honored your duty to him."

"Thank you, sir," Dustin said, thinking it a strange thing for the man to say.

He turned away from the young man and looked again on Lucy. "Now that you have Dustin here to look after you, I'll be on my way." He picked up his heavy leather coat that was lying over a chair by the door and pulled on a wool skullcap that had been stuffed in one sleeve. "Have another cup of that tea and you'll be just fine."

She reached out her hand and he took it in both of his. "I really don't know how to thank you. You quite possibly saved my life."

"You have already thanked me in ways I can't explain," he said as he kissed the hand he was holding.

"I hope if you're back this way, you'll stop in for a cup of tea."

"If that is my fortune, it will be great," he said softly, looking into her eyes as he backed away, letting her hand slip slowly from his. A chill swept upon her again.

Dustin saw him to the door. "Thank you again, sir. Do you need a lift somewhere? I didn't see a car when I drove in."

"No thank you, son. I don't have far to go."

"I meant what I said. If I can ever be of any assistance, please let me know." Dustin reached to shake his hand one more time, but the stranger did something that caught him totally off guard. Instead of taking his hand, he embraced him for a moment and spoke into his ear.

"Son, you will be of great assistance some day to a lot of people." He winked at Lucy, turned, and walked out the door. They watched him stride down the drive and out onto the road. Neither of them spoke until the snow banks swallowed his form.

"Now that is one strange dude," Dustin said. He looked at his mother. She had a big smile on her face and a dazed look in her eyes, almost like she'd been drinking. The lines of an old Irish ballad were waltzing through her head:

> *I know my love by his way of walking*
> *and I know my love by his way of talking*

"Hey Mom, are you feeling all right?" He hadn't seen her smile much since his father was killed.

"I feel wonderful," she said. As she stood up, the plastic bag that was still balanced on her head slid off and hit the floor. Its contents, now liquefied, splashed all over. She laughed and went for the mop.

"Here, give me that," he said, grabbing the mop from her hands. "I'll clean this up and put the groceries away; you go get dressed. I'll drive you into town and we'll have a doctor look you over."

"I'll take you up on part of that offer. I will go get dressed and let you drive me to town, but I'll pass on the doctor, thank you very much. How about buying me lunch at Clementine's instead?"

"Are you sure you feel up to it?"

"Honey, I told you I feel fine."

"Good, because I want to talk to you about something and the drive into town will be a good time for it."

"Aren't you spending the night?"

"No, sorry, can't this time. I should leave by eight. I've got a lot going on right now."

"Of course you do," Lucy murmured under her breath as she turned and headed for her room. She couldn't remember the last time he had stayed the night. "Maybe I just shouldn't expect it," she thought. But she always did.

They both went about the tasks they had agreed upon and within half an hour were in the car backing out of the drive. "Okay, let's have it," Lucy said as they started the twenty-minute journey to town.

"Mom, you know that I'm busy and can't get out here much," Dustin began.

"Of course I know that, honey."

"I really don't like it that you stay way out here all by yourself."

She became defensive. "I'm sorry you don't like it, but I love being at Twin Willows."

"I know. I know you do. But I worry about you."

"Well, don't. There's nothing to worry about. I'm fine out here."

"Fine? You're Fine? Mom, you could've died today if Mr. McKellen hadn't come along."

"He was a really nice guy, wasn't he?"

"Don't change the subject. See it from my side. I come walking in today and find some stranger with an eight-inch blade hanging from his belt sitting with my mother, who is in her nightclothes and has a nasty lump on her head. For all I knew at first, he could have bopped you on the head and was threatening you in some way."

"Yeah, he threatened me with a cup of tea," she chuckled.

"Mom, I'm being very serious."

"I know you are, honey, but I like where I live and accidents can happen anywhere. God watches over me."

"Like He watched over Dad?"

She hadn't expected that. "Yes, exactly like He watched over your father." She reached out and touched his arm. "You're not angry at God about your father's accident, are you?"

"No, mom, I'm not angry at God. I'm just trying to make a point."

"Well, you're going to have to make it some other way. I appreciate your concern, but really, I'll be fine."

"Okay, Mom, if you're happy, I'll drop the subject for now. Just explain one thing to me: What were you doing outside in just your night clothes?" They rode in silence for a moment. Lucy wasn't sure if she wanted to open this can of worms after the discussion they'd just had, but she didn't want to lie either. "Mom?"

"I... Well, I was..." She stopped then started again. "I went out to... to see..." She stopped again. She was trying to formulate some way to tell this tale without making it seem quite so odd. She decided there was no good way to spin it, so she just blurted it out. "I went outside to see what happened to the little man who tapped on my window and woke me up this morning. He told me he had a message for me, but he wouldn't give it to me unless I gave him whiskey. So I got a thimble and..."

"Mom!" Dustin said loudly. "Slow down. I can't understand you. Did you say a little man woke you up?"

"Yes, that's right."

"You mean a really short guy, like a midget?"

"No, smaller."

"Smaller? How small?"

"Oh, maybe the size of a small rabbit."

"A little man about the size of a rabbit woke you up this morning?" Dustin was squeezing the steering wheel tightly. His whole body had tensed and he was squinting.

"Small rabbit, yes. Look," she said, "I know this sounds nutty, but just listen to me and then we'll talk about it, okay?"

"Go ahead," he said in a deep, authoritative voice that sounded nothing like the way he usually talked to her. She had heard him use this tone once to an older board member in a meeting just after he assumed the position of president of the company. The guy was trying to test his grit, and she was sure he never tried again.

"Well," she continued, "the little man woke me up by tapping on the window. At first I thought it was the cardinal. You remember, I told you about that bird that taps on my window when the birdfeeder goes empty."

"Yeah, sure, I guess. Go on."

"Well, when I opened the curtains, there he was, this little man in a red hat sitting on a branch of the ornamental elm. He motioned for me to open the window, so I did." Dustin stuck his hand out to feel her forehead. "Stop it," she said, swatting it away. "I'm fine. Just listen. I opened the window and said hello, then I told him my name and that I was happy to see him, and he stopped me mid-sentence and told me to hush."

"Oh boy," Dustin blurted out. "Mom, are you being serious?"

"Yes, of course. Please, just listen. He was very rude and told me my blabbing made him forget the message he came to deliver."

"A message? From whom?"

"That's what I asked him. He said his brain got cold and whiskey would help him remember. Thank God I had an old bottle of your father's in the kitchen. I had to find a thimble to put it in so he could drink it. I used your Great Grandma Josephine's little silver thimble with the flower designs pressed into it. Anyway, he drank it right down and then asked me for another because he said he still couldn't remember. I thought to myself, 'he's just being a rascal, and if I...'"

"Mom," Dustin interrupted, "I'm going to ask you one more time: are you for real telling me this?"

"Yes, Dusty, I told you I know how it sounds." He suddenly made a left hand turn onto Blue Star Highway. "Hey, why are you turning here? Clementine's is straight up Phoenix Street. Don't you remember?"

"We're not going to Clementine's right now, Mom. We're going to the emergency room. I think you must have a concussion. You're talking out of your head."

"Oh," she huffed, "I am not." She was hurt and angry. "I knew you wouldn't believe me; that's why I didn't tell you about the little man before when I first saw him."

"Please don't argue with me, Mom. I just want them to check you out. It can't hurt, right? And I'd feel a lot better."

"Oh, all right. I'll go, if it will make you feel better. But I'm not delusional or making this up. You could have at least listened to the whole thing." She sniffed and wiped her cheek.

"I will, Mom," he said, pulling the car up to the emergency entrance, "just as soon as they have a look at that knot on your head."

For the next three hours the South Haven Community Hospital held her captive. After the doctor listened to her explanation of how she'd been knocked out by the garage door and Dustin's accusation of how she was talking out of her head, he examined her and ordered x-rays. She lay in a cold room waiting for someone to take her to radiology, watching as orderlies rolled sick or hurting people past her. She felt dreadful taking up time they could use to treat others. She resigned herself to make the best of it and forgave Dustin for bringing her there. "It was just bad timing," she told herself. "If I could've told him without this other incident looming in his mind, he may have believed me."

Meanwhile, Dustin had gotten hungry and walked to the cafeteria in the basement. He asked the guy taking orders if they would make him a grilled cheese sandwich with a fried egg, grilled onions, and tomato, on whole-wheat. "I don't see why not. It seems to be our specialty today. We'll call you when it's up."

Dustin picked up a carton of milk and set it on his tray, paid at the register, and turned to find a table. It was a small cafeteria: it had a counter with six stools, and five were filled with hospital workers taking their breaks. There were four or five tables in the center and booths along one wall. Visitors or other hospital personnel sat scattered about. As he looked around the room, he noticed a man sitting alone in the very back booth. "What a coincidence," he thought. He walked over to him. "Mr. McKellen," he said, putting out his hand.

"Hello again, son," the man said as they shook hands firmly.

"This is a small world," Dustin remarked.

"Small town, big world, much bigger than most people can even conceive. I'd be most pleased if you'd sit down here with me."

"Sure," Dustin said, sliding into the green plastic-covered seat opposite his host.

"You brought your mom in to be checked out?"

"Yes, sir."

"Did her headache start up again?"

"No, she said she felt fine, but she started talking out of her head about some little man that woke her up this morning. The story was so crazy I thought it was best to have her looked at."

"Just remember, son, what one person thinks is crazy may be someone else's reality."

That response surprised Dustin. "Yeah, sure."

"So how is she doing?"

"They're taking her for an x-ray now."

"No, I meant how is she doing since she lost your father?"

Dustin thought that was a strange question coming from someone who had only met her a few hours ago. "Oh, she's, well, you know, it was hard on her at first, but she's getting on with it."

"Getting on with what?"

Another funny question, but it made him think. What was she getting on with? She had always been all about her family: her husband and her boys. She hadn't really had a job in his lifetime, though he knew she worked before she married his father. She had done a lot of volunteer and charity work over the years, but since she moved to the country, he couldn't think of anything she was doing right now. "Well, she's living out at the farm, and I guess she likes it. She was born in that house, her father—my grandfather—built it, and she says she wants to be there till she dies."

"So is she getting on with living or with dying?"

Dustin felt somehow like he was being scolded. "I don't like her living out there all by herself. I talked to her about it just today. But she's set on it. That's where she wants to stay."

"I've always felt the country is a much better place to be lonely than a city filled with people. Is she seeing anyone?"

"Sir?" Dustin looked hard at him. "You mean like another man?"

"If there isn't one, there can't be another."

"Quite frankly, I don't see where that's your business."

"Why not?"

"Look, I appreciate that you helped her out this morning, but…"

"But you don't want me seeing your mother again?"

Dustin didn't know what to say. He didn't know this guy from Adam. And what he did know seemed odd. He was trying to formulate an eloquent answer when the counter bell rang and the cook called out: "Your chow's ready." He put two plates with sandwiches on the pass bar. Dustin jumped up to get his, thankful for a moment to think.

"Which one is mine?" he asked the cook.

"Doesn't matter. Made 'em both the same."

"But I only ordered one."

"I only made you one. The other one is for your buddy over there."

"You mean he ordered the exact same sandwich as I did?"

"No, you ordered the exact same sandwich as he did."

33 – Waiting

Lucy lay waiting for her turn to again see the overworked doctor, feeling guilty to take up the time he could obviously use to help someone who needed him more. There was a man who rammed a stick in his eye while out hunting and another man who needed stitches because, while splitting firewood, the axe he was wielding careened off a knot and nicked his leg. There was an elderly lady with pneumonia and a local teacher who had the flu. There had also been an accident at the Bohn Aluminum plant downtown; a man severed part of his finger. They rolled him past her holding his injured hand, with its bloody bandage, high in the air. The severed part of his finger was lying on ice in a clear plastic container sitting on his chest.

Lucy prayed for them one by one as she lay there waiting her turn. She prayed for herself too. She asked for wisdom and guidance on how to tell Dustin about the little man. *That little rascal has certainly turned my world upside down,* she thought. How absolutely astonishing he seemed to her now. No wonder Dustin thought she was delusional. But her thoughts didn't stay focused on the spry little fellow. They turned to the other man that had appeared suddenly in her life that day. She wondered if she would see him again. She closed her eyes and saw his lean form leaning over her, those green eyes peering into her more deeply than anyone had looked in quite a while. She opened her eyes all of a sudden. A feeling of guilt had come upon her. Was she betraying her husband by thinking about this man?

"Nonsense," she said aloud. She knew who authored such thoughts, and she knew how to dispense with them. She closed her eyes and prayed once more. She thanked the Lord for sending the stranger to save her. She prayed for his wellbeing, and that the meeting with his son would be soon and go well.

A young nurse roused her. "Mrs. Donegan?"

"Yes. Oh, hello, dear."

"Hi, I'm Julie. How are you feeling?"

"I'm fine, really. I told my son I didn't need to come down here, but he insisted."

"He's concerned for you. I met him out in the hall while you were in radiology. He seems sweet."

Lucy just nodded her head while holding tight with her lips the thermometer Julie had placed under her tongue. *So, Dustin, enchanted another one, have you?* she thought. Then she spoke to her love. *Maybe he didn't inherit your good looks, my darling, though he is just as strikingly handsome in his own way. But he surely inherited that easy charm you had, which the ladies found so irresistible.* This she spoke with her thoughts to the world beyond as she looked at the beautiful young girl who stood before her. She sighed, remembering her lost love. She missed him in so many ways, but especially at a time like this.

Julie went about her duties taking Lucy's temperature, pulse, and blood pressure. "The doctor is looking at your x-rays right now. He asked me to tell you he'd be coming by in about ten minutes."

"Wonderful. Then I can get out of your hair. You all have more important things to do than nurse my tiny bump."

"It's not so tiny. Your son was right to bring you here to get checked over." She recorded Lucy's vitals on the chart. She turned quickly to leave and slammed right into Dustin, who was just entering the little partitioned cubicle.

"Whoa! Hey there," he said, laughing as he grabbed hold of her.

"I'm so sorry," she blushed. They both stood a brief moment smiling at each other. She finally took a step back and smiled at Lucy. "I just told your mom that the doctor would be in shortly."

"So how's she doing?" he asked.

"Hey, I'm right here. You could ask me that?" Lucy thought, watching the two of them dance around each other.

"All her vitals are good and she says she feels fine. So if her x-ray is negative, I'm guessing you'll be out of here soon."

"That's great." Dustin's smile followed her as she started walking away.

She stopped, turned and said to them both, "I'll be back when I see the doctor is here."

"Fantastic," he said. He continued watching her as she carried her tray into the next partitioned space and disappeared behind its curtain.

"Where did you get off to?" Lucy asked when he finally looked at her.

"I went downstairs to the cafeteria to grab a bite."

"Oh, I'm glad you got something."

He bent down and kissed her cheek. "I had a grilled cheese toe sandwich." She knew it was his favorite, for she had made him many while he was growing up. He had given it that name when he was little: the *toe* stood for tomato, onion, and egg.

"Was it good?"

"Not as good as you make, Mema, though it was their specialty today."

"Really?"

"That's what the café guy told me. I thought he was being sarcastic until I ran into your friend Mr. McKellen, and guess what? He had just ordered the same sandwich."

"You're kidding?"

"No. Weird, isn't it?"

"Mr. McKellen is here?"

"Yep, and did you hear me say he ordered the exact same sandwich?"

"Odd."

"That's what I thought."

"Did you talk with him?"

"Of course. He invited me to sit with him and we had a good old heart-to-heart."

"Really? Why was he here? Was he visiting friends or family?"

"No." Dustin paused, shaking his head. "He said he was here to see me."

"To see you?"

"Yep. Wait, it gets better."

"Mrs. Donegan?" Dr. Buck said, walking up to Lucy's bed. "Oh good, your son is here."

"Hello, Doctor," Lucy said half-heartedly, turning her attention toward him. Although she had been waiting for him to show up, now she wished he could have waited a few more moments; she was anxious to hear what Dustin had to say.

The doctor didn't notice her response anyway. He was tired and had three other things on his mind. He picked up her chart and looked at the results Julie had written down. "Well, everything looks fine: vitals are good, and your x-rays show no sign of fracture." He passed the chart off to Julie, who had rushed to his side at that moment. "With this type of head injury, there's always the possibility of concussion. It's hard to say if anything will come of it. You may be just fine. But then again, something could come up." He continued talking as he shined a light in her eyes again. "After all, you took a hard enough blow to render you unconscious. That's quite a jar to the brain. What I would like to do is admit you to the hospital for a brief period of observation. I'm mostly concerned about the confusion you experienced."

"I didn't experience any confusion," Lucy said sharply, shooting an icy look toward her son.

"Mom," Dustin retorted, "you were talking about seeing a little man."

"Yes, Dustin, I was. But I wasn't confused about it, you were." Lucy knew she had an uphill battle to fight, and she had supplied the other side with ammunition.

Another nurse came rushing up and tapped the doctor's shoulder. She said something softly to him that Lucy couldn't hear. "Okay, folks, decide what you want to do. I'll be back in a few moments." He went off with the other nurse while Julie remained at the end of the bed.

"Mom, look, I don't want to argue with you. I think you should stay, just overnight maybe. You heard him say that you may have a concussion."

"Or not," Lucy shot back.

"I don't want you going back to the farm and staying all alone tonight; I've already told you I can't stay."

"Dustin, I'll be fine. You can call and check on me later."

"Not good enough, Mom. I'm leaving around eight, and you shouldn't be alone tonight."

"Well, I'm not staying here overnight, and that's that."

"Yes, you are, Mom. Please don't argue with me on this."

"No, I am not," she said through clenched teeth. She needed a diversion to give her time to think, and she spotted one. "Julie, you see how stubborn this man is. It's a trait inherited from his father."

"I thought maybe he inherited it from you," Julie smiled.

"Way to go Nurse Julie. Give me five on that," Dustin said, holding his open hand up for her. Julie swatted it gently away with the back of the clipboard she was holding.

"Oh, you are a traitor to your sex," Lucy joked.

"But not to my profession."

"That a girl! Tell it like it is," Dustin hooted.

"Cheer all you want, Dusty, but the fact is I'm not staying," Lucy declared, crossing her arms on her chest.

"The fact is, Mother Dear, you are."

"Dustin," Julie interjected, "it *is* up to your mother. I know you're concerned about her, but she is lucid and it is her decision."

"Hey, whose side are you on, anyway?" Dustin protested.

"That's a good girl," Lucy said. "Slip me that five."

"Mom," Dustin chuckled, "It's 'slip me some skin' or 'give me five.' She's always mixing up sayings like that," he explained to Julie, shaking his head.

"You can't blame me for that. I'm talking out of my head, remember?"

"Yes, Mom, I do remember; that's why I want you to stay."

"Oh, back to this, are we?" Lucy sighed.

Dustin was tired of arguing. He was ready to give up when an idea came to him. "Julie, I'm wondering if you could help us out here. Do you know of anyone I could hire to spend the night with my mother, a nurse perhaps?"

"Dusty, I don't need a nurse," Lucy exclaimed.

"Mrs. Donegan, please. You shouldn't be alone tonight. To be honest, I could use some extra cash; they've cut my hours back here at the hospital and I'm still paying off my school loans. I would be happy to stay with you if you'd like."

"Oh honey, really? That would be wonderful, though I don't think it's necessary. But it would certainly settle the issue between me and my son."

"Yes, ma'am."

"I don't live here in town; it's about a twenty minute drive on country roads. Dusty can draw you a map."

"That's not necessary. I see here on your chart that you live on 62nd Street."

"That's right, just off 102nd Avenue."

"I think I know right where you are. There's an old school on that corner, right?"

"That's right, Crow school. I'm the first house north of the school, on the west side of the road. The mailbox says 'Twin Willows.' How do you know that area?"

"I'm living with my Aunt and Uncle in Lacota, on 60th Street."

"I'm only three miles from Lacota. Who are your aunt and uncle?"

"The Coles. Do you know them?"

"Heavens, yes. I went to Crow school with just about all your aunts and uncles. You must be Ray's girl, am I right?"

"Yes, I am. But I don't remember him at all. He was killed when I was only a baby."

"I remember, dear. I was heartbroken when I heard. Your father was a real sweetheart. Your Aunt Ginny and I were best friends in grade school. I see her from time to time when she comes back to visit her family. I recall she showed me a picture of Ray once holding you when you were just born."

"Small world," Julie said.

"Small town, big world," Dustin murmured.

"My shift is over at five. I'll go right home afterwards and pack a few things." She turned to Dustin: "Here's my number. Call me when you're just about ready to leave tonight. It will take me less than ten minutes to get over there. I'll stay tomorrow until your mom can arrange for someone else."

"I have a better idea," Dustin said, tucking her number into his pocket. "Come about six thirty and have dinner with us. I'm cooking tonight so Mom can rest. How's baked salmon with fettuccine Alfredo sound?"

"Is the sauce from scratch? I'm part Italian and pretty particular about my pasta." She smiled playfully.

"Yes, ma'am. I make it with fresh garlic and real cream."

"It's a deal then."

"Oh, good," Lucy said. She noticed the looks the two younger people had been giving one another and decided that everyone was getting something they wanted from this arrangement. It should be a lovely evening.

Doctor Buck came back, and after giving her a list of symptoms she should watch for and advising her that she should see her own doctor as soon as possible, he signed the chart to release her. She thanked him, dressed, and waited for an orderly to come wheel her to the front door. She tried refusing the wheelchair, but was told it was the hospital's policy. Finally, a young man showed up and pushed her to the front of the building where she again sat and waited. This time she was waiting for Dustin to bring the car around. She knew it would be a few minutes because he had lingered behind to have another word with Julie to make sure everything was set for dinner.

People came in and out, hurrying by her without a nod or a hello. She smiled, but no one seemed to notice her. She felt as if she were becoming invisible, like she didn't really belong in this world anymore. This feeling had been growing in her for some time now, ever since the little man waved to her.

She hated to leave home in case he showed up again. Her hunch that he might have a message for her had been right. But what did it mean? Who was coming for her? Who was she waiting for?

"Waiting for someone?" A voice roused her from her deep thoughts.

"Pardon me?" she said softly, turning to see if someone had indeed spoken to her.

"Are you waiting for someone?" Mr. McKellen repeated, taking another step to stand beside her.

She was surprised to see him. "Dustin," she answered. "He went to get the car."

"He is a fine lad. We had lunch together."

"Yes, he told me." She wanted to say more, but she felt tongue-tied, like a schoolgirl encountering a boy she had a crush on. In the awkward silence, he broke into a wonderful smile. It was as if all the sunlight that had made its way into the drab lobby gathered around him.

"How are you feeling?"

She realized she was sitting in a wheelchair and hopped up. "I'm fine, really. They insisted I sit in this thing. It's their policy." Even as she said it, the blood rushed to the top of her head and she started to sway.

"It's a fine policy, don't you think?" he said, taking her under the arms and helping her to sit back down.

"Whoa," she said. "It's a wonderful policy," she laughed at herself. He squatted down next to her chair so she wouldn't have to look up at him. "I was wondering, Mr. McKellen..." She hesitated then found the nerve to ask, "if you would be free to have dinner with us this evening?"

"Us?"

"Yes. Dustin has hired a nice young nurse named Julie to stay with me this evening. He'll be leaving to get back to the city after we eat, and he didn't want to leave me alone."

"Good on him."

"She's coming over around six-thirty. Dusty insists on doing the cooking tonight. I think he mentioned baked salmon. Do you like salmon, Mr. McKellen?"

"I do, yes, though I usually have it alone, cooked on a stick over a camp fire."

"Then you should try it baked in the company of friends."

"Well now, that is a mighty tempting offer."

"Dusty is an excellent cook, really." She continued to plead her case.

"Is he now? Does he take after you on that count?"

She didn't get the chance to answer. Dustin came rushing in through the door. "Okay Mom, let's go." He noticed the man crouched down beside her and stopped short. "Mr. McKellen."

"Hello again, son."

"Dusty, I've just invited Mr. McKellen to dine with us tonight."

"You have, hunh? And did he accept?"

"No, not yet. You go on and talk him into it, will you?"

"Mom, he may have something else to do. Maybe we shouldn't twist his arm." Dustin stared at the man uncomfortably.

He held Dustin's stare as he said pleasantly, "I am afraid my arm cannot be twisted, not tonight." He then gazed back at Lucy and said softly, "So then, will you give me a rain check on that dinner?"

"Of course I will."

"Fine then, I'll be in touch. Meantime, don't put a lot on your stomach tonight. Drink what is left of that tea I made for you and get plenty of rest. Your body will heal just fine if you don't overdo it for a couple of days."

"Thank you." She was disappointed, but she knew he was right. She hadn't eaten anything all day, and yet she didn't feel at all hungry.

Now that the strange man had refused the invitation, Dustin relaxed. "Okay mom, let's get going." He went behind her chair and started pushing her toward the exit. Mr. McKellen walked to the door and held it open for them. He winked at Lucy as she rolled by.

She smiled and blushed. "Go with God," she whispered.

"And you," he mouthed back.

After a quick stop at the market just across the street from the hospital—to pick up a head of fresh romaine for the salad—and another brief stop at the wine store, they were finally on the way home. Lucy waited patiently in the car while Dustin completed his shopping. She felt as if she had been waiting all day for one thing or another. She wanted to finish telling him about the little man and his strange message, and she wanted to hear more about his lunch with Mr. McKellen.

"So what did Mr. McKellen have to say, Mom?" Dustin asked.

"I was just going to ask you the same thing," she giggled. "You started to tell me about what the two of you talked about at lunch, remember?"

"I remember," he said uneasily.

"Well?"

"The guy is strange, Mom."

Lucy took offense. "What do you mean?"

"I mean like psycho strange."

"Dustin, it's not like you to say such a thing, especially about someone who has been so kind."

"I know. But mom, the guy is... Let's just say, very unusual."

"Oh for Pete's sake, just tell me what he said."

"Well, first off, he asked me if you were seeing anyone."

"He did?"

"Yeah."

"So that's why you think he's strange, because he showed some interest in me? Must be a real lunatic, hunh, to show interest in me?" Now her Irish blood was rising up against the part that was English, and she felt her face getting hot.

"Come on, Mom. Calm down. You know that's not what I meant."

"Well, please get on with it, then. Just what did you mean?"

"For instance, I asked who it was that he came to the hospital to see, and he said me. He had come to see me. I asked how he knew I would be there, and he said because he knew I would be concerned about you and would want to have you looked over. I thought, 'Okay, so here it comes: he's thought about it and he's going to ask me for money or something for helping you out.'"

"Did he?" Lucy asked.

"No, he didn't ask me for anything. He said he wanted to give *me* something."

"Give you something? What?"

"This." He reached into his pocket and pulled out a wonderful, old ring. He dropped it in her hand. She gasped; its magnificence took her breath away. She turned it over and over in her palm. It was amazing—platinum, she guessed, finely engraved with symbols and runes up both sides and around a stunning blue gem set in the center. The gem was cut so as to magnify the coat of arms engraved underneath it. "Spectacular," she said.

"Isn't it?" He snatched it from her hand and put it back into his pocket.

"I don't understand. Why did he give that to you? It must be worth a fortune."

"I think it must be. I'm going to take it to Ian Collier tomorrow and let him take a look at it. Mom, think hard. Have you ever seen it before?"

"Me?" She *had* gotten a weird sensation when he handed it to her, like she had indeed held it before. But she would certainly recall if she had ever seen such a magnificent object in the past, wouldn't she? "Why?" she asked.

"Well, when I saw it, I told him I couldn't accept it and tried to give it back. He told me it was mine, that my father wanted me to have it."

"Your father?" Lucy questioned.

"That's what he said. I asked him, 'If my father wanted me to have it, why hadn't he given it to me himself?' He said that I would understand someday, but for now I needed to keep it safe. Now this is where it gets even further out there. He said if I wore it, it would attract knowledge—and anything else I needed from the universe—to complete the task I was created for."

"Wow!" Lucy gushed.

"See what I mean about him, Mom? Strange!"

"Okay, okay, maybe a little. But that doesn't make him evil. I'm going to ask him about all of this when he comes over."

"What do you mean 'when he comes over'? I thought he turned down the invitation for dinner tonight."

"He did. He took a rain check. I'm going to cook dinner for him when I'm feeling stronger. He said he'd be in touch."

"Mom, I don't want you alone with him. Do you understand me?"

"Dustin, don't talk to me that way. I'm not a child, and I'm not that old either. If I want to keep company with Mr. McKellen, I will. He may be different from most people, but that doesn't make him evil or dangerous. Let's not forget, he probably saved my life this morning."

"You're right, Mom. I'm sorry about my tone of voice. How's this?" He began again, "I would prefer if you aren't alone with him."

"That was much better, and I have noted your concern." Lucy's head was throbbing. They were almost home and she had not yet discussed the little man with him. It would probably be better to wait now. Besides, there were still some questions she had for him about his lunch meeting. "Did he tell you where he lives?"

"No. He did say that he's only visiting this area, and while he's here he's staying at the Spicebush not far from Twin Willows. Have you heard of it?"

"Of course I've heard of it. That's the name of the little river back in the woods, across the road from the farm."

"He's staying in the woods in the middle of winter?"

"Well, he does look the rugged, outdoorsy type."

"I'll say," he smirked.

"What else did he have to say to you?"

"He looked at me sort of Svengali-like and started talking in a language I've never heard before. He said it would take too long to translate, but it would all come to me in time. Poor guy, maybe he's one of the 'Nam vets who saw too much action." They were pulling into the drive now, so Lucy decided to wait on her tale until after she had a cup of tea and time to think about everything.

The tea was from the pot Mr. McKellen had brewed earlier. She warmed it in the old kettle and sat down in the rocker by the fireplace. She sipped it as she watched the sun send ribbons of color over the western horizon. After only two sips, she felt relaxed and rejuvenated. Her headache was gone, and she felt a warm glow inside her.

Dustin went outside to shovel the drive and walkways. He also wanted to make a space for Julie to park so she wouldn't have to move her car when he got ready to leave that evening. Lucy turned the rocker so she could watch him out the east windows. He was working on moving a snow bank that she had piled up a few days ago. He was widening the drive for two cars to fit side by side, up close to the north end of the garage. As she watched him, she saw something fall into the snow near to where he was working. He didn't seem to notice it. She got up and moved closer to the window to get a better look. It was a small hunk of ice. She crooked her head to see from where it had fallen, and she almost fell over.

"Oh God," she said aloud as she watched the little man jumping up and down on a large chunk of ice that had formed on the roof of the old garage.

"Oh God," she said again, making a beeline for the door. She ran outside and screamed her son's name. Surprised, he stopped shoveling and took a step in her direction. A rumbling caught his attention and he looked up to see a large block of ice slide from the garage and land with a thud right in the spot where he had just been standing. "Whoa!" he said. "Thank you, Jesus."

"Dusty, are you all right?"

"I'm fine. Boy, that was a close one. Look at that hunk of ice." He kicked at it with his foot. "What is it you wanted, Mom?"

She thought it might not be such a good idea to tell him right now just what she had seen, so she simply said, "Oh nothing, it can wait."

"I'm almost done here. I'll be in soon. Go back in the house; you don't have a coat on." It was cold, so she obeyed. She sat back down in the rocker and offered Jesus her own thanks. She wondered if the little man had actually been trying to hurt him.

Dustin came in the house a few moments later, took off his boots, hung his jacket, and walked to the fireplace. Rubbing his hands in the heated air above the hearth, he asked, "Mom, what did you want when you came out and called me?"

"What did I want?" *Now is as good a time as any*, she thought. "I wanted you to move so we wouldn't have matching lumps on our heads."

Dustin looked puzzled. "How did you know that ice was going to fall?"

"Because I saw..." She stopped herself. She took the last sip of tea for courage and said, "Because I saw the little man jumping up and down on the roof." Dustin stood like a statue with his hand clasped mid-rub in front of him.

Lucy rose, went to him, and took hold of his hands. "Honey, I know this is weird, but would you please just sit down and listen to me?" He backed up and lowered himself slowly into a chair at the table. "Good boy," she said. "Here, before I tell you about what happened this morning, read this." She handed him the small, green velvet journal in which she had recorded the other sighting she had had of the little menace.

He opened the journal and read the entries. As he did, he thought to himself, "My mother is losing her mind. I better call Uncle Freddie. He'll know what to do."

She stood next to him waiting for him to finish reading, and when she saw his eyes stray from the page, she exclaimed, "Oh good, now let me finish telling you about this morning." He sat quietly listening as she laid out all the events as they had occurred. "When I opened my eyes, I was lying on the couch, and Mr. McKellen was here." She waited for a response, but he said nothing. "What do you think, Dusty? Do you believe me now?"

He took hold of her hands. "I think this is like one of the fairy tales you used to tell Mike and me when we were little. Remember when we would drive down here from the city to see Grandma and Grandpa or go to Aunt Sue's?"

"Sure, I remember." She was hurt. "But Dusty, I'm not making this up."

He ignored that. "You told some great stories, Mom. We always said that you should write them down. So why don't you do that. Why don't you write all this down." He picked up the journal and handed it to her. "I need to go get cleaned up and start dinner. Julie will be here in about forty minutes. Do you want me to get anything for you before I start? More tea?"

"No, I'm fine." She felt disappointed by his comments. But then again, what did she expect him to say. "Maybe I *will* write it all down," she thought. "I'll write all of it, whatever happens from here on out. Who knows where this is going. It may get even stranger, but at least there'll be some record of it." She didn't know if he believed her or not, but she realized it didn't matter. This, after all, was her story.

34 – Birthday

It had been a week since her accident with the door. She had had no further interactions with or sightings of the little man nor heard from Mr. McKellen. Lynn came to stay with her for a couple of days, so Dustin was appeased. Now he was visiting again; it was his birthday weekend. Although she knew he was concerned, she also knew he hadn't come just to see her. He once again invited Julie for dinner.

Lucy liked Julie very much; she was down to earth and had a really sweet heart. She was happy that Dustin was showing interest in someone again. She had worried about him. Soon after he went off to school in Dublin, the girl whom he had dated all through high school—and whom everyone assumed he would marry someday—met someone else. Lucy could tell he was heartbroken, though he never admitted it. He poured himself into his studies and sports and had little time left over to think about dating. She knew he had dated other women from time to time; you couldn't be a young, good-looking top executive in a big city without getting mentioned in the social columns of the local newspapers and magazines whenever you stepped out with a beautiful woman on your arm. But there was never anyone he was serious enough about to bring home to Mom. Until now, she thought.

At his birthday dinner, Lucy sat quietly eating her meal and letting the young people get to know each other. After they had desert, a German chocolate cake Lucy baked especially for him, she mentioned that she'd read in the *Lakeshore Flashes* that a salsa band was playing at the Dutch Mill that weekend. She knew that he loved to dance like his father had. He passed the idea by Julie and she readily agreed to go. They asked Lucy if she'd like to come with them, but she knew it was only out of politeness. So she bid them run along. Besides, it always left her melancholy, missing Michael, when she watched others dance.

After the dishes were done and food stored away, she sat by the fire, stared into the flames, and thought about another dinner she hoped to have soon.

Dustin told her that he showed the ring Mr. McKellen had given him to an acquaintance of his who dealt in fine jewelry from around the world. Ian Collier had been a close, personal friend of his grandfather's as well as a trusted colleague of his father's, so Dustin had no doubt as to the quality of the man's word. He confirmed what they already suspected, that the ring was extremely valuable. It was of the finest platinum, and the gem was a very rare azure diamond, masterfully and unusually cut to display an ornate coat of arms, skillfully reverse engraved, on the underside. "I am quite sure this ring must have been made for a king or otherwise prominent person," Ian told him. He took several pictures of it and promised to show them to some other experts he was acquainted with, top appraisers and curators from around the world, to see if they had an idea of its origin. Dustin requested that his identity and the ring's whereabouts be kept secret.

In the meantime, Lucy had taken Dustin up on his suggestion to write a book and worked diligently on it, sometimes into the wee hours. She began it by simply describing what her days were like since her husband died and she'd moved to Twin Willows. She recorded everything she could remember about the little man who had, at her first glance of him, changed her life. She also made mention of the man who had saved her from freezing to death and of the ring he had given to her son. As she wrote, she realized how very little she knew about him and how much more she wanted to know. "How can I be so enthralled with someone I hardly know?" she asked herself.

She brought the tale along in her book as far as she could and now sat waiting for the next chapter to reveal itself.

The fire was dying down and a chill was coming on the air, so she rose from the rocker to get more wood. Dustin had left the heavy garage door up, and as she walked by it to the woodpile she heard footsteps crunching on the cold snow in the driveway. She glanced out into the night. Resting in the dark sky over the drive between the two twin willows, the crescent moon hung luminously, and under it walked a man. Lucy knew immediately who it was and her heart leaped. "Mr. McKellen, what a nice surprise. How are you?"

He removed his hat, laid his hand on his heart, and bowed to her. "Standing here before you eases any burdens that I may carry." He took her hand in his and brought it to his lips. A chill ran through her. "You are cold. I shan't keep you in the chill of this night."

"I just walked out to get more wood for the fire. Would you like to come in for a while?" He smiled and she nervously added, "I'm waiting for Dustin to get back from the Dutch Mill. He took Julie dancing. There's a pot of tea steeping on the stove."

"Go on in out of the cold. I'll fetch the wood." She smiled and cheerfully nodded.

She rushed through the house into the kitchen and poured two cups of tea. When she carried them into the breezeway, he was kneeling at the hearth tending the fire. "Your house smells wonderful. It reminds me of my mother's house in Ohio when I was a lad."

"What a nice thing to say, thank you. It's probably the pot roast lingering in the air. I made one for dinner tonight because my son was coming and it's his favorite."

"Mine too."

"Would you like me to fix you a plate?"

"I wouldn't want to cause you any trouble."

"Oh please, I would be happy to do it." He smiled and nodded. He was staring into her eyes, looking deep into her. She was caught in his gaze and didn't move until he blinked. Slowly she backed away, then turned and rushed into the kitchen.

After turning on the oven, she pulled an iron skillet from the drawer under it. Into this she put a heaping scoop of leftover mashed potatoes and a good-sized pile of baby carrots, then she slid it into the oven. On a top burner she set a small pot of gravy into which she sank two thick slices of the roast, making sure to capture as many of the onions and mushrooms as she could find to cover them. She lidded this pot and turned the burner to medium. She set the timer for seven minutes and walked back to find her very welcome guest sitting in the rocker in front of the fire. She thought she saw a tear rolling down his cheek.

"Mr. McKellen, what is it?"

"Please, call me Lance," he said, turning to face her and holding her again with his eyes. She saw in them great joy and great sadness. She reached out her hand and touched his cheek. He put his hand on top of hers and moved it to his lips. Closing his eyes, he kissed her palm over and over then folded her hand around the kisses and moved it from his lips, putting his other hand around it as well. "I've not stopped thinking about you."

"I've been thinking about you too," she whispered breathlessly, her body atingle. Suddenly feeling guilty, she put her head down and stepped back away from him.

"What is it?" he asked.

"I was thinking of my husband."

"Ah yes, Michael. Of course you were, for he is part of your heart. That is as it should be. I have held in my heart a woman that I could not be with for many years while she loved another."

"Is she the mother of your son?"

"Yes, that's right." He smiled now and his eyes twinkled. "Today is my son's birthday."

"Really? It's Dustin's birthday today as well," she proclaimed. "My, we certainly seem to have a lot in common." Again he held her with his eyes. "I better go in and check on your plate."

"This night I am truly blessed," he said as she retreated into the kitchen.

When she took the mashed potatoes from the oven, she put in three of Myra's special recipe soda biscuits to warm while she prepared his plate. She mounded the potatoes on one side, making a well to hold the gravy. Then she laid the meat slices on the opposite side—one staggered on top of the other—and spread the mushrooms and onions on top. Over these she poured the gravy. She made a neat little pile of the hot carrots in the room left on the plate and sprinkled them lightly with a mix of brown sugar and cinnamon. On a separate, smaller plate she placed a scoop of Irish butter and the three nicely warmed biscuits.

"Come wash up," she called to him, "and I'll set out your plate." They passed each other coming in and going out of the kitchen, and her body felt drawn to his. She sat at the table waiting for him, sipping her tea. She ran her thumb over the palm of her hand where he had kissed it.

When he sat down, he spread his hands over his plate, lifted his head, and spoke quietly in a foreign language: "*Tika wa potu noturum. Aved noturum. Da avid tika nu da avid camra tiju.*" She lowered her head as he spoke, assuming it to be a prayer, and visions filled her thoughts. First she saw the vegetables growing and being harvested, and then she saw a cow grazing and then being slaughtered. She even saw herself preparing the food. When he was done, he winked at her and smiled.

"What language was that you were praying in?" she asked.

"It is the old language of our people, spoken aloud now by only a few. I pray over my meals with it lest I forget how blessed I am."

She watched with joy and contentment in her heart as he devoured the food on his plate. When he was finished, he thanked her and she carried his plate to the sink, bringing back the teapot. "I have not had a home cooked meal like that in many years. It is a good thing, I suspect, for if I knew a meal like that was waiting for me, prepared by the hands of a beautiful woman, I fear my work would go untended." He winked at her again and hoisted his cup.

"And what work is that again?"

"'Tis the work of a Guardian."

"A guardian? Do you mean like a security guard?"

He laughed. "Yes, I guess that's right. I am a security guard."

"Where is it you work?"

"Well, tonight I work here. I'm guarding you."

Now it was her turn to laugh. "Guarding me? From who?"

"Not from who, from what."

"From what, then?"

"Loneliness," he said softly, looking into her eyes. "Am I doing a good job?"

"Yes," she whispered. "You're doing a very fine job."

"Good. Then let's not talk." He fell to his knees in front of her. "I have waited so long for this night. I want to kiss you. May I?"

Her eyes answered yes as his lips moved toward hers. He gently captured her mouth, filled her with himself until her thoughts did not exist; only the kiss between them was real. As his mouth left hers, she fell back to her body. She gasped for breath. He stood and took her up in his arms. She knew what he wanted. She wanted it too. He carried her to her bed, and they lost themselves in each other. She denied him nothing and he gave her everything. She was remade.

She lay in his arms in the afterglow of their lovemaking. "Are you happy, my lady?"

"I am more than that. I am renewed."

"Joy is once again mine," he said. "I was wondering if I may have yet another recompense."

"Whenever you are ready."

"I am ready now." He kissed her tenderly. "Ready for a piece of that chocolate cake I saw in the kitchen." His eyes twinkled.

"I baked it for Dustin's birthday. It's German chocolate, his favorite."

"Mine too." He rolled on his side, raising his torso and resting his head on his hand. His other hand played with her hair. "I cannot tell you how long it has been since I have had a slice. When I was young, Mrs. Lundy, the lady who played organ at our church, would bake one for my birthday every year. Dear sweet woman, I haven't thought of her in ages."

"I'm so glad you've had good memories and that you're sharing them with me. I hope you'll have another to carry with you from this night."

"You don't have to hope for that. It is already so." He leaned forward and captured her mouth again.

The kiss over, Lucy stood, wrapped in her housecoat, slipped into her slippers, and went off to the kitchen leaving him to dress. As she was cutting the cake, Dusty and Julie came laughing through the door. Lucy had forgotten about them. "Mema, you're up and sneaking a piece of my cake, I see. Cut me one while you're at it, please. Would you like a slice, Julie?"

"No thanks, I should be getting home. Thank you very much for dinner, Mrs. Donegan."

"Did you have a nice time tonight, love?"

"I had a wonderful time," Lance said, entering the kitchen from the opposite direction still buttoning his shirt, unaware she had been talking to Julie. He walked up behind Lucy and kissed her neck.

Dustin's eyes almost popped from his head. "Mr. McKellen!"

Lance looked up and smiled. "Well hello, son."

"What are you doing here?"

"I stopped in to see your beautiful mother. She fed me, bedded me, and now she's giving me cake." He put his arms around her waist. "Happy Birthday."

Dustin started to rush toward him. Julie grabbed his arm and Lucy stepped in front of him with a plate of cake. "Here's your slice, lovie," she said anxiously. "Let's all go sit in the breezeway, shall we?" Julie tugged on his arm and he backed out of the kitchen, still eyeing the man that stood by his mother.

"Lance," she whispered, turning to face him, "I don't think it was such a good idea to tell Dusty about…"

"About our lovemaking?"

"Well, yes. I am his mother after all."

"Aye, and I'm his..." he paused abruptly. "I'm his mother's lover, am I not?"

"Of course you are."

"Would you have me lie about it?"

"No, Lance."

"Lucy, there is no time to play games. Time is getting very short. If people would realize that, they could start setting things right."

"Of course you're right, my love. But I am his mother and he doesn't know you that well, so please forgive his behavior."

"Dustin is a man. He can make his own apologies." He squeezed her to him. "May I have my cake now?" He smiled at her and it made everything right again.

He ate the cake like he was making love to it. You could tell his mouth celebrated every bite. Lucy sat watching him; they all did. When he was done, he stood, took up his plate and Dustin's, and carried them to the kitchen.

"Mom, I'm going to follow Julie to Lacota then keep on going back to Detroit. I'll call you tomorrow."

"But I thought you were going to stay."

"Under the circumstances, Mom, I think it's best if I leave."

"Dusty, please don't."

"Dustin, I think you should stay with your mother tonight. I'm leaving in a little while, and I know she wants you here," Lance said, returning to the table.

"You're leaving in a little while? It's almost 2:00 a.m. Where are you going? You don't even have a car here."

"Not all things can be told right now."

"Not all things can be told? Well, I wish you would've thought of that one before you told me you bedded my mother."

Lance looked him in the eyes. "I'm sorry if my telling you that offended you. I've been away from your type of civilization for a long time. I guess I've forgotten the convention of 'beating around the bush.' Please accept my apology. I only meant to speak the truth. I love your mother very much."

"Well, excuse me for saying so, sir, but you've only known her—or more to the point," he gave a sideways glance at his mother—"*she* has only known *you* for a little more than a week."

"We aren't children, son. Time is an enemy to us."

"I'm not sure what that means. I'm not sure what half the things you say really mean." He looked down and shook his head. "Julie, toss me your keys. I'll go out and start your car so it warms up. I need some air."

Lance watched him as he walked out the door. "He's a good lad. I hope he'll understand someday and forgive me. God knows my will would have had things differently." Now it was Lucy who didn't understand what he meant. He saw her confused look and smiled. "I was wondering if I might have another cup of tea before I leave."

"Certainly, I'll go make some. Julie, would you like a cup?"

"No thanks, Mrs. Donegan."

"So Julie, it's a nurse you are. That's a noble profession. I'm Lance McKellen; they've forgotten to introduce us." He bowed his head to her.

"I think they had other things on their mind." She smiled and bowed her head to him.

"I guess so," he said. His eyes showed himself to her and she smiled.

"Dustin has told me a little about you."

"I'm afraid that's all he knows. Just what is it you think of our young lad?"

"He's very sweet." She felt the need to defend him. "Please don't take his reaction to you as being a harsh judgment. He's taken on a lot since his father died. He worries about his mother and her living alone. I'm sure once he's had time to think about it, he'll be happy she has someone now."

"Ah yes, but alas I cannot stay. I'll be gone again this night."

"You're going away?" Lucy asked. Suddenly sickened, she slumped into the chair next to him.

He took hold of her hands. "I only had a small window of time to see you, and I did not want to waste even a second of it." She saw the same happy sad look fill his eyes. Julie sat watching, wishing she could disappear. She liked Lucy and understood her to be an unusual woman, but these were private moments.

"Will you come back?" Lucy whispered, afraid to hear his answer.

"Yes, my love, but not for a while. When I do, I'll ask you to go with me. I had to see if it could be more than just a memory you loved." She looked confused again. "You will understand all this very soon, I promise." He took her hands to his lips and kissed them.

Dustin came in the door and Julie jumped up and grabbed her coat. "Is my car ready? I should be getting home. It was nice meeting you, Mr. McKellen. Good night, Mrs. Donegan." She hurried out the door.

"I'm going to follow her home, Mom. I'll be right back." He didn't wait for a response. As soon as the door closed, Lucy fell into Lance's arms. He gave her a kiss to seal his promise to return.

Dustin made sure Julie got home safely over the icy roads and returned straight away. When he turned down 62nd Street off 102nd Avenue, he saw a man in the headlights of his car standing atop the stone across from the old school. It was Mr. McKellen. He stopped the car, rolled down the window, and asked, "Do you need a lift somewhere?"

"Good lad," Mr. McKellen said, reaching through the window to pat his shoulder. "I was hoping you would stop. I wanted to speak with you privately."

"Come on. Get in the car."

What was said to Dustin that night he never revealed to his mother, so it does not belong in this tale.

Lucy was waiting at the window for him when he returned, and when he saw her apprehensive smile, he went to her and gave her a kiss. "Mom, I'm sorry if I acted like a jerk. I was just caught off guard. If you're happy then I'm happy for you."

35 – Leaf Message

༄ The time of winter was drawing to an end. March came roaring in like a lion, and in its midst came a blustery snow storm to rival any that had preceded it that season. Lucy had not seen nor heard from Lance, but her days were joyous holding his promise in her heart.

One afternoon, just after the winds of the last storm had died down, there came a soft knock at the front door. No one that knew her well ever used that door, and she wasn't expecting anyone. She first went to the window that looked out onto the porch, but she saw no one. There was no car in the drive and no tracks in the fresh white snow covering the yard leading up to the door. Not wanting to let the heat out nor the cold in by opening the door for no good reason, she turned away and walked back to the kitchen, thinking maybe the knocking she'd heard came from a bird or squirrel in the rafters of the open porch.

The knock came again. She turned around and went through the same motions as before, surveying once again the porch, the yard, and the drive. The results were the same: nothing. This time she opened the door cautiously and stepped briefly into the frigid winter air. There was no one there, no bird, no squirrel, nothing. She stepped back inside, and as she did her glance caught something on the worn, smooth planks of the porch floor. She pushed the door back open, stepped out again, bent down, and picked up what appeared to be a big oak leaf. It wasn't brown, as the season should have dictated; it was fresh and green. It was folded in thirds with the stem end folded up and the pointed tip folded down and slightly overlapping. It was stuck together with sap to form a seal. She scanned the yard once again. Still she saw nothing. Holding on firmly to the leaf, she backed into the house, shut the door, and made sure to lock it.

She walked through the house to the breezeway and sat down in her grandmother's old rocker before a crackling fire. Carefully she began to unfold the leaf, loosing the tip first with her fingernail and folding it upwards, then carefully folding the bottom down. To her amazement, there appeared to be something on it, tiny markings like writing. She squinted at it. It looked like some sort of symbol. It also looked familiar. A sudden panic gripped her. She threw it down on the coffee table and jumped up. "Wait, wait a minute," she said aloud. "What's going on?" She felt like she had a cramp in her brain. The mark looked familiar, but she couldn't quite remember. It was the same feeling as having a word on the tip of your tongue. She paced around the room. She circled the coffee table once, stopping a moment, then again, all the time unable to take her eyes off the leaf. She sat down, cautiously picking it up again. "I'm letting my imagination get the better of me," she thought. "This is probably the sort of mark left by the eating pattern of an insect or a worm." But it was not her imagination.

As she examined the leaf, she carefully traced the pattern with her finger. Suddenly it came to her like an explosion in her mind. Her heart raced as she recalled where she had seen the mark before. "Lance!" she gasped aloud. She fell to her knees as the blood rushed to her head. Her heart pounded violently in her chest. In every labored exhalation the name *Lance* was mixed within the whooshes of her breath. Again and again she repeated the name, finally falling silent to look within. The door to a secret closet in her mind had been blown wide open. Thoughts, images, sights, and sounds were invading her. Her heart was a swollen lump lodged in her throat. Memories once lost now flashed before her. She remembered him now.

She returned to her feet and with rubbery legs ran back through the house into the dining room. She picked up a chair from the table and carried it into the long hall that lay between bedrooms. She placed it on the floor midway through the hall. There in the ceiling, painted to match its color, was the hinged door for the attic opening.

Her father had built a closet along the wall that extended the whole length of the hallway. It served as a linen cabinet on the top and a wardrobe on the bottom. He built the shelves out of heavy cedar planks that could be used, with the doors opened, as a ladder to climb into the attic. She opened one of the four equally-sized doors above where she had placed the chair. She stepped atop the chair then grabbed a vertical beam for support while she climbed upon the first shelf. Standing there gave her enough height so that when she extended her free arm, she could push up on the attic door. It was stuck tight from years of disuse in the hot and humid summers followed by the cold and dry winters, which expanded and contracted the old wooden door and its frame.

Lucy pushed and pounded, and after many heaves of a determined heart it finally came loose with a loud crack. She gave one final push with all the strength she could muster, and the old trap door swung back on its creaky hinges. It came to rest with a loud crash on the attic floor. A cloud of dust rained down on her and made her cough. She brushed herself off then reached for the flashlight that was kept on the shelf where she was standing. Laying it inside the opening so she could use both arms, she climbed upon the next shelf, which placed the top of her torso into the dark cavity. Fixing her hands flat on each side of the frame and leaping up, she lifted her body, bent forward, and dragged her butt through the opening to sit upon the edge. Then she brought her legs up until she was all in.

Resting a moment from this unaccustomed activity, a terrible thought came to her: what if her mother had found the box and thrown it out? She soon dismissed this fear, remembering that her dear mother never threw anything away. Her mom had lived through the shortages of war and the Great Depression, which made her afraid to get rid of anything that could be of use some day.

Lucy had not been in the attic for years. It was terribly cold and full of cobwebs. She grabbed the flashlight and turned it on. A beam of light shot up overhead. "Thank God, the batteries are still good," she thought. Immediately an image startled her. The first thing she saw, hanging like a horse thief from the rafters, was a big old Raggedy Ann doll. The poor thing was in terrible shape. It had hung there for "Let's see, fifty years," she thought. It had belonged to her older sister, and when she was done playing with it, her mom stuffed moth balls in the pockets of its dress and asked her dad to string it up to keep the mice from ruining it. Lucy recalled that while she was growing up she had begged her mother on several occasions—whenever the attic door was opened and the old doll came into sight—to take it down and let her play with it. The response was always the same: "No. It belongs to your sister and one day when she has a little girl, it will be hers." But that promise was unfulfilled. Long forgotten on the gallows, the poor doll never escaped. Not that there weren't grandchildren—Shirl, Lucy's older sister, had five girls that could have inherited it. But no one seemed interested in the longsuffering Raggedy. They opted for Betsy Wetsies and Barbies instead. As the years went by, the banished doll was forgotten by all but the mice. Lucy now saw they had visited it often. She stood surveying with her flashlight the heaps and piles of boxes and bags covered with dust. She wondered what other useful things had been stored with an intended purpose of *someday*, only to be forgotten and left to deteriorate into un-usefulness.

After several moments of searching, the flashlight beam fell upon an old wooden box. Her heart jumped. "Eureka!" she exclaimed. She picked it up in her free hand and blew the dust from its top. The pine box was about ten inches long by six inches wide and six inches deep. There were grooves in the top of each side for the lid to slide in. Lucy didn't know where the box had come from in the first place, but it had been around that house for as long as she could remember. When she was little, she used to keep spinning tops and marbles in it. Later, in her school years, it held secret notes from her friends. Finally, it was designated for the purpose of storing what Lucy hoped its contents would soon reveal. She clutched the box to her chest and let out a big sigh. Her knees felt weak.

She remembered the day she had stuffed the box with what she hoped still remained in it. She had come home to see her folks, for maybe the last time. She was on her way to the Serpent Mound in Ohio where she hoped to find a tunnel into time to search for Lance. If she found him, she hoped to convince him to let her stay with him. If she didn't find him, chances were she wouldn't be able to come back anyway. Whichever way it turned out, she wanted to make sure her most prized possessions would be safe.

She took a deep breath and then coughed it back out, her lungs rejecting the cold and the dust. She climbed back down with the little box tucked securely under her arm and struggled to replace the heavy attic hatch. When it slammed into place, another dust cloud fell upon her. She didn't worry about cleaning up any of the mess; her thoughts were on the contents of the box. She hopped off the chair, picked it up, and replaced it on her way back through the dining room.

She carried her treasure box to the table by the fireplace and put another log on the fire; she had gotten chilled from searching through the freezing attic for the prize now before her. She was shaking not only from the chill but also from the life she now remembered. She sat again in the comfortable old rocker and picked up the box. She placed it on her lap and laid her hands lovingly on top of it. She looked to see if the leaf, with its invitation into the past, still lay upon the table. It did.

She held her breath as she carefully slid back the thin pine lid. Revealing the precious contents was like exposing a wound that had never healed. She felt the old pain creep into her heart. There they were, gathered together and tied with a frail, brown ribbon, all of Lance's letters. She took the stack from the box, closed her eyes, and pressed them to her chest, falling in her mind into his arms as she had done so many years ago on the day they parted. She then sighed deeply and untied the ribbon. She almost forgot what she was looking for; seeing the letters brought back such a flood of memory and feelings. Tears welled in her eyes as she sorted through them, viewing the postmarks on each one.

"Let me see," she thought, "it was from Scotland, I think." The letter she was searching for was the very last in the date-ordered stack. She removed it carefully, lovingly from the envelope. Unfolding it, she gazed once again on Lance's handwriting. It was so beautiful and yet so strong. She had read these letters so many times in years when he was missing that his handwriting had become him.

So there he was again:

Lucy Darling,

This will be short because I have much to do tonight before I sleep and dream of you, my love. We are breaking camp in the morning and moving from the Highlands, heading for Cornwall. I've talked to an old clansman from the Findhorn area. He told me a story about being taken by the fairies when he was a child into a stone circle, which transported him into their realm. He has traveled the U.K. seeking other circles and portals for entry into other dimensions. I've learned much from him. I think I am very close now to a great discovery. I wanted to jot you this note and give it for posting to my friend, Sean McDun. He is leaving in moments and will not continue on with us. He has gotten word that his wife has had a very tough delivery of their newborn seventh son, and she lies near death in his home near Edinburgh. Sean is a good brother and has promised to post this letter the very first chance he gets. I pray God's good grace on him for the health of his wife and their new little one.

I dream of the day when you will carry my son. I pray for God's protection on you while I am away. Please know that you are always in my heart.

I feel I am very close to finding an answer to what our true purpose may be.

Sleep well and dream good things. We'll be together then.

My love everlasting,

Lance

P.S. The design I'm putting here I've copied from an etching on the stone the old man found in the circle. I do not yet understand its meaning, but I am sure it is key and will play a part in our story.

She stared at the letter, tears rolling down her cheeks. She looked up and over to the coffee table. Picking up the leaf, she moved it to rest upon the page next to the marking. "Identical," she said. Here after all these years, the same symbol that caused her to forget was here to cause her to remember.

"Lance, oh my God, Lance," she whispered. "So you've returned as you promised after all these years." And Angus, she remembered him now too. The little man she had been seeing; it was Angus. Now she understood everything: he was preparing her for this time to give her back to Lance, to give her back their memories. It was Angus that brought her this leaf. There was no doubt of that. She silently wept, tears spilling onto the pages of his letters as she read each one and remembered.

She awoke in the early morning, still in the old rocker with the letters on her lap. The leaf was gone.

She fixed a pot of coffee and made her way to what used to be her bedroom as a child. It was at present her writing chamber. Her story now took on a new dimension. Her fairytale life once forgotten was again coming to life on the pages of her book. The periods of missing time dating back to her early childhood spilled out into the dark void of her computer screen: the secret school she'd attended with Michael and Lance, the history of the Tuatha De Danaan that was given her by the watchers, the strange and beautiful Shalala and the magnificent Arro, all spilled from her now opened mind. The story of her loves, her wonderful husband Michael, and the man she was made to forget, now remembered—the fathers of her children. She now knew that Lance was Dustin's father, something Dustin would only learn about on the pages of this book.

Michael had come in from the garden at Glen Eden one night with a strange expression on his face. She now knew why. He told her he was planning a business trip to England and Ireland and would like to take her and the baby along. "We'll ask Myra to go too. She can visit her people and help you with Mikey." Baby Michael was just a month past his second birthday at the time. Michael told her most of his business would be in Cornwall, and so he rented a cottage in the country where they would stay. She remembered how uncharacteristically distant he seemed to her on that trip. He told her he was just under stress with the business negotiations and that it was nothing she should worry about. She understood now exactly what stress he had been under and that it had nothing to do with his business. It had to do with delivering his wife into the arms of another man.

When he left her at the cottage that morning, he told her of a dolmen near the ruins of Chûn Castle. "I'm told it's a lovely walk up the pathway behind the cottage. Maybe you can go today when Mikey takes his nap. I'm sure Myra won't mind staying with him."

"I'd rather wait and go with you."

Michael was insistent. "I'm not sure when I can get back, and I'd hate for you to miss it. Take your camera along and get some shots for me."

"Okay, but only if you promise to go for a stroll with me in the moonlight when you get back."

"I promise, my darling." She recalled now seeing a tear in his eye when he said it. He held her especially long, kissed her especially tenderly, and left her standing in the door.

That afternoon after the baby went down for his nap and Myra sat dozing in a chair, Lucy hiked through the fields of the castle to come upon the dolmen her husband had spoken of. As she approached it, she heard the faint sound of harp music. She walked around the ancient structure, peering inside as she did. At one point she thought see saw a sparkling light come from inside. She squeezed through an opening and sat staring at the dark, stone surfaces. As the music became louder, the chamber in which she sat started to spin. She felt as if she were falling. Colored lights blinked and spun around her. She closed her eyes to steady herself, and when she did the falling sensation stopped.

When she opened her eyes, she was in the center of a stone circle. She recognized it as the one Lance had once taken her to. Yes, she remembered him fully now, for her mind was back to the day she'd been there with him. It was Michael she had no thought of. Lance didn't want to tear her heart in two, so he took her mind back to a time they had shared in the past. Here he would plant the seed of the future king. Then he would give her back to Michael without memory of the day so his child could be raised by its mother and the man who had faithfully kept his word.

Lucy was overwhelmed as she remembered this now and realized the depths of Michael's love. Never once had he shown any evidence that Dustin was not his son. She knew him to love both boys equally and now marveled at his noble heart. As she wrote, she recalled the time she'd spent with Lance in the circle on Green's Farm on the night he sealed her mind and caused her to forget him. Lucy somehow knew that all was as it should be, that she was living and fulfilling the life she had agreed to long ago when the mist was upon the land.

She wrote it all down, and as she did she realized that she was recreating the life that she had lived. Night after night she wrote and she waited, finally bringing what was her tale to tell to an end. She knew Lance would be coming for her soon and she knew why. Her cough hadn't gone away. It had gotten worse, and she knew it wouldn't get better, not if she stayed.

The phone rang.

"Hello"

"Lucy, what's going on with your book?"

"Funny you ask. I just finished it."

"You did, huh?"

"Yes, I just wrote the last chapter. Why?"

"Lucy, stop screwing with me?"

"What do you mean?"

"I mean your book. You've already written it, right?"

"Stacy, how many glasses of wine have you had? I just told you, I finished it today, just before you called."

"Oh God, you are good. You really had me going."

"Stacy, what are you talking about?"

"I'm talking about your book, Lucy. You know, the one that tells about the little man and your mysterious lover from beyond this reality."

"Wait, Stacy, how do you know about that?"

"How do I know about it? I know about it because I told *you* to read it," she laughed. "That's a good one; I told you to read your own book. I have to admit, using the name Vlee of Twin Willows threw me off."

Lucy couldn't believe her ears. How did Stacy know the pen name she was going to use? She had only just decided on it. "Stacy, wait, I'm confused."

"You're confused? I told Greg I was a little mad at you. He's the one who told me to call and get it straightened out. He said we'd been friends too long, and if you wrote the book and didn't tell me there must be a good reason for it. So come on, spill. Why didn't you tell me?"

"How could I tell you? I only just finished it?"

"Lucy," she began, her voice raised now, "you mean to tell me that you didn't write this book I'm holding in my hand right now? This book that I read three months ago and asked you to get? The one you said the library didn't have and that you would have your son check on? You didn't write it?"

Lucy felt a very strange feeling sweeping over her. She had been leaning against the wall as she talked with her friend. Now she slid down it and came to rest on the floor. "Stacy, do me a favor and read the first page to me, will you please?"

"Oh God, what for?"

"Please, just do it for me."

"Oh, for Pete's sake… just a sec. Greg, do you see my glasses over there? By the computer. Bring them here, will you? Lucy wants me to read the first page of her own book to her."

"Why does she want you to do that?" Greg asked, fishing through a stack of papers by the computer. "Are these the glasses you want?"

"Yes, that's them. Give them here. I don't know why she wants me to read it. Maybe she wants my creative input." She laughed again. "Lucy, Greg wants to know why you want me to read this to you?"

"I need to know where I am in time, or maybe where you are."

"This is really strange. You make me feel like I'm tripping again, like that time in Grand Rapids."

"What?"

"You know, that Easter when you showed up with 'Guide' written on your hat. You said you were taking us on a trip and gave us each a plastic egg with a hit of acid in it."

Lucy's brain was breaking. She did remember that now. But when was that? Wait a minute. That Easter would have been the spring she was in California with Lance. So how could she remember being in Grand Rapids with Stacy. "Something is wrong, Stacy," she cried into the phone. "Time is all wrong."

"There is nothing wrong with time, Lucy. You're just trying to screw with my head, as usual. Do you want me to read this or not?" Lucy struggled with the question. Did she really want to know? Did she want the life Stacy was remembering, or the one she'd written on the pages of her book? Stacy didn't wait for an answer. She cleared her throat and began reading:

"She sat staring into her teacup at the spent tea leaves laying about the bottom. She lived alone, and with no one to talk to she spent most of her time remembering things from days past. Today she remembered that her grandmother used to read tea leaves…"

"Lance, you've come for me."

"What? What did you say, Lucy? …Lucy? …Hello? Where did you go?"

Epilogue

Dustin was coming out to Twin Willows every weekend now. He had fallen in love with Julie, and she with him. Besides wanting to see her, he also wanted to keep tabs on his mother. Her cough was getting worse, and beyond that ever since the day of her accident she seemed different. He couldn't quite put his finger on it. She seemed happier, resolved in some way. He thought maybe the fact that she was writing gave her a newfound purpose. He didn't allow himself to think her new air may have come from her evening with Mr. McKellen. He asked her from time to time if she'd seen him again, and her answer was always the same: "Not yet."

He tried to get in touch with his father's friend, whom he had always called his Uncle Fred, when his mother first told him of the little man she was seeing. But Fred Loch, PhD was out of the country lecturing and promoting his new book. It had to do with people he'd treated whose lives had been affected by their belief that they were having encounters with aliens, fairies or other spirit beings. Dustin started to read it out of respect for the man who wrote it. But the subject matter didn't pique his interest, so he hadn't finished it. Aunt Shannon, who wasn't really his aunt but who had worked with his father for many years, was traveling with her husband and so Dustin left messages with their offices asking them to contact him when they returned stateside. Since his mother hadn't mentioned the little man again, he thought maybe that whole business was just the result of the head jolt she'd received from the garage door. After all, she could have written the journal entries that same day while he was outside shoveling the drive.

Ian Collier phoned to say he had some news on the ring. He had sent the photos of it to a colleague of his, a curator of Breton artifacts. After studying the photos, the man phoned Ian rather excited by the prospect of examining it for dating purposes. He told Ian the ring fit the description of one told about in tales carried around Brittany by traveling storytellers dating as far back as the twelfth century. The minstrels told of a race of Fae who were facing destruction by a cunning enemy fixed on capturing their prized treasures. This story, like the Irish myth of the Tuatha De Danaan, told of a chalice, a sword, a spear, and a very rare and pure blue stone, each having a special power. A group of the bravest and best among them was sent off with the treasures into a cave in the heart of the Brocéliande forest, there to find a wizard who would use, by the oldest sorcery, the fire in the belly of the earth to meld the objects—with their powers—into a magnificent, magical ring.

The ring, it was told, bore etchings on its blue stone of the pieces that were melted to form it, with runes on the band containing an enchantment that when uttered by the true king would unleash the powers it contained. The story goes that the noble band that had taken the treasures to the wizard were on their way back to deliver the ring to their king, thus giving him the power to defeat their enemy. But alas a heavy fog came upon the land causing them many missteps and injuries, which lengthened their journey and delayed their homecoming. By the time they returned, they found their lands laid waste, the royal palace destroyed, and their king dead. Rumors were many about the fate of the king's wife and newborn daughter. Some had them slain with the king, their bodies fed to their enemy's foul wolf beasts. Still other reports had the baby taken to a time portal by a Guardian gnome. Thereby she was transported to a future time to conceive a royal heir, who would one day return and, aided by the ring, claim the throne and rid the land of the evil that had fouled it. With the hope that the latter was true, the band of brave souls entered time portals themselves to search for their queen. They would become guardians of the ring and their queen until the time of the rebirth of their paradise was at hand. This story could never be verified as true. No ring had ever been found to lend credibility to it. Until now.

Dustin was anxious to share this story with his mother. He knew it was right up her alley. He tried calling her, but her phone rang busy. After a few attempts, he gave up and decided to wait and tell it to her in person since he would be at the farm by six that night anyway. She'd promised to have a pot roast waiting for him, and he had a date to take Julie to a movie at the Michigan Theater in South Haven later that night.

The last of the winter storms came up suddenly, slowing traffic and delaying his arrival at Twin Willows. When he pulled in the drive at 6:30, he had an odd feeling. His mom wasn't in her usual position, watching for him at the window. The garage door was up and the door to the house unlocked. When he entered he called to her, but she didn't answer. He walked through the house, but she wasn't there. He found her purse on the dresser in her bedroom, with her wallet and the car keys in it. The car was in the garage. Her coat hung on a hook by the back door, and her boots sat nearby on the drip mat. He discovered an overdone roast still cooking in the oven, and he found the phone off the hook, the handset on the floor. His concern rising, he walked outside around the house, but the new fallen snow had covered any tracks of where she may have walked or evidence that she may have had a visitor.

Julie came over and they started phoning everyone they knew who might have had contact with her that day. Dustin's first call was to his Aunt Sue, his mother's twin, whose farm was near the small town of Bangor, about seventeen miles away. She told him that she usually talked with her sister every evening and had done so the night before around ten. She had not heard from her since then. Not wanting to alarm her, he played down his concern telling his aunt that a neighbor had probably taken her to the grocery in Pullman to pick up something she wanted to serve at dinner. But none of her friends or neighbors had heard from her either—not Lynn, not her cousin Leona, no one who she normally talked to on a regular basis. He finally decided to call Stacy and Greg, whom he had only met one time when he was young but whom he knew kept close contact with her.

Stacy told him she'd been talking to his mother around 4:30 when she suddenly said the name *Lance* and then nothing more; she assumed the line had gone dead. After learning this, Dustin phoned the South Haven police. They told him it was too soon to file a missing person report since there was no sign of forced entry or of any foul play. They reassured him she'd probably just gone somewhere with her friend and would be getting in touch with him later. But as a favor to him, they promised to send out a car in the morning if she hadn't returned by then.

After no one heard from her for three days, an extensive search was launched in the area. The fields, orchards, and woods around Twin Willows were filled with friends and neighbors wanting to help find her. A photo of her was broadcast on the local television stations—WKZO in Kalamazoo and WOOD in Grand Rapids—along with a description of Lance McKellen, the man she may have been with. But still no good leads came in.

There was one person who claimed he had seen her: her nephew Gorby, Sue's son. He was fifteen years old, a Down's syndrome boy with limited hearing and thus no verbal skills save grunts, snorts, and an occasional hoot. He spent many weekends with his aunt at Twin Willows since she had moved there. And even before that, whenever Michael and Lucy came out to the farm for a weekend they would stop and pick him up to give his parents a much needed break. Michael always called Gorby his "little buddy" and would take him for long walks in the woods or to the beach in South Haven. Gorby loved being in or near the water as much as Michael did, and the two of them could work for hours building sand structures.

As the search for Lucy went on, Sue remembered that the day she went missing, Gorby was outside playing with his pony. He suddenly bolted in the house, making all sorts of excited sounds. He grabbed the picture of his Aunt and Uncle that sat on the buffet and brought it to her. He tugged on her arm until she followed him outside. Tapping on the image of his Aunt Lucy, he pointed to the sky over the woods and made his special sound for *horse*. Sue saw a strange anomaly there. It was like a hole in the sky with rainbow-like pink and blue bands around it. As she watched, it shrunk and disappeared. Gorby was all worked up, hooting and snorting and pointing at his aunt's image. He calmed down only after his mother interpreted what his gestures meant: he had seen his aunt riding a horse in the sky. Of course most people, including Dustin, didn't put any stock in this. But Gorby's mom and dad knew he was not capable of making up a lie, and they always wondered about what he had actually seen.

The following summer Dustin married Julie. His brother Mike returned from Romania with his family for the wedding and stayed at Twin Willows. While searching through Lucy's things for photos of her husband's mother and father to use for a memory board at the ceremony, Mike's wife Domnica came across a brown envelope. Inside was the manuscript of the book Lucy had been writing when she disappeared, with a special note to her sons:

My Lovies,

This is the strange tale of your mother's life.
There are many tales in the mind of God,
but they are all connected and go on forever.
It is time now for your part in the evergoing story.

Dustin's mind and time were consumed with the wedding and honeymoon plans, so he put the manuscript back where it was found to read at a later time when he could give it his full attention. That time didn't come for several months. It was when Julie went off to Texas to attend a nursing seminar and visit with her mother that Dustin decided to spend a long weekend at Twin Willows.

After eating lunch, he settled in his great grandmother's rocker by the fireplace in the breezeway and pulled the manuscript from the envelope. The first thing that seemed strange to him was the title: *In the Shade of a Shadow of Reason*. He was sure that was the title she had asked him to look for in book stores in the city well over a year ago.

He began reading and was made a captive. He was learning about a woman he thought he had known, his mother. The question he asked himself, remembering the stories she told him as a child, was "Is this all just a fantasy from her creative mind?" Just how much of what he was reading was the truth? Her mention of the little man brought back memories of the night she first told him about seeing it. His memory of what she told him matched exactly what she wrote.

Her mention of Lance McKellen and their love affair in the early chapters disturbed him, especially since he always suspected this man had something to do with her disappearance. As he read more, he began to recognize some of the characters she was writing about. He recalled meeting Ashley once when he went to the races with his father. Michael told his son he was the man his mother had been in love with before they met. He remembered seeing a photo of his mother with a girl named Peggy and was told at the time the two used to be best of friends. The story of Myra being his grandfather's mistress was of course something he learned when he had gotten older. When he was young he simply knew her as Granny Myra. He was getting sleepy when he came to the chapter revealing the fact that William was actually his father's father and not Aidan, as he was led his whole life to believe. He found himself getting angry at his mother for either writing treachery or, worse yet, lies.

Reading about Glen Eden made him wonder why his family never went there while he was growing up. Why after Granny Myra died hadn't his father sold the place? He held on to it, even paying a caretaker to stay and keep it up. Why hadn't his mother moved there instead of Twin Willows after his father died? Dustin made a mental note to visit even as early as tomorrow to find an answer to these questions and see how much of her description of it was factual.

He found it very difficult to stop reading, though the time was now well past midnight. He brewed a pot of coffee and stoked the fire. Settling again into the old rocker, he read on. Now he was learning about the occasions when his Uncle Freddy hypnotized his mother and she gave accounts of her lost periods of time.

She indeed had a fantastic mind, and Dustin wondered where all this came from. He thought it was odd how she used an event he had learned about from his cousins—namely that her Aunt Nellie had dropped dead right after she had kissed Uncle Claude at his funeral—to describe how Lance's mother died. He began to wonder which accounts were made up and which were based on the truth. He contemplated whether his mother had struggled with that same problem.

Now he read Lance's note delivered to his father by the little creature Angus. The line—"Nevertheless she must also bear my son"—caused Dustin's breath to catch. He suddenly felt a tug at his heart that made him want to read faster. He leaned forward in the rocker, resting his elbows on his knees and bringing his face closer to the words.

Now came the account of Angus at her bedroom window, the day the garage door knocked her out and Lance McKellen came back into her life.

After reading the chapter titled "Leaf Message," Dustin's life changed forever. Lance McKellen was his father? He thought about the ring Lance had given him. He rose quickly and ran to get his jacket. Fumbling through a pocket, he pulled out the magnificent gift. Though he had the ring for over a year now, he had never put it on. As he held it up, the first rays of the rising sun were caught in the breathtaking blue stone. He suddenly found he was able to read the words written in the strange runes. He uttered them for the first time as he slipped the ring on his finger: "Come forth now powers that would defeat all evil." The stone shown forth a flash of light and a voice proclaimed, "Hail Dustin King!" He turned to see a little man bowed before him.

"Angus?!"